STEEL DRAGON 1

STEEL DRAGON 1
STEEL DRAGONS SERIES™ BOOK 1

KEVIN MCLAUGHLIN
MICHAEL ANDERLE

This book is a work of fiction.

All of the characters, organizations, and events portrayed in this novel are either products of the author's imagination or are used fictitiously. Sometimes both.

Copyright © 2020 LMBPN Publishing
Cover Art by Jake @ J Caleb Design
http://jcalebdesign.com / jcalebdesign@gmail.com
Cover copyright © LMBPN Publishing
A Michael Anderle Production

LMBPN Publishing supports the right to free expression and the value of copyright. The purpose of copyright is to encourage writers and artists to produce the creative works that enrich our culture.

The distribution of this book without permission is a theft of the author's intellectual property. If you would like permission to use material from the book (other than for review purposes), please contact support@lmbpn.com. Thank you for your support of the author's rights.

LMBPN Publishing
PMB 196, 2540 South Maryland Pkwy
Las Vegas, NV 89109

First US Edition, October 2019
Version 1.03, April 2020
eBook ISBN: 978-1-64202-515-6
Print ISBN: 978-1-64202-748-8

THE STEEL DRAGON TEAM

Thanks to the Beta Team

Erika Everett, James Caplan, Crystal Wren, Larry Omans, Kelly O'Donnell, John Ashmore, Chrisa Changla, Daniel Weigert, Mary Morris

Thanks to the JIT Readers

Jeff Eaton
Dave Hicks
Micky Cocker
Tim Adams
Jeff Goode
Dorothy Lloyd
Peter Manis
Nicole Emens
Deb Mader
Misty Roa
Jackey Hankard-Brodie

If I've missed anyone, please let me know!

Editor

The Skyhunter Editing Team

CHAPTER ONE

Kristen Hall stepped out of her car, careful to avoid a puddle slick with oil—no easy task, considering the parking lot was more cracks than concrete. Despite being surrounded by a chain-link fence and a guard seated near the back of the building with a shotgun resting across his lap, she didn't feel like she was in any danger. On a day like today, her family wouldn't go anywhere else. Buddy's Pizza offered the best food in Detroit.

She opened the door to the diminutive building and the smells of perfectly crispy crust and melted cheese washed over her. Her smile was instinctive. She loved this place.

As she stepped inside and savored the aroma, her younger brother blocked her path. "I thought police were supposed to look tough. Shouldn't you wear a scowl with your hair in a bun or something?" Brian enveloped her in a bear hug.

Although he was taller and wider than her, she still wrapped him up and leaned back to lift his feet off the floor. "I could still wrestle you to the ground and make you eat bugs, Brian," she whispered sweetly.

Despite being treated like a big doll, he merely grinned as she placed him on his feet. "You always were a terrible bully, but bugs off the floor at Buddy's would still be better than your cooking."

"Ha-ha." She laughed dryly. Everyone in her family seemed to be able to cook except her. Even Brian, as lazy as he was, could roast a chicken and vegetables. She was basically a master of the microwave and nothing more.

Her mom approached from the back of the restaurant and threaded her way through the narrow spaces between tables. "I think you look lovely, honey." She kissed her daughter on the cheek. "But Brian's right, if you let that red hair of yours run loose at your new job, you'll distract the entire force. Now, come on. Let's go find your father. He's holding a table like he's pinned down."

Kristen followed her through the crowded pizza parlor. Smiling people crammed around tiny tables with red and white tablecloths, argued over the Tigers' latest loss, or scarfed pizza. The walls were covered with photos of celebrities who'd come to Buddy's to do the same. Eminem, the Temptations, and even Aretha Franklin had all eaten there, and those were only some of the more famous celebrities. She had been coming here since she was a little girl. It was her family's go-to celebration venue when her mom didn't want to cook.

She located Frank Hall at a table in a corner, pouring over the menu as if he hadn't seen it a million times already.

Her grin wide, she shifted her posture so her feet would fall silently as she approached. "It looks like you need a spotter." She poked her dad between the ribs with a finger.

He flinched but as soon as he heard her voice, he broke into a smile. "Aw, Kristen, now that you're an honor grad, I can finally let my guard down." He studied her affectionately. "You look beautiful, sweetie. The police don't deserve you."

Kristen pulled a chair out and sat down beside him. "They didn't deserve you either." This wasn't the first time she'd had this conversation with him. He was proud of her for following in his footsteps—at least on the surface—but he was still an old cop. And he was a dad who didn't want to see his little girl hurt, even if she was more athletic than he'd ever been.

"Yeah, well, an old baldy who won't ever shave his mustache is a far cry from the woman you've become." He threw an arm around her shoulder. "I still say you could do anything you want."

"Being a police officer is what I want." She raised an eyebrow. "I want to protect people and help this city become even better than it has in the last ten years. Exactly like my old man did."

His only response was a smile. Despite his misgivings, she could see that what he felt most of all for his daughter was pride.

"Come on, can't we get a pitcher of beer before we get into all the mushy stuff?" Brian plopped into an empty seat and gestured toward a server.

"We're proud of you, too," his mom said to him.

"Yeah, those high scores don't set themselves," Kristen quipped, unable to help herself.

He laughed. "Oh, my God, do you have any idea how you two sound? High scores? No one's cared about a high score since pinball machines were popular." He scratched his hair and shook his head. Brian took after his mother with brown hair and plain features. Kristen was the only one in the family with red hair or a figure, despite her eating virtually as much pizza as the rest of them.

"From the rumors I've heard, Kristen knows more than enough about high scores. Honor grad, huh?" Her dad beamed. "You know I barely scraped through. You've already done well for the family name." He finally put the menu down as the server approached.

"We'll have two pizzas. One pepperoni mushroom, one ham and pineapple, plus an antipasto salad," Kristen ordered before he could speak up. "Oh, and a pitcher of something hoppy from Founder's."

The server nodded and vanished into the noise and hubbub of the restaurant.

Brian grinned. "At least you know how to order food."

"It's not her fault she likes her meat raw on the inside and blackened to a crisp on the outside."

"Mom!" she exclaimed, shocked that her mother would say that until she remembered it was exactly what had happened the last time she'd cooked chicken.

"Nice one, Mom. Get in on the action before her and dad start going at it." Her brother chuckled.

"Now that you're a member of the force, you won't have to cook ever again if you don't want to," her dad stated matter of factly. "Christ knows I don't."

He was lying, of course, and could grill a mean burger. Even that was beyond his daughter's skill in the kitchen.

"I'm not a member yet," Kristen reminded them. "Only a graduate."

"A graduate with honors, honey," her mom added quickly.

"A graduate who was hand-picked by a dragon," Brian said incredulously. "It's not like you won't actually get a job."

"I was not handpicked," she protested.

Her parents shared a look that said they thought that was exactly what happened.

"I still think it's insane that you bumped into one at all. You'd think I'd have seen one by now. After all, enough come through Detroit to perform or whatever."

"Honey, you have to leave the house if you want to meet people." Their mother turned to Brian. "Or dragons," she added after a moment.

Kristen laughed. "Nice one, Mom!"

"But that's kind of how it happened, right, Krissy?" Her dad leaned closer over the already cramped table. She'd told him the story so many times and yet he always wanted to hear it again.

"No. I mean, yes, I bumped into a dragon at a concert—"

"What did it look like? How big are its wings? Did it buy you a drink?" Brian winked.

"It was in human form, duh, and he was…well, handsome, obviously. We talked for a few minutes at the end of the show and he gave me a card with an address."

"So what you're saying is he literally handed you a job." He had skipped every recounting of the story and preferred to spend his time working his way up leaderboards.

She shook her head. "No, not at all. I arrived there and had to take a number of tests. I still don't know the point of half of them. There were physical activities like running on a treadmill, an obstacle course, and things like that. I enjoyed that part of it."

"Yeah, well, no surprises there," her brother said.

"Brian!" their mom chided. "We should be proud someone in this family is athletic. I don't know where you get it, honey, but whoever it came from, I'm happy they gave it to you."

For a moment, she wanted to press her on what that had meant. She sometimes said things like that—like Kristen had history that was different than the rest of them. She certainly looked different. But before she could say anything, the server returned with the salad and a pitcher of beer which broke the moment. Not that she intended to complain. She was starving.

Everyone scooped piles of salad—and didn't skimp on the cubes of salami or cheese—onto their plates and dug in. For a moment, they simply ate and let the sounds of the cozy little pizza place wash over them. As usual, though, Brian couldn't stay quiet for long, "So, what parts did you not like?"

"Well, I still don't really like olives," Kristen mumbled around a mouthful of salad.

"Not the salad, stupid—the tests. You liked the physical stuff, obviously, so what were the parts you didn't like? Did you have to play videogames? I told you that you should've practiced."

"No videogames, Brian, sorry." She shrugged. "I honestly didn't understand much of it. There was some weird history stuff. Questions about dragons in America during colonialism and the Civil War. All kinds of other odd things too. What was strange is that they hooked me up to monitoring devices to measure my brain waves or whatever."

"And they were able to find some? I'm impressed, Kristen." He grinned like a fool.

She put an elbow on the table and flexed her bicep. "Do you want to arm wrestle, or what?"

"Pizza's here." He evaded her question neatly because obviously, he'd lose like he did every single time.

Their server put two rectangular pizzas on the table and the Halls wasted no time in digging in. It tasted exactly like it had for her entire life—perfect. Baked on a steel pan, the crust of each square piece of pizza was perfectly crispy. A lake of sauce covered the cheesy bread and toppings and more cheese were sprinkled on top of that. It was heaven on a plate.

"So uh…did they uh…tell you anything else?" her dad asked around bites of food. Kristen shot him a look. That wasn't really like him. Frank Hall was a direct man and always had been. When he wanted something, he demanded it, whether it was the TV remote or a crook to be prosecuted to the fullest extent of the law.

She shrugged, swallowed another cheesy bite, and washed it down with cold beer. "Well, not really. The tests were kind of all over the place."

"Did they let you ask questions, or did you have to fight your way out of there?" Brian had already wolfed down three slices of ham and pineapple and now reached for a fourth. She snatched it from him before he ate the whole pizza himself.

"That was the weirdest part, actually. They said I could ask anything I wanted to, so I did."

Her brother lowered his voice. "Did you ask the big one?"

"The big one?" her dad whispered, concern in his voice.

"Yeah. Are they always smoking hot in their human form or can they choose how they look? If I could change shape, I know I wouldn't keep this." He slapped his round gut and laughed.

Kristen and her parents all shared a groan.

"No, I didn't ask them about their glamor. I don't like it when people ask why my hair's red and curly instead of brown and straight like Mom's, so I assumed they wouldn't appreciate it either."

Her dad straightened in his chair. "Did you ask to be a cop like your old man?"

"Because if you did, you'll be in big trouble, Krissy," her mother huffed. "I spent thirty years staying up late wondering if Frank would come home, and I don't look forward to spending another thirty worrying about you."

"No, I didn't ask about joining the academy. I asked about the tests, mostly, and why they selected me. I...well, this will probably sound stupid, but I asked if they thought I was a mage or something."

Brian spat out a bite of pizza. "You asked what?"

"Why else would they be so interested in me? Seriously, think about it. I barely bumped into this guy in a concert and suddenly, I'm doing all this crazy stuff and taking these tests. I thought there must be a reason I didn't know about."

"Maybe dragons like redheads." Brian ran a finger through his brown hair and pouted his lips in a poor impersonation of her.

"Brian!" his mother snapped.

"It's fine, Mom. They answered that question anyway. No. I'm not a mage. They almost laughed in my face when I asked it."

Her parents shared another look.

"What?" she demanded.

"We worry about you is all, honey." Her mother dabbed the corners of her mouth with a napkin. "I mean, two rebellions, both led by mages—"

"Marty's right, Kris. One of those wars made Canada, for Christ's sake. I hope you're not a damn mage. You'd either have to serve them or… Is it true they can really breathe fire?" Her dad shook his head. Everyone had heard rumors, but dragons were rare and fairly secretive, especially about the extent of their powers, so most rumors remained exactly that—pure conjecture.

"I don't know, Dad. Like I said, they didn't answer most of my questions, and it's not like the one at the concert transformed and took the time to show me his powers. They merely took more notes on what I asked. Honestly, I think that was one of the tests too."

Brian—having devoured a fifth slice of pizza—rejoined the conversation. "Why would you be a mage, though? Doesn't that run in families or whatever? Unless mom and dad are holding out on us, the Halls are basically normal."

"You're definitely not normal, Brian," she retorted and drew a look of mock indignation from him.

"Halls aren't magic," their dad stated in a tone as frustratingly opaque as the dragons had been.

Kristen nodded. "That's what the dragon said too."

"So, then what happened? They popped you off the diodes and you felt compelled to join the police academy?" Brian gestured at the ridiculousness of his sister being selected instead of him. "They do that, right? I've read about it on the Internet. Compulsion or whatever."

"No. No, not at all. They took a few minutes to look at the results, then told me I'd be a great fit for police work. It wasn't like they forced me or whatever. Dragons aside, you guys know I've always wanted to be a cop like Dad."

"Which is still not okay," her mother said, but her voice lacked the fervor it had possessed when Kristen first applied to the academy. Marty Hall might not be happy her daughter was following her father into the force, but she'd accepted it.

Her dad reached for another slice of pizza. If they waited, Brian would eat it all. "It'll be fine, honey. With a pretty face like that? They'll put her on meter maid duty for a few years before they promote her to detective. Before long, she'll run the force without so much as a scratch on her."

As they usually did, her parents fell into their familiar patter about the job. Since she'd joined the police academy, dinner often devolved into the two of them debating her choice. She might have had second thoughts about her decision—she had always loved her parents and wanted to make them proud—but since they weren't in agreement, she knew she couldn't please them both. The choice was ultimately hers to make.

She'd always been athletic and wanted to help people, so being a police officer made sense. Still, she hoped her mom didn't continue to stress eat.

Kristen's phone buzzed in her purse and she glanced at it. Brian had already tuned out of reality and now played a game on his phone, so she knew her parents wouldn't say anything.

"Oh, my God—Dad, it's an email from the force. They've given me my first assignment," she blurted before she'd even read the whole thing.

"That's great, honey!" Her mom obviously tried to be enthusiastic but sounded like she didn't think it was great at all.

"Now, Krissy, remember, the force is still a man's world," her dad began. She'd heard this speech before too, but beer often made him repeat himself. "I'm sure that once they see what you're capable of, they'll get you into more action, but there's nothing wrong with starting out as a meter reader or a traffic cop. The force has to make money."

She almost couldn't hear him. Not because of the noise of the restaurant or because his words were slightly slurred, but because of the four capital letters that glared at her from the screen of her phone.

"I've been assigned to SWAT."

For a moment, he didn't say anything. He merely blinked at her like she'd short-circuited him. "SWAT?" He looked like he'd found a rat in his beer after he'd already consumed half.

"Is that good?" her mother asked. Despite being married to a cop for more than thirty years, she still knew next to nothing about the police force and its many different departments. She'd always maintained that discussing such things at dinner was uncouth.

"Special Weapons and Tactics." Brian didn't look up from his game. "Nice job, Krissy."

"No, no, Kristen. That can't be right. It must be a mistake. I know you did great at the academy, but you don't have the training for the SWAT team, not yet. Shit, I never even made it to SWAT."

"Frank! Language!"

"For fuck's sake, Marty. If Kristen's really going to be on SWAT, it merits a few choice words."

"I am, Dad. Look." She passed her dad the phone and leaned back while he stared at the screen.

For a moment, he merely read in silence, obviously confused. Kristen could see his lips moving to mouth the same words she'd already read twice. He stopped reading and sat in silence for a moment as if utterly devoid of words.

"Holy crap," he finally managed, which essentially summed up exactly how she felt.

Finally, he took a deep breath and bellowed, "Check, please!" over the din of the restaurant.

"Frank!" Her mom put a hand on her husband's shoulder and looked around the restaurant, obviously embarrassed.

Frank shrugged. "Krissy's supposed to be at work tomorrow morning." He turned to her and looked her dead in the eye. "And you'll need some rest. They say SWAT makes the academy look like kindergarten. And that's without dragons watching."

CHAPTER TWO

A little nervously, Kristen stepped from her car into the parking garage of the Detroit Police Department. She walked past police vehicles and massive slate-black SWAT vans and paused only once to check her uniform in the reflective rear windows of one of the cars. Her red hair was in a tight bun and her uniform still crisp from being starched. When she glanced at her shoes, her face reflected in the shiny leather.

She took a deep breath in an effort to silence the flutter of nerves and pressed the button for the elevator.

Her head held high, she emerged from the garage and crossed the small breezeway to the station. The Detroit river shone blue in the early morning light, and out in the water between the USA and Canada, picnickers already flocked to Belle Isle. One of the auto company's headquarters towered nearby. To her, it looked like a giant pair of batteries held together with enormous bolts.

Despite the fact that she was right there in the flesh, a part of her couldn't believe this was happening. Not only was she a police officer like her father, but she was also stationed there in the newly thriving downtown of her city? Her heart swelled with pride and when she entered the station, she grinned from ear to ear.

She approached a woman seated at a large antique wooden desk and introduced herself.

"Kristen Hall, reporting for duty."

"Let's see your orders," the officer said and held a hand out without looking up from her computer.

In silence, she passed the woman the printed orders.

While she marveled at the desk, the officer examined her printed out email. The furniture had to be a hundred years old and was so well polished that the dark wood shone. There were a few bullet holes here and there, but they looked like they had been added decades before in a harder time. Maybe being on SWAT wouldn't be so bad. She'd had moments when she'd questioned whether it was the right place for her, but now that she was actually there, the doubts seemed foolish.

"You're with Sergeant Jones." The woman finally looked at her. "Good fucking luck with that."

"Excuse me?"

She smirked. "You'll see. He and Butters—that's Sergeant Goodman—are in the lounge." She directed her past the front desk and through the innards of the station to where she would find the squad.

Kristen had thought—based on the state of the vehicles in the parking lot and the well-maintained antique in the entryway to the station—that she had been assigned to one of the more prestigious units. As she made her way through the building, however, she could see the assumption had been mistaken.

Most of the desks were piled high with paperwork—an obvious indication that the force was understaffed—and the few officers she did see barely gave her crisp uniform a second glance.

Holding cells against one wall looked almost comically out of place in the office setting. The bars were brightly polished at about chest level, no doubt from decades of prisoners' taking hold of them while they complained to police officers about their incarceration. The sight of the cells made her realize that in the grand scheme of things, the desks and paperwork were the temporary fixtures of this space. The cells were the real reason why the building had been built there.

Beyond these and near two bathrooms that smelled like they were in need of a good scrub, she found the lounge.

She entered the dingy room and made a quick survey. The floor suggested it was long overdue for replacement and the walls faded from white to yellow as they approached the ceiling. It smelled of stale coffee and fresh donuts—which, she had to admit, wasn't the worst smell in the world.

Sprawled on a tiny sofa was an overweight man who sucked powdered sugar from his plump, brown fingers. His uniform stretched tightly across his middle, although he didn't look sloppy, merely round. Still, she found herself thinking back to her training. How had this man made it through all that? He had her father's physique and Frank Hall hadn't worked out once since he'd retired.

Another man paced near the coffee maker, his back still to her. He was skinny, but she could tell from the way he held himself that he had hidden muscles and could probably handle himself in a fight.

"Do you think this freshmen bitch is ever gonna show up?" the thin man shouted over the gurgling sounds of the coffeemaker as it transformed the last traces of fresh water into drinkable caffeine.

"That all depends, Sergeant Jones," the larger man replied and raised his eyebrows at her in obvious embarrassment. He had a southern accent she immediately found endearing. "Did we get two new recruits or only this one?"

Sergeant Jones poured himself a cup of coffee. "Jesus, Butters, do you do anything around here besides eat this damn breakroom junk? Only one. Some woman, they said. Like I have time to put the fucking toilet seat down."

"Jonesy!" the larger man snapped. So there really was a man named Butters? That couldn't be right. He pushed himself to his feet and approached her with his hand extended. "I presume you are Kristen Hall. I am Sergeant Hank Goodman. Welcome."

Jonesy startled and spilled his coffee. "She's here? Shit, Butters why didn't you warn me? Were you too busy stuffing that fat mouth?"

Kristen took the sergeant's hand and shook it. "Nice to meet you, Sergeant Goodman." Fortunately, he had eaten the donut with his left hand so her fingers stayed dry and she escaped having to transfer sticky sugar to her pristine uniform. She didn't think he'd appreciate it if she'd asked for a cloth to wipe her hand.

"Butters is fine. Everyone else can't help but use the name so I don't expect you to call me Goodman for long anyway. This is Sergeant Jones. He prefers Jonesy."

Kristen could tell from the way Butters raised an eyebrow that Jones did not prefer the moniker.

The other man turned and revealed no surprise at all when his gaze settled on her, despite having insulted her not once, but twice. In fact, he glared at her, sniffed twice, and flared the nostrils of his freckled nose. "Do you smell that Butters? Starched sheets and group showers. When did you leave the academy, Miss Hall? Twenty damn minutes ago?"

"Jonesy. Be proper. Clearly, Miss Hall is in the right place."

Jonesy snorted. "I didn't realize we was in a butcher shop. This is no place for fresh meat, sister. Get out now while your hair's still in a nice little bun. We'll tell them you never showed and we can all forget all about this."

Fury immediately kindled inside her chest and she fought the urge to clench her fists. How dare he talk to her this way. She wanted to slap him across the face with her orders but knew that wouldn't win someone like this over. And that was what she wanted—to win.

"Why should I leave? Did you suddenly realize that no one will want a rancid piece of flank steak or a record-setting turkey if I'm here?"

For a moment, neither man said a thing. They simply stared at her and both their mouths hung open in shock at her retort. Then, making it clear that the two had worked together for some time, they reacted almost in unison and began to talk. Well, Jonesy did. Butters merely laughed—a deep, hearty laugh that made her think of a Baptist church with a charismatic preacher instead of a cop who licked powdered sugar off his fingers.

Jonesy, though, was less than amused. He yelled over his companion's laughter. "A piece of flank steak? If I was a piece of meat, I'd be a T-bone."

Kristen had never heard such a bizarre rejoinder before. But before she could say anything about the strangeness of a man comparing himself to a piece of meat, Butters cut in, "Boney is right."

"And what the fuck do you mean by rancid?" the skinny man continued. "It's not like you can smell anything over those flowers you soaked in rubbing alcohol that you're trying to pass off as perfume."

"Thank God one of us remembered to bathe last night." She smiled. "And it's not perfume, actually. It's called soap. You might want to try it sometime. They make it for uniforms too. It helps with the map of stains you're working on." She waggled her fingers at his chest.

He looked down and found the coffee stain she pointed at. The scowl on his face was worth everything she might have to endure as a result.

Butters threw back his head and laughed so hard that he almost plopped on the couch once again. "Miss Hall, you'll fit in here just fine, I think."

"Bullshit she will," Jonesy said, still fuming. "This is SWAT, not a fucking playground. So you can throw a few fucking insults around, so what? This isn't grade school."

"Yeah, obviously, otherwise you'd have dropped out." Kristen could see she wouldn't win the man over, but she couldn't help herself. She had been raised not to take shit from anyone and could hear her dad now, telling her not to start fights but damn well make sure she finished them. That particular maxim had been one she'd always applied to verbal sparring as well as physical confrontations.

"She has more spine than you, Butters, I'll give her that." He sneered at her. "But it doesn't change the fact that you're not qualified to be here."

"I was assigned—"

"Bullshit. Someone made a mistake." He stared at her with hard, unrelenting eyes as he continued to speak. "When I heard we were getting a grad fresh from the academy, I assumed it was an ex-military type, maybe one of them survivalist freaks. Someone with experience, not some pretty little fawn hoping to make the world a better place."

"You know what? I hope you're right. I hope this is some kind of mistake." Kristen felt another wave of emotion rise within her. This time, it was fear mixed with rage. The problem was that she didn't feel qualified either, so everything he said struck home. Still, she couldn't let him win. "Because at least if there's been a mistake, I won't have to worry about my sense of dignity slowly burning away from being forced to share airspace with you."

There was a heavy moment of silence. She could tell she'd struck a nerve but she wasn't sorry. The man had behaved horribly and didn't deserve her respect. He stared belligerently at her and she returned it without flinching. She wouldn't let him see that he'd gotten to her.

"Do you have your orders?" Butters asked. His question broke the moment but didn't ease the tension in the room at all.

"Of course I do." She pulled out a printed copy of her orders and handed it to him.

He read it for a moment, his eyebrows furrowed, then looked at her. "Well, I must admit this is quite a surprise. Congratulations on high marks in the academy and…and, well, I guess we'll be working together soon." He nodded cordially at her. Although much more polite than his colleague, he didn't look openly excited about her being there. She could understand that. Even her own father had said she was underqualified.

"Let me see that fucking piece of paper." Jonesy snatched it from his teammate's fingers.

"The little marks are called letters. Together, they form words," Kristen all but purred. She'd traded insults with her brother for years. This idiot simply didn't know what he'd gotten himself into.

"Yeah, yeah, I know what a fucking word is. Try these ones—shut the fuck up for a goddamn second and let me read." With that, he stopped glaring at her and actually read the document in front of him.

It took some measure of control from her not to comment on how his lips moved as he read the words.

For a moment, she thought the orders might actually work and he might calm somewhat, but this proved to be wishful thinking.

"And what, you expect me to believe this shit because it's printed on a piece of paper?" Jonesy waved the offending document around like it was hazardous to his health. "This doesn't change a damn thing. Some bureaucrat who doesn't know what the day in the life of an actual cop is like saw your fancy little resume and put you on SWAT. It doesn't change the fact that a new academy grad will put the whole damn team at risk. I already have to manage Butterball's snack breaks. Now, they want to add another liability?"

"Just because I can eat and still snipe better than anyone in the force doesn't mean you need to take it out on Miss Hall," the other man said.

"No more devil's advocate, Butterball!" The skinny man practically spat the words. "Let's go talk to the captain and get this damn mess straightened out."

Kristen folded her arms and shrugged. "That's fine with me."

"Right this way, my lady." Jonesy left the break room and she followed.

As they walked through the police station and past mountains of paperwork, framed photos of dead police officers, and the few tiny holding cells, her mind raced. She honestly didn't like Jonesy—Sergeant Jones? She already thought of him as Jonesy, as his demeanor hadn't exactly earned him any respect from her. He was rude and sexist and yet, part of her—not a small part either—worried that he was probably right.

She shouldn't have these orders. She had done well in the academy, that was true, but she also knew that police work and schoolwork were quite different and that SWAT was another step beyond that. While she tried to rationalize as the man led her ever closer to the captain's office, she constantly came up against one idea, again and again.

Did the dragons have something to do with all this? Why had they sent her to that strange testing place? And why had they recommended her for the police academy? She didn't think it was because they knew she wanted to follow in her father's footsteps. And if the dragons did have a hand in all this, did that mean the captain would be honored to have her on the force or furious to be jerked around by a race of beings who held themselves above humanity?

There was only one way to find out.

Jonesy knocked on the door to the captain's office. Kristen was a little impressed that he'd actually knocked. He seemed the 'knock down the door and ask questions later' type of police officer.

A voice called out, "Come in."

She walked into the office to meet her new boss and honestly felt like she was walking into a dragon's den.

CHAPTER THREE

Despite Detroit's recent regrowth, there was still much of the city in need of repair. Of course, that was the current line pedaled by the pawns on the city council. John Murray knew better. The city was best as it was—with new money pumping through it but still not enough to clean up every dark alley and abandoned factory.

There were more police, but despite his profession, he liked them. He really did and often argued their merits to the other members of his gang, the Breaks. For starters, police couldn't drive half as well as anyone in his gang. As long as the gang members continued to maintain their cars, they could outrace any set of flashing lights and sirens out there. Plus, police made going downtown seem safer for the tourists, which in turn was good for business. But most importantly, they knew their place and followed orders, and that kept them to the newly gentrified parts of the city.

They left abandoned steel mills to the rats who infested them.

Murray looked at the inside of the derelict factory their contact had chosen for this meeting. A crumbling incinerator was the centerpiece of the room. Its sooty bricks reached all the way up through the cavernous space and eventually vanished beyond the ceiling. Broken steel molds and smelting buckets big enough to hide bodies lined the other walls. Shattered windows admitted more than enough light, and the aroma of generations of rats fought with the exhaust fumes from the cars idling in the middle of the factory.

Ahh...to him, these remnants of the once-great metropolis felt like home.

He decided his gang looked like they belonged in the space. The four men he'd chosen to accompany him to this meeting all wore their very finest ripped denim dotted with spikes and rivets. The Breaks were ostensibly punk rockers, but their clothes served a purpose. It was difficult to stab through rivets and wearing metal made metal detectors basically worthless.

It was, however, something of a surprise that the two men who stepped from the van across from them had chosen to meet there. They wore black suits and sunglasses despite the fading light and were—undoubtedly—merely tools.

But that was fine, all things considered. Rich tools tended to have far more money than regular folk and better toys.

"Are you sure we shouldn't simply fuck 'em up?" Lemar whispered to him. "We get in our cars now and run 'em down. No fucking way that van and the asshole inside can escape."

He considered the idea. There was something absolutely delicious about running people down in the Motor City, especially with the cars the Breaks used. All were classics and all American with steel parts that didn't dent from something as brittle as bone. Powder-coat paint jobs that washed clean from even the most incriminating of fluids was another impressive feature.

"Keep the cars running, but let's hear what they have to say."

Lemar nodded.

Although Murray liked the idea of keeping their money and getting new toys, there was something about the way the two suits behaved that made him cautious. Something about how carefully they moved around the third man who'd stayed in the van made him hesitate.

Obviously, the man in the van had all the power. While the other two busied themselves with cargo, the third one had only cracked his window and exhaled a cloud of smoke. The gang leader thought it smelled like a cigar and yet part of him—the part that was still a scared little boy who'd grown up in the projects fighting for his lunch money every damn day—wondered at that smoke. Could it be...a dragon? Had the Breaks finally gotten big enough to be noticed?

The two suits came to stand in front of the door to the vehicle and framed the mostly rolled-up window. The man inside spoke, his voice deep and arrogant with its richness. He hated dudes who talked like that. "You have followed instructions and had each of your lackeys bring a vehicle. This is good."

"You said you had supplies so the boss brought transport. Don't act like we're your stupid little dogs or we'll bite," Lemar retorted before Murray could reply, his tone a near-growl.

A deep inhalation from the man inside the van was immediately followed by a great plume of smoke that erupted from the car. It floated through the still air of the factory and surrounded the man's head and he coughed.

"Nice trick." Murray directed a look at his gang, then bowed. He had been right. They had been noticed. It was time to make sure the boys didn't fuck it up. Fortunately, they all followed his lead and bowed, even Lemar. "Your excellency. Tell us, what brings your business to the Motor City?"

"Believe it or not, it's you, Murray of the Breaks." A smoke ring curled from the van, drifted between the suits, and dissipated lazily against his chest.

He nodded. "You flatter me, sir." He hoped he was doing all right but really knew he was out of his league. There must be a dragon in there. The damn things lived insanely long—long enough to explain why anyone in their right mind would call him Murray of the Breaks.

"He's civil enough," the voice said to one of the suits, who nodded. "Let's see if we can change all that."

Before he could say anything—truthfully, he didn't know what to make of that—the henchmen opened the van.

In that moment, he forgot about the stranger smoking in the passenger seat. He forgot about the derelict factory and its crumbling incinerator and even forgot to close his mouth while he stared. Inside the vehicle—lining its interior on classy little racks, in fact—was more firepower than he or anyone else in the Breaks had ever seen in their entire lives.

There was everything a man who knew the value of force and the worthlessness of pacifism could want—assault rifles, handguns, shotguns, enough body armor for the whole gang, plus a few crates that were tantalizingly labeled *explosive.*

Murray wished he could have said something cool or even had remained standing in stoic silence but instead, he blurted, "Holy shit," and took a step toward the armory.

The suits made no effort to stop him.

"Please, handle the merchandise," the voice drawled from the front seat.

He needed no second invitation and reached for an assault rifle. Although he stole a glance toward the front as he did so, it was walled off and its occupant hidden. Not that he was surprised, of course.

To his surprise, the weapon was loaded. He raised the assault rifle, took aim at one of the last few unbroken windows, and pulled the trigger. The sound of gunfire echoed through the cavernous space and the glass shattered. He grinned.

Temptation loomed and he glanced at the two suits while he made some quick mental calculations. Maybe the gang could take them. It was a bad idea if the guy inside was a dragon, but if he was merely an asshole who liked to smoke it would be doable. The windows might be bullet-proof but still, it was doable.

"A fine shot, Mr Murray," the voice stated, and he felt his plan slipping away like a bad dream upon waking. Why had he thought they could attack these men? They hadn't even flinched when he'd fired the weapon.

"Thank you, sir. We'll…uh…we'll take five of these for the boys here, some of those pistols for the rest, and all the body armor you have. Lemar, get the cash."

The other man moved toward one of their cars but stopped when the voice spoke again.

"I'm not interested in cash, Murray of the Breaks. Not yet, anyway."

Murray was confused. They didn't have the cash for more and he didn't know what the men wanted. Then it occurred to him. "We... uh... I guess we could trade a car for those guns then."

"Fuck no, Murray," one of the boys complained. He made a note to make sure it was his car they traded.

"You'd have to trade all five for the contents of this van and then what would you transport them all in?"

He replaced the assault rifle quickly. "Look, I don't know what the fuck you expected, but you should've told me you had merchandise like this. I could've had the boys call in some debts."

"I'm not interested in your petty debts. They represent the past. What I'm interested in is your future. Do you know what represents the future, Murray of the Breaks?"

"Uh...no?" he stammered.

"Credit. That is what represents the future. I will supply the contents of this van to you and your gang on credit."

"You're uh...very generous, sir, but my old lady's swimming in credit card debt. What's the catch?"

"There is no catch. However, you are correct in enquiring about the payments for this credit. I am—first and foremost—a businessman, so I expect to be compensated, of course." Another plume of smoke issued from the van.

"Uh-huh." Murray nodded and waited for the catch.

"I believe that by providing your organization with these assets, my investment will prove itself. We could dither about the price and set up a timetable with interest payments and penalties for defaults and all that nonsense. However, it would be difficult for you to fully understand the effort it took to bring these weapons here, as I'm sure it will be difficult for me to understand how exactly you might decide to use them."

"Sir, you can bet your ass that however we decide to use these tools, our business has nothing to do with you." Was that what the man behind the glass wanted? Plausible deniability? He could promise that. After all, promises were free, but that couldn't be it.

"Indeed." The man paused as he inhaled more smoke. "It seems you understand business very well, Murray of the Breaks. And I'm pleased to hear that you know the first rule of business is to mind your own."

"But what do you want?" Lemar took a step toward the van. The suits blocked him. "There's obviously something in it for you. What is it?"

"A man who understands the importance of time. I respect that as well. What I want is simple—to see you in action. I tire of these petty operations you've worked so hard at. Robbing liquor stores. Laundering stolen cars. This has got you to where you are today, but it can't sustain your growth in the future. I want to watch you grow like the roots of an oak tree that cracks through the foundation of this city."

"Bullshit." Lemar spat derisively. "No one gives weapons away like this. Do you expect us to think you're the fucking Red Cross?"

Murray's heart dropped into his stomach. This was it then. He knew he should've run Lemar over. The asshole was smart but he had a fat mouth. Now, it would get them all killed at the hands of someone who could change their lives and make the Breaks into something great.

For a long moment, no one said a word. The suits didn't step toward Lemar but none of the gang came to his defense either.

Finally, a long exhalation of smoke wafted from the van. "He's right, of course. This isn't charity. I want to see you grow because I want a piece of the action."

"How much?" Lemar asked.

"Tsk, tsk, Murray of the Breaks. Once, they chopped out the tongues of those who didn't know when it was their time to speak. Now, we must settle for more humane treatments."

One of the suits brought a fist up and the gang member dodged, only to take a knee in his crotch from the other man. He crumpled and moaned pitifully.

Murray glanced at him. The man writhed in pain but was still conscious. He'd live. For a moment, he wished otherwise.

He turned his attention to the vehicle. How odd it was to have this conversation with cigar smoke and his own reflection. "How much of the action are we talking here? Ten percent?"

The man behind the glass laughed at that. "No! No, no, no. I would like to make my investment back within the next century, so obviously, ten percent is much too low. I want fifty."

"I knew he was fucking crazy." One of the Breaks laughed. "Ain't no gang in the Midwest that can pay fifty percent."

"Indeed. Gentlemen, it seems our demonstration went unnoticed. If you will."

On the command from their hidden leader, the two suits marched toward the man who'd laughed.

"Whoa, whoa, whoa!" Murray held his arms up placatingly. "We get the message loud and fucking clear. Ain't no reason to come to blows over a little negotiating between bosses." He snarled the last words at the scowling Breaks. "Now, it seems to me fifty percent is a tad high, but you're right in that ten's too low. Let's meet somewhere in the middle. Say twenty-five. See, twenty-five percent of profits will give us enough liquidity to continue to operate our various schemes, grow our organization, and operate at the high level of efficiency that earned your attention."

"Fifty percent," the voice said in a voice that chilled him to the very bone.

He looked at his gang, who all attempted to look tough behind him. It was easy to tell from their faces what he knew in his heart—they were hopelessly outclassed by these guys. Whoever was in there knew who they were and what they could do, while he didn't know a thing about him. Suddenly, letting them choose the meeting place seemed like a bad idea. Still…fifty percent?

"We can do forty, but that's as high as—"

"Fifty. Percent." In that moment, the sun either slipped behind a cloud or below the horizon because the room plunged into shadow and all he could see was the red ember of the cigar smoldering in the van. He suddenly felt very, very cold.

"Right. Right then. Fifty percent sounds fine," Murray muttered.

Apparently, it had been only a cloud that had blocked the sun as the room brightened once again, although to him, the chill didn't go away.

"It's a pleasure doing business with you, Murray of the Breaks, and remember—I'll be watching. Credit only functions when you work to pay it off. I expect to hear much of your organization in the future."

Before he could respond—not that he had a clue what to say—the window rolled up to seal the man inside with his cloud of smoke.

"Let us give you a hand with all that," he said to one of the suits, but the man didn't even bother to respond. He simply glared at him and went about unloading the arsenal.

Rack after rack of weapons came from the vehicle.

Murray pulled the semi-recovered gang member to his feet and rejoined his men. Despite the discomfort he'd felt when talking to the man behind the glass, he couldn't help but be excited at the prospect of the arsenal before them.

"What's the plan, boss?" Lemar wheezed, still reeling from being kneed in the crotch.

"The plan? With weapons like these, we won't need a plan unless they call in the fucking National Guard to stop us."

"Come on, boss, that's not like you," one the Breaks said. "John Murray always has something in mind."

He snorted at that. It was true enough, after all. "It's time to think bigger, boys. Plans were when we lived from paycheck to paycheck. Now, we've gone and got ourselves a proper salaried position. It's time we got ourselves a goal."

"So what's your fucking goal?" Lemar said. He apparently now felt good enough to talk shit, then. Murray supposed that was good, although part of him still wanted to run the shit-talker over. But that could happen in time.

"My goal is for the Motor City to quake at the sound of my bannermens' engines. I want to be a goddamn king, and you'll be my princes. From now on, The Breaks make the fucking rules."

CHAPTER FOUR

Captain Juanita Hansen barely had time to shove the file she was looking at into her desk before Jonesy entered her office and all but dragged the new recruit—Hall, that was her name—behind him.

She considered giving the man an earful for practically barging into her office—she had no doubt he would have if she hadn't responded immediately to his knock—but decided against it. Despite her inclination, she thought it better for the recruit to see her captain do something besides chew out one of her new teammates before they had even worked together. That tended to not do much for team morale. Not that she would put his reprimand off the table. Sergeant Jones was more than capable of earning an earful, but she'd give him the benefit of the doubt for the moment.

So, instead of ripping into him, she gave the new recruit a moment to take in her surroundings.

Juanita had never furnished her office with fancy chairs or unusual art. She didn't go in for expensive things, but her office wasn't barren either. Instead of worldly pretensions, she simply let her work speak for itself.

On the walls were pictures of her working her way up through the force. There she was, smiling after chasing down her first runner. She'd fallen and broken a tooth and had always thought the blood on her face in that photo was charming in an understated kind of way. In another, she grinned from ear to ear immediately after she'd lit a thousand pounds of confiscated cocaine on fire. That little stunt had earned her a promotion and revealed the priorities of a few of the less scrupulous members of the force. Others showed her with the mayor, with her state representative, and with one of Michigan's two senators.

The pictures were arranged in such a way that as the new recruit craned her neck to take them all in, she saw the decades-spanning career before her. When she finally locked eyes with the captain, Juanita was reasonably confident that the girl understood that the woman before her wasn't merely an appointee with political connections but a cop who'd worked hard to earn her current position in command of all the special operations in Detroit.

Although truly—much as she hated to admit it—being a short Latina woman who'd put on a few pounds since she'd moved to working primarily behind a desk was usually enough to make people understand that she'd worked her way into this position. The few women who actually took handouts tended to look like...well, the attractive redheaded woman standing before her.

"Is there a reason why you've accosted me in my office when we both know you have a mountain of paperwork to catch up on?" she asked coolly. That might have counted as a reprimand for some officers, but Juanita and Jonesy both knew it was fairly tame for the captain. Some officers complained about paperwork, but she genuinely didn't mind it as long as it was done. Paperwork was the grease that kept the engine of the Detroit Police Department running smoothly.

"Paperwork's exactly why I'm here, Captain." He obviously made no attempt at all to keep the hostility out of his voice. "This little princess thinks she's SWAT because of a damn email, and I wanted her to get a reality check from the queen of protocol before she gets comfortable."

Juanita folded her hands in front of her. "Is that why you're still here, Jonesy? Because being on SWAT makes you comfortable?"

His expression darkened. "Damn it, Captain. Are you telling me you really did select her?"

"She has a name, you know. Use it." It was a power move, certainly, and perhaps a little petty, but she genuinely couldn't remember the woman's name at the moment. Chrissy? Christina? She'd been as frustrated as he was when the orders came in and hadn't paid as much attention to the details as she would usually have done.

That might've been too much, though. Jonesy turned bright red and betrayed his Welsh roots. "Sorry, ma'am. This is Kristen Hall, the new recruit who has been ordered onto our team via e-mail." Ah… that was more like it. His words were formal enough, but the way he said "e-mail" made it sound like he was in the process of severing his own finger with a rusty hacksaw. It conjured an intriguing picture that almost made her smile.

"I'm glad you've made her acquaintance," Juanita responded with a smile she normally reserved for visiting politicians. It looked good in photos but he, better than anyone, knew exactly what it meant. "It's good to meet you, Kristen. I like to put a name to an order. Your record from the academy is impressive enough, so I'm sure you've realized that I'm your boss, despite us not actually ever interviewing."

"It's a pleasure to meet you as well, Captain Hansen. My dad told me all about you."

"Your dad is?" She hated to be rude but maybe she'd missed something in the girl's family history.

"Frank Hall?" Kristen stammered. "He was an officer on the force for over thirty years. He's the reason I wanted to become a police officer."

"Ah. He never made SWAT, did he?"

"No, ma'am."

"That explains why I haven't heard of him." The young woman's face fell when she said that but it couldn't be helped. The captain continued. "Still, it's good to know you have some kind of expectation for what police work can be. Normally, appointees who come with your kind of references don't have any familiarity with police work. At least you understand that there will be long days and late nights in your future."

Kristen fidgeted for a moment before she replied, "Of course, ma'am." It was obvious something was bothering her.

"Is there a problem?"

"Who the fuck are her references?" Jonesy interjected. Juanita had been waiting for him to interrupt. It was not Patrick Jones' style to keep his mouth shut for long. Really, she was thankful. Him swearing meant she could tear into him without losing any face in front of Kristen.

For a moment, she considered not telling the man anything—she also liked to use silence to make him sweat—but she relented. He'd find out soon enough anyway, and better to hear it from her rather than through the grapevine. "The email I got from Dragon Special Operations made it quite clear that they wanted Kristen on SWAT and that they would not take no for an answer. Not that they ever do."

"Dragon Special Ops?" He turned to Kristen, incredulous. "You're telling me a fucking dragon referred you to the SWAT team? What, did one of them fuck your grandma or something and feel guilty enough to give you a job?"

"Just because the grandmothers you can afford to pay to have sex feel bad after they're done with you doesn't mean that's always how it goes." She sneered and fixed him with a challenging stare.

Juanita was careful not to let a smile show. Not many people—let alone women—could maintain verbal sparring with Jonesy, but she seemed capable enough.

"Jonesy, I'd tell you to shut the hell up, but it looks like Kristen did that already."

"I... Damn it, Captain," he muttered. She didn't know if he was bewildered by the woman's references or that a rookie had burned him with a multi-level bomb of an insult. "Dragon Special Ops? Really?"

The captain raised an eyebrow at Kristen. She didn't want the new recruit to think she'd won. "Indeed. It seems Kristen has friends in high places."

"With respect, Captain, I don't. I bumped into a dragon at a concert, of all places. He told me to take some tests, and they sent me to the academy. I'd always wanted to be a cop, but I never thought I'd make SWAT, especially given my inexperience."

She let Kristen's statement hang in the air for a moment. From the girl's expression, she thought she was being honest. But if she really didn't have a connection to the dragons, there must at least be something unusual about her, but what? She was too good a cop to jump to conclusions, however. She'd give it time and let the evidence reveal itself.

What was important currently was making sure Jonesy understood that her place on his team was not up for debate. "See, Jonesy? What more could you ask for? She's honest, down-to-earth, and doesn't intend to have her friends light you on fire for wasting both her and your captain's goddamn time."

"Captain?" Before, Jonesy had looked like the flames that powered his anger had been diminished. Now, he looked like he'd had cold water tossed on him. It made her proud that she could do that to him in only a few sentences. She used to have to scream at him loudly enough for the whole building to hear to get him to shut up.

"In answer to your original question, no, Jonesy, I did not choose her to be on my force."

"Then—"

"In answer to the question you were about to ask, yes, she is on your team."

"But—"

"I don't expect you to like it. But we both know I'd rather spend my morning writing parking tickets than concern myself with thinking about what you like and don't like. What next? Do you plan to complain that Sergeant Goodman ate all the jelly-filled donuts?"

"He does eat all the jelly-filled donuts." He huffed petulantly.

"And yet, somehow, you live with this injustice." Juanita smiled at him. He swallowed, fear in his eyes. She continued, her voice saccharine sweet. "I expect you to live with this as well, Sergeant Jones, exactly like I expect you to get out of my office and get back to your job. And remember, Jonesy, if you don't like it, you can always quit." She smiled, crinkled her nose, and squinted her eyes just so.

Jonesy scowled at her. They both knew he'd never be able to go above her head with anything because when he got pissed, he cussed people out, and when she got pissed, she merely smiled until she won. So, he simply scowled and stormed out of her office, no doubt to yell at Sergeant Goodman about eating too many donuts. That was fine, though. Someone had to help the sniper keep the weight off, and his boss did not have time to babysit.

Normally, that attitude would extend to fresh recruits as well, but Juanita thought she owed the newcomer a minute—or not the girl herself exactly, but the questions that her presence called into existence. "Please, sit." She pointed at a chair in front of her desk. "So, if you don't know a dragon, why are you here?"

Kristen took the proffered chair. "Honestly, Captain, I hoped you'd be able to answer that question. When I told my dad I'd made SWAT, he was even more surprised than I was. He said I should have had at least a year on the force before they promoted me here. Okay, I did well in the academy—"

"Not that well. I've looked at your physical examinations and you were top-notch there but still, you haven't been tested under real conditions. SWAT's quite different than regular police work. We like to select from those with experience that applies to the position."

"So, if it wasn't the academy, why am I here?"

Juanita pushed herself to her feet. When Kristen moved to follow, she shook her head. "Sit." She paced slowly through her office as she spoke. "The only clue I have is that Dragon Spec Ops want you here. But it can be tricky to get into the head of all-powerful, ancient, shapeshifting dragons."

"Have you met one?" the girl asked. "A dragon, I mean."

She shook her head, then walked behind Kristen as she crossed her office. "No. The closest I ever came was meeting that senator." She gestured at the framed photo. "There were rumors he took orders directly from a dragon, but we didn't talk about that, of course. Believe me when I say that if I knew what the dragons wanted with you—or with anything, for that matter—I wouldn't keep it a secret. You met one, though, and you went to one of their testing facilities. What was that like?"

The captain moved to stand in front of the picture of her and the senator. She kept her back to Kristen. While she wanted the recruit to know her place, she also hoped to get her talking. Maybe there was a clue as to why she was there and she didn't know it.

The girl shuffled in her seat. "The physical tests seemed normal enough—not that different than the police academy anyway."

"You didn't have to shoot an arrow into a target from a thousand paces or pull a sword from a stone?"

Kristen laughed at that. *Good,* Juanita thought, *let her trust me more than the dragons.*

"No, no feats of strength. But do you really think they would want people to do stuff like that? If you think about it, the last two times people rebelled, the dragons crushed us."

"Us?" she asked.

"People, I mean."

"Right." She returned to sit in her chair when she realized she'd rather be able to read the newcomer's face than passive-aggressively assert her power. Besides, she'd made her point. "You said the physical stuff was normal. Was there non-physical stuff that wasn't?"

Kristen shrugged. "Maybe? I don't know. They asked about the rebellions."

"What did you tell them?"

"Essentially what I learned in school. That in the first rebellion, human mages made dwarves to fight against the dragons. They might have been able to stand against them since they're stronger than people but instead, they made a deal with the dragons and they still own Canada because of it."

"What did they say about that?" She scratched her head. That was basically what the history books said had happened.

The young woman laughed. "Nothing really. Honestly, it felt like I was taking a history test and barely passing. I got the sense that—never mind, it's silly."

"You got the sense that?"

Kristen straightened in her chair. "Well, like I said, this will sound silly, but I got the sense that they were fishing for details—like they thought I was hiding something from them. Like, for example, they kept asking me these weird questions about pixies."

"Pixies?" Juanita raised an eyebrow.

"Yeah, pixies. Mages made them in the second rebellion, but they failed to overthrow the dragons even worse than the attempt with the dwarves."

"I'm familiar with the things. What did they ask about pixies?"

"At first, it was only regular things like have I seen a pixie? If so, where? What do I see them doing? Stuff like that."

"Have you?"

"Yes, actually. Hasn't everybody?"

It was the captain's turn to shrug. "I suppose I've seen a few."

Kristen nodded. Juanita thought she looked relieved. "Right, so have I. I'll see them sometimes if I get out of the city or if I go to Belle Isle. Pixies like greener spaces, I guess. I told the dragons that whenever I see them, they do what pixies always do—stare at me awkwardly with their big eyes that are all one color."

"Pixies stare at you, huh?" She tried to make the comment sound casual. In all honesty, she'd never seen a pixie sit still long enough to make out their eye color.

The girl laughed and seemed to be completely oblivious about how odd what she had admitted was. "All the time. Brian—that's my brother—used to joke about it. This one time, we were camping and one watched us build the fire. It started yelling at us about not needing kindling."

"Not needing kindling?"

Kristen smirked. "Yeah, that's pixies for you, right?"

"I…suppose so," Juanita said cautiously and filed the comment away for later. There was something to that, she was sure of it. "And you told this story to the dragons? What did they say to that?"

Her face told the captain she believed every word that she was saying—she had been in enough interrogation rooms to identify a lie when she heard one—but there was definitely something unusual going on.

"Nothing, really. They made notes and looked at each other and then asked me another question. That was really all they did for the entire interview. They asked some other questions about pixies too—like if they had ever listened to me or done magic for me, stuff like that—but of course they never have."

"Of course not," Juanita said. At least she could relate on that point.

Pixies were twitchy little things. She had never liked them. They could perform magic but were…odd. It was like they didn't have the same relationship with reality that humans did, despite originally being made from people. They also didn't have any kind of attention span. Pixies didn't stare at people. They didn't stare at anything because they didn't sit still long enough. She had never heard of a pixie fixating on anything, let alone a human.

There was something unusual about this Kristen Hall, but she couldn't say what. Pixies focusing on her was certainly odd, but that didn't exactly explain why she'd been chosen for SWAT. She might have felt differently if Kristen was able to get the pixies to do magic for her. Imagine being able to make an enemy's weapon turn into a stick or better yet, disappear.

Juanita took a deep breath and decided she'd do what she did for every complex case she'd ever been presented with. Pay attention, wait, and gather more evidence. She'd find out what was going on with her new recruit. Of that, she was certain. She only hoped to discover it before the dragons moved forward with whatever they were playing at.

She looked at Kristen and realized she hadn't spoken for a few moments. The girl tried not to squirm in her seat, but—despite being singled out by dragons and pixies—she obviously felt about as awkward seated across from her boss as anyone else did.

The captain set her jaw. It was time for the 'new kid' speech.

"Dragons or not, I want you to understand I won't allow anyone to take it easy on you."

"I wouldn't expect you to—"

"Now's the part where you listen."

Kristen nodded. She was impressed with that. Jonesy would have already whined about being told to shut up.

"SWAT is serious," she continued. "Lives are at stake here on a regular basis. In fact, that's part of the job. It's different for everyone, but you need to understand that you will see people die. Whether it's a perp, a civilian who happened to be in the wrong place at the wrong time, or your own partner, you need to prepare yourself to face it."

The girl kept her mouth shut, but her jaw hardened at the mention of death. That was good. The fact that she didn't look surprised meant that she had thought about this already.

"On top of that, I expect you to stay in shape and stay sharp. I know you met Sergeant Goodman, but believe you me, his skills are the only reason I let his gut stay on my force. Sergeant Jones too. He may have a mouth on him, but he's damn good at his job. I demand the same from you, do you understand?"

"Yes, Captain. I appreciate being held to a high standard. I excelled in the academy because they pushed me, and I'm ready to work hard here as well. I was an honor grad there, and I hope to do even better here."

Juanita chuckled. "SWAT isn't the academy, but if you come at it with that attitude, you might make it. Or you might wash out—which, honestly, would be fine with me."

"Excuse me?" That had thrown her for a loop.

"If you decide this isn't for you, you're merely one less problem I have to deal with. Believe it or not, the city of Detroit keeps SWAT busy enough without me having to worry why Dragon Spec Ops sends me recruits I didn't ask for."

Kristen clenched her jaw at that. The captain didn't let her amusement show, but she already liked the newcomer. She seemed to have a steel heart, and when exposed to heat and pressure, she used it to make her stronger rather than let it melt her away. That was a good attitude to have in the motor city and an especially good outlook for the newest member of the Detroit SWAT.

"Don't think I want you to fail or anything like that. God knows we could always use more women on the force, but I definitely won't do you any favors either. I'll try to set you up for success like I have for every recruit who's come through my office, but if you don't step up? Well, that's on you, not me."

"I understand, Captain," Kristen said. Her smiles and shrugs had given way to a hard jaw and a stubborn look on her face.

Juanita found she really liked this kid.

"All right, now let's get out of my office and go meet the rest of the squad."

"Yes, Captain Hansen." She stood and followed her to the door.

They were about to leave when the older woman cleared her throat and turned to her. "And Kristen, if you see any dragons loitering around my station, tell them to keep the fuck moving and that there's nothing to see here."

"Yes, sir!"

CHAPTER FIVE

Kristen tried to pay attention to where they were going as Captain Hansen led her through the station, but her mind wandered constantly. Why had the dragons forced the woman to take her on at SWAT? Why had she asked her about the pixies? Dragons and pixies were facts of the world she lived in, but that didn't mean they had anything to do with her...right?

She felt like pieces were moving and shifting all around her and yet she couldn't see what shape they would ultimately form. It was beyond frustrating but, as the captain showed her to the squad room, she forced herself to push it all from her head. Now was not the time to wonder about dragons. She would work with the people she would meet in this room. It was their lives she would need to protect, first and foremost, and it was the people in this room who would protect her life—not any dragons and definitely not any pixies.

"You've already met Sergeant Jones and Sergeant Goodman," Captain Hansen said cordially. Jonesy only scowled at her as he put a bulletproof vest on that—despite being a vest—still managed to look baggy on him. Butters merely winked at her.

She smiled. At least one person wanted her there.

Captain Hansen gestured at a tall man who was even skinnier than

Jonesy. "The man with the glasses is Sergeant Jared Polanski." He currently looked through the aforementioned glasses into a book.

"Beanpole is my spotter," Butters said with a nod at Polanski. "And don't let his glasses fool you. He needs them to read but has damn excellent vision when it comes to keeping me alive."

"I simply try to do my job," Polanski—Beanpole—said.

"It's nice to meet you, Beanpole." She assumed that if everyone was introduced with nicknames, she might as well use them too.

"Likewise. I look forward to us working together."

There was at least one normal person on her team anyway. She found that to be a huge relief.

"This is Corporal Lyn Hernandez, demolitions." Captain Hansen pointed to a woman in a tank top who pulled a long-sleeved shirt over her tattooed arms.

"What, no nickname?" Kristen said after a minute.

"No. No fucking nickname," Hernandez retorted. "Is that what you think this is? Some kind of fucking club where we all hang out with decoder rings and jerk each other off?"

"You'll have to pardon Hernandez," Butters said, his calm southern accent a welcome change to the vitriol in the woman's voice. "We think she blew her sense of humor off with C4 a few years back."

"Fuck off, Butterball." She turned her back to Kristen and snapped on a belt that had a few more compartments than the standard issue.

"Hernandez's bark is worse than her bite," Hansen whispered to Kristen. "But tread carefully. Her bite is fairly bad too. I'd have kicked her from the force a long time ago, but the woman has a way with forced entries. We have never seen a building she can't get into."

"Or a pair of pants." Hernandez flicked her tongue crudely at the newcomer.

"Oh, now you're a lesbian?" Jonesy scoffed.

"I don't make such distinctions, Jonesy. The flesh wants what the flesh wants."

"Are you coming on to me?" He smiled. Kristen found she preferred his scowl.

"Not if you were the last lump of flesh on earth," his teammate returned smartly.

"You'll get used to those two," Captain Hansen said. "They're both a huge pain in the ass but they mostly only insult each other so it cancels itself out."

Kristen smiled. Jonesy and Hernandez would be tough, but at least the captain seemed to be in her corner.

"Speak for yourself, Captain. You don't have to ride in a van with those two," Butters interjected.

"I guess there are perks to being captain after all," his boss said cheerfully. She turned to a young, attractive man with an athletic build. He had a square jaw, a clean haircut, and looked exactly like Kristen had thought a cop should look like when she was eleven years old. "This is Corporal Keith Wentworth. He was our rookie until you showed up."

"Welcome to the force, rookie," he said, proffered his hand, and proceeded to use it to attempt to crush her fingers in a vice-like handshake.

She had been raised by a cop, however, so she squeezed right back. At first, he looked impressed. Then, he squeezed harder so she did the same until finally, he flinched and released her. He rubbed his hand surreptitiously.

"The rookie thinks he's my fucking shadow, so if you find yourself tangled on some clumsy fuck when you thought you were following me, it's him," Jonesy said.

"Now that she's here, you can't call me rookie anymore," the other man protested.

The sergeant raised an eyebrow at him. "Red crushed your hand like the Sox do the Tigers every damn year, and you think that means your days as a rookie are over?"

"The Red Sox do not crush the Tigers," Keith complained. "The last game was close."

"Who gives a shit?" Jonesy shot back. "They lost."

"No one. No one gives a shit," said the only man in the room who had not been introduced.

"And this..." Captain Hansen walked over to the tall man with a furrowed brow and threw an arm around his shoulder—no easy task considering how short she was and how broad the man's shoulders were. "This is your fearless squad leader, Alexander Drew. Sergeant Drew has already been briefed on the...peculiarities of your arrival, isn't that right, Drew?"

"Yes, ma'am," he said and his gaze rested on Kristen. It was obvious to her what his opinion of her place on his team was, but at least he didn't cuss her out about it like Jonesy and Hernandez.

The captain removed her arm from his shoulder and addressed the room. "Everyone, this is Kristen Hall, your new squadmate. Make her feel welcome and make sure she's ready. As of this moment, she rides with you. Someone with far more brass on their uniform than me thinks she's hot shit, so you all better make sure she makes it through the week without being shot."

"What if she's blown up?" Hernandez asked and almost sounded hopeful.

"Then it will be your responsibility to clean up the mess, Hernandez."

The woman considered it. "That doesn't sound so bad."

"Cleaning up messes includes paperwork," the captain reminded her.

The demolitions expert wrinkled her nose at that, but she only nodded. Kristen was beginning to fear paperwork.

And with that, Captain Hansen nodded to the squad and left her with her new team.

For a moment, no one said anything. She thought that was a good sign until she realized that everyone was staring at the team leader.

She was about to say something to break the silence, but Drew spoke first. "The Captain showed me the orders. They made it sound like you were fresh out of the academy."

"Yes, sir, just graduated."

"Were you in extracurriculars or something?"

Kristen had no idea what he was talking about. "You mean like... sports? I played soccer, volleyball, basketball, lacrosse—"

Jonesy snapped at her before anyone else could. "No! He means like were you in a marksman class? Maybe a human psychology class where you focused on talking down deranged fucking maniacs? Maybe a driving course where you learned how to dodge gunfire while one of your best friends tries to stop one of your other best friends from bleeding out in the neck?"

Kristen swallowed. "No…no, nothing like that."

Butters came to her defense. "Jonesy, I dare say you hadn't done any of that stuff before you got here either. We were all green once."

"Not your plate." Hernandez snorted at her own joke.

"Butters is right," Drew said and inspired his team to return to silence. "Some experience can only be learned on the job. But can you tell us the difference between a covert and a dynamic entry?" He had a deeper voice than the rest of them—softer too, so he was almost hard to hear—but when he spoke, everyone on the squad stopped talking.

She thought back to the academy. "Uh…covert means you sneak while dynamic means you break the door down?"

"Lucky guess," Hernandez said.

"Do you know how to run the wall?" Drew asked.

"That's um…staying at a ninety-degree angle from each other when you break in?"

"We don't break in," Hernandez corrected waspishly, "we force entry."

"And you've done that?" he asked and ignored the other woman.

"Well, no, but I've read about it," she replied honestly.

"Ah. A reader. Good." Drew turned away from her as if what he said had made sense.

Jonesy took up the challenge. "What about sectors of fire?"

"Or, uh…what does it mean if a room is green or red?" That came from Keith, who stood behind the skinny man and tried to look tough. Kristen thought maybe she could understand why everyone called him rookie.

Kristen knew that one. "Red means danger and green means safe."

Jonesy ignored her and instead, turned to snarl at the other man. "Damn it, rookie, of course she knows that one. Anyone who has ever been to a goddamn roller-skating rink knows what red light and green light means."

"Wait…does that mean that Sergeant Patrick Jones of the Detroit SWAT has been to a roller-skating rink?" Butters' grin was even more massive than his belly.

"Of course I've been to a fucking roller-skating rink. Who hasn't gone skating? Christ."

"I've never been skating." Hernandez's smirk said exactly what she thought about Jonesy admitting to how he spent his free time.

"I haven't either." Beanpole looked up from his book and also grinned.

"We all know that if I started skating, I wouldn't be able to stop rolling." Butters guffawed at his own joke.

"Listen, you fucking smartass wannabes without a drop of class between you, pardon fucking me for not treating a lady to another boring night at a fucking restaurant and going out and doing something fun for a fucking change."

"That's enough, Jonesy." Although Drew hadn't raised his voice, the other man practically flinched at the sound of it. He scowled at everyone on the squad and went off to polish his gun, although Kristen thought it already looked like it was extraordinarily shiny.

That left the leader standing in front of her with a massive stack of textbooks in his hands. The muscles in his neck bulged at the weight and for a moment, she wondered if she'd be able to even lift the stack. This had to be some kind of test.

"These are for you," Drew said and dumped the stack in her arms.

Kristen took a step back, caught her balance, and looked him in the eyes. He wasn't smiling—he honestly didn't seem like the type of person who ever smiled—but there was something in his gaze that was close to amusement. The stack of books really had been a test then, and not dropping it meant she'd passed.

"What do you want me to do with them?" she asked and wondered vaguely if she was about to participate in some kind of hazing ritual. Despite not having bulging muscles like he did, she most definitely worked out. The building they were in couldn't have been more than a couple of stories. She thought she could take the steps with the books in her arms.

He frowned at her. "They're books. Read them. Learn every word, concept, and acronym in them. You're done when you know the information in there like your ABCs. I don't want my team to waste time explaining how to ODS in the middle of the mission."

"Or KISS." Hernandez blew a kiss to Jonesy's back.

Kristen looked at the stack of books she held. Her arms were fully extended so the lowest book was below her waist, yet the stack still came up to her chin. This would be enough reading to keep her occupied until it snowed. "By when?"

Drew looked at her without blinking. She noticed his eyes didn't shift a little like most people's did. His simply stared and didn't move at all, frozen and looking as immutable as stones. "Every other person in this room learned all that before they were allowed through the door to even try for a place on a team. You have some catching up to do. A ton of catching up to do."

She forced a smile. "So, two weeks?"

The man did not return the smile. "More like yesterday."

Really? He had to be kidding, right? Kristen waited for an awkward moment. There was no way she could get through all this in a week, let alone a day. When he didn't move or say anything else, she realized he was serious. *Great welcome to the force, huh.*

Finally, she put the stack of books on one of the benches, took a seat beside it, and took the top one of the stack. She opened it to a diagram of people breaking into an apartment and clearing it room by room. At least it would be interesting reading, she thought.

"What are you doing?" Drew asked and jerked her attention away from the diagrams.

"Getting to work." She looked at him and again, he stared in return, his gaze as still as a boulder. "Sir," she added and hoped that was what he'd waited for, although she very much doubted that it was.

"Today's not a paperwork day," he said.

Hernandez cut in, "And if it was, you can bet you'd be helping your team fill out their forms, not doing your homework."

"I thought I needed to know all this to better serve the team," she protested.

"Oh, you do," Drew said and his stony visage finally chipped to reveal the barest hint of a smile. "But you have to learn the physical part of SWAT training too."

"Lucky for you, we were about to train for five or six hours." Jonesy smirked.

Kristen simply resigned herself to the inevitable and stood. "Well, then, let's get to it. How bad can it be?"

CHAPTER SIX

It turned out there were many differences between covert and dynamic entries—far more than she'd dreamed of. Kristen worried that if they tried to do any more variations of a dynamic entry, her brain would collapse like the doors they repeatedly broke down.

They were outside, across town and in a training area that had a few empty buildings in it. A small house, a large house, and a tiny apartment block were all surrounded by a sweltering parking lot. Much of Detroit had been abandoned, then reclaimed as the wealthy moved back into the city. SWAT could have scooped up a few abandoned houses in actual neighborhoods, but it seemed they preferred to work in the desolate parking lot.

She knew she was merely bitter. The sweat that poured constantly was a major contributing factor to that.

Each exercise was basically the same—break in, make sure each room was clear of hostiles, secure any hostages, and get out—and yet her new squad knew endless variations on this simple theme.

"Breacher up!" Jonesy instructed.

Hernandez grunted in affirmation and pounded into the door with what Kristen could only describe as a miniature battering ram. The door flung open, which meant it was time—yet again—for her to spring into action.

She ran into the tiny house with Keith and Jonesy at her side.

"Living room's clear!" she shouted.

"Take the kitchen, Red," Jonesy ordered.

Without question, she obeyed, left her team behind, and entered the kitchen.

She found Butters bent over and digging around inside the fridge, his huge butt protruding into the kitchen.

"Butters? What are you doing?"

"I'm a hostage," he said as if it was the most obvious thing in the world.

In the next moment, she felt the hard punch and immediate sting of a rubber bullet in her shoulder.

"Ow! Fuck!" She yelped.

"You're dead." That was Drew. He'd played a hostile, which meant he basically hid in the house and shot at her. The man really was way too good at his job.

"The hostage?" she protested. "Butters was rooting around in the fridge. I thought he wasn't ready."

The team leader stood from behind the kitchen table. "Do you expect every situation we enter to have hostages on their knees with their hands behind their heads?"

"No, of course not, but digging in the fridge?"

"It does happen." The rotund man closed the fridge. "Sometimes, a hostile demands a sandwich. Do you think a barbarian with a weapon will actually take the time to spread mayo on his own bread?"

Kristen clenched her teeth. It took everything in her power not to roll her eyes. She'd already been shot by countless rubber bullets and now, they talked to her about sandwiches?

"Reset," Drew said.

"Haven't we done enough?" She didn't want to quit but felt like she had to. It had been a long, hard day and she was hot, tired, and wrung out. She could do more of this tomorrow, or the next day, or any time but now.

"That wasn't a request."

Wearily, she trudged to the front door. Hernandez kicked it in. Jonesy and Keith entered with her again. This time, the skinny man took the kitchen, which left a hall to the bedroom for the other two.

Shoulder to shoulder, they moved down the corridor and kicked doors in as they went, looking for Beanpole, Butters, and Drew. In an actual dynamic entry, the first two would be somewhere nearby, probably across the street—Butters with a sniper rifle and Beanpole with binoculars to watch his back—but Drew wanted them in the building today so they could more properly fuck with her.

She kicked a bathroom door open to find Beanpole sitting on a toilet.

"Hands up!"

Beanpole—his pants thankfully still at his waist—threw his hands up.

"I'm checking the next room." Keith stepped back and was about to lift his leg when he stumbled. "Shoelace," he yelled and crashed to the floor.

Kristen dropped to one knee. "Keith, you okay?"

When she turned, Beanpole had a handgun trained on her forehead.

"Reset!" Drew yelled.

"Oh, come on!" By now, she was truly frustrated. "A shoelace?"

"Believe it or not, that happens," the team leader said as he stepped from the next bedroom down the hall.

"We added that to the routine thanks to the rookie." Jonesy stepped out of the room after him.

Keith was tying his boot. "Now she's the rookie."

"She hasn't botched one of these entries because she forgot to tie her shoe," Drew said. "Now, reset."

Again, they went back to the front door, kicked it down, and entered the house. This time, she found Beanpole with a gun to Butters' head.

"Back off, pig!" When Beanpole gestured with his pistol, she leapt into action. She stepped low, put the hostage's girth between her and

Beanpole, then moved around him and struck the skinny man in the back of the leg hard enough to knock him to one knee.

"Good one," he wheezed. It sounded like the wind had been pushed from him.

Drew stepped into the room. She had no idea where he'd been hiding. "You have good instincts. Now, reset."

Back at the door, Hernandez kicked it down and Kristen entered. This time, the fridge was rigged with C4 and they all exploded.

"Reset."

Yet again, the front door was kicked in. Kristen found two hostages—Drew and Beanpole—before she was tackled by Butters, who'd hidden behind a door like a kid playing hide and go seek.

"No hostile will do that. They'd have to know we were coming," she complained from beneath his weight.

"It's happened before. Reset."

Kick down the door and race through the living room. Someone shot her through a door.

"Reset."

Kick the door…living room…man hiding a gun behind a goddamn bouquet of flowers.

"Reset."

Door…living room…one of her squad was struck in the head with the leg of a chair and died.

"Reset."

Door…living room…hallway…weird smell…gas leak sparked when the hostile fired a weapon…everyone dead.

"Seriously?"

Drew nodded. She had really begun to hate his nods. "It happened once in ninety-six."

"It was a fucking tragic one." Jonesy grinned. "There was a pie in that oven. Apparently, the hostiles had stopped fighting and had made up, but when they heard a knock on the door, the man grabbed his gun instead of answering. Police kicked it in. He fired. Boom. I guess the pilot light was out."

"Then it didn't happen to SWAT," she grumbled as she trudged yet again to the front door for another practice run.

"It didn't happen to SWAT because we train." Keith clenched his jaw and tried to look tough. She understood why everyone else on the team called Keith rookie—he seemed so much like a kid who tried to act like a cop instead of an actual cop—but she didn't find it annoying like Jonesy and Drew seemed to.

"All right, ready." Kristen sighed. They'd been at it for hours. She was exhausted but she wouldn't quit. Not on day one and not doing an exercise the rest of the squad found to be important enough to spend a day doing.

"Let's switch gears," Drew said. "You've had enough forced entries for the day and you've shown some improvement."

"I died nearly every time."

"True. But not every time. That's better than Keith's first day." From Drew, that almost seemed like a compliment. "You really do have good reflexes. That'll get you a long way. You merely need to keep practicing these drills so the movements are second nature. You'll get there."

She beamed. Now that was an actual compliment.

"What is she going to suck at next?" Hernandez smirked. "Target practice? Disarming explosives?"

"Combat exercise?" Jonesy suggested wryly.

Drew considered it for a moment, then nodded. "Why not?"

They all scrambled into a SWAT van. Beanpole drove, Drew rode shotgun, and the others sat in the back. The van was blessedly air-conditioned but the ride was too short. She was so tired she almost nodded off, but before she could actually do so, they arrived at a gym.

They separated to change and Hernandez begrudgingly showed her the way to the women's locker room.

"Don't expect them to go easy on you because you're a woman," she said as they found open lockers. "They sure as shit didn't go easy on me."

Kristen wanted to see if that was why the woman had been so hard on her but decided this was probably not the time. Besides, "Is that why you've been such a bitch?" was rarely a question that went over well with anyone.

Instead, she remained silent and simply stripped her body armor off—relieved to be free of it not so much because of the weight but because her skin could now breathe—and changed quickly.

She slipped on a pair of sweats, a fresh sports bra, and a tank top, and turned to find Hernandez staring at her, slack-jawed.

Instinctively defensive, she folded her arms in front of her chest. "I don't really care if you're a man or a woman, sexual harassment is still sexual harassment."

"No. It's not that. White girls aren't my thing, anyway." The woman seemed genuinely dumbstruck.

"Then why the fuck were you watching me change?"

"How many times did you get hit with a rubber bullet today?" she asked.

"I don't know. A lot?"

"Where are your bruises?"

Kristen looked at her arms. They were bruise-free. She peeked inside her tank top—she'd been hit once right above her boob and that one had hurt like hell. There wasn't a bruise, though. "Maybe the Kevlar—"

"Kevlar is there to make sure there are bruises. Even from rubber bullets."

She shrugged. "I'm a fast healer."

"Yeah, no shit," Hernandez muttered and headed to the door. "Come on, and uh…sorry for staring. I… I didn't mean to."

"It's fine."

"Good. If you're fine that means I don't have to take it easy on you." And in an instant, her vinegar was back.

They found the rest of the squad in a large room with a padded floor. A sparring room, obviously.

"Partner up," Drew instructed and folded his arms in front of him.

She found herself working with Keith. They went through a few light exercises, practiced a few kicks, and generally warmed up. After a few minutes, it was time to fight.

Hernandez and Jonesy went first. Kristen didn't think she'd ever seen a fight so dirty before. Neither of the combatants had any issue with gut-shots, hair-pulling, crotch-hits, or anything else. The fight was supposed to end in a pin, but it ended in a stalemate. He had a fistful of his opponent's hair, and she literally had him by the balls. "Nice fight, for a Mexican." He groaned.

"We both know I would have beaten you faster if I could actually find the shriveled little blueberries you call your nuts."

The team leader broke it up. "All right, you two, good fight. Well, good for you two anyway. Let's see Kristen and Keith."

Kristen hoped the way they fought was an exception, not the rule.

"Rookie vs rookie," Butters said. Somehow, when he said it, it didn't sound quite so bad.

Her opponent stepped into the center of the room. He put his mouthguard in and punched his gloves together.

She nodded, flexed her back, and moved to stand opposite him.

"Fight!" Drew commanded.

If Keith had any reservations about fighting a girl, he'd overcome them long before. He attacked immediately and threw a punch as soon as he was in range. She dodged and retaliated with a jab of her own, but he was taller than her and outside her reach.

He attempted another punch but she blocked it, then rocketed a leg into his ribs.

Although he grunted and stepped to the side from the impact, he wouldn't be defeated so easily. He brought both fists down on her back with enough force to make her stumble, but she didn't go down.

Kristen had wrestled her brother since she was a little girl. Her current opponent was obviously stronger but he did not compare in mass to Brian trying to squish the air out of her.

She used the distance between them to rush forward, stepped left to dodge his punch, and caught him the jaw with an uppercut that was strong enough to knock the man on his ass.

Keith didn't stay down, but he didn't exactly get up either. He tried to push himself to his feet but fell again.

"She knocked the balance right out of him," Butters exclaimed.

"I don't fucking believe it," Jonesy added as if his expletives truly contributed to the conversation.

Her opponent finally managed to get back to his feet—technically there hadn't been a pin—but Drew called the fight for Kristen.

"Let me have a round with Red." Jonesy licked his lips. It seemed that Hernandez had only threatened to crush his nuts. He looked formidable as he stepped in front of her and tilted his head from side to side to crack his neck.

Drew shook his head. "No way, Jonesy. You have an ax to grind. We're not doing that today."

Much to her surprise, though, the team leader stepped up in front of her.

She swallowed. Keith was big, shorter than Beanpole but broader too, and definitely broader than Jonesy. But compared to Drew, he looked average. This man made her feel like she faced off against a brick wall, or maybe a gorilla—or better yet, a gorilla made of bricks.

"Are you ready?" He slipped his mouthguard in.

All she could do was nod.

"I'll give anyone three to one, any amount you want, if you put your money on the redhead." Suddenly, there was a fistful of cash in Hernandez's hand.

"I'll bet fifty bucks, but you gotta give me five to one," Butters countered.

"Done!" The woman beamed.

Kristen didn't know whether to be flattered that Butters had put money on her or offended that he'd demanded a five to one payout to be willing to do so.

"I have twenty bucks that says Red goes down in twenty seconds," Jonesy said and tossed cash on the mat.

"She's a fighter." Beanpole added a twenty to Jonesy's. "My money says she lasts a minute."

"Ten seconds." Hernandez added a twenty to the pile.

"A minute thirty." Butters winked at Kristen. "I have to hedge my bets."

"Ready?" Drew said around his mouthguard. She didn't know if he was asking her or Keith, who stared at the pile of money but seemed incapable of choosing a time after losing to her.

She nodded again.

Drew surged forward.

Kristen tried to use her smaller size to her advantage and bounced away on her feet, assuming he wouldn't be as quick as she was.

She was wrong.

He swung after her and made her think of the mountain goats that—despite weighing hundreds of pounds—could balance on rock shelves only inches deep.

When she tried to tuck around him, he responded with a punch and she was forced to stop and block.

It was like being struck with a hammer fired from a cannon, except this cannon had rapid-fire mode. He punched again and again, each strike powerful and each one from a slightly different angle and she realized he was testing her defenses.

Kristen caught each blow on the back of her gloves and felt the strikes in her bones.

On his fourth punch—fifth or maybe even ninth, she couldn't be sure—he drew back, but she could tell he was aiming for her gut.

Quick on her feet, she moved out of the way and pounded him in the kidney with every ounce of force she could muster.

Drew grunted and shoved her back with both hands.

She almost fell but managed to stay on her feet. That was a good sign. A push meant he wanted distance from her, which meant he was intimidated…maybe.

"Nice hit. You're strong. For a girl."

He returned to the attack. This time, she didn't try to avoid him. Instead, she wove between his piston-like punches and delivered one of her own at his chin. He leaned back to dodge the blow, but she could see the surprise on his face. He had thought he'd had her and was surprised that she'd made it so close.

Without hesitation, she went on the offensive. She rained punches on his arms in an attempt to get past his gloves to pummel his middle, but she couldn't find an opening.

As soon as she realized she'd overcommitted, a gloved fist collided with her ear and she stumbled.

"You're good. Fast."

Kristen decided she'd had quite enough of his sparse little compliments.

She rushed in and feinted a few times. Drew blocked lazily and she dropped to one knee and tried to sweep his legs out from under him.

He jumped over the kick like he'd seen it coming a mile off. Before she could get back on her feet, he shoved her from behind and she sprawled across the mat.

A mad scramble brought her back to her feet but not quickly enough. By the time her gaze settled on Drew, all she could see was a gloved fist. It caught her in the face and her feet left the floor exactly like Keith's had.

The mat offered scant protection and before she could so much as move, he was on top of her.

Jonesy counted, "One…two…three!" It was all over.

He pushed himself off her, then reached down to help her up with a gloved hand.

"That was damned impressive," he said after he removed his gloves and his mouthguard.

"I guess. But you won," she mumbled.

"But you won me sixty bucks." Butters collected the stack of money.

"You owe me fifty, Butterball, so don't go thinking you'll go out for a nice dinner or anything."

Butters paid Hernandez but he didn't seem to mind. "Ten dollars is enough for chicken and waffles. That's one thing this city does right."

The two began to argue about the best place to get chicken and waffles and if ten dollars really was enough to pay for it. Kristen ignored them. Her stomach felt sour. She'd honestly thought she could win.

Drew fixed her with a solemn look that held no trace of mockery. "Seriously. You have real potential. Your form is rough—obviously—

but if you're willing to put in the work, well, you might actually be able to beat me one day."

"You never said that about me," Keith whined.

"Because that wouldn't be true, rookie," Jonesy interjected.

"Honestly, though, Kristen. You might have what it takes, but it won't be quick and it won't be easy." The team leader gave her a long stare. "You'll have to put in some work."

"Sir, there's nothing I like about quick or easy. I joined the police because I wanted to work. My father did this job for thirty years. My goal here is to make him so proud he'll be a little jealous."

"Even it means having your ass kicked every day?"

Kristen grinned at that. If this was what they called an ass-kicking, she could handle it. The rubber bullets had hurt and yes, her pride had been bruised after he'd knocked her to the mat, but that didn't mean she intended to give up.

Not now and not ever.

The dynamic entry drills had been hard, but she was ready for a challenge. The police academy had been tough, but she had still passed with flying colors. Maybe SWAT would finally present the challenge she had searched for her entire life.

"Sir, if that counts as an ass-kicking, don't be pissed when I kick yours."

Drew finally smiled at that—actually smiled—and slapped his gloves together. "Good. Let's go again. Your eyes need to follow my core. That'll help you anticipate my movements."

They got back to work and she tried—and failed—to work his body as well as he did hers. By the time they were done—after what felt like hours later—she felt good but exhausted. Her ribs ached, and she knew that no matter how rapidly she healed, she'd feel this workout in the morning.

CHAPTER SEVEN

The decommissioned SWAT van pulled into the parking lot and made no effort to slow despite the bumpy gravel road. How Jonesy had come to possess the vehicle was something Kristen didn't even want to guess at. She hoped that however he'd acquired it, Captain Hansen had overseen some part of the exchange. In the back of her mind, she had visions of him sneaking into a parking garage and boosting the van, but she told herself that was a fantasy. Probably.

They'd driven the old clunker for miles, ostensibly to a bar, but she could now see that she had been way off on that mark.

"I thought you said we were going for a 'pleasant, relaxing evening.' An airsoft range doesn't exactly sound relaxing," she said to Keith before the van hit a bump and she had to shove her red hair out of her face. She and Keith were in the back of the van—along with Hernandez and Butters—on a bench that ran along the side and had decidedly unimpressive seatbelts. Jonesy and Beanpole were up front.

At least she had chosen to wear jeans and flats. She'd dreamed of joining the police for years so she preferred pants to skirts anyway, but this was still something of a surprise after being invited to "happy hour" for the first Thursday on the job. She had thought her new team knew somewhere with decent drink specials.

"We'll relax afterward," Keith said and tried to sound tough.

"You sure didn't," Hernandez said. Besides the single moment in the locker room, the woman still hadn't shown Kristen anything approaching kindness. It was vaguely comforting to see that at least she didn't show anyone else much respect either. "Keith cried like a baby for a week. He said the welts were too painful on his *pompis*." She slapped her butt—helping to translate from Spanish. The woman glared at her. "We'll see if you do any better."

"Do you really think I've never played airsoft before?" It was pure bluster, of course, but because she hadn't didn't mean she or anyone else had to know that.

"You look like the only exercise you did before this was Pilates and CrossFit," Hernandez sneered.

She wasn't exactly sure how that was an insult, but the woman chuckled as if it was so she tried to look offended.

"Don't be scared of Hernandez. She'll more than likely blow herself up out there," said Butters.

"Oh, shut it, Butters. We both know you're the easiest target to hit on the whole damn field."

"What we all know is that —despite my love of all things fried—I'll hit you long before you hit me." He patted his big round stomach like it was only a joke but Kristen was eager to see the sniper in action, even if he would only use airsoft guns.

The stripped SWAT van stopped with a jerk and a moment later, Jonesy swung the door open with enough force to explain the state of disrepair his vehicle was in.

"Are you fuckers ready to rock or what?" The sergeant grinned.

"Watch your language, Jonesy, there's a lady present," Hernandez said and elbowed her way past Kristen as she did so.

Kristen climbed out of the back of the van. As she waited for Keith and Butters, Beanpole stepped out from the front seat.

"Are you ready to enjoy your evening?" he asked Kristen pleasantly. After a few days of working together, she already found his unceasing politeness to be at odds with everyone else.

"Battle Royale in five minutes," a voice yelled over the PA.

"Wicked! We have enough time to get suited up," Jonesy said as he hauled airsoft rifles from the back of the van and passed them out. "I'll settle up with the greedy bastards while you guys get suited up. Which one of you pussies wants a canvas shirt?" He pointed toward the booth where they had to pay to use the course.

Hernandez hooked a thumb at Kristen. "White girl does."

"Anyone else?" he asked.

Butters chuckled. "There's no way they have my size."

"I'm fine, thank you," Beanpole said.

"Keith?" Jonesy raised an eyebrow.

"You know I'm with you, sir. I don't need a shirt unless you advise…that is—" Keith stammered until the other man cut him off.

"Yeah, yeah, yeah. For fuck's sake, you little kiss-ass. I'm not gonna get one so you better not either. Only Red, then?"

"I'm fine," Kristen said quickly.

He grinned. "Are you sure? These guns are right at the legal limit. The shit stings."

"Tell me what rules you play by," she said, hoping there were multiple sets of rules and she didn't sound like a total phony.

"Everyone will have ninety seconds to get to whatever position you want to be in before I come to shoot you, then it's a free for all," he said. "If you are hit, you raise your dead-flag so no one will shoot you while you get out of our way and make for the sidelines." Jonesy tossed her a red bandana. "Last man standing wins."

"Or woman," Hernandez grouched.

"Yeah, I'll believe that when I see it," Jonesy said and hurried off to pay for the round while the rest of the team checked their rifles and put goggles on.

A few minutes later, a claxon blared, and they all ran into the arena.

Kristen had to admit it was a cool space. About as big as a football field, the arena was filled with structures made of wooden pallets— one of which was multiple levels high—plus barrels, and even a pair of burned-out dumpsters in the center. It felt delightfully post-apocalyptic to run into the area, get away from her co-workers, and turn to try to hunt them.

Except she had never hunted anything that hunted her as well.

The claxon blared again, and the soft *pop-pop-pop* of airsoft rifle fire erupted in the arena. She had to dive and slide behind a pile of pallets to avoid being hit but rolled easily back to her feet. Thankfully, she'd played almost every sport there was, so sliding through the dirt was second nature to her.

She poked the barrel of her rifle out through the pallets and tried to get a feel for where everyone had gone. There were other people on the field too—teenagers, mostly, and a few hunter-types—but she didn't really care about them as it quickly became obvious that her team was there to dominate the match.

A huge shadow moved through the upper level of one of the pallet structures. Butters?

It had to be. Anyone who approached the fort was picked off the second they raised their rifles.

Kristen would save him for later.

For now, she had to—

"Surrender!" Keith had his rifle trained on her back. He'd snuck up while she attempted to get a feel for the field.

"How does that work?" she asked and turned slowly to face him.

"You, uh...surrender?"

She smirked. *Fat chance.*

With the hope that she could catch him off guard, she dove into a roll and tried to bring her rifle to bear, but he had the drop on her. She had to still raise her rifle and aim while all he had to do was pull the trigger. He did so, of course, and fired dozens of tiny pellets that rocketed toward her at hundreds of feet per second.

Kristen blocked them with her gun—all of them. She simply held her weapon up and deflected the rounds until Keith—his jaw practically on the dusty ground—stopped firing.

While he stared in shock, she raised her weapon and shot him in the chest.

"Ow, shit! Okay, okay. You got me," he said and rubbed his chest as he walked toward the side, muttering, "My fucking nipple. Ouch!"

Beyond her grin, she realized she had also learned her first lesson of airsoft. Much like an actual combat zone, it was suicide to sit still.

She didn't know where the rest of them were, but because she knew Butters was probably in the tower, she headed that way and dodged from pallet to barrel, crouching and sprinting. It was a ton of fun. It was weird how she had basically done this all week—sprinting through cover while she infiltrated locations and pretended to face off against hostiles—and yet with a toy gun in her hand, it didn't feel like work.

Perhaps halfway to the tower, she found more of her team.

"Fucking suck it, Beanpole!" Jonesy shouted as he leapt out of one of the dumpsters and fired at the other man, who tried to get a bead on his boss.

"Oh, dear, enough. Enough!" Beanpole protested as he was pelted with pellets.

"Hey, Sarg," Kristen said, her weapon raised and ready.

The look on the skinny man's face when he turned to see the force's newest recruit already unloading pellets into his chest was priceless. It slid from shock to horror to a mere smidge of amazement before it settled into straight-up laughter.

"You fucking got me," he said and rubbed his chest where the pellets had struck. "Two left. If you win this, you'll officially be tougher than Keith or Hernandez."

But she barely heard him and already ran toward the pallet tower where Butters was hiding. If she couldn't get inside, there was no way she could beat him.

She dodged from a barrel to another stack of pallets, then low-crawled over.

Shots rang out and she scrambled behind a barrel. Damn it. He had seen her.

Still on her feet, she sprinted to the next available cover—two barrels with a third on top—but it was too far. Her opponent fired and led her expertly and Kristen—with nothing to hide behind—brought her gun up and used it once again to block the pellets.

The string of colorful profanities that erupted from the two-story pallet fort all but confirmed that the southerner was indeed in there. She didn't think anyone else could possibly use the word "declare" with as much emotion and vitriol that he put into it.

Kristen made it to the three barrels and paused to catch her breath.

"Come on out and I'll fry you like a battered drumstick," Butters shouted from his hiding place.

"More like you should come to me. Isn't that what a southern gentleman is supposed to do?" she yelled in response.

"Now why would I do a fool thing like that?"

"Because you're cooked, Butterball." Someone darted away from the bottom level of the fort. She had forgotten all about Hernandez. The woman dashed out from the two-story structure and laughed maniacally as what sounded like a string of firecrackers detonated inside.

Except firecrackers wouldn't have been able to cause the entire structure to groan and finally collapse in spectacular fashion. A brilliant flash flared from the bottom floor, followed by the wood cracking loudly as the entire structure came down. Before the dust had even settled, Kristen darted in, found Butters amidst the wreckage, and aimed her rifle at his big belly. "Do you surrender?"

"Ha-ha, nope. Not to someone 'bout to get shot in the back."

"Shit!" She flung herself onto the pile of broken pallets beneath her as Hernandez opened fire. It had clearly been a mistake to assume that the explosives aficionado would wait for her destruction to be complete before she darted in, but she'd obviously underestimated the woman. She wouldn't make that mistake again.

But what Butters had said earlier about Hernandez was true. Despite her having the advantage, she didn't manage to hit her. Kristen again used her weapon to block—and drew the same confused look from the woman that she'd received from everyone else who'd seen her do so—and shot her.

"Okay, Okay. You fucking got me." Hernandez threw her death-rag up in disgust.

Kristen didn't take any time to gloat. Instead, she turned and shot Butters.

He grunted in pain but quickly began to laugh. They both knew he deserved it because he'd been reaching for his weapon while she was otherwise occupied.

She helped him to his feet and they made their way out of the airsoft arena.

They found the owner—or manager or someone who obviously cared about the place—chewing Hernandez out. "I told you not to come back here, goddammit. We're holding you liable for the damage you caused."

"What damage? She knocked a bunch of fucking pallets down," Jonesy argued.

"Those fucking pallets were insured."

"Show us the paperwork," Kristen said. "I'd be interested to see how that structure passed inspection."

The sergeant raised an eyebrow at her. That was as close as he'd come all week to actually saying she'd done a good job. But, as usual, he didn't actually say anything complimentary and instead, turned to the pissed-off manager. "I have your paperwork right here," he said and slapped a wad of twenties on the table.

"You already paid with a card for the first round…" the manager said cautiously.

"And for the second round too. This is only so you remember the night when a goddamn newbie beat what I thought was the best squad in SWAT in a private match."

The man nodded and made no effort to count the twenties. The stack was thick enough that he didn't need to. "This should cover the pallets—"

"It fucking better," Hernandez said.

He scowled at her. "But it doesn't cover her entry. We've been over this, Mr Jones. She can't bring bombs in there."

"You call those bombs? If I'd brought a bomb, you would've known it," the woman protested.

"It's fine. I was gonna sit this one out anyway. You can keep me company," Jonesy said.

She scowled but she didn't object.

"What do you say? Do you boys want a rematch?" Kristen asked. Despite the intense gameplay, she wasn't really winded, merely warmed up. It felt way too good to shoot the people who'd shown her what she'd done wrong all week long.

Butters shot a look at Beanpole, who nodded. Both men looked at Keith, who glanced indecisively from one man to the other until Butters finally cleared his throat suggestively.

She understood what they had in mind before Keith did—haze the new kid and all that. That was fine with her. She'd known she'd get this kind of treatment as both a rookie and a woman but simply hadn't thought she'd be armed when it first happened. As things stood, she almost pitied them.

"Unless you boys are chicken?"

"The only one of us who is chicken is me, and that's simply because I ate some for lunch." The rotund man chuckled but it sounded hollow. Oh yeah, they definitely intended to team up and take her down a peg or two—or try to, anyway.

The claxon sounded and they sprinted into the same arena. It was unchanged except for the pile of rubble at one end.

The boys immediately separated, and she had no doubt of their strategy. Butters would try to get into position while the other two attempted to distract her.

For now, she kept an eye on the sniper. He vanished among the dumpsters, some of the only cover in the arena big enough to hide his bulk completely.

The other two hastily found suitable positions. Keith ducked behind a couple of barrels and Beanpole behind a wall of pallets that in no way hid his height. She would have thought him foolish if she hadn't known they had a deliberate intention to lure her to attack.

Well, the best way to defeat an enemy was to use their strengths as weaknesses, so Kristen played into their little ambush. She approached in a crawl until Keith caught sight of her and opened fire. Quickly, she rolled behind a pile of pallets, found a loose one, and picked it up with her left arm and wielded it like a shield.

The man gasped—actually gasped—when she held the pallet with one hand. She used the opportunity his astonishment provided to pepper him with pellets. Her accuracy was slightly out with only one hand free to fire the rifle so instead of a tight circle on his chest, she delivered the barrage to his entire torso, legs, and face.

He fell and moaned in pain.

One down. She made a mental note to get him a beer later. While her successful "kill" was satisfying, she hadn't meant to shoot him in the face.

Beanpole fired at her before she could raise the pallet to block, and one of the pellets bounced off her arm. Did that count as a hit? It hardly hurt at all. Surely it was merely a glancing blow.

Kristen brought the pallet into position before the tall man landed any further shots but of course, that was what Butters had waited for.

A line of pellets rocketed toward her. She barely had time to drop prone and go beneath the fusillade.

"That's downright impossible," the sniper yelled.

She had no idea what he was talking about—the pellets hadn't been that fast and she assumed his gun must have been low on air or something—but she didn't waste his surprise.

On all fours, she scrambled toward Beanpole, came up in a crouch, her gun aimed, and fired at her tall teammate.

"I surrender, please! We always do this to newbies, not only girls," he said and held his gun and his death-rag together in one hand. He touched the growing welts on his neck and chest tenderly with the other.

In that moment, she honestly didn't care about that. She simply wanted to win and there was only one person left.

"To the death," Butters shouted.

Kristen shook her head at his mistake. His voice had echoed, which meant this would literally be like shooting fish in a barrel.

She approached the dumpsters and found—unsurprisingly—that Butters was not positioned between them.

"Gee. I wonder where Butters is?" she said as loudly as she could without it sounding obvious.

"Right here, ya Yank—" He wasn't able to finish. As soon as he'd darted up from the dumpster she'd already guessed he was hiding in, she sprayed his giant belly with pellets.

He immediately collapsed into his hidey-hole with a clang that rang through the arena.

The sound was quickly swallowed by Jonesy's uproarious laughter. "That was pretty damn good, Red! I'm glad I sat that one out."

Kristen smiled and started for the exit.

Butters caught up to her. "Hey, no fair," he said. "You were hit." He pointed to the welt on her arm.

"I thought you said it would hurt."

"It does," Beanpole said. He and Keith waited for them at the exit and both were covered in welts.

"Next time, I think I'll go for the canvas shirt," Keith said weakly.

Jonesy laughed even louder at that.

She merely smiled. Their antics tonight—and her success—made her think she'd make it with this team after all.

CHAPTER EIGHT

A little stiff, Kristen dragged herself out of bed on Friday morning. As she limped through her early-morning routine, she wondered if she was in better or worse shape than anyone she'd faced during the week.

She made her way to work, parked, and headed past the front desk and to the lounge for a dose of coffee. There hadn't been time to make herself a cup at her apartment as she'd slept in.

Keith, Beanpole, and Butters had gathered in the lounge, all slumped together on the couch and nursing cups of coffee. Butters had a donut.

"Well, look who it is, the bringer of welts," he said by way of greeting.

"Good morning," she replied brightly as she selected a mug with a bulldog wearing a police hat and fixed herself a cup of coffee.

The peppy greeting had been the right response. Keith and Beanpole both glared at her and she could understand why. Their arms were basically all welts. Ah…nothing tasted as sweet as gloating with kindness.

"Be a dear and get me more coffee?" Beanpole asked her.

"It's right there." She nodded at the coffee maker.

"I know, I know. Forgive me for asking." He shoved himself to his feet and groaned mightily as he did so. The movement was pained and he looked about as limber as an eighty-year-old. He bumped into Keith, who uttered an equally pitiful moan of protest.

"If I've bumped you, then pardon this." Beanpole put a hand on his shoulder and used it to push himself up. The other man practically writhed in pain.

Kristen watched the entire pathetic spectacle. She didn't think she'd seen anyone so sore since Brian had tried out for the football team in ninth grade.

"Are you as beat as us?" Keith asked her once he had his whining under control.

"Not really, no. But I guess you have to be shot for it to hurt, right?"

Butters laughed at that. Keith and Beanpole smiled indulgently at her, but either they didn't have the energy to laugh or they simply didn't find her overwhelming victory very funny.

Sergeant Drew entered the lounge, frowned at the grown men on the couch, and grabbed a donut. "What the hell happened to all of you?"

She raised an eyebrow at the team, eager to hear how they'd spin this one.

"Rough night," Keith managed as if that explained anything.

"Did you have a good time at the airsoft course?" Their leader appraised their welts and bruises. "Were other cops playing too or something?"

"We definitely faced a cop." Butters glanced at Kristen.

"You should've seen these fuckers." Jonesy burst into the room, his grin wider than she had ever imagined was possible. He swooped in front of Beanpole, who still hadn't managed to hobble to the pot of coffee despite it being literally across the room.

"Is this your work, then?" Drew asked.

"Ha! I wish." Jonesy fixed his coffee languidly while Beanpole tried to get past him.

"Pardon me," the tall man said.

"Just a moment, my man." Jonesy slapped his teammate on the back in what might have passed as a friendly gesture if the man hadn't gasped as if he'd been stabbed.

His reaction seemed to be what the sergeant had wanted as he stepped out of the way of the coffee maker and leaned against the counter to grin at his boss. "These three numbskulls tried to triple-team Red. It was fucking epic. She fed them their asses on a goddamn silver plate."

"Is that right?" Drew looked impressed.

"I wouldn't put it that way," Beanpole hedged.

"She's played before," Keith protested.

"We were beat pretty bad, yes," Butters admitted.

"She strung them along like fish on a line." Jonesy laughed. "It was like watching Wonder Woman—no, wait, more like Captain USA or whoever the fucker it is with the shield. She picked up this pallet and *pop, pop, pop.*" He mimed using a shield to block gunshots. "It was fucking wicked."

"She was with you and Hernandez, then?" The leader's eyes didn't leave Kristen. He seemed to be appraising her.

"No fucking way. Hernandez blew shit up in the first round and was DQ'd. She's probably gonna be pissed about that today, by the way. Anyway, me and her sat the second round out. It was literally Red—fresh out of the academy, first week on the force, look-at-my-beautiful-fucking-hair Red—versus three of Detroit's finest. Well, two of its finest plus the fucking rookie."

"I'm not the rookie." Keith protested, but his heart wasn't in it. Last night had proven he still had far too much to learn.

"She peppered them more than Butterball's famous white gravy." Jonesy laughed.

"There is such a thing as too much pepper, by the way," the sniper added.

"I'm surprised you got them all so bad," Drew said, but he didn't look surprised. He looked impressed.

Kristen tried not to let herself smile too broadly. "Thank you, sir."

"Are you paying for it in bruises today?" he asked.

She shrugged. "Not really. I was only hit once."

"Yeah, but the day after my first time playing airsoft, I felt like someone had remodeled my thighs with ice cream scoops," Butters said.

"Eh, I do squats and all that every day. My legs are fine."

"Plus, you were diving around. Aren't you bruised?" Keith asked.

It was as if the memory of her dodging him and getting back on her feet flitted across his face like a replay. It was a different dynamic but a satisfying one—to be in the station and see these people's work faces and yet know she'd whooped them all in a sport they had far more experience in.

Kristen took a sip of coffee. "I heal quickly."

"You don't seem to have a mark on you," Drew said.

"I don't. I took a shower, had some sleep, and I'm as good as new."

"That's good. But I guess we haven't pushed the training hard enough. Today, we'll—" He fell silent when the radio on his shoulder blared to life.

"We have a ten-forty-five in progress at a pawn shop. Three hostiles and four civilians reported. One officer is down."

"Where is it?" he asked.

The radio operator gave him the directions.

"We're on it, but isn't someone else closer?"

"They have firepower beyond what the police are equipped to handle. The building is locked down and officers are maintaining a perimeter until SWAT arrives." The radio crackled.

"On our way," Drew said. Jonesy was already running to the parking lot.

Keith and Beanpole dragged Butters to his feet. The three men groaned as they did so but not one of them complained.

"I hope you'll do as well with real guns as you did with toys last night because you're coming too," their leader said to Kristen.

She nodded. Her confidence from the night before had evaporated like a cup of lemonade spilled on a sidewalk in July.

They hurried through the station toward the parking lot to find Jonesy and Hernandez already there and suited up.

"Get the fuck in," he said.

"Everyone, armor up. Even you, Butters," Drew ordered. "Apparently, the hostiles have heavy-duty artillery. I want helmets on the whole time unless your eye is pressed against a scope."

Kristen snatched a bulletproof vest up.

"Dress as we drive. We have potential hostages." The team leader climbed into the passenger seat in the front of the van.

"There's no time to make yourself pretty, Red." Jonesy took the driver's seat.

She ignored him and climbed into the back of the SWAT van with Keith, Hernandez, Beanpole, and Butters. This one was in noticeably better shape than the decommissioned vehicle the team had used the night before.

The tires screeched and they lurched into motion before she'd had time to buckle up. She barely managed to snap the clip in place and avoid being hurled off the seat. Safely strapped in, she heaved a breath. They were on their way.

"Are you all right?" Butters asked as soon as they'd cleared the parking garage.

Kristen shook her head, then nodded. "I'm fine," she blurted.

"You don't look fine. You look chicken-shit scared," Hernandez said as if they were about to go on a particularly exhilarating roller-coaster ride rather than face people who would try to kill them with advanced weaponry.

"Do you really think that's appropriate right now?" Beanpole asked as they jolted over a bump.

"There's nothing wrong with being scared." The woman made herself sound casual. "I was scared my first time out—so scared I nearly pissed myself. That reminds me, Kristen, did you use the potty before we left?"

"Oh, hush," Butters said.

"I'm fine. This is what we've trained for," Kristen said.

"A good point." She loved Butters. Despite only knowing him for a week, he always seemed to have her back.

That was a welcome change from Hernandez, who seemed determined to get into her head. "Yeah, but we trained in an empty building, not a pawnshop. There might be a perp waiting in there with a chainsaw."

"Girl, hush." The sniper huffed his irritation.

"Don't listen to her. They'll have guns, exactly like they always do," Beanpole said as if that was supposed to make her feel any better.

"I remember my first time," Keith ventured.

"When was that exactly—last week?" she quipped.

"No, not that. Last year. I had been on the force for about two weeks."

"Oh, so we're not talking about sex?" the woman yelled over the screech of the van's tires as they took a turn.

He turned bright red, which inevitably made Kristen wonder what exactly Hernandez was referring to.

Kristen wanted to learn how to channel the demolition expert's energy. Despite them being moments away from armed combat, she looked calm and in control. Although maybe she could learn to be that way without putting everyone else on edge.

Keith looked distinctly uncomfortable, but like her, he seemed to try to force himself to stay calm. "It was a liquor store hold-up. The hostile had a shotgun. You'll never guess the value of the whiskey this guy blew to pieces."

"A tragedy." Butters nodded.

"I didn't get hit, though. I managed to dodge a shot and the guy's gun jammed. That was plain luck. I bashed his head in with a liquor bottle."

The sniper chuckled at the story. "The mountain of paperwork on that one."

"What about your first time?" Kristen asked Butters. She hoped the man's sense of calm would also apply to combat stories.

"Now there was a lesson to be learned there," he started to reply. But before he could begin the actual story, the van squealed to a halt and Jonesy yanked the back door open and yelled at everyone to get in position.

"Places, people—on the double!"

For a moment, Kristen thought Jonesy and Drew had set this all up as some kind of elaborate drill. When everyone poured from the van like ants, though, she knew this was the real deal.

They were parked in the back of a strip mall's parking lot. Housed within were the typical businesses of low-income neighborhoods—liquor store, dollar store, a payday loans place with barred windows, a pawnshop at the end, also with barred windows, and a row of bicycles with a chain threaded through their wheels.

Butters and Beanpole immediately jogged away from the pawnshop. It occurred to her that they were panicking like she was, but then she remembered—duh—that one was their best sniper and the other his spotter and they would obviously move to higher ground—presumably on the roof of the fast-food burger joint across the street.

"Hernandez, I want you at the door. It's plate glass, so they'll see us coming. We'll need a plan for that. Keith, you have my back," Drew ordered.

"Where should I go?" Kristen asked, but that only earned a glare from him.

"Jonesy, take Kristen around back. See if there's another exit and check if they have a getaway vehicle. I don't want any heroes, you understand? You find an unlocked door, you let me know. Take it slow, everyone. I'm not sure what kind of firepower they have in there, but we know it's big, whatever it is."

As if those inside had listened to his orders, gunfire erupted from the pawnshop. In less than a minute, a hail of bullets had obliterated the front of the store and the police car the Detroit Police Department had left parked there.

Kristen was amazed at how well the gun disassembled the barriers in front of it. In one moment, there was a plate glass window and in the next, it was full of holes. Spiderweb fractures raced out from the punctures before it all shattered and fell in a spectacular shower of glass.

A part of her doubted the criminals' wisdom in destroying this wall of glass, but there were two reasons this wasn't the tactical blunder she first thought. The first was that bars still blocked the entrance across the front of the store, where the glass had been only moments before. The second was what happened to the police car.

She would later be unable to describe the destruction of the vehicle without using the words 'chewed up.' To her, it looked like the car was simply devoured by bullets. Its wheels deflated and paint and glass flecked away in a fountain of destruction. One of the bullets found a home in the engine as well and steam began to spray from the now-demolished vehicle.

Its utterly wrecked state seemed to suggest that it should, by rights, have exploded.

"Consider that your warning to not go inside. These guys are packing heavy heat," Drew said and nodded for them to go around the back.

Jonesy nodded impassively as if he'd been sent for water refills instead of possibly to his death. Kristen nodded as well, but she was shaking. Suddenly, her bulletproof vest seemed less than adequate. She tightened the strap holding her helmet on and jogged after Jonesy.

They hurried around to the back of the strip mall—fortunately, the pawnshop was on the end—and only then did her companion stop.

"That's a baby-blue mint condition 1971 Dodge Charger parked out back," he said.

"Yeah, so?"

"Do you know who would rob a pawn shop with a mint condition Charger?"

"Someone who's not trying to steal much big stuff?"

"The Breaks."

"Who?"

"A local street gang. They mostly boost cars, tear 'em to pieces, and sell the parts. Last time I heard, the Breaks didn't have weapons like what these fuckers have."

"Yeah, well, last time I checked, they actually obliterated the front of a building. Should we check the door and tell Drew about the car?"

He nodded and approached the door, hugging the wall of the back of the pawnshop. Fortunately, there was no plate glass there, only good ol' one-hundred-percent opaque brick.

As they edged forward, her teammate turned his radio on.

"Drew, we have a fucking mint baby-blue Charger back here so it's probably the Breaks inside. We're checking the back door now."

He inched his hand toward the back door to the pawnshop. To both his and Kristen's surprise, the handle turned.

It wasn't locked, not even from the inside.

"Drew, the hen house is not secured," he said into his radio. There was no response, only static. "Drew?"

Jonesy took his radio from his shoulder and smacked it with his hand. Obviously, he wasn't an engineer. He seemed to know this as well and when his plan to simply thump the technology didn't work, he turned to her and told her to try her radio instead.

Hers didn't work either.

"Something's jamming the system?" she asked, as weird as it sounded. Criminals jamming radio signals was not something they ever touched on in police academy.

"We're on our own here." Jonesy smiled. He didn't look half as nervous as she felt.

"Should we go out front?" she asked and immediately wanted to kick herself for sounding like a coward.

Fortunately—or unfortunately depending on one's perspective—he didn't pick up on her fear.

"No way, Red. We have an unlocked back door. What we do is wait for the next round of assault rifle fire, the sound of breaking glass, and we go in. They're obviously focused on the front."

"But what if one of them is back here?"

"Then we eliminate the fucker. This is the Breaks we're talking about. If we were driving, I'd advise caution, but these assholes don't know a firecracker from a firefight. I don't know where they got these guns, but there ain't no fucking way that whoever gave them the arsenal trained them on how to use it properly."

More gunfire erupted from inside the building. Jonesy glanced at her. "Are we ready?"

"No!"

He ignored her and flung the door open, waited for a heartbeat, and stepped into the opening with his shotgun raised.

She regretted that she only carried a pistol, but she followed him all the same.

It took a moment for her to adjust from the bright sunlight and drab tan paint of the outside of the pawnshop to the dim fluorescents and crowded space of the interior.

They were on the other side of a freight door that opened into the back of the showroom—or whatever the hell one called the makeshift corridors made by shelves crammed with guitar amps, yard equipment, TVs, and microwave ovens. From their position, they could see out the damaged front of the shop but didn't have visuals on any hostiles.

Her teammate motioned for her to stand beside him so that when they reached the end of the little aisle they were in, they could look in both directions and cover each other. Kristen—extremely pleased with herself for reviewing the SWAT operations manuals and therefore able to understand his hand signals—moved into position. Her training and the fact that they weren't under fire yet both helped her to feel a little calmer.

She was still definitely freaking out but was now maybe at a nine thousand, five hundred percent level instead of her earlier ten thousand.

More gunfire erupted. Inside the pawnshop, it was deafeningly loud but also confirmed that the hostiles had absolutely no idea that the two of them had infiltrated the building from the rear.

Their advantage was short-lived, however. One of the gang members spun into the front of the aisle that the two used to sneak forward and leveled a massive handgun at Jonesy.

Kristen didn't have time to think, only to act. She felt a wave of protectiveness wash over her—this was her partner, her mentor, and maybe even her newest friend—and she body-checked him into a shelf.

"Damnit, Red!" he said as he bounced into the shelves and fell.

The hostile didn't seem perturbed about missing his original target. He fired his cannon of a handgun into her chest instead.

She fired her weapon and in the same moment, felt the force of the hostile's bullet strike her in the chest and tumble her forcefully.

A splash of blood confirmed that she'd hit her man, but one of the shelving racks sagged and overturned above the SWAT duo.

Not that she really noticed. The bullet felt like a freight train had pounded into her lungs. It was hard to think, let alone breathe.

"Cover your head, Red!" Jonesy shouted before he immediately disregarded his own directions and crawled on top of her. Instead of simply power tools and musical instruments falling on her, it was those plus him.

The shelves themselves connected painfully with his back and he grunted at the collision.

Apparently, the rest of the team outside had been watching. Once the shelves had fallen, she heard voices of men and women as they rushed into the pawnshop. They sounded so far away, though, and all Kristen could really hear was her own labored breathing.

"Lemar's down! Let's fucking go." That had to be one of the criminals.

Two men—Kristen thought it was two but it was hard to tell while pinned under both a man and a shelf—raced past them toward the back of the store.

As soon as they were gone, Jonesy pushed himself off her and used his back to lift the shelf. Now that the crap that had been on it was all over the floor, it wasn't particularly heavy.

That was the moment when she realized she might've cracked a rib. The skinny frame pushing on her should not have hurt nearly as much as it did. She gasped in pain.

He thrust the shelf over the other way. "Drew will be here in a minute. Tell him about the fucking car. We should've slashed the goddamn tires. That was fucking dumb of us."

"Wait…for me," she wheezed. It seemed that in addition to a possibly cracked rib, the gunshot had slowed her reaction time. He was her partner and she couldn't let him run off without her, even if all she wanted to do was put her head between her knees and breathe.

"For fuck's sake, Red. You already took a goddamn bullet for me on your first fucking week. Stay here, okay?"

"Jonesy—" Kristen gasped but he had already scrambled through the wreckage of the shop and headed to the back door.

Despite her aching chest, she shoved herself to her feet and stumbled after him.

She made it to the exit in time to see him stop firing at the retreating form of the Charger.

He reloaded his weapon as the car raced down the back of the strip mall. "The fuckers think they're smart. They knew they couldn't go this way or we'd blow their asses to kingdom come, but you better fucking believe Drew has that way blocked too." He grinned.

The blue Charger raced past the back of the tan strip mall.

Suddenly, her radio blared to life. Obviously, whatever had blocked the signals was gone.

"Hostile vehicle escaping. Should be at choke point in three… two…" Before Drew could finish his countdown, an explosion detonated at the far end of the mall. It didn't touch the getaway vehicle at all.

"Officers down. I repeat, officers down! Careful moving in. There might be more explosives."

"Those fuckers set a trap," Jonesy said as he watched the blue car turn onto the street and accelerate away, leaving the annihilated police vehicle behind it. A few wailing sirens followed, but Kristen knew they'd escape. The thought of that made her head swim.

Her teammate rounded on her. "You know you shouldn't have fucking done that, Red. I have armor, too. It's not your goddamn place to take a fucking bullet. Okay, it was brave—real fucking brave—and stupid enough for me to be impressed but it's not something that —Red?"

Kristen tried to keep up, but it was all too much. Being shot at, almost crushed, shooting someone, and actually taking a bullet finally overwhelmed her. She sat on the curb, tried to catch her breath, and only succeeded in fainting.

CHAPTER NINE

When Kristen regained consciousness, her first order of business was an attempt to protest what her boss was doing to her, but Captain Hansen was adamant. "You're bruised to high heaven and you have two ribs cracked in three places. You're on leave until you can take a breath without coughing, and that's final."

"But Captain—" She tried to argue but that only made her cough again. Having the wind knocked out of you and cracking ribs was apparently not much good for one's debate skills.

"My point exactly. You did well out there. I won't risk losing you because you're not at full strength."

"My training—"

"Can wait. Take a few days. Call me when you can hold a conversation. That'll still be too soon to come back but at least I'll know you'll be ready in a few days after that."

She took a deep breath to protest further, but it hurt so she shut up.

Captain Hansen nodded at that, pointed her to her clothes folded on a chair in the hospital room, called her a cab, and left.

Resentful, she forced herself to dress. She wasn't that hurt, other than not being able to really talk, or so she thought until she actually saw the injury. The entire left side of her chest—from her collarbone down past her breast, from sternum to armpit—was an enormous bruise of various colors.

Kristen touched it to find—big surprise—that it hurt like hell. She wisely decided to obey the captain's orders and at least not call until the bruise had mostly healed. Knowing her body, that wouldn't take long. Or she hoped so, anyway. She'd never been shot before.

Finally, she checked out of the hospital to find a cab waiting for her. He had her address but instead of agreeing to be sent home, she told the cabbie to take her to her parents' house.

The drive took about thirty minutes from the hospital nearest the pawnshop in Eastpointe to where her family lived in Dearborn.

She tipped the driver well—both for the ride and for not bothering her with any attempts at conversation when she slumped in the back seat—and entered her parents' garden.

In her mind, the home she grew up in was an archetypal Michigan suburban house and she had no problem with that.

A massive pine tree anchored the well-manicured front lawn. A small hedge of green mountain boxwood battled lilacs for dominance below the front window. The boxwoods were her father's preferred landscaping plant and the lilacs were her mom's favorite. She had always found the longstanding argument kind of cute, but currently, she found it insane to think that people could spend years arguing about the merits of various landscaping choices in the same world where people shot others and knocked shelves filled with chainsaws onto those who tried to stop them.

Kristen rang the doorbell twice in rapid succession, then once more after a moment—the family's secret ring. She stepped into the screened-in front porch, took her shoes off, and found her dad watching the Tigers on the couch.

"Krissy, sweetie! Have you come here to bust your old man? Let's hear you do the Miranda rights."

"I think I'm a few steps above that," she wheezed. It was already less painful to talk but still not easy. It mostly only hurt to take a deep breath now.

"Is that right? Did you earn some PTO or something? Well, why not get us a few brewskies and regale your old man with your first week on the force?"

She fished a few beers out of the fridge and frosty mugs from the freezer. Despite her dad working in law enforcement for years, he was not above stealing mugs from bars. "What about the game?"

"Fucking Tigers. They were up six—six goddamn runs—in the second, and now it's the ninth and they're down three."

"They could still come back." Kristen poured the beers. She poured one too fast and the foam overflowed, then froze solid as it tried to race down the outside of the ice-cold mug. As a little girl, she had always found the effect magical. She licked the outside—who was she kidding? Frozen suds would always be magical—and handed the licked mug to her dad.

"I don't give a shit if they do come back. This should've been an easy win, but sloppy play put them in a hole. Serves them right. Thanks, by the way," her dad finished sarcastically and grimaced at the tongue-print on the mug, but he didn't reach for the other one. His kids had licked his frosty mugs since they were old enough to get them from the freezer for him.

Kristen sat on the couch beside him. He muted the TV but didn't turn it off or turn to look at her—a classic Dad move that didn't faze her at all.

"How's Mom?" she asked.

"She's fine, probably wondering what SWAT's newest member is doing at her parents' house in the middle of the day."

She swallowed. "Okay, I assume Captain Hansen didn't call you."

Her dad belched. "Tell me what?"

Carefully, she put her beer down. "Dad...I was shot."

Frank Hall dropped his mug and it shattered loudly in the startled silence.

"For fuck's sake, Krissy! When? Why the fuck weren't we notified?"

"It only happened today." Kristen darted up and went to find a rag. "Some assholes tried to rob a pawn shop."

"Jesus! And you're here?" He seemed distracted and looked from her to the spilled beer as if not sure what to focus on. Kristen realized dimly that she could have given her dad a heart attack. She wisely ignored the spilled beverage and broken glass for a moment and sat again.

"Yes. It hit my Kevlar, so I'm fine. Dad, take a few deep breaths and calm down."

He nodded. "Right, yeah. Get me an aspirin, will you?"

She stood quickly and retrieved an aspirin and a glass of water. He swallowed the pill, washed it down, and leaned back on the couch. She wiped up the beer and the glass, then took her place at her dad's side.

"Well...what happened?" he asked. "And go slow, for Christ's sake."

"The important thing is that I'm fine. Okay? I am bruised fairly badly, but it should be fine in a few days." She pulled her shirt down to show him the massive bruise on her collarbone.

"Where did you get shot? In the boob or something? Krissy, you're beautiful but I don't want to see that. Show your mother."

"No, Dad, I was shot here," Kristen pointed to the place below her collarbone, only to find the bruise had shrunk from where it had been only an hour before.

"I guess I can understand why you're not freaking out," her dad said hesitantly.

"But... That's impossible. I...it was right here. I have two cracked ribs too." She felt her ribs. They still hurt, but she realized she wasn't short of breath anymore.

"It doesn't look like you were shot, Krissy. It looks like you dodged a goddamn bullet. Maybe this is a sign or whatever, like your mother says."

"A sign of what?"

"That you should ask for a different assignment. You've been on SWAT for a week and you've already been shot. There's obviously been a mistake."

"Dad, I saved my partner's life today."

"Oh, you're telling me he wasn't in a vest and you were?"

"No, of course he had a vest too, but if I hadn't acted—"

"Kristen, if you'd have been a second faster or slower, you'd be dead right now."

"I don't know why you're freaking out. I'm following in your footsteps and only trying to be a good cop like my dad."

Something came over Frank's face when she said that. A whole series of somethings really—doubt, guilt, shame, and finally, resolution when his gaze found her face again.

"Kristen…" He looked away, took a deep breath, and made himself look at her again. "I'm not your father. Not biologically, anyway."

For a moment, she felt nothing at all. This was like when Brian had told her she'd been left at their house by pixies—it was a joke, obviously—but her dad's expression didn't seem to suggest humor. Besides, jokes weren't really Frank Hall's thing.

"Mom…had an affair?"

He snorted. "Do you think she'd go out for a slice of bacon when she could have the pork roast at home?" He rubbed his potbelly.

"Dad, are you seriously saying I'm adopted?" She pushed off the couch with her beer and began to pace.

"Yeah. Well, kind of. Look. You should probably sit for this. I don't want to have to steal another pair of pint glasses. It's easier to walk out with only one."

She slammed the glass on the table and whirled on him, her hands on her hips. "What the fuck is going on? Are you telling me I'm not family?"

Frank smiled and she immediately regretted saying that. It was the same smile she'd seen when she'd first learned how to swim, or when she'd scored her first goal, and that had sent her off to prom. Whatever Frank Hall intended to say, she was certain of one thing—he was still her dad.

"No," he told her and the steady smile she knew so well never left his face. "If there's one thing I am certain of, it's that you are my family."

"Then what are you telling me? Where did I come from?"

"I honestly don't know, Kristen."

"You don't know how some random baby came into your life?"

"No, I know how we found you, but I just don't know if we're actually family. My sister Christina brought you to us. You were still so tiny so you must have been only a few days old."

Kristen couldn't speak. In fact, despite her driving need to pace, all she could do was hold onto the table and attempt to stay standing.

"She asked if we could protect you." Frank uttered a weak laugh and shook his head as he looked at her. "Your mom said yes before I could even get my head around what was happening.

"So…so I'm your niece, not your daughter?"

Her Dad—Frank? Uncle Frank? Her head was spinning—only shrugged. "I asked Christina when she'd gotten pregnant. We weren't all that close and saw each other for the holidays and sometimes talked on the phone. But still, I think she would've told me if she was knocked up, you know?"

"What did she say?"

"She didn't answer me and only told us to keep you safe. Then, as soon as she saw Marty pick you up and smile, she left."

"You never called her?"

Frank shook his head and snorted, his go-to response when he didn't want to cry. "She died in a car crash that same night. Some asshole ran her off the road—at least that's what the evidence looked like to me, an experienced fucking police officer. The official report said it was an accident. It was bullshit is what it was."

"Did you investigate?"

"I could have. I sure as shit wanted to, but Marty talked me out of it."

"Why would she do that?"

"Because she loves you, Krissy. She loved you the moment she saw your bald little head with that weird little tuft of red hair on top of it. I was ready to raise holy hell for Christina. She was scared, Krissy, damn scared. Of what, I don't know, and I wanted to find out. But your mom wouldn't have it. She said we should name you Kristen in her memory and forget all about it."

"But…but how could you? You don't even know if she was my real mom."

"Marty's your real mom," he said pleadingly as if he tried not to allow his heart to break. "She was from the moment she laid eyes on you."

"You mean she's my real mom despite the fact that she's lied to me for my entire life?" she snapped.

"We both did, Krissy. We had to. Your Aunt Christina…she was as smart as they came. She studied to be an evolutionary biologist or something—I never really understood half the shit she talked about. She worked at one of the only places that didn't shut down when Detroit hit rock bottom. Rumor was it was funded by…" He looked around as if there might be people listening in his own living room. "By dragons."

Kristen finally sat. Her dad wasn't actually her dad, and her mom wasn't her mom? Kristen was their niece or…or…something. She didn't know what to think.

"So, you can see why I've been nervous about all this police academy stuff and your assignment to SWAT," Frank said. "I think maybe your mom—that is my sister Christina—was trying to protect you from the dragons for some reason. Maybe they've found you again and are…I don't know, doing something to my little Krissy that I don't like. I think that, given what's happened, you have an opportunity to get out. Your captain will understand. Not everyone can take getting shot."

"Yeah, but I can," she yelled. While she hadn't meant to lose her temper she was unable to help herself. "You're telling me that you hid this from the world for my entire life. You let them cover up your own sister's murder and you think I should simply walk away?"

"I can't let you get hurt, Krissy."

"I'm a grown woman and I'm not even your daughter. You don't get to decide what I can and cannot do."

"But Kristen, you are our daughter. You were from the moment we took you in."

"Then why did you lie?"

"We didn't feel like we had a choice. We did it to protect you."

"Well, I don't feel like I have a choice about sticking with SWAT."

"It's not the same thing at all," he countered and his face grew red.

"Stop trying to control me." She almost screamed the cliché of how he wasn't her real dad but didn't. Instead, she burst into tears and headed to the door.

"Krissy, goddammit—Kristen!" Her dad—Frank, his name was Frank fucking Hall—yelled after her. "Kristen, come back here. Please."

Kristen shut his pleas out. Instead, she snatched up the keys to his car—a problem of the suburbs was that bars were rarely in walking distance—and got the hell out of there.

By the time she made it to the bar, the baseball game Frank had been watching was over. Normally, the Sports Bar would be full, but given that the Tigers had lost, it was mostly empty. That suited her down to the ground.

She pulled a stool out, dropped her elbows on the lacquered wood in front of her, and ordered a whiskey and a Labatt's blue to chase.

The bartender put her drinks in front of her and opened her tab. "Cheers."

After a curt nod of thanks, she swallowed the whiskey, followed by half the beer. Ugh. She should've asked for something from a higher shelf. Even with the beer to chase, the whiskey wasn't great. She ordered another from a different bottle. Her bartender grunted a "good choice" at her selection and served her the drink.

"Now there's a woman who knows how to drink," a man said and gestured at her whiskey.

"Yep, well, it is one of the body's primary functions. It's actually fucking amazing that women know how to do it as well as men when you think about it."

He obviously didn't know what to do with her rebuttal, so he smiled a little nervously. She studied him openly and tried to decide how far up his own ass she should tell him to go fuck himself.

The stranger was handsome in a roguish kind of way with short, almost white, gelled hair. He had keen eyes and what she would later describe as a pointy smile. Surprisingly, he wore a blue seersucker suit, complete with the vest but no tie—a screen-printed t-shirt hid under the shirt—and his dress shoes looked like they'd been polished moments before he'd stepped into the bar.

"Do you mind if I join you?"

Kristen wanted to tell him to buzz off, but something about him made her think he was something more than a creep trying to pick up a drunk woman. The suit, for starters. Creeps tended to wear clothes that were less…conspicuous. Also, she was something of a sucker for a British accent, even though he tried to hide his.

"Sure, have a seat, but if you think you'll get me drunk, it absolutely won't happen."

"I saw you down that whiskey. You hardly flinched. I wouldn't be surprised if you could breathe fire."

She didn't know what to make of that. It was a figure of speech, obviously—dragons were a regular touchpoint when it came to idioms as they'd shepherded human culture since the beginning, after all—but the comment coming so soon after her conversation with her dad was…well, eerie.

"Get this man two whiskeys and a Labatt's. My tab," she said.

"No, please—really, I insist."

"You can get the next round if you can make it through that."

He nodded politely and took a seat, downed the two whiskeys back to back, and sipped the Labatt's blue. It must have been a trick of the light, but she could almost see smoke pouring out his nose as he put his beer down.

"I'm Chadwick, by the way—Chadwick Kensington."

"Chadwick Kensington? You must be joking."

"I'm afraid not. It can be a bit much in this day and age and indeed, this country, but there was a time where it was as a common a name as…"

Kristen looked at him. He smiled with an eyebrow raised at her. Oh, right, duh. "Kristen Hall." She raised her beer and he did the same. "My friends call me Kristen."

"I've been trying to get my friends to call me Ken."

"Ken, I like that. But it's not working?"

"No." The man's expression soured. "They insist on Chadwick, despite it being decidedly unusual."

"Well, I'll call you Ken, Ken." She grinned and realized that the whiskey had set in.

"Much appreciated, Kristen. So, what brings you to a sports bar after the game is over?"

She pointed to the wall of whiskey.

"Ah." He nodded. "Point taken. Tony, can we trouble you for another round? My tab this time."

"Of course, Mr. Kensington." The bartender retrieved a bottle of whiskey from a cabinet and poured them each a drink in a crystal tumbler. She had no idea the bar actually had crystal, but at least she now knew that Ken had been there before. If he turned out to be a creep, the bartender would be able to corroborate his description to the police. She paused when it occurred to her that she was the police now.

They sipped their whiskey and Kristen tried not to let her face show how good it was. It was amazing that the same ingredients—in this case, grain alcohol, treated barrels, and time—could produce products of such different quality. The whiskey she had first drunk tasted like gasoline, the next like smoke, and this one tasted of fine tobacco, chocolate, and hazelnuts, with a heat that dried the mouth and left her with the taste of oatmeal smothered with brown sugar. She was happy he had put this round on his tab. That one drink of whiskey probably cost more than all she had ever drunk in her whole life in total.

"So, what brings you here?" she asked him.

"I love the feeling of bars once people have left. You can still feel the people and sense their presence, but it's not as loud." He chuckled.

She decided she really didn't know what to make of this guy but thought perhaps his appearance began to make more and more sense. The kind of guy who snubbed his nose at cheap whiskey, wore seersucker suits, and complained about noisy bars seemed like the kind who would have his ass kicked on a fairly regular basis. She was certain of one thing though—she didn't feel threatened by him. Something about him was simply…calming.

"Feel their presence, I get that." She took another sip of her whiskey.

"How do you mean?"

"Have you ever thought you know someone, only to find out you really don't and that they've lied to you for all the time you've known them?"

"I must admit, I know the sensation. Tell me, is it friends or family bothering you?"

Kristen scoffed at that. "Neither? Both? I don't know anymore, honestly. My family situation suddenly became more…complicated. Okay, I love my dad, but it turns out he's not… Well, let's say he's not the man I thought he was."

"Fathers rarely are. They're only human, after all…mostly."

She nodded. "You have a point, I guess. He's not a monster."

"Then consider yourself lucky. My father is—by virtually every definition of the word—as monstrous as they come, but at least he made me who I am."

After a moment's thought, she shook her head. She didn't like it, but what he said struck home. She was who she was because of Frank, and she liked who she was—well, mostly. For one thing, she didn't like how hard her first week of SWAT had been. Things were supposed to be easy for her but her last week had definitely not been that.

"What do you do for work, Ken?" she asked, hoping to change the subject. She could already see she'd have to apologize to Frank, and she'd have to talk to her mom too.

"Ah, Americans…never one to bandy about with simple conversation when we could talk personal economics."

"Sorry. I didn't mean to make you uncomfortable."

Ken waved her apology away. "Please, it's fine. I've grown up with means. My father made very savvy investments a long time ago, so I've never had to work. It's a defense mechanism of the wealthy to avoid talking about wealth. If you like, I could regale you with tales of me sailing my yacht around the horn of Africa or of parties with prestigious English playwrights."

"I doubt I'd know who the hell you were talking about. I don't know any playwrights."

"Oh, I'm sure you've at least heard of one or two of Bill's plays, but that's fine, I'd rather hear about what you do for a living."

"I'm on SWAT."

"SWAT?" Kristen couldn't tell if he was impressed or was asking for clarification.

"Special Weapons and Tactics. You know, the police in the armored vans with the big guns."

"Yes, I've seen the television programs. Is it really like it seems? Seizing caches of weapons and stopping robberies?"

She shrugged. "I don't really know. I've only been on the team for a week."

"Ah." He sounded slightly disappointed. "So only paperwork, then?"

Her smirk crept in unbidden. "Well, earlier today…"

For some reason, she trusted him and told him all about her last week of work. The tale covered her hostile team members, her gives-no-shits boss, the headache-inducing training sessions, and taking a bullet at the end of it all. Putting it all together in one half-drunk explanation made her realize exactly how crazy it all was. She'd been there a week—a week—and so much had already happened. It made her feel like she'd slept through the police academy and indeed, most of her life.

"I honestly don't know why it's so hard," she finished. "I've always been a star athlete. I did well in school, and for whatever reason, SWAT is somehow way harder than all that put together."

Ken chuckled. It was a pleasant, polite kind of chuckle that mostly came through his nose. "One thing I've learned from my…er, position is the value of patience. Maybe you'll need more than one week to be as good as the people who have been there for years."

"Yeah, well, when you put it like that, it sounds obvious. I guess I need to keep training."

"Sometimes, it's hard to see what's obvious in one's own life." He shrugged. "We often need a different perspective—a dragon's eye view, as it were."

"Yeah…the view from above," she said and lost herself for a moment while she stared at the bottom of her glass and the amber liquor therein before she downed it. "Tony?" she raised her glass for a refill.

"Is that wise, Kristen?" her companion asked.

"I thought you were trying to get me drunk. Alcohol is a necessary ingredient in that formula."

"I thought you'd decided you need to keep training. A bar isn't exactly the best place to hone your skills."

"My dad was a cop for thirty years and he knew how to drink."

He raised an eyebrow at her. "I don't mean to speak out of turn, but isn't this the man you say has lied to you? Are you sure you wish to follow his advice on drinking, of all things?"

"He's still my dad."

"But, unless you left out a crucial detail, he was never on SWAT."

"What's your point?"

"Me? I have no point. I merely wonder if your father found his job easy."

"Of course he didn't find it easy. He was a cop. In Detroit. He used to say if he was only shot at once, it was a good day."

"And yet you expect to master SWAT—a level of intensity your own father never made it to—in a week and with the help of whiskey?" He looked tactfully into his own glass of whiskey before he finished it quickly. "Because if you are, the least I can do is get you another round."

"No. You know what? You're right. Tony, let me close my tab and call me a cab while you're at it."

The bartender nodded.

"You know what, Chadwick Kensington? Thank you."

Ken smiled. "For what, pray tell?"

"For reminding me that this is what I've looked for my whole life. I've never backed down from anything before and there's no point in starting now. I've been there a week and already took a bullet for my partner. That's not so bad."

"Indeed not."

"I'll head to my parents' house, hope to hell my mom and dad are asleep, and pass out on the couch. Tomorrow morning, I'll run the four miles here to get the car and burn off the hangover I'm sure will come."

"An admirable plan. I believe that I—having a job far less demanding than yours—will have another whiskey and wish you the very best of luck."

Kristen nodded and left the bar. Somehow, his statement made her goals that much clearer. There were people in this world who had an easy life—she'd had evidence of one such entitled person seated beside her—but she didn't want to be one of them. She'd worked hard to be successful for her entire life and had no intention to quit now that she finally found something that was an actual challenge.

Her taxi pulled up and she gave the man directions and returned to her parents' house. She found her dad passed out on the couch with a dozen beer bottles on the coffee table in front of him.

It reminded her that she could do better than that. For Frank's sake, she had to.

At about the same time that Kristen fell asleep in her old bedroom, Chadwick Kensington finished his second whiskey, tipped the bartender handsomely for continuing to care for the bottle after all these decades, and stepped out of the bar.

The night was cool and absolutely perfect, with a clear sky and tendrils of mist that hugged the street despite there not being any grates spewing vapor from Detroit's steam tunnels nearby. He considered calling a cab himself. Even after all these years of the vehicles being around, he still found it exhilarating to race along the streets like a mouse with wheels. But the night was far too beautiful to not take to the air.

He stepped into an alley, looked at the sky, and discarded his glamor. First, his head changed. His white hair grew into white horns and his skin filled with pockmarks that separated into blue scales. Then, his fingers elongated, knuckle by knuckle, and black claws grew where nails had been. His clothing changed at the same time as his skin, fissured into scales. and expanded as his body grew from the size of a man to something that could eat a man. Finally, at his full size, he spread his wings and leapt into the night sky.

Briefly, he considered flying past the Hall girl's house to ensure that she was sleeping in preparation for another day of training but decided against it. If she saw a dragon flying through the night it might change her immediate priorities, something he didn't want to do and especially not after how well his manipulations had gone.

After speaking to the girl, he thought the others were right. If they were, her priorities—and indeed, her entire life—would change soon enough.

CHAPTER TEN

The door flew open and thunked against the inside wall. Kristen wasted no time, rushed in, and scanned to her left and then right using the light mounted on her gun to pierce the darkness.

"Clear!"

She moved to the next room. "This is SWAT. Open the door."

When she received no answer, she kicked the door open.

"Clear!"

In the next room, a hostile held a woman hostage with a gun to her head.

Without hesitation, she shot him between the eyes.

"Now just a fucking second."

The voice had come from her radio and she almost jumped out of her skin. She hadn't expected it as she knew it was after hours and she was alone in one of SWAT's training buildings.

After a quick, deep breath, she pressed the talk button on her radio. "Who's there?"

"Who the fuck do you think is there? It's me, Jones."

"Jonesy?"

"Yeah, Red, fucking Jonesy."

Kristen scanned the room, moved quickly to the kitchen, and

checked there but couldn't locate him. She'd cleared the house, after all, so should have seen him. "Where are you?"

"I'm outside. Do you think I'm hiding in the kitchen cabinets or some shit? Come on. I'm not an idiot, especially not after the way you've put down cardboard cutouts."

"How can you see me?"

"For fuck's sake. They're called binoculars. Have you heard of them?"

Her face flushed and no doubt turned as red as her hair. She made her way out of the house to where Jonesy walked toward her from somewhere out in the parking lot. Exactly as he'd said, he had a pair of binoculars around his neck.

"What are you doing here?" she asked.

"I could ask you the same question."

"Drew and Captain Hansen are right. I'm inexperienced and I don't have a right to be here like the rest of you. I don't know why I have this opportunity, but I don't intend to waste it. I'll run these drills until its muscle memory. What about you?"

He shrugged and managed a half-grin. "Sometimes, I like to come out here and shoot the windows out." He gestured at the empty apartment block that loomed in the dark.

"But that's police property."

"I know. That's what makes it perfect. They always think it's some stupid kids taking potshots." He laughed. "Speaking of which, you can't take a shot like that."

"At a building in the dark?" She had lost what he was talking about.

"No, that last shot you took inside. Someone had a hostage with a gun to their head. You can't pop 'em between the eyes."

"Protocol says if you have a shot, you take it." She was quite sure of that because she'd read the manual anytime she'd stopped her evening of training for a break.

"Yeah. You're right—technically. But you still can't take that shot. For starters, a hostile will see you kick the door in and all he's gonna have to do is pull that trigger to end it."

"Which is why I need to be faster."

"I admire your resolve, really. I totally fucking do, but you still can't take that shot. Even if you get to be as good a shot as Butters, you still can't."

"Why not?"

"Because even if you make it every goddamn time, you'll still get a hostage covered in some asshole's brains, which is a fucking nightmare of paperwork if there ever was one."

Kristen laughed at that. "Are you saying I should let a man go because of paperwork?"

"I mean you should think about it. If your choices are to take a shot and possibly kill some poor woman or make the shot and cover her in brains, you have to try some other options."

"Like what?"

"SWAT's not about one person doing the right thing. It's about a team effort. You can't ever take a building by yourself. That's like a wolf running solo. That shit doesn't happen."

She shook her head. "I know. I know you're right, but I don't know what to do. I need to be better, but I can't ask people to stay after work and help me train. I'll simply have to continue to run the drills on my own until I'm decent."

"That's a fucking waste of time and we both know it."

Finally, she sighed and nodded. He was right. This wouldn't really work.

"Give me a second to get a vest on and we'll run some drills together."

Kristen looked quickly at him. He merely shrugged and cocked an eyebrow. "Jonesy, that would mean so much to me."

"Just shut the fuck up, okay? I'm not doing it for you. I'm doing it for that lady who you'll cover in brains."

"That's still kind of noble."

"Ah, fuck you," he retorted. "I told you it was a mountain of paperwork. Besides, if I can teach you to not fuck up so much, you won't make me look bad by taking more goddamn bullets to the chest that you have no right to take."

"Thanks, Jonesy."

The man waved her gratitude away with a dismissive gesture. "Seriously, don't mention it. I… Look, you have talent, okay? It's obvious to Drew and it's obvious to me. The way you've approached all this makes it damn obvious you want to graduate with honors or whatever."

"SWAT's not like the academy."

Jonesy smirked. "See? You're learning already. The point, is I think you have what it takes. You were shot, but instead of tucking your tail between your legs and quitting to go be an accountant, you chose to put in extra hours. That shows resolve."

They ran drills together after that and he set the house up with different scenarios. It was way more useful to her than her doing it on her own. For starters, she didn't know where every hostile would be. Plus, with him beside her, every mistake she made was corrected with enough profanity to make her remember to not do it again.

"For fuck's sake, Red. Don't kick a door open and simply stand there. Are you waiting for some asshole to give you another one?"

"Jesus Christ on the cross, do you think every damn person without a gun is innocent? You were shot in the back by an old lady packing heat in her purse. And don't give me that 'she was an old lady,' shit. I've seen any number of men shot by old bitches. If you bust in somewhere, you make sure every damn person gets on the fucking floor. But don't let her break her hip in the process."

"That was a test, and you fucking failed. If you find a suspicious package with wires sticking out of it, you don't go MacGyver on that shit. You call Hernandez in."

After each drill, they'd do it again. Jonesy really seemed to know what he was doing because he worked in each mistake she'd made to another drill but never the one immediately following. As a result, she had to continually absorb his profanity-laced advice and apply it not only to the next mission but all the following ones.

They worked that way for a few hours until he claimed she had begun to lag, although she'd seen him panting when they'd descended the stairs of the apartment block.

"Let's call this shit a night. Your form's starting to slip, and you need to be fresh for tomorrow. Go drink some water and get to bed."

"Do you want to go get some food?" Kristen asked.

"Ain't nowhere gonna be open this late."

"I was thinking White Castle. I skipped dinner."

He looked at her for a moment and finally shrugged. "Sure, let's do it, but don't order any fucking French fries. That shit's only fat and carbs. Get a couple of burgers if you're hungry. I learned that shit from watching that fat-ass Butterball. He's practically made of French fries and soda. Eat lunch with him for a week and it'll change your life."

She nodded sagely as if this advice were every bit as valuable as how to properly sweep a building for hostiles.

They caravanned to the nearest White Castle—she had noticed one on the way over and had thought about it for way too long—ordered their food at the drive-through, and drove a few more blocks until they looked out across the Detroit River at the lights of Canada's illuminated skyline.

"Holy shit, you really took my advice," he said as he sat on the curb beside her. He took two burgers from his bag.

Kristen had ordered eight. "I get hungry."

The man nodded and looked like he wanted to say something else, but when she began to virtually inhale her food, he shut up. Still, it was obvious from his face that he'd never seen a woman eat the way she did. She merely smiled. At least in that particular way, she would always be a Hall. No one could eat faster than her family—no one.

"It's weird to think that across that water is a country that's not run by humans," she said.

Her companion shrugged. "Eh. Our country is hardly run by humans, at least that's what I think. The fucking dragons have pulled our strings for centuries without us even knowing it. At least in Canada, it's common knowledge that the dwarves are in control. I think the weird part is that right now, we're looking south across a river into Canada."

She glanced at Jonesy, who munched busily on his second burger.

By this point, she had already eaten five. "Jones, thank you for this. Seriously, I really mean it."

He shook his head and looked decidedly uncomfortable. "I'm not trying to get into your pants or anything, Red, so calm the fuck down. I don't even like you—fucking upshot academy geek who thinks she can simply walk in here and join my damn team—but well, I'm a cop too, right? I'm only doing my part to make sure you don't get anyone killed."

"Well, whatever your motivation, it means a lot to me."

His expression frozen in a half-scowl, he lobbed the last bite of his burger into the river. "I'll get the fuck out of here before this shit gets any more like a goddamn Hallmark special. And look—don't call me Jones, okay? Everyone's gonna start thinking we're friends or some shit. Call me Jonesy like the rest of those assholes."

"You got it, Jonesy."

Even that seemed to be too heartfelt for him as he only sneered once more at her, slid into his car, and drove away.

Kristen smiled before she started on her next burger. The man was a grouch, but he wouldn't have bothered if he didn't care. And if he believed in her, she knew she could do this.

Now, if she could only get Hernandez off her case…

CHAPTER ELEVEN

Drew burst into the lounge and his precipitous entry made those who'd already drunk their coffee jump. Those who hadn't scowled. "All right, everyone. Strap your boots on and get to the van. We have a bomb threat."

"Fuck, yes!" Hernandez pumped her fist in the air.

Kristen had completed a few days of high-intensity training and Jonesy had appeared every night to help her. This would be her first contact with hostiles since she'd been shot.

"Who's under threat?" the skinny sergeant asked. He'd yet to have his coffee. "Because it might help them to think about how badly they need SWAT for an extra five minutes."

"A payday loan place. There's been a hotrod seen nearby, so we think it might be the Breaks again, even though this shit doesn't fit their MO. Why are you still standing? If you need coffee, take it black and get in the fucking van. If you're not loaded up in ninety seconds, I'll replace everything in this room with decaf. Now move." Their team leader's tone brooked no argument.

Everyone complied hastily. Jonesy drained his coffee, while Hernandez and Keith pushed past on their way out the door. Kristen assumed that Beanpole and Butters were already outside.

She stood quickly and turned to the door.

"Not you, Hall. You're staying here."

"What? No way! I've been training."

"Not with bombs, you haven't. We don't need you. Plus, you were shot less than a week ago. I'm sure you're still as sore as hell. It'd be better for you to wait here."

"I'm fine, really—my bruises are all healed, look." She yanked the collar of her shirt to down show him her lack of bruises.

He put a hand up so he wouldn't see the skin below her neck. "Jesus, Hall, keep your shirt on. You're grounded. That's it."

"I can help."

Jonesy stepped past her. "You wanna help, Red? Fix us a nice fucking lunch. Watching Hernandez defuse bombs always gets me hungry."

Kristen felt the words like a slap to the face. She thought Jonesy had her back and shot him a resentful glance when he walked past and she caught his eye. He mouthed the words, *not yet. Just wait.*

She was pissed because she had trained hard, but if he thought she should wait, she could sit this one out. After all, Drew was right. She didn't know anything about bombs.

So, as much as it rankled, she watched them go. Orders were orders, she told herself, but that made her think.

Jonesy had told her to fix lunch. What if she made her mom's famous chicken cacciatore as a surprise?

Her first step was to tune her radio to her team's frequency—she needed to make sure they were okay—before she poked her head in the captain's office.

"Captain Hansen, is it all right if I fix lunch for everyone?"

The woman didn't so much as look up from whatever form currently held her attention. "Whatever you want, Hall. As long as your paperwork's up to date and you don't burn the place down, I don't really care."

That, she decided, could be taken as a vote of confidence. If the captain was worried about her new recruit not knowing what she was doing, she surely would have given her a task to do or something to study—or she still hoped she would simply wash out. She tried not to think too much about that possibility.

Instead, she hurried to the store, purchased the chicken, pasta, and ingredients for the sauce, and set to work.

As she chopped the onions, garlic, celery, and beets for the sauce — her mom used beets for it, right? She couldn't remember—she listened to her team over the radio.

By the time they'd reached the payday loans store, any sign of the hotrod that had driven around was long gone. The team set up a perimeter and Drew told Butters and Beanpole to keep an eye out, but neither saw any sign of the vehicle.

Hernandez made quick work of the bomb and volubly insulted whoever had made it over the radio the entire time. Although once she'd defused it, she did admit that it contained enough explosives to level a city block. Drew was pissed at that and began to lay into her for risking her life instead of letting the bomb squad handle it. She simply continued to assert that the device was so poorly put-together, it probably wouldn't have detonated, even if she hadn't defused it. With no other leads to follow and no sign of any hostiles, the team headed back to the station.

It would be close, but she had enough time to finish the meal.

She removed the chicken from the oven. It was a little…darker than when her mom made it, but it had only been in the oven for a few minutes so it couldn't have burned. She boiled the pasta next but was distracted by sauce—she couldn't seem to get the balance of spices perfect—so by the time she turned to the pasta again it was cooked well beyond *al dente*. Well, that was merely a weird preference her mom had. She thought the meal smelled good, and that was what mattered.

By the time her team returned, she had the meal plated. A breaded chicken breast atop a bed of pasta and freshly made sauce awaited each member of her team.

"The parmesan cheese." She remembered the final detail and dusted everyone's plate hastily as she heard them come down the hall.

"Did something die in here?" Hernandez entered the lounge, her nose wrinkled at the smell.

"No, ha-ha." Kristen smiled. "I fixed lunch. My mom's famous chicken cacciatore."

"Blackened chicken, huh?" Butters pushed past Hernandez at the mention of food. "Normally, I think that's better for catfish and whatnot, but I'll try anything once, especially if it's an heirloom recipe." He settled at the table and eyed his plate.

"It's a good thing we didn't stop at that diner, huh, Jonesy?" Keith nodded at the sergeant.

"What the fuck ever, rookie. Let's get a sense of Red's culinary prowess before we insult Louie's. They have the best damn corned beef in the motor city, I'm telling you." Jonesy sat and scrutinized his plate with suspicion.

Beanpole and Drew sat down without comment, although Beanpole did poke his noodles and raise an eyebrow. She realized she had over-cooked them a little because even she knew they weren't supposed to fall apart like that.

"How's our health insurance?" Hernandez said as she finally sat.

"It's fine, why?" their leader said.

"Because if I get sick from this white bitch's weird fucking cooking, I want to make sure I'm covered."

Kristen forced a smile. The woman hadn't even tried it.

Butters attempted to fill a fork with pasta but had a little difficulty. It really was overdone. She could at least recognize that, but it should still taste good and that was what mattered.

"Mmm..." The rotund man chewed. "You know, I don't think I've had pasta sauce with both chili powder and cinnamon."

Jonesy laughed uproariously at that. "That's the worst fucking thing I've ever heard him say about any food he's ever eaten."

"It's not that bad..." Beanpole took a bite of the chicken. "Although how you managed to burn the pork and leave it cool in the center is um...impressive."

"She said it was chicken, not pork," Keith pointed out.

Beanpole spat his food out. "Yeah, yeah...that explains the color."

"Drew, I think her culinary skills are far more dangerous than taking her with us on a fucking mission." Jonesy laughed again. He made no attempt at all to eat his food.

"Seriously though." Hernandez nodded. "I defused enough explosives to bring the bridge down from here to Canada, but there's no fucking way to make this plate safe."

"Okay, okay, cut her some slack," Drew said. Kristen smiled. At least someone liked her cooking. "The chicken must've been spoiled or something."

Her face dropped. She'd just bought it.

"All in favor of going to Louie's?" Jonesy raised his hand.

The rest of the team did as well like a table of third-graders voting on who liked pudding more than Brussel sprouts.

Everyone stood and headed to the door. She tried not to let her shoulders slump, but she felt dejected. It seemed like the ultimate failure that she couldn't even fix lunch for her team. They'd never accept her. Well, at least she could clean up. That was the job her mom had always left for her.

She cleared their plates, wiped her chicken cacciatore into the trash, and started on the dishes.

"Hey, what are you doing?" Drew asked. Everyone else had left the room.

"Cleaning." She tried not to let her bad mood come through but she was certain she'd failed at that too.

"Worry about all that later. The team's going for lunch."

"You mean…me too?"

"Yeah, of course. You're on the team, aren't you?"

Kristen went to lunch with a smile so wide that both Hernandez and Jonesy made sure to insult it multiple times during the meal.

CHAPTER TWELVE

It was impossible to fall into a routine working for SWAT. The day to day demands of the job were simply too varied, and yet Kristen did her best to adapt to her new life.

Days were spent training—and training hard—while nights were spent working out and honing the skills she needed her body to understand without thought. Of course, no schedule was perfect when part of one's job description was to pile into a van and confront assholes with weapons. Still, she became used to transitioning from break-room banter to life or death situations as well as anyone could adjust to that kind of situation.

The constant need to be ready to spring into action certainly made her more appreciative of the days when that didn't happen. Of course, the down days were predictably spent inside sweltering, ramshackle apartment buildings and practicing breaking into rooms.

"Kristen, you take point on this one. We have a hostile who's taken one of our officers hostage. He knows he's surrounded so there's no point in going quietly into the dark." Drew's voice crackled over the radio.

She gestured for Butters and Beanpole to watch exits. Her sign language had improved along with all her other skills. She told Hernandez to force the door and readied herself to save the massive teddy bear they used as a hostage.

"Gee, I would, but all my supplies were left at the base," the demolitions expert protested blandly.

"Time's wasting, Kristen. What do you do?" The team leader had obviously planned this.

A snarky retort was tempting but she wasted no more time. With a grunt, she kicked the door and splintered the wood around the two deadbolts that had locked it.

Before the door had even swung wide, she was in the room with her weapon raised. "Living room's clear. Jonesy, get in here."

"I'm trying. Red—waiting for the sawdust to clear."

She waited for a few heartbeats and as soon as she heard his footsteps, she moved forward. They cleared the kitchen and started on the hallway. She kicked the first bedroom door open and it catapulted off its hinges.

"Holy shit, Red."

"Keep up, Jonesy." She moved on to the next room.

"If you come in here, I'll blow the teddy bear's goddamn brains out! Cotton stuffing all over the ceiling—do you want to live with that?" Keith hollered through the door. He played the part of the hostile and did a damn good job. He even worked a trace of terror into his voice. Drew had said that was the most dangerous thing to hear in a hostile's voice. Fear made someone unpredictable.

From his voice, though, she could tell he stood almost directly behind the door.

That was his first mistake.

Before anyone could say anything else, she spun into a roundhouse kick and the door careened into the room. She'd already tested the hinges on the last one and found them flimsy, so she had a fairly good sense of what she could do with this one.

"Ah! Shit!" her teammate cursed from under the door.

Kristen lunged forward until she was on top and effectively pinned him beneath it.

"Nice try, but—" Before Drew could finish his sentence, she tucked into a barrel roll, snatched a pillow up from the bed, and hurled it to where she'd heard his voice come from.

A muffled *whump* confirmed that the pillow had struck him in the face and in the next second, she reached him. She grasped one of his arms, wrenched it behind his back, and attempted to take hold of the other.

"Yeah, right, you redheaded bitch." He thrust an elbow at her face.

The team leader had said he believed that insulting her was an integral part of training because hostiles tended to hate cops, so it was good that she got used to it.

She agreed wholeheartedly. Being called a bitch made any guilt she might have felt for punching him in the ribs as she dropped and dodged his elbow evaporate.

He grunted at the blow, so she released the arm, then—in one of her brother Brian's favorite moves—threw the man back over her outstretched leg and knocked his legs out from under him. He sprawled in an ungainly heap and—as the cherry on top—she drew her handgun and aimed it in his face.

Drew nodded and started to smile.

Before she could question it, Keith hammered a chair onto her back. He obviously hadn't held back at all because it splintered into pieces on her athletic frame.

The force of the blow made her stumble but she caught herself using Drew's body instead of the ground, which earned another grunt from the man.

Kristen snagged one of the chair legs and spun to whip it into her attacker's body. Or, at least, that was what she'd planned but instead, she caught him in the face.

"Ah!" he cried at the moment of impact and staggered back, tripped on the broken door, and crashed into the bed.

"Oh, my God—Keith, I'm so sorry!" she spluttered, finally unsure of what to do. She didn't want to abandon the drill but she could see him holding his nose while blood streamed. Quite obviously, she'd hit him way harder than she'd intended to.

"Ith fine, ith fine," he said, speaking through his mouth as he pinched his nose and attempted to stop the flow of blood. "Thith ith what I get for improvithing."

She braced herself for another strike from Drew, but none was forthcoming.

The team leader merely pushed himself up from the ground—groaning as he did so, which made her feel way more proud than anyone should for punching their boss in the ribs—and told them to call off the practice session.

"Holy fucking shit, Red. That was goddamn incredible." Jonesy nodded as he surveyed the wreckage she had left behind her. It was fairly impressive—three broken doors, a splintered chair, and two injured officers.

"Try not to break anyone's nose next time," Hernandez said, and Kristen frowned. Even after all these months training together, the woman still hadn't shown her any kindness besides that one time in the locker room. "Unless it's Jonesy's. Someone's gotta snap that thing back to normal."

She grinned and relaxed. From Hernandez, that was basically a hug and a pat on the back.

"Thorry about the chair," Keith mumbled, still pinching the bridge of his nose.

"Don't apologize," Drew said and rubbed his rib where Kristen had punched him. "Hostiles often improvise, and it's not like you hurt her. Right, Kristen?"

"I was lucky." She shrugged. "That chair must've been fairly old."

The other team members shared a look that said the chair was definitely not old.

"Luck doesn't have anything to do with it. You've trained damn hard, and it shows. You're faster and stronger than any woman I've ever met," Drew said.

"Any woman?" Hernandez interjected. "I've never seen anyone—dick or no dick—fell our fearless leader with a rib punch."

He tried not to smile at that but failed miserably. "Yeah, well, I guess Hernandez is right about that. I've never seen anyone outside a wrestling ring stay standing after having a chair smashed on their back."

Kristen tried to look modest. "I told you guys I used to play sports."

"Bullshit." Jonesy shook his head. "You've put in extra hours with me every damn night—we can stop that and switch to simply getting beers by the way—and you've studied too. You're better with the fucking hand signals than I am."

Hernandez snorted. "Everyone's better with the hand signals than you are."

"Yeah? How's this for a hand signal?" He extended his middle finger and stuck it in the woman's face.

"One of my favorites. Do you want me to snap it off? You could tape it to your crotch and watch your dick double in size."

"Enough, you two." Drew motioned at them to cut it out. "The fact is, you've improved. I'll start having you take point instead of Jonesy," he said.

"Oh, come on. Really?" the sergeant protested.

"I'm surprised you're complaining, to be honest. But you're right, fair's fair. Keith, grab that chair and smash it over Jonesy's back. If you can stay standing, we'll all know Kristen still has much to learn."

"As long as we know she's on point because she likes getting shot and having chairs broken over her. I have no fucking problems with being partnered with a meat shield."

"Thanks, Jonesy," she said. Like Hernandez, his compliments didn't tend to sound like compliments but after a few months, she had learned to recognize them.

Butters' voice spoke over the radio. "I hate to break up the lovefest, but we're wanted back at the office. It looks like our little star has a visitor."

"Roger. We're heading down. Get the car running and the AC blasting," Drew ordered.

As Kristen descended the steps of the apartment block, she beamed. She'd overcome the first challenge—proving herself to her team. Now, it was time for the altogether more difficult task of stopping criminals who wanted to shoot her instead of slow her down with chairs.

CHAPTER THIRTEEN

When Kristen returned to the office, she immediately headed to the showers. She knew she'd done well in that last session, but that didn't mean it wasn't hard work that made her sweat enough to soak her clothes. But before she could make it to the locker room, Captain Hansen's voice echoed through the station from her office. "Hall, get in here."

With a grimace—but determined to continue her so far almost perfect day—she obeyed the order.

She entered the captain's office and immediately paused to take in the two strangers. Their presence alone was unusual, but even odder was the fact that one of them sat in Captain Hansen's chair while the other—even more baffling—was smoking.

"Hall, meet our guests, Mr Lyra and Mrs Damos," Hansen said. Despite having someone else in her seat, she seemed like her usual herself.

"A pleasure to meet you, Kristen Hall," Mr Lyra drawled from the captain's chair. He wore a black suit with a silver tie, and—the weirdest thing of all—a silk shirt with elaborate cuffs and frills on the chest that ruffled from beneath his jacket. She thought he looked like a business pirate, for want of a better expression.

Mrs Damos nodded in acknowledgment, "We've heard so much about you." She wore a garish purple skirt suit with a red scarf. Either color was far too bright for the SWAT offices but together, they almost made her eyes hurt. "Captain, an ashtray?"

"Yeah, I have your damn ashtray right here," Captain Hansen said, brought the wastepaper basket over, and held it while the woman knocked the ash from her cigarette.

Kristen had no doubt that the two guests were dragons. No one else dressed this way, for one thing. Plus, their slow and almost lethargic movements belied a hidden power. Then there was the fact that her boss allowed one of them to sit in her chair. Dragons had an aura that made most people obey their desires. Even those with strong will like Captain Hansen obeyed, albeit with an attitude and her share of grumbling. That was simply her normal demeanor.

None of this impressed her, though. "What the hell can I do for you?"

The visitors shared a look and a smile that thoroughly pissed her off.

"We simply came for an update on your progress," Mr Lyra said and put his feet lazily on the desk.

The captain glared balefully at him, but she said nothing.

"Do you mean you came to tell me what the hell is going on?" She leveled a glare at him.

"Whatever do you mean?" Mrs Damos asked and moved closer. Her high heels—that matched her scarf—clacked irritatingly.

"You're dragons, obviously. No one else wears frills and whatever the hell it is that you're wearing." She gestured to the woman's bright colors. "So, are you here to tell me why you put me on SWAT?"

"But Kristen…" When the visitor smiled, it became apparent that her teeth were weird too. Not unattractive or anything but more like flawless and sharp. "We didn't have a thing to do with your placement here. It was your hard work at the academy and the tests you passed that earned your place on the force. We're simply here to inquire as to how you're doing. The tests aren't always accurate, unfortunately."

"She's doing well," Captain Hansen volunteered, unable to resist the dragon's request for information. "Better than expected, in fact. Hall's performance in training is almost up to the minimum standards. And quite frankly, I don't expect that from recruits who are dumped on my team without my permission." She paused for a moment to glare at the dragons. It was odd to see her still trying to express herself despite the power the creatures had over her. She ostensibly treated them like the intrusive, unwelcome guests they were, and yet she didn't protest Mr Lyra's feet on her desk nor Mrs Damos smoking in her office.

"Well, I suppose that answers all our questions, then. Mr Lyra, shall we?"

"Indeed, Mrs Damos, we shall."

With that, he removed his feet from the desk, stood, and smoothed his suit. Mrs Damos extinguished her cigarette on the bottom of one of her high heels—and demonstrated an incredible sense of balance—placed the butt in the wastepaper basket, and preceded him out.

"Hall, the door," Captain Hansen ordered as she reclaimed her chair.

"Yes, sir." Kristen closed the door to the captain's office.

"I fucking hate those things. Being around them is like being in a damn fog. You seemed all right, though."

"Sir?"

"Cut the shit, Hall. Who the hell are you really and what the hell did you do to attract this kind of attention? I've never had a dragon in my office before and now, I've had two. Spill it."

"I honestly don't know." She tried not to shrug but failed at that endeavor. "I've told you everything I know. I met one at a concert, he sent me to their testing facility, then the academy, and then here."

"So it's a mystery?"

"Yes, sir, I suppose so."

"I fucking hate mysteries." The captain took a deep breath and exhaled through her nose. "And I don't like dragons or anyone else meddling with my people."

"Sir, does that...am I one of your people?"

"Oh, come on, Hall, you've been with us for months now. You've taken a bullet for Jonesy and somehow turned Hernandez to your side. Of course you're one of my people."

Kristen grinned. She honestly couldn't help herself. "Hernandez said she likes me?"

Captain Hansen snorted. "Of course not. With Hernandez, it's more what she doesn't say."

"Of course, sir."

"Your record speaks for itself. You've done well here, but with these dragons… I don't want the rug pulled out from under me."

"Me neither, sir."

"Well, I guess we don't have any choice but to press on, for now. You're dismissed, Hall."

"Yes, sir!" She turned to go but stopped when the captain cleared her throat.

"Oh, and Kristen? Take a shower. You stink."

"Our presence didn't affect her at all," Mrs Damos said once they made their way out of the station.

"Indeed not," Mr Lyra replied.

"That's an indication that she is one of us."

"Which is what I have said since she took our tests."

"The results of those were inconclusive."

"An inconclusive result means she's not obviously human, which indicates that she must be a dragon."

"Pah!" His companion snorted. "There have been false positives before. An inconclusive result means only that. Even if she is one of us, where did she come from? How did she come to be?"

"You ask the questions I have been asking. Do not expect me to have the answers now." He growled his annoyance. It was a low sound more fitting to a tiger or a bear than the shape of a man, but the sound had not been made by a man at all.

"Questions swirl around her like smoke in the wind," Mrs Damos muttered.

"Which is why the police academy was the proper choice for her. We were able to monitor her easily, and she has excelled there as few humans do."

"And you stand by your decision to put her into SWAT?"

"Of course, I do!" He did not like being questioned. "Already, she can resist our aura. The more dangers she survives, the more her powers will manifest. If she is a dragon, her abilities will not let her die, bleeding into the gutter like a common animal."

"And if you're wrong? If the tests were inconclusive simply because she's more gifted than most of her kin?"

"No one will grieve over the loss of one more human."

Mrs Damos nodded. Trial by fire was effective at cooking meat if nothing else.

Together, the two dragons shed their human glamor and took to the sky in their true forms—a purple dragon with claws of red and a great black dragon with silver ridges that caught the wind and propelled him high above the city. The pair had ruled from the shadows since it had been founded by their kind centuries before.

CHAPTER FOURTEEN

When Kristen left the captain's office, Jonesy was waiting for her. "What the fuck was that about, Red?"

She pushed past him. "If I knew, I'd tell you."

He fell into step behind her. "Ah, come on, Red. Were those two motherfucking dandies friends of yours?"

"No."

"Family, then? Perhaps a former boss?"

She reached the break room where most of the team had gathered. "I'm telling you, I don't know."

"Don't know what?" Butters asked.

"Who those two puffs were who just left," Jonesy explained.

"You must have some idea," the sniper said. "Even their outfits demand a story."

"Dragons?" Beanpole ventured.

"Yeah, probably." She forced herself to take a deep breath.

"Dragons, huh? And what the fuck did they want with you? Fashion advice?" Hernandez grinned.

"I was telling Jonesy I don't know what it was all about, okay? I tried to ask them why they put me on SWAT when I'm not qualified but they didn't tell me."

"You weren't qualified, but you are now." Butters winked at her.

"Thanks, Butters. I appreciate it."

"Maybe this is why you're on SWAT and not working for the regular police. Your detective skills are shit." Jonesy smirked. "You really have no guess why dragons are checking in on you, Red?"

"No, Jonesy, I really don't."

"Maybe she talked to them about helping her out the next time we go for a round of airsoft."

"I don't need help in airsoft. I whooped all of you, remember?"

Just then, Drew stepped into the room with Keith on his heels and surveyed the room. "Whatever this is about, drop it."

"We have more important stuff to worry about," Keith added.

"Shut the fuck up, rookie." Despite the harsh words, Jonesy was smiling.

"You shut up, Jonesy," the other man retorted.

"Children, enough." The team leader's glare finally silenced the room. "A call came in. There's a bank robbery in progress and the hostiles are heavily armed. We're talking serious firepower, top-notch body armor, and a bomb threat. This is as big as it gets, so gear up and meet the van."

"Yes, sir!" The response was unanimous and the team left to retrieve their gear.

Jonesy marched beside Drew. "Do you think it's the Breaks?"

"Given the increase we've seen in activity from them lately and the weapons we saw at that pawnshop, yeah. I think so, which means no time to dawdle. No getaway car has been identified yet, but them making a break for it is the expectation."

"Ah, fuck yeah. I have a bone to pick with those hotrod fuckers."

"Not today, you don't. There are hostages."

Kristen's heart dropped. Despite her months on the force, she hadn't been in an actual hostage situation yet. She'd practiced forced entry into buildings with civilians but that was very different than people actually taking hostages in reality. If they messed up today, people would die—innocent people.

They scrambled into the van and drove to the bank. It was one of the nicer ones—a downtown branch on Griswold street. The lobby was on the ground floor with offices stretching into the motor city's skyline. Classic American architecture defined the entranceway with its glass doors set behind a brick arch that was framed by unnecessary pillars that hugged the brick walls.

The bullet-shattered glass windows and two police cars that were absolutely destroyed by gunfire on either side of the stone archway added a decidedly post-apocalyptic look to the building. This kind of activity wasn't supposed to happen in Detroit—not anymore and not since its rebirth.

"All right, listen up and look alive. We're team A for this one. Butters and Beanpole, that means you'll be across the street, two or three stories up. Keith, Jonesy, and Hernandez are with me. We'll go loud and rush the front door—at least, that's what we want it to look like. While team A holds their attention, Team B will sneak in through the back."

"And the bomb, sir?" Hernandez asked.

"These assholes said there's a bomb in the building, but we have no idea where. It could be in the offices above or the bank itself, or could simply be a bluff. For now, Hernandez, you're with us. As soon as we have any intel on it, that's where you'll go."

"Yes, sir."

"What about me?" Kristen asked. "Am I on team B?"

"Absolutely not. I want you in the van. You'll bring it closer when we go in to give us a fall-back point as well as provide better cover than these police cars they have shredded."

"But Drew, I've been practicing! I can go in."

"Not today you can't."

"But—"

"That's an order."

She cursed under her breath but nodded.

"Right. Let's go."

Within three minutes, Butters and Beanpole confirmed they were in position for the team to move forward. Team A ran in a crouch to the police cars—everyone except for her—and drew more gunfire from inside the bank.

She sighed and put her foot on the gas to inch the van forward. More shots were fired but they pinged harmlessly off the front of the vehicle. A few months before, she might have been relieved but now, she merely found it a waste of her talents. Why had she trained so hard if they simply intended to bench her?

More shots from the bank were answered by Butters and Beanpole. The plan seemed to be working. Chatter on the radio indicated that Team B was inside and moving through the bowels of the bank.

An explosion roared over the radio and for a moment, only feedback followed it.

Finally, after what felt like an eternity, a voice spoke over the comms. "We have men down. A goddamn bomb went off. We…we need support. I have people bleeding all over the fucking place!"

Drew spoke over the radio. "Change of plans. We're going in. Kristen can you—"

His words cut off abruptly, replaced by only static. She immediately thought back to the pawnshop. Hadn't something jammed the radios then too?

Butters began to shoot in earnest and peppered the front of the bank with covering fire while Jonesy, Keith, Drew, and Hernandez moved from one of the wrecked police cars to the edges of the brick arch.

They had no sooner reached it when one of the police cars detonated. It was one hell of an explosion too, powerful enough to flip the car upside down.

Drew gestured for everyone to fall back but a volley of gunfire from inside pinned the team behind the brick walls. There was no way they could get out. Without that police car, there simply wasn't any other cover.

"We request immediate support," the officer from Team B said over the radio. "Mitch is coughing blood and Garcia… Garcia's out. He needs a goddamn doctor. Maybe a fucking priest. Fuck!" Gunshots chattered in the background, followed by more static. Whatever was jamming the radio had been turned on again.

They had to act and they had to act now.

But they couldn't, she realized with growing frustration. The entire team was pinned down and there was nothing Butters could do from his vantage point.

Another bullet from the bank pinged harmlessly off the van.

Kristen tried not to smile as a plan formed in her head. By the time she shoved the vehicle into low gear and thrust the gas pedal to the floor, she grinned like a maniac.

The armored vehicle accelerated in response and she hurtled toward the building while bullets rebounded off the armor. She was right about the space between the pillars—it wasn't enough—and when the van tried to pass between them, it simply destroyed them completely. Obviously, they were ornamental and not load-bearing.

Beyond them was what was left of the glass windows at the front of the structure.

There was no resistance and the van careened through and released a shower of glass into the lobby, but she didn't ease her foot off the accelerator. Gunfire continued from behind the long wooden divider that normally separated tellers from patrons of the bank and now gave the criminals cover.

Her expression grim and focused, she crashed the van through the wooden wall as well and barely lost speed until she impacted the wall behind that. This was obviously load-bearing as her forward momentum stopped abruptly.

The airbag deployed and she blacked out for a few seconds.

She opened her eyes and blinked at her surroundings before she realized dumbly that if someone had wanted to put a bullet in her head, she had provided them with a golden opportunity.

Fortunately, Team A had pushed in behind her and now had their weapons raised and trained on the robbers. It probably helped that the criminals had been even more stunned than her own teammates when she'd destroyed their cover.

"Drop the weapons, assholes, or we tell the van to back up." That was Jonesy, her brain told her.

A clatter of weapons followed but no gunshots, so she assumed they had complied.

"The building's secure," Drew said into his radio. "I need EMTs in here ASAP. I have three officers in need of medical attention."

"What if there are more bombs?" someone asked over the radio.

"These guys don't have time."

"This bomb is on a button trigger anyway," Hernandez interjected. "We have the hostiles. Now get in here and save our officers."

Footsteps echoed in the odd bubble that seemed to surround her and people ran past with stretchers. Before she could see if they returned, Drew leaned into the window.

"How many fingers am I holding up?"

"One. The mean one."

"That's right, Hall. Now get the hell out of that van."

He helped her with the seatbelt, checked her briefly for wounds, and —finding none—proceeded to dress her down with more energy than she'd ever seen from him. "That was the stupidest damn thing I've ever seen, and I work with both Jones and Hernandez. You destroyed a piece of architecture that's decades old, not to mention the antiques you turned into kindling. And then there's the van. If the transmission is ruined, Captain Hansen will dock your pay for that. I've seen it before and I'll be damned if I'd argue for anything less for someone so irresponsible."

"Sorry, sir," Kristen said and followed him through the trashed lobby. The van really had done a number on it. Where before, the room had been mostly intact except for the bullet holes, there was now a van-sized path of destruction from the front door to the back wall.

"Look out there." He pointed through the hole she'd made in the front of the building.

She obeyed and looked at where the three B-team members were being loaded into ambulances. Two of them already had IVs inserted. She felt a pang of guilt. Had that been her fault?

"They're alive because you took action. Stupid, reckless action, yes, but you saved at least three lives today, maybe more."

Startled, she glanced quickly at him to find him smiling, his eyes moist. A tear—an actual tear—ran down his cheek. He cleared his throat. "Mitch's wife has a baby girl due in a month. Their first. It's all he ever fucking talks about. Now, she'll still have a daddy, thanks to you."

Kristen nodded, thought of her own father, and fought back tears of her own. Before she could speak, though, Drew told an EMT she might have a concussion and she was rushed to the back of an ambulance for monitoring.

They hooked her up to machines she didn't understand and asked her questions she didn't want to answer but at that moment, she didn't care about any of it. She had saved lives today. After her months of training, she finally got it. This was why her dad had worked such long days and given so much of himself to his job—because saving people felt good.

For the first time since she'd joined SWAT, she didn't question her placement or wonder about the dragon who had set her on this path. And also, for the first time, she felt like she belonged.

The EMT asked her a few more questions, but apparently satisfied, let her get out of the ambulance.

Jonesy waited for her with what she could only describe as a shit-eating grin on his face. "Fucking great work back there. I always hated the front of that butt-ugly bank." He led her over to the rest of the team. "I think you need a new nickname, Red."

"How about Speed Racer?" Keith smirked.

"I like it, I like it," Butters said and rubbed his chin before he burst into song. "Go Speed Racer, go Speed Racer, go Speed Racer, go!"

"Don't quit your day job." Hernandez put a finger to her ear like his singing might have caused permanent damage.

"I am a little parched. Perhaps we should discuss it over a bite." The sniper grinned.

"I got one, I got one," Hernandez had to stop herself from laughing. "She came in like *wrecking baaaaaall!* Motherfucking *Kristen Haaaaaall!*

All they wanted was to rob a bank, but they should have let her crazy ass in! Let her crazy ass in!"

Everyone laughed way too hard at that, and Kristen was forced to consider that this might be the moment that would define her career —and more importantly, who she was to her new friends.

She decided she was okay with that.

CHAPTER FIFTEEN

The last time John Murray had taken the Breaks to this warehouse, he had felt like he was in control. Detroit was his city, after all, and whoever the rich asshole behind the mirrored glass windows was, he would have to learn his place like rich assholes inevitably did.

But things had changed. He no longer felt in control. The last few months had started off well enough. There was nothing quite like strong artillery to make raiding pawn shops and liquor stores easy. He'd lost Lemar, which he had to admit hurt him more than he'd expected, but things had gone well—or rather, he thought morosely, well enough. But when they'd robbed that bank... It was a miracle he had even made it through that shit show to tell the tale.

Most of his gang hadn't.

That was another reason why he no longer felt in control, despite this being the same warehouse he'd first chosen for his meeting with his armed benefactor. The Breaks were no longer the only gang present for this meeting.

He stood in front of a 1971 corvette with brown leather seats, copper paint, and chrome highlights. Behind that was a 1965 Ford Truck in blue-and-white with a brand-new engine. He'd brought the truck and hoped to fill the bed with new supplies, but looking at the other gangs present made him wonder if there would even be enough to go around.

It was bullshit, really. The Breaks had lost men—too many men—trying to prove themselves to this mysterious financier, and this was how they were rewarded?

"Where the fuck is your man, Murray?" That was Lee, leader of the Dead Reds. He picked up Chinese immigrants who were down on their luck and mostly did work with gambling, he seemed to recall. He drove a stupid tiny Honda that was more plastic than metal.

"He'll be here," he grumbled.

"He fucking better be," a wannabe-thug named Marcus said. "You promised us the hook-up for the same stock you've been getting."

"I didn't promise you shit. I said I had a meeting with the guy and he wanted you there. We didn't hook little pinky fingers like schoolgirls."

Murray hated the man. He was covered in shitty tattoos that you could hardly make out on his dark skin and ran with the Knights, a group of crack-dealers and pill-pushers. Worse, the asshat drove a goddamn boat of a Chrysler from the eighties with dropped suspension and subwoofers he had neglected to turn off. It was less of a car and more of a traveling fucking entertainment system—a goddamn embarrassment for an American-made vehicle.

It had pissed him off to no end when the man who'd sold him the weapons had ordered him—ordered John fucking Murray—to contact the drug dealer. He didn't want to stoop to their level but he also needed more firepower, so he'd made the damn call.

A few other gang leaders were present too, but he didn't know their names. They were amateurs, all of them.

"He gonna show, or what?"

He scowled at Lee and returned to his corvette. He had something in the trunk for all these goddamn posers. Maybe this was a test—a last-man-standing kind of thing. He looked at his boys and was about to give them the signal when a noise from the far end of the warehouse caught everyone's attention.

A door slid open and the black van drove in and stopped.

The man who'd opened the door to the warehouse climbed into the van and it drove forward. It turned so the passenger side faced the assembly of criminals, then stopped in the middle of the semicircle of gang leaders and their most trusted cronies.

Murray had to admit the man behind the glass had balls. Driving the van into the middle of the group was akin to a seal belly-flopping into a ring of sharks.

Exactly like before, two men dressed in black suits, ties, and sunglasses stepped out and stood on either side of the passenger door.

Again, he found himself wanting to cap these assholes. They didn't wear armor. There was obviously no way they could fit it under their goddamn tailored suits.

"Are you here to give us some actual decent weapons this time?" He sneered.

The passenger window opened a crack and a cloud of cigar smoke poured from the gap.

"I seem to recall that I already gave you a cache of weapons, Murray of the Breaks."

"Yeah, and we used them exactly like you fucking said. We chose bigger and bigger targets, and what did that get us?" He looked around the ring of criminals and back to the van, daring anyone to say a word. "A fucking headache, that's what. We raid one bank—one bank—and the goddamn SWAT team showed up with armored vehicles and machine guns and snipers. We need better tools to even the odds."

"Bullshit," Marcus interjected. "You had your opportunity. It's time to see if the rest of us have what it takes. That's why we're here, isn't it? To break the Breaks?"

"You will not speak to me that way again, Marcus of the Knights," the man said from the vehicle.

"Marcus of the Knights? What the fuck do you think this is—the round table in King Arthur's Court?" He snorted at the members of his gang and they laughed. No one else made a sound, though, and the silence soon swallowed the Knight's attempts to make light of the situation.

The window of the van rolled up.

The thug laughed again, although it sounded forced. "Fucking pussy."

One of the men in black suits opened the passenger door.

Out stepped the largest man Murray had ever seen.

He was tall like a pro basketball player, and his shoulders looked like they could support the roof of a barn. His skin was tanned and his black hair was pulled into a tight ponytail that somehow seemed at odds with his black goatee. He wore a black suit with a red silk shirt beneath, a tie of the identical shade of red, and black gloves with strips of red on each finger. The Breaks leader might have described the man as a giant puff if he didn't look like he could snap anyone in the warehouse in half. In his massive hands, his cigar looked like a cigarette.

"Approach, Marcus of the Knights and Murray of the Breaks."

Murray glanced at Marcus, who seemed about as reluctant as he felt.

"Now," the man said and drew languidly on his cigar.

He approached and the other gang leader did as well a second later.

"Now kneel."

"Who the fuck do you think you are?" Marcus stood belligerently in front of the goliath of a man.

"Your superior," he responded and kicked the man in the chest with a shiny black shoe hard enough to sprawl him on his ass.

Murray didn't need to be told twice. He knelt.

"Now. Approach and kneel, Marcus of the Knights. Others here have made mistakes as well, yet I am one who believes in forgiveness."

"I bet you fucking do," the Knights leader muttered but he approached the man who'd felled him with a single kick and knelt before him. The stranger extended a hand with a massive ruby set in a gold ring. Marcus frowned but he got the message and kissed the ring.

"Your...uh, honor," Murray stammered, unable to endure the

silence. "I know we have failed you but please, give us another chance. If we have better weapons than the police, we can take whatever we want in this city."

"Stop speaking," the man said and he complied. "You may call me… what is the affectation of this time?" He turned to one of the men still standing in front of the van.

"Mister."

"You may call me Mr Black."

Murray nodded. "Yes, Mr Black."

"I am not pleased with you because I do not like failure and you have failed me. It might be wisest and simplest to have my men simply kill you and be done with it."

The two men opened the van, and each selected an assault rifle. Every gang member in the warehouse recoiled visibly. These weapons were military-grade, a few steps up from what the Breaks had been given before.

"We done nothing wrong," Lee said. "Let us serve you." Murray's jaw almost dropped to the floor when the man approached and knelt in front of Mr Black. Lee didn't work with anyone. The two other gang leaders followed him a few moments later. They also both approached and knelt.

"I accept your fealty but understand that those who serve me must be willing to truly serve me."

The sound of wind swirled around Murray's ears and a cloud moved to block the sun that came in through the windows of the derelict warehouse. Thunder boomed and shadow writhed around Mr Black. Two enormous black wings unfolded from his back, a tail of shadow whipped in the darkness, and his face—his face was too terrible to behold. It was all spikes and teeth and horns and horrible red eyes that looked like they held only hunger.

Murray tried not to think about the fact that he was merely a man made of meat and that the being before him seemed like so much more.

In the next moment, the clouds shifted, sunlight flooded the warehouse once more, and the illusion was gone. Mr Black stood before them again, seven feet of muscle and control but a human at least, or a human form anyway. Murray had wondered if the man was a dragon. Now, he knew.

"Make no mistake, if you were gobbled up by this city, no one would miss any of you. But I find that would be a waste of resources. Even with your failure, I believe you to be the best tools for the job. After all, you have sown discord and fear. Those who sit on the hidden thrones that control this city do not like the disruptions you have caused. Even in failure, you have made them begin to fly about rather than remain in their roosts. Besides, one uses the tool one possesses, not the ones one wishes one has. Isn't that right, Murray of the Breaks?"

"Yes, Mr Black." When the dragon didn't speak, he hurried to continue. "And with better tools, I assure you I can lead everyone in this warehouse to take this city from the pigs and the corrupt city council." That must be why the other gangs were there, right? So he could introduce them to the big game.

"Do not presume to know my orders, you infantile speck of a mammal." He hadn't yelled or raised his voice, yet the words echoed through the warehouse.

Murray's voice caught in his throat.

"Why would I trust you to be my general when you can't even rob a bank with the bounty I have provided you? Why feed the dog that fails to catch his dinner?"

As the man spoke, terror grew in Murray's gut and spread into his chest. In moments, his entire body shook in fear. And he wasn't the only one. The smell of hot piss come to his nose and he knew he wasn't the only one who felt what he did. He'd heard that dragons could do this—that they could make a human feel a certain way—but it was one thing to hear a rumor and another entirely to feel it in your very soul.

Even if the monster before them didn't eat him, he never wanted to feel that terror again.

"Please, sir!" He threw himself prostrate before the being of power that stood implacably. "We won't let the police catch us off guard again. We hadn't faced SWAT before. This time, we'll be ready."

"He's had his chance, Mr Black. Please, let the Knights serve you." Marcus too put his forehead to the concrete floor of the warehouse.

"The Dead Reds will do you great honor with the tools you gave the Breaks." Lee also put his head to the floor.

The leaders of the other two gangs followed suit and mumbled empty promises and tried to place the blame on Murray for his failure.

"Please, sir, please," the Breaks leader begged. "You came to us because we're the most organized club in Detroit. Let me lead us all against the corruption in this city. Let me set the Motor City on fire for you." He honestly had no clue exactly where the words came from, but when he said them, he believed them. At that moment, there was nothing he wanted more than to please the man, even if it meant burning his hometown to the ground—no, especially if that meant burning his hometown to the ground

"Arise, Murray of the Breaks, and take my blessing."

He stood slowly. Mr Black stepped toward him and cupped his face with one of his massive gloved hands.

"Yes, sir. Thank you, sir."

"You will be my general." His boss—or perhaps owner was more apt—removed his glove to reveal fingernails sharpened into points. Again, he cupped the gang leader's face but this time, his thumb scratched a bloody line on his cheek.

"Thank you, sir. Thank you so much," Murray stammered, startled at the sight of his own blood on the massive hand as the man stepped back to where he had stood before. One of the two men in suits handed him a handkerchief and he wiped the blood away.

"Understand that this will be the last time I reward failure because if you do not succeed, there will be no next time. There will be no pleading and no forgiveness. You will be bled, and you will be burnt." Mr Black raised his voice and filled the cavernous warehouse with his orders. "Arise, Marcus of the Knights, and take my blessing."

Marcus stood, and the man scratched a line on his forehead with one of his fingernails. The Knights leader thanked him for the wound.

"Arise, Lee of the Dead Reds. Arise, Hector of the Eskeletos Muertes. Arise Jane of the Stray Cats." The gang leaders complied, and he marked each of their foreheads in turn. "I believe in each of you. With Murray at your head, I am sure you can disrupt the broken rails this city runs on. And if his leadership is lacking, I am sure one of the four of you can save me the trouble of putting this dog down."

Murray swallowed hard as the four leaders of the other gangs in town nodded at one another. Despite the fear he was certain they all felt, they wore smiles at the idea of betrayal. They really were nothing more than animals.

"Now, come. Behold the gifts I bring thee."

The two henchmen opened the van. The last time Murray had seen the inside of the vehicle, it had been the greatest cache of weapons he'd ever laid eyes upon. This treasure trove, however, was enough to take over a country.

There was better body armor with helmets to match, military-grade assault rifles, two heavy machine guns that he thought would look fucking fantastic mounted on top of one his cars, and best of all, a rocket launcher.

He looked at his benefactor like a kid on Christmas morning. They couldn't fail, not if they worked together. With this arsenal, they wouldn't have to stop with the police, those lapdogs to the politicians. They could destroy the entire damn establishment and make the people who ran this city finally understand injustice.

Mr Black smiled, lifted the rocket launcher from its stand, and placed it in his hands. "You will have to share, Murray of the Breaks, and you must be careful. This city is a fireworks factory and I have given you the match." Despite his words, he did not seem at all concerned about the implications of this statement. In fact, he looked even more eager than his new general felt.

For a few minutes, the man said nothing and merely smoked his cigar while the gangs loaded the weapons. In the end, Murray got one of the heavy machine guns to mount on one of his cars, plus the rocket launcher. After all, it had been put in his hands and he didn't want to lose it. He'd agreed to share the other heavy machine gun and divide the assault rifles between all the other gangs.

But were they still other gangs? He had been put in charge, and that meant everyone there was his…as long as he didn't fail.

"Now, go, all of you. I will return to you once the sickness that has choked this city for decades has been burned out. You will be the wildfire that cleanses the land before the rain." Mr Black's red eyes gleamed.

Murray nodded. He could see the vision reflected in his red eyes, and it was beautiful. The city would soon be in chaos. The gangs would wreak havoc on every corner until those in power felt the foundation of their towers of steel and concrete tremble. Together, the five gangs would make a fist that would smash the windows of this city. They'd light every business on fire. After all, only the corrupt could flourish in the Motor City. Those who were successful had only achieved that by taking from people like him.

And then, once it was all broken and burned, Mr Black would come.

And he would be there, his loyal general.

CHAPTER SIXTEEN

Kristen parked in the parking garage, jogged down the stairs—a habit she'd picked up from training with her team—and walked into the police station.

The front desk stood empty. She approached with her hand on her hip, already reaching for a gun she hadn't strapped on yet.

She found only a tiny web camera facing the entryway to the station. Odd, that.

Her months of training kicked in and threw her into high alert and she scanned the station quickly.

It was empty, she realized. No one shuffled paperwork or wandered to the lounge or even moved at all. Her heart began to pound. She took a deep breath and forced it to slow so she could focus and try to determine what was going on.

Cautiously, she moved deeper into the office, past the cells—which were empty too—and toward the lounge. She'd peek in there and if she found no one, she'd run like hell to the gear room, arm herself, and return to try to get to the bottom of it a little more prepared than she was right now. Could the whole force have been abducted? It couldn't have. That was impossible, right? But what else could explain the lack of people?

A noise caught her attention from deeper in the station—hushed voices perhaps? Hostage scenarios from months of studying began to race through her mind.

After a long, slow breath, she approached the lounge in a crouch, not sure of what she'd find but knowing that she wanted to be ready for whatever it was.

She put her ear to the door but heard no more voices. There was, however, a rustle that made her think of a press of bodies.

Kristen nodded, took a deep breath, and kicked the door open.

"Surpri—"

Her momentum from kicking the door took her cleanly into a roll. She darted up and caught hold of the closest body to her. The room was dark and she couldn't make out a damn thing, but she was determined not to let anyone get the drop on her.

"Someone, get the lights!"

The lights flickered on and she gaped at Keith, who she held firmly by the lapels.

"Uh...surprise?" He smiled.

A hasty glance around her confirmed that the entire station was crammed in there. The lounge had been decorated—well, a single banner had been hung that said *Happy Birthday Chris* but she would take it. They'd thrown her a surprise party.

Jonesy was already laughing. "Goddamn, rookie. You can't make this shit up, can you? Only you could get ambushed while waiting to ambush someone."

She released Keith and smiled. "Sorry. I thought, uh... How did you all know it was my birthday?"

"Jonesy looked in your personal file. Don't worry. We've locked him out of the computers. Happy Birthday!" Drew clapped her on the back and handed her a card.

Still smiling, she looked at the card in her hand. It said, *Breaking Expectations* and had a picture of a wrecking ball on it.

Her smile broadened. "You guys! I don't know what to say."

"Thank you is the go-to when people go out of their way to do something nice," Hernandez snarked.

"Thanks, Hernandez." Kristen tried to put as much girlish goofiness into her voice as possible. The woman cringed, which was exactly what she had hoped for.

"All right, you assholes. There's nothing to see here. Get yourself a piece of cake and get the hell out before we drag your asses back to the station," Jonesy yelled at the other people in the lounge. It really was impressive how many staff members had fit in there, only for her to ruin the surprise.

People shuffled past and gave her congratulations or wished her happy birthday as they did so. She noticed the woman who normally worked the front desk, who had a tablet in her hand with a video that displayed the entrance to the station. Ah, that explained the webcam, then.

Once only her team remained, she finally served herself a piece of cake. It had presumably said *Happy Birthday* but apparently, whatever bakery they'd purchased it from had decent frosting because almost all the slices with letters were gone. She took the *H* for Hall, sat on a couch, and dug in.

"You're lucky we're even celebrating at all. I lost money on you, you know." Jonesy said around a mouthful of cake.

"Is that right, Jonesy?" Hernandez interjected and her eyes gleamed. "Did all those late nights helping the wrecking ball cut in on your time on the pole?"

"What the fuck are you talking about, Hernandez?" He retorted smartly. "Male strippers don't pole dance."

The woman laughed. "Oh, spoken from experience then?"

"Fuck off. Just because no one would pay to see you naked doesn't mean— You know what? Just shut up." he glared at her and took a bite. Kristen didn't think she'd ever seen someone look so pissed-off while eating cake. He finished chewing. "I bet you wouldn't last a month, let alone four, Red."

"I wouldn't have made it this far without you, Jonesy. It means even more to me now that I know you had money riding on me washing out. I can cover that bet."

"No, no." He tried to wave the offer away.

"No, really, I insist." She dug in her wallet. "What do I owe you—ten bucks? Twenty?"

"More like a hundred." Butters chuckled.

"You bet a hundred bucks that I wouldn't last a month?"

"Don't look at me like that, Red. I wasn't the only one who lost money because you turned out to be a fucking wrecking ball."

Kristen looked at her team. They all shoved cake in their mouths and tried not to look guilty. "So, who won?"

Silence followed and everyone seemed determined not to look at anyone else.

"Seriously, though. Who bet I'd last four months?"

Awkward glances were exchanged before finally, Beanpole stood. "I bet ten weeks, but you beat me too so take the money." He took his wallet out, withdrew a stack of cash, and thrust it into her hands.

She counted the money in disbelief. "This…this is almost a thousand dollars."

"Happy birthday." He nodded and moved aside quickly to help himself to another slice of cake.

"You assholes bet almost a grand that I would wash out?" She might have been pissed if she'd known about it months before, but it didn't bother her now. After all, these people had trained her—especially Jonesy, who she had no doubt was the first to make a bet against her. They'd sweated together, been hurt together, and she had taken a bullet for one of them and saved most of their lives.

"I didn't want to, but…well, the odds were good." Butters shrugged.

"Bullshit, Butterball. You were the one who wanted to raise the buy-in to a hundred bucks." Hernandez raised an eyebrow as if to challenge him to argue, but he merely hid behind his piece of cake.

"Look, honestly, if things had gone differently, I might have washed out and one of you would be all the richer." She held the wad of money up. "Like, say for example, if Jonesy could actually take a bullet or if any of you were halfway decent at airsoft."

Everyone laughed, especially Jonesy. "Leave it to Red to stay on the force because she got fucking shot."

"But seriously, guys. Thank you. I know I joined the force under weird circumstances, but you still helped turn me into the officer I am today."

"You had more potential than any of these punks. Don't think otherwise," Drew said and earned another round of laughter from the team.

"Still. I'm thankful. Really, from the bottom of my heart, I am. This job is damn hard, but you guys make it all worth it. It means so much to be a part of the team, even if I did have to kick down a thousand doors before I earned my place."

"It was our pleasure to watch you fuck up so many times, Red." Jonesy smiled.

Hernandez shrugged. "I still think you're an uppity, privileged white bitch, but at least you're not another privileged white male. Plus, you're definitely better than the rookie."

"I'm not the rookie," Keith protested and again, the room filled with laughter.

"It's good to be here."

"Okay, Jesus—someone turn on the blinking light or whatever so Red knows her fucking speech is coming to a close," Jonesy said.

Butters cleared his throat. "Kristen, if you'd truly like to thank us, promise us you'll never cook for us again. I'll cook any dish that's ever been served south of Tennessee if you'll please promise to refrain from attempting any more creations."

Everyone collapsed at that.

"Holy shit, do you remember the smell when we got back to the station?" Hernandez held her sides and could barely speak around her laughter.

Jonesy nodded. "You thought an animal had died in the vents." He managed to regain a little control, but that seemed to set him off again.

Kristen let it wash over as she sank into the couch. After all these months—no, it was longer than that—after years, she finally felt like she was home. These people, her new team, pushed her to succeed in ways she never had before. They challenged her, protected her, and believed in her. In her short time in SWAT, they'd already transformed from co-workers, to teammates, to friends, and now, she finally felt like they were family and that this was home.

She took a deep breath and soaked in the continued shit-talk they didn't seem capable of stopping. The most important thing was that she was home—she was finally home—and she was committed to protecting her new family, even if she had to make Jonesy look bad and take another bullet for him.

CHAPTER SEVENTEEN

Jonesy and Kristen were out in a squad car when the call came in.
"We have something happening downtown. Armed robbery."
"Where at?" Jonesy asked.
"We don't have a specific location yet, only multiple reports of armed gunmen. The damn phones are flooded with conflicting information."

That in itself was odd. The dispatchers were great at pointing them in the right direction. How many calls would it take to overwhelm them?

"We'd better get back to base." Jonesy put the car's siren on and pressed the accelerator.

They made it a few blocks through downtown before something shattered the glass of one of the back windows.

"What the fuck was that?" he hollered and ducked involuntarily.

"I think—" Before she could answer, more gunshots clattered and the bullets *pinged* as they struck the passenger door to the vehicle—her door. Their impact could actually be felt through the metal. "Some asshole shot at us."

"Un-fucking-believable," he swore but he didn't turn the car.

"Jonesy, shouldn't we show these assholes whose boss? Contain the threat?" she protested.

"Listen to the damn radio, Red." He turned it up.

"Active shooters on Grand Boulevard and Woodward. Reports coming in of hostiles at the DIA, please confirm. Requesting all units to mobilize. Repeat, all units."

"We're a unit, Jonesy. Where the fuck are you going?"

"It sounds like there are more than a dozen damn shooters out there and you want to take them down in a fucking police cruiser with a couple of pistols? We're SWAT, Red. The police gotta hold these assholes until we get there."

Her heart plummeted into her stomach. The city might not have a few minutes. If people were already shooting at police, the tipping point might have already been reached.

Jonesy sped toward the station and for once, he was silent. Instead, he cranked up the radio so they could hear it over his sirens.

"There is no apparent pattern to the attacks. Most are in the Riverton Warehouse district but there's no focus on targets. All officers mobilize, repeat. We need all officers."

"It sounds like a fucking warzone," he mumbled.

Kristen tried to think of what could have triggered it all but was cut short when a copper corvette screeched around a corner and raced up beside them.

"Jonesy!"

"I know, I know!" He tried to accelerate but was no match for the corvette. It pulled easily up to the driver's side of the police car.

Two men in denim jackets studded with spikes sat inside. The man in the passenger seat held an assault rifle the likes of which she had only ever seen in movies.

"Your days of corruption are over, you fucking pigs," the man screamed over the roaring engines of the two racing vehicles.

He punctuated the vitriol with a fusillade aimed at their vehicle.

"Fuck!" the sergeant hollered and jerked the wheel to the right to hurtle them down another street. The corvette tried to follow but they were going too fast and the turn was too sharp. The tires screeched before the driver adjusted their course and careened on down the street they had been on before.

Even though the guy in the corvette had only a few seconds to fire, he'd obliterated the side of the police cruiser.

"The motherfuckers are packing." Jonesy clenched his jaw as they neared the next intersection with both officers on high alert.

The corvette reappeared and fired wildly. It raced past the back of the police vehicle—the damn corvette must've been going ninety—and a rattle of bullets impacted the trunk.

"Red, do you think you can handle these assholes?"

"I can try." Kristen drew her pistol, took her time, and fired. Her first three shots caught the windshield before she got lucky and hit one of the front tires.

The corvette veered to the left and gave up the pursuit.

"Nice fucking shooting, Red. I don't know if Butters could have made that shot."

"Yeah, well, almost being annihilated by fucking motorheads is like old hat for me now."

"No fucking joke. Did you see any more of those assholes?"

She looked behind them. "Yeah. Holy shit, Jonesy. There are so many people on the streets back there. It looks like…it looks like a goddamn war zone."

He responded with another push on the accelerator and the vehicle surged forward. The thought of leaving the violence behind instead of facing it head-on made her feel sick, but she knew he was right. If they went into a warzone, they needed to be better equipped.

They made it the station in less than five minutes. She was half-surprised to find it still standing. It was close to downtown, after all, and according to the reports that flooded in, it sounded like downtown attempted to blow itself up.

Jonesy parked in front of the station and the duo raced inside.

"About fucking time. Now, saddle up!" Drew yelled at them as soon as they reached the gear room. He chucked a bulletproof vest at her and another at Jonesy. It was a small miracle they'd made it back alive and she hadn't realized how much danger they'd been in. Thankfully, she had no time to dwell on their lucky escape and snatched a helmet, shoved it on, and tightened the chin strap while she shoved the disquieting thoughts aside.

The team raced through the station to their SWAT van. They scrambled in with Jonesy at the wheel, the team leader in the passenger seat, and the others in the back.

"What's the plan?" the sergeant asked Drew.

He answered through the window to the back of the van so they could all hear.

"Right now, we don't know who these assholes are or what they want. All we know is that there is a considerable number of them, they're heavily armed, and they seem to be converging on the warehouse district. We've created a blockade on the bridge to Belle Isle. The big brass think they're using the warehouse district as a staging area and that they might try to take the island and use it as a permanent base. It'd be damn hard to dig them out if that is the case because there's only the one bridge on and off."

"Who is telling us go to Belle Isle if the warehouse district is the focus?" Kristen asked.

"That's above our paygrade, Hall. We're a team and every member of a team needs to play their position. Our job is to not allow the assholes to take the island."

They raced down Lafayette St, banked hard on East Grand, and crossed about halfway on the bridge to Belle Isle before they stopped. Three police cars were drawn up there already, plus another SWAT van. They unloaded and Jonesy turned the vehicle to join the blockade.

She sighed a breath of relief. There was no way anyone could get through that.

It was almost like her thought was some kind of bizarre trigger.

"Places, people, keep it neat and keep it clean," Drew commanded when the gunfire started.

Fourteen members of SWAT plus seven more police officers took positions behind their vehicles and tried to hold the bridge.

It boggled her mind to think there were at least ten more SWAT blockades like this. How could that be? She knew there were gangs in Detroit, but this was ridiculous. Had they all joined forces and decided to…what? Burn the city down? It simply didn't make sense. Gangs did things for money. This was purely destruction.

"We have forces converging on the warehouse district. All unit—"

The radio chatter was abruptly replaced with static.

"For fuck's sake!" Drew cursed.

"What do we do?" Keith asked.

"Hold our fucking position, rookie." Jonesy nodded toward the mainland. Three cars raced toward them. A machine gun was mounted on the roof of one of them.

Kristen braced herself for it to get within range but apparently, whoever manned the weapon had far less patience. He opened fire and sprayed the line of vehicles with bullets.

Butters delivered a clean shot into his chest and he fell from the top of the vehicle.

The other two cars continued their headlong approach. They didn't seem to be slowing.

The car's tires squealed as it stopped. Another man climbed out and took control of the mounted machine gun.

The sniper promptly shot him in the chest.

He stumbled but didn't fall—bulletproof armor, obviously—so he adjusted his aim calmly and fired a perfect head-shot.

That seemed to discourage whoever else was there to try anything else but already, a mounted machine gun seemed a low priority. The other two cars now rocketed toward the blockade and their engines roared. The police officers already took potshots at the rapidly approaching vehicles, hoping to get lucky.

"Tires," Drew ordered, and Beanpole, Keith, and Jonesy launched a concerted volley toward the car on the right. They managed to damage its front tires and it slewed to the side, pounded through the small wall on the side of the bridge, and splashed into the Detroit River.

The third vehicle collided with the front of a police car and forced the stationery vehicle into a spin while it simply continued through their blockade.

"Red, Hernandez, Jonesy, you watch those fuckers who made it through. Everyone else, we have more coming this way."

Kristen turned to fire at the car that had broken through their barricade. She noticed in shock that two officers had been run over and immediately tried to use her radio to call for EMS. Only static met her efforts.

Rather than fall prey to her growing frustration over what she couldn't do, she clenched her teeth and fired at the car that limped toward them. Jonesy and Hernandez also opened fire and targeted the wheels and windshield. After a moment of concentrated gunfire, it was disabled.

Two men exited, and one of them lobbed something at the blockade.

"Grenade!" the sergeant yelled and everyone flung themselves down.

The ordnance rolled under the other SWAT van and exploded. No one was hurt but the vehicle obviously wouldn't run again.

"We have more coming," Drew yelled and pointed across the bridge to where more cars raced toward them. These didn't look like they belonged to the Breaks, though. One was a souped-up Honda and another a low-rider with music loud enough to be heard over the now constant crackle of gunfire.

The radio sputtered to life. "All units converge on Chene and Guoin. We've triangulated whatever's interfering with our radio. Repeat, if you can hear this, there's an abandoned warehouse on Chene and Guoin, half-covered in vines. All units—"

The broadcast was swallowed by a wave of static again.

"You heard the woman—get in the fucking van," Drew instructed. Two SWAT teams and seven police officers obeyed but immediately encountered difficulty.

It was soon clear that they couldn't all fit, so their team plus the other SWAT team and two regular police officers crammed in the van while the other cops took the remaining cruiser and gunned the engine.

Jonesy threw the vehicle in gear and they began the race toward the warehouse.

It was lucky that it wasn't the Breaks who now barreled toward them. Kristen doubted that Jonesy would've been able to outmaneuver one of the motorheads, but since these clearly lacked the other gang's skill and enhanced vehicles, she thought they might actually survive.

The low-rider was easy enough to lose. The sergeant merely pounded into the side of it and that was enough to ruin its suspension and render the vehicle useless.

The little Honda was trickier because of its speed. But it was also light, so it couldn't do much to a larger armored vehicle. It swung against them a few times, but Jonesy had obviously driven in situations like this because he anticipated each strike and managed to keep them moving. Someone in the Honda was armed too, as bullets struck the side of the van, but none punched through the bulletproof armor.

Still, it was a harrowing few minutes in the back. They were crammed tightly in there, so every turn pushed her against someone. More than once, she thanked her lucky stars that whoever was in the Honda didn't have explosives.

One lucky grenade would be enough to obliterate two SWAT teams.

"He's behind us," Drew shouted. "Who wants the shot?"

"I'll take it," one of the members of the other SWAT team yelled. Two of his teammates held his shoulders and a third opened the rear of the van.

Behind them, the Honda approached rapidly in determined pursuit while the person in the passenger seat fired an assault rifle.

The officer didn't so much as flinch. He took aim, exhaled like he was on a gun range instead of in the back of a speeding vehicle, and fired.

He struck the driver and the Honda slewed wildly with no one at the controls.

"You're not the only hotshot, Goodman," the man joked.

For a moment, Kristen didn't know who the hell he had spoken to, but she remembered that their sniper had an actual name and the man had used it.

"You're letting out all the cold air!" Butters replied mildly and one of the shooter's teammates swung the door shut.

They continued for another few minutes and fortunately avoided any other armed vehicles before tires squealed into an abrupt halt.

This was it. They had arrived at the warehouse.

She clenched her teeth as she made herself the promise that she would save her city, or she would die trying.

CHAPTER EIGHTEEN

A single SWAT van stopped dramatically outside the warehouse.
"Should we blow it to high hell, your honor?"
For a moment, the black dragon forgot to shrug the arms of his human glamor. It was demeaning to spend so much time in human form. Worse still, he constantly had to learn their expressions and the changes in body language over the decades. It didn't have to be like this. After all, human ranchers didn't show this much respect to cows.

"Mr Black, your orders?"

He couldn't even use his real name with these pathetic, short-lived rats. They couldn't pronounce it, for starters, but there was more to the dragon who called himself Mr Black's fake identity. It wouldn't do for the other dragons of Detroit to find out he was the one who had stirred trouble up in their city. Not until after tonight anyway, he reminded himself—not until it was too late.

"Sir? Should I shoot the SWAT van?"

He turned to the man. Murray of the Breaks was a pathetic excuse for a leader and yet, he was the best available in this wretched excuse for a city. Still, with the weapons the dragon's henchmen had procured, even he and his pathetic little band of petty criminals could inflict real damage on the city as long as they remained in the dragon's aura.

"Wait," he said.

He'd flexed his innate power for the entire night. It hadn't taken much to push the rats who called themselves gangs over the edge. They were obviously already worthless excuses for humans, more prone to violence than the average man. A dragon's aura—even one as powerful as him—couldn't alter someone's fundamental nature. A dragon couldn't turn a saint into a sinner was an often said and fairly accurate idiom, but you could push people in the direction they were already inclined toward. Conveniently, none of these people had been saints.

The fact that it had taken so little effort to compel the gangs to attack their homeland and their own neighbors further demonstrated how badly this city needed to be razed and rebuilt. He hadn't told them to kill or filled their hearts with rage or terror. Instead, he had simply freed them from their fear and inhibitions against harming their own kind. They had taken up arms like birds learning to fly.

But it did take concentration to exude an aura like that over multiple city blocks, and when one concentrated, one often missed things one should not otherwise miss.

Like the dragon who stepped out from the SWAT van.

Mr Black's eyes locked on the woman who fitted a helmet over her red hair. She was a dragon. He could sense it. Her human body glowed with energy, strengthened her muscles beyond what the human frame should be capable of, honed her reflexes, and quickened her reactions. But how could there be a new player in town he hadn't known about? Who was she, and why didn't she use her full powers? This could ruin everything. She could literally send months of planning up in smoke.

He had planned to take this city from the two spineless worms who'd been in control for centuries but apparently, he wasn't the only one who'd hidden in the shadows.

Whoever this dragon was masquerading as a police officer, she obviously didn't want to reveal the full extent of her powers. If she was on the police force, she must have been undercover for some time, but why? Obviously, she must have machinations of her own—ambitions beyond the scope of what most humans dared dream—and she'd set her sights on this city.

Mr Black could use this. Tonight was to be his grand reveal but at the end of it all, it would inevitably come down to a fight—two versus one. But with another player on the board, perhaps he wouldn't have to reveal himself. Whoever the newcomer was, she must be hiding for a reason. Perhaps she wished to rule the Motor City herself. Perhaps she worked undercover for those worms Damos and Lyra. Whatever her plans were, they clearly relied on her remaining undercover as a human.

It was well within his ability to ruin those plans.

There were two options he could see. He would force her to reveal herself or kill her in the process. Whatever cover she'd built would be burned away. Perhaps Damos and Lyra would see fit to deal with her themselves, thus evening the odds when he chose to finish his coup.

"Turn the radio scrambler off," he ordered.

Murray obeyed and fidgeted nervously with the controls. The dragon could understand his concern. The last man who had operated the scrambler had messed up and let the police reveal the location of this warehouse, although it seemed that in the end, only the one police carriage had heard the call and come to investigate. Still, failure was failure. He had hurled that man from the rooftop. It seemed Murray of the Breaks understood the implications of the not-so-subtle threat.

"It's down, sir," the gang leader said, his hands shaking.

"Tell everyone to converge on the warehouse. I want that carriage full of officers to eat lead. I want them to be roasted alive by the weapons I have given this city."

"Sir, if I give those orders, the police will come too."

"Let them come. More bodies means more bullets means more carnage." Mr Black didn't know this hidden dragon's game, but he knew it involved deception. He would force her to reveal herself and once he understood who she was, he would either enlist her to his side or leave her corpse in the shadows when he took this city from her.

"Breaks, Dead Reds, Knights, Eskeletos, Stray Cats—return to the roost."

Immediately, orders came from the human police to notify their officers to go to the warehouse.

Mr Black smiled. It was a good thing he could fly. He very much doubted this building would be standing by the end of the night.

CHAPTER NINETEEN

The team surveyed the warehouse before they stepped from the van. It was made of brick, about three stories tall, and in obvious disrepair. Most of the windows were broken. The walls at ground level sported graffiti, tags, and curses that had been written in spray paint over the years and never painted over. The only sections of the structure that didn't have spray paint were covered in vines.

Kristen marveled at how truly choked the building was with creepers. It was a wonder it still stood under all that weight. Two large metal hangar-style doors on one end of the warehouse were ajar. A few smaller doors dotted the one side of the building.

"All right," Drew said and assumed command of the van full of people. "I have no idea if anyone else heard us, which means we might not have reinforcements until after we've done our job."

"What's the plan?" one of the members of the other SWAT team asked and seemed willing to defer to his authority.

"We'll check the side doors first. If we can get through one, your team will go in and assess the scene while we look for another door and try to flank these assholes."

"That sounds about as smart as anything else," the leader of the other SWAT team said. Everyone nodded. It was either that or rush in through the slightly open hangar doors, but every single person in the van felt the same way about that. The open doors could only be a trap.

"Let's fucking do this thing," Jonesy said.

They kicked the back of the van open and poured out.

Apparently, subterfuge was lost on the hostiles inside the building. No sooner had they stepped from the vehicle than they began to take fire. A nest of snipers on the roof seemed eager to spill blood.

"Inside—get the fuck inside," Drew shouted and everyone in the group obeyed without question. They sprinted toward the hangar doors as shots rained from above.

They made it inside without a casualty. Kristen counted that a huge victory until she realized what they were up against.

Despite the recent gentrification of the warehouse district, the building they entered was still a crumbling reminder of Detroit's industrial past. An assembly line of some kind snaked back and across the floor. A conveyer belt at the center of all the machinery made her think the place used to make car parts or shoes or something else relatively small. Every now and then, a workstation broke up the snaking conveyor belt. She didn't know what any of the machines were exactly, but they looked long-unused and obsolete. A catwalk across the top of the building overlooked the entire operation. The walls were piled high with crates and other stacks dotted the floor, either abandoned there long before or moved there recently.

She leaned toward the latter because hostile gunfire clattered from all these places. Weapons teams were posted at the assembly line and the machines spaced sporadically around it, on the catwalk above them, and behind the crates spread around the factory floor.

"Get back outside," Drew yelled. They had been right about this being a trap.

The SWAT van exploded before they could even turn to obey.

"There's cover." She pointed to a stack of crates perhaps twenty feet ahead and to the left.

"Follow Red!" he ordered and she surged forward.

She sprinted as fast as she could, dove, and connected hard with the concrete floor, but at least it was smooth enough to allow her to slide and crash into the crates.

Quickly, she looked behind her. Her team, the other SWAT team, and the two police officers followed, but they were slow—too slow. One of the two police officers who'd been in the van with them took a shot in the chest and crumpled. One of the SWAT was hit too but fortunately, he wore Kevlar so he only stumbled, cursed louder than the barrage of gunfire, and pushed on.

Gunshots nearby were loud enough to almost deafen her. She realized that a hostile used the same stack of crates for cover, albeit on the other side.

Kristen scurried around the edge of the crates but stopped when she came under fire. The hostiles knew she was there, then.

She glanced once more at her team.

The other cop was down too.

"Goddammit!" she cursed and rage swelled in her chest. She didn't know either officer personally, but she knew they had friends and family and had died protecting their city from a mob of violent lunatics. No matter what, she couldn't let their deaths be in vain.

Fully committed to her course of action, she crouched and leapt up with every ounce of strength she had. She cleared the first crate and hooked her fingers over the top of the second. Quickly, she hauled herself up and peered down at the two hostiles who'd killed two police officers.

It was a simple fact that she could shoot them and no one would blame her. They were cop-killers, after all, and heavily armed, but she chose not to. She didn't need to, not yet. If she fired at one of the other assholes who actively tried to eliminate her team and she killed them, fine. This was different. Stupid, maybe, but different because they weren't actually firing at present. Somehow, that made a difference.

So, instead of two quick shots, she vaulted off the top of the crate and landed between the two men. Her decision had been made none too soon as the warehouse of criminals seemed to collectively notice she had presented herself as a target when she stood on the crates.

Fortunately, she had already begun her descent by the time they tried to respond.

"What the fuck?" one of the gang members managed to say before she kicked him in the face hard enough to break his nose and knock him unconscious.

The other man raised his weapon and she grasped the barrel.

For a moment, intense heat flared in the palm of her hand as she held the burnished steel but the sensation faded quickly. She yanked the weapon from the man's hands and struck him across the face with it.

He catapulted away and struck the concrete at an awkward angle. He'd live but he'd also remember the impact for a long time.

Kristen doubled back to where her team hunkered behind the stack of crates.

"We have to split up." Drew had to yell to be heard over the gunfire that kept them all pinned. "We need someone to draw fire—my thought is they make for the assembly line in the middle of the plant—and the other team will use the crates on the side of the warehouse as cover as they work toward the catwalk. If we can get Butters above these fuckers, we'll be all right."

"I'll go with him," Beanpole said.

"Me too," volunteered the sniper who'd taken the shot from the back of the moving van.

"I'll take the assembly line." Kristen gritted her teeth.

"Oh, for fuck's sake, Red, you beat me to it." Jonesy grinned as if they'd both ordered the same kind of ice cream cone instead of having both agreed to use their bodies as bait.

"I'll come with you two as well. Hernandez, Keith—"

The woman darted out from behind the crates and fired her assault rifle at someone on the catwalk. A scream and crash confirmed that not only had Hernandez hit her target, but she'd knocked him from his post. "Yeah, fucking yeah. We're right behind you."

"That means the rest of you will take the crates to the catwalk."

"Yes, sir!" the other members of SWAT replied.

"Watch how's it done, Red," Jonesy said.

Hernandez, Keith, and Drew each selected a target and laid down cover fire while Jonesy sprinted toward the conveyor belts in the middle of the factory. He made it without taking a bullet from the dozen or so gunman who fired at him and immediately began a retaliatory assault.

"Keith?" Drew said between rounds of gunfire.

The other man nodded and raced toward Jonesy. While the sergeant had run in a straight line, he swerved in a zig-zag pattern, hoping to confuse the gunmen.

It was a bad plan and a burst of red erupted from his left calf. He'd been shot.

"Rookie!" Jonesy yelled but didn't move. Too many people had him pinned down.

Kristen sprang into action. She hurtled across the open floor, caught her teammate by the collar of his Kevlar, and dragged him to their teammate.

"Holy fuck, Red. You didn't even slow down."

She looked at him in confusion. What he'd said was true, but the floor was smooth and Keith wasn't that heavy. Really, it was kind of crazy that the man could think about such a dumb thing with lead raining down all around them.

"Am I gonna die?" Keith asked from under the conveyer belt.

"For fuck's sake, rookie." The sergeant shook his head. "They got you in the damn calf. You might bleed out in maybe nine hours, but we'll probably all be dead by then."

"Ready?" Drew yelled from across the floor.

Jonesy and Kristen responded by laying down a wide spray of cover fire across the room while their two teammates raced over to join them. As soon as they reached the factory machinery, they turned and joined the barrage against the hostiles.

She stole a glance at Butters and Beanpole. They'd left the crates and attempted to reach the wall. One of the SWAT team fell when the group made it perhaps halfway.

Relief that it wasn't Butters or Beanpole surged briefly but she pushed it back, furious at herself for dismissing another man's life.

This had to end.

"What now, sir?" she yelled at Drew.

"We keep moving, follow this belt, and try to draw their fire and eliminate as many as we can."

It seemed clear enough and she didn't need to be told twice. She crouched under the conveyer and when she realized there wasn't enough height to even do that, dropped on her belly and army-crawled until she reached the next piece of machinery on the assembly line. She darted out, found a hostile reloading his weapon, and kicked him so hard in the chest that she felt ribs break under her boot.

"Nice fucking moves, Red." Jonesy emerged from under the belt and fired at a hidden gunman. Drew and Hernandez followed.

Their distraction wouldn't be enough, though. They only had limited space in which to move before they either ran out of cover or had to double back. The plan would only work if Butters, Beanpole, and the other snipers could make it to a proper vantage point.

Which meant they had to keep the pressure on the enemy.

Her gaze settled on three men who hid behind a nearby stack of crates.

"They're mine," she told Drew and sprinted toward them.

Her plan worked. Every eye in the abandoned factory found her and redirected their fire as she left cover.

Thankfully, they were too slow.

By the time the barrage started, Kristen had already careened into the stack of crates. They wouldn't fire on their own men, which meant she could deal with these three in relative safety. Unfortunately, while the logic was sound, the hostiles disregarded what seemed obvious to her.

A maelstrom of bullets continued relentlessly. She felt something smack her head and realized that if she hadn't worn a helmet, she'd be dead.

The men she'd targeted were already dead—killed by their own allies.

Still, the fusillade continued with no respite.

Another shot struck in her the back and she was saved again by her armor.

She couldn't keep taking that risk, though, so she punched a hole in one of the crates. The wood splintered under her fist and she crawled inside.

Now in relative safety, she peered out. It was dumb luck that she could see all the way across the floor to where Butters, Beanpole, and the rest of the officers scaled a ladder on their way to the crosswalk.

She froze, a hand to her mouth as a silver rocket careened overhead and directly toward the group.

It struck a few rungs below Beanpole, engulfed everyone below him in flames, and shook the ladder hard enough to almost dislodge him.

Butters—already on the catwalk—turned and caught his teammate, but it was too late for the others. They'd either been obliterated or had fallen more than twenty feet onto a concrete floor. One way or the other, an entire SWAT team had been eliminated from this fight.

Which meant their plan had gone from stupid to suicidal.

At least the explosion had distracted most of the warehouse.

Kristen crawled from the crate and sprinted to her team.

"With that little stunt, I think we're down to six hostiles," Drew said and deliberately didn't acknowledge that they'd lost so many of their own men. "We can finish this if we keep our heads on straight. The plan's the same. Keep eyes off Butters and Beanpole."

She nodded. They really had no other choice, and the sniper was a good enough shot to take out six men, of that she was certain. They could do this and would mourn the dead when they made it out alive.

The team froze and looked at one another when tires squealed and vehicles revved outside. She looked through vines that had grown over the windows of the warehouse to see car after car after car come to a halt. Men and women poured out of each one, obviously pissed-off and armed to the teeth. Suddenly, instead of being in a building with six hostiles, they were surrounded by sixty.

Her jaw clenched. It didn't take a veteran to realize that things had become a whole shitload worse.

CHAPTER TWENTY

Drew instructed them to direct their fire at the entrance to the factory. Kristen reasoned that even this would keep the hostiles already inside sufficiently distracted so Butters could at least eliminate them without taking fire himself, but the plan wasn't fated to work.

The problem was that there were multiple entrances to the building and the hostiles knew this. As a result, while Kristen and Jonesy peppered the entrance they'd come through with consistent fire, Drew, Keith, and Hernandez had to try to keep another group from entering the building from the opposite direction.

That worked for about thirty seconds. There were far too many crates placed around the area. To her, it was obvious that the gangs had repositioned the junk in this abandoned factory to provide maximum advantageous cover. She and the sergeant each managed to shoot an entering gang member, but too many made it behind a pile of crates and immediately returned fire.

Worse still, Drew was equally unsuccessful, so they went from barely being able to hide from six people around the room to being the targets of closer to fifty.

"We gotta get the fuck out of here!" Jonesy shouted over the now constant roar of gunfire.

"All right, here's the plan—" His words cut off abruptly when another team burst through the door and unleashed a concerted attack on the trapped SWAT team.

"These assholes are getting close," Jonesy warned. "That pile of crates we were at—Kristen, watch out!"

He pounded into her and time seemed to slow.

One moment, she stood and focused on the enemy.

In the next, his body shoved her hard and she fell, her gaze locked on his fully extended torso and the grimace of pain on his face.

The bullet struck him squarely in the chest.

She was so high on adrenaline that she actually saw a shockwave spread from the point of impact on his chest.

In the same breath, another bullet struck, followed by another.

Seven shots in total pummeled the man before he crash-landed, and only five of them had been blocked by the vest.

"Jonesy!" she screamed as she returned to the regular flow of time. Her gun was up and the man who shot her teammate was dead.

Kristen dropped to her knees. He looked at her and blood seemed to ooze between his teeth. One of the bullets had grazed his neck and the other under his armpit—or, at least, that was where the most blood seemed to be coming from.

"He's going to be okay, right?" she asked and looked at Drew with wild eyes.

He didn't answer but he didn't need to. The set of his jaw and his cold stare told her everything she needed to know.

"He needs a fucking medic," Keith shouted and fired at what now seemed like an unending stream of foes.

"What's the fucking plan to save Jonesy?" Terror crept into Hernandez's voice.

"We crawl under this conveyer belt, get as close to the door as we can, and we run for it. Then, we wait for reinforcements to get here so we can go back in for Butters and Beanpole."

"He doesn't have that kind of time," she said. "I'm taking him out."

"Hall, you'll never make it," Drew protested.

"The fuck I won't."

She had always been athletic and recently, she'd trained damn hard. Not only that, her best friend—for that was what she realized Jonesy had become—was dying. She simply scooped him up in her arms, looked at the exit, and ran.

The entire factory and the whirlwind of bullets faded to something abstract. All she could hear were her own footsteps, the sound of the bullets that struck the concrete around her feet, and Jonesy, who continued to talk despite the fact that she'd told him to shut the fuck up.

"You know you're not supposed to carry victims like this." He coughed. "I might have a spinal injury." He laughed.

"I'll get you patched up." She hammered into a pile of crates and felt the other side of them torn to splinters as the hostiles focused their weapons on her.

"Make sure you tell Hernandez to go fuck herself at least once a day. Otherwise, she doesn't feel appreciated."

"Will you shut up?"

He nodded and coughed up blood. "That's good, but you really need a 'fuck' in there. Otherwise, she won't believe it."

"You hang on," she retorted and when there was the briefest lull in the shooting, she sprinted the rest of the way to the door. Something caught her in the back—a bullet, no doubt—but her armor enabled her to continue. Why hadn't it protected Jonesy? Why had she failed him?

Finally, they were outside.

Vehicles of every make and model surrounded the warehouse. There seemed to be an endless variety of old hotrods, tiny street racers, boats of cars with tricked-out suspension, and even pink scooters.

Kristen wanted to slash the tires of each and every one.

Instead, she continued to run to the next ring of vehicles—police cars, SWAT vans and—blessedly—a pair of ambulances.

"We're almost there, Jonesy. Hold on, please."

CHAPTER TWENTY-ONE

One of the EMTs threw open the back of an ambulance when he saw her race forward with Jonesy in her arms. He directed her to lay him on a stretcher.

"He was shot!" Kristen shrieked.

"Yes, ma'am."

"In the neck."

"We know ma'am," another EMT said as he dressed the wound on her friend's neck.

"And his side."

"Ma'am, I need you to step back and let us do our job."

"Give 'em some fucking breathing room, Red, for fuck's sake."

"Sir, please don't talk."

"Shut the fuck up." He laughed. "See? Like that. You gotta mean it."

The EMTs removed his bulletproof vest and shirt to reveal a number of shitty tattoos and a hole in the left side of his body. She almost threw up when she saw the size of the injury and the dark-red blood that oozed out of the wound.

"That bad, huh?" He grinned.

One of the EMTs put a bandage over the injury. In moments, it was soaked through with blood.

"We need an IV," the man said. "Sir, your blood type?"

"O fucking negative."

One of the medics hurried to call that in to the hospital trauma team. She had somehow assumed they'd anticipate the need and have it with them—or that they always carried it. Kristen had no idea. She was supposed to call EMS for hostages or people who were caught in the crossfire, not need their services for her damn friend.

The other EMT poked Jonesy's arm with a needle connected to a tube. He attached it to a bag of clear fluid. Painkillers, she hoped. The other man continued to examine the armpit wound and scowled, his face anxious.

"You did good back there, Red. Seriously. You have what it takes." He grimaced.

She shook her head. "No, I don't. I didn't see that shooter until it was too late. I could've shot him and you'd be fine."

"Don't be so fucking greedy, Red. You took a bullet for me, which was a real dick move, by the way."

"Well, you took seven for me. If taking one makes me a dick, then seven—"

"Makes me a real fucking asshole."

"You're not an asshole. You're my friend."

"Oh, cut the Hallmark crap. We're not friends."

"Yes, we are."

"We're not friends. I don't want to get a fucking tangerine martini with you for Christ's sake. We're teammates…we're partners." He fell into a coughing fit.

"I think we have internal injuries here," one of the EMTs said. "His BP is dropping rapidly, and the blood I can see from the side wound isn't enough to account for that. How they could stay so calm when a man was bleeding out in their hands was utterly beyond her comprehension.

"We're more than friends, Red. How many of your friends have you taken bullets for?"

"I don't know. A couple?"

A joke was the wrong move. He laughed and the EMTs cursed as the bandage under his armpit shifted and he lost the pressure he'd attempted to apply.

"You need to lie still and stop talking."

"Fuck you, you fucking pissant. I've seen enough men die to know that I am completely and irretrievably fucked."

"Jonesy!" Kristen gasped.

"You thought I was gonna make it? Maybe you are the fucking rookie."

"Jonesy, stop talking."

"No way. Fuck you and fuck them and fuck everyone." He laughed again. "You took a bullet for me, Red. That's what a team is all about. We look out for each other, take care of each other, and take bullets for each other if that's what it takes to keep each other safe."

"But you're not safe."

Jonesy smirked. His bloody teeth made her shiver with real fear that she struggled to keep at bay because losing him was unthinkable. "But you are, and we both know you're the only one who can save the rest of our team."

"I'm not leaving you."

"I knew you'd say that, but don't worry. I won't make you. Remember, though, the team needs you… You need to…go to them…to keep them safe… Only…only—" He coughed and it was bad this time. Flecks of blood tinged his spittle. It was only then that she realized one of his lungs must have ruptured. That was where the blood was coming from.

"Only what?"

"Only don't get shot again… It…it fucking… It fucking sucks…"

He exhaled, his chest fell, and it never rose again.

For a moment, Kristen heard nothing but a high-pitched blare. She realized after a moment that it was the heart monitor to tell the EMTs his heart had stopped.

"We're sorry, officer," one of the EMTs said but she couldn't hear him. She couldn't hear anything beyond the sound of her failing Jonesy and the sound of his heart stopping. Her own heart had pounded in her ears in mockery while his had ceased. It was completely unfair. He shouldn't have done that. If he hadn't have done that—

An explosion rang out and sliced through the sorrow that threatened to grasp her by the throat and never let her go.

The people who'd killed Jonesy were still in that warehouse.

Her team was in there with them—vastly outnumbered, pinned down, and to quote Jonesy, fucked.

Kristen dragged in a breath and looked around. The SWAT teams outside the building were preparing an assault. They didn't have time to prepare. They needed to act and do it now. Her team was in there, surrounded by a horde of damn lunatics, and the rest of the police force was out there talking about taking prisoners and zones of defense?

She wanted to scream that didn't have time for this nonsense and needed to act.

But it was pointless. They wouldn't, not in time.

Only she would.

Her sorrow blossomed and burned away. Rage swept in behind to fill the space. It came from the loss of her friend and it pointed itself at the bloodthirsty morons who thought they could take a city—her city—from the people who lived there.

As her fury grew, she balled her hands into fists.

It settled into an implacable determination—she wouldn't allow these assholes to take her city, but she wouldn't let her anger blind her, either. All those months of training had readied her for this moment. She channeled her white-hot fury into what she knew and let it cool and harden into ice.

A moment later, she ran back into the warehouse to save her friends.

CHAPTER TWENTY-TWO

Someone had closed the door to the warehouse, but it didn't matter. Kristen kicked the giant metal door with enough force to dent it and force it off its hinges.

Voices cried out in surprise, then fell silent.

Good. She'd already snuffed out the lives of two of these murderers and wounded a few others. Let them see she was unafraid.

A moment of silence settled over the space as every gun turned to aim at her. That was also good. The more they focused on her, the less they'd focus on her team.

She didn't want to think about what she'd do if they hurt anyone else. God help them all if it was anyone on her team, but if they hurt Butters... Well, she simply wouldn't let them.

A moment before every weapon opened fire, she sprinted forward to a stack of crates. Two hostiles were hidden on the far side. She ducked around it, picked one of them up by his throat, and let his allies shoot him in the back while he shielded her from their bullets. Despite the fact that she used one of their own as a shield, the barrage didn't even slow. She swung his corpse at his ally with enough force to hurl them both through the crates they'd huddled behind.

Part of her wondered vaguely at the strength needed to do it, but people were trying to kill her and she let the thought leave her mind.

Her cover was destroyed, so she snatched up the lid of one of the crates and raced deeper into the building. She wielded it like a shield to intercept bullets intended to kill her. Oddly enough, she could feel that she moved faster than she'd ever done before. She couldn't dodge bullets but she knew enough about how people used guns to keep out of their way as she sprinted toward her team.

To confuse the enemy, she alternated between direct burst and zigzag maneuvers, which brought her closer and closer to her destination while she held the lid of the crate between her and the army of thugs. Occasionally, small jolts of pain made her think of the airsoft range. Surely getting shot hurt more than this? Maybe she had merely been grazed.

An unfamiliar instinct inside her told her to keep going. She felt a power she'd never felt before. Whatever it was, it was fueled by the loss of one of her friends and the threat of losing more. She wouldn't let that happen. The power inside her told her that she didn't have to.

Something caught her squarely in the chest and Kristen whirled to careen the lid of the crate across the arena. It spun, easily as fast as a circular saw, and decapitated a man. She felt nothing at the carnage. He'd tried to kill her team and got what he deserved. It had been quick, at least, which was more than she could say for Jonesy.

Two men bounded into her path, both armed with shotguns. Kristen flung herself aside, rolled, and came up behind another stack of crates. The two men tried to come around either side—she could somehow hear their voices over the gunfire—so she shoved the entire pile of crates and toppled them to crush both men and kill them instantly.

Hexagonal nuts spilled from the broken boxes and for the briefest of moments, she wondered how she'd been able to move them. Each one must have weighed close to a ton. She'd heard of people being able to tap into reserves of strength in situations like this, but it seemed beyond what should be possible. There was a power inside her, though—the same power that had always been there and that had propelled her through the police academy and had earned every trophy on her wall. Only now, she really used it.

She wondered how she knew it was there or even how to tap into it, but that wasn't important. Not now. Her team was still in trouble and she'd use this strength she hadn't known she'd possessed without asking unnecessary questions.

Gunshots ripped into the wooden crates she'd been hiding behind in almost the same moment that she broke from cover and ran toward the conveyer. She reached it with a headlong sprint through the middle of the warehouse and located her team. They were still crawling under the belt, following it as it snaked through the now deadly warehouse floor. They had barely made it twenty feet, and Keith was still bleeding.

"Hall, get the fuck under here," Drew said.

"Get ready to run," she replied and kicked the entire conveyer belt—metal frame and all—over onto its side to give the team a shield that protected them from half the warehouse as they made their exit. She would protect them from the other half and the twenty hostiles on that side.

"There are still people on the other side," Hernandez protested. "We'll never make it."

"They're mine."

"You're not a one-man army," Drew blurted.

"You're right. I'm not a man," she replied.

Something between fear and awe entered his eyes. "We'll go for it. Butters is still up top but we'll be back with reinforcements to get him. Hall, you cover us and follow us out."

"Go," she said, took Hernandez's assault rifle, and fired at the enemy who could still target her team effectively. They retaliated but the constant barrage of gunfire seemed to have slowed. They'd realized they couldn't hit the redheaded warrior, so had changed tactics. That was fine with her.

Drew, Hernandez, and Keith stumbled out of the warehouse, over the damaged doors, and to safety. "Hall, come on!"

Kristen looked at the sunlight streaming into the warehouse and considered it. She might have to leave. There were too many of the criminals, and she didn't know where Butters was. She could kill more of them—surely she could—but she didn't know how many. What mattered wasn't vengeance—not yet. What mattered was saving Butters.

Then, she saw the man with the rocket launcher.

He'd already aimed at her—he must have already aimed at her team—but now that she had kicked the conveyer belt on its side, he had an easy shot.

Before she could move, he launched the rocket unerringly at her. She leapt over the conveyer belt and tried to use it for cover, but barely a half-inch of steel and less of rubber padding might be able to slow bullets enough to make them non-lethal, but it wouldn't do a damn thing against a rocket.

The last thing she saw before the heat from the explosion forced her eyes closed was her scanty barrier blown to bits and she was engulfed in flames.

CHAPTER TWENTY-THREE

Kristen Hall stepped from the flames. She had thought being hit by a rocket would have hurt more but she had hardly felt it.

Curiously, she looked at her arms. The sleeves of her shirt had burned away and her skin was visible but it was different. It gleamed like polished chrome. She turned her hand and stared at it from all sides. Every speck of it was the same—shiny, gleaming metal. She looked at her chest. Her body armor was still there and her police belt, although they too were now made of steel. Her pants were mostly intact, although her shoes were gone. Steel toenails reflected a face made of metal.

I did this. Somehow, she'd turned herself and her clothes to metal. Well, most of them anyway. Obviously, she'd let the sleeves of her shirt and her shoes get burned in the explosion.

What did this mean? What was she?

A bullet struck her in the chest and her moment of self-reflection was over.

It didn't hurt, not at all. In fact, it didn't even dent her steel skin but it reminded her why she was there. The pathetic excuses for human beings in this warehouse had killed Jonesy.

She flinched when something struck her face. It was like being sprayed with a water hose—annoying, distracting, and uncomfortable. She held a hand up to block whatever it was, looked through the torrent, and realized it wasn't water, but bullets. Someone was firing a mounted machine gun and its ammunition felt like water to her.

Kristen smiled. Vengeance would come easy this day.

Roused from her distraction and spurred into action, she raced forward. Her metal body didn't slow her in the least. She didn't feel heavy or sluggish, either. In fact, she felt great. Reflexes honed in the last few months kicked in and she moved easily as the barrage of gunfire tried to pin her down. They couldn't even hit her, not that it would have mattered.

When she reached the vehicle with the mounted machine gun, she punched the hood simply to see what she could do. It crumpled like aluminum foil.

"Get me the fuck out of here!" The woman operating the weapon yelled and was immediately lifted into the air by a pair of chains connected to a platform. The machine gun went with her.

Kristen vaulted upward but fell short and landed on the vehicle. Her steel body crushed its roof.

More bullets pounded into her from behind and she turned to face the men on the floor. They were on her level. She'd kill them all, then get up on the catwalk and finish the job.

Someone fired another rocket.

It missed her but impacted the truck beneath her feet instead. When the crate of explosives in the bed blew up, she knew that had been the intention.

The blast was much larger than the last one. It catapulted her through the warehouse and into another pile of crates. These splintered when her steel body plowed into them and scattered their contents on the hostiles who'd hidden behind them.

They tried to flee, but they still carried their weapons. If they managed to scurry away, they'd be a threat to her friends. She struck each only once and the force of her blows was enough to end their fragile lives.

More shots ricocheted off her and she sprinted toward their source.

"We surrender!" one of the men who'd fired at her seconds before shouted.

She hesitated for a moment, unsure how to take a prisoner in the middle of this mess. The man used the opportunity to draw a pistol from the back of his waistband.

He never had a chance to fire it. She surged forward, picked him up by his shirt, and flung him across the room. He careened into another woman who'd been firing at her. She didn't know if they'd live and honestly didn't care.

When another volley was released from above, she looked up and located a ladder to the catwalk.

Quickly, Kristen ran to it, stepped on the bottom step, and felt it shift beneath the weight of her steel body. It held, fortunately, so she climbed steadily.

At the top, the man with the launcher attempted to load another rocket. His nerves obviously had the better of him, though, and he shook and cursed as he tried to shove the missile in place.

She picked him up as if he weighed no more than an insect and pitched him off the platform. He screamed as he fell but abruptly went silent.

Her gaze settled on the rocket and she picked it up and considered crushing it in her hand.

"Don't. Someone might be able to use that to understand who was behind this."

Startled, she looked at Butters. She had completely forgotten he was there and that he was the reason she had come back in. Vengeance had blinded her and almost cost her the life of a teammate. He was all right. She smiled. He was all right. A surge of relief washed over her and in a moment, her skin flickered from steel to flesh. "Where's Beanpole?" She immediately felt guilty for not asking sooner.

"So, this is weird," the man said and peeked over Butters' shoulder.

At another flurry of fire, the two men both dropped to the platform and yelled at her to do the same. She ignored them—she was impervious to gunfire, after all.

Except she'd transformed from steel to flesh once again.

She held up her hand to stop the barrage of bullets and as soon as the hot slug of metal met her skin, her body transformed. Instantly, she was made of steel and the bullet bounced off.

"Stay here," she said. "I've cleared the back of the warehouse. I'll finish the job."

Kristen expected Butters to protest but instead, he pointed ahead and to the right. "Whatever machine they have that's blocking the radios is over there. We tried to get to it, but we're not…uh…well, we're not made of steel."

"Here." Beanpole thrust his assault rifle in her hands. She hadn't realized she'd lost Hernandez'. She took it with a nod of thanks.

Once she'd moved past Butters and Beanpole, she watched them start down the ladder and she continued her assault on the people who'd killed Jonesy and tried to take her city from the people who called it home.

Armed with an assault rifle and protected by her steel skin, she was an unstoppable force of destruction. She turned toward every shot that struck her and returned fire. So much of her SWAT training had been about firing at hostiles while remaining behind cover but now, she didn't have to do that. She simply turned, took aim, allowed bullets to glance off her, and fired at her attacker. Even though her aim wasn't perfect, she found her marks after a few attempts. After all, they ducked constantly behind crates and the ruined conveyer belt and craned their necks up to see her. She stood still and breathed carefully like she was at the shooting range.

She continued forward to a branch in the crosswalk and turned to the right. Ahead of her lay a strange machine and one of the mounted machine guns. She approached while the man operating the machine gun released the full force of the weapon against her.

The bullets proved futile and simply *pinged* off her as she approached like harmless distractions. She reached the machine and pounded it with a steel fist. Immediately, her radio came to life with voices.

"We have radio."

"The machine's down. Hall destroyed it." That voice belonged to Butters.

"I have eyes on her, Drew. She's on the catwalk. Hostiles are unloading a machine gun into her chest."

"Hall, get out of there!" Drew bellowed.

Kristen didn't respond.

"I don't think she needs to, sir," someone said. She assumed it was one of the snipers who no doubt had eyes on her.

"Then we'll go in." A shout erupted from the front of the warehouse as SWAT poured into the building and assumed defensive positions near the door.

The man with the machine gun continued to fire at her. It was shocking how little she felt it and she again wondered what was happening to her. Was someone on SWAT a mage who had cast some kind of a protection spell on her? She knew next to nothing about the humans who could wield magic, but she didn't know how else to explain this.

She was a girl from the suburbs of Detroit. Her mom and dad were normal people—except they weren't her mom and dad, not biologically and had been entrusted with her and told to keep her safe. They'd done so and even kept her safe enough to never have to fully reveal whatever this power was inside her. Now, it was her turn to protect their city.

She stepped forward and flipped the machine that had jammed the radios off the catwalk like it was nothing more than an empty cardboard box.

The hostile maintained the machine gun fire, so she rushed forward and thrust him from the catwalk with a single kick.

"Sir, she walked into over a hundred goddamn bullets. I don't know what we can do to help her," said a voice over the radios. "She's...she's not human!"

"I don't give a shit what she is because she's my damn teammate. We can cover our goddamn teammate," Drew replied. More gunshots followed. The hostiles now focused their firepower on the SWAT members who entered the warehouse.

Perhaps, if they'd surrendered, Kristen could have been talked into sparing their lives. But instead, they insisted on killing more and more people. Even in the face of defeat, they refused to lay down their arms.

The rattle of heavy machine gunfire joined the sounds of radio chatter and assault rifles. She looked ahead of her and across the catwalk that traversed the warehouse. The woman with the mounted machine gun who had escaped her earlier was there and aimed at the SWAT team.

"No!" she shouted and sprinted forward as the weapon began to fire.

The woman smiled with gleeful malice. Kristen remembered the expression from a boy she'd been in fourth grade with. He took pleasure in ripping the legs from insects. This woman's expression was the same—satisfaction derived from the suffering of others was a sick thing, truly.

She thought of the people she'd killed but reminded herself that she'd done it because they were intent on destroying this city and her teammates and because they'd killed Jonesy. Had they deserved to die? Maybe. But was that her role? To decide who lived and who died?

No. No, it couldn't be. Not if she wanted to think of herself as different than this woman.

"Hey!" she hollered at the hostile. "Stop now, and you live."

"Fuck you, fucking dragon-bitch! I might not be able to kill you but I'll bleed your friends out like the fat fucking piggies they are. We'll burn this place down and the whole damn city will smell like bacon." The gang member laughed maniacally and resumed her assault on the men and women below her.

Furious, she bounded forward and pushed her new abilities to their absolute limit. She ignored what the woman had called her and how much sense it made. The catwalk shook beneath as she raced forward, running faster than she'd ever thought possible.

Despite the threats to kill her friends, she still turned the machine gun on Kristen as she approached.

Exactly like the other one, it did nothing to her. She embraced the gunfire because she knew that each shot fired at her was one not fired at her teammates below.

In the span of a few heartbeats, she was inches away from the gun.

"I said stop." She grasped the barrel and twisted it in her hands, bending the steel up back around like it was a pipe cleaner.

"Fuck you!" The woman drew a knife and darted toward her.

She vowed to herself in that moment not to become like this woman—obsessed with murder and nothing else. Her willingness to continue to kill, even in the face of obvious defeat, was disgusting.

The thought gave her pause. She honestly didn't want to kill her— she didn't want to kill anyone else, not unless she had to in order to protect the people she loved.

Instead of catching her by the throat or kicking her in the chest or any number of other simple maneuvers that would now be lethal because of her steel skin, she simply punched the machine gun with all her force and repeated herself. "I said, stop!"

The blow was enough to destroy the weapon like it was made of playdough rather than metal. It was also enough to sever the catwalk from whatever supports had suspended it.

The entire structure groaned, then lurched.

"Hold on!" she shouted to the woman, but she obviously didn't have the necessary reflexes.

When the platform lurched, she jolted off the edge and plummeted to a messy death in the middle of the SWAT team.

"Get out of here!" Kristen screamed at the people below her.

"You heard her. Go!" Drew ordered the officers around him and no one argued.

As the catwalk ripped free, Detroit's SWAT team left the building and moved clear of the falling piece of metal with moments to spare.

She rode the twisting network of platforms, railings, and ladders to the floor. Her weight was such that when she landed, she cracked the concrete.

The catwalk followed with a thunderous crash to shatter everything and release a great plume of dust.

Calmly, she stood and walked from the building.

CHAPTER TWENTY-FOUR

The team waited for Kristen when she stepped out of the warehouse. Jonesy's absence left an enormous hole in their ranks that she felt immediately.

"Hall," Drew said by way of greeting. His voice was shaky.

"Thanks for checking that we cleared the building," Butters said. She didn't think she'd ever heard the jovial southerner sound angry before. Right now, he sounded furious.

She swallowed. In all the violence, she'd forgotten about getting him and Beanpole out. While she'd told herself that was why she went back in, was it true? Once inside, all she had wanted was vengeance.

"We left through one of the other exits," Beanpole said. "A while before you crushed every man and woman in your path."

"Seriously, Red. We've all eliminated a hostile in the line of duty. It comes with the fucking territory, but fuck…there's limits, you know?" Hernandez shook her head.

"There will be an investigation into what happened here," Drew stated and made a visible effort to return his voice to normal. "What you've done—"

"Was fucking rad!" Keith interjected. He was the only one of the team who'd been substantially injured. Besides Jonesy, of course. He was dead and her team was chewing her out?

"It was not," the team leader countered. "You used a level of violence beyond anything the police would normally allow. You killed—we don't even know how many people you killed."

"Those thugs killed Jonesy." Kristen could feel her rage rising again. She clenched her fists involuntarily and realized she was still in her steel skin but didn't change it. "They intended to burn the whole damn city down. They didn't act like people. They acted like a pack of rabid dogs."

He nodded. "I know. Believe me, I do, and everyone here knows we would have lost even more people if you hadn't…stepped up. But the fact remains that we had the enemies contained. They were all in that warehouse and we had them surrounded. You didn't have to—"

"Save your asses?" she cut in.

Drew shrugged. He seemed conflicted but ultimately thankful for his life. "I'm only saying you've made a mess, Kristen. Captain Hansen will have to punish you. One death—even of a hostile—means a mountain of paperwork. This? Well, this is like the goddamn Rocky Mountains of paperwork."

"Are you saying I shouldn't have done it? Even after they killed Jonesy? Are you saying I should have simply let them kill Butters and Keith and you because the paperwork will be too much to deal with?"

"Fuck that!" someone yelled, an officer from another SWAT team. "Those fucking dogs killed Donnie. If you hadn't had…uh…" The man paled when he realized he was talking to a woman with steel skin. "That is…uh, thank you, ma'am. My wife and kids will thank you too."

"I don't care if I'm in trouble. I did what needed to be done. I killed the people who killed one of my people." She removed her helmet. When she did so, it turned from steel to normal.

"They didn't all kill Jonesy," Butters said.

"They tried to. Everyone in there was hell-bent on murder. I did what had to be done to save this town. I don't know if any of you looked into their eyes, but I did. There was no remorse there, not in any of them. All they wanted was blood and death. I ended this conflict the only way I could."

"Hall, that's total horseshit." Drew clenched his jaw. "You could have fallen back and we could have kept them bottled in there for days."

"And how many lives would we have lost?"

"Not as many as you took."

"Watch how you talk to her, human. You're on the verge of setting her off again, which I don't think any of us want."

Drew turned to look at the person who'd interrupted. Kristen realized immediately that it was a dragon in human form. An aura poured off him and washed over her team, and they all took a slow step back. It swirled around her like water around rock. She didn't fear these dragons any more than she had the thugs inside the building.

She looked the man in the eyes and noticed they were orange with black slits like the eyes of a snake or a crocodile.

The Dragon—Stonequest, the name on his uniform read—stood tall, unintimidated by her despite her steel skin. "Do you know who we are?"

A quick appraisal of the other three with him confirmed that none of them were people either. She wasn't quite sure how she could tell, but she was absolutely certain these were dragons as well.

"You're dragons. Slow ones."

"Not merely dragons, you little runt, but Dragon SWAT." A woman with gorgeous steel-blue eyes hissed a warning. Her eyes were framed by perfect cheekbones and extremely long, platinum-blonde hair that was tied in tight French braids. To Kristen, she looked like a princess, not a member of a SWAT team.

"Easy Heartsbane," Stonequest said. "This one obviously doesn't know how things work around here."

Heartsbane only clenched her jaw at that, but she said nothing further.

Her companion continued. "Like she said, we're Dragon SWAT. Obviously, humans could never police dragons, so that's where we come in. We're the law above the law. When one of us breaks the peace or catches our leaders' attention, my team brings them in."

"So, what will you do—breathe fire on me? In case you didn't know, I survived a blast from a damn rocket launcher. I'm not scared of three dragons." She stepped forward and pushed past Stonequest, still in her steel skin. "You want me? Try to take me." She checked him with her shoulder and he took a step back to let her pass.

"She doesn't know." Heartsbane laughed derisively.

The two other dragons laughed as well.

"We're not here to bring you in. You've done nothing wrong—at least not for a dragon." Stonequest's voice rolled over her like a cooling wave.

She walked on as the words sank deeper and deeper into her mind. He didn't actually say… He couldn't have meant that she…that Kristen Hall was… She wasn't a dragon. Was she?

Kristen thought back to what her father had told her, about his sister working for the dragons at some kind of bioresearch lab. Her thoughts wandered to her training and how impressed everyone had been with how quickly she'd picked it all up. And she'd always been strong and fast. And then there was the matter of her steel skin. She looked at her hands. They shone in the streetlights that had come to life. But that simply meant…it meant she was a mage or something. Not that she was a dragon.

"Dragons are above ordinary police rules of engagement," Stonequest said and raised his voice. "Those thugs killed someone you considered yours. For a dragon, that's all the reason necessary to end a human life. An attack against someone under a dragon's protection is a direct affront and will never be tolerated. You only did what any dragon would have done in your situation."

Kristen stopped. "But I'm not a dragon."

The two who hadn't spoken shared a curious look. Heartsbane snorted and shook her head. Stonequest merely nodded. "Yes, you are. The steel skin is a sign that you are. It's unusual, certainly—an indication that you're different. A steel dragon, but a dragon all the same."

"So, you are here to bring me in?" She turned to them. "Try it. I won't go without a fight. I've never heard of a steel dragon and I'll bet you've never fought one." Her mind raced. Could this really be possible? Could she really be a dragon? But how could she have been one her entire life and not known it? How had she not discovered it sooner? A dragon had sent her to the academy, after all, and they'd been behind her assignment on a SWAT team. How long had they watched her?

Stonequest shook his head. "As I said, you've done nothing wrong. The people you killed"—he gestured to the building filled with dead thugs like they were nothing more than farm animals—"don't matter."

"Of course people matter!" she protested.

"Not those," Heartsbane countered. "We heard what they tried to do to the city. They were nothing more than beasts who needed to be put down. They couldn't have done all that themselves anyway. They must have been under the control of one of us. Monkeys don't know how to organize—"

"Heartsbane!" Stonequest cut her tirade short. "Watch your tongue or I'll have it out."

She stuck her tongue out. "Oh, for fire's sake. It would grow back in a month."

"Then I'd have a month of quiet."

Heartsbane regarded her leader and finally acquiesced. He focused on Kristen.

"Do you think that I… Do you think all this was my fault?" she asked.

He shook his head. "No. And we're not supposed to talk about open investigations." He directed a sharp look at Heartsbane. "But since she already spilled the coals, I think it's safe to say we sensed a dragon here and assumed it was responsible for what was happening. When we arrived, though, we found you. The trail of bodies you left behind does a fairly good job of convincing me that those people weren't under your sway."

"Then whose sway were they under?" she asked.

"We don't know." Stonequest didn't shrug so much as crack his neck. He was even bigger than Drew, and—if his powers were anything like hers—was probably far stronger than he looked. "We sensed a disturbance and came here. By the time we arrived, the only aura we could sense was yours."

"But you said I didn't do anything wrong. Why didn't you pursue whoever was behind this?"

"Your aura was stronger than anything else around here. If there was another dragon—and that's still an if—he must have fled, using your own aura for cover."

"But that doesn't explain why you're talking to me instead of trying to find the man, er—dragon, who tried to take this city over."

"Whoever the snake was, he failed against an inexperienced dragon who hasn't come into her powers yet. He's—what's the human expression? Small potatoes." Heartsbane smiled way too sweetly.

"When we realized you were in there, we told our superiors and they ordered us to make contact with you. New dragons don't simply appear out of nowhere and besides, you've been watched. Apparently, there was quite a betting pool on whether you were one of us or not." Stonequest grinned and made it obvious that he had money on that bet and also which side of it he'd placed his wager on.

"I heard Damos bet an entire chest of Spanish doubloons on you being human." One of the other two dragons laughed. "She's gonna be pissed."

"So what do you want from me?" Kristen asked. She clenched her fists. Okay, so maybe she was a dragon. It kind of made sense. Maybe...kind of. And on top of that, she was a steel dragon. Which apparently was unusual. Which meant if these assholes wanted a fight, they'd get one.

Stonequest shook his head and held his hands up, the palms down in a soothing way. "We'll want you to join us eventually, once you've come into your powers fully. When that happens, you'll be reassigned to Dragon SWAT. Until then, you are to remain with the human SWAT team to continue learning more and improving your skills."

"I...you can't simply pull my life around like I'm a puppet on a string."

He smiled indulgently. "Kristen, who do you think put you on SWAT in the first place?"

She had nothing to say to that and besides, he had raised another question in her mind.

"What did you mean by come into my powers fully?"

"This is like talking to a child," Heartsbane protested. But before Stonequest could reprimand her, she took a few steps back and transformed.

Wings sprouted from her back, spikes appeared down her spine, and she grew a tail. Her uniform and flesh transformed into scaly skin and for a moment, the image of a white demon stood before them—a man-sized, winged beast with scaly skin and glowing eyes—until she grew in size to become a dragon bigger than a car. Even in this form, she was beautiful. Her scales were as white as ivory, and ridges down her back caught the wind coming in off the river. With a pump of her wings, she became airborne and soared above them.

"There's more to being a dragon than being quick and strong."

"But my steel skin—"

"Is interesting," Stonequest said and cut her off. "Perhaps even unique. If the world were made only of humans, you could rule, no doubt, but we are dragons who have slain dragons. As long as you are stuck in your human form, you wouldn't stand a chance against us."

"Bullets bounced off me," she protested.

He narrowed his eyes. "I'm not here to threaten you, but don't think you're above us either. As long as you're in this form, you are weak and cannot challenge us. All I would need to do is order Heartsbane to snatch you up and drop you in the river. Steel sinks."

"I can change back—"

"And we could try other things. The volcanoes of Iceland aren't terribly far for beings such as us. We could drop you in one of those. It's not like you could fly out."

Kristen paled.

Stonequest smiled, although it was hard to tell if it was genuine with his slitted orange eyes. "But like I said, we're not here to threaten but to welcome. For the time being, you are to stay with the humans and continue to grow. Once you begin to realize your full potential, we'll be in touch."

She nodded. There really didn't seem to be anything else she could say.

He seemed to know this as he gestured at the other two dragons behind him. They all transformed from their human shape and took to the skies.

Numbly, she watched them vanish into the night.

After a moment, she realized that the rest of her team had watched the entire exchange.

For a moment, no one spoke. Finally, Hernandez broke the silence. "And I thought I was a bitch."

"They weren't so tough," Keith added and limped over to the group from the back of one of the ambulances. "Okay, yeah, they can fly and breathe fire and probably pick up a police car, but can they play airsoft?"

"I bet they wouldn't know gumbo from jambalaya," Butters added.

"Come on. Let's get back to the station," Drew said. "I heard that asshole say you're stuck with us humans for a while, which means none of us will do your paperwork for you. After all, great powers to manifest and all that shit."

"I don't think he meant I had powers over paperwork," she protested but laughed. She realized her steel skin had reverted to normal. Suddenly, she was exhausted.

"Why else would he wish you to stay with us?" Beanpole asked. "You defeated a small yet extremely well-equipped army. What more is there to learn than how to properly file a report?"

She shook her head and smiled at the insanity of it all. While she had no idea what the future held, she was glad her team would continue to be a part of it.

As soon as he had seen the police officer rise with steel skin, Mr Black had left his human form and the warehouse of gang members behind.

He'd become the black dragon, leapt across onto another nearby warehouse, and transformed into human form in a swirling cyclone of shadow and smoke. When he descended the stairs of this adjacent warehouse, his two personal guards waited for him with an armored getaway vehicle. He had expected to be successful, so it was a little frustrating when one of his men proffered a chilled bottle of champagne.

"Not tonight," he muttered angrily at the human. "Get me out of here."

"Sir?" The device that blocked the radios was useful when fighting coordinated human forces, but there were disadvantages like having to explain to his guards what happened.

"Another dragon was forced to reveal herself this night. In doing so, she unraveled my plans for this wretched city. Still, I don't believe she wished to reveal her powers, and even after all these centuries, information is still the most precious currency."

"Where to, sir?" one of them asked. The other guard offered him a cigar. The black dragon told himself he'd give that one a raise.

"Take me to my den. Her aura is giving me a headache. Also, there's...yes, dragon SWAT will be here soon. I'd hoped to deal with their masters from a place of power, but now—with this steel dragon emerging from nowhere—I don't wish to reveal myself yet. If I know anything about them, Dragon SWAT and their masters will try to keep the presence of this new steel dragon quiet, which suits me perfectly. After all, the dragons I know will be very interested to hear about a new player in the Motor City...very interested indeed."

CHAPTER TWENTY-FIVE

Drew had not been lying about the paperwork. By the time she was halfway through with it, her right hand ached from holding a pen for three days straight. Time spent on the shooting range was less physically demanding, she'd thought morosely more than once. Worse, there was the fact that she'd had to confront the identities of all the people she'd killed.

Despite them being criminals who'd killed Jonesy, after three days of reviewing their files, she felt guilty at ending all their lives so quickly. A few of them had kids. Some had wives. More had girlfriends or boyfriends. Kristen knew all but a few of the truly wretched would be missed. Hell, even the monsters would probably be missed. Human beings were funny when it came to emotions.

But the hostiles having friends and family only made their behavior even more confusing. These had been people who had tried to take over with guns and explosives. They would have burned the whole damn city down—their own city. What compelled people to take up arms and turn them against their homes? Detroit certainly had its fair share of protests in the past, but people armed with machine guns and rocket launchers trying to entrap SWAT was a level far beyond protests that turned violent. Had a dragon made them all behave so monstrously?

She didn't know and as far as the paperwork was concerned, it didn't matter.

Her team leader put a hand on her shoulder and broke her from the paperwork-induced stupor. "Hey, Hall. It's time."

Without a word, she nodded, stood, and followed him out of the station and into a police car. Butters was in the back seat. He remained silent and simply looked at her with a stoic grimace.

Drew turned the lights on but not the sirens and pulled out. Keith eased out behind them in another cruiser with Beanpole riding shotgun and Hernandez in the back. They drove in silence for a time until they made it to the funeral parlor.

"The viewing should be over soon," Drew said.

He was right and after a few minutes, people carrying a casket emerged from the funeral home and loaded it into a hearse. But it wasn't an "it" they loaded. It was Jonesy.

Kristen had already been to see the body. The coroner obviously hadn't known the man. He'd put makeup on him to cover his pockmarked face and persuaded his mouth to show a wry smile. Jonesy didn't smile. He sneered, he scowled, and he spat, but she had only seen him smile when he cussed someone out—and he wasn't cussing at anyone now.

The hearse pulled out and Drew followed it, leading the procession of police cars through the Motor City. She tried to keep herself from crying—they were driving in a funeral procession, after all, so there was no reason to weep yet. But when she heard Butters sobbing in the backseat, she stopped pretending like losing Jonesy didn't hurt and let herself mourn. The tears stung at first. It was like admitting he was dead all over again, but after a minute of pain, she began to feel better. It was amazing what a human could adapt to…or a dragon, she thought dully, still in shock at what she'd learned about herself.

"He was a pig, you know?" the sniper said.

Drew nodded. "It's Jonesy we're talking about. Show some respect. He was a fucking pig. A goddamn fucking pig." He stopped and dragged in a breath. "I... God, no one could curse like him, not even Hernandez."

"Don't mention that to her. She's in worse shape than anyone else," Butters mumbled.

She didn't know how it was possible for anyone to feel worse than she did. Jonesy died because of her—he'd taken those bullets for her, and he'd died because of it. And to think that if he hadn't jumped in the way, her steel skin probably would have stopped them anyway. "At least she didn't kill him," she blurted.

"Neither did you," Drew said with a sharpness that surprised her. "A criminal with a gun did. Don't forget that. I've seen too many officers blame themselves for the actions of a moron with a gun."

"But if I hadn't blocked that bullet in the pawnshop, maybe he wouldn't have tried to protect me and I would've transformed sooner. No matter how you look at it, his death is my fault."

"Don't you fucking do that Hall." His curse sounded as fierce as Jonesy's ever had.

"But it's true. If I had used my powers, I could have—"

"I don't give a shit about your powers, but I guess you're right. We all could have used a bulletproof dragon warrior a little earlier in the fight."

"Then why are you screaming at me?"

"Don't you dare act like Jonesy wasn't a goddamn hero. He would've taken those bullets regardless of whether you'd taken any for him. He was a hero. A goddamn hero." That cracked the man's stoic façade. He clenched his teeth and wiped his eyes before the tears could spill from them.

"Of course he was a hero," Butters said from the backseat. "Do you think we would've put up with his bullshit if he wasn't? He was a loud, disrespectful—and if I'm totally honest—racist son of a bitch. He made more enemies than friends and was a constant pain in my ass, but damn if he wasn't a good cop. He didn't let that shit get in his way either. He didn't curse out shoplifters or shoot black kids in the back like some cops do. He left his politics at home but not his damn tongue."

"Exactly," Drew said. "He was a fucking asshole, but he was a great fucking cop." He shook his head and forced himself not to cry.

They arrived at the cemetary, and the six of them—Kristen, Drew, Butters, Beanpole, Hernandez, and Keith—carried Jonesy's casket to his grave.

There were speeches and tears. She listened but all she could think about was the man about to be lowered into the grave. In the end, she threw a handful of dirt on the casket.

It almost broke her heart, but she knew Jonesy had lost people. Everyone on SWAT had lost people, so she didn't let it overwhelm her. She'd continue to fight and keep this city safe for the people he had left behind.

Brian had refused to go to Buddy's and instead, insisted that she pick up one of the pizzeria's uncooked pizzas so they could eat at home.

She hadn't minded until she'd realized that her brother had ulterior motives.

"I still don't believe it. There is no way my sister is a dragon."

Kristen rolled her eyes for what felt like the thousandth time. "Brian, what's there to believe? Look." She'd practiced changing her skin to steel and back and had gained some measure of control over it. After a deep sigh, she held her hand up in his face and turned it to metal.

He shrugged. "Big deal. So, you learned a trick. I'm not impressed."

"It's not a trick, Brian. Watch!" She snatched one of her mom's kitchen knives and stabbed her palm—or she tried to anyway. The blade broke.

"You could've weakened the knife. And besides, I've seen gloves that can do that on the Internet."

"Then you choose a knife. Stab me anywhere and see what happens."

"If you two think you can ruin all my knives over some sibling squabble, you have another think coming," their mother snapped. "Now, dinner is ready. Wash your hands and come to the table ."

They obeyed her, washed up, and sat at the table. Kristen felt more relaxed than she had in days. Being home felt normal again. Brian still treated her the same as he always had, and her parents? Well, they were still her mom and dad, exactly like they'd always been.

She'd been adopted but so what? She could deal with that. At the end of the day, that wasn't what mattered most. The love and care her parents had shown her all her life were what truly counted.

"I thought dragons were supposed to have, like, super-great reflexes." Her brother tossed an olive at her face. She batted it away.

"Brian! Don't pester your sister," their mom protested.

"I do have good reflexes. I beat you in everything we've ever played."

"Not video games. You can't even win at Mario Kart!"

"I can too."

"No fucking way."

"Brian! Language!" their mother said, venom in her glare.

"What? Dad talks that way."

"Your father was on the police force for thirty years. He has earned the right to swear every now and then."

"Did I hear that shit right?" Frank swaggered into the room.

Marty smiled her smile that said it was not the time to argue. "Of course you may swear, you know that, but not at the dinner table. And Kristen, you are a lady. You'd better not pick the habit up."

"But, Marty, I'm not a lady, I'm a dragon. That's what I've been telling you." She turned her skin into steel and back to flesh.

"Mom, Kristen's showing off," Brian complained.

"Kristen Hall, if you call me Marty again, I will throw you out on the street and let your brother eat all your pizza."

"That's your name."

"Not to you it isn't, young lady. I don't care if you're a dang gold dragon, you will respect your mother," Frank said, but the heat wasn't in his voice. He grinned even wider than Brian did. "But, for your old man, do the silver skin thing again. It's too cool."

She smiled and flickered her steel again, which drew an even bigger grin from her father. Kristen shook her head. He wasn't Frank to her and he never would be. The man was her dad and he always would be.

It made no difference to her that she was adopted. She didn't care that this wasn't her biological family, and—under this roof at least—she didn't care that she was a dragon. She knew her family didn't end here, though. Not being related by blood to these people made her new bonds with the SWAT team feel all the more important, but she would never forget where she came from.

Although, if Brian didn't shut up, she would totally use her powers to beat him at video games.

CHAPTER TWENTY-SIX

For Kristen Hall, facing hostiles and the real possibility of coming under fire felt like déjà vu. The entire situation seemed like an almost-duplicate of her first live action as part of SWAT, although with a couple of notable exceptions.

Exactly like the first time—which had also been her encounter with hostile fire—the criminals were in a pawnshop. Also like her first time, it was her job to sneak into the back through an alley. This time, she didn't wear a bulletproof vest or a helmet. Her somewhat naïve rookie self hadn't known what it felt like to kill someone. Now, she knew and didn't like how easy it could be.

But the biggest difference was that her partner Jonesy was dead.

She had taken a bullet for him in that too-similar assignment, only to have him foolishly return the favor to save her life at the cost of his own. Except he hadn't saved her life, not really, because neither of them had known she was a dragon—and not merely any dragon, but a steel dragon. If he hadn't jumped in the way, Kristen's powers might have activated and he'd still be—

Consciously, she dragged herself away from that line of thought. There was no point in dwelling on what she couldn't change. Not now and not on a mission when she could damn well make sure nothing like that ever happened again.

"I counted two hostiles back here," Keith murmured. "We enter. You take the one on the left and I'll go right. Butters should be able to hold down the last guy in the front."

Kristen nodded, even though she had absolutely no intention of doing what he said.

They stalked forward through the back of the store between rows of bicycles, lawnmowers, and work-out equipment people still hoped to buy back from the pawnshop before the items made it onto the showroom floor. At the end of the room, a door opened into a tiny armored airlock of a room where the pawnbroker usually worked.

Currently, the access was wide open and the two hostiles had their heads turned away from the SWAT duo to look into the store itself.

"We should have the drop on them—" Keith said but stopped when she sprang into action.

She rushed forward and tapped into the increased speed that being a dragon gave her. It brought her to the first guy before he so much as turned toward her. She caught him by the shoulders and hurled him overhand toward the back of the storage room she and Keith had come through. Fortunately for him, he collided with a punching bag rather than the wall, but the impact made enough noise for the other hostile to turn toward her.

He fired before she could reach him. The shot would have been wide but he was armed with a sawn-off shotgun, so a hundred midsized BB's peppered her abdomen.

His gleeful anticipation of what he obviously considered the inevitable outcome faded to an expression of shock. "I hit you!" he whined and almost sounded petulant.

"You forgot to call no tag-backs." She transformed her face and arms into steel to match the part of her body the hostile had tried to injure. He yelped and dropped his gun when she grasped him by the right shoulder and squeezed.

"I think technically, that makes me it," Keith said and sauntered toward her.

"Hmm?" she turned to him and lifted the criminal off the ground at the same time.

"One of the BB's got me," her teammate said, wiped his brow, and showed her a bloody hand.

Kristen's stomach twisted. Keith had gotten hurt—he was actually bleeding—and it was all her fault. Without thinking, she tightened her hold on the man's shoulder. A bone crunched under her grip before she hurled him across the room. He catapulted into a row of bicycles that clattered on top of him. Although he groaned in pain, he didn't move any more than the man she had thrown into the punching bag.

Keith approached. "Damn, Kristen, calm down. I'm fine."

"Sorry. When I saw the blood, I... I won't let anyone else on the team get hurt, especially not our Rookie."

"I've been here longer than you," he protested. It was true, of course. He'd been the Rookie since before she had joined the team, but a steel dragon—even one that hadn't known what she was or the extent of her powers—could skip a few steps in the nickname hierarchy. "And besides, it wouldn't have happened if we'd taken those goons down together."

"I can't allow that. Not after what happened to Jonesy."

"I don't like that he's gone either, but we lost him in what was practically a war zone, not a pawnshop robbery."

"There's still no reason to risk your life when I can turn my skin into steel."

Keith clenched his teeth and shook his head but he said nothing more to her. Instead, he spoke into his radio. "We have secured the back room. The hostile is holed up behind the bars. He's not going anywhere."

"Roger that," Drew replied. "We'll tell him to surrender and Butters will light up his location with a few warning shots if he doesn't comply. I want you two stationed behind cover. Be ready to nab him if he tries to make a run for it."

"The fool thinks broken glass and a few metal bars count for cover. I'll shave his damn beard with a few rounds." Butters laughed over the radio. Kristen didn't doubt that the man could do it. He was the best shot out of any officer in Detroit.

"Roger. Moving behind cover." Keith crouched behind a riding lawnmower that was near the back door of the storage room.

Kristen moved to stand directly in front of the door that led to the showroom.

"Kristen, Drew said to take cover," her teammate protested.

"Then stand behind me. I won't let this guy get away."

"He won't get away. We disabled his getaway vehicle and he's lost his two cronies. He'll surrender as soon as Butters fires his warning shots. And even if he doesn't, we can catch him when he tries to run through here. I won't even complain if you use your dragon speed."

"I won't let you get hurt twice in one day."

"For fuck's sake, Red!" Both the curse and the nickname sounded false coming from him. Those were Jonesy's words. Keith couldn't say them with the same casual vitriol. "The bleeding has already stopped and besides, I volunteered for SWAT. I'm here because I believe in being a police officer. Someone has to risk their life to keep our communities safe and I'm willing to do it, not hide behind my partner."

"Things have changed, Rookie. I can't let you get hurt for no good reason."

"Protecting our city is a good enough reason to get hurt."

She shook her head. On the one hand, she could understand what he was saying. After all, she had signed up for the police academy and spent her first few months on SWAT without knowing the extent of her powers. She had been willing to risk her life for the safety of others and she respected Keith for being willing to do the same.

On the other, though, those risks were no longer necessary. As a dragon, she could protect her friends—she had to protect her friends. She wouldn't let one of her own die and didn't have to, not anymore and not ever again. While she could understand Keith, she also could not step aside. Something in her gut simply wouldn't let her.

"We have you surrounded!" Drew's voice sounded odd, amplified by his megaphone but muffled by the brick wall between them and the showroom area. "We have the back covered and we both know you won't come out the front with that damn rifle in your hands. Put your weapon on the counter where we can see it and your hands up behind your head, and the judge will be more likely to take a plea deal."

"In your fucking dreams, copper."

No sooner had the hostile yelled the words than Butters took his shot. Keith had overreacted by moving to the back of the storeroom. The bullet didn't penetrate the brick wall.

Kristen retained her steel skin all the same.

Gunfire erupted from inside the pawnshop.

It wasn't the singular shot Butters had made but a cacophony of blasts. The sound triggered a mental image of the man wielding his assault rifle in a wide arc to shoot from the hip like a stupid movie villain.

Even though it was unlikely he would hit anyone—they were all most likely behind cover—she felt immediate pangs of dread for the safety of her team. One of the shots might somehow catch someone in the neck or one of the major veins in the leg. She had to step in.

"You're gonna need your fucking steel dragon to take me down," the hostile bellowed before he resumed his indiscriminate fire.

Well, that settled it.

She kicked the armored door to the showroom open.

"Butters, hold your fire," Keith yelled over the radio at the same time that a shot rang out.

The flash from the barrel was vivid, even across the parking lot, and she realized she was in the way. Rather than try to avoid it, she simply faced it stoically and took the bullet in the chest.

"Kristen!" Butters screamed from his distant vantage point.

Of course, she was fine. She had hardly even felt the high-powered round.

"Well, if it isn't the steel bitch!" the hostile said and swung his assault rifle toward her. She made no effort to stop him.

The look on a criminal's face when they shot her and saw that their bullets did nothing filled her with a perverse sense of glee. She loved the power she felt in that moment and how obviously terrified it made her adversaries.

He delivered six bullets into her chest before he stopped, panic in his eyes. Not only had his shots done absolutely nothing, but his gun had jammed. That was a good sign, which also might indicate that whoever had armed the men who'd tried to take Detroit over and killed Jonesy hadn't returned yet. Those guns had been far more effective than the one the man in front of her now tried desperately to fix.

"I give up!" he said finally and flung the useless weapon aside.

"It's too late for that," she replied and moved toward him.

The felon screamed and tried to run—something that more and more of them seemed to do, which she thought was a good thing.

Kristen darted forward and caught him by the collar as easily as a snake catches a rat. She kicked his legs out from under him, slammed him to the floor, then put a foot on his chest to pin him in place with the weight of her steel body.

"I…surrender," he wheezed as if he hadn't fired at her friends at all. For all she knew, one of them could be dead or dying, bleeding out into the parking lot because of the pathetic, desperate actions of this worm. It would be so easy to stop him from ever hurting another soul. All she had to do was press a little bit harder with her foot—

She shook her head, knowing she couldn't do that. Keith was barely hurt and the man she held trapped beneath her steel foot hadn't been the one to hurt him. Her friends were probably fine too. But if they weren't, she would be well within her rights as a dragon to— Angry at herself, she stifled the thought. She wasn't above the law. In fact, she served the law, exactly like her father had done before her. Being a dragon did not mean she could kill at every opportunity—not unless she had to, she reminded herself—even though most dragons would completely disagree with the sentiment.

So, instead of crushing the man's ribcage, she took hold of the steel bars that separated the showroom floor from the vault-like space. She bent them as easily as a child would bend pipe cleaners. Once she'd made a roughly man-sized hole, she picked the hostile up from the floor, stuffed him through the hole, and bent the metal back around his arms so he was splayed and trapped and escape was impossible.

Only then did she respond to her radio. Drew had yelled over it for a while now.

"Damn it, Hall, report. Did you take fire? Is the hostile in custody, injured, or dead?"

"It's all clear in here, Drew. Is Butters all right?"

"For fuck's sake, Red, that's not your goddamn business," Hernandez bellowed. Lyn Hernandez knew how to swear properly but of course, she was mistaken. Butters was Kristen's responsibility. If he'd been shot, the guilt would rest on her shoulders.

"Yes, everyone is fine. We're coming in now." The team leader did not sound amused.

Drew, Beanpole, and Hernandez approached the front of the building. Butters shifted his bulk in his vantage point and continued to guard the team from behind his sniper rifle. It was unnecessary—she had told them she'd eliminated the hostiles—but she appreciated it all the same. Also, if he was still taking aim, it meant he was fine, which meant the man she had wrapped into the steel bars could live.

She shook the idea from her head. The inner conflict seemed to be ongoing. She didn't want to be an executioner, but the urge to protect her own seemed to be growing stronger every day. Humans were simply so defenseless compared to her.

Kristen swallowed.

Had she actually thought that? Seriously, had she really thought of herself as something more than human?

Before she could explore this new revelation of how her powers were affecting her, Drew strode through what remained of the front entrance of the pawnshop with Hernandez and Beanpole on his heels.

Despite the fact that the front of the store was all shattered glass and therefore easy to see into—and her telling them it was clear—they still spread through the room to check every corner and cubby until they could verify for themselves that it was secure. It was protocol and made sense—unless you had a steel dragon on your team. Still, they did what they had trained to do and what had now become instinctual.

Only then did they look at her handiwork.

"For fuck's sake, Red. Why not crucify the asshole and be done with it?" Hernandez demanded disdainfully.

Kristen opened the door that led from the caged-off area to the showroom and looked at the hostile. She snorted a laugh. Hernandez was right. "Okay, maybe that was a little too much."

He was vertical, his legs in front of the counter and suspended about a foot above the floor. He'd tried to scramble across the counter after she had released him but he'd only made it that far before he realized his arms were securely trapped in the steel bars. Each one extended like he was ready to do jumping jacks, or—as Hernandez had said—he had committed a crime in Rome thousands of years before.

"You know, you do have handcuffs," Beanpole said. That was the closest thing he had ever said to actual criticism.

"But what would the reporters say then?" Hernandez jerked a thumb toward the parking lot.

Three news vans and a handful of reporters armed with microphones had been joined by a small crowd of people with their smartphones up, no doubt recording Detroit's most famous police officer. Some of the more desperate reporters were already interviewing the pawnshop clerk, but Kristen could be fairly certain he'd be edited out of the segment before it aired.

Drew sighed. "They'll say what they always say—that SWAT's dragon cop disabled another sack of criminals all on her own without letting anyone else get so much as a scratch."

"The Rookie was shot," Kristen protested.

"That's bullshit. I'm fine," Keith called and stepped through the doorway from the storeroom. "It hurts more to have a flu vaccine. You didn't need to—holy shit, that's awesome." He pointed to the man held by the steel bars. "I cuffed the two goons back there. They're fine by the way."

Drew chuckled and shook his head. "It is…something else, Hall.

The captain will be pleased that no one was hurt. But next time, you need to work with your partner and your team. We could have talked this guy down."

"You can still get me down," the hostile complained from his place on the wall.

"I couldn't let anyone else get hurt," she responded.

The team leader clenched his jaw. "Part of our job is getting hurt."

"It doesn't have to be, not anymore."

At that, the rest of her team shared a glance. Obviously, they felt similarly to Keith.

"And is part of our job straightening metal bars after you've turned them into a one-man cage?"

Drew looked like he wanted to say more but Beanpole jumped in. "Not to mention media relations."

The other man sighed at that. "Ugh, thanks for the reminder. We'll talk later. Beanpole, Hernandez, I want you on the front of this building. Don't let any of the media in here but if they want video of this asshole, I don't see how we can stop them."

The criminal struggled against his steel bindings but it was a futile gesture.

All business once more, Drew turned to Kristen. "Hall, you're not to say a thing about any of this. We don't comment on open investigations and all that."

"What's the investigation, sir? These assholes tried to rob a pawnshop and the security cameras caught the whole thing. Our dragon stopped them," Keith said. He was undoubtedly the most excited to have her on their team. Despite his earlier protests, he loved taking pictures of her aftermath. The captain had already had to order him to stop posting images of her missions on social media.

"Okay, maybe you can take a few questions." Drew relented reluctantly. "But seriously, Hall, you are part of this team. You can't continue to run into every situation like a one-woman army."

"Of course, sir." She nodded, even though she damn well knew she could.

Still, he was at least right with the concept of teamwork. She found the media was the most impressed when she talked about the efforts of her team and let her work speak for itself. She had a feeling that the hostile trapped in the steel bars of the business he tried to rob would quite likely go viral. If so, those who wished to strike fear into the heart of the Motor City would have another reminder of who they'd face if they tried.

CHAPTER TWENTY-SEVEN

The reporters came armed with ever more barbed questions. Kristen was certain they'd play the story about the criminal who'd tried to rob the pawnshop and ended up as wall decoration. Unfortunately, it seemed she was now famous enough that if they could get a good sound bite from her, that might be the bigger story. She tried to keep a cool head as the wave of microphones and cameras accosted her.

"Ms Hall, how does it feel to do more for the city than the Detroit police department has done in the last twenty years?"

"I think that's a mischaracterization of the men and women who serve our community."

The reporter looked disappointed at her textbook response.

"Ms Hall, does your team like knowing that they're the most protected SWAT squad in the city?"

"My team protects me as much as I protect them." It was a white lie but it sounded better than the truth—that over the last month, she had personally eliminated or apprehended every hostile armed with a weapon more dangerous than a letter opener.

"I'll take that as a yes, then."

She shrugged. She'd already been misquoted dozens of times. What was important was that there no sound bite.

"How does it feel to be the Lost Dragon?"

That was a new one. "Excuse me?" she asked, hoping for clarification. The reporters calmed, eager to get an answer.

"You grew up thinking you were human, only to discover you were a dragon while on the force. How did you find out you were a dragon, and do you think there might be another Lost Dragon out there?"

There was a moment of silence as every microphone pointed toward her.

Kristen knew she had to be careful with her answer. She didn't want to explain what had really happened—that one night, Frank Hall's sister had shown up with a baby, begged the Halls to care for it, then vanished, only to die that same night under mysterious circumstances. No one had looked deeply enough into her family to ferret out that Aunt Christina had worked for some kind of biology lab that was run by the dragons, and she wanted to keep it that way.

"I don't know if there are other hidden dragons out there, but I will say I discovered my powers when pushing myself to the limit. Maybe the best way to find out if we have the heart of a dragon is to push ourselves past our comfort zone to inspire the ones we care for."

"You're saying kids should risk their lives and hope they have steel skin like you?" one reporter asked.

"No! No, not at all."

"If there are more Lost Dragons, will you all work against the current dragon-dominated system?" another reporter asked.

Now that was a loaded question. Answering that one wrong would not only draw the ire of her team but maybe the dragon community.

Fortunately, before she could answer, two police cars arrived with officers to collect evidence and photograph the crime scene. They promptly pushed the reporters away, which only pissed off those who'd yet to properly record the man dangling in the pawnshop.

Drew put a hand on her arm. "Come on, let's get out of here."

She nodded and seized the opportunity to escape. They strode quickly to their SWAT van, but before she could get inside, Hernandez thrust herself up close and glowered at her.

"Ms Hall, Ms Hall, how does it feel to be even more self-centered and stuck up than the average white girl?"

"Cool it, Hernandez," the team leader said.

"No, fuck that. I worked hard for my reputation as a mean-ass bitch, and now—thanks to little miss Lost Dragon—everyone thinks I'm a goddamned damsel in distress."

"No one thinks you're a damsel in distress." Kristen tried to smile and assumed the woman was joking.

"Oh yes they fucking do." The demolition expert's eyes were wide in disbelief "You're not the only one the media's been hounding. They only ask questions about you, of course, but it's still pretty fucking annoying to be stopped every time I go to my damn car."

"I didn't know that," she responded. She'd been so focused on avoiding the media herself she hadn't really thought about her team.

"Yeah, well, no fucking shit you didn't notice," Hernandez snapped.

"That's not what's important, though," Keith said.

"The Rookie's right," Butters interjected and his southern accent immediately cooled the heated conversation.

"I am?" The other man looked startled.

"I'm as surprised about it as anyone else, but indeed you are." Butters chuckled. "I had that shot, Kristen. And Keith knows how to disable a hostile better than any Rookie. You can't continue to act like you're alone out there."

She sighed. "I understand where you're coming from, I really do, but how can I let you take a bullet when they simply bounce off me?"

"But what if they don't?" Beanpole inquired. "What if there's a limit to your power and you merely haven't found it yet?"

That gave her pause because she knew there were limits to her power. She was faster and stronger, of course, but not fast enough to dodge bullets or strong enough to lift a van. Still, turning her skin to steel and back didn't seem to take any effort.

"I guess I hadn't thought of that…" she began tentatively while she tried to think of what could possibly hurt her considering she'd already withstood being shot with both a rocket launcher and a mounted machine gun. "I guess someone might try to crash a couple of busses into me."

Butters and Keith laughed at that, and Drew and Beanpole smiled. Hernandez shook her head but that was positive coming from her. She didn't laugh out loud unless someone was insulted with gratuitous curses.

A rich peal of laughter joined the voices of her team and Kristen turned to face the intruder. Her skin became steel in an instant, readying her to protect her friends from a new threat.

"Oh, beg your pardon." The man bowed. He had blonde hair that fell to his shoulders, tanned skin, and a golden suit.

"Hey, buddy, maybe you're new here, but once we go to the fucking van it means we're involved with police business. Kindly go back to whatever pawnshop you came from. They're paying good money for eighteen-carat these days." Hernandez flashed her 'go-fuck-yourself' smile.

"Ah, you've misinterpreted my intention. I'm not a reporter you see, but a—"

"Dragon," Kristen said hastily. She could sense his aura, although he tried to keep it neutral so as to not affect the humans around them, namely her team.

"Yes, Lady Hall, a dragon. And I come bearing tidings."

"Will you talk like that soon?" Keith laughed.

When she felt the man's aura surge with anger for only a moment, she had a sense of what he really was—a dragon with golden scales who was incomprehensibly old and immeasurably powerful. She wondered if he could sense her dragon form even though she'd yet to actually transform. While she didn't want to piss him off, he'd also intruded and interrupted them.

"What are the tidings, good sir, and who—may I ask—the hell are you?" she asked with a wink at Keith in the hope that humor would defuse the situation.

Goldenrod looked at her team. His upper lip twitched with the faintest hint of disdain but he immediately became all smiles again. "I did not mean to interrupt official…ah, police duty, Lady Hall. Perhaps we can talk for a moment in private. I am Vincent Goldenrod, ambassador of the dragon council." He bowed with a flourish worthy of his name.

"I'm on the job. Anything you want to say to me you need to say to my team," she said, a little affronted by the way he looked at them.

"Very well." The dragon nodded and turned so he faced the entire team instead of only her. "I wished to invite you to a party held in honor of all of your recent successes. It is a private affair arranged by some of the dragons who would wish to personally thank you for what you've done for our city. It will be held on the rooftop of the Detroit Marriot in the Renaissance Center tomorrow night, just before sunset."

Hernandez laughed. "Do you expect us to fly up there?"

"I have arranged transport for Lady Hall."

An extremely awkward moment followed, in which Goldenrod shot Kristen a glance so pointed it could have stabbed her. Obviously, the invitation had been intended for her, and her only. The venue itself screamed dragon. Part of her wondered if being up that high and surrounded by a number of dragons might help activate her ability to transform into her dragon body. But that really wasn't the issue here. If the dragons of Detroit wanted to thank her for work, they needed to thank her team as well.

"We'd love to come!" she said and spread her arms in a wide gesture that encompassed her teammates.

Keith grinned and nodded like a fool and Butters seemed to already imagine the spread. Beanpole and Drew looked indifferent, while Hernandez couldn't hide her shock.

"Ah, yes, excellent. We'll have to adjust some of the festivities to account for your…ah, friends. But that is well within our power."

"Sorry, Butters, that probably means no whole cow roasted by dragon's breath," Keith said and waggled his eyebrows.

"Dragon's fire is not used for cooking," the dragon reprimanded in a tone that was more a snarl than human.

When Kristen narrowed her eyes at him, he blinked, clearly unsure of what he had done to offend her.

"That is unless we wish to eat fresh meat." Goldenrod laughed, a prim and proper sound that did little to assuage her or her team's visions of dragons roasting human beings alive throughout history. Things weren't like that anymore, though, or so she believed. She'd find out soon enough. If anyone could decide what to say to make sure they were burned alive, it was Lyn Hernandez.

Anyone living, obviously. Jonesy could probably have already made this dragon mad enough to roast all of them.

"We'll see you there, then," she responded and hoped it was the right thing to say.

Vincent Goldenrod bowed once more. He took a few steps into the parking lot and transformed into an absolutely gorgeous golden dragon—complete with a lion's mane and a tuft at the end of his tail—and took to the skies.

The reporters pointed their cameras upward and recorded the dragon's exit before they returned their attention to Kristen. They probably wanted her and the gold dragon in the same shot.

She sighed. At least she could be reasonably certain there'd be no paparazzi at a dragon party.

CHAPTER TWENTY-EIGHT

Unfortunately for Kristen, she had over twenty-four hours to agonize about what to wear and how to behave at a dragon party. Fortunately, she already had dinner plans for that evening.

She parked her car in front of her parents' house in Dearborn—a suburb of Detroit—and plodded inside, careful to avoid stepping on her dad's freshly mowed lawn.

Part of her told her that Frank Hall wasn't her father—not her biological one anyway. She had no clue, of course, whether dragons actually had parents or anything about their reproductive cycle for that matter. But whoever her dragon…uh, sire had been, he certainly hadn't come forward or even made his identity known. On the other hand, Frank Hall remained the loving dad who still demanded his little Krissy come home for dinner once a week.

With her new schedule, she didn't make it home every week, though. She often put extra hours in when someone from her team was called out on assignment—a habit her captain had yet to complain about—but she had to be home tonight.

Her mom was making lasagna. No Hall would miss that.

She walked up the front steps, removed her shoes, and stepped through the doorway.

Immediately, she was struck in the chest with a two-by-four. She turned to steel on reflex and the piece of wood cracked in half.

"Brian Justin Hall, you apologize to your sister this instant!" their mom roared. "You could have hurt her."

Brian was already running out the back door and shrieked with laughter.

"No, he couldn't, Mom."

Marty groaned in a tone that clearly said, "You may think you're tough because you're all grown up but I remember when I had to kiss every boo-boo and ouchie for you to stop crying and I'll be damned if anyone hurts you now."

Kristen had heard that groan more frequently since she joined the police academy, but it was the number-one sound now that she was the so-called Lost Dragon.

"You know I can catch you, right? Super-speed, remember?" she hollered out the kitchen window.

"You're a dragon, not a superhero. And I'm not afraid of you until you have fire breath instead of halitosis. I can smell your breath from here, by the way." Her brother stuck his tongue out from the security of the very back of the yard. Despite legally being an adult, he had a long way to go before anyone actually thought of him as one.

"Mom, make him apologize. I do not have bad breath."

Marty didn't even glance at her as she took the lasagna out of the oven and carried it to the table. "Oh, so he can attack you with a board but if he says mean things you still need your mommy?"

"Uh…yeah? Obviously." She held her hands up at the injustice of having a younger brother.

Her mom laughed and set the lasagna on the table.

"How about this. You can have a corner piece since he called you mean names."

"Mom, there are four corner pieces. We can all have one."

She pinched her cheek. "Look at my little clever girl. That used to work, you know, before you were all grown up. Now, set the table." At least Kristen knew where Brian got his sarcasm from. Before she could protest that he should set the table because he still lived there, her mom cupped her hand to her mouth and bellowed, "Fraaaank! Dinner!"

Petty revenge would have to suffice. She busied herself with setting the table and made sure to give Brian a salad fork instead of a regular one because he hated it when his was too small. Her mother added the finishing touches—salad with feta cheese and olives and a Hall family classic, pesto garlic bread.

It was a recipe that was said to be fool-proof, yet Kristen had burnt it every single time she'd ever attempted to make it.

"Frank, put a shirt on," Marty chided.

"I will honey. Give me a minute." Kristen's dad waltzed into the kitchen in running shorts that he'd obviously not actually used for their intended purpose, given the size of his gut. He planted a fat kiss on his wife's cheek and vanished into his bedroom after he snatched a piece of pesto garlic bread.

Kristen reached for one only to have her mom slap her hand. "It is not dinner time yet. Oh... Kristen, I'm... Did I hurt you?"

"What? No, of course not." She glanced hastily at her hand and realized she'd turned it into steel. "No, it's only a reflex. I've worked on it to hone it so if anything hits me, I turn to steel automatically. It's safer that way."

"It's a good thing you don't have a boyfriend to surprise you." She hadn't noticed Brian come inside but she wasn't at all surprised by his timing. "Can you imagine? He sneaks up behind you with a bouquet of flowers for his beloved, and you turn to steel and roundhouse kick him into the Detroit River."

"You're hardly one to talk about romance, Brian. When was the last time you asked out a girl? Fifth grade?" she retorted waspishly.

"Ninth grade, for your information. I asked a foreign exchange student out during my freshmen year," he said rather snootily as if that did anything other than prove her point.

"It's so great to know that your parents' marriage has inspired a sense of romance in both of you," Marty said sarcastically.

Her children both laughed. Neither had ever been very romantically inclined. She was too competitive and he wasn't competitive enough.

"Frank!" their mom yelled once more before she sat at the table and proceeded to serve herself salad and bread.

Kristen helped herself to the lasagna so Brian stabbed her with a fork, which made her skin turn to steel.

"Brian, damn it. Stop that!" Marty snapped.

"Mom, it's fine," Kristen said, shocked at her mom's outburst. Martha Hall did not swear.

"No, it is not! It is disrespectful and dangerous, and I won't allow it in my house and especially not at my table."

"Yes, ma'am." He sniffed and acted as if he wasn't the one who'd tried to stab his sister.

Fortunately, their dad appeared and the tension in the room evaporated. "Krissy! How nice of the Lost Dragon to grace us with her presence," Frank said cheerfully as he settled at the head of the table. "So, tell us about who you busted this week."

"Come on, Frank, at the table?" Marty wheedled.

"What do you want me to talk about? Edging the damn front lawn? I'm retired, your part-time job at the grocery store is hardly nail-biting excitement material, and Brian, well—"

"I'll have you know I teamed up with a band of barbarians to storm the Necromancer's Gate. We defeated over four hundred skeletons and I came away with the Golden Blade of Avalon. That gives a charisma boost to any allies within range and looks fricking sweet with my armor."

"Right, see? That's my point. I didn't understand a word of that besides skeleton." Frank rubbed his temples. He'd confided to his daughter more than once that he really, really wanted Brian to move out and get his own place.

"Well, earlier today there was this raid at a pawnshop—" she began but Brian cut her off.

"Yeah, that's all over the Internet You wrapped that dude's arms in those bars? That was legit Kristen." Brian took his phone out and showed their dad the picture of the hostile, his arms trapped in steel while his legs dangled above the floor. The photographer had caught the guy in mid-curse so he looked pissed rather than pitiful.

"Why did you have to do that? Did your handcuffs break or something?" Frank asked.

"No. I wanted to teach him a lesson."

"Did you take any shots at that one?" her brother asked eagerly.

She shrugged. "A couple. Maybe ten or so. That guy shot me six times from three feet away. You should have seen his face when it all bounced off."

Her mother almost choked "Ten or so? Kristen, are you okay?"

"Yeah, Mom, of course."

"Is your team okay?" her dad asked, concern obvious in his voice even though he spoke around a mouthful of lasagna.

"Yeah, they're fine. I moved in so none of them got hurt."

"That is killer-bad. The Lost Dragon saves the day." Brian pumped his fist in the air. "What else did you do? Any car chases?"

"Only one. The guys almost lost us too. They took an entrance to the highway and we missed it. Drew was going to turn, but I jumped and turned to steel. I crashed through the back of the car. I think maybe more than only my skin turns to steel because I get way heavier."

"Cool, a cop with transmutation," he enthused.

"Did Drew tell you to do that?" Frank asked.

Kristen shook her head. "No. He was on the radio, calling for backup. They would've gotten away if I hadn't—"

"Risked your life?" Marty cut in.

"No, Mom, I didn't risk my life. I can turn to steel whenever I want." To prove her point, she made her entire body—clothes and hair included—transform before she reverted to her normal form. "What's there to worry about?"

"Your team getting sick of your shit, for one," her dad said.

"Frank! Language!" The woman corrected foul language—her words—on reflex. She was probably faster at it than her daughter was at activating her steel.

"Marty, I'm serious. Back when I was on the force, that was a huge issue."

"Gee, Dad, I somehow don't see you as the super-soldier." Brian waggled his eyebrows and stared pointedly at Frank's round belly.

"Ha-ha-ha, Brian, because you're the spitting image of health."

"Mom, Dad's calling his son fat," he whined.

"We all know your mom's cooking is better than any of our willpower against seconds."

"True that," Kristen said and served herself another slab of lasagna. She saw the injustice of it because she'd probably be overweight too if she didn't have a dragon metabolism.

"But I wasn't talking about me," Frank continued. Over the years, the couple had become adept at remaining on point despite their children's constant interruptions. "I was a good cop, don't get me wrong, but I was nothing like Raymond."

"Oh, Raymond," Marty said wistfully.

"Yeah, see? My point exactly," Frank grumbled.

"Who is Raymond?" his daughter asked.

"He was the goddamn closest thing I ever saw to a super-soldier—well, present company excluded. He never lost a perp in a footrace, never lost his temper—not with the public and not with the captain—he was in shape, and he knew the drills. He was everything you wanted in a cop."

"So, what was the problem?" she pressed. "He sounds like an inspiration."

"The problem was he thought he was the whole damn force. He didn't work with a partner, not the way we were supposed to. Any time there was a bust or a traffic problem or anything at all, he took lead. He always had to be the first inside and always the first to jump into danger."

"And let me guess, he got shot," Brian said with a nod.

"No, actually. He never did."

"Again, Dad, I don't see the problem," Kristen said.

"He's dead. That's the damn problem."

"I thought you said he didn't get shot"

"He didn't. They pulled a truck over on the interstate. Despite being in the driver's seat, he hopped out before his partner could and was run over by a truck. That was it for Raymond."

For a moment, no one said anything, and only the sound of silverware clinking on ceramic plates could be heard.

But Kristen couldn't stay silent forever. "But that could have happened to anyone."

"Of course it could, Krissy. I'm not saying it couldn't. I'm only saying that if he had followed procedures or listened to his partner for five seconds, he'd still be around."

"Dad, I can turn to steel. It's a little different."

"No, it's really not. Look, I know you think you're hot shit—"

"Frank!"

"Damnit, Marty, this is important. Krissy, I know you think you're hot…uh, manure, and you are, but you've allowed yourself to become arrogant. As long as you're part of a team, everyone needs to watch each other's back. If you continue to take unnecessary risks, you'll either make a mistake or someone on your team will."

"But even if they make a mistake, I'll be fine. I can protect myself."

"You need to protect each other. Everyone on the team is safest when the entire team works together in concert. You can't let your team rely on you because they'll become complacent and make a mistake that might cost a life. They all have more experience, and even though you're…uh, the Lost Dragon or whatever, they're still SWAT."

"I merely think the situation is different. I am literally bulletproof."

"Don't forget rocket-activated," Brian added.

"I know you are, Krissy, I really do, and I've never worried about you, not even when you were still merely a puny mortal like us." Frank chuckled at his own joke and tried to lighten the mood, but no one else joined him. "But you've also talked to Dragon SWAT, right? They said as your powers develop, they'll want you on their team. I don't see why they'd make you wait unless the threat level is that much higher there. It's never really been a part of my world but damn,

Krissy, what if you find yourself in a standoff with a dragon? I would think dragon fire could melt steel."

The thought was sobering. When Kristen had met Dragon SWAT, they'd basically spelled out how they could stop her if they needed to. Even though she was faster, stronger, and in better control of her steel skin, she still couldn't transform into a dragon.

Her dad seemed to sense his words were finally getting through to her because he leaned back as he continued speaking—that was basically Frank for "thanks for listening."

"I don't want you to become careless. As soon as people start acting like they always know what to do, people make mistakes. That's simply how it goes. I know losing your partner was hard on you—it'd be hard on anybody—and I don't want that to happen again."

"But I can protect them."

He shook his head. "Not by taking away their ability to protect themselves. Think about it. There's no way you can protect every person in this city. Maybe if you could, I dunno—"

"Teleport? Fly? Make copies of yourself? Psychically control the entire city?" Brian held a finger up as he listed each impossibility.

"Right, yeah, one of those. But that's not your power, and even if it was, you couldn't protect the whole state or the whole country. The fact is that you'll need help. This city needs help, and I for one will sleep better when I know people are helping to protect it."

"Dad, I'm still a person."

"I know you are. I wouldn't eat lasagna with you if you weren't, but your team is people too. And if you treat them like they're children, they gonna start acting like children and they'll make a mistake and there won't be anything you can do about it."

"He's right, sweetheart." Her mom nodded sagely. "Look at Brian. We treat him like a man-child and look where it's gotten us."

Brian stuck his tongue out, put a single olive from the salad on it, then snapped it out of the air like a dog performing a trick.

"Point taken," Kristen said, which drew a sneer from her brother and appreciative nods from her parents. "I'll do my best to keep all that in mind. I wouldn't want my team to get sloppy."

Frank looked like he wanted to protest further—like maybe that wasn't his point—but instead, he asked for more pesto bread and began to complain about the Pistons not playing as a team either.

CHAPTER TWENTY-NINE

Kristen very much enjoyed having dinner with her family. The sense of familiarity and comfort she felt was even more obvious when, twenty-four hours later, she arrived at the Renaissance Center with her team.

Everyone was dressed up. Well, almost everyone. Drew and Beanpole looked good. They both wore tuxedos that fit, anyway. Butters wore a seersucker suit with suspenders. He joked about wanting everyone to know he was from the South, but he looked nervous and more than a little uncomfortable. Keith wore jeans, a blazer, and a button-up, and was pissed that no one had told him to rent a tux. Hernandez, however, shocked everyone the most.

Her white high-collar dress sparkled with sequins. She had teamed it with gloves and white hose. Not a single tattoo was visible.

"Wow, Hernandez...er, Lyn. You look amazing," Drew said.

"Can we calm down and not talk about it? I've never seen a tattoo on a dragon, and I wore this atrocity to my Quinceanera so I assumed it'd cover all the ink. Red looks pretty fucking hot too."

"Hell yeah, you do," Keith said as they walked through the parking lot toward the ground floor of the Renaissance Center. "Red looks great on you, obviously, and that necklace is...well..." He grinned, looked at her boobs, then realized that she looked at him looking at her boobs, so shifted his gaze to her legs. "Your legs look good too. Uh…healthy."

Butters put a hand on the man's back. "Do yourself a favor, Rookie, and stop talking."

"Right, er, of course. Yeah, good plan," he mumbled.

They entered the ground floor of the building and were greeted by a dark-skinned man with an elaborate pattern shaved into his short hair. He wore red robes trimmed in gold and a symbol around his neck that Kristen didn't recognize.

"Lady Hall, I presume," he said. His deep, rich voice held a touch of an accent that seemed to indicate that he had at least studied overseas.

"Yes, um, how did you know?" She couldn't sense an aura coming from him so she didn't think he was a dragon.

"Your face is all over the news, Lady Hall. Everyone in this city knows you, even those not working the door at the most prestigious party in the Midwest."

Right. Of course. Kristen made a note not to ask any more stupid questions. Fortunately, Keith had that covered.

As they stepped into the elevator, he pointed at the whirls and lines shaved into the man's head. "So, are you a dragon, then? Is that why you have those swirls?"

"Lady Hall is a dragon, and her hair has not fallen out in the pattern of runic spells," the man pointed out dryly.

"So…you're not a dragon?" the Rookie continued and his idiocy made every floor they rose to seem twice as awkward as the one below them.

"I am a mage." The man bowed toward Kristen, not toward Keith. "You may refer to me as Enfuegus."

"Wow, holy shit, Enfuegus, that's quite a name. Did your mom give that to you when you were born or did you choose it later or what?" Keith grinned but no one else did.

"Dammit, kid, my real name's Daryl," Enfuegus said and his accent slipped away so he sounded exactly like any other Detroiter. "That breaks the feel of the night, though, which is something the dragons hate, so I use my mage name. You are way underdressed, by the way."

"Aw, dammit, I knew it!" Keith protested.

"If you knew it, why didn't you dress up?" Beanpole adjusted his cufflinks.

"Don't worry about it. Consider this the blessing from Enfuegus," the mage said and used his deeper, slightly accented voice once more. He looked at Keith, raised a finger heavy with jeweled rings, spoke an incantation, and suddenly, the Rookie wore a bow tie, slacks, and cummerbund under his jacket.

"Hot damn! Would you look at that." He appraised his new digs.

"Unfortunately, there is nothing I can do about interjections such as that," Enfuegus said. "Please, be on your very best behavior. Remember, the guests of this party have practiced speaking correctly for centuries. Some leniency might be given to the dragon, but humans—especially rude ones—are not tolerated."

"Are you saying we're in danger?" Drew's posture changed as the elevator came to a stop.

"I don't know, man," the mage replied. "It's not like they've ever thrown anyone from the roof who can't fly. They might remember to call me to escort your ass out first, but don't count on it. Be cool. They never tip as well when someone causes a scene."

"All right." Drew nodded and slipped into SWAT mode. "Remember to watch each other's backs. I'll take the open bar with Beanpole. Butters and Hernandez, you're on food. I want to know if we have tapas, if it's serve yourself, or what. Keith, you're with Hall—scratch that. Keith, you're a damn liability. You stick with Butters. Hernandez, you're with Red. The two of you look…uh, well, the Kevlar doesn't do you justice."

Everyone saluted.

Enfuegus rolled his eyes. "Good luck," he said as the doors to the elevator opened onto the roof of the hotel.

They stepped out into the most decadent and elaborate party Kristen had ever seen. Obviously, their guide was not the only mage working that night. Golden globes floated above the roof, remaining stubbornly in place despite the breeze and the fact that nothing anchored them to anything.

Between these, strings of flames danced and threw bright sparks while they followed some invisible pattern she couldn't quite identify.

Below this heady atmosphere were the guests and—despite wearing the most expensive dress she could find—she immediately felt out of place. Her clothes fit well enough but compared to those at the party, she might as well have worn a burlap sack.

Every woman on the roof had a form-fitting dress in fabrics and styles from through the centuries. Kristen wondered if the clothes were real or if they were simply projections of the dragons' own bodies, that was how good everyone looked.

The men mostly wore tuxedos but few opted for a standard black jacket with a white shirt. Instead, they wore fabric in sparkling silvers, radiant golds, garish purples, fiery reds, and a dozen other colors. The cut of their clothing was unusual as well. Rather than simple collars, many of the men had fancy, elaborate additions that, to her, seemed very much like the tuxedo's equivalent of horns and spines.

Other mages moved between the guests and levitated trays of food and drinks. When a dragon wanted refreshment, they didn't have to glance at a server, only the drink. Kristen tried not to let her eyes bug out when a dragon gestured at a glass and it simply floated off the tray and landed in his hand without spilling a drop.

The pixies surprised her a little. She had seen them before but they were still a sight to behold—aside from the fact that she somehow hadn't expected them there. They were short—the height of kindergarteners—with big eyes and huge black pupils that caught the light. Despite the range of skin tones, most were heavily freckled, and they all had long pointy ears and extremely long hair. They wore light, flowing clothing that did little to hide their skinny arms or legs and did nothing to conceal their wings.

For a moment, she simply stared at their wings. She was at a party with creatures with wings. It seemed almost incomprehensible. The pixie's wings were all vaguely insectile. Some tended more toward butterfly and others were more translucent like a beetle's. As she stared, one of the pixies fluttered their wings fast enough to make them appear as nothing more than a blur. It—she? Kristen couldn't tell—elevated sharply and bellowed, "New guests."

An instant silence descended and everyone on the rooftop—every mage, every pixie, and every dragon—turned to stare at the team.

All in all, it was the most overwhelmed Kristen had ever felt on stepping from an elevator.

"Uh… Hi, I'm Kristen," she managed to say.

The pixies laughed, the mages returned to work, and the dragons turned to their conversations, which was both simultaneously depressing and a huge relief.

"All right, stick to the plan," Drew said. He and Beanpole wandered away. Keith and Butters went in pursuit of a swarm of levitating shrimp, which left Hernandez and Kristen to mingle.

Almost immediately, a woman approached them. Her black hair had been arranged in elaborate braids and a purple dress with all its fabric sewn into the train left little to cover her chest. She smiled—and exposed perfect teeth with the exception of her canines, which were perhaps a little too sharp—and extended a hand gloved in black satin to Kristen.

"Well, if it isn't the Lost Dragon. I am Marliana Seasdeep. Charmed."

She took the proffered hand and shook it firmly. The woman barely grasped hers at all and she realized she'd probably made her first faux pas. Apparently, one didn't try to crush someone's hand during a handshake at elegant dinner parties.

"Tell me, how does it feel to still have to cram into human clothes?"

"Probably about as comfortable as it feels to cram your scaly dragon hide into whatever century you're currently inhabiting," Hernandez said with a smile.

Marliana hissed strangely through her nose. It took them a moment to realize that she was laughing. "Clever girl. Clever, clever. I didn't expect humans to be so…sharp. Perhaps you're right, though. It is time for an update."

She grasped her hair, undid it, and shook it loose. Kristen was glad

Keith wasn't there. He would probably have fainted. Hernandez gasped audibly as the purple dress transformed into a more modern, form-fitting variation. It barely covered her thighs and had a window cut into the front that—despite showing less skin—even further accented her impressive cleavage.

"Is this more to your liking?" she all but purred.

Hernandez nodded. "Yes, ma'am."

"Lyn, you're drooling," Kristen whispered.

The demolitions expert snapped her mouth shut so fast her teeth clacked.

"It is a pleasure to have you join us. I know you're new to the community but do let me know if there's anything I can do to either of you."

"Do to us?" Hernandez mumbled and sounded hopeful.

"For you. Pardon, a slip of the tongue." Marliana winked at the woman, then excused herself.

"They have auras, remember. You need to keep your head," Kristen said to her teammate as they pushed deeper into the party.

"It's easy for you to say. You're immune or whatever. She was… I normally don't go for chicks, but damn, she made me happy to be bi." She shook her head and tried to clear the dragon from her mind.

"Ah! I hoped you'd come to the party," said Vincent Goldenrod, the dragon who'd invited her.

"Why's that? Because otherwise, everyone here is a senior citizen?" That was Keith, who'd appeared through the crowd and currently crammed a floating deviled egg into his mouth.

"What? Of course not," Goldenrod replied. "What would even make you say such a thing?"

"Well, isn't Kristen here the youngest dragon in the room by a few hundred years or something?"

The dragon looked a little nonplussed. "We… Sir Trevor Lance won't make his first century for another few years…and there…ah, are a few others, I'm sure. But by dragon standards, many of us are still quite young. Most of the room is less than five hundred years old."

"Not really selling it, Grandpa," Keith replied, which earned a giggle from Hernandez that was the most out of character thing Kristen had ever seen her do—besides wear a Quinceanera dress. The night was full of firsts.

"Keith," Butters chided, "this gentleman is our elder. Some respect is owed." The sniper gave Goldenrod his friendliest smile, but the dragon continued to look a little aggrieved. He blinked a few times and studied them as if to make sense of them. He was saved from having to comment when another dragon entered the conversation.

"It is as I said, Goldenrod, she has been with the humans too long." The man who spoke wore a green suit that fit perfectly. Beneath it was a silver shirt with a rather elaborate waterfall of frills down his chest. He had a thin mustache that lent him an imperious demeanor.

"She hasn't lived with people as long as you have, because…you know, she's not a dinosaur," Hernandez said to the man and earned her first scowl of the evening. She looked proud to have received it.

"She's right," Butters declared cheerfully. "After all, you've been with people far longer than she has."

"And yet I have retained a degree of separation that your dragon has not," the mustachioed man replied.

"She's not ours," Drew said as he stepped into their little circle, two drinks in each hand. He gave one each to Kristen and Hernandez, and one to Butters. Beanpole—tall and silent behind the team leader—had one for Keith. "People don't think of each other that way."

"Oh, they most certainly do." The green dragon sneered. "After all, slavery was your invention."

"And these mages you have here are free to do whatever they please?" He didn't break eye contact with the man.

"And tell me, human, is that what you want? Magic to run unchecked? The powers these humans wield is far more formidable than even your most devastating weapons of war. Without dragons, you would beg at their knee for scraps."

"How is living in a world serving dragons different?" Kristen asked, not sure if that would elicit an answer or get her chucked off the top of the building.

"It is precisely because of our longevity that we are fit to advise your leaders," the dragon said. "We are able to see trends in your species—the invention and implications of electricity, or the political will to end slavery—and help you along those paths. We are not interested in despotic rule because we live long enough to achieve any freedom we need."

"I think you live long enough because you don't actually risk your lives for the people who provide you with air conditioning or the ingredients for these fancy drinks." She held her glass up to emphasize her point.

"Which is precisely why I wanted to have this event for Lady Hall," Goldenrod interjected. He looked nervous. Clearly, he was concerned about the conversation and probably envisaged the night as a whole slipping away from him.

"I see nothing noble in risking one's life unnecessarily," the green dragon replied rather snootily.

"I agree," she said and earned a raised eyebrow from him. "But risking my life to protect the men and women of this city is definitely not unnecessary," she finished icily.

He twitched his mustache in contempt, excused himself, and vanished into the crowd.

"Cheers!" Beanpole said, his voice ever so slightly slurred. "To making enemies who could obliterate us if they weren't so proper."

"Indeed." Goldenrod nodded. "It's considered quite poor form to eat a human when there are so many well-cooked hors d'oeuvres floating around."

Hernandez raised her glass. "I'll drink to that."

The team clinked glasses, then drank—after being reprimanded by Goldenrod for not making eye contact. Apparently, he'd spent a few centuries in Europe and still found the American habit of toasting while staring at one's glass instead of looking into the eyes of one's friends quite pointless.

The drink was—quite simply—the most incredible liquid Kristen had ever consumed. The first taste was the sweetness of molasses, but that brightened fairly quickly as alcohol and cinnamon battled for dominance on her tongue. It warmed her entire body when she swallowed, and a slight spicy burn lingered in her mouth to finish the effect.

From there, the team split up again.

Goldenrod followed her for a while, asking her questions about living with people and what it felt like to defend them. Even his questions seemed odd to her. She still thought of herself as human so defending people seemed natural, but as the night went on and he called for more drinks—the dragons seemed to be able to get the attention of the servers in a way the humans could not—her head spun and she began to feel less and less human.

The first thing she noticed was the auras that poured off the dragons. They didn't use them to affect each other, not in the way they used it to affect the behavior of mortals. Instead, they used it to underscore points in conversation.

As she moved from conversation to conversation, she felt different shades of disgust directed at her—this aura often came from those who tried to politely tell her to stop wallowing with the humans. Others, however, simply found her fascinating. Goldenrod wasn't alone in his interest in her. Many of the dragons were equally curious about her and their auras betrayed only that.

The worst encounter of the night came after a few hours and a few drinks, and she later wondered if the offensive dragon had planned it that way.

Kristen had separated from Goldenrod and stood near the edge of the room in conversation with Butters and a fairly short female dragon with a Spanish accent and an amazing ruffled orange flamenco dress.

They talked about travel and how the airplane might never have been invented without dragons to inspire flight—or, at least, the dragon in the orange dress held that opinion. Butters argued that people had been inspired not by dragons but by birds because most people saw birds every day of their lives, while few people ever saw dragons.

The woman obviously disagreed but she was polite enough about it. Kristen was about to pull herself from her drink-inspired haze and intervene when someone pushed through the crowd.

"Please, not now," Goldenrod called from behind them, but the person would not be deterred.

A man—a dragon in man form—emerged from the crowd. He wore a slate-gray suit and an eyepatch, of all things. He strode toward Kristen over the continued protests of Goldenrod and came to a stop, swaying as he did so.

"Admit it. You're a damn fake," he said bluntly.

"Pardon me?" She turned to him, suddenly painfully aware of how far above the streets of the city she really was.

"Pardon the interruption, Lady Hall. This is Sir Thomas Ironclaw."

Ironclaw raised the eyebrow above his normal eye and brandished a fist at her. It turned to iron—the dark, light-sucking black of cast iron.

"Sir Thomas believes—"

"Shut the hell up, Goldenrod, before I knock your damn jaw off. I can speak for myself."

"Can you?" Butters asked mildly.

The newcomer faced him and his aura swept like a tidal wave. She realized that she was supposed to feel fear—no, terror—at being in the presence of this dragon. His purpose was that she would be so frightened, she would want to throw herself from the rooftop rather than face the ire of the god-like being in front of her.

Kristen, of course, didn't feel that at all, and before Butters could react to his aura, she flexed her own. She'd never done that before but after being surrounded by dragons the entire night, she felt she had some idea of how it worked. Until that moment, she'd blocked their auras with her own sense of confidence so she simply tried to expand that feeling into her teammate.

It worked perhaps a little too well.

The sniper set his jaw and took a step toward Ironclaw. "I do believe you owe Lady Hall an explanation."

A crowd hadn't gathered—the dragons were obviously much too polite for that—but they didn't ignore the exchange either. Every eye that could discreetly glance at the two dragons did exactly that, and every eye that couldn't watched the faces of those who could.

"You're a fake," he reiterated.

"A fake what?" she asked and transformed her entire body into steel.

"You're some mage's little project let loose, or you have a piece of tech the humans invented. You're not one of us. You're not a dragon."

"And yet, for some reason, I feel like my steel body would still beat your metal hand in a fight."

Ironclaw threw his head back and laughed loudly enough to silence what little conversation continued. A chill nipped at her as a cold breeze cut across the rooftop. A few of the floating golden globes flickered while a couple of the threads of flame were extinguished.

"You wish to fight, girl? Fine, let us fight."

Kristen raised her fists.

He laughed even harder. "Do you think I'll fight you in this pathetic form? What will you do when I lift you from this roof and let you fall?"

"You couldn't knock me off," she said rather lamely. She lacked confidence because it had started to rain—only lightly, but enough to slick the surface and cause her hair to slump. Her and Hernandez were the only women whose hair was affected by the drizzle.

"You may weigh more with your shiny little shell but my wings have pushed my iron claw to such speeds as to make gravel out of stone mountains. I helped the Mongol hordes smash the great wall of China, girl. Do you think you can stand against me because you have stood against bullets? Only one dragon has ever been killed by a bullet, and it wasn't the pathetic variety you humans so love to hurl at each other."

A blinding flash sizzled when a bolt of electricity struck the lightning tower at the top of the skyscraper they all stood on. The crack of thunder was powerful enough to shake the rooftop and shatter glasses.

"I think that's quite enough, Thomas," a man said as he stepped from the crowd. He was difficult to see as the globes closest to him had all gone out and he wore a black suit that drank what light did fall upon it.

"Sebastian—please, I have this quite under control," Vincent Goldenrod protested.

"I disagree. Thomas has seized the night and offended our guests in the process." He was much taller than anyone else at the party and broader too and his large frame made even Drew seem slight. His black ponytail and goatee were the same midnight-black as his suit. As he approached, lightning struck another building and for a moment, he was fully illuminated. The only color besides his tanned skin was the blood-red of his silk shirt, tie, and highlights on his black gloves. Kristen had the sense that he was at least partly responsible for the lightning. Ironclaw's scowls at the weather seemed to confirm her suspicions.

"Don't tell me you feel differently now, Shadowstorm! When we spoke earlier—"

"I played devil's advocate, you fool," the dark dragon growled. "This is uncivilized, especially in front of humans. You owe our guest an apology—a proper apology."

There were gasps at that, and she had the sense that simply saying sorry would fall far short.

"You insult me," Ironclaw protested and wings unfurled from his back to the sounds of chains and gears clanking.

"You insult yourself. You challenge this young woman to combat despite knowing full well that might does not always equal right. Or shall we replay the events of the American Revolution?"

"Your actions weren't sanctioned by the council. And the battle you fought wasn't clean."

"I don't know. I think history and I tend to see things differently." Shadowstorm winked on the same side of his face that the other man hid behind an eyepatch. Kristen didn't think that was a coincidence.

"We fight, brother," Ironclaw roared.

Lightning seared the sky again and blinded her. In the darkness that followed, Shadowstorm moved in front of Ironclaw and snaked one hand around his neck. She couldn't tell if he had run there using his dragon speed or had moved somehow with the darkness.

"Kneel, brother, and beg forgiveness of our guest."

"Never!" The other dragon spat in his captor's face.

In response, Shadowstorm simply lifted him by the neck, caught his cummerbund, and threw him off the side of the building and into the strengthening rainstorm.

He plummeted for perhaps forty stories before a sound like a steam engine coming to life preceded a dragon's sudden appearance in the rain. Ironclaw's wings caught the air and he flew into the city and demolished the smokestack of an abandoned factory with his iron claw as he moved.

The party began to break up. The rain hadn't actually made anyone wet but it had turned the floating hors d'oeuvres to mush and doused the strings of flame.

"Oh, dear, I do apologize," Sebastian Shadowstorm said to her and bowed deeply.

"You have nothing to apologize for," she said.

"No, I do, really. For you see, I was talking to Thomas earlier about the peculiarities of your powers and he must have taken my curiosity too far."

"And then, of course, there's the rain," Goldenrod added. He frowned at the other dragon.

"Yes, indeed, and I fear that losing my temper has caused the party to break up. Let me see if I can..." Shadowstorm closed his eyes and took a few deep breaths. When he exhaled, great gusts of biting wind blew across the roof. So he could control the weather. She had never really wondered what dragons could do but now, she found it was the only thing her brain wanted to know.

The wind didn't cause her still-steel body to stumble, although she was relieved it was Butters who stood with her near the edge of the skyscraper and not Hernandez.

Still, it was too late. Goldenrod was right in that the ambiance was ruined.

At least for some of the more well-behaved dragons.

A pixie flitted over to a small table she hadn't noticed, put on some headphones, and began to spin records while he pounded out a deep bass beat.

"This is crazy," Keith said as he staggered up to them, a drink in each hand. "Suddenly, I can get service!"

Kristen smiled. That was hardly surprising. More than half of the party had either retreated to the elevator or simply leapt from the edge of the building. Dragons of different colors flew away in every direction. She had never seen so many in one place. There must have been close to a hundred!

Drew and Beanpole arrived a moment later. The team leader looked moderately amused—which meant he'd had two drinks, the most she had ever seen him have—and Beanpole weaved a little.

"Give me back my fucking shoes, you damn pixie!" Hernandez screamed. "I need those to walk home."

"Like, on the ground?" the pixie replied in a high, buzzy voice and tossed the shoes from the rooftop. It began to fly around and dance to the music with a few other pixies. Kristen didn't think it was an accident the pixie stayed well above the woman's reach.

Dragons joined the pixies on the dance floor—although they didn't float above it—and soon, the rooftop was no longer a dinner party but a rave.

"Whatever. Those damn heels were killing my back anyway," Hernandez grumbled and her wet feet slapped on the roof as she approached the group.

"Thank you for your help, Sir Shadowstorm," Kristen said to the towering man.

"It was nothing. Ironclaw and I have been at each other's throats for centuries. Really, I should thank you. I haven't had an excuse to fling him from a building in decades. And please, call me Sebastian, Lady Hall."

"Kristen's fine. And…thank you, really. If he had knocked me from the building, I don't know what would have happened. He's right, you know. I still can't transform into a dragon."

"I'm sure that myself, Goldenrod, and half of the guests here would have thrown ourselves after you in a race to see who could be the dragon that saves the damsel in distress."

Goldenrod nodded in affirmation but before he could speak, Hernandez hiccupped and spoke.

"Damsel in distress?" The woman laughed. She was drunk as well, that much was obvious. "How 'bout we call her that instead of Red?"

"I'm so glad that you're all still enjoying yourselves," Shadowstorm said. "But neither flight nor transformation is something that comes easy for a young dragon. It's true, most of us spend our first decades in their dragon form rather than human, but the process of changing shape is the same either way. I'd be honored to help you with it."

"It's not hard," Goldenrod said and flicked his hair back. By the time his golden mane had settled on his back, he was a dragon and shook his tail to the beat.

"Nor is it easy, Vincent," Shadowstorm said. Kristen had the sense that he could tell Goldenrod was drunk as easily as Kristen could tell Hernandez and Keith were.

"I don't know how long you intend to stay. These parties can run fairly late, but please take my card and call me if there's anything you need." The dark dragon proffered his card. It was as black as his suit with his name and a phone number printed in dark red and nothing else.

"Thanks, yeah. I will."

"Now, shall we dance?" He extended his hand like they were about to waltz to something composed by Mozart instead of the dubstep that pounded them with drums and bass.

She shrugged and took his hand.

CHAPTER THIRTY

After dancing, Sebastian led the steel dragon to a lounge area and gestured for one of the mages to dry the sofas and bring them drinks. The mage obeyed hastily, blew hot wind over the seats, and bowed to him exactly as the little runts were supposed to.

"That was great," his companion said and smiled at him.

He smiled indulgently in response. It was nothing short of amazing. This woman had unraveled months of his work. She'd almost unmasked his alias as Detroit's hidden crime lord, Mr Black. He'd ordered men to shoot her with sniper rifles, machine guns, and even a rocket launcher. There was no person who'd done more to hinder his plans, and he now plied her with alcohol. But she wasn't a human, was she?

"I thought that since…well, you know, you've been around for a while so this kind of music wouldn't be your thing." Kristen laughed.

But she was so very human. There she was, talking to one of the most powerful dragons in the western hemisphere—at least according to his own calculations—and she asked about his dancing? If the discovery that she was a dragon was an act, it was a very convincing one.

"Honestly, staying up to date on music trends isn't the forte of many of my brothers and sisters, but—living in Motown—I find it enjoyable as well as essential to understanding the people who live here. Plus, it's easy. Simply ask the pixies what they listen to. They have the attention span of children so only like the newest musical groups."

"Band," the steel dragon said—Kristen, her name was Kristen, he reminded himself.

"Pardon me?" He didn't know what exactly she was talking about. He accepted a drink from the mage and took a sip, hoping to feign intoxication.

"Musical groups are called bands…oh, never mind, it's not important. Can I ask you a question?" She plucked the levitating drink from the air and actually thanked the mage for bringing it over. It was so quaint it was almost cute.

"Of course you may ask me a question—with the caveat that you will, in turn, tickle my curiosity."

"That seems fair." She sipped her drink. "This is good." She smiled broadly. Ferreting out this enigma of a dragon's secrets would be all too easy. "Are they all really your brothers and sisters? And if they are, does that mean I am too?"

"All dragons are brothers and sisters in that we're equals, but our family tree is as complicated as humanity's. Calling them brothers and sisters is merely an expression, I fear, and yet it does bring me directly to my question."

"And that is?" she said after he paused. It was good to make people want to answer questions. It helped to assuage suspicion.

"I must admit, I'm terribly curious about how you came to be the Lost Dragon the media has gone on about," Sebastian said casually. Guests had hopefully pumped her for information all night and she wouldn't think anything of another dragon asking about her past.

"You and me both!" she blurted and giggled. The drink after their time on the dance floor had gone straight to her head.

"What do you mean?"

"I have no idea how I came to be a dragon or whatever." She sipped her drink. "All I know is that some asshole shot a rocket at me and bam! Steel skin."

"Yes, I'm afraid I'm quite familiar with that part of your story. But what about before that? Don't you have any clues as to your origins?"

"My origins? You mean like Spiderman?"

"Pardon me." He hoped he could recover. That sounded much too specific. "I simply meant that you cannot be born of the man and woman who raised you, for then you would not be a dragon."

"Are you sure about that?" She waggled her eyebrows.

"Yes. Absolutely. Human women cannot birth a dragon, not without crushing the egg."

"Oh. You hatched then?"

"Indeed."

"Well, I guess I did too." She shrugged and spilled her drink. He gestured for another. "Well, you probably heard what I told the media. Some lady dropped me on their doorstep when I was born. My mom had fertility problems so they saw it as a blessing. My folks pretended I'd been born overseas. I guess that's maybe illegal or whatever, but I have my driver's license so too late now."

"And this woman who abandoned you—do you have any idea who she is?"

That question seemed to sober her. "No. No, I really don't. Why? Is that important?"

He shrugged and assumed a wry smile. "I don't know about important, but interesting? Certainly."

Kristen frowned more deeply at that.

Perhaps she wasn't as drunk as he'd thought. He would have to end this conversation soon, but he thought he could still recover. "You're a steel dragon, something no one has seen before. That old drunk Ironclaw was the closest thing anyone has to your powers, and he earned that relic in a fight he lost to a mage. On top of your unique powers, you're the media's darling because you're human, so therefore relatable. Plus, your powers manifesting must make many people think they might be a dormant dragon. Right now, you're the most interesting thing in the world."

"Well, thank you Sir…uh…Shadowstorm, right?"

"Yes, that is correct, but please, call me Sebastian. Or do you prefer I call you Lady Hall?"

"God no!" She laughed.

One of her little friends chose that moment to interrupt their chat.

"There you are, Kristen." It was the large one, he noted.

"Hey, Butters. I was talking to Sebastian here," she said.

"Do pardon me, sir," the man said and bowed. At least this one knew proper deference to his superiors.

"Please, the apologies are all mine. I've basked in your friend's attention instead of letting her enjoy the party. I really should be going, though. No rest for the wicked and all that." He stood, nodded his head slightly at Butters—a gesture of acknowledgment that fit his higher station in life—and made his exit.

With his back to them, he didn't have to hide his scowl when he heard the man begin to yammer about the other human trash who had attended the party.

"Beanpole got Hernandez's shoes back from the pixie. I think he bet three pixies that he was taller than them combined, but Keith puked all over the shoes. Hernandez wants to go, and we should probably get Keith out of here."

"Ugh." Kristen groaned in response. "Can we get burgers?"

Sebastian shook his head as he transformed into his dragon form and leapt from the side of the building. Clouds of shadow enveloped him as he fell and obscured his body until a fully formed dragon burst from the clouds. Much like their appearance, each dragon's transformation looked a little different. His clouds of blackness were anything but common. Once transformed, his scales were as black as coal, his claws like obsidian, and his eyes the color of molten lava.

With a single pump of his wings, he rose above the skyline of Detroit. Those below him would see nothing but shadow and feel nothing but a touch of dread as he soared overhead on wings as silent as clouds.

The girl had seemed genuine. He very much doubted that she was a dragon who had somehow created the deception. Instead, he believed she had actually been raised by humans—poor thing—and had only now come into her powers. And what powers they were.

In his hands, he could transform her into the most powerful weapon the world had ever seen. There had to be limits to her abilities, of course, but if she could withstand a rocket blast as a human, once she had unlocked her dragon form, she would be truly formidable.

Or a true threat.

She obviously had some sense of justice and was loyal to her human friends—a feeling he had always been careful to not cultivate for others, and especially not humans. Many a dragon had met their end after caring about a human and letting their emotions make their decisions for them. It was far too late to teach her such caution. Better to remember that she had a vulnerable family and use her emotions against her if it became necessary.

And it might. If Kristen unlocked her dragon form and was somehow capable of flight while in her steel skin, she would be close to unstoppable.

Still, he was excited at the prospect of finding out more about her and bringing her into his careful machinations that she'd ruined so completely once already.

The question was how best to obtain a hold over her so she could be manipulated. If he could somehow position himself as a mentor while simultaneously testing her abilities, that should serve his purposes. It would be difficult, but Sebastian Shadowstorm did so love a challenge.

He alighted in the back of an old car lot. It hadn't been entirely a lie when he'd told Kristen he had work to do, but it would be far earlier in the morning than dawn.

Alone in the darkness, he transformed into his hulking human form. Size was one thing dragons couldn't change about their human bodies but fortunately, clothes were. Rather than a tuxedo, he created a simple black suit with a red shirt. He retained his black gloves—how he hated getting his hands dirty. That was one thing he and his alias, Mr Black, had in common.

He looked around the lot but saw no one and checked his watch. It indicated that he was five minutes late, which meant the damn mercenaries had better be here.

"Put your hands up," a man in black tactical gear and night vision goggles said, rolled out from behind a car, landed in a crouch, and trained an assault rifle on the disguised dragon.

"I told you I wanted to see what you were capable of. I'm hardly impressed." He cracked his knuckles, his tone bored.

"Go." The man said dispassionately from behind his night vision goggles. A bullet struck the ground a few inches from Mr Black's left shoe. Another struck a few inches from his right, although it came from the opposite direction.

He immediately looked up—dragons could see in the dark, so he didn't need night vision to see the snipers—and located one.

"Your man is in the cab of that semi-truck. I could end him before he drew another breath. The other—"

"Has orders to shoot you if you turn to try to identify him. We know your kind can see in the dark. That's why you hired us."

"I'm slightly more impressed. But surely you know I can transform in the blink of an eye, and bullets…well, they haven't changed the balance much, have they?"

"Not lead bullets, no," the man said. His smirk was the only visible part of his face under his night vision goggles. "But like I said, that's not why you hired professionals with our reputation."

"Indeed." Sebastian smiled. "Very well. You will have to do. It's not like your target will expect anything anyway."

"Do you want to accelerate the plan, then?"

"Not at all. Continue as we discussed. The targets I chose for you should make it look like some kind of a hostile real estate takeover for anyone who pays close attention. I have other agents buying that land up. Together, this should create quite a stir in the ranks of those who own these communities."

"Very good sir," the mercenary said and finally lowered his weapon. "And the news is correct about her?"

"As far as I can tell, it is. She's yet to activate her full potential, but she might quite soon. Either way, you need to operate on the understanding that SWAT has a dragon and that successfully encountering that dragon will determine the size of your bonuses."

"Oh yes, sir. I'd like to thank you for the opportunity. We can't wait to meet her."

CHAPTER THIRTY-ONE

The next Monday, a new recruit arrived at the station—a replacement for Jonesy, Kristen thought bitterly. Their team Rookie quickly tried to brand the guy with the moniker before he arrived but no one was interested in calling anyone but Keith that.

She was in the lounge, arguing with Butters over who could eat the last jelly-filled donut when Drew walked in with the new guy at his heels.

"Everyone, this is the new guy. New guy, this is Butters and Hernandez. That's Kristen, of course, although I'm sure you've seen pictures of the Lost Dragon or whatever on TV."

"Hi there. My name's Jim—Jim Washington." He was on the shorter side, African American, and looked fit, although he didn't have Drew's gym-sculpted muscles. He stuck his hand out.

Hernandez took it and promptly tried to crush it in her grip but was ultimately unsuccessful. "Welcome," she said enigmatically. Kristen wondered if she was already thinking about playing against him in an airsoft battle.

Jim reached for her hand next, but it was covered in powdered sugar. She wiped it hastily on the leg of her uniform, then tried to shake but he didn't look too pleased with the prospect.

"So you're her, huh?" He studied her with open curiosity. "I gotta say, even though I've seen your picture, this isn't quite what I expected."

She wiped her hand more vigorously on her pants. Maybe he avoided shaking because of powdered sugar, although she was sure she'd removed it all.

"I've heard of you too. Wonderkid, right?" Butters interjected before she could ask what exactly this wonderkid had meant by not shaking her hand. Had it only been the sticky fingers?

Jim grinned. "Apparently, twenty-four years of age don't count for much, even though I spent four years in the marines and another two working for Detroit PD. They still call me the kid."

"It sounds like you've been in a few hostile situations before," Drew commented.

"Oh, yes, sir. I spent some time in the Middle East fighting someone else's war. I'm glad to be here where I can actually make a difference."

"What do you mean by that?" Hernandez said. She'd lost a brother in Iraq.

"Well, quite frankly, our international system would be much simpler if someone besides the most powerful was in command." His gaze drifted to Kristen as he said this and barely managed to contain a sneer.

"Do you think I have something to do with terrorists attacking our country because I'm a dragon?" she asked, not liking the hostility in his eyes at all.

"Not you, no, but your kind? Yes. If the ruling dragon class wasn't so damn ostentatious with their wealth and power, maybe the common man wouldn't be screwed so damn often."

"You're saying war is all the dragon's fault?" Hernandez raised an eyebrow.

He shrugged. Kristen had the sense the gesture was extremely calculated. "I'm saying people in this country profit from war. Sure, some of those are regular people, I guess, but most of those at the top don't care about regular folk. They'd as soon eat the poor."

"Are you worried I'll eat you?" She smiled and flashed her teeth.

"I'm saying if you try, I'll be ready," he replied.

Drew cut in. "That's enough politics. Jim's on the team because he was the best nominee for selection. You have big shoes to fill, Wonderkid, but your record says you should be able to fill them."

"I certainly plan to." Jim still didn't take his gaze off Kristen.

"Well, all right then. Wonderkid, have a donut. We'll go through some paperwork in a minute. I gotta talk to Captain Hansen." The team leader left Butters, Hernandez, and Kristen alone with the newcomer.

"So, you said dragons started our latest foreign engagement, yet we have humans in congress who authorized the war. Discuss." Hernandez smiled, obviously pleased with herself for tossing a lit match into a tank of gasoline.

"Look, all I'm saying is that I've seen what it looks like when the rich and powerful try to take wealth that doesn't belong to them." He raised his hands as if to show he had merely stated the obvious. "Most of the time, they get it and most of the time, regular people are shot in the process."

"Except by the rich and powerful, you really mean dragons." Kristen placed her hands on her hips.

"Well, for starters, every damn dragon I've ever heard of is rich and powerful. They've manipulated regular folk for all of history simply because they're more powerful and think that makes it right to ignore regular humans."

"Do you think I'm rich and powerful?" she snapped.

"Not yet," he retorted. "But I also heard you made it on SWAT directly out of the police academy."

"That was before anyone knew I was a dragon."

"I read on the Internet that Dragon SWAT intervened in that promotion, though," he retorted smartly. He'd obviously been sitting on that one.

"And if you read it on the Internet, it's true?" Butters asked incredulously. "Not exactly the most reputable of sources, the Internet."

"It's not true, then?" Jim asked her pointedly.

She shrugged.

Hernandez laughed. "You'd better fucking believe it's true. She got here as green as her hair is red."

"I've put in my time—" she protested.

"I'm sure you have, but not for six years," Jim replied.

"So, you didn't go to college then?" Butters asked.

"No, sir. But that doesn't mean I'm stupid. I've seen something of the world when I was on tour. I chose to come back here to make my hometown better. I don't want Detroit to become as bad as some of the places I saw when I served."

"There are dragons here, though," Kristen said. "Isn't that a problem for you?"

"My job is to make sure dragons are not a problem."

They locked gazes, then, and she could feel her aura begin to bubble up. She wanted to make this man feel scared, to feel regret for how he had judged the Kristen Hall from news stories without even meeting her. Part of her wanted to make him feel terror for the woman who could walk through bullets, but the other part of her knew he was at least kind of right.

When the gangs had teamed up and tried to take over Detroit, a dragon had been responsible. When she—a dragon—had put down their little rebellion by killing damn near all of them, the dragons who'd come to stop the incident hadn't cared about the loss of human lives.

But she wasn't like that. She wasn't raised by dragons but by people and had wept when Jonesy—a human, and a flawed one at that—had died. Despite what he thought, she wasn't like the other dragons who cavorted and partied high above the city they ruled from the shadows.

She took a deep breath and silenced her aura. Using her dragon powers on him after just barely meeting was not the way to achieve anything worthwhile. She wanted Jim to respect her, not fear her.

"Look." He shook his head to clear his mind of the aura she had unintentionally built and had deliberately silenced. "I'm from Detroit.

I'm here to help the people of this city. So long as we're all doing that, I don't have a problem."

Her intention was to say something about her keeping an eye on him as well, but Drew hollered before she could.

"We have a weird one," he shouted down the hall. Footsteps indicated that Keith and Beanpole were out there too.

"What seems to be the problem, officer?" Butters grinned.

"Get this—we have a team of perps holed up in an abandoned building. There are no hostages and no demands, but apparently, they are heavily armed and Detroit PD has requested SWAT. I want everyone geared up and in the van in less than five minutes. That means you too, Wonderkid."

"Yes, sir." The shouted response was unanimous, and Jim followed Kristen to the gear room. She wondered if he resented her for walking down the hallway before he did.

CHAPTER THIRTY-TWO

They arrived to find an abandoned five-story building surrounded by police.

"Bring us up to date, officer," Drew said to the cop who walked up to meet them as they exited the van.

"There hasn't been any shooting for a while," the officer said—Johnson, according to the name on his uniform. "We've maintained a respectable distance and kept our heads down. That's what happened when we got too close." He hooked his thumb at a cruiser behind him. The windshield was shattered and the hood of the vehicle was riddled with bullet holes. A few other cruisers had damaged windows as well.

"They must be well-provisioned if they're taking potshots at your windows," Jim said like he'd been on SWAT for years instead of for all of thirty minutes.

"Potshots? What the fuck are you talking about?" Johnson protested.

"Instead of simply destroying the one cruiser, they demolished the windows on a couple. That shows they have ammunition to spare and the skill to only hit the targets they want. This looks like a message to me."

"Look, Wonderkid, just because you got promoted to SWAT

doesn't mean you get to act all high and mighty over your old force." The man's face said he'd had problems with Jim Washington for a long time.

"Tell us what happened leading up to the stand-off," Drew commanded and ended the argument.

"Yeah, sure, but there ain't much to tell. Someone noticed a B and E and we sent a cruiser in." The man pointed again at the only cruiser with significant damage. "He took fire and called for backup. They tried again when there were three cruisers but were pushed back by gunfire. They tried again—despite orders not to—when there were six cruisers here, but with the same result. We pulled back, cordoned the building off to make sure those assholes stay inside, and called in SWAT."

Drew nodded. Apparently, he knew all this already.

"Casualties?"

"Zero." He half-grinned at that.

"I thought you said you took fire multiple times."

"We did, but no one's been hit. Believe me, it's a fucking miracle. They have assault weapons up there too—cop killers—plus, they're spread out. We located one at a window and shot it out but they were already at another one a few stories up. My boys have them bottled up, though."

"This supports my theory that they're trying to send a message," Jim said. Kristen was learning quickly why everyone called him Wonderkid.

"I don't know about all that," Johnson started to argue but Drew began to issue orders and the man wisely shut the hell up.

"Butters and Beanpole, I want you in…" The team leader scanned the nearby buildings. "That one. Actually, on the roof. Beanpole, do you think there's cover up there to keep our star sniper safe?"

The man held his binoculars up, scanned the rooftop briefly, and nodded. "There are quite a few air conditioners that need to be replaced. The old models are big enough to hide him."

"I resent that, and thank you," Butters said over his shoulder. He was already assembling his weapon.

"All right. The rest of us will go in under the cover of smoke. Wonderkid, if you want to sit this one out, that's fine with me. I don't want anyone to rush into this kind of thing on their first day."

"This ain't my first day. I've used smoke grenades before and besides, I've waited for a slot to open on SWAT for months. I've itched for action." He strapped an assault rifle on.

Kristen frowned briefly at the idea that Jim had basically waited for someone to die, but she quickly shook that thought out of her head. That was unproductive nonsense. Jonesy was gone and nothing could change that. Her goal now was not to lose anyone else, and that included the Wonderkid. She'd protect him like she had everyone else on her team, and that would make him feel differently about dragons.

"Hernandez, Keith, if you'll do the honors?" Drew said after he'd handed out gas masks.

"Let's do it, Rookie. Remember to pull the pin and then throw." Hernandez mimed pulling the pin and lobbing the grenade.

"I know how to use a grenade," Keith complained but he did pay careful attention when Hernandez counted them down.

"Three, two, one, puff, puff, pass," the woman shouted and she and Keith each hurled their devices at the building. Before they'd even begun to smoke, they each followed with another one. In moments, the parking lot between the police and the five-story building was filled with smoke.

"Let's do this. Watch each other's backs. On point, I want—"

"I got it, sir," Kristen said before he could finish, turned her skin to steel, and led the way through the smoke.

Gunshots erupted from above. Mostly, she couldn't see them but sometimes, one came close, pierced through the smoke, and left a swirling wake in the acrid clouds. She ignored the gunfire. Her self-appointed role was to reach the building first and force the hostiles to retreat so her team could enter safely and guard the exits while she cleared the building.

Something glanced off her chest and she grinned. It had been a bullet, obviously, but the interesting part was that it had come from ahead of her. There were hostiles on the ground floor, which meant she had made the right choice to rush ahead and leave her team behind. She had work to do.

Moments later, she entered the building. The ground floor had been stripped of its interior. The entire level was open with rows of concrete pillars that supported a roof that was about twenty feet high. Very little light came in through the windows, and every single pillar was large enough to hide anyone with the exception of Butters.

Whoever had fired at her through the smoke clearly didn't want to give their position away because, at the moment, the interior was completely silent. She didn't hear gunshots from the higher levels either. Maybe everyone had come down thinking they'd trap the SWAT team.

Too bad for them. They couldn't stop the Steel Dragon.

It was dark—too dark for her steel skin to reflect much light—so Kristen moved into the cavernous space with her gun up so she presented an obvious threat. With any luck, she'd come across one of the hostiles hiding behind a pillar, he'd see her weapon and try to shoot, and it'd all be over for him. If that interaction sparked others to attack, she would be able to pick them off one by one while they panicked and failed to hurt her.

It worked. After less than a minute, someone broke cover near the far side of the room. The person—she assumed it was a man because those who wielded guns for power usually were—darted out, unloaded as many damn rounds as he could into her, and ran farther into the open room before he ducked behind another pillar.

She smiled. This would be too easy. Despite being shot by dozens of bullets, she was unharmed. Hadn't these guys watched the news? Guns couldn't stop the police anymore, not with Kristen Hall—the Lost Dragon, the Steel Dragon—on SWAT.

"Give yourselves up now and we'll take you in peacefully," she said and flexed her aura as she spoke.

It worked too well. Three men broke from cover this time, each paused to shoot at her, and all vanished through an open doorway. She had meant to make them afraid and thought she had, but maybe too much. Maybe she had overdone the idea of terror she had infused into her aura. Rather than make them surrender, she'd made them flee for their lives.

She sighed morosely—she really wished she could control her dragon powers better—and set off in pursuit.

"Hall! Damn it, Hall, hold up," Drew yelled over the radio. She glanced behind her to confirm that the rest of her team had made it through the smoke. Drew and Wonderkid were in the lead, followed by the Rookie and Hernandez. Everyone was still moving fine, which meant no one was hurt. So far, so good.

"They went through here," she shouted and ran toward the doorway the hostiles had taken.

"Hall! Stop! I repeat, stop! For fuck's sake, that's an order!" Drew bellowed as he sprinted across the open room.

Kristen ignored him. She reached the doorway to find the stairs leading up had been demolished. Her first thought was that there had to be another way up, but then she heard something from the stairs leading down into the basement—footsteps.

The idiots had given themselves away. Despite having snipers on the upper floors, they tried to hide out in the basement. They must have hoped she would try to climb the broken path or—and this was more likely, she thought—there was another set of stairs somewhere in the building that led directly into their trap.

They could spring that one in a minute, but right now, she intended to eliminate the assholes who thought they could outsmart a dragon by hiding in the basement.

"Dammit, Hall, don't you fucking move!" Drew was halfway across the room now.

If she didn't hurry, she might find him in the firefight with her, something she definitely did not want to happen.

She plunged down the stairs toward the darkness below.

CHAPTER THIRTY-THREE

There was sufficient light to enable her to take the stairs two at a time but she had to hold the railing for the last section. Each step took her farther and farther from the light and soon, she could barely see at all.

From what she could make out, the floor was essentially the same as the one above it. Although the ceiling wasn't so high, concrete pillars ran in rows that vanished into the gloom.

Kristen took a step forward. Footsteps echoed through the room and something greenish bobbed through the dark. Night vision goggles, she realized. Maybe they had wanted SWAT to come down there, after all.

Of course, that meant she had already walked into a trap. But it also meant it was all the more important to make sure her team didn't follow her down.

"Hall. I need you back on the ground level now," Drew ordered, his voice crisp and cold over the radio. Her expression resolute, she silenced the device.

She heard more footsteps and peered into the gloom. Suddenly, it was as if someone turned a dimmer switch up. She could see—albeit not very well—someone's shoulder protruding slightly from behind one of the pillars in the sixth row.

Her thoughts returned briefly to the dragon party. Hadn't Shadowstorm said something about night vision when they were dancing? Was this another of her dragon powers manifesting?

Someone darted from one pillar to another. Movement seemed fairly easy to make out. Her eyes were adjusting but she didn't have time.

From behind her, footsteps and the heavy breathing of people trying to move quickly reclaimed her focus.

She had to move and she had to move now if she wanted to prevent her team from getting hurt. They had night-vision goggles in the van, but the police had said the shots had been fired from above. She thought about alerting Drew but knew that would only encourage the team to join her. No one had thought about the basement. It was a stupid mistake, and she would not let it cost them. Not when she could end this before their trap hurt any people.

Her radio still inactive, she walked into the darkness, still in her steel skin, and tried to use her aura to dare these assholes to attack her.

After five steps in with no response, she paused and waited.

She continued to ten steps but still, nothing happened.

At twenty steps, she caught movement from the corner of her eye.

They'd taken the bait. Her senses deepened. With each passing moment, her eyes could pierce more deeply into the gloom. Her ears seemed keener too, and she realized she could tell fairly easily which way the people moved simply by the sounds of their footsteps.

Confident in her ability to succeed, she let them move into position until they had her surrounded. Perfect! This meant the hostiles were occupied with her, and that meant her team would be safe. Even Jim would have to admit that having a dragon working with people changed things.

One of the hostiles leaned out from behind a concrete pillar and fired at her.

She smiled and made no effort to dodge. It wasn't like weapons could hurt her.

The projectile from the weapon struck her forearm. As expected, it didn't hurt. It did stick, however. She looked down quickly. Two barbs wound with copper wire extended back to the shooter. For a moment, she could actually feel the tickle of the magnetic field from the little devices. A split-second later, electricity surged into her skin and for the first time since she'd known she was a dragon, she felt pain.

The sensation was excruciating—worse than the time she had tried to unplug the old clock in her grandfather's garage and touched the live wire or the taser she had felt during an extremely unpleasant day of training at the police academy. It was even worse than being hit by a rocket—for her anyway.

Her teeth gritted, she fought the urge in her body to clench up. Her gaze followed the cables to the man who had shot her. It was harder to see now—apparently, severe pain didn't do much for one's concentration. She determined that the barbs were connected to some kind of high-powered taser rifle in the hands of a man dressed in tactical gear and equipped with night vision goggles.

By sheer force of will, she took a step toward him, followed by another. It was hard—damn hard—to make any progress with the electricity that coursed through her skin and made her muscles twitch, but she could do it. They obviously wanted her to drop her steel skin, but she wouldn't fall for that.

That was what she thought until another two barbs fired from her left and stuck to her ribs. She tried to knock them away but between her twitchy muscles and the magnetic fields, they didn't budge. Instead, they released more electricity into her steel skin. She took another step forward, even though she now moved away from one of her attackers. It was the hardest step she'd taken in her entire life.

A third pair of prongs struck her, this time in the small of the back. More electricity flooded her system like a forest that was already burning struck by additional lightning.

Kristen tried to take another step but fell to one knee.

When a fourth taser struck her in the neck, she could see the cords extending into the darkness—darkness that was much deeper than it had been moments before—and she tried to swat them away. Her arms were completely unresponsive.

She fell heavily, her steel body clanging and echoing off the concrete floor and pillars.

Desperately, she tried to stand—no, that was an enormous overstatement. She tried to think about standing and could barely manage even the idea of it.

Her body wasn't her own. It was a twitching mess of pain. She felt like she was on fire, except this was far worse. Fire didn't make someone's muscles loosen so they pissed themselves. It didn't make someone's legs buck and kick while it immobilized them.

The sound of gunshots blasted into her awareness.

No. No! No, no, no, no, no, no! She was unable to even close her mouth. Drool trickled out and electricity coursed through it to sting her teeth.

She tried to turn to see what was happening, but even that proved futile. Still, she could think clearly enough to know that she'd failed her team. She'd tried to rush in to protect them and now, they were engaged with the enemy while she was reduced to nothing but a quivering pile of metal.

But she was stronger than that. She wouldn't let this defeat her. After all, her dad was only human, and he'd been shot and survived. She was a steel dragon and could overcome this.

Somehow, despite all the twitching, she got her arms under her and pushed with every ounce of strength she had.

It wasn't even remotely enough. The additional strain on her arms only made her twitch more, and she couldn't raise her steel chest barely an inch off the ground. She collapsed into a writhing mess, completely powerless.

Kristen couldn't even turn her head to see behind her. She didn't know if the gunshots were from her own team attempting to rescue her or from the hostiles executing them.

Beyond her growing despair, she realized that the nature of the gunfight had changed. Instead of the quick bursts of fire—the regular exchange as two teams of combatants tried to pin the other down—it became the longer, steadier shots of one side pursuing another. Kristen could almost hear her team control their breath as the hostiles —cowards!—ran deeper into the room.

They'd done it. Her team had done it. Despite her running stupidly in to protect them, they'd saved her.

Kristen tried to turn her head to face them but that only sent shockwaves of pain through her body.

She closed her eyes, fought tears back, and opened them again to see the red digital numbers of a clock in front of her. Was this all a dream, then?

No, it wasn't. She wanted it to be, but that wasn't an alarm clock. It was a timer—and one connected to something attached to one of the pillars.

Oh. A bomb, her brain told her. *Of course.*

"Hernandez!" She tried to call out but her vocal cords ignored her.

Instead, her gaze traced a wire that ran from the timer to another pillar, and another and another. Many of the supports had bombs on them—maybe all of them.

The gunshots stopped and Drew and her team arrived. She tried to tell them what was happening, that she'd seen a bomb—no, bombs —but all she could manage was to stutter and drool while she stared at one of the pillars.

Hernandez waved a hand in front of her face. She blinked, looked hard at the woman—though even that motion was painful—then returned her stare to the bomb.

Her teammate caught the hint, looked up, and cursed. "We have a fucking bomb."

"That's not important right now. Get this shit off Hall," Drew said and kicked away one of the magnetized barbs. Apparently, the hostiles had left their fancy tasers on the ground when they'd fled. He and Keith quickly kicked them all away.

Kristen sucked in a breath of air when the last one was removed. Her muscles no longer felt like they were controlled by a kid flipping a light switch, but she still hurt. It felt like she'd been cooked. Her muscles were hers once more but they were completely drained. She tried to speak but couldn't even manage that.

"They escaped into the sewer," someone said. Jim? That was the new guy's name, Jim. Even her brain seemed to be barely functioning.

Drew looked her in the eye. His face was full of pity and concern. Was this how her team saw her when she rushed in somewhere to protect them? She didn't like it. "Hall, you'll be okay. Keith and I will catch these creeps and make sure nothing like this happens to you again—"

"Not a good idea!" Hernandez shouted before he could finish.

"You can't disarm the bomb?"

"Not in the forty seconds left in the timer. Plus, it's not one bomb. It's a goddammed demolition rig, at least as far as I can tell." She sounded as nervous as hell. Kristen didn't think she'd ever heard her sound scared of anything.

She wanted to say something about how Hernandez was a chicken after all, but she only managed a gurgle in the back of her throat and more drool.

"How big are we talking?" the team leader asked as his gaze settled on the timer.

"They're trying to take down the whole damn building, Drew."

"Then we follow these assholes into the sewer. They'll lead us to a safe place," Washington shouted.

"There is no way we're leaving Kristen," Drew replied almost viciously.

"She has steel skin so she'll be fine," the man responded.

"There must be limits to her power."

"But—"

"Damn it, Wonderkid, now is not the goddamn time. Get over here and help me with her."

There was a moment—a second really, because she saw it run out on the timer—before Jim moved. That felt like an eternity. Even though she couldn't see him, she could imagine his posture from his tone of voice. He itched to run into the sewer and catch these people, not because they'd hurt her but because that was his job. He saw her simply as collateral damage. She couldn't help but wonder, if he had his way, whether he'd let the building drop on her because it would be one less dragon.

But he knelt in front of her and helped Drew to roll her onto her back.

"Hernandez, are you gonna be able to stop it?"

"No, sir. I don't have the time or the tools. Shit, this thing looks good!"

"Then get the hell over here and help us with her. Keith, take her legs."

Keith and Hernandez each grabbed a leg, while Jim and Drew took hold of her shoulders. Together, the four of them were able to lift her off the ground—barely.

"Red, if you can turn your fucking steel skin off, now would be a damn good time," Hernandez said through gritted teeth.

She tried to explain that she couldn't, that her body felt like it had been run over by an oil tanker and deep-fried, but she only managed another gurgle.

Her team dragged her toward the stairs while she watched the timer.

Twenty...

Nineteen...

They made it to the stairs.

Eighteen...

They hauled her up and cursed mightily all the while. She lost sight of the timer when her steel head clonked against a concrete step with enough force to chip a piece of the building off.

Seventeen...

Sixteen...

When they reached the first landing, she could tell they needed to catch their breath but they all knew there wasn't time.

Fifteen...fourteen...thirteen.

At last, they heaved her onto the floor of the building.

Twelve...

Not speaking a word, they raced past the pillars.

Eleven…

Someone tripped and they lost their grasp. Her body struck the floor with a clang.

Ten…nine…eight…seven…six…

They scrambled and lifted her again to push on.

Five…

Closer to the door meant closer to safety.

Four…three.

They would make it.

Two.

The team pushed outside, their breathing labored

One…

"Get back. Everyone, get the fuck back!" Drew yelled between ragged, rasping breaths. He should have used his radio to tell the police there was a bomb, but he'd needed both hands to carry Kristen. His kindness might have killed dozens of men.

Zero.

The expected detonation failed to materialize.

They grunted with effort now and shuffled her along while her steel body dragged on the concrete but still, nothing happened. She heard nothing and the building was still intact. Had it been a distraction?

Dozens of explosions answered her unspoken question. The sequence started at the bottom floor and rippled up through the building. She had the perfect view as her team hauled her backward away from the warehouse. Obviously, her count had been off.

In a few seconds, the blasts were over and the structure began to fall.

To Kristen, in her pain-induced delirium, it reminded her of the magic trick where the wizard held a curtain in front of a woman before he dropped it to reveal that the woman had gone. Like a curtain, the building fell straight down. Nothing came from the perimeter of the five-story structure besides a scattering of gravel and a large dust cloud. It looked as if the structure had literally vanished into a cloud.

"Fuck," Hernandez cursed. She dropped her teammate and panted as she watched the explosion. "Fuck, fuck, fuck!"

"What?" Keith panted hoarsely. Her entire team was completely out of breath.

"Bombs don't blow things up like that. That was definitely a professional demolition job."

"Are you sure?" Drew asked.

"Yes, I'm fucking sure. Do you know how many times I've fantasized about wiring a building like that?"

"But who would take the time to demolish a building?" the Rookie asked. He stood, forced his hands into the small of his back, and tried to stretch after carrying her out from the building that was now nothing but rubble.

The team leader took a deep breath before he spoke. When he did, his voice lacked its usual stone-like resolve. He was shaken and tired, two things Kristen rarely saw in the officer. "Someone who hoped to drop every damn pound of it on the steel dragon immobilized in the basement."

CHAPTER THIRTY-FOUR

The drive back to the station was beyond awkward. No one talked much. Kristen still couldn't. She managed to revert to her normal skin, but even that had been a huge effort. Everyone else seemed to be lost in thought—about her, no doubt.

By the time they arrived and unloaded, she was actually excited at the prospect of being yelled at. And she had no doubt that it would happen. It was written on every muscle of Drew's face.

"Do you need a hand?" he offered and she took it.

"Thanks," she wheezed.

"You all go on ahead," he said, and everyone obeyed without even a backward glance. In moments, it was only the two in the parking garage standing at the back of the van.

"Are you all right, Hall?"

"Yes, thank you. I'm sore but it's feeling more and more like I only had a really good work-out. I think Bruce Lee used electroshock to train." Even as she said it, she knew it was a poor attempt at humor.

He nodded and continued to do so for what seemed like an unnaturally long time. All the while, the scowl on his face grew meaner and meaner. "Then what the hell were you thinking back there? You rushed ahead like you had a damn death wish. What happened to the months of training we did together? What happened to your team? And it was Wonderkid's first day. What if he thinks that's how we do things and he starts rushing in?"

"Washington is not a steel dragon." She tried to keep her voice cool.

"So what? Now that you're a dragon, you're above the rules of us puny humans?"

"No, of course not. Drew, you know that. My dad was a cop for thirty years. I'm a person."

"Well, the people on my team follow my orders." He was red in the face and she had honestly never seen him this worked up.

"And what would have happened if one of those tasers had a hit another team member instead of me?"

"They'd be dead, most likely."

"See? I had to go in." She held her hands up to emphasize her point. Even that motion hurt after having so much electricity pumped through her.

"What would have happened if we didn't get you out of there? Could you survive a building dropped on your head?"

She looked down.

"Hall. Hall! Damn it, Kristen, answer the damn question."

"I don't know," she murmured, mostly to herself.

"What was that?"

"I don't know!" she finally yelled at him. The effort made her head hurt and she rubbed her temples.

"That's my point, Hall. You don't know your limits. I've seen you do some amazing stuff—we all have—but you're not invincible."

"Yes, I am," she retorted sharply, surprised at the ferocity in her own voice.

"Are you? Are you really? And what if someone hit you with a rocket right now, like right at this moment? Could you survive that?"

Kristen clenched her teeth and looked away again. They both knew she couldn't. The tasers had totally worn her out. "Even if I couldn't survive, I would have to try. Like you said, those tasers would have killed everyone else. It had to be me."

"You know, I've seen survivor's guilt before but this is beyond that."

"Survivor's guilt?" She hadn't thought much about the term, but the implications struck her in the chest like an arrow.

"You couldn't have saved Jonesy. No one could. It's not your fault he died. It's not anyone's fault except the hostile who pulled the trigger."

"You're wrong!" she shouted. "I have to protect my people. I must protect my people."

There was a long moment in which he simply watched her, his arms folded and eyes narrowed.

"You're still changing, aren't you?" Drew finally said.

She sat on the rear bumper of the SWAT van. It collapsed beneath her weight with a dull crash. She hadn't realized she'd turned her skin to steel again. It took some effort but she returned to normal, stood again, and began to pace. "I don't know…yes? Okay, I know there are still powers I can't use, but I don't really know what they are. There are these feelings too, sometimes. I don't have kids but, that's what it feels like. Like you're all these defenseless little children and I have to protect you because you're mine."

"We're not yours, Kristen. We're not anyone's. We're people. That means we're our own."

"I know. Believe me, I know! And the last thing I want is to treat you the way the other dragons treat people, but… Ugh, it's different. I think there might be a reason dragons are all manipulative or aloof. It's either to protect people or remove themselves from mankind and ignore that urge completely."

"But you can't protect us."

"Yes, I damn well can," she snapped without meaning too. She shook her head and put it down to weariness. This tired, some of her reactions didn't even feel like her own.

"No, Kristen, you protecting us from every encounter will not keep us safe. These are adults you're talking about. And probably the most capable adults in all of Detroit."

"But they can't stop bullets." Kristen turned her hand to steel and gestured to Drew.

"But you can't stop every damn bullet. What if things had gone differently today? What if, when you ran into the cloud of smoke, those snipers simply unloaded on the whole force?"

"But they didn't."

"No, they didn't. But I'm saying that there are many situations where you can't protect your team. Look, the fact is that we're all SWAT. We've all been shot at. We all signed up for this shit. If you want to keep us safe, you need to do the same thing the rest of us do—work together and trust each other to do our job."

"But—"

"Face it. You went on your own this time and that put us all at risk. We might've all been crushed today. How would you feel then?"

She clenched her teeth and shook her head. That was a low blow. "If the building came down I could have—"

"You couldn't have done a damn thing. You were incapacitated. It was a damn miracle we got you out of there. When we busted that step with your head—" Drew snorted and uttered a single short laugh. Kristen knew the sound. It was the laugh you made in the face of death but also the one you made when death took someone from you for no good reason. It was a laugh of desperation, of looking loss in the face and being able to do nothing more. She'd laughed that way when thinking about Jonesy dying in her arms.

"Thank you," Kristen said. The words drained some of the tension from her body she hadn't realized she'd been carrying. "For saving me, I mean."

"You're welcome." His red face lost some of its color and he actually smiled. "We saved your steel ass back there."

It was her turn to laugh. "Yeah. Yeah, I guess you did."

"And don't make us do it again," Drew yelled loud enough for it to echo in the parking garage, but he didn't sound angry anymore.

"Yes, sir." She nodded smartly.

"You weigh a goddamn ton. Why do you think I always keep Butters outside the perimeter?"

She laughed for real this time—An honest, that-was-actually-funny-and-kind-of-rude-laugh. "You know, I bet I could carry him if I needed to."

Drew snorted. "That's good to know. If I decide to use you in that regard, I'll tell you. Those are the kind of skills we could use on our team. What we don't want is you trying to save the whole damn world one bust at a time."

"Yes, sir."

"You're not our dragon overlord. Not yet. You'd better continue to take orders, watch our backs, and let us watch yours until you are."

"Yes, sir."

"All right, then. Now, let's get inside. We have things to discuss."

They walked to the lounge in companionable silence. Kristen could hear from the hallway that they hadn't been the only ones having a heated discussion.

"Because, for fuck's sake, I'm an explosives expert!" That was Hernandez, obviously.

"And that means you know their intentions?" That was the new guy, Washington the Wonderkid.

Drew stopped in the doorway. She peered around his massive shoulders to see Hernandez and the Wonderkid toe to toe. Both had bulging neck veins and her face was red, while Jim's headed toward purple.

"Hernandez, Washington, sit down and have a donut." Drew's voice was like water on flames.

Both backed down immediately. Washington settled into a chair. Hernandez snatched a donut and crammed in beside Butters on the couch. Her scowl remained, but she always scowled so that was no indication that of any continued aggression.

"Now, Hernandez, tell me what you're arguing about." The team leader sounded as if he had asked a fourth grader to explain their science fair project.

"I said it in the van and I'll say it again—those were professional-level explosives. The way that building came down was absolutely perfect."

He nodded. "It's hard to disagree with that. Washington, what was your argument?"

"That if those explosives were so damn professional, why didn't they use them to kill any cops? They had enough power in there to kill every damn officer, but they didn't. How is that professional?"

"Maybe their target wasn't your average cop," Beanpole said from the wall. His arms were folded and he had remained completely silent and unmoving. Kristen hadn't even noticed him.

"That's what I thought too." Butters gestured with a jelly donut and sprinkled powdered sugar on Hernandez. Fortunately, she didn't seem to notice.

"What do you mean?" Drew asked the sniper even though he probably already knew exactly what he was getting at. He was simply trying to involve the entire team. Kristen had no doubt it was either for Washington's benefit—it was his first day, after all—or for hers. Obviously, the man valued teamwork in all things.

"Well, the perps must've set that place to blow long before any officers arrived." Butters' accent made her think of a southern lawyer pontificating before a judge. "On top of that, they had weapons that could hurt a steel dragon. The Rookie said the barbs on those tasers were odd. Did anyone else notice them?"

Drew nodded. "They were magnetic. I noticed that too."

So had she, what with them sticking to her steel skin instead of bouncing off.

"And then there's the fact that they kept the regular cops away and didn't even attempt to hurt even one of them."

The sniper let the evidence linger in the room for a moment. She had a feeling that everyone had the same thought, so when she cleared her throat and spoke, she wasn't surprised to see everyone nod with her. "The whole thing was a trap for me."

"And we walked right into it," Drew agreed.

"More like the dragon led us into it." Washington glared at her.

No one said anything for a moment, and she understood that they'd all had similar thoughts about how it had played out. She was about to swallow her pride and apologize to the whole group but thankfully, Drew spoke first.

"We've already discussed Hall's recklessness. She's now on probation and we've agreed there will be consequences if she tries to play rescue the damsel in distress again."

"Probation?" she whined.

Everyone laughed.

He hadn't said anything about that but she realized he hadn't intended to. His purpose was that he wanted her reaction to be genuine because it would remind the team that she was still one of them. He really was a good leader.

"Seriously, next time you want to pull shit like that, let me know so I can at least bring my magic fucking sword." Hernandez snorted.

"And my ax," Keith added.

Everyone laughed and some of the tension drained from the room.

There was a pleasant moment for a second before Washington effectively shattered it. "So, the question then becomes why are hostiles trained with straight-up military tactics and targeting Detroit's Lost Dragon?"

"Do you think they were military?" Keith asked.

Jim shrugged. "Their movements were. I doubt it was an actual military force, of course, which means they were probably hired professionals, and—given their gear—not cheap ones."

"Maybe it has something to do with whoever was behind the gang violence," Kristen said.

Hernandez shook her head. "For fuck's sake, Hall. I miss Jonesy too, but not everything's about him."

"No…no, I think she might be on to something." Drew rubbed his chin and frowned in thought. "We know that whoever was behind the gang violence is still out there. Dragon SWAT said it was a dragon and we never caught one."

"Neither did they," Hernandez added.

"Right, exactly. Which means there's someone out there who tried to take over the city and was stopped because of one person. The same person who was almost crushed today by a professional hit team."

"Fuck," the woman said and perfectly summed up how Kristen felt.

CHAPTER THIRTY-FIVE

Captain Hansen was openly skeptical about the idea that a criminal mastermind was trying to maneuver their dragon into a position to hurt her. She still, however, ordered the team to spend their week training at the abandoned apartment complex where Kristen had first learned the many nuances of forced and dynamic entries.

Drew was far more committed to the idea of her being the target than the captain was, and he designed drills to reflect it.

Honestly, she was impressed with his creativity.

"Right." He addressed them in a brisk tone that demanded they stand at attention despite running drills all morning. "We have a report of people's cutlery sticking to the ceiling and TVs not working. We think it's on the third floor."

"Sir, I thought we were practicing entries, not solving episodes of the Twilight Zone," Washington complained.

"In case you didn't realize it, we live in a city a dragon used its psychic powers to try to attack. We need to be ready for anything," the team leader replied, his voice terse.

"We wouldn't if we didn't have a dragon on the team." He glared at her.

She very politely flipped him off.

"You know, that gives me an idea. Wonderkid, Hall, you two are together until further notice."

"No way," Jim complained.

"I agree with the Wonderkid, sir." She tried to keep any emotion out of her voice, even though she thought this was ridiculous. "He's perfectly capable. I need to be with Keith or Hernandez to make sure nothing happens to them."

Drew smiled at that and shook his head. "And you were so close, Hall. So close." He held up two fingers a hair's breadth apart. "But you're still too focused on keeping your team safe and not on the mission. Maybe if you're with Washington, you'll focus on the task at hand instead of babysitting."

She groaned but didn't argue further.

"Sir, it's a waste of my talents to partner me with her."

"See, the thing is, I don't give a shit about your prejudices," the other man said. "I don't care if a dragon ate your grandmother, Hall is one of us and now, the Wonderkid is too. You both need to accept that."

They raised their voices to protest further, but he simply put a whistle to his lips and blew it until they shut up.

"Now, like I said—hostiles inside, silverware flying everywhere. And…go!"

"Right, you take the east stairs and we'll take the west," Kristen said to Keith and Beanpole.

"Got it."

"Drew, can we assume the power to elevators has been cut?"

"Elevators not working but the building still has power."

"Is that important?" Washington asked.

Drew only smiled. That meant he was up to something. "Time's ticking. If you do this in less than five, the next box of donuts is on me."

"Let's move, people," Butters shouted, and everyone laughed as they ran into the abandoned practice building.

Jim followed her toward the west stairway and she made a

conscious effort not to race ahead although it wasn't easy. She was used to moving fast in these situations. To have to move at his speed felt like being in molasses.

"Here, I'll get the door," he said when they made it to the entrance.

She shrugged but let him do it.

He had to kick it three times before it opened. She tried not to let him see how much time she knew he had wasted.

They raced up the three flights of stairs without stopping. When they made it to the top, her partner had to suck in a few deep breaths to steady himself. Kristen wasn't even faintly winded.

"Okay…I'll take point," he said between breaths.

"No way. You're winded and I have better reflexes."

"Because you're a dragon."

"So what? Do you want to get shot when you don't have to?"

"Drew said—"

"Drew said he wants us to work together," she reminded him sharply. "He didn't say anything about you doing everything while I watch. Now, I'm taking point."

"Okay… Okay, that's fine, but don't turn to steel."

"Why not?" she asked and fought down the reflex to transform.

"Because Drew said the TVs are messing up and the silverware is sticking to ceilings. It sounds like a magnet to me."

"That's ridiculous."

"Drew cares about you. I don't know why, but he does. I'm telling you, don't use your powers. Well, not if you can help it. Do you mind getting these doors?"

Kristen nodded and wiped her face. He was exhausting to work with. In one second, he told her not to use her powers, then he wanted her to use her strength to open the doors. It was inconsistent and annoying. Still, it was better than watching him tire himself out opening everything in the hallway.

They started down the corridor. The building was old so it wasn't particularly appealing. Old tile, stained in a few places where water had gotten in, greyish walls, and cheap fluorescent lights all made the place feel decidedly grimy. Not that it was much different than how many people lived in the United States.

The only thing that set this apartment complex apart from any number of other aging structures that needed to be updated or demolished were the doors. SWAT chewed through doors, so they were constantly replaced. In this hallway alone were three bright red doors, a purple one, a green one, and—oddly—a screen door.

She made a point of trying each knob before she kicked them open. The first three rooms were abandoned but the fourth showed light under the green door.

"SWAT! Open up," she yelled.

"Die, bitch! My mutants will rule this world in a way you have not," Hernandez shouted in response. She played the hostile on this practice mission and apparently, her teammate was more into role-playing than she had realized.

"I'm gonna force the door," she said.

"Do it, but don't turn to steel," Jim reminded her.

"Like if I need to stop you from getting shot?"

He glowered at her but didn't respond.

"I'm coming in," she yelled and kicked the door in the middle, using her dragon strength despite her partner's admonishment not to do so. It snapped and the pieces catapulted inward. Whoops, maybe she had overdone it.

She stepped inside the room, her weapon up, and moved to the left. Washington entered directly behind her and went right. It felt sluggish to have to move at human speed, but she could do this. She could work on a team.

"I have you now, you stupid fucking dragon. I will smash your eggs and extinguish your flames," Hernandez shouted from the other room. Apparently, she was playing a Russian mobster or, at least, that's what the accent suggested.

They followed the voice down a tiny hallway and into a bedroom.

Hernandez waited there, armed with a gun. She held it up and fired at Kristen's face.

"You forgot your helmet, Red," the woman chided as Kristen held up a hand to block the airsoft.

"Hall, don't."

She ignored Washington. If he was such a great partner, he should have told her to put her helmet on before they entered the building—not that it would have mattered. The face shields on the helmets were hardly bulletproof.

Her hand blocked the airsoft pellets easily. They stung, though, so she turned her hand to steel.

"Gotcha, dragon capitalist pig," Hernandez crowed and stamped on some kind of foot pedal from which black wires ran to the wall behind her.

A hum was immediately followed by a strong pull that drew her steel hand back.

"Change, Hall," her partner yelled.

She resented him for telling her what to do. That tiny ping of anger plus the sensation of her hand out of her control made her act reflexively. She transformed her body to steel. There was no way that whatever force dragged at her would be able to move a steel body.

Unless, of course, it was a bank of electromagnets.

Their power was immediately apparent when her body turned to metal.

They pulled on every inch of her and hauled her inexorably backward. She tried to lean against them and fight her way free from the force using her muscles that could lift her tremendous weight, but the magnets were too strong.

She was yanked into the back wall.

"Bang! Bang!" Hernandez said and pretended to execute her, then Washington. "Democracy dies in darkness, you stupid Americans."

Kristen tried to pull off the wall, but she couldn't. She was stuck until the other woman stamped on the foot pedal that had activated the magnetic contraption. It killed the power and she was free once more.

"How'd they do?" Drew's voice asked over the radio.

"Not good. Kristen turned to metal and was trapped." The demolitions expert sneered somewhat smugly.

"I told you not to turn to steel," Washington said.

"Oh, whatever. You merely don't want me to use my powers because it makes you look bad," she retorted.

"I said there was something magnetic. The silverware and TVs were a damn clue."

She clenched her jaw. Dammit, he had said that.

"You could have simply changed back to human," Hernandez said, obviously quite pleased with herself and her wall of magnets.

"Yeah, yeah, whatever. I guess if we have a fight in a garbage dump, I'll keep that in mind." She waved her hand dismissively at the other woman and started out of the building.

Her two teammates were right, of course. If she'd only turned her steel skin off, she would have been free to pursue Hernandez. The problem was, she'd spent every day since she'd learned that she was a dragon honing her reflexes to turn her steel skin on if there was a threat. It clearly wouldn't be easy to unlearn that.

They walked down the three flights, collected Keith and Beanpole who hadn't made it to the room because Hernandez had locked the door to their stairwell with a couple of chains, and went out to the van.

"We still have training to do," Drew said. "Which means no donuts today."

"I can buy," Butters protested.

He shook his head. "Doggies don't get treats when they can't sit."

"Come on, Drew, magnets? Really?" Kristen complained.

"You were literally stopped because of magnets." He shrugged and looked way too proud of himself for her taste. "I'm not so thick as to think they'll use the identical trap again, but we'd be foolish to overlook the possibility. This is a very specific threat to you. I think we need to be ready in case they try to use it."

"But a wall of magnets?" She snorted. It was ridiculous.

"They were fucking slick, right? Those were mostly car speakers, plus like every volt of electricity running through that building," Hernandez said smugly.

"Right, but who will have time for something like that?"

"The same people who demolished an entire building in hopes of eliminating you," Washington said, his brow furrowed like it was obvious.

She sighed and finally accepted that it was possible.

"Plus, I may be handy, but I don't know how to design a damn magnetic taser to practice with." The other woman shrugged but looked disappointed.

"But we have their tasers," she pointed out.

"The batteries are all dead and the tech is weird. I don't even know how they charged them," Hernandez explained.

"Can we go back to the station?" Kristen said. "I want a damn shower."

"I bet. I had to cut the power to the air conditioning to have enough juice to run the magnet. You stink."

"Gee, thanks."

She was frustrated, tired, and yes, stinky. She thought they were supposed to be training to be on a team, and yet it felt like Drew simply tried to come up with ways to stop her from using her powers. It was exhausting and it felt petty and childish.

Did other dragons let humans do this to them? Test them for weaknesses? Boss them around? Hold them to a double standard? She doubted it and couldn't exactly imagine that Stonequest guy from Dragon SWAT letting people chip away at him with chisels or whatever.

With a heavy sigh, she realized that she didn't know if Stonequest's last name meant he had different powers than a regular dragon. There was still so much she didn't know, and her team wasn't helping by limiting her powers. They should be embracing her abilities, not trying to find loopholes.

These thoughts filled her mind and distracted her all the way back to the station. When they arrived and exited the van, she was almost surprised that they were already there.

"Okay. Showers, then I want you in the lounge in twenty. I have more ideas for team building," Drew sounded like he was really enjoying coming up with specific ways to torture her.

Kristen nodded and headed toward the showers. It had been a long morning and she simply wanted to go home. There were still hours of the day left, however, which meant time to review more tactics or whatever else their team leader would demand they look at until it lost all meaning.

She removed her bulletproof vest—Drew had insisted she wear it—her gun belt, and her boots and crammed them in a locker. Her uniform shirt drew a grimace of distaste when she noticed that she'd managed to sweat through her undershirt and through the outer one as well.

Gunshots echoed through the building as she was about to strip down and get into the shower.

"Code red. I repeat, code red! Hostiles in the—" Her radio began to blare feedback.

Instinctively, she turned her skin to steel and raced from the locker room.

As she ran—despite using her dragon speed to go as quickly as possible—she heard multiple weapons unload tons of rounds.

By the time she made it out of the hallway and into the main office space of the station, it was a mess. Bullet holes riddled the walls, computers were destroyed, and loose paperwork was everywhere. The hostiles were still at the doorway, all wearing ski masks.

No sooner did she stop to scan the scene than they began to shoot at her.

She ducked back—training to not use her powers had worked to some degree—and took a moment to assess the situation. She was unarmed, underdressed, without bulletproof armor or even shoes, and she was alone. It seemed like the perfect time to activate her powers and show these assholes what happened when they brought the fight to her territory.

Kristen flexed to confirm that her entire body was steel and prepared to race across the room when she felt a hand on her shoulder.

"Wait. Butters and Beanpole are almost in position." Washington had made it farther along in his shower than she had, obviously. He was shirtless and smelled pleasantly of soap, but he hadn't put his shoes or armor on either. Fortunately, he wore more than a towel.

"I can take them," she said and turned away from him.

"Give your team a chance."

She scowled but she waited.

A second later, Beanpole darted out of the lounge with a shotgun and fired it three times to force the hostiles to take cover behind the front desk. As soon as they did so, Butters emerged with a rifle.

He took two shots—and missed both times—before the intruders tried to flee out the front door.

One of the men slipped on one of the papers, landed hard, and pushed himself up. He slid again, then pulled his ski mask back to reveal a light-skinned face and a brown mustache.

"I got him," Butters said.

"No, wait." Washington stumbled toward the sniper and blocked his shot.

"Dammit, Wonderkid!"

Kristen glared at Jim. He didn't return the look and seemed too distracted to notice. There was something odd in his expression, though. Surprise? Fear? Recognition?

The invaders used the opportunity created by the brief moment of confusion to race out the door and the advantage was lost.

"I got them," she said. They'd barely cleared the front door and she could make it there no problem. If she put her steel skin on, she could even stop their getaway vehicle.

"No! No, wait," Washington said and scrambled in her path.

"They'll get away." Kristen put a hand on his shoulder as a reminder that she could fling him across the room if she wanted to.

"Exactly. Even though they didn't do shit besides make a mess, they're already running off. This has to be a trap."

"He might be right," Drew said from down the corridor. "Hall, don't pursue."

She obeyed, but she also made a note to talk to their team leader about Washington later. Why had he stopped Butters from taking that shot? What had she seen in his eyes? Could she trust him?

In the moment of stillness that followed the attack, her mind raced. He had been there on that day in the demolished building. In fact, he'd wanted to leave her behind. Now, he covered for hostiles brazen enough to attack the station?

Given all that, she decided she didn't mind having him as her new partner. At least this way, she could keep an eye on him and snap his neck if she found out he couldn't be trusted.

CHAPTER THIRTY-SIX

Kristen had the next two days off which, with Drew's new obsession with them being a team, meant that she wasn't allowed to come into work. Apparently, part of being a team meant letting her team do their jobs without her babysitting them. Captain Hansen might have still allowed it—she liked the publicity their dragon brought in—but she didn't want to go above Drew's head. She respected him too much for that.

So instead, she moped around her apartment, called her mom on the phone, and in a moment of true desperation, dropped in to visit her folks and play videogames with her brother.

After destroying her mercilessly in three different games, Brian threw his controller down. "You're not even trying. You used to be good at Pro Skater."

"Yeah, I know. Sorry." She put her controller down as well and stood to get a snack from the freezer. Despite the fact that her mom often joked that her brother was a man-child, they still fed him like one. She found a freezer full of ice cream sandwiches, corn dogs, and frozen burger patties.

"So, what's up?" he asked as he loaded a one-player first-person shooter. He seemed to like that style of game more now that she was on SWAT.

She selected a corndog and put it in the microwave. "You know how in Pro Skater, there are some levels where you can't use your special bar?"

"Yeah, the worst levels. I hate that shit. The best part of the game is using your cool moves, so why limit it?"

"Exactly! Well, that's what it's like at work right now. They don't want me to use my dragon powers, even though I know that if I had more, I would be a bigger asset."

He shrugged, his gaze still fixed on the screen. "It makes sense to me. Leveling up makes everything easier."

"Right? And yet they act like that would make me vulnerable."

"Well, you are vulnerable, right? For one thing, you found out that steel skin and electricity don't get along. Or magnets."

"Right. Or magnets, so my boss wants me to forego using my powers so I don't rely on them."

"That's stupid." Brian paused the game when the microwave beeped. Apparently, she wasn't the only one who wanted a corndog.

"I don't know…I guess it makes sense. After all, there are levels without special, right?"

"Yeah, but not in real life. I guess if you're fighting in a powerplant or something you'll need to not use your steel power, but that only means you'll need to be even better with your other powers, right?"

"I guess? I don't even know what my other powers are." Kristen sighed. It was so frustrating.

"Obviously not videogames," he said, slid his corndog into the microwave, and fixed his special sauce—mayo and ketchup with tabasco.

"I don't know if dragons can have powers like they do in videogames." She shook her head at the ridiculousness of it. "Honestly, I don't even know if dragons can really breathe fire. I've yet to see it myself. And they have these weird names. Like maybe they're clues about their abilities. I simply don't know."

"You need a tutorial," he said sagely.

"A what?" she asked around a bite of corndog.

"You know, like in fighting games? A tutorial shows you all the moves, the combos, how to block, that kind of stuff. You need to take a dragon tutorial."

"Adults call that training, Brian."

"Sure, whatever. You need training then. Dragon training." Brian removed his corndog from the microwave and bit it as if that emphasized his point.

"But I can't train with Drew and the others."

"Right, that'd be like using a fatality in Street Fighter."

"What?"

"You know, it's a real shame you never got into fighting games. I simply mean…" He scratched the pathetic growth of peach fuzz on his chin. "You're using the wrong move set is all. You need someone who can show you what it means to be a dragon. Which probably means—"

"A dragon," Kristen said and finished his thought.

He nodded, his corndog already reduced to only the stick.

"Too bad you're a huge loser who doesn't have any dragon friends." He selected a different game, loaded it, and selected a fighter. "I will show how you to kick someone's head off, though."

"I have dragon friends!" she said and immediately regretted it. If there was anyone who knew how to get under her skin, it was her brother.

"Yeah, I don't know, Kristen. Does that Stonequest dude from Dragon SWAT really count as a friend? Didn't he say to stick with SWAT until your powers fully came in? That doesn't exactly sound like the kind of guy who has time to train a total noob."

"No, no, you're right. I don't think Stonequest would help. Also, he didn't give me his card or anything. I'd have to go through proper channels and that might piss Drew off."

"So, you're stuck then."

She nodded, even though it wasn't true. At the dragon party, the black dragon had offered to help if she ever needed anything. Sebastian Shadowstorm was his name. He'd been a real gentleman.

Thoughtfully, she finished her corndog, poked the stick in one of her mom's potted plants, and dug in her purse for the card. She withdrew it and looked at the phone number. There was no address.

"Hey, Brian, I'm going to make a phone call."

"Oh, yeah? Did some other dragon swipe right?"

Kristen ignored him and stepped into the back yard. She dialed the number. It rang three times before a man's voice answered.

"How may I help you?" It wasn't Shadowstorm.

"Hello. Maybe I have the wrong number. I'm trying to speak to Sebastian Shadowstorm. Do I have the right number?"

"Who is calling?" the man asked rather rudely and didn't answer her question.

"This is Kristen Hall. I met Mr Shadowstorm at a party. He said to call if I needed anything."

"Ah, yes. Lady Hall. The master has been awaiting your call. Would you like to come to his residence this afternoon?"

She glanced inside. Brian clenched his teeth as he pounded buttons, deep in the clutches of a fighting game. "Yes. That would be great."

The man gave her the address and she wrote it down. She poked her head inside, said goodbye to Brian, and left through the side gate.

"Enjoy your hot date," her brother called after her.

After a perfunctory and somewhat distracted wave in his general direction—which he obviously wouldn't have seen anyway—she slid into her car and headed to the address.

The journey took her through a part of Detroit that, decades before, had been one of the wealthiest and most opulent. Every house was a mansion made of brick complete with a sunroom and tower. The street had been laid almost a hundred years before by the capitalists of the last century, although in the years since then it had fallen from what it was.

Still, she knew it was in better shape than it had been. It used to be that every third mansion stood crumbling with sagging roofs, broken windows, and overgrown lawns but now, it was more like one in ten was in disrepair. Before long, even those last few places would fall to the wave of gentrification that had swept the city over the last ten years.

She continued until she found Shadowstorm's address. As soon as she saw the mansion, she knew it was his without the need to verify the address.

While most of the houses in this neighborhood—and compared to Shadowstorm's residence, the mansions she had driven past were little more than houses—had gone through a phase of disrepair, his looked like he'd spent the last hundred years adding to the splendor of his property.

The house was in absolutely perfect condition. She wasn't sure how, but the wood siding looked original—although the black paint might have been a more recent affectation—and the red brick chimney wasn't sooty or crumbling anywhere along its towering height. There was another tower as well, this one ringed by windows.

The front yard was amazing. Perfectly trimmed grass pushed up against flowering hedges and well-manicured oak trees. She even saw a wisteria in bloom. Odd, considering they usually bloomed in spring and it was late summer, but whoever took care of Shadowstorm's landscaping obviously knew their stuff.

Kristen parked, got out, and approached the wrought iron black gate that surrounded the property. Walking past the extensive gardens, she realized that there probably used to be more houses there. It looked like he had bought the properties and demolished them to create more space for a garden filled with marble statues of people and bronze sculptures of parts of dragons.

Here was a dragon's head and there was the skeletal arm of a dragon that pulled itself from the earth. All over were people, done slightly smaller than life-size in bright marble, which only made the pieces of dragon seem all the larger. A woman crouched, protecting a child, while a man stood with a raised sword—although the stone weapon was broken—and terror on his face.

She didn't think there were this many sculptures in the Detroit Institute for Art. And it was all so specific. Parts of dragons and people in various states of terror. Had Shadowstorm had it all commissioned? It certainly looked as if he had.

What did that say about him? Did he like people's fear? Did he wish to protect them? Did he wish to see dragons torn to pieces? Did he find their anatomy fascinating and beautiful?

Impatiently, she shook her head. She was overthinking it. Her parents had a statue of a peacock in their front yard for years until she had caught a football and plowed into it. They'd bought it because they could afford it and kept it because they hadn't known what else to do with it. Surely Shadowstorm had a reason for the specific collection of art, but it might be a reason that made no more sense than her parents' peacock.

Finally, deciding she could wait no longer, she approached the gate and looked for the buzzer, only to be confronted by a guard, who asked to see her ID.

Kristen showed him her police badge—it was, after all, valid identification, and besides, Shadowstorm had met her because of her face being plastered all over the news. The guard studied it, glanced at her once more, then closed the window to his station and spoke on his radio.

CHAPTER THIRTY-SEVEN

"A human girl is here, flashing a Detroit Police Department Badge," the guard said over the radio.

Sebastian Shadowstorm frowned. A human girl with a police badge? Who else could that possibly be? The damn guards could sometimes be incredibly dense.

"Is her name Kristen Hall, by chance?" he asked.

"Yes, sir."

"She's not a human, you fool, but the SWAT's Steel Dragon. Do you ever go home and read the newspaper or do you spend all your time in that guard shack?"

"Sorry. sir. My apologies, sir," the man blubbered. Even over the radio, Shadowstorm could tell he was terrified. Excellent. Security needed to know what they were fighting for. "Shall I let her in?"

"You said she flashed her badge?"

"Yes, sir."

"Very well. We must not stand in the way of official police duty. Let her in, lock the gate behind her, and engage the moat." If she was on police business, she might have discovered his secrets or be close to it anyway. But if she was alone? Well, he could take the steel dragon so long as she was stuck in human form.

"The…moat, sir?" the guard asked and broke into Shadowstorm's thoughts.

"Damn it, you fool, you know what I mean. Not the moat but the… perimeter defenses. To stop any vehicles."

"As soon a she's inside, I'll bring up the tire spikes sir," he replied, obviously not happy at all to correct his boss.

"Yes, the tire spikes. Do that!" He growled his annoyance. Times changed so rapidly and humans could rarely see the long picture of their development. Call a car a carriage or even an automobile, and they looked like the foundation of their very existence had been questioned. Now with the invention of their infernal jabbering television, it was even worse.

His residence reflected what he thought of the revoltingly fast turnover of technology. He left his tower and walked down his carpeted stairs past oil paintings of kings he'd deposed and princes wise enough to swear secret fealty to him.

Various suits of armor stood strategically, still blackened from the knight being cooked alive inside. He passed treasure taken from five continents and furniture that had supported some of the documents that now governed the world.

Sebastian did have a telephone—he could see the value in that invention anyway, even if he couldn't stand the cursed ringing of its bell—and he had electric lights, of course. That aside, he'd never purchased a television and didn't quite understand the obsession with computers.

But none of that was important now. Incompetent guards merely had a way of reminding Shadowstorm of humanity's priorities and why they needed to be usurped or at least guided with a stronger hand than the weak wrist of the Dragon Council.

He wondered again about this Kristen Hall. He'd invited her and yet she had waited over a week to come and visit. That didn't exactly sound like a social call. It sounded more like a sheriff following up on unanswered questions.

But how could she have discovered anything so quickly? Still, it didn't matter. If she knew, she knew, and that meant she would be destroyed. He considered taking a sword from the wall but decided against it. With her steel skin, his dragon form would be all but essential in defeating her.

But was that her purpose? To apprehend him? He couldn't be sure.

If the whelp intended to challenge him in his home, he'd destroy her himself. Invading another dragon's stronghold was quite improper, after all.

Shadowstorm considered meeting her in the garden to prevent any possible damage to his residence but decided against it. It would be better for her to come inside. If she turned against him, it might cost him a few walls but the collateral damage would be more convincing if other dragons questioned what might happen today. If it looked like a home invasion, no one—not even that moron Ironclaw—would challenge his decision to slaughter the little steel runt.

At a knock on the door, he gestured for his two servants to open it. Each took hold of one of the huge iron and oak doors and pulled them open.

Kristen Hall stood in the doorway, framed by the massive opening. In her jeans and t-shirt, she looked entirely out of place like a piece of modern art that had somehow made it into the renaissance collection.

"Mr Shadowstorm, hello," she said.

He hid a smirk. She didn't sound like a sheriff on a case, she sounded…perhaps intimidated was apt. "Ms Hall. I thought I asked you to call me Sebastian."

Her nervousness cracked and she smiled. "Right, Sebastian. Sorry. It's simply that this place is…well, it's amazing."

"Indeed, thank you. Please, won't you come in? You honor me with your visit."

Kristen nodded, glanced quickly at the chandelier, then at the polar bear rug on the floor, and stepped across the threshold and into his stronghold. "Well, you said if there was anything I needed, I should call you, so…here I am." She tried to smile, but her nervousness made it a little shaky.

Shadowstorm, meanwhile, simply beamed. He could barely believe it as he'd all but given up on trying to build a relationship with the

Steel Dragon. Humans, he'd learned, had the attention span of any of the lesser animals. Some had focus, true, but if they didn't return a call within a day or two, they simply forgot about it. Apparently, he'd been on her mind.

"But of course, Kristen, but of course. Please come in and make yourself at home. Tyler, libations, if you please. Our guest looks like she's in need of something to calm her nerves."

The two servants closed the door behind her and one vanished to fetch drinks.

The other man—Shadowstorm could never remember his name, Mitchell? McDonald? Something like that—escorted his visitor across the spacious entryway to the sitting room.

Sebastian gestured for her to sit in the last chair Mussolini had sat in before he'd died, while he made himself comfortable on Napoleon's couch.

"So, how may I be of assistance?"

"Well, to jump right to it, I want to unlock more of my dragon abilities."

"Yes, of course." It was time for a gamble, but he had always believed in playing the odds. "But hasn't Dragon SWAT shown you some of our methods?"

Kristen laughed derisively. "I wish. They—or he, I guess, a guy named Stonequest—ordered me to stay where I am until my powers develop."

Shadowstorm hid his glee. His gamble had paid off wonderfully! "Stonequest… Yes, I must say I am familiar with the gentleman. He's quite committed to his job of bullying the rest of us around. I can't say I'm surprised that he's not taken the time to properly welcome you into our little community."

She sighed. "So, what? He'll simply keep me at arm's length until I learn what I'm doing?"

He shrugged slowly and delicately like he wanted to avoid saying something against Stonequest although really, he only wanted her to ask more about him. "That might be his intention."

"Oh yeah?" She raised an eyebrow. "Well, what else might it be?"

"Well, Kristen, I know you're quite new to all this, but…well, how do I put this delicately? Not all dragons can be trusted."

That seemed to startle her. Shadowstorm found it an actual challenge not to smile. How could she be so gullible? His effort to defund public schools might be paying off.

"So you think he's…he's been lying to me or something?"

Again, he shrugged delicately. He pushed himself to his feet and began to pace in the sitting room before he paused to admire the crossed swords hanging on the wall. "I don't think he's evil or anything like that, but…well, Stonequest works for the police, and police like stability. But you know that, of course."

"Of course. But there's nothing wrong with that."

"Of course not. But, look at it from Stonequest's view. His job is to police dragons, beings that have been around for centuries or even millennia. Not all of them keep up with the times or like their motives questioned." He snorted playfully. "Why, even I have yet to purchase one of the new portable phones."

"Okay, but so what? I know how to play Xbox, but what does that have to do with ignoring me?"

He had no choice but to ignore the Xbox comment. It must have been some kind of amusement game like the pinball machines humans were so fond of. "It's not that he's ignoring you, it's that he has a balance to maintain between many different powerful and stubborn forces. You—by your very nature of being raised by humans and being so young—will have a new set of ideals. And then there's your ability. I've never seen anything like it and although Stonequest's fingers reach farther than mine, he probably hasn't either. From his perspective, it's probably simpler if you stay a human sheriff who can stop bullets."

"A sheriff?" She laughed.

Shadowstorm waved his hand at her tinkling laughter. This was honestly too easy. "Officer, keeper of the peace, whatever you call yourselves. I will help you, but you must promise not to drag me into this century. It's too loud and far too bright."

"You will help me?" she asked.

"Of course. Although, I wasn't kidding about Stonequest. It would probably be better if you don't tell him about this."

"I won't. He probably has—what did you call them? Fingers?—in our offices too. If you can train me to be a better dragon, I'll let the results speak for themselves."

In that moment, Tyler returned with the drinks. Shadowstorm took his and raised it in a toast to her. "A toast, to our new alliance."

She smiled and raised her glass. "To new friends."

They clanked glasses and a wave of satisfaction washed over him. It was so overwhelming he almost felt it himself. It was her aura pushing against him with the strength of a rising tide. Who was this girl? How was she this powerful? He glanced at his servants to see them both smiling as well. She had overpowered his own effect on them without even trying.

Yes, he decided, he'd done the right thing. By working with the Steel Dragon, he could get a feel for her powers, her strengths, and most importantly, her weaknesses. "Shall we begin?"

"What? Today?"

"Yes, right now. I'd love to get a sense of what you're capable of… to better tailor my lessons. There's no point in wasting time on developing your speed if you're already faster than me." Shadowstorm chuckled and Kristen smiled. He didn't even have to lie about his interest in her strengths.

"Uh, sure."

If she became an ally, he'd have to work on her manners, but that would come later. He took a sword from the wall and started toward the door. "Please, right this way."

She followed him through his mansion and out to his garden.

They strolled past his sculpture collection. If it made Kristen uncomfortable, she did a good job of hiding it by jabbering away. "So, do all dragons basically have the same powers, or what? I know that one guy could turn his hand into metal, so is that more common than I realized? Are we all more or less the same strength, or can working out affect that? I guess I can't imagine a dragon doing pushups or going to the gym, though. Do your two forms line up? If

I'm super-buff as a human does that mean I'll be extra strong as a dragon?"

"Kristen, please, calm yourself. There is much to learn but I can't simply tell you everything."

"Why not?"

Shadowstorm sighed and tried to sound endearing. She was such a human with no sense of patience or propriety. "To begin with, I have another engagement this evening and do not have the hours needed to fully answer all your questions. Beyond that, I simply don't know all the answers."

"What? But you've been around for like… Wait, how old did you say you were?"

He waved the question aside. "Old enough, my dear, old enough. I've been around long enough to know that we dragons are private beings. We could rule this world if we would only reach out and take it—there was a time when it bent to our will far more than it does today—and yet my brothers and sisters prefer to give their counsel from the fringes of society."

"Well, isn't that for the best? I find it commendable that human democracy has flourished considering only one of you could rule a state if you wished it."

"Is it best, though? I understand that humans wish to oversee their own affairs, but surely some level of direction is needed. Look at Hitler and look at the brutal history of slavery in the United States. Democracy is only as good as its majority. Sometimes, I wonder if there would be less violence in the world if we simply had a ruler who did not allow it."

She paused to consider that. "I never thought of it that way before. I guess, from your perspective, that might make sense."

"From our perspective, Kristen. I know you've yet to feel fully comfortable as a dragon, but I've read about you in the papers. You single-handedly stop criminals from committing violence in your town. Tell me, how do your human peers feel about that?"

Shadowstorm left her to think about that as they walked out onto his training arena. It was a large sandy court that was often used for volleyball matches when he wanted entertainment—human games were always such fun to watch—but his servants had understood his intentions and removed the net for the two dragons. One of them was still raking the last corner of the sandy square smooth. The man would be punished later if he distracted his guest.

He stopped and turned to face her. She looked like she'd almost prepared an answer to his question, but he didn't want to hear it. He merely wanted her to think about her new place in the world. If she was to become his ally, she would need to come to her own conclusions about what was best for the humans who claimed this planet for their own. He knew how he felt about the vermin, but many balked at such judgments of the wretchedly irresponsible beings who called themselves intelligent.

So, instead of letting her answer his question, he drew a line in the sand at his feet with the sword, pointed the blade at her, smiled, and said, "What's important is that you learn your abilities, so please, try to cross this line."

Kristen grinned. "That's it? That's how you want to train me? No theory and no guidebooks?"

Shadowstorm laughed indulgently. "We are dragons, not basketball players. Our power is inherent in our form. In answer to your questions about our strength, I do not know all the details of every dragon. I think that each of us has different levels of abilities, and yet few of my brothers and sisters realize their full potential."

"And you wish to help me realize my full potential?"

Again, he laughed. "I think we should start with you crossing this line. Come, as quickly as you can. Use your speed." He stabbed the sword into the sand and raised both hands in a defensive stance.

She nodded. No sooner had her head moved than she raced forward.

He had to restrain an instinctive gasp. *Fire above, she's fast!* In a blink, she had halved the distance between them and in another, she was about to cross the line.

Shadowstorm drew the sword and swung it at her shoulder.

"Hey!" She turned her arm into steel and deflected the blow effortlessly. "You put the blade in the sand. I thought that meant it was off-limits."

"I never said any such thing and besides, I didn't expect you to be so fast."

His praise brought a broad smile to her face.

"There were dragons at the party who don't move as quickly as you do."

Kristen shrugged. "You seemed fast and blocked me with no problem."

He smiled and hoped it was a warm gesture. Most of his smiles were used to threaten, after all. "I have never taught a dragon how to use their powers before. Do not assume I am a teacher of such quality as to make you better than my own humble skills."

She nodded and seemed to parse the deeper meaning of what he'd said. That was a mistake. His statement had been too close to the truth.

Hastily, he changed the subject. "Let us test your strength. We clasp hands and try to shove the other to the sand or pull them across the line."

"You mean like pro wrestling?" She grinned.

Shadowstorm didn't even vaguely understand the reference—wrestling was one human sport he found to be quite dull—but he nodded all the same. His instructions had been clear enough, even to someone raised by humans.

They stood on either side of the line, caught hands, and each tried to move their opponent.

The first two matches went to him quite easily. He was simply larger than her and had wrestled in both his human and dragon form for centuries. The first time, he simply shoved her back into the sand and the second, he pulled her toward him, lifted her off her feet, and threw her down.

In the third contest, though, before he could lift her, she turned herself to steel. He thought he could still lift her, but not with the hold he currently had and not with her pulling so hard.

Shadowstorm gave a few inches and when she slipped back, he

readjusted himself, lowered his bulk closer to the ground, and yanked again.

She came toward him but didn't topple forward. Instead, she maintained her balance and yanked back.

He used one of his most well-guarded secrets and turned himself insubstantial for only the briefest of moments. It was not easy to do so he rarely did the trick, but it worked. Kristen—unable to hold on to pure shadow—fell and tumbled through the sand.

"Again," she said, grinned, and pushed herself up. "I don't know how you broke my grip, but it won't happen two times in a row."

Shadowstorm saw the wisdom of that and changed activities.

Over the next hour, he tested her in every way he could think of. She was strong, fast, and had almost mastered her ability to turn into steel. He showed her a few tricks, mostly how to increase her healing speed and how to use her aura to affect his servants. While he didn't wish to divulge anything, she already had a powerful aura that undoubtedly affected the people around her, so she might as well know how to use it properly. Besides, auras didn't work on other dragons, so she wouldn't be able to turn it against him if she decided to.

And she might very well decide that he was her enemy. He was forced to admit that to himself. She was a fast learner and smart. When she saw that her opponent would beat her, she tried to find other ways to win.

If she discovered that he'd rallied the gangs to attack the city—that dear old Sebastian was, in fact, Mr Black—he had little doubt she would turn against him. Yet she would be a potent weapon if she could be properly tempered.

In the end, he invited her back for more training. It would be a dangerous game of Dragon and Knight but he felt the risks were worth it. She had to see him as an ally and hopefully, a partner. Only then could he unleash her as a weapon upon this worthless city.

CHAPTER THIRTY-EIGHT

The next few days at work would have been relaxing if Kristen worked for anyone but Drew. There were no major incidents and no more of the odd baiting from the specters who'd attacked the station. None of the detectives were able to learn a damn thing about the hostiles who'd come in and attacked, though. They'd escaped in a car that had been found abandoned an hour later with no prints, no DNA, and no clues at all.

She would have worried over their escape if she hadn't been so certain they'd attack again. All she had to do was wait and they'd target her once more. The thought made her both giddy and terrified.

The team leader used the opportunity to push them hard during training and obviously relished having Washington as a new recruit and Kristen working at being human again.

In an effort to adhere to the commitment she'd made to him, she kept her reservations to herself. She understood where Drew was coming from. He simply didn't understand the extent of her powers, and—if Dragon SWAT was honest—she wouldn't be with them forever. And yet, after meeting with Shadowstorm for another session, the training felt stifling. It was more like the team was adjusting to being themselves again and how to behave without a dragon on the team—which was a total waste of time, in her opinion.

While she didn't know how long she'd be on SWAT, if they used her abilities—really used them—they could actually effect real change in the city.

They finished practicing non-lethal, hand-to-hand takedowns and Drew told everyone to hit the showers. She smiled as she turned the hot water on. Shadowstorm and her had been practicing the same kind of fighting, and he was a much tougher opponent. Working with regular humans was more of a challenge in control than it was in learning the skills.

After training with the much more powerful dragon, she fully understood that she could quite easily defeat any human in hand-to-hand combat, even without her steel skin. While she'd seen glimpses of it before, it had never really settled in as a certainty. She was much faster than a regular person and strong enough to crack bones with her bare hands.

Still, she decided to not tell her team these tidbits. As little as she liked to admit it, Shadowstorm was right. She was different than a regular person and she could see the wisdom of keeping some of these differences a secret, especially when her boss was so determined that she act human while at work.

Kristen finished her shower, dressed in her regular clothes, and went to join everyone in the lounge. There was a heated debate going on about what to do for after-work relaxation.

"I'm telling you, the finest hot wings you've ever tasted this far north." Butters stood with his feet apart and pontificated to the room at large.

"Hear, hear," the Rookie shouted. "Happy hour with beer and hot wings."

"We can do that later," Hernandez argued. "I'll spring for the fifty cents you're saving per beer if we do airsoft first."

"I thought you were banned after what happened last time with—" Drew didn't finish the sentence. They all knew that he was going to say, "with Jonesy," but he didn't. Sometimes, it was better not to scratch the wound.

"There's a new course." The woman's eyes gleamed, which convinced Kristen that she'd hidden low-powered explosives and wished to bring another play fort down on her team's collective heads.

The team leader considered that and shrugged. "Airsoft has my vote. We can practice with different partners and new strategies while we're there. Beanpole, thoughts?"

"Airsoft sounds enjoyable. I'd like to show Butters what happens when I don't have his back."

"All right, three to two. Hall, do you want to push this into a solid majority?"

She thought back to the last time she'd played airsoft and shook her head. "Sorry. I'm with Butters and the Rookie. Beer and wings sound fantastic after all the drills you've made us run this week." She didn't mention that airsoft wasn't much fun when she knew she could move faster than the plastic pellets. And that had been months ago. It wouldn't even be a challenge for her now.

"Damn, three to three. I guess it'll be up to the Wonderkid. Where is he, anyway?" Drew poked his head out into the hall. "Washington! You wanna shoot your friends or drink poison?"

"Shoot my friends, always," he called in response.

"Hot damn," Hernandez said. "Four to three. do you guys want to carpool or race there?"

The group left the lounge and headed to the front of the station and past the armed officers who were on duty at all hours now.

"Wonderkid," the woman who worked the front desk called in a sing-song voice as they passed.

"Yes, ma'am?"

"Did you piss the missus off or something?"

"Ma'am?"

"I've never seen a bouquet of flowers this big come for anyone unless a was fight was involved." There was indeed a huge bouquet of flowers on her desk.

"Or a funeral," Hernandez quipped. Everyone laughed. Sometimes, gallows humor was all those who had lost still had against the world.

"I'm still single...and alive," he said with a grin.

Everyone laughed at that too. It really had been a good week for the team. There really was nothing like training way too hard under Drew to make a team work together.

"Well, they're still for you. You're the only Wonderkid we have here."

Washington furrowed his brow. "Are you sure? Who are they from?"

"It's signed 'your secret admirer.' There's a poem too. You never told us you were the romantic sort, Jim."

"Let me see that." He snatched the note as the woman was about to start reading.

"Yay!" Butters exclaimed. "A performance. Please, project. We'd all love to hear whatever sappy nonsense it takes to get in the Wonderkid's pants."

Everyone laughed except Washington, who read the note with his eyebrows drawn together and his lips moving slightly. He paused and read it again.

"Okay, Washington, you can dump those on your desk. We can carpool out and you can collect your fancy flowers in the morning."

"Nah... Nah, you know what? I think I might...uh, take these home. Airsoft's not really my thing anyway."

"What? I call bullshit. You said you wanted to shoot your friends." Hernandez sounded as if she'd been betrayed on her deathbed instead of having a friend back out of a few hours of fun.

Keith chuckled his rookie laugh. "Damn, man. Flowers and a poem and you come calling? I guess I would too. That's not exactly discreet for a booty call."

Everyone absolutely lost it at that one. He beamed at their laughter until Drew slapped him on the back. "Come on, you guys," the team leader said. "Don't resent the guy for getting some while the rest of us have to vent our blue balls by shooting each other with tiny plastic balls."

More giggles ensued. It had been a long week but Kristen didn't think that had anything to do with their teammate's changed mind. Washington didn't look like he was about to go get laid. He looked nervous—scared even—and he glanced constantly from the flowers to the rest of the team. He tried to hide it, but something was amiss with the Wonderkid.

"Now hold up!" Butters said. "The vote is tied. Three to three. There is no reason for us to go to airsoft without a proper debate or a recount."

Hernandez put her hands on her hips. "Bullshit. Washington's vote counts. What, you don't believe in absentee voting?"

"No, I cannot say that I particularly do," the sniper responded smartly.

"I still say drinks sound better than more airsoft," Keith said.

"Either way, let's load up," Drew said and led the way to his car—an SUV that, although newer, wasn't nearly as homey as Jonesy's decommissioned SWAT van had been.

As they walked beneath the darkening sky, Kristen surveyed the Motor City. The SWAT station really was located on a prime piece of real estate. On the appropriately named Atwater street, it sat directly on the river with downtown at its back and a view of the water in front. She looked behind them to see the sun sinking between the buildings. And there was Washington, huffing down Bates Street toward the city center with his bouquet in hands, moving like he was on a mission.

Something about that didn't sit right with her. She thought back to the team of assholes who had tried to demolish a building on her head. He had wanted to leave her to pursue them. At the time, she had thought he wanted to catch them but now, a different idea struck her. What if he had known the building would come down? What if he'd merely tried to get to safety and leave her behind? His dislike of dragons was no secret, and this gang of thugs also seemed to have their sights set on her.

Except they were not thugs. They were obviously professionals and most likely military—exactly like Washington.

And then there was the incident when they'd attacked the station. That had been a well-coordinated, precise strike, in and out with no casualties on either side. They must have known the layout of the station for their assault to go so smoothly. But it shouldn't have, she recalled. She could have pursued them but someone had stopped her. He had stopped her and he'd also prevented Butters from taking a shot he could have probably made blindfolded.

What if Jim Washington, Wonderkid extraordinaire, was a mole?

"You know what?" she said as she watched him walk toward the lights of downtown with his bouquet. "I think I want to go home and veg out. If I hurry, I might be able to watch twenty whole minutes of TV before I fall asleep."

"That means the vote is three to two again. Airsoft wins." Hernandez pumped her fist in the air.

"What? No way," Keith whined. "Come on. I want to drink a beer with the Lost Dragon and maybe put some money on some dude beating you in an arm-wrestling contest. I could watch his face when you turn to steel and make him buy me wings all night."

"Gee, how could I miss the Rookie using my mysterious steel dragon abilities to win free hot wings? I'll see you guys tomorrow morning, okay?"

Hernandez snorted and entered the SUV. If she was pissed, she'd take it out on the rest of the team. Kristen felt maybe a little bad about that, but she had to see where Washington was going.

The rest of her team loaded up in the vehicle. She dilly dallied around her car until they drove off because she didn't want them to see her leave on foot. It would arouse suspicions she didn't want.

Once they were out of sight, she jogged back and looked down Bates street. Despite it being a fairly long way before there were any turn offs, she didn't see any sign of Washington.

"Damn," she cursed quietly and sprinted after him.

Oh, it felt good to run at her full speed. She raced down Bates and her muscles pumped faster than they ever had before. Her training with Sebastian had helped her understand what she was capable of. She could move faster, her legs firing like pistons, but she could also leap farther with each step. It wasn't that she had super-speed. She wasn't the Flash and couldn't vibrate her whole body so fast the world slowed down. It was more that if she learned to control herself properly, she could move somewhere in fewer steps than a regular human and make each step much faster.

She did that now as she sprinted down the road. The concrete walls on her left blurred and the iron fence with its tips bent toward the street flickered past on her right. She had a sense of how Sebastian moved. He couldn't vanish into shadow—she didn't think he could, anyway—but simply knew his abilities well enough to fully exploit them. She aspired to that level of control.

Obviously, she wasn't there yet. When she made it to Jefferson and tried to stop, she almost careened all the way across the street. She slowed herself enough after one lane, which drew a blaring car horn and a few profanities from the driver who had to swerve to avoid hitting her.

Kristen cursed and scrambled back to the sidewalk. A young couple laughed at her. And old man shook his head, but there was no sign of—there he was.

Washington had already made it down Jefferson and now crossed the street. She checked for traffic and hurried across as he vanished inside Millender Center.

She reached the other side, checked for pedestrians, and ran with everything she had—fast enough to blow the newspaper out of someone's hand. If she hadn't been so focused on her need to see what Washington was up to, she would have been thrilled.

Moments later, she reached Millender center as Washington left Ashley's Flowers, now without a bouquet.

There was no way he had hurried all the way there only to return the flowers. Who did that? She felt like her suspicion was proving to be justified. No one returned flowers so something was definitely up.

He didn't exit the building but instead, took the stairs to the People Mover station two at a time.

"Shit!" The People Mover was a rail car that ran on a fairly small loop in downtown Detroit. Some people joked that it was faster to walk than it was to use it, but she had always found it endearing. Although she might miss her ride if she didn't hurry. A train was moving over her head and would be in the station in less than a minute.

Kristen darted inside, hopped the turnstile—wondering if cops ever bothered to pay for civil services like that—and took the stairs three at a time, four at a time, then five at a time. She made it to the top not even slightly winded.

Which was good, because she had to throw herself behind a trashcan to not be seen. She held her breath until she heard the hiss as the doors opened, then stood and tried to act casual. It occurred to her that she had no idea what the man would say if he saw her now, but she knew that her plan to spy on him would be ruined.

He had been near the front of the platform, so she walked onto the rear car.

Her gamble paid off. While her teammate wasn't on it, she could see him through the window. He looked around nervously but hadn't noticed her.

The People Mover lurched into motion. He didn't get off at the next stop, which was the Renaissance Center. She exhaled when he didn't stand up to exit.

That was where the dragon's rooftop party had been held. If he had gotten off there, she would have been certain that he was working with a dragon. He didn't, which meant…exactly nothing. It didn't mean that he wasn't working with a dragon, only that he wasn't definitely working with a dragon.

She shook her head and focused. There would be time for speculation later. Now was the time to obtain the facts. Hypotheses would follow when she had information.

They rode the People Mover past Bricktown and the stop near the Greektown Casino, then past the Cadillac Center and Broadway Street stations.

Kristen was about to give up and chalk his adventure up to merely another nostalgic ride on the elevated train—she had certainly taken her fair share of those—when he stood at the Grand Circus Park Station and exited.

Fortunately, he didn't look around and she waited until the last possible moment, then darted through the doors as they closed. She leapt through them like a grasshopper. One moment she was inside the train and the next, she stood ten feet in on the platform, all in one jump. She looked to her right. Washington was already heading down the stairs. After a few moments to give him a little lead time, she followed.

He was easy to see as he crossed Park Avenue. He glanced back and she ran behind a bus and kept up with it easily enough. By the time she stopped, she wasn't behind him anymore but a block over. She watched him move deeper into the park toward the Edison Memorial Fountain.

Her dragon powers were definitely growing stronger. Despite it being dark and Grand Circus Park being less than well-lit, she could easily tell him from the other late-night visitors to the park.

She darted across the street and wove in and out of the speeding cars with ease. One honked at her and she had to put on an extra burst of speed to get out of the way. She was glad she did. The close call had activated her steel skin. If she'd been struck by the car, she would probably have been fine but it would have destroyed the vehicle and her quarry would've seen her.

As it was, she thumped onto the sidewalk and her weight pulverized the already crumbling surface. She made a mental note to not complain about her taxes—after all, she'd done some damage to the city—and followed him into the park.

He was more nervous now and looked around almost constantly. In fact, he looked damned paranoid, which made him more difficult to follow but also convinced her that she couldn't give up now.

Cautiously, she moved from tree to tree, trying to get closer and closer without being seen, but he suddenly stopped.

He stood in a bubble of light, illuminated by the Edison Memorial fountain and the lights in the park.

Kristen couldn't get any closer without the risk of betraying her presence. She accepted that despite her impatience, waited in the shadows, and watched him.

It was a little surreal to be there on a stake-out. She had seen the fountain on dozens of postcards while growing up, always with the jets at full blast and a rainbow of lights reflected in the water.

It wasn't quite as grand in real life as it was on the postcards, but it was still a sight worth seeing. She also noticed that pigeons—honest to God pigeons—were sculpted into the fountain itself, when someone stepped out of the gloom on the far side of the park and approached Washington.

The two men nodded and her teammate looked both uncomfortable and angry while the other man looked more guilty than anything else. She strained to hear what they were saying, but the fountain was too loud. Maybe that was why they had chosen it as a place to meet.

She squinted through the gloom and strained to hear but with little success. Her dragon abilities meant she had better sight than humans, but should she have better hearing too? She didn't know and it wasn't like she could call Sebastian and ask him how to activate more of her powers, so she resigned herself to the fact that all she could do was watch.

The stranger was light-skinned, had a neatly trimmed brown mustache, and seemed familiar to her. She could almost place him but not quite.

After a few minutes of conversation, Washington's expression turned to anger. "That's unacceptable and you know it," he yelled at his companion.

The man scowled and ran a hand through his hair. The gesture triggered the memory and she recognized him immediately. She'd seen him do the same thing—rub his face with his hand and push his hair back—but the last time she'd seen the gesture, it was because he'd pushed a ski mask off his face.

It was one of the men who'd attacked the station—the one who had slipped on the papers and the man Washington had stopped Butters from shooting.

His outburst seemed to have ruined the conversation, though, because the man muttered something. Jim protested but whatever he said apparently had little effect as his contact mumbled something else and vanished into the park. Washington didn't follow.

Suddenly, she didn't care so much that she hadn't been able to hear them. He was working with the enemy. Instead of arresting this man, he had chatted to him. What more evidence did she need?

Jim Washington felt like eyes were boring into the back of his neck, but he didn't see anyone following him and ascribed the sensation to still working through PTSD. Sometimes, the worst part of being in a hostile situation was the waiting. At least when you were shooting, you knew where the enemy was. It was the rest of it that could make a man's mind itch and eat itself alive.

Jim exited the People Mover and hurried off the platform, checking once more to make sure he wasn't followed. He didn't see anyone and hurried down the stairs before he heard the doors hiss shut.

He crossed Park Avenue and headed to the center of Grand Circus Park and the Edison fountain.

"Where the elephants play and the lights go away," the poem had said.

Except it wasn't a poem, but a rap lyric he and a buddy from Detroit had written when they were overseas together. It was supposed to be a dumb song about how nothing ever was what it promised to be when you grew up poor in Detroit—no elephants at the circus and lights that looked better on a postcard than in real life because they were out half the damn time.

That wasn't the case anymore, of course. The city had changed.

So had his friend, apparently. Dwight Olsen was a noncommissioned officer Jim had met while serving in the Marines. They were both from Detroit but hadn't known each other until they'd met overseas.

He had almost had a heart attack when he'd seen Dwight pull his mask off after the attack on the station. He had been a good man—not perfect because no one who grew up on the wrong side of the poverty line could afford to be perfect, but good all the same. Now, he tried to be a goddamn cop killer?

It simply didn't make sense. Jim had reached out to him through back channels and hoped to meet at a bar where he could maybe get a few drinks in his old friend before he grilled him to discover his role in all this. Dwight, however, had seen right through that and sent the flowers with a note that only he would have understood.

Which meant that his friend was deep in this shit, deeper than he had wanted to believe.

Full of misgivings, he'd waited at the fountain and looked for the man he was supposed to meet. Part of him worried that he looked paranoid, but there were a handful of people waiting to meet someone, so he told himself he was merely being jittery.

Finally, after what felt like an eternity, Dwight sauntered out of the dark.

"Dwight, how are you, my man? What's with all the cloak and dagger stuff?" he said, hoping to play on their friendship.

"I wanted to make sure you were still the Jim I served with."

"I couldn't forget those damn lyrics if I wanted to."

"Oh, so you don't want to?" Dwight smiled. It looked mostly genuine, although it was forced near his eyes.

He laughed all the same. The boot hadn't dropped…yet

"So how long you been in the city, Dwight?"

"Jim, we can cut right to it, man. I know you saw me at the station—shit man, you saved my damn life back there."

"Yeah, man, just returning the favor," he said. The forced casualness of the statement worked as intended. Dwight flinched at the words. He continued. "The thing is, I now have all these other people who depend on me to protect them, and you came in there and tried to blow all their damn heads off."

"We weren't trying to blow all their heads off, Jim, and we both know I wouldn't have let any of them go in there if I knew one of my old buddies from the Marines might get hurt."

"The thing is, I was in there. And we both damn well know that when you bust in shooting, people get hurt—innocent people."

"They're cops, man."

"So am I."

Dwight simply stared at him for second as if sizing him up. "We won't hit that place again. But Jim, man, you should really get out of town."

"And why's that?"

"That's need to know information. The people I'm with…let's say they make the Marines look like a gaggle of first-graders. Organization like you would not believe. You and that fat cop who almost shot me can't stop them. And I tell you what, you talk to them for ten minutes and you wouldn't want to."

"Oh yeah? Are you offering me a meeting?" It wasn't what he had planned, but if he could meet someone higher in this well-organized group, he would exploit that contact.

"Do you think they're gonna come sit down with a cop? Come on, Jim. You're supposed to be smart."

"You're the one who said I needed to meet with them." He was getting frustrated. The man was giving him the runaround.

"What you need to do," Dwight continued and put a hand on his shoulder, "is get the hell out of Detroit."

"We both know I won't do that."

"We go back, Jim, way back. That's why I'm here, man, because I don't want to see you hurt. Get out of here, take your girl if you got one, and forget all about the Motor City. It's gonna get messy for a while."

"That's unacceptable and you know it," Washington yelled, losing his composure. He was reasonably certain Dwight had chosen to meet there because the sound of the fountain would make eavesdropping difficult, but anyone could've heard that.

His companion ran his hand through his hair. He used to do that when he was given an order he didn't like. Shit. He had fucked this up.

"I gotta go, Jim. Nice talking to you."

"Dwight, come in with me. I can get you immunity."

"After trying to shoot a cop? Yeah, right. Plus, I told you it was a damn tight operation. If I'm not back in thirty… Well, I gotta get back or some of the boys I told you about are gonna get theirs."

Jim nodded and let him go. He thought he could take him, cuff him, and bring him in if he needed to, but Dwight wasn't one to lie. If he said the folks he was running with had threatened his friends, they probably had.

He sighed and looked around once more—he still felt eyes boring into his back—then shoved his hands in his pockets and headed home. He could get a cab or take the People Mover again, but he'd always liked to think when he walked, and he had much to think about.

CHAPTER THIRTY-NINE

It was Kristen's day off, which meant she was at Sebastian's training court.

The dragon had her doing weight drills. He'd set up a number of the sculptures in the sandy arena and she had to lug them around. At first, it had seemed impossible, but once she learned how to balance them, it was easier. Not easy, merely easier than impossible.

She was supposed to move the one she currently held from one side of the arena to the other without stopping. It was a sculpture of a woman carrying a bouquet of flowers. She had a look of pensive dread on her face, and she thought the frozen features suggested she was searching for someone.

The flowers made her think about Washington. How could he work behind their back? It was disgusting to think that he'd betray his own damn team. They were supposed to be working together, not—

Her foot slipped and the stature teetered out of her grasp.

"Kristen!" Sebastian yelled and rushed forward. He shoved one hand under the sculpture and prevented it from crashing to the ground. It irked her that he caught it as easily as she would've caught a can of beer.

Although he didn't exactly look happy about it. "Kristen. I chose these statues to work with because I thought it would help you focus on not breaking them."

"I am focused!"

His raised eyebrow told her exactly what he thought of her bald-faced lie.

"I am focused. Only…not on this."

"Then on what?"

She hesitated. Washington wasn't his business. It was police work, but she couldn't exactly tell her coworkers she'd tailed him through the park, could she? She was certain Drew would freak out and the captain would—at the very least—demand a mountain range of paperwork. Still, she reasoned that she should probably tell them, but would it hurt to tell Sebastian? It wasn't like he had made his feelings about regular people a secret. Some drama on the force was probably beneath his notice. Maybe it would be better to tell him first. She could present what she'd found to him, see how he took it, and use his reaction to do a better job of convincing the captain and Drew.

"I…I'm sure this kind of thing isn't that interesting to a dragon, but… Well, I don't think I can trust one of my teammates."

He looked taken aback. "Trust is indeed important to dragons. And I can see with your profession and your alleged superior's insistence on you not using your powers how this would upset you. Is it him? Is it the tall one you don't trust?"

"No. Drew's great. It's a new guy. You haven't met him, actually. He didn't come to the party."

"Ah," he said.

Kristen almost let it drop. Telling him about it made her realize she should tell Drew and the Captain, but there was something about the man standing across from her, something about the way he looked at her… She couldn't help herself and simply let it all out.

"There are these mercenaries in town. At least we think they're mercenaries. They're why I wanted to train with you, honestly, because they're professionals. They used magnetic tasers on my steel skin before they tried to bring that building down on my head. Later, they attacked the station."

"And what is the issue with this new fellow? Is he a coward?"

"No…no, I think he might be a mole." She looked at him with guilt in her eyes. While she felt bad even thinking this kind of thing, she had to know the truth, which meant she had to share her ideas with others.

Sebastian's expression was completely blank. "A mole?"

Her laughter cut the tension of the moment. "Right, that expression must still be fairly recent."

He took a deep breath and seemed to study her. "No… No, I believe I know what you are talking about. Do you believe this new teammate is a spy? That he is undercover?"

"Yes, exactly. Sorry, when I said it you looked…uncomfortable. I assumed that you didn't know the expression—like doing the dab or whatever."

At the word "dab," he only blinked. He really did live in another time decade, or maybe century. "You believe this to be the case because…they attacked the police station?" He scratched his chin.

"No. Well, yes, they must've known the layout, but that's not all."

He raised an eyebrow as if to encourage her to continue.

"Last night, I tailed Washington. That's the new guy. He received a big bouquet of flowers with a note in it, and it freaked him out. He left in a hurry and I followed him using my dragon speed. Thanks for that, by the way."

Sebastian nodded and waved his hand dismissively. "It's nothing, merely your birthright as a dragon. Tell me more. The suspense is killing me."

"He met one of the assholes who attacked the station."

"How can you know?" he countered. "Weren't these mercenaries masked?"

She paused and frowned at him for a moment. She had not mentioned that the mercenaries were masked. "This guy's ski mask came up when he stumbled so I saw his face. But how did you know that? I didn't say they covered their faces."

Sebastian smiled. "Kristen, I may be an anachronism of a dragon, but you said these were professionals. Even I know enough of technology to assume your police station has cameras to catch photographs of their faces. Only a complete and utter moron would reveal his face there." The way he had said moron gave her pause. He'd snarled the word as if the accused had insulted him and needed to be dealt with directly.

"Well, moron or dumb luck, I saw his face. Then, when I followed Washington, it was the same guy. The flowers must have been a code or something. Dammit! I should've taken pictures. Either way, talking to you makes me realize I should simply tell Drew. Even without photos, I think I have enough evidence to at least make them ask the Wonderkid some questions."

He nodded slowly. There was something about his body language, though, that had changed. He seemed more guarded. Was he merely worried for her? If that was it, dragons had an odd way to show concern. "When did this all happen?"

"Last night."

"At what time?"

"Why does that matter?"

His grin was disarming. "As you may have realized, I have rather formidable resources at my disposal. It bothers me to no end that a mercenary is fraternizing with a dirty police officer. If you tell me the time and the location of this clandestine meeting, perhaps I can ferret out more information about this…leak, in your organization."

"I guess so. I think I'll tell Drew, though, and we'll go from there."

"I don't think that's wise, Kristen."

"I trust Drew with my life."

"Yes, of course," he said placatingly. "It's merely that the police are police. There are procedures they must follow—procedures that might very well spook the target. If he is a mole—and at the very least it sounds like he is keeping secrets from his superiors—he will know how to escape into a tunnel and vanish if things go wrong. We must tread lightly, discover who his handler is, and perhaps we can unravel this thread from the tatters of these mercenaries. I assure you, I'll be discreet. All I need to start is the time and place, please."

"It was at Grand Circus Park, the Edison fountain, about eight in the evening," she told him.

Sebastian nodded and his smile widened. He made her think of a cat that had caught a mouse beneath an ottoman and left it with nowhere to run.

"I still think I should tell Drew. I need to know who the assholes are."

"You need to be careful. I'm sure you can trust Drew, but do you trust everyone he trusts? Besides, where would you tell him? If there really is a mole, they could have planted those infernal monitoring devices. They could fetch the tape and find out everything you know. Give me forty-eight hours. If I find nothing, bring them the mole. Does that sound all right?"

She nodded. "Should we keep training?"

"I think not. We'll both be quite distracted. Let me get to work. I'll be in touch."

"Sure," she agreed, but she didn't think she could simply ignore Washington. Still, if he thought it was best for her to conceal the truth from Drew and Captain Hansen, there was obviously value in subterfuge. It might be better if the Steel Dragon came at this from a different angle than Shadowstorm—an angle she didn't need to tell him about until she found out more or he gave her satisfactory answers.

CHAPTER FORTY

An absolutely massive bouquet flowers arrived for Washington the next evening. Kristen didn't know much about flowers, but these looked expensive. Fortunately, she didn't have to sneak around to see the poem because the whole damn station wanted to read the message from the Wonderkid's secret admirer.

When she stepped from the lounge into the office space, Hernandez was already standing on a desk, brandishing the missive like she'd captured the flag. Judging from the Wonderkid's scowl and ashen face, he seemed to think so too.

"Where the big cats roar, till throats are sore, I'll see you from where I stand. Where boys and men play together, snatch them balls with your hand."

The entire office roared with laughter.

"Nothing wrong with being bi." She hooted to the crowd. "But no matter how you slice it, flowers and poetry is for princesses, not police. Plus, Wonderkid, this isn't exactly discreet. Can you show some class, at least? You gonna go give a handjob or something? Even if it's consensual, you still can't do that shit to little boys."

Howls of laughter erupted from everyone except Washington, who only smoldered. Keith laughed so hard he couldn't breathe. Even Beanpole giggled at it all.

"Give me the damn note, okay?" Jim said.

Hernandez relented and handed it over.

"What does it really say?" one of the officers shouted out over the crowd of cops.

"Hey, Anderson, I'm in demolitions, not a goddamn poet laureate. Do you think I made that shit up?"

Everyone laughed again, Anderson the hardest of all. Kristen kept her eyes on Washington, who clenched his jaw so tightly she thought he might crack a tooth. So that was what the note really said, then.

"All right you animals, back to work! I'm paying you to protect this city, not listen to standup comedy and romance poems," Captain Hansen ordered and the crowd dispersed, still giggling amongst themselves.

Kristen busied herself with paperwork. There'd been a convenience store robbery earlier that she'd busted. No, helped bust. They'd done it by the book with no dragon speed or using her steel skin as a shield. It had gone well—no one had died—but that didn't mean the paperwork filled itself out.

While she typed the data in, she thought about the words of the poem. Obviously, they were clues about another meeting. If they contained actual information, Washington wouldn't have gone to the park. Did that mean the poem told him the location?

If so, where did it point to?

"Where the big cats roared till throats are sore," seemed to point to the Detroit Zoo. There wasn't anywhere else in the city that had big cats, but the thing about the sore throats didn't make any sense. There were lions at the Zoo, of course, and a tiger as well, but they didn't roar until their throats hurt. Mostly, they only slept.

Then there was the part about boys and men snatching balls. Honestly, she was somewhat relieved that Hernandez had turned it into a sex joke. That would be at the forefront of everyone's minds, not any other hidden meaning. But what did it mean? She didn't think he was gay, and even if he was, he hadn't met a clandestine lover in the park.

No, it was another clue. It had to be. But where would one go in the city to hear big cats roar and also catch balls? Maybe the boys and men was a father-son reference?

Finally, she slapped her forehead. "Duh!" She'd cracked it and she couldn't believe how obvious the answer was. Her dad would have been ashamed that it took her more than a second to solve it.

Her teammate would meet his contact at Comerica Park, where the Detroit Tigers played baseball. Now that she'd found the answer, it seemed almost painfully obvious. Every single Tigers fan went home with a sore throat, and the line about catching a ball ruled out the Detroit Lions. No one ever went home with a foul football, but that was expected in baseball.

There didn't seem to be a time specified, so she assumed he would simply head there after his shift.

An hour later, she followed him to the People Mover. This time, though, he was much more careful and watched the stairway where she crouched until the doors closed. Only then did he turn away, which meant it was too late for her to get aboard.

No matter. She was a dragon, and she knew where he was going.

As she sprinted down Randolph street, she moved faster than some of the cars. Her training with Sebastian had really made a difference. Not only had he helped her increase her speed but he also helped her use her reflexes better. That meant she could run faster simply because she wasn't worried about tripping over every little thing.

She was actually surprised when Randolph turned into Broadway as she'd run so fast, she'd arrived there sooner than she'd realized. Broadway took her to Witherell, where she turned right and reached her destination.

And not a moment too soon. The People Mover had pulled into the station in almost the same moment. It amused her that she was virtually as fast as a train. She hid behind a dumpster and waited for Washington to come down the steps.

When he did, he looked around and immediately headed toward Comerica Park. She'd cracked the code, then. Missing the People Mover had made her nervous. If she'd misjudged and he'd stepped off somewhere else, she would have had to wait for the next bouquet and would have probably told Drew.

As it was, she'd brought a better camera than the one on her phone. She planned to get pictures and record audio if possible. It was too bad the stadium was so big and she couldn't get ahead of him and set the phone to record. She'd simply have to tail him.

Washington hurried to the front entrance, then turned right. He followed the wall of the massive stadium for a while, almost to the back where the scoreboard was. As soon as the barrier gave way to a black, wrought iron fence, he removed his leather jacket—she had been wondered why he'd worn it as it wasn't cold—and threw it over the spikes at the top. He took a few steps back, ran at the fence, vaulted up to grasp his jacket—and tore it in the process—and hauled himself over.

He left it there, presumably for a quick escape, and moved deeper into the stadium.

She considered taking the jacket and calling Drew but decided against it. If a number of cops arrived, Washington and the mercenary would get spooked.

No, it was better to get what information she could. Then, when he came to work in the morning, he'd walk into a trap.

Kristen stepped up to the ten-foot fence, crouched, and leapt over it. Apparently, a ten-foot vertical leap was still beyond her abilities, but clearing the fence wasn't. As soon as she realized her feet wouldn't make it over the top, she turned her hands to steel and caught hold of the spikes. She pulled herself over effortlessly, landed, and jogged into the darkness where her quarry had vanished.

It was a passageway to the stands—specifically, the part near first base and home plate. Foul ball country. What better place was there to snatch a ball?

Washington approached a man who sat in the stands with a hood up. All she could see of his face in the moonlight was a brown mustache. Everything else was in shadow.

She moved four rows back, dropped to her hands and knees, and crawled after him. Fortunately, he walked at a normal pace and she was able to keep up without too much difficulty. By the time Wonderkid sat beside his handler, she was behind them, albeit four rows back.

Once the conversation began, she crawled over a chair so she was only three rows back and close enough to hear him. She turned her audio recorder on her phone on and waited for an opportune moment to snap a picture.

"What's up, Dwight? I thought I wouldn't hear from you again."

That was a weird thing to hear from a mole. Of course he'd hear from his handler.

The other man didn't respond.

"Two times in a week is a little much, man. And that lyric? Shit, dude. It's a little too obvious, don't you think?" He uttered an odd chuckle she'd heard from him before and knew he was trying to ease the tension.

"I had no choice," Dwight said and clapped a handcuff on Washington.

"What the fuck is this, Dwight?"

"I'm sorry, Jim, really," his companion said, pushed himself up, and took two steps back from the man he'd fastened to a chair. "I told you they would kill my people. I told you that. Why'd you have to look under rocks?"

"I didn't, man. I'm telling you. I didn't lift a fucking finger." He struggled against the handcuff. The rattle of the tiny chain sounded loud in the quiet stadium.

"I told him everything, Jim—about the lyrics, how we met, how I tried to save your stupid fucking ass. He has this effect on people. You simply can't say no. He said he'd let me get my people out of town. That's…that's more than he does for most people."

"And you believed him?" Washington demanded incredulously.

"Fuck, yes, I believed him. He knew about our meeting at the

Edison fountain. He fucking knew, Jim. And I sure as shit didn't tell him, which means you did."

"No, I didn't, Dwight. Someone must've tailed you. But it's all right. I can get you to safety. With your intel, we can stop these assholes and protect your family and your friends. You gotta let me go."

But the other man had no opportunity to respond. Instead, a bullet caught him in the temple and his brains exploded out the other side of his head.

"Shit!" Washington cursed and tried to drop in his seat. He couldn't hide, though. Kristen could still see his hand. Now that Dwight had cuffed him to the chair, the mercenary had obviously served his purpose.

The shot had come from behind her, which meant the sniper would have to move to get Jim in his sights. Her teammate was crouched on the floor and struggled frantically with the restraint.

Kristen was about to sneak forward when a man darted up from the front row. Another appeared from the next stand over.

There wasn't only one sniper, then, but a goddamn death squad.

She turned her skin to steel and sprang into action.

"Wonderkid, get ready to fucking move." She leapt over the rows between them and thunked onto a chair that collapsed beneath her weight.

Shots struck her but did nothing to her steel skin. She dropped down so she was at eye-level with him while the mercs closed in.

Washington looked at her with terror in his eyes but the bullets that *pinged* off her seemed to sober him. "You followed me."

"You're goddamn right I did, and a good thing too. Are you armed?"

"With a pistol."

"Not good enough. Get ready to follow me out of this place."

"I'm cuffed."

With a deft movement, she snapped the chain connecting him to the seat as easily as if it had been made of tissue paper. Gunshots rang out. One struck her in the back. "Change of plans. I'll eliminate a few of these guys, then you'll run to the field."

"The field? There's no cover."

"There is in the dugout."

"You can't take these assholes on by yourselves. They are who tried to kill you."

"These assholes are nothing if not well prepared, but they didn't know I'd be here. Now, I'll stand and they'll shoot me. I'll kill one of them and then I'll move. That's when you run. Got it?"

"But—"

"Do you understand the plan?" She hissed and flexed her aura. Jim was immediately compliant. He had no choice and felt what she felt—a desire to complete her plan.

She stood up to find that the mercs had indeed moved closer. They opened fire but their bullets continued to do nothing to her.

"We have you surrounded, steel bitch!" one of the men said. "You ain't got no gun, so what you gonna do? Come at me?"

So, they did have tasers then. Idiots. She might have tried hand to hand, but not anymore. Not with one of them baiting her.

Instead, she ripped one of the chairs from its moorings and hurled it the mercenary who'd tried to goad her.

It pounded into him and hurled him back. Her strength and accuracy training with Sebastian had dramatically improved her aim.

She ripped up another two chairs, one in each hand, and threw those at two other men. One managed to dodge but the other caught the projectile squarely in the chest. He sprawled and tangled in the seats.

"Washington, go!" she said, and he obeyed, sprinted down the stands, and hurdled over the guard rail to land on top of the dugout. He scrambled down and was lost from sight.

At least she wouldn't have to worry about him.

With him safely out of the way, she yanked another chair loose. Something pinged nearby and she spun and managed to catch the taser with the seat.

The assholes really had prepared for every scenario.

Kristen darted to her left, found a handrail, ripped it free, and threw it at him. It spun like a frisbee despite being a six-foot-long piece of steel.

The mercenary barely managed to dodge and therefore kept his head.

She paused, alert for the next attack, but her adversaries obviously decided on a strategic retreat. Three pairs of men each ran toward different exits. She considered following them but she had to assume each had a taser and that they'd know how to set a trap for her.

Plus, there was Washington. If she left him in the dugout and vanished into the bowels of Comerica park, she had no doubt that one of the teams would double back and execute him. That had been their primary goal—this time, anyway. She felt certain of that.

Rather than pursue, she jumped down onto the field, found her teammate huddled in the dugout, threw him over her shoulder like a damsel in distress, and got the hell out of there.

His jacket would be the only clue that they'd been there in the morning—besides the seats she'd had yanked out of the concrete and the bullet holes everywhere.

She shook her head. It really was a good thing they were cops. She wouldn't want to be the detective tasked with discovering what had done that to the foul ball zone.

CHAPTER FORTY-ONE

The duo took the People Mover back the station. It would have been awkward, she thought, but nearly dying together had a way of making uncomfortable moments seem unnecessary.

"Thanks for saving my life back there," Washington said.

"It was nothing," she replied, feeling guilty.

"No, seriously. I've given you shit for being a dragon, and if you weren't… Well, you saw what happened to Dwight."

"Look, Washington—"

"Call me Jim, seriously."

"Jim, sure, look. I…there's something I need to tell you."

He nodded. "For sure. We should probably call the team, though, right? I know I won't be able to sleep after all that shit."

She nodded, even though she wanted nothing more than to sleep. "Yeah, you're right. I'll call Drew and the Rookie. You call Butters and Beanpole. The first one done calls Hernandez."

"That sounds good."

They spent the next few stops calling their team. By the time they stepped off the People Mover and made it back the station, the others had assembled.

Except for Keith, who had apparently answered his phone without realizing it. He had been watching a romantic comedy and laughing uproariously. Despite her yelling at him from his pocket, he would not be distracted.

"Why am I out of bed right now?" Drew asked.

"Same here, and where the fuck is the Rookie?" Hernandez grumbled.

"Okay, I've followed some leads on my downtime," Jim said and ignored the demolitions expert. Kristen found that she couldn't help but think of him as Jim. Saving someone's life after putting them in danger did funny things to the brain.

"Is that what you call it when someone sends flowers for a booty call?" Hernandez asked.

There were a few chuckles but the looks on Kristen and Jim's faces silenced them quickly.

"The flowers were a code. Old lyrics from some raps me and a buddy made."

"So...you're a SWAT officer moonlighting as a gay rapper?" The woman looked incredulous. This time, no one laughed.

"No. The flowers were from one of the people who attacked the station," he said.

For a moment, the words seemed to simply hang there while everyone let the weight of them sink in. Kristen still hadn't told Jim everything, but he'd insisted on telling the team what he'd been up to first. Apparently, he felt guilty and wanted to come clean. She knew the feeling. While she also wanted to confess, she knew the team would need his information for hers to make any sense.

"Is that why you stopped me from incapacitating that clumsy asshole?" Butters finally asked.

Drew said nothing but the tightness of his jaw spoke louder than words. He was a moment away from tackling the man and throwing him in a cell.

Jim nodded and looked as guilty as hell. "Yes, sir. That was my buddy, Dwight. We were in the Marines together. He's also from Detroit—was from Detroit."

"So you chose your old team over your new one?" Drew snapped.

"Please listen, Drew," she said placatingly.

"That first bouquet of flowers he sent me had a code for a location for us to meet. He told me to get the hell out of Detroit. I didn't listen."

"Why did he want you out of the city?" Beanpole asked.

"He was trying to protect me. The perps who've been running around are definitely mercenaries and highly skilled ones at that."

"Yeah, no shit. I could have told you that the moment that building almost crushed us," Hernandez said. She looked about as pissed-off as Drew did.

"What else?" the team leader asked.

"They're working for someone, but Dwight wouldn't tell me who."

"Maybe he'll tell us."

"I doubt that," Kristen said. "You need a head to talk."

"What are you talking about, Hall?" he glared at her as if he tried to understand what her place in this was.

"Dwight is dead. I went to meet him again tonight, but it was a setup," Jim interjected before Kristen could answer. "They used him as bait, then killed him and tried to kill me. I'd be dead if not for the Steel Dragon."

"Baiting cops? That smells like the shit that went down with the gangs." Hernandez rubbed her face. "Do you think that asshole Dragon SWAT was talking about is back?"

"I don't know about that. In fact, I don't know how they found out Dwight was the leak. Both meetings were on his terms, and he used lyrics that no one would know but me. It's not like we released an album."

"That would be me," Kristen said, the words like knives of guilt in her chest. "I followed you the first night."

"No way," Jim blurted. "I know how to watch for a tail."

"Yeah, well, not when they have dragon speed you don't," she said.

"That doesn't explain—"

"Please listen, Jim." She cut him off. The trust he placed in her was killing her. "I tailed you the first night, and tonight—well, actually, I worked the code out this time but that's not what matters."

There was a collective raising of eyebrows as everyone looked at her. She swallowed. "I told someone that I suspected you."

"Not your superior officer," Drew said angrily.

"Or your friend." Butters sounded hurt.

"No. I intended to do that, but you're right. I didn't."

"Then who?" Beanpole asked.

"Sebastian Shadowstorm."

"I'm sorry, is that a cartoon character?" Hernandez snapped.

"That is that dragon I met at the rooftop party. The one who threw Ironclaw off the roof."

"Keep talking," the team leader said. Everyone else nodded.

"He offered to help train me, and…I took him up on it. It's been tough at work, trying to clamp down on my powers. He offered to teach me about my dragon abilities. I know I need to be more of a team player, but…well, I couldn't say no. It's helped too. I'm faster now and know how to use them with more precision."

"Damn straight," Washington said. "Hall stopped six armed mercs from braining me using nothing but chairs."

"That's not entirely true," she protested.

"Oh, that's right. You ripped a damn handrail off too."

"Now, that's a story I want to hear," Butters said.

"Oh, I'm sure Officer Hall will include all the details in the report she'll write up and leave on the captain's desk for the morning."

"Yes, sir." Kristen looked at the floor. It would be a long night.

"Why do you think it was this dragon? He sounds like an ally," Beanpole said, ever the pragmatist.

"He said he would 'look into it.' That next day, the bouquet arrived." She shrugged. While she'd wanted to trust Sebastian, it wasn't like he'd made his disdain for people a secret.

"It could be a coincidence," Beanpole suggested.

Drew shook his head. "I doubt it."

Jim also looked unconvinced. "The last thing Dwight said to me was about the guy having some effect on him. Dragons can do that, right? Compel people to do stuff or whatever?"

She nodded. That was one of the skills Sebastian had helped her with. He was an expert in using his aura.

"We need to operate under the assumption that your friend Sebastian is Mr Black," the team leader said.

Hernandez sucked a breath in through her teeth. "Shit. Do you really think so?"

Mr Black was the only name they'd obtained from the few remaining gang members after the assault on the city.

"Maybe he's the real culprit, maybe not, but it feels like he's a part of things."

Kristen agreed with him. If Sebastian didn't have a part in this, she'd be shocked. She simply didn't know who else could have unraveled that there had been a leak and had the ability to manipulate Dwight into divulging the lyrics he'd used as a code.

"So...not to be a pussy, but this means we turn this shit over to Dragon SWAT, right?" Hernandez didn't look proud of her suggestion, but there it was.

Drew scratched his chin. "Yeah. Yeah, technically, that's what we're supposed to do. Dragons are their jurisdiction."

"That'll leave the mercenaries loose, though, won't it?" Butters asked.

"For a little while, at least." He nodded, his expression grim.

"How fast will Dragon SWAT deal with accusations about Shadowstorm?" Beanpole asked.

Kristen shrugged. "That's a good question. From what I understand, he's fairly well known. He threw Ironclaw off that roof and no one even blinked. I don't think Dragon SWAT will take an accusation at face value. Especially not if...well, especially not if it comes from humans." She looked at her team and tried to hide her embarrassment at no longer being human.

"You're saying we need proof," Jim said. "Not circumstantial evidence."

Drew, Beanpole, and Butters nodded at that. Hernandez scowled, stood, and began to pace. She cursed under her breath the entire time.

"Well, how do we get that? It's not like we can send him a dropped pin and expect him to come into the station willingly," Butters said.

"No. He wouldn't even check an email," Kristen said but the beginnings of a plan formed in her head. It would be risky—damn risky—but mostly for her. Given how this was all her fault, she found that more than acceptable. For it to work, a couple of her assumptions had to be true. If she was wrong, she knew it would go poorly, but she didn't think she was.

"I was only kidding, Kristen."

"But you gave me an idea. I think it's time for us to lay a trap of our own."

CHAPTER FORTY-TWO

Drew burst into the lounge, despite having barely left with a cup of coffee. "Okay, people, get your asses in the van. We have a situation."

"Our guys?" Butters asked.

He nodded. "It's gotta be. An officer reported a perp who backed into his car and flipped him off for no apparent reason. He must have been baiting him. The officer called it in but still gave chase. He followed him to another abandoned building and tried to approach, but…" He mimed a gun being fired with his hand.

"It definitely sounds like our guys," Jim agreed.

"Right, so stop staring at me and move." Everyone bounded to their feet. It was an odd feeling to go willingly into a trap. They had the beginnings of a plan, but she felt a pang of dread in her chest. The people they pursued were hunting her. They would undoubtedly have a trap prepared and specifically designed to eliminate her, the strongest person on SWAT. If anyone on her team made even the slightest misstep, it would be disastrous. Weapons that could harm dragons would kill people. That was a given. But that didn't mean they could stay home.

They ran pell-mell through the station, geared up, and were in the van in less than two minutes. Tires squealed and they were on their way.

After a minute of the tense silence that often led up to an action, Jim cleared his throat. "Hey, Kristen, I wanted to tell you, I'm sorry." It was one of the most awkward sentences she had ever heard spoken aloud. He meant it, at least she thought he did, but there really was so much going on in the veteran's mind. She wondered if maybe he'd seen a dragon when he'd served overseas.

All that didn't matter, though. What was important was keeping her team alive and stopping these criminals who thought they could play games with the Detroit Police Department.

"No, Jim, you have nothing to apologize for." She meant it too.

"I really do, though. I treated you like shit because you're a dragon and lost focus on the dragon who's actually trying to hurt our city."

"I shouldn't have followed you." She wasn't entirely sure she'd meant that. If she hadn't followed him on the first night, his friend might still be alive. But if she hadn't followed him on the second night, he would almost certainly have a bullet through his head already. What she regretted most was her dishonesty with the rest of her team.

"Bullshit. I would've done the same thing. That wasn't dragon behavior—you tailing me—that was good police work. Besides, I'd be dead if you didn't use your dragon powers." Admitting that seemed to take something out of him, some nugget of resentment and vengeance he'd clung to.

"Welcome to working with the Steel Dragon." Keith grinned. "Don't worry, you get used to being saved by magic powers fairly quickly."

"Are we done playing pat your back and hug it out?" Hernandez looked like she'd watched grandparents make out—mostly disgusted but slightly impressed.

The van halted a few moments later and Drew shoved it into park. "We're here."

Kristen climbed out into the parking lot of an abandoned motel. This one was only three stories high with concrete corridors and stairways on the outside. It looked like it had been left to the forces of nature for quite some time. The roof sagged in places and vines made a valiant effort to pull one side of it down.

A half-dozen police vehicles waited in the far corners of the parking area. Two of the cars had their windows destroyed, but that was the full extent of the damage. There were no fatalities reported, either.

"Jesus," Hernandez grumbled. "This place is a fucking dump. It's like they're taunting us by attacking and destroying sites that are worthless. These guys are capable enough to probably fuck a bank up. But instead, they're focused on a damn motel that even the rats don't like."

Kristen thought that was a good thing. As little as she wanted to admit it, these people scared her. At least by using these old buildings, there weren't any hostages involved.

"Do we all remember the plan?" Drew said.

Butters and Beanpole nodded and pointed to the nearest building. They were eyes.

Keith pulled a tablet out. He had already brought up the floorplans of the building. "There's an exit in the basement. It's the old entrance to a steam tunnel."

"That's where the trap will be then, not to mention the control center for their bombs," Hernandez said.

"Then that's the last place you two go." Drew looked pointedly at Kristen.

She nodded in understanding. There was no way she'd let anyone else get hurt, not by her trying to rush in and play the hero.

"Right, let's do this," the team leader said.

"Wait, wait, wait," Keith sputtered.

"What?"

"Hernandez was right. They're using wireless to communicate with their bombs or whatever."

"Are you saying you can shut them down before we even go in?" Hernandez asked. A shot pinged off the side of the SWAT van. "Because I don't think they would like that," she finished.

Keith fiddled with the tablet but eventually shook his head. "No… no, I can't turn them off, but I think I can locate them."

"Excellent work, Rookie!" Drew said.

"You know, I only know how to do this because I've been on the force for more than a year—"

"What's the plan, now?" Butters cut off his protests. He would always be Rookie.

"The same as before. You—Butters, and Beanpole—watch our backs. Hernandez and Keith, disable the bombs but don't go near that entrance to the tunnel on your own. I'm with the Steel Dragon and the Wonderkid. We're gonna make some damn noise and get these fuckers to run."

They separated and focused on their roles.

Kristen turned her skin to steel—the enemy expected to face the Steel Dragon, so they'd make sure that was who they believed they faced—but she didn't rush ahead.

Instead, she, Jim, and Drew hurried to the far side of the building opposite the entrance to the basement and the mercenaries' escape route.

The anticipated volley was delivered and the bullets struck the ground in front of her, but none of them actually made contact. When she considered the situation for what it was, it seemed obvious that the perps didn't want to hit them yet. The bullets wouldn't hurt her and if they injured one of her teammates, there was a good chance she wouldn't proceed into the building. Their actions were all designed to drive up the adrenaline levels in the SWAT team in order to rile them up and push them into doing something stupid.

They wouldn't fall for it, however.

Instead, Butters would let them think they were. He opened fire on the gunman. Windows shattered and the cursory assault on his three teammates ceased for a moment. Having a sniper like him on the team had enormous advantages. While the plan wasn't to simply shoot the hostiles, he was good enough that he could.

They reached the far side of the building and ran up the stairs to the third floor so they were as far away from the basement as possible.

"It's time to make noise of our own." Drew kicked a door open and fired inside. It was empty, but his shotgun was damn loud.

"My turn." Jim mirrored his team leader at the next room and peppered the back wall with assault rifle fire.

"They heard you and want to come to the party," Beanpole said over the radio. "Hernandez and Keith, move on my mark…" There was a long pause. It couldn't have been more than ten seconds but to Kristen, it felt like hours. "Mark!"

They'd worked all this out beforehand, or something close enough to it anyway. When Beanpole gave them the cue and a hostile darted out from one of the empty rooms and fired his assault rifle at the trio, she wasn't surprised.

She blocked the bullets with her steel skin.

"Funny, they didn't use a taser despite having an open shot," she said once the hostile had vanished into a room.

"Not with you on top of the building, they didn't." Drew grinned. So far, they were winning the mind game behind the actual firefight.

Jim cut the conversation short when he stepped out from behind her and fired at the attacker, who'd poked his head and the tip of his weapon into the hallway again. He retreated hastily into the room he'd emerged from.

They followed and found the door closed, so the team leader shot the doorknob, careful not to stand in the actual doorway. The force of the blast swung the door inward. A taser fired through the open space. It missed because the Steel Dragon hadn't forced entry and didn't stand in the aperture. The hostile inside cursed. They really had been right about this whole thing being a plan to eliminate her.

Too bad for them, it wouldn't happen.

"Wonderkid?" Drew nodded.

Jim ducked, stepped into the doorway, and fired into the room. No shots were returned. "We're clear, but I have no idea where the asshat went to."

His teammates entered cautiously behind him. They searched quickly and found it empty, but something was odd about it. Kristen couldn't quite place her finger on it.

"Hey, Drew," Hernandez said amidst a crackle on the radio.

"Talk to me."

"These aren't bombs."

"Then what are they?"

"Some kind of incendiary device. But I don't get it. I can't see them trying to burn the building on the Steel Dragon."

"Roger that." No sooner had he responded than one of the devices ignited in the room the three of them were in.

It had been hidden under the bed so they hadn't seen it. Now, it poured enormous clouds of white smoke into the room.

"Get out!" Jim yelled and stumbled into a framed poster of a shitty painting on the wall. He fell right through it.

"Shit!" he shouted. "Secret tunnels."

"Kristen—outside. I'll get Jim."

As little as she wanted to obey Drew, she left the room and stepped onto the outdoor walkway of the motel.

A moment later, the team leader dragged Jim out. Wonderkid coughed violently but pushed himself to his feet, so she assumed he would be all right.

"It's exactly like we thought. This is all for you, Kristen." Drew gestured toward the smoke that poured from the motel room. "The hostile in there was hiding behind that picture. He had sights on me and one of those tasers but didn't shoot. I think they want to stun you, then suffocate you. Obviously, the insides of your lungs don't turn to steel or you wouldn't be able to breathe."

"New plan?" she asked.

"Nope. It's time to come up with a different strategy. We'll follow them to the basement. Don't go into any of the motel rooms. I bet they knocked holes in the walls of all the ones they're in. If we stay out here, Butters has our back."

"That makes sense," Jim said and wiped his eyes. "That shit's nasty, though, whatever it is."

Drew nodded and activated his radio. "Hernandez, Keith, fall back and get gas masks. Are any of these devices at their exit?"

"Oh, yeah," Keith replied. "That's where they're mostly clustered."

"Then that's where I want you to be. Hernandez, disarm as many of these damn things as you can. Keith, you know what to do."

"Drop the pin."

"That's right. Now, if you'll excuse us, we have noise to make."

Kristen grinned and started down the concrete balcony. She punched the next three doors open, careful to never stand in the doorway. In the third one, they found another mercenary, who didn't make his escape as quickly as his ally had. He tried to vanish behind one of the shitty prints of a painting, but Jim shot him in the leg, and he cried as he fell.

She caught him by the scruff of his neck and pulled him out of the room.

"Gas mask," she said to him.

He shook his head so she lifted him by the shoulder and dangled him out over the parking lot.

She returned him to solid ground when he hastily became much more compliant. He removed the gas mask and gave it to her.

"Drew?" She handed it to her leader.

"No, you take it."

"Oh, come on," she protested, unable to help herself. She didn't want any of her people to choke to death while trying to save her life.

"No. They want you to choke on this shit. Let them know that won't happen and it should speed up their exit."

Kristen didn't like it but she saw the wisdom of it. She was their target and their entire reason for using smoke instead of explosives. It made sense to render their plan obsolete so she put the mask on.

They proceeded along the balcony and opened the rooms as they went. The fifth one contained another hostile. He cursed loudly when he saw her gas mask but that didn't stop the incendiary from detonating.

"Do you want to go get him?" she asked Drew.

"No, no. There's no reason to be rude. Let him tell his friends what's up." He spoke into the radio. "Butters, let us know if you see movement. Keith, make sure you have Hernandez's back."

"Sir, it looks like migration season from over here," the sniper responded after perhaps fifteen seconds.

"Shall we corral these assholes?" Jim asked.

"That's the plan. Kristen, you take point. I want you with us. If any of these assholes are watching—and they're pros, so I'm sure they have at least one guy on overwatch—I want them to know you don't rush into shit anymore. We need to look like a team so they know their only option is to retreat."

She nodded and the three of them ran toward the stairwell above the entrance to the basement. They encountered no more hostiles.

Butters, meanwhile, seemed to take great delight in shooting at those who fled from the second floor. She wished she could watch him work. Drew had said he didn't want them to kill anyone and definitely didn't want prisoners, so each of the shots must have been placed on the hostiles' tails. The idea was to keep them moving.

There was still the guy whose leg they'd shot. Although they hadn't cuffed him or anything so hopefully, he'd escape. She didn't like the idea of him bleeding out so they might have to take at least one prisoner with them if he was left behind. They simply hoped it wouldn't make whoever was behind all this skittish. But there was time to worry about that later.

"Here they come," Drew shouted over the radio.

Kristen tensed when gunshots sounded from the first floor. That was part of the plan, she reminded herself, but she still felt a pang of dread in her chest when she thought about her teammates down there.

A moment later, Keith yelled and it was over. "Goddammit! They got away. Those motherfucking professional hitmen outsmarted us yet again and got away."

Drew put a hand on his shoulder and pulled him away from the entrance to the basement. "Maybe a little ham-handed with the dialogue in the end there, but the delivery worked, Rookie."

They retreated to the SWAT van and simply watched while smoke poured from a few more motel rooms and dissipated on the wind.

"We disarmed a good number of those things, but whoever goes in to take out the rest will need to be careful," Hernandez said.

"It's a good thing these assholes chose another abandoned building. I don't want to think what that smoke would've done to regular folk," Butters muttered as he joined the group.

"Or the Steel Dragon," Beanpole added.

Kristen nodded. It felt damn good to have her team back. Although she'd never physically left, she now saw what they were talking about. They could never have accomplished what they had if they hadn't worked together. The training they'd put in had them working as a team again. She had thought that would make her weaker, but after this operation, it made her proud that she hadn't gone it alone. And then there was the fact that the hostiles had again used weapons that would've made steel skin an obsolete defense.

She only had one question.

"Keith?"

The Rookie grinned and stuck his tongue out. "Oh, not to worry. I dropped the pin."

"Then what are we waiting for?" Drew asked.

Keith opened the tablet. A map of Detroit displayed on the screen, and there—only a block from where they were—a red blip moved farther and farther from the SWAT team.

CHAPTER FORTY-THREE

From a safe enough distance to keep their pursuit undetected, they followed the tracker to a warehouse. Along the way, Drew shared the location with every SWAT team in the Detroit Metro area.

They waited a few blocks distant from the target until enough teams were in place to surround the building. A dozen vans, each filled with at least six heavily armed members of SWAT was a good start, but that wasn't all. Hernandez had watched the mercenaries' retreat closely and located the steam tunnel they'd used to enter the warehouse.

She'd then—with perfectly understandable glee—collapsed it so they could no longer escape underground. The explosion was intended to be loud enough to cue the hostiles into this fact. If they tried to escape the way they had come in, they would find their path blocked with rubble.

Minutes later, another twenty or so police cars had joined the SWAT vans. Drew ordered everyone to close in, and they advanced like a pod of orcas hunting fish. They all reached the building within a minute of one another. There were so many damn official vehicles that Kristen didn't think they'd even need officers to arrest the mercenaries. They could simply open the car doors and if they tried to flee, they'd be caught like fish in a net. It was another example of why teamwork was so important. The people inside obviously knew what they were doing, but against a force like this, even professionals would be intimidated. She had no doubt that if she had tried to face them alone, she'd have been defeated.

"We have you surrounded," Drew declared over the loudspeaker once everyone was in position, obviously enjoying this bust. It was almost comically one-sided.

Still, part of her thought about how it could go bad. If the mercenaries were able to escape despite their exit being collapsed and every available police car and SWAT van in the metro area bottling them in, there'd be nothing they could do.

"Someone's making for the roof," Butters reported and gunshots responded from the tops of all the nearby buildings. Snipers pinned down the dragon who tried to escape. She was quite certain there was a dragon inside and could feel an aura. Plus, who else would try the roof except for someone who could fly? It wasn't like there was a helicopter there or anything like that.

But whoever the dragon was, it didn't have steel skin. The volley of sniper rounds kept it inside.

Drew waited about thirty seconds before he picked up the megaphone connected to the loudspeaker again. "By now, you've discovered that we collapsed your tunnel." Feedback echoed from the megaphone for a moment and he fiddled with the controls, then held it up. "We'll open the front door from out here. If you throw your weapons down and come out one at a time, you'll actually get to talk to a damn lawyer. If you shoot, we'll simply blow you to hell. Oh, and thanks for choosing an empty building by the way." He sounded downright cheerful.

They waited perhaps ten seconds before they pulled open the larger hangar-style door on one side of the warehouse. About ten seconds after that, a hostile emerged, his hands clasped behind his head. He didn't look particularly scared, only pissed.

Kristen thought that was good. If he was afraid, he might try something desperate or his boss might try something. Pissed meant he understood the gravity of the situation.

Five seconds after that, another hostile followed, then another. She was surprised when the procession stopped after only nine people. It seemed impossible that such a small force could have caused the city such a headache—which only served to indicate how professional they actually were.

Her surprise at that, though, was nothing compared to the shock she felt when Sebastian Shadowstorm exited the building with his hands raised and a smug look on his face.

At first, she thought she was mistaken. She wished that was the case, but she wasn't. His hulking frame, ponytail, goatee, and black-and-red gloves left little doubt as to his identity.

They'd talked about him working with the enemy but to actually find him there with the mercenaries directly after a mission still felt like a true betrayal. She knew that he had played some kind of role in the attack on Jim, but she'd told herself that he must have poked around in the wrong places. Her assumption had been that he had asked questions that had alerted the real mastermind to Washington's clandestine meetings. Now, however, she saw that wasn't the case. Sebastian Shadowstorm's presence could only mean one thing—he was Mr Black, the dragon who had already tried to destroy the city once.

It was Mr Black who had killed Jonesy—and who had been training her.

Everything she'd learned—her new abilities, her understanding of her dragon aura, the precision with which she could wield her dragon strength and speed—all came from the dragon who exited the building.

She simultaneously hated him and owed him a great debt. More than anything, she hated that he'd set up this contradiction inside her mind. She hated him for what he'd done and yet he had made her stronger too and showed her things about her true nature while the rest of the dragon community had ignored her. Had it all been part of a plot? Was she merely a pawn? The idea of being manipulated so effectively cut her to the core.

Kristen couldn't help herself. She strode forward to confront the dragon. "You spineless lizard. I trusted you."

Sebastian smiled. "Yes. I suppose you did. It's unfortunate that this is how you found out about my training methods for the Steel Dragon. I must admit, I continue to be impressed. You've learned more than I realized, especially about your limitations." She couldn't decide if he meant to look vicious or endearing and assumed that was exactly what was so damn dangerous about him.

"Your…what?" She wanted to trust him but was that simply his aura? He'd said it didn't work on dragons, but she obviously could no longer trust him fully.

"My methods. I apologize for killing your friend, Kristen, really, I do. I didn't know there was a new dragon in Detroit and if I had, I would have been more careful not to take what is rightfully yours."

"That's appalling. You can't talk about people like they belong to dragons," she said icily.

"But of course we can. That's why the world is stable, after all. No one likes it when our pieces are taken by another. If I had known at the time, I wouldn't have done what I did."

"Bullshit! You've tried to kill me!" she shouted, her face inches from his.

"I protest, Kristen. I've done nothing of the sort. Did you not notice that these mercenaries appeared around the same time as the party I threw in your honor?"

"You didn't throw that party—" she began in protest.

"But I did. This is my city, Kristen, as much as it's yours—or as much as it will be yours once you fully come into your power. Nothing happens here without my knowledge. You were the first thing to surprise me in some time, and discovering that you were raised here only made me wish to help you thrive and grow stronger despite the muck and the filth all around us. I knew that training you wouldn't be enough. You learned with me, yes, but the team of men I hired was to help you evolve and come into your powers. It is only in fire that steel can be tempered. I sought only to give you that which is rightfully yours—power."

"People were hurt—"

"No, they weren't—well, no one except the people you hurt in the baseball arena and the man you left behind at the last building. They were under orders not to hurt anyone."

"Because they're your people?" she challenged.

"Because they're yours." Sebastian smiled imploringly as if there was nothing more important in the world than that she understand the sincerity of his words.

"That…that makes sense," Keith said and nodded.

She looked at her teammate. He stared at the dragon with wonder in his eyes like an older sibling had confirmed the existence of Santa Claus.

"Total fucking sense," Hernandez added and also nodded, her expression one that suggested she was enraptured by his explanation of the events.

Kristen looked at Sebastian, this criminal mastermind who masqueraded as a member of society, and raised an eyebrow. He might have convinced her. He'd been right, no one had gotten hurt, but Hernandez? That had been too much.

She flexed her own aura and felt her team's trust for the dragon seep away. Keith shook his head like he tried to wake up.

Hernandez's look of shocked understanding immediately settled into her more typical scowl. "Fucking asshole."

"Don't listen to him, Hall. Like you said, he's a damn snake," Drew said to her, apparently oblivious to the fact that he'd been under the dragon's control as well. She knew he was a snake, and the team leader felt that way as opposed to trusting him because she used her aura to influence her team.

She hated doing that because, by using her aura, she only confirmed that Sebastian was right. To protect people—her people—she needed to use her dragon abilities, and her ability to control her aura with any level of precision came from Sebastian. No, she couldn't call him that. He was Mr Black or Shadowstorm but not Sebastian, never again.

"Indeed," the dragon said. She could see that he understood what had gone through her head and that she'd recognized him using his aura and pushed back. He looked less than amused but turned away from her and faced Drew. "Don't you have rights to read me or something? There will be lawyers and trials and all that, yes? I must say, it's been quite some time since I've run afoul of human law. Don't ruin your chances by insulting one of your captives."

"Let's go. asshole. You have the right to remain silent. I recommend you use it while you can." He resumed reading Mr Black his rights.

Kristen nodded. Drew was right. He was a snake and had outmaneuvered her. Worse, she now realized that he knew everything about her—the exact limits of her powers and what she could and couldn't do. All their training had been a ploy to learn about her and to find out how to hurt her. It was almost too much to comprehend. Compared to his Machiavellian plotting, she really was a child.

In response to her inner frustrations, she scowled at the prisoner and flexed her aura as she did so. The slight effort she put into it whipped the police around her into a frenzy of curses and jeers at the disgraced dragon. Some of those who hadn't known about the operation and had been called away from lunch even threw their drinks at him.

She sneered at him. "Whoops. I guess I haven't quite learned the finer points of control." It hadn't been her intention that the cops throw fountain drinks at him but rather that they simply feel her anger toward the man who'd lied to her and led her on for weeks. The police had taken that anger, combined it with what they knew of the man who'd tried to start a war inside the city and killed a number of their ranks, and this was their reaction.

The dragon didn't even flinch when he was showered by sticky beverages and the curses of people she had no doubt he saw as beneath him. "You're welcome," he said to her and extended his huge arms to be handcuffed.

Keith did the honors, although the restraints barely closed around his thick wrists. They put him in the back seat of a cruiser and his massive frame barely fit.

Kristen swallowed. They'd won the battle and the mercenaries were now off the streets but obviously, Mr Black had another card up his sleeve. He could have snapped the handcuffs like paper—and, for that matter, probably shredded the car like cardboard. In fact, he could have simply flown away. She didn't know the extent of the dragon's powers—he had quite conveniently kept that information from her—but she did know that a dragon had never been shot and killed by a gun. Injured perhaps, but not for long, and never killed.

And yet, he sat in the backseat, slightly stooped, with a grin on his face like he knew the punchline to a joke he hadn't bothered to tell them.

CHAPTER FORTY-FOUR

Mr Black, seated at the table in the interrogation room, almost looked like an optical illusion. He was simply so big. At well over six feet and with shoulders that brought the word "oxen" to Kristen's mind, she didn't see how the room could actually hold him. Even if he wasn't a dragon, he looked like he could snap the handcuffs apart, although he'd made no effort to do so.

She almost wished he'd use his powers to trash the place. At least she would have known they had actually got to the bastard.

Drew paced in front of him and demanded answers, but the dragon made no response at all. The man tried every tactic he knew to intimidate the prisoner, but she knew none of it would work. Sebastian Shadowstorm was a master of controlling other people's emotions with his aura. Less than a year before, he'd whipped every gang in the Detroit area into open rebellion. The team leader's bluster about being locked away without a key simply didn't make any impression on him—and especially because she had no doubt he could bend any bars they put him behind.

After ten minutes of this parody of an interrogation, Mr Black cleared his throat. Drew turned too quickly and she could see the desperation in the gesture. The dragon could have asked for a steak dinner and would most likely have been given it. Still, the officer retained a little of his bluster. "What? You want your damn lawyer?"

Kristen shook her head. He had probably compelled Drew to ask that.

"Lawyers. Pah. My lawyer isn't versed in criminal law, only real estate. Those men who work with me, though, will all need a lawyer. You'll find there's a substantial sum set aside for their defense. You'll also find that the people defending them are quite well-versed in how humans and dragons are supposed to interact."

"Then what do you want?" Drew asked.

"I want you to shut up. I won't talk to you, you insufferable simian simpleton," Mr Black stated officiously. "I simply wanted to let you know that if you continue to blather at me, I will use my abilities to make you and everyone in this station piss themselves. You bore me. Your questions are dull and your posture is obvious. Ugh." He waved a hand dismissively at the man like he was nothing more than a fly.

"This isn't a time for puerile threats," he retorted sharply.

"Puerile? What a clever word, human. You know, I remember when the English first adopted it from the French in the late sixteenth century."

The team leader scowled, left the room, and slammed the door behind him. "I can't believe this asshole." He shook his head and moved to stand beside Kristen behind the one-way glass. Mr Black stared at them both. She wondered if his dragon senses empowered him to look through the mirror. The expression of contempt on his face certainly made it seem like he knew he was in control.

"I know you don't really have the experience but, Hall, I think you should go in." He didn't sound too proud of the suggestion.

"Me? I've never interrogated anybody," she protested.

"Yeah, I know. Most people on SWAT never do, but…well…" He uttered a strangled laugh. "The asshole said he won't talk to humans, and, uh…"

"I'm not human," she finished for him.

He shrugged and forced a smile. "I'd say try to get a confession, but he's right in that our laws don't exactly apply to him. Still, if you get him to admit to giving orders to the mercenaries, maybe that'll prove he's involved enough in human affairs to drag him down with them. They have crimes to answer for—destruction of property and possession of illegal weapons and hazardous materials. Maybe a conspiracy charge. If you can get him to talk about them, maybe you can bring up what happened with the damn gangs. Cops died. Maybe we can get a murder charge to stick."

"Do you really think so?" she asked.

His expression didn't look confident. "I don't know, but dragons don't normally hire teams of mercenaries. The world would be far more fucked up if they did. Maybe he broke one of their rules by doing all this shit. If you can get him to confess, maybe we can transfer him to Dragon SWAT."

After a moment's thought, she nodded. "Okay." It was worth an attempt.

She got two cups of herbal tea—Sebastian had always been partial to jasmine—and walked into the room. She knew—and Mr. Black knew—that there was no way she could intimidate him. After all, he'd trained her and sent mercenaries to kill her. Maybe that meant he couldn't kill her with his bare hands, but it also meant she didn't inspire anything even remotely like fright in the dragon older than the city she'd been born in. He must see her as less than him. Then again, he probably saw everyone as less than him. Maybe she could use that arrogance.

"So you won't talk to humans? Then talk to me. Dragon to dragon." She pushed a cup of tea across the table and sipped her own.

Sebastian laughed. Mr Black, she reminded herself irritably, but it was hard to think of him as the criminal mastermind when he laughed in the same way he did when she told him stories about growing up human.

"So you are," he said with a smile as he studied her for a moment before he picked his cup of tea up and took a small sip. He looked like a kid pretending to be tied up while playing cops and robbers. The handcuffs really were comically undersized. He closed his eyes, inhaled the aroma of the beverage, and set it down with a look of satisfaction.

Kristen wondered if he'd had the same look in his eyes when he'd ordered the rebellion that had killed Jonesy. Remembering her partner made it much easier to think of him as the enemy he was. Suddenly, she knew that any attempt to be the cliché good cop wouldn't work. She was the Steel Dragon and definitely would not sit there and wheedle information from this asshole while he sipped his tea. "How long have you known the mercenary team that tried to kill me?"

"You mean those brutes who stormed into my abandoned warehouse? I think that maybe those thugs destroyed my property." He said it all in a phony, saccharine-sweet tone that made the lie painfully obvious and took another sip of tea.

"Bullshit. You may not be talking to the cops, but your little cronies are. We have confessions from most of them and are working on the others."

"A human's words don't carry weight against a dragon, Kristen. Face it. You have nothing on me. We've faced rebellions like this in the past before—a team of pathetic humans conspires together to try to oust their superiors. It always turns out to be a lie. Always. Their kind isn't trusted, Kristen, not by our kind." He put the cup down and raised his hands in a gesture of absolution.

"So you're saying you didn't have a part to play in the gang rebellion that almost burned this city down and killed my partner."

Mr Black smiled indulgently. "What would you like me to say? That my aura affected those criminals? That somehow—without speaking, mind you—I inspired a horde of worthless criminals to show their true selves? Forgive me. You know I'm somewhat out of date, but are auras something that counts as evidence in your human courts?"

"We have multiple confessions from them as well. I'm sure some will identify you as Mr Black. You'll pay for Jonesy's death and all the other officers who died that day."

He laughed. "Why do you think your criminal system hasn't made laws that apply to the full range of our abilities? Why do you think there are jurisdictions that one can simply fly away from and leaves their crimes behind? It's not a terribly convenient system for a human. It's hard to flee a city, after all, but for a dragon? Come now. Surely you can see how this system wasn't designed entirely for the people at the bottom. You say I'll pay for your partner's life. Tell me, how much is the life of your partner worth?"

"More than yours."

"Is it? Last time I checked, bullets were cheap and that was all it took to kill your friend, wasn't it? A couple of slugs of lead you weren't able to stop? Think about it. If you had worked with me sooner, I could have shown you how to better use your reflexes. That is so ironic it's almost poetic—thanks to me, he might still be alive."

"You bastard!" Kristen said and pounded the table so hard her fists made dents in the burnished metal. Both cups of tea clattered to the floor. She hadn't realized she'd turned her hands to metal.

Mr Black didn't so much as blink at her outburst. He only chuckled and lowered his cuffed hands to his lap. "Calm yourself. I simply meant that if I had made your acquaintance sooner, I could have helped you. You make a fair point about your friend's life, though. Other lives were lost as well. A shame…a real shame." He sucked a breath through his teeth and shook his head. "Perhaps a charitable contribution to the families of the deceased would fix things? It can't be easy to lose the breadwinner. How about a hundred thousand—"

"That's a goddamn insult and you know it."

"Let me finish, please. Let me finish. How about a hundred thousand a year for the rest of their mortal lives? I imagine some of them even had kids. A hundred thousand dollars will cover their expenses for a long time. Therapy, college, housing, food—almost anything they could think of. This is what dragons do for people. This is what you do for people, Kristen. You help."

"You're the one who needs help. We have multiple confessions linking your identity to the criminal Mr Black. We have your fingerprints and those of your servants on unopened crates of weapons we found. We also have confiscated the payments you made to mercenaries. Spanish doubloons? Really? That doesn't scream dragon at all."

He paused as if to consider all this for a moment. "So those rats kept their nest right here in the city?"

"Those desperate men you exploited were more than happy to share what they knew when they saw the writing on the wall for multiple life sentences."

"Which together would still equal less than mine."

"Just because a human's life is shorter than a dragon's doesn't make it less valuable," she retorted sharply.

The dragon snorted at that and obviously found the comment ridiculous. "You know," he said, raised his cuffed hands, and scratched his check languidly before he lowered them to his lap again. "For a human, you might have had enough. The evidence you have spoken of sounds compelling, even in this country with its ridiculous 'innocent-until-proven-guilty' laws. Maybe with one of your lawyers and a jury from this city, you could've made something stick."

"There's nothing to make stick. We already have everything. You're going down, Sebastian."

He clucked his tongue and shook his head again. Oh, how she loathed that sound. "Kristen, how can you be so naïve? For a human, this might have worked. But I am a dragon, so this has all been nothing more than a waste of both of our afternoons. Now, here's what will happen. In a moment, a knock will come at the door. The person will say that a call came in and that you are to release me without charges. You'll release me, return my gloves, and we'll be done here."

"Bullshit. You haven't made any phone calls."

Mr Black merely smiled. "When you so valiantly appeared at my warehouse to apprehend those terrible criminals, I might have had one of my chauffeurs call Tyler. He does more than fix drinks, you know."

"Like I said, bull—"

A knock came at the door. She answered it and tried not to let herself turn to steel and trash the entire station when Keith explained to her that what the prisoner had predicted had indeed happened.

Five minutes later, she watched Sebastian Shadowstorm saunter from the station, transform into a dragon in a dark cloud of shadow, and fly into the approaching evening. She was so angry, she thought she would be physically ill.

"I can't believe that fucking monster. I want to blow his goddamn brains out," Beanpole all but snarled from where he leaned on the front desk. Kristen had never heard him talk that way before.

"I know what you mean," Butters agreed fervently. "I want to rip him limb from limb."

Reality kicked in and she shook her head and tried to calm herself. She'd let her aura get out of control and could see the ripple effect throughout the station. Everyone seemed angry and on the verge of violence. She tried to settle her own rage but only succeeded in bringing her aura under control. Beyond that, she was still utterly furious. Separating her emotions from her aura was an important ability—yet another she'd learned from Sebastian.

She returned to the interrogation room to find it empty and finally located Drew in the lounge, eating a donut and staring into the distance.

"This is bullshit, Drew. He's the reason Jonesy is dead."

Drew shrugged. It was a weak gesture, and in that moment, she hated him for it. "There's nothing we can do about it right now. He's a dragon and out of our jurisdiction, and we didn't really gather much evidence. I liked the line about the fingerprints on the weapons, but he must have known you were bluffing. When we busted the asshole, he was wearing gloves. He even asked for them back."

"The gold coins weren't a bluff."

"Yeah, but a few coins in a few pockets doesn't unequivocally pin them to Mr Black."

"He was there, Drew. Can you even hear yourself?"

"I know he was there, Hall. I was there too, goddammit. Do you think I like this shit? If we want to nail him, we'd practically need him to confess—and even then, I have no idea if that would be enough."

How odd it was to hear her own rage come back at her from another person. She'd let her aura affect him.

"Do you think a confession would work?" she asked, the gears already turning in her mind.

"I don't know. Maybe? It's happened before. I've looked into it. There have been cases where a dragon admitted wrong-doing and has been punished for it."

"Then what's the damn problem?" she said. "We have enough already."

"Not for a human court, we don't. They've been punished in the past, but not by us. He's a dragon, Hall. Shit, the only reason he talked to you was because you're one too."

"I am not."

"Yes, you are, goddammit, and if you weren't, we'd all be dead a hundred times over already." He looked so beaten, she could hardly bear it.

"So you think a confession plus our evidence would do it?" she asked after a minute.

"I don't know if the evidence even matters. I think that if—and this is like the biggest damn if of all time—if he confessed to other dragons, maybe he'd be held responsible. At least I damn well hope he would be. Otherwise, we'll know those monsters can simply wreak havoc on our cities anytime they want."

Kristen sank onto the couch and rubbed her face. It was all so damn exhausting. She stood, snatched a donut, and sat again. Was this really how the world worked? Justice meant something different depending on who you were, on your connections, and how much money you had? It was disgusting—absolutely disgusting—that people rotted in jail because they'd been desperate and done something stupid like rob a convenience store while at the same time, the most powerful of all could get away with almost anything. If one was powerful enough, laws didn't matter. All that mattered was prestige. And Shadowstorm had cultivated his for centuries.

He could do anything he wanted. Well, Kristen thought, not anything. He'd said he'd wanted to throw that dragon Ironclaw off a building for a long time, but he hadn't. There was some kind of code dragons lived by. There had to be laws too—if there weren't, why would there be a dragon SWAT?

"You know, I think… I think there might actually be a way," she said in mid-bite of her donut.

Drew smirked. "I gotta say, I love that you don't know how to stop."

"No. No, I'm serious. I know, he learned about me during our training, but I've learned about him too. I think we could do it."

"Oh yeah?" He raised an eyebrow. "Do you want me to go to tell the captain to ready a cell for a goddamn dragon?"

"No, no, not at all. Listen." She looked hastily around the empty lounge and lowered her voice. "For this to work, I'll need a team."

"Yeah, well, you obviously have one of those. I'm sure even Jim would fight for you now. You're Detroit PD's Steel Dragon. You know that."

"Not for this. Are you willing to work outside our normal modes of operation?"

He inclined his head as he considered that. "Absolutely. If it means bringing down the shitbag who's responsible for Jonesy's death, you have my support."

"Do you think the team will go for it?"

The question drew an immediate laugh. "Are you kidding? Hernandez would do anything for Jonesy's memory, and the others would do anything to make the Steel Dragon proud."

"Dragon or not, I want Black to know he's not untouchable, not in our city."

CHAPTER FORTY-FIVE

The team took to Kristen's plan far more quickly than she'd anticipated. Which possibly meant they should have spent a little more time developing it, but no one had wanted to wait.

Mr Black had said he was above the law, but if he left town, he really would be. Maybe he was nervous, too, although she couldn't be sure. He had raised the matter of jurisdiction so perhaps he might consider running. At least, that's what she had told her team. The result was that in less than twenty-four hours, they already began to put the plan into action.

She told herself it was because she'd convinced them and they'd seen the logic of acting quickly before he could adjust to the new status quo, but she really couldn't be sure. It was preferable to believe it wasn't her aura that had made her team agree so quickly, even though she knew she still didn't have perfect control of the ability. She wanted to catch Mr Black so badly and knew they did too. He'd taken one of their own, after all, but for her, it was more than that. She wondered if her team felt the way she did because she forced them to. It wasn't a pleasant feeling but she decided she could feel guilty about it when her city was no longer in danger from a monster who'd tried to compel it to consume itself with violence.

The team pulled up to the gate of the dragon's mansion in a SWAT van disguised to look like a utility truck.

Kristen wasn't inside. She waited a block away for the right moment with a radio on to hear the conversation.

"We had a report of a gas leak?" Beanpole said from the driver's seat. It was amazing how completely disinterested he sounded—like every repairman called in for every false alarm ever all rolled into one dude who simply wanted to get home.

"We didn't report any gas leak," the guard said. She could practically hear him frown.

"Are you sure about that?" her teammate replied, his voice thick with sarcasm. "I told you this was another waste of our time. If we're outdoors and can smell it, that normally means it's already at a dangerous level." He turned to Butters, who was in the passenger seat. "Do you smell anything I don't?"

"Of course, I smell it. You can't miss the stink. And I also told you that the gentleman who lives here wouldn't waste our time." His mock outrage at his companion slighting Mr Black seemed to work. The guard cleared his throat and sniffed loudly enough for her to hear him over the radio. If he had to side with one of the repairmen, the thinking was he'd go with the one who called his boss a gentleman.

"You know, now that you mention it—"

Part of the fence exploded in a shower of white sparks. They had hoped the guard wouldn't be able to recognize different kinds of explosions and it seemed the gamble had paid off.

"Holy shit! Holy shit—what do we do?" he shouted so loudly it forced feedback.

"Let us in! We need to shut the mainline off before this whole place goes up. Do you guys have a control switch in there?"

"I...I don't know!"

"That's fine," Butters said. "Let us in and we'll take care of it."

The guard turned to his controls and opened the gate.

When he looked down, Hernandez and Kristen snuck in through the hole in the fence the demolitions expert had created and ran through the garden, keeping the truck between them and the guard.

Kristen had never learned the full story behind Sebastian's collection of cowering human sculptures. But she found that she no longer particularly cared about them either. She knew she didn't like them, so when they began to blow up, one by one, from the explosives her teammate dropped at each of their feet, it filled her with nothing but a sense of pleasure at seeing those tortured faces freed from their master's gaze.

At the third explosion, she felt him. Either he'd heard the explosions or the guard had told him. His aura—normally so calm and controlled—had ignited with rage.

The servants poured out of the house but Mr Black wasn't with them. That suited her perfectly.

She'd given her team a plan, but she didn't know if she would stick to it. While her purpose was to defeat Shadowstorm—she had to defeat him—if she had an opportunity to do more, she would take it. If she saw an opening to kill him, she would do so. She'd killed the men who'd worked for him. Why did their leader deserve anything different?

There was no way to be sure how all this would play out, but as she raced across the manicured grounds that now erupted in flames and used her dragon abilities to quickly outpace the rest of her team, she became sure of one thing. She would make the dragon pay for what he had done to her city and she would make him answer for what he'd done to her friend.

CHAPTER FORTY-SIX

Her body already transformed to steel, Kristen barreled through the mansion and tracked the other dragon's aura. It led her through his home and she followed the direct route and simply pounded through walls as easily as football players ran through paper banners.

She bulldozed a path through room after room and crushed treasure after treasure until she thrust through the final one and found Mr Black outside.

He stood on his sandy training court, wearing nothing but black pants and black gloves trimmed with red. She hated those gloves.

His posture stiff and rigid, he glared at her. "I knew you were coming, Steel Dragonling. I've waited for you outside, in the obvious place to have this fight."

Thunder cracked, and an eerie darkness gathered on the horizon. She never had asked him if he could control the weather, but it looked like she had her answer.

"Oops? Did I track mud through your house?" She stepped onto the sandy court and kicked her shoes off.

"You do understand that I didn't teach you everything I know, correct? That for you, this will be the fight of your life, and for me, this will be but another demonstration from a student destined to live in my shadow."

She snarled her defiance. He had taught her a considerable amount, this was true, but he hadn't taught her anything about her steel abilities that she didn't already know. And one of the things she'd learned from him might be his downfall. After all, it was Shadowstorm who had delivered the lesson of what it felt like to lose a friend. She wasn't so naïve as to think she could make him feel the pain of it but she could still take something from him. The arrogant look on his face would be a good start.

Without warning, she raced forward and her steel toes propelled her through the sand until she moved at a blur.

He anticipated her, clasped his hands together, and raised them above his head. She veered at the last moment, but he had anticipated that too and twisted his body so he could still strike. His fists caught her on the shoulders, and she catapulted out of the court. Her steel body scraped a groove into his manicured lawn.

Kristen stood. She'd hardly felt the blow. Being made of steel had advantages, after all. She attacked again and this time, leapt into a flying kick. Something about being in the air felt right. She had a moment of exhilaration like a foreshadowing of that other still-elusive dragon part of her as it tried to break free.

But the feeling was a distraction. Shadowstorm caught her leg and hurled her away with a roar. Once again, she careened away and the feeling of weightlessness was quickly replaced by the knot in her stomach from momentum she couldn't control. She impacted a marble statue that shattered in the collision.

Unperturbed, she picked a broken hand up and threw it at him, followed by a woman's crying head and a torso.

Her adversary deflected the first two, but she could tell they hurt his forearms all the same. His skin wasn't steel and she had thrown chunks of marble at him as fast as most of the pitchers for the Tigers could. The third piece—the torso—caught him in the shoulder with sufficient force to make him stumble.

She had already begun to sprint when that thunked into him. He recovered quickly, though, and she only managed to land a few punches to his gut before he grasped her by her throat and threw her across the sandy arena.

Shadowstorm was breathing hard. Obviously, tossing her around wasn't easy for him. So much of her training with him had been focused on using her speed and strength rather than her steel abilities. He obviously hadn't taken into account how much heavier it really made her. She realized that she might actually be able to win the fight.

While she wasn't stronger than him, she carried far more bulk and weight. If she could use that difference in their bodies, she could finish this.

Encouraged, she took a few steps back until she stood near one of the metal dragon statues that looked like it was rising from the ground. She caught hold of the clawed hand and pulled it loose. While she didn't quite have the strength to lift it directly, her adversary had taught her how to use leverage.

It took effort but she managed to yank it free and swung it as he launched himself onto her. She powered a blow across his head with the arm and he tumbled with a curse.

He stood and spat blood. The grass ignited with hissing flames where his spittle touched it. She swung the arm again. He dodged, darted forward, and kicked her in the groin.

The strike accomplished little except to hurt his foot.

Kristen tried to swing the arm for another assault but she was too slow. By the time the weapon arced toward him, Shadowstorm had clamped a hand on her forearm. He squeezed hard and despite that it wasn't particularly painful, the pressure was still enough to make her drop her impromptu weapon.

She tried to kick him and thought she managed it, but the blow went past him. Or through him? She couldn't be sure but she felt certain it should have landed.

Her opponent used her confusion to his advantage. He caught her by the neck and tightened his grasp.

Although she was made of steel, it wasn't exactly rock solid. She could move, after all, which meant his grip on her neck compressed her flesh exactly like it had when he'd squeezed her forearm.

The dragon grunted and lifted her from the ground. Veins bulged in his neck and his arm flexed so tightly, she thought it might burst. Still, he didn't drop her to the grass and instead, lifted her higher and squeezed.

Involuntarily, she choked around the crushing hold around her throat and began to hammer on his shoulders with steel punches and kick his chest with steel feet. He really was a huge opponent. Her feet were nowhere near the ground.

"Enough of this!" Shadowstorm bellowed and dropped her. She landed hard and managed to keep her feet under her, but he simply shoved her to the left and over his outstretched leg. Her ass hit met the sand but he didn't release her. Instead, he followed her down and drove her throat to the sand as he did so. He tightened his hold and dragged her by the neck toward the outside edge of the training court.

"You still don't understand leverage," he said while she gagged and tried to cough. The advantage didn't come without a price for him, however, and he panted with the exertion required. The weight of her steel body was considerable, even for the hulking man. If she could go back on the offensive—if she could only breathe and fight back—she could do this.

Kristen found it more and more difficult to believe those thoughts.

When her adversary heaved her over the edge of the training court, his hand faltered and she struck him in the thigh. He cried out in pain and dropped her. Instead of a punch, she'd tried a karate chop. The smaller surface area of the blow had worked well and magnified the force of her blow. Given that her skin was made of steel, it didn't hurt her at all. Funny, he had never shown her that.

She rose, her hands held like knives in front of her and told herself she could do this. Truthfully, she had no choice. If she lost, she knew he would slaughter her friends in a heartbeat and it wouldn't even matter to him. They were only people, after all.

Shadowstorm roared and attacked. She lashed out with chops and tried to get inside his greater reach and work his torso. He adjusted his attack and attempted to grab her, so she retaliated in kind. For a moment, they simply pulled at each other, each dragon trying to displace the other and seize the upper hand. In the end, the victory was hers.

Her greater steel mass worked to her advantage and she threw a shoulder against him and managed to unbalance the taller man. As soon as one of his feet lifted, she wound her arms around his torso and pulled back with every ounce of her dragon strength. She managed to hoist both his feet up and used the full power of her weight to pound him into the sand. Before he could recover, she simply fell on top of him and he gasped from the abrupt force and pressure.

It really was odd how effective wrestling moves were when one's body was made of steel.

The other dragon struggled to escape from beneath her bulk, but he couldn't. Brian had made her watch enough wrestling that she knew the real holds from the fake ones.

"Give up, Sebastian. It's over. You've lost." Kristen hissed her annoyance at his obduracy.

"Foolish…girl," Shadowstorm wheezed between breaths.

In the next moment, her hold on him was gone and she lay in the sand.

A dark mist drifted around her like a cloud. Flashes of lightning cracked and she narrowed her eyes against the flare of brightness. For a moment, she thought the storm on the horizon had descended onto the battle.

The roiling mass of shadowed cloud resolved itself into her adversary's dragon form.

He was utterly enormous—bigger than an elephant or even two—and was covered in black scales that looked as hard and impenetrable as her steel skin. Red, angry eyes glowered with hatred above white, pointed teeth. Spines covered his back and jutted from the joints of his knees. His claws were like butcher knives on the ends of hands bigger than her torso. He might not be able to use them to slice her steel skin, but then again, she didn't actually know what dragon claws were made of. She knew they were capable of punching through suits of armor, though, and had seen a relic in his house that bore marks of exactly that.

She couldn't beat him. Not like this. He was too big and too powerful, and he could fly. He knew her limitations better than she did. Panic surged in her chest and she realized he'd simply toyed with her.

Kristen pushed herself up to run. She made it perhaps four steps before a bolt of lightning struck her.

Everything went white-hot for a second before she tumbled into the sand, her shoulder aflame with pain that made the tasers feel like nine-volt batteries. It felt like someone had stabbed a sword through her shoulder, attached a powerline to it, and turned on all the electricity that powered Detroit.

The pain was so intense that she couldn't even writhe. It took everything she had to merely stay conscious.

She had no idea if the lightning had come from the approaching storm or from Shadowstorm himself. It confirmed to her that the dragon could definitely either control lightning or create it and either option was equally as terrifying as the other. She had no idea if he could do it again or if it had been a lucky strike.

It very quickly became a moot point, however. Before she could scramble to her feet, a claw lashed into her back and pinned her to the ground.

The sensation of being crushed was almost a relief compared to the lightning. At least she had some recourse against that. Against lighting…well, steel skin certainly wasn't an advantage.

It took every ounce of strength she possessed and she managed a push up—at least she thought she did—but as soon as her chest raised off the ground, his tail whipped into her and twisted her onto her back. She understood then that the only reason she had been able to get her face out of the sand was because he had allowed it.

Before she could attempt to move again, he drove a claw down onto her chest. He began to apply pressure to pin her in place and force the air from her lungs.

A great gust of wind buffeted her—a harbinger of the storm that had finally reached them—and was immediately followed by only stillness.

Kristen couldn't feel much besides the increasing pressure on her chest from Shadowstorm's claws. She saw nothing but the red eyes, the ridge of spikes, and the gaping mouth of his true form.

"You're a shitty teacher," she sputtered.

The dragon merely laughed.

CHAPTER FORTY-SEVEN

"What's the matter, Lady Hall? Have you not learned how to transform yet?" Shadowstorm roared with laughter. Thunder boomed above him as he did so and echoed his amusement.

"Like I said, I had a shitty teacher."

"Most of us learn the full extent of our powers when we must. But apparently, being raised as a human instilled their sense of worthlessness in your psyche. I had thought that even now, in this fight, I might release your true potential and we could take to the skies together. Then you would see that we could be allies, but I realize now how much of a liability your past truly is. Although you may not be a pathetic human, your heart will always belong to them." He laughed and again, the thunder boomed.

Kristen struggled against his claw but couldn't move. She hoped it would rain. Perhaps the slickness would enable her to slip free, but given that the thunder mirrored her captor, she seriously doubted that would happen. "You're a monster," she managed to say in a voice ragged from her exertions.

"No, my dear. I'm a dragon. I thought you were too, but I begin to doubt that. I thought I could make you into one of us, but I was wrong. My only regret is that a mongrel like yourself was the one to disprove me after so much time. I think I might have preferred it to be a human instead of a runt trapped between worlds. At least then, I'd know these creatures were learning."

"Whatever I am, at least I fight for something besides myself. You care about nothing except this pathetic palace and your own stupid machinations."

Shadowstorm threw back his head and laughed hard at that. His throat swelled and collapsed with each breath. He really was huge —like swallow-a-person-without-chewing huge. When he brought his face back to hers, a gust of wind came with it and blew sand into her eyes and mouth. His aura affected the weather then, or had he planned that?

Even for someone with steel skin, the sand was irritating. It also served to emphasize how much more powerful than her he was. Given his enormous stature, the sand hadn't even reached his face.

"Do you hear yourself, human?" He pitched his voice in a crude impersonation of her. "You only care about your own stupid machinations." He laughed again. "Only a human could say that. My machinations will give me this city, this country, and one day, the world."

"Bullshit."

"Lady Hall, my machinations already killed your friend. I was there, you know, at the top of the warehouse, and tried not to laugh while he bled out in your arms."

"Fuck you!" Kristen hissed her fury and struggled against his claw. She thought it might work as she felt it raise but then realized he had merely picked her up.

He wrapped his taloned fingers around her steel body and held her above the sand. If the weight bothered him, it didn't even vaguely show.

"Even now, I feel your aura trying to make me feel terror or fear." Shadowstorm chuckled. "But you're so weak I don't even feel nervous. My aura, on the other hand, inspired the gangs of this city to come together and fight against the yoke of their human oppressors." He tightened his grasp.

"I stopped you," she wheezed. She would have said more if she had enough oxygen but his hold crushed her like she was nothing more than an insect. Dimly, she wondered what would happen if he applied more force. Would her organs simply rupture inside her or would her steel skin crack like a peach to release her blood?

"Once, yes, you stopped me when your powers were so weak, I could hardly sense them. But my mercenaries led you on a merry chase through the city to an abandoned warehouse, did they not? You even managed to catch us. And yet, here we are, on my land. How clever you must feel."

"None of your friends will ever see the light of day."

"Friends?" Shadowstorm laughed so hard the rain began to fall—a slow drizzle that didn't loosen his grip at all but only irritated her eyes. "Do you think those pathetic humans were my friends?" He hurled her into the sand and leaned on her with the weight of his dragon body. "Have you really learned so little from me? I will shed no tears over the loss of human lives. They're worthless to me. Less than worthless—insects or ants. No, that's not quite true. Humans can be useful tools. They're worth at least a little more than simply poisoning them. After all, once I snap your neck, they'll give me the city."

"And that's what you've been after this whole time? This city? Detroit and the people you lord it over? You want it to be yours instead of whichever dragon runs it now?"

"I thought that was obvious, Kristen. You were to rule it at my side."

"Like I said, fuck you."

Shadowstorm smiled, a predatory gesture. "You are true to the pathetic moral cloth that raised you, I'll give you that much. But unfortunately for you, I have no place for short-sighted human morals. Do you wish to turn back to flesh so I can snap your neck quickly or shall we see how flexible steel really is?"

Kristen clenched her teeth as he brought his other claw closer and wound it through the steel filaments that were her hair.

"I wonder if your hair will come out or the vertebrae in your neck will snap first." He tugged her head to the left. "It's an interesting question that I haven't been able to answer despite our training together. How deep does your steel skin really go? If it's all the way through, surely your hair will come out first. But if it's only skin-deep—that's my hunch, by the way—your neck will probably snap before you lose any hair."

She tried not to let him see how much pain she was in but that was impossible.

In the next moment, her tormentor flinched and released her hair, although the clawed hand that pinned her to the sand remained firmly in place.

He looked up.

"Hey, lizard breath. Let our partner go."

"Yeah, asshole. Or else!"

Kristen craned her neck, thankful it could still move at all.

Drew and the team had arrived.

CHAPTER FORTY-EIGHT

Shadowstorm laughed and the rain fell harder.

"Was that supposed to hurt me? My scales are as strong as steel, you fool, and my flesh has power greater than any creature that walks this earth. I cannot be harmed by your tiny weapons."

"Yeah, yeah, I know all that. I merely wanted to get your attention," Drew said almost casually and lowered his handgun.

In response, lightning struck the tree closest to the team. The thundercrack was deafening and in seconds, the tree was engulfed in flames.

"You have it," the dragon said.

"You missed," Kristen snarked. Maybe the lightning had only struck her because she was made of steel. He could direct it but not completely. Otherwise, she had little doubt Drew would be dead right now.

"Don't interrupt, child," he said and struck her across the face. His claws didn't actually hurt her skin, but the force of the blow twisted her neck and that was beyond painful. She realized the folly of her plan. The dragon really could crush her insides like jelly. He knew this, obviously. That was why he'd trained her.

Another shot rang out. Even though she saw the spark of the bullet striking his chest, he didn't flinch in the slightest.

"I told you, your weapons are useless."

"Guns, maybe," Drew said and strolled away from the burning tree before it collapsed—which, given the roar of the flames, probably wouldn't take long. "But humans do have weapons that can hurt you, Mr Black."

Shadowstorm grinned. All his expressions were terrifying in dragon form but this smile was especially malicious. "You amuse me, human. What weapon could you have that could possibly hurt me? I have outlived empires and turned castles to rubble with my own hands. Tell me, did you get one of those tasers to work? You'll find they don't particularly bother a dragon who often soars amongst the clouds that breed lightning."

"It's all about values, right?" The man took another casual step forward. "Humans are vulnerable because we care about each other. You only value yourself and your power."

"Neither of which can be taken from me," the dragon responded dismissively. "I grow tired of this. You are stalling. Did you only stop me to get a better vantage point before I kill your friend?"

"We stopped you because you already confessed," Keith said and held a cell phone up.

"We have it all on video, Mr Black," Drew explained. "In Hi-Def too, but of course, you're a dinosaur who probably understands that less than my Nana does."

Shadowstorm chuckled and the thunder rumbled. "Yes. Video. This was one invention I paid attention too. When you're working in the shadows, one can't have people shining lights and filming."

"Okay, cool. So you understand that you're fucked, then?" Hernandez said.

"Such crude language." He shook his head and sucked a disapproving breath between his teeth. "I won't feel bad about roasting you alive and destroying your little video strip with you."

He inhaled and leaned even more heavily on Kristen.

"Yeah, except I've actually live-streamed the whole thing." Keith grinned. "We tagged Dragon SWAT. Stonequest seems really pissed, and Heartsbane? Dude, her comments have been hilarious."

"Stonequest?" The dragon balked. It was the first word he'd said since Kristen had confronted him that wasn't laced with confidence.

"Yeah. Although he hasn't said anything in a minute. I guess dragon hands can't hold a phone? I dunno. They should be here… Hold up, let me close the app." Keith frowned slightly and tapped the screen of his phone. "Sorry, I couldn't see the clock. Yeah, really soon. I'd say he'll be here really soon."

Washington smiled at Shadowstorm. "In other words, fly away little birdy."

"You can't expect me to believe this—" he began and stopped abruptly.

Kristen had felt it too—the slightest tinge of another dragon's aura. Stonequest was still far away, but he was moving closer by the second and he wasn't alone. Other dragon auras pushed into her consciousness.

She also felt Shadowstorm's aura change from confidence to anxiety rather rapidly. One day, she told herself, she'd thank him for the ability to sense such things. Maybe a day when her throat wasn't crushed by his giant hand. Maybe when he was chained up in a hole he couldn't crawl out of.

"Cursed humans." The dragon raised his claw high enough off the ground to pound her into the sand, then pumped his wings and was airborne and she was free.

"See you around!" Drew shouted after him.

"Indeed, human! This isn't over, and now that I know where the Steel Dragon's alliances lie, she will pay."

He pumped his wings, gained speed, and fled in the opposite direction from which the other auras were approaching.

When he left, the storm followed. In a moment, it had stopped raining and in another, a rainbow appeared.

"If that's not like the fruitiest damn thing I've ever seen outside of Keith's apartment, I don't know what is," Hernandez said.

Everyone laughed. Kristen pushed herself to her feet and limped over to her team. Every inch of her hurt except for her skin. She didn't know that bruised bone could be so painful.

"So, this is where you've trained, huh? What was the end game here? To become a chunk of a dragon or a tiny scared white woman?" Butters gestured at the sculptures around the mansion. "It seems like a lose-lose situation to me."

"I don't mean to be rude, but the garden décor kind of screams super-villain," Beanpole said.

"You trained here in the sand? Too bad he doesn't have cameras. That would've made for a sick Steel Dragon training montage." Keith scanned the house for security cameras and found nothing.

Hernandez apparently thought that was hilarious because she laughed so hard, she snorted.

Jim stepped out in front of the team, his head hung in shame. He cleared his throat. "Hall, I'm sorry about all that anti-dragon shit. We couldn't have done anything to that guy without you," he said and raised his chin so he could look her in the eye with his shoulders straight. He really was the Wonderkid and even apologized like a professional.

"Yeah, well, I'm sorry for tailing you. And I'm sorry about your friend back there. He…that was my fault."

"Hall, you were supposed to learn that it's not always about you," Drew said. "Don't let this be Jonesy all over again."

"Yeah, share the load with that guilt." Jim forced a laugh. Everyone else laughed too. It was the kind of thing you did for each other when part of your job was trying to stop people from killing each other and inevitably failing sometimes.

The screech of a car's tires caused the team to all turn toward the driveway.

A car raced away from the mansion. Either the butler was still under Shadowstorm's aura or the dragon had actually inspired some degree of loyalty.

"Do you want me to shoot his tires?" Butters had already raised his sniper rifle. He sounded like he could have made the shot even if he was half-drunk.

"It might be smart to let him go," Keith said with a shrug. "Shadowstorm's untouchable but his henchmen might leave a trail."

"I say aim higher than the tires," Washington said.

"Drew?" Butters said.

"Take out his brake light," the team leader said.

The sniper did and everyone laughed when it shattered and the man cursed loudly enough to be heard all the way across the grounds.

"Thanks, you guys." Kristen grinned sheepishly. Despite having been almost killed by the most powerful being she had ever encountered in her entire life, it still made her feel silly to have asked for help. Even as a kid, she'd detested needing help. She wondered now if that was an inherent dragon trait or her mom's stubbornness raised into her.

"No problem," Keith said cheerfully.

"Seriously, Kristen, the pleasure was all ours," Butters assured her. "I get to put 'shooting a bitch-ass dragon' on my resume!"

There were few chuckles before the weight of the joke settled around them.

"You probably shouldn't actually include that," Jim said. "Kristen's cool, but most of them probably won't like it at all."

"Yeah, I know. Dragon jurisdiction," Butters said glumly.

"How will those assholes react, Red?" Hernandez said to her. The nickname finally felt fine coming from her.

"I have no idea. Dragon SWAT will be here soon."

"You weren't bluffing?" Drew asked.

She shook her head. "They answered our call. I can feel their auras getting stronger, which means they're getting closer, I think. I don't know why they'd come unless it was to help us with the job."

"Gee, I don't fucking know." The other woman's words positively dripped sarcasm. "Maybe they're less than thrilled that some uppity Detroiter the media's obsessed with took on one of their own in combat and showed the whole damn thing on the entire Internet."

"I thought you said you would only share it with Dragon SWAT," she said.

"Whoops?" Keith shrugged. He didn't look regretful, though. "The only bummer is I didn't get his human face. Only the brawl, then him, uh…"

"Pinning Kristen like a cat with a bird?" Butters asked.

There was a moment of silence in which they all thought about how the world might react to a dragon beating the crap out of one of the most famous people in the world right now. She was a dragon too, so the dragons said, but she'd yet to actually transform. It could quickly spiral into a PR nightmare.

"Hey, everyone, I had an idea. How about we get the hell out of here?" Hernandez suggested.

Everyone agreed. Suddenly, standing on a dragon's estate waiting for more pissed-off dragons to arrive didn't sound so great. While those approaching were supposed to be pissed-off at the same people the team was, something about an angry being that might or might not be able to breathe fire wasn't that appealing.

They scrambled into the van, Drew started the engine, and they left without seeing any sign of the dragons.

"Do you think there'll be repercussions, Red? You can be straight with us." Hernandez stared at her from across the back of the van as if she actually knew anything about any of this.

"I have no idea, but I don't really care. We did the right thing. If they don't see that…" She sighed and tried not to sound despondent. "I'll hold them off long enough for you guys to get out of here."

No one laughed.

"That was a joke!" she said.

That still didn't make anyone laugh.

"Look, whatever happens, happens." She shrugged. "All I know is that I want a beer."

"I know a wings place," Butters added quickly.

"The first round's on me," she said.

"Rookie mistake," Keith said. "Butters will buy out every damn wing in the place as soon as a waitress looks at him."

They laughed and fell into companionable silence after the sniper told Drew the name of the place.

Tomorrow was another day, but for now, she had her friends and a cloud that loomed over her city had blown away. For that, she was thankful.

CHAPTER FORTY-NINE

Kristen hadn't thought she was too badly hungover. That theory was sorely tested when the captain bellowed for her to get in her office.

She pushed herself from her desk, hurried down the hallway, and wished she wasn't hungover at all. This meeting with the captain was inevitable, but she'd have preferred it to be after lunch. A fool's dream, obviously.

When she passed the water fountain and had an irresistible urge to drink water, she succumbed and no doubt drew the ire of the captain even more. When she drank, the hangover simply vanished. One second, she had a headache and felt like a sheet hung between her eyes and her brain and the next, her world was clear and her headache gone.

It was her healing power at work, a skill she learned from that traitor Mr Black. She was simultaneously thankful and furious at the idea that her dragon powers would always feel like they'd come from him. While she really had learned from the dragon, there was obviously much he hadn't shown her either.

The captain's door was closed so she knocked. It sounded gentler than she'd intended—like she was scared, which was way too close to the truth. She didn't want to lose her job but couldn't exactly fault the woman. Their escapade had involved an officer dragging a SWAT van and a team out on an illegal bust, after all.

When she entered the office, it wasn't Captain Hansen who made her heart pound in her throat.

Stonequest was the first person she saw. The captain of Dragon SWAT nodded at her, his orange eyes with their black slits unblinking.

"Hall. Thanks for finally joining us. You've met Stonequest, correct? I believe he was the one who laid into you the last time you acted completely outside protocol." Captain Hansen glowered from behind her desk.

"That's putting it strongly, Captain," Stonequest said mildly.

The woman calmed immediately.

"Don't use your aura on her," Kristen snapped and flexed her own aura—anger and surprise and a trace of indignation. It struck the woman like a slap in the face and she immediately scowled.

"Whatever you two are doing to me, cut it out." Hansen shook her head and tried to push the residual effect from her head.

"Yes, sir," she said and let the aura drop. She'd wanted the captain to be free from outside influence but had used her aura to enable her to do so. It was deliciously ironic that her superior officer was only able to get angry because she had intervened and removed Stonequest's aura, and that the captain had taken it out on her as well.

"I'm sure you want to know why I'm here," Stonequest said and his orange gaze leveled on her. It felt like being watched by an anaconda.

"More like how long until you haul me off to dragon jail," she replied. She had meant it as a joke—one of those that are only funny because they have a ring of truth to them.

He cracked a smile at that. "Dragon jail?" He snorted. "There are no little boxes that can hold our kind. The penalty for those who won't heed the dragon council is death."

She swallowed and glanced at Captain Hansen, who also looked nervous.

"Which is what we'll do if we ever catch Shadowstorm."

Relieved, she released the breath of air she'd held. Okay...so at least she wouldn't die today. That was nice. "You're...not mad?" she asked.

Stonequest frowned a little. She thought he might have looked curious but it was damn hard to read his eyes with his slitted pupils. "I'm a little upset that you abandoned Shadowstorm's home before Dragon SWAT and I arrived and shared that stream on the internetwork—which isn't exactly the best for publicity—but my displeasure isn't why I'm here."

Oh...well, that was good. He smiled when her aura of relief reached him. "So then... I'm not in trouble?"

His smile broadened. "You're a dragon and didn't do anything wrong. You felt Shadowstorm had wronged you, so you challenged him. That's been legal for dragons for millennia."

Another relief, she thought. "So you believe Shadowstorm's confession then?"

Stonequest smiled even more broadly and this time, it even reached and softened the weirdness of his eyes. "I've felt your aura. It's powerful, but Shadowstorm was a master of subtlety. No one who has met him believes that he could be coerced by anyone. I believe the confession was his own."

"And my team?" She asked the question of him but it was really for Captain Hansen.

He shrugged and dismissed the question with a wave of his hand. The subtext was clear. The concern was beneath him. "The humans acted under your orders. You had a legal challenge against a dragon so, by obeying you, they did not act outside the law. In fact, technically, humans who swear fealty to a dragon must obey. At least that's how it works in dragon law. I understand there are different rules amongst your kind." He nodded at Captain Hansen as if he were giving her permission for something.

"So they won't be punished, Captain?" Kristen asked and hoped she understood the gesture.

The woman only shrugged. "Hazy legal grounds are better than breaking the law. I'm with Sir Stonequest here about the live streaming, though. That was unprofessional."

Again, the dragon shrugged. "It was…embarrassing, but it might ultimately be for the best. My kind often ignore technological developments. There have been big ones, recently, of course—electricity, the photograph, automobiles, and whatnot—but most dragons have failed to see the difference between television and the Internet. Television is easy enough for us to control. The hierarchical power structure of the major companies allows us to…filter that which we believe to be too disruptive, but the Internet is a different beast. A decentralized network of uncensored content creators is dangerous in a way television was not."

Stonequest chuckled. "Ugh, sorry, you got me monologuing. Let's forget about it. That kind of talk is for the Dragon Council," he added with a gesture toward the captain. Kristen felt his aura like a surgeon's blade. A knife of forgetfulness sliced into the captain's consciousness and she shook her head.

She was awed and once again realized that there were many things Shadowstorm hadn't shown her. Still, she didn't like that he'd manipulated the woman and wanted to protest but before she could, he stood.

"To make things very clear, Dragon SWAT is thankful for the help of your officers, Captain," Stonequest said to Captain Hansen.

"You'll go after him then?" she asked, oblivious to the little trick that he had played on her mind.

"Oh yes. We haven't caught him yet, but we will. Now that his slight against the Steel Dragon is public knowledge, quite a few dragons have come out against him as well. Enough have taken offense that we'll investigate him. There will be a list of grievances brought to the council, of this I am certain."

"Wait…a list of grievances?" Kristen was dumbfounded. "Are you saying the only reason you'll pursue him is because other dragons have filed complaints?"

Stonequest looked surprised and his orange gaze bored into her.

"That is how dragon law works. I take it Shadowstorm told you nothing of our ways?"

"No, not really. But am I really supposed to believe that him riling up a horde of gang members into trying to blow Detroit up and hiring mercenaries to literally blow it up is fine?" She felt anger curdling in her gut like hot bile.

"No, of course not. Damos and Lyra—the two dragons in charge of this region—have taken offense with him for those very reasons. The people in this part of the world are theirs to protect and punish. Shadowstorm can't usurp a city for no good reason."

Her fury began to escalate and it took considerable concentration to not become steel. "But there's no law against slaughtering people?"

"No. No, of course not." Stonequest seemed amused "Dragon laws don't apply to people. We operate on another level of power. That would be like your kind making laws to protect the birds or the fish."

"We do have laws to protect the birds and the fish."

The dragon chuckled. "Do you really? How curious. I really am looking forward to you coming into your powers, Lady Hall. There is much the dragons can learn from one who grew up amongst humans. Do humans actually respect these laws of fish and birds?"

"No…not always, but that's not important right now. Shadowstorm killed dozens of people. He could have killed hundreds."

"And do your politicians go on trial when they go to war? There was a time when dragon kind had killed more humans than you had each other, but as we've moved into the background—of our own accord, I might add—humans have been more than willing to take up the mantle of committing atrocities on each other. The atomic bomb, the world wars, firearms, and swords are all things your kind have perpetrated on itself."

Her skin rippled to steel and quickly reverted. This was…this was disgusting. Dragons thought of people as little more than fish? Except there were dragons like Shadowstorm who manipulated people from behind the scenes, and Stonequest thought these manipulative ones had simply decided to sit out the entirety of human conflict? That was like absolving a politician for a war they'd called for simply because he hadn't been the one to fire the guns. It was absurd.

"So, because I complained, Shadowstorm's in trouble? If I hadn't, he would have walked free."

"The information you shared is more than enough to infuriate quite a few dragons," Stonequest said. He still seemed rather oblivious as to how angry she was at his thoughtless carelessness. "Lyra and Damos want his head, obviously. Many of the other North American dragons had sworn not to harbor him as well. As I said, his shadow is a long one." He chuckled at the pun as if they were discussing some celebrity's gaff instead of the potential slaughter of innocent human lives.

"So, to be clear, if Damos and Lyra decided to simply burn Detroit to the ground, that wouldn't be doing anything wrong?"

He frowned at her and looked genuinely appalled at the thought. "Of course that would be wrong. There would be no reason for such slaughter. So many of us would call their ability to rule into question and besides, it would represent a huge loss of resources. If Damos and Lyra burned the city, many of the dragons in North America would turn against them."

"Because of a loss of resources?" She sneered.

"This is how it's done, Hall," Stonequest stated and his voice lacked emotion. "We have no laws about humans because we don't wish to interfere in every decision their kind makes. With autonomy comes the freedom to hurt each other."

"This is unacceptable," Kristen retorted. "You know there are dragons interfering with human affairs. There are dragons paying off politicians and piloting corporations from behind the scenes. You turn a blind eye to the fact that because of the power you wield, you've influenced mankind from the beginning."

"Maybe that's true but we've taken steps back," he snapped. Apparently, she had struck a nerve. "No one agrees with you more than I—although it is perhaps not wise for me to admit that—but it can be difficult to change minds that are literally hundreds of years old."

"So why bother?" She couldn't help herself. By now, she was furious.

"We struck a blow today. Shadowstorm is lying low. Already, many of the leaders on this continent have sworn not to harbor him, and as the news spreads, others will probably do the same. He will pay for his actions—for what he did to you and yours." He paused, his expression inscrutable, but she sensed a slight softening, a hesitation that suggested he might not entirely be the uncaring, emotionless dragon she assumed him to be. "There are dragons—not many, I concede, but a couple—who believe that humans have…unexplored potential. It may be that more and more will respond to that idea. And yes, it will take time, but I think progress can be made. What we've done with ousting Shadowstorm proves that."

"And what do you want me to do in the meantime? Sit on my hands while I wait for justice?"

"Honestly, we'd like you to stick to human issues for a while." Stonequest smiled. It seemed genuine because his aura matched the expression, but it was still hard to read him with those eyes.

"I thought we weren't supposed to interfere with human affairs," she said and wished it had sounded less petulant than it had.

"That's been the arrangement for a long time, but our ways are not set in stone." He smiled at the pun on his own name.

Kristen wondered for how long and in how many languages he'd made inappropriate plays on words.

Stonequest continued. "Your situation is unique, and the world is beginning to watch the Steel Dragon from the Motor City. You are aware of human issues in a way no other dragon is, simply because of your upbringing. Even the most…liberal of us often have difficulty empathizing with your kind. For example, I'm in law enforcement and had no idea that you actually made laws for the fish.

"On top of that, you are an adult by human standards, and a sheriff, as most of my kin still calls the police. By dragon standards, you're a whelp, but you are certainly old enough to make judgments on humankind."

"Make judgments?"

He raised an eyebrow. "I've seen what you've done to some of the humans who threatened your city. The thief you left hanging in the bars he tried to hide behind was especially poignant."

"And especially outside what SWAT is supposed to do, Hall," Captain Hansen added. She sat at her desk, her arms folded, and Kristen had almost forgotten about her.

"Of course, ma'am. It won't happen again."

Stonequest smiled. "And you defer to human judgment. That alone makes many of us think that you continuing to work on human affairs while you wait to come into your powers fully will give you a wisdom most of us lack."

"Fine. It's not like I have a dragon teacher right now anyway. I'll keep working on making this city safer. But you need to understand that if I hear about a dragon hurting people, I won't send in a complaint and wait for some kind of consensus. I'll protect the people in my city. If that's a problem, take it up with me. You're not as big as Mr Black was and you saw the video." It was more of a threat than she had intended, but now that she'd said it, she didn't regret it.

He sighed although he didn't sound particularly upset. "I wouldn't expect anything less from the Steel Dragon, and I've told Damos and Lyra as much. You've proven yourself capable of causing headaches on a scale I thought impossible."

"You call injustice a headache?"

Stonequest chuckled. "No, but invading a dragon's home rather than coming to me was problematic."

"If I'd come without the confession, would you have raised a finger against Shadowstorm?"

"Perhaps. As I said, many have already sworn not to shelter him. That doesn't happen unless there was already resentment there. However, you're correct in that coming to us would have taken longer. Shadowstorm is tricky. If his network had obtained the information, he could have taken action we'd have been unable to stop."

He rubbed his head. She had seen the gesture from every superior she'd ever frustrated—which, when she thought about it, was virtually every boss she'd ever had.

"You should do what you feel you must. I'm sure you will anyway. But please, let us know before you blow another dragon's house up next time."

She left the meeting feeling strangely vindicated. That aside, she'd learned something of dragon culture and how unjust it was toward humanity, but she couldn't do anything about that…yet. She could, however, continue to protect her city, and that was exactly what she intended to do.

CHAPTER FIFTY

A few days later, there was enough normalcy in the air for Hernandez to bug everyone about airsoft again. "Come on, you punk-ass chumps. We haven't gone since Jonesy died. If we don't go soon, we'll never go."

Kristen sighed. She hated to admit it, but him not being there made airsoft simply sound less fun and she said as much to the other woman.

"That's fucking bullshit, Red. Jonesy loved airsoft. Shooting us, watching us complain about our welts, shooting Keith first, again and again." The demolitions expert sighed wistfully. "We owe it to him to keep playing. Every time we shoot the Rookie, Jonesy laughs about it, wherever he is."

"I'm in," Keith said. "But only so I can shoot your ass, Hernandez. You never win either."

She laughed. "Right, we'll see about that. Although I'm not sure if that's the best plan." She winked and Kristen felt the beginnings of a conspiracy start to stir.

"I'm in." Butters sauntered into the lounge. "Those wings gave me heartburn."

Beanpole looked up from his coffee. "I'm there too."

"Washington?" Hernandez asked the Wonderkid.

"Absolutely. I'd love to try some new tactical maneuvers."

Kristen shook her head. "Leave it to the Wonderkid to make a game sound like work."

"Are you guys talking airsoft?" Drew entered the lounge—or tried to although Butters still blocked the doorway.

"Yes, sir," Hernandez said quite formally. "Would you care to join us, sir, or are you still a fucking pussy?"

Everyone laughed but Drew. He turned a shade redder and gritted his teeth. "I'll meet you all there. I'll bring someone else too—is that cool? I'd like to even the odds. I heard about what happened last time. It sounded like a massacre," he added with a pointed stare at Kristen. Oh, so he wanted to team up against her too?

"You can bring whatever bimbo you want to watch me take you down," Hernandez said and glanced at Kristen. "Or to show the power of teamwork. But don't be pissed if she wants to go home with me instead of you when it's all done."

Keith looked put out at the idea of her taking another woman out after the game, but he didn't say anything.

"Great. We'll meet there at six." The team leader nodded. "Now, my whole damn team needs coffee at the same time? That paperwork won't complete itself. Get to it!"

The rest of the workday passed uneventfully. Captain Hansen was marginally less furious with them after Stonequest's visit, but there was still a ton of forms to fill out to put the entire investigation in Dragon SWAT's hands and out of hers. Unsurprisingly, she wanted this paperwork done even more thoroughly than usual.

When the day finally finished, Kristen actually looked forward to airsoft. If they all decided to team up against her, she'd have no choice but to use her powers to show them what happened when you messed with the Steel Dragon.

She drove to the location Hernandez had given her and stopped only once for burgers. They'd probably go out to eat after the game, but being the Steel Dragon and a Hall meant she had a killer appetite.

Apparently, no one else had her appetite. When she reached the airsoft course, the team was already there, huddled together and talking in hushed voices. They grew even quieter as she approached, which meant she knew exactly what they were talking about.

"So it's the humans versus the dragon, huh?" she said.

Hernandez, Beanpole, and Butters actually blushed. Keith only grinned and stuck his tongue out.

Drew raised an eyebrow but didn't look embarrassed at all. "We've been practicing tactical maneuvers with you on the team but now, you can try going solo." Obviously, the idea of airsoft being fun totally escaped his mind.

"I'm not gonna lie, I'm excited about putting a dragon in her place." Jim grinned at her. "Although everyone needs to be careful if she picks a chair up. I've seen her stop a professional death squad with nothing more than that."

Kristen rolled her eyes at her friends. "You know what? Bring it. I'll keep my skin normal so I can feel if any of you actually hurt me but if it's the six of you, I won't slow down."

"We wouldn't dream of it, Hall," Drew retorted. "Now, mind your sightlines. We'll come at you from every angle."

Oh, wow, it really was no wonder he didn't come on these little excursions.

A shadow fell upon them as something massive flew between the setting sun and the ground.

"What the shit was that?" Keith stammered, held his hand up to block the sun, and tried to see whatever had flown over.

Wingbeats generated great gusts of air. Beanpole and Butters looked at each other, then aimed their airsoft guns like they were assault rifles. Hernandez only squared her jaw and glanced toward her bag. There were explosives in there, then. Jim sneered. He seemed to understand that if a dragon chose to attack them, airsoft guns and firecrackers wouldn't do a damn thing against it.

Only Drew looked unalarmed.

Another flap of wings was followed by the smell of powdered limestone and a cloud of dust, and a dragon landed before them.

Kristen sighed a breath of relief. It wasn't Shadowstorm. She had panicked, thinking it was him, but now that it wasn't, she was merely curious. This dragon was smaller than him, with mostly orange scales with touches of black here and there, almost like a tiger. What was most unusual, though, were his scales. They reminded her of the marble in the Fisher Building's lobby and looked like they were made of stone. Marble maybe, as they had flecks of crystal in them and sparkled in the setting sun.

The dragon took a step forward, then another, and flapped its wings to release another burst of dust that smelled of limestone. The cloud billowed, but when she was about to hold her hands up to protect her face, it dissipated and a man stood in its place.

"Stonequest." Drew grinned like he'd completed a perfect bust. "I'm so glad you could make it."

"This is your guest?" Hernandez demanded in a strangled tone.

"I thought we could use some help on the team," the team leader said and caught the woman's eye.

Kristen understood before she did. They would all go against her, Stonequest included. Everyone else finally seemed to understand as nods and grins passed between her team. *Not my team, a group of chumps who are about to learn what's what.*

Stonequest was oblivious to this communication of nudges and glances like the humans were oblivious to the auras exchanged between her and the newcomer. Her aura was one of surprise, then confidence, and finally, challenge.

His aura attempted to make her feel outnumbered while he simultaneously drummed up courage in the humans. A useful ability that, she thought, to be able to make an enemy feel one thing and allies another. She realized he was smiling at her. He wanted her to see what his aura was capable of.

"Neat trick," she said.

He nodded, impressed. "I know you went to Shadowstorm for additional training. I had assumed he taught you something about auras after the captain's office."

She held his stare, unsure of what to say, and simply went with, "Sorry." She wasn't able to put any emotion into the word at all, so it sounded hollow and fake. "If Shadowstorm hadn't trained me, I'd never have been able to take him on."

"I understand. Dragons usually learn their abilities under the supervision of a senior…although it's been a while since anyone's needed to learn the basics."

"So, you're not mad I worked with him?" Kristen had wondered how all that worked. In a political system that rested on reputation like the dragon's world seemed to, she had wondered if learning at his wings would have been disastrous to her reputation, fresh as it was.

"I understand why you did it. We shouldn't have kept you at arm's length, but your position as a human is…interesting. We wanted you to learn how they enforce their laws," he explained.

"She didn't exactly go by the book," Jim interjected.

"I know, and I don't like that Shadowstorm knows more about you than I do. From here on out, I'd rather you work with someone I trust."

"Great." She tried to keep the sarcasm out of her voice and failed spectacularly. "Who is this Mary Poppins of the dragon world you've found to babysit the Steel Dragonling?" She hadn't intended all the sarcasm, but Marty—the queen of sarcasm—was her mom. Sometimes, she couldn't help it any more than she could help taking seconds at dinner.

Stonequest hesitated, then scratched his head. "I've been called a lot of things over the centuries, but what is a merry popping?"

Everyone laughed, Kristen included.

"When do I meet the coach?" she asked again.

He looked confused. "We start tonight."

"Oh," she said rather dumbly when she realized she'd been talking to her new teacher for a while now.

The dragon—noticing that she finally understood—held his airsoft rifle up. "Are you ready to see what a dragon can do with one of these things?"

Drew also held his rifle up. So did Butters and Beanpole, who barely hid their grins. Keith and Hernandez looked downright diabolical.

"So…seven against one?" she said and studied her team and the dragon they now surrounded. "That sounds good to me. Maybe, just maybe, now that you all have a ringer, you'll last more than a minute against me."

"This is what you've wanted, right, Hall? A chance to test your dragon powers?" Drew asked.

"Well…I guess? You guys are so whiny when I beat you, I'm merely not sure it'll be any different this time. I'm not sure I can stand the blow-back if I beat all of you by myself." She laughed. If there was one thing she'd learned on SWAT, it was how to talk shit.

"Then let's even the odds," Jim said and left the team to stand at her side.

"I thought I was a dragon and you didn't like my kind," she joked.

"I still don't like dragons much." He eyed Stonequest as he said this. "I think history shows what they've done with their power to people and that many of them are callous and cruel, but it'd be foolish to keep acting like all of you are the same. You saved my life, Kristen, more than once at this point. I'd be a fool not to fight on your side."

He lowered his weapon and reached out for a handshake. She could see the respect in his eyes fighting against his own prejudices. But whatever he felt internally, he did his best to treat her respectfully and that was what mattered.

But a handshake? What was he, her boss?

She wrapped him in a great big bear hug, lifted him off the ground, and squeezed, flexing her dragon strength to do so.

"So…we're cool then?" He wheezed from the crushing hug.

Kristen put him down and shook his hand anyway.

"That all depends on if you can take down that dragon over there." She gestured to Stonequest.

"He's mine. You handle all the puny mortals." Jim fake-sneered.

"Who are you calling puny?" Butters laughed louder at his own joke than anyone else.

The speakers in the arena came to life. "All right, all right, all right. Tactical teams into position. Round one of the evening is about to start."

Kristen and Jim ran into the arena and prepared to defeat their friends.

"I really do owe you," he said as they took cover behind a canvas tarp stretched between two trees.

"You can start your debt by pretending to shoot the folks who saved my life."

He grinned wickedly. "Sometimes, I really fucking love being a cop."

She found that, hard as it was, she really liked it too. There was nothing she'd rather do with her life or her abilities than protect the people around her.

Especially if that meant giving all your friends welts and making them buy you a beer afterward.

The klaxon blared for the match to begin.

CHAPTER FIFTY-ONE

The foolish beasts crowded in front of Sebastian Shadowstorm displayed nothing resembling intelligence. They were cattle to be herded, nothing more. One day, he would rule them—or roast their flesh and make them suffer for not asking to be ruled sooner. How anyone could think these creatures were worthy of anything more than being fed table scraps by their betters was beyond the black dragon's ability to comprehend. Yes, they used tools, but so did crows, and at least crows understood that they were scavengers.

A blaring horn dragged him from his thoughts.

"The light is green. Let's fucking go."

He scowled into his rearview mirror. "I am going, you plebian cockroach," he roared out the window of the 1982 VW bug he currently drove. Humans lauded their inventions, their mastery of machines and medicine, electricity, and frozen pictures, and yet for all their ingenuity, they had invented traffic.

"Well, go faster or I'll cram my fucking truck up your asshole."

Human beings were disgusting, crass creatures. And yet, this ape had the right of it. The traffic light was green, and it was his turn to go. He admired the efficiency of the systems humans used to govern their day to day activities. At this intersection, all of them bowed to the color of the streetlights without a second thought. Soon, they'd put the same colors on pine trees they'd bring into their homes and virtually worship the things. It really was pathetic.

His scowl deepened as he eased his foot down onto the gas pedal and the car lurched out and across the intersection. No sooner had he moved forward than the man in the truck behind him raced around his vehicle and leaned pointedly on his car's horn as he went.

Sebastian stuck his massive arm out the tiny window of the VW bug and raised his middle finger at the man. It was a human gesture that worked as both an insult and a threat. He found it was rather delightful to use.

Or it was until the man in the truck's passenger seat threw a cup of carbonated sugar water out the open window at him and soaked the sleeve of his black suit.

In that moment, it took every speck of control the dragon had learned over his centuries of life to not transform into his true shape, spread his wings, peel the man out of his truck, and devour him like a human would a canned sardine. How pleasurable it would be to reach out to the clouds and summon the rain and the wind. It would begin to storm and the man in the truck would start to worry about the road. In the blink of an eye, a shadow would eclipse the lightning raging in the sky and the man would be no more than dead meat.

But he didn't transform, nor did he summon a storm or bolts of lightning. He didn't even flex his aura and make the man fail to pay attention to the road and crash his obnoxious vehicle.

He was in hiding among humans, so he had to behave as one, as demeaning as that might be. Fortunately, he understood the gravity of his situation enough to control himself. The man in the truck was merely a human. Not an enemy, simply an annoyance. Sebastian Shadowstorm had enemies who could do far worse than make his suit sticky. Until they could be defeated or undermined, he would deal with the insults.

Besides, traffic wasn't that bad a behavior for humans. The dragon had lived through both the Inquisition before he'd left Europe and the slavery in the new world. Compared to their own past, humans of the modern era were downright peaceful.

Unlike his enemies.

They thought they'd driven him from the Motor City, and he couldn't betray his position for petty revenge. He'd been in hiding for a few weeks, and Dragon SWAT didn't seem to have any inkling about where he was. Centuries of practice had taught him to control his aura better than almost any other dragon, which meant he could hide it from most of them. Currently, hiding his abilities was the only skill he was able to practice, and even that hadn't always worked, not against everyone anyway.

But it did seem to work against Dragon SWAT, and that was what mattered. As long as he remained in Detroit, he was in a position of power. He'd spent decades building up his network of humans to serve him here. This was where his base of power was, and this was where he could most easily take action if he wanted to.

Or if it was demanded of him.

Another driver—apparently fed up with the VW bug's reasonable speed of twenty-five miles an hour—accelerated around him and cut him off, honking its infernal horn the entire time.

How he wished he had his chauffeur and his limousine right now, but he'd been ordered to come alone and come discreetly, and he had no choice but to obey. Besides, he hardly fit in the tiny car on his own. If Tyler were driving, he wouldn't have fit at all.

Plus—although he didn't really like to admit it—he liked Tyler. No, not liked but appreciated his service. He was an efficient, well-trained servant who was more loyal to his master than he was to his own pathetic species, and it would be a pity—no, not a pity, he told himself, but a waste of resources—to lose the man over a car ride.

Sebastian turned down Sand Bar Lane and drove to the end of the street. He parked his car, squeezed out of the small door of the tiny vehicle, and assessed the meeting place. It was humiliating. He'd been told to keep a low profile and remain discreet and yet he'd been ordered to meet at a restored steam-powered paddleboat—the only one in the city, in fact.

The vessel had been built close to a century before, but one wouldn't know that by looking at it. A fresh coat of white paint practically sparkled in the afternoon sun, the perfect foil for a red paddlewheel and two gleaming smokestacks. Despite the boat being more than twice as old as his VW bug, it looked newer, nicer, and far more glamorous. From its interior came the sounds of a string quartet and the smells of roasted meat. It was the most garish spectacle he had seen in weeks, and it filled him with pangs of jealousy.

He'd abandoned his mansion and moved into a tiny, roach-infested motel. For too long, he had eaten fast food and done nothing for entertainment besides watching television and trying to familiarize himself with the phenomenon that had taken his power from him—the Internet. Now, he was confronted with all he'd lost. There was something absolutely decadent about living the luxuries of decades past while the world raced forward. Obviously, the owner of the paddleboat felt the same way and wanted him to see it and suffer.

Or maybe not.

Maybe—just maybe, if everything went right—he could earn his place back and more. It wasn't his fault, after all. It was Kristen's. How he hated the steel dragon and her allies on Dragon SWAT. He could have defeated her and had been tantalizingly close, but she had outwitted him with that infernal smartphone. But he'd learned from that and knew it was her understanding of the modern world—the human world—which had given her an edge. He would simply have to make it clear that it wouldn't happen again and he was sure that the Masked One would understand. After all, a string quartet playing from a gilded paddleboat wasn't exactly typical human behavior.

Dragons looked down on the obsession with inventions humans had taken up in the last century or so. Every year, there seemed to be something new. The Masked One undoubtedly knew the new kinds of music and transportation in the world, but he chose to live in the past. Hopefully, he could make the powerful dragon see that they shared the same faults.

Sebastian straightened his shoulders, rubbed the crick in his neck that had come from cramming himself into the tiny VW, and walked up the gangway and onto the ship.

The interior of the vessel was even more garish than the outside. Meticulously carved pillars supported a ceiling that was painted with images of dragons guiding humans through their own history. The winged creatures stood over fields of battle, on ships sent to discover new lands, and above the kings and politicians who derived their power from the scraps of the dragons' table.

If only those idiots honking their horns could see this. Maybe then, they'd understand how insignificant their species truly was.

He started down a gorgeous winding spiral staircase that led to a ballroom with a marble floor. On the far side of the ballroom, the string quartet played beautifully for a room full of dancers. Men and women danced elegantly to music that had existed for centuries. Despite their fine clothes and graceful movements, he didn't sense a dragon among them. He smiled slightly at the show of power. The Masked One's power was such that he could conduct his business in front of all these people. They would obey his every whim and corroborate every story. The scene was a discomforting reminder that the thugs he had employed were little more than disposable muscle.

It was an irritating thought and he pushed it aside as he walked across the dance floor, looking for the man who had summoned him. He couldn't be dancing, right? No. He looked at the clock on the far side of the room. 6:01. Technically, they should already be talking but he couldn't find who he was looking for. Still, he wasn't naïve enough to think that his superior wouldn't hold that against him.

"Shadowstorm," a man all but growled, a human dressed in a tuxedo with a pointed mustache.

"What?" he snapped in response.

"Do not speak to the servant of your master thus. You have failed. Do not forget this."

"He's summoned me."

"The Masked One waits above. He likes to watch the dancers to see which of them does not fit into the choreography. Such carelessness makes a thing of carefully planned beauty into a flailing mess."

Sebastian nodded. The parallels to his own situation were not lost on him. He followed the man up another staircase to find the Masked One seated on a throne.

Well, not a throne exactly, more like an overstuffed red velvet chair with gilded, clawed legs and elaborate armrests. The chair stood beside a small table on which rested a single drink in a martini glass. He wasn't foolish enough to think he would be offered one until the dragon wished to make a point. Nor was he foolish enough to complain about the metal folding chair the servant gestured at him to sit on.

He ignored the human.

The Masked One wore a dark, blood-red robe with the hood up. His skin was middling-brown, although he could see little of his facial features as he wore the front part of a human skull over his face. This, of course, was why he was called the Masked One. Despite Sebastian's disdain for mankind, it was still uncomfortable to see one of their skulls worn like a mask.

"Sit," the Masked One ordered.

Sebastian sat.

"My lord, forgive me," he begged, took the other man's hand, and kissed one of the golden rings.

"I am not one to forgive, Shadowstorm. You know this. I occasionally give second chances, although I see little reason to do so now."

"My lord, I beg you, one more chance."

"And why should I do this? Detroit was supposed to be crumbling into chaos by now. They've had their little time in the sun, but for my plans to continue, this city must fall."

"Yes, my lord, of course it must."

"Then why hasn't it?"

At that moment, the string quartet stopped playing. He hadn't listened to the music enough to know if the song had ended or if this was some kind of code. Silence descended as he scrambled for things to say. What would the Masked One believe? The truth? But the truth was dangerous in that it was not what had been planned. It had been his own plan, and it had failed. But should he lie to the Masked One? What if the other dragon saw through his deception?

A burst of impatience pulsed from the Masked One's aura. It was a powerfully uncomfortable thing to be swayed by another dragon's aura, and rare too. He'd thought himself immune to such things and yet now, the words poured out of his mouth as quickly as the fingers of musicians in the string quartet when they started their new song.

"My lord, it's all the Steel Dragon's fault. I had the city on the precipice of chaos. Gangs were ready to raze the place and she appeared and… Well, I failed to anticipate her."

"Failed. Yes. That is the word for it, isn't it?"

He slid off his chair and knelt at the Masked One's feet. Even bowed, he was massive and much larger than the seated dragon's diminutive frame, but he knew there was far more to power than brute strength.

"Please, my lord, please. I beg you—only one more chance. One more. I will finish what I have started."

"Can you even do such a thing? Now, Dragon SWAT knows who you are. They know your face. The identity of Mr Black is worthless. You have masked your aura thus far, but they will find you in time."

"No, my lord, not with the gifts you've given me, not with the powers you've opened up to me. I can evade them. I can finish the mission."

"And how will you do that? Buy this pesky Steel Dragon a cup of coffee and try to convert her to your cause?" The Masked One laughed at his words. Clearly, he found them ridiculous.

"I was wrong, my lord, truly I was." Sebastian spoke to the floor, not daring to look up and face the skeletal mask of the stronger dragon. "I thought I could sway her to our side, that I could get to her before the other dragons infected her mind with their laughable moral codes and humane principals. But she is too far gone—worse even than Dragon SWAT. She believes herself to be a human and I was not able to make her see the truth of the matter."

"And could you find out where she was from? What made her?"

His heart began to pound in his chest—harder and harder, faster and faster, repeating the same message again and again. *You failed. You failed. You failed.*

"I...I did not find out that information, my lord."

"We have spoken much of your failure today, Shadowstorm. Tell me now of how you plan to fix this mess."

The pounding in his ears began to lesson. He would be given another chance. But he wasn't out of the caverns yet. If he said something wrong, he had no doubt that his position of privilege in the Masked One's organization would crumble and make his current lodgings at a cheap human hotel look downright decadent.

"Detroit will fall, my lord. There is a history of inequality here. The city is ripe for destruction despite the false wealth it currently displays. It was only the Steel Dragon who stopped me. I will stop her now, though. I underestimated her and thought I could manipulate her, but I see that I cannot. I have already found a tool capable of removing her. Once her work is done, the rest of the city will fall."

"And if your tool fails? What then?"

"She will not, my lord. I assure you, she will not."

"And if she does?"

"Then I will finish the job, my lord. I will kill the Steel Dragon with my own talons if I must, and I will light this city on fire."

"That will have to do, then, Shadowstorm. And truly, it must. If you continue to slow my plans, you are useless to me—worse than useless. If you think this tool of yours will do the job, by all means, wield the tool. But if it fails, you will complete the task. If you don't, I will show you how to deal with this steel dragon and it is not a lesson I have ever given twice."

"Yes, my lord. I understand."

"Do you? Let me be crystal clear. Failure is no longer an option for you, not if you want to keep your scales intact. Understood?"

Sebastian nodded.

"Good. Rise, Shadowstorm. Have a drink, and if you'll excuse me, I must dance."

There was nothing he wanted less than to sit in that uncomfortable chair and sip a drink while he watched the Masked One, but the alternative was far worse.

So, he sat and accepted a drink. He sipped it slowly while the Masked One walked down the spiral staircase to the ballroom floor.

He could at least admit that the drink was good. While he had never been one to get drunk and preferred to be in control, the taste of alcohol—that delicious burn—was something special. Not that the dragon would have guzzled grain alcohol from the bottle like humans did when they reveled in their pathetic mortality. The drink in front of him was far from that, though.

It tasted of cinnamon, orange peel, and a hint of cherry. That combined with the whiskey was something heavenly. Humans did have their inventions that were worth keeping. It amazed him that the same creatures who let their grain rot into alcohol had also learned how to elevate the intoxicating poison to such levels of beauty.

The Masked One reached the bottom of the staircase and discarded his red robe to reveal a tuxedo of the same dark-red color beneath. The skull mask covered his entire head and looked like it had been cobbled together from different skulls over the years and fused with dragon fire. The horrible helmet of death was both garish and grisly, marvelous and macabre.

He approached a pair of dancers and gestured for the man to approach, which of course he immediately obeyed. Sebastian had felt the pulse of power. There was no way the man could have resisted the dragon lord's power in that moment.

The dancer stood in front of the Masked One.

"Sixteen measures back, you had a misstep," the dragon said to the human.

"Yes, sir, Alicia's dress tangled on my shoe, and I—"

"This is when you stop talking, boy."

The man wisely shut up. Perhaps boy really was a better word for him, though. He couldn't have been more than twenty years old.

"When you are dancing, the man must be the dragon and the woman the cattle that is humankind. You are to lead her and steer her.

Her clothes are your clothes, her body your body. A failure to properly control her is a failure of yours."

"What should I have done, sir?"

"Shut. Up. Boy," the Masked one snarled. "I was speaking. You should have slit the little whore's throat and demanded better."

"But, sir, it was only a mistake!"

"Enough," the dragon said and waved his hand almost lethargically in front of the dancer's face. At least it would seem lethargic to a human. Sebastian saw the hidden movements, the godlike speed, and the hand that transformed into a dragon's claws and severed the front of the skull and face from the rest of the boy's head.

The victim, though, saw none of this. One moment, he stood in silence and the next, his face was simply gone, a bloody hole where there had once been the young features of a boy, soon to be a man.

He fell back screaming and writhed in pain while blood poured from the wound and down his throat.

The Masked One peeled the skin from the skull as easily as a human peeled a banana, removed his own mask—he turned away when he did this, of course—and put the fresh skull to his face, connected it to his bizarre helmet, and gestured for the string quartet to begin playing again.

They complied as if nothing at all had happened. In fact, none of the dancers screamed or ran despite the dance floor now being slick with one of their group's blood. Instead, they danced, and Sebastian understood that they had all seen this horrible display of brutality before. Yet they had returned because they understood that to not return was to die equally as horribly.

The Masked One reached out for the dead boy's partner, Alicia. She swallowed, took his hand, and waltzed through the remains of her last partner. If she felt anything, she did a better job of hiding it than Sebastian did.

The ice in his hand clinked because his hand shook. He swallowed, wiped his brow, and downed the rest of the drink. Surely the Masked One had made his point. He possessed a level of power that he could not match and a level of influence that was almost absurd.

Throughout the centuries, ballroom dancers had consistently come from the upper class. They were typically a larger part of society than the thugs and cretins he had employed. His mind marveled at the boy's death. Surely the child had family, friends, probably professors and classmates in a university, or contacts at work. To all those people, he would simply disappear. He knew this simply because no one talked about these things. People would go missing and go uninvestigated, and it was because of dragons like the Masked One and the power they held.

There were forces of power in the world that Sebastian Shadowstorm had always resented. The Dragon Council and their childlike morals and creeds. Dragon SWAT with their pathetic attempt to mimic human law enforcement. Even the Circle of Mages was an obnoxious force of rule-keepers.

But as he watched these humans waltz through the blood of their dead companion, he thought he would have preferred all their arguing and proselytizing to this wanton display of death.

And yet this was who he had thrown his lot in with. He'd made his choice long ago, and he couldn't change it any more than a human could hope to become a dragon.

Sebastian snarled at the thought. For centuries, that phrase had kept humans cowed. Even their bravest leaders—warriors and kings, politicians and poets—had never dared challenge the power structure the dragons had built. They'd conducted their wars with each other, gobbled resources, and built their cities, all because they'd known that to do otherwise was impossible. Humans were not dragons and never could be. They understood that they were but rats.

Or they had.

The Steel Dragon's emergence from the human population had changed all that. The Masked One was right about her. They needed to unravel her past and reveal it to the world. Then, humanity would see what had always been true—that dragons were born of dragons, and that humans would forever be beneath them.

He believed this with all his heart and yet, to see it displayed so grotesquely on the dance floor below him was beyond his ability to enjoy. Humans' place in the world was to serve dragons with their clever little monkey minds. It was a waste to treat them as nothing more than dancing meat.

When he regained his position, he could restore them to their place as the preferred servant of dragon-kind, but not if Kristen Hall continued to live. Not if the world continued to think of her as a human with dragon powers who was capable of thwarting the true rulers of this world.

Terrified and more certain than ever of his mission, he left the boat when the next song ended. He would destroy the Steel Dragon. There was no other option.

CHAPTER FIFTY-TWO

"I wish I could do that when the nurse tries to give me a needle."

Kristen Hall smiled at the eight-year-old patient in the hospital and turned her body back to skin instead of steel. The little boy gasped in awe. He'd obviously heard of Detroit's famous Steel Dragon, but hearing wasn't quite the same as seeing. "But then you couldn't get your medicine."

"My medicine makes my hair fall out. I hate it."

She nodded and honestly didn't know what to say to him as she'd never had a family member suffer from cancer. Her grandparents had all died from heart disease, so this was an ailment she wasn't familiar with, and it seemed especially cruel to be affecting kids.

Even being in a hospital wing was relatively new to her. She'd been once when her brother had broken his arm, but her grandparents had died when she was little and her parents were still blessedly healthy—although her father would end up there soon if he didn't change his diet and start exercising.

This room was weird. There were beds up and down the sides of the room and sheets with cute printed designs of animals, princesses, or spaceships. Beside each bed was some kind of monitoring machine. Most were turned off. Many of the kids in the room didn't need them

STEEL DRAGON 1

while they were there, but the message was clear—death is nearby, children. Never forget it.

The center of the room had a large, brightly colored carpet with the alphabet printed on it. Most of the kids sat on it, choosing some semblance of normalcy despite being stuck in the hospital. The little boy in front of her looked up and scratched his head. Before her very eyes, another patch of his buzzed hair fell out.

She was aghast. It was difficult to admit that such suffering still existed in the world. While she spent her time trying to help people, things like leukemia still took lives. It made her wonder if the mages the dragons controlled could use their magic to heal this little boy's blood disease. She didn't know, nor did she know what to say.

He touched her beautiful red hair and smiled wistfully as he did so. That gave her an idea. "I wish my hair would fall out sometimes."

"Nuh-uh," the boy said, but he smiled.

"No, really, I do. The last time I fought a dragon, he pulled me by the hair. If my head was nice and smooth like yours, I might've won that fight."

"Can't you just transform into a dragon?" the boy asked. Despite his innocence, the words still hurt.

It was a barb under her skin that she hadn't yet learned to transform into a dragon. At the same time, a part of her didn't want to.

"I like being in a human body. It reminds me that I'm related to cool people like you."

His face soured. "I'm not cool. I'm sick."

Kristen nodded. She didn't know what to say, only that she'd gone too far. She felt like this always happened. Fortunately, another kid chimed in before she had to justify herself.

"There's no way you lose fights," a girl with two broken legs said. She'd watched from her wheelchair and inched forward slowly when she thought the dragon trapped in a human body wouldn't notice. Her dragon senses had detected each scoot forward, though.

"Oh, she most certainly does. She may be the Lost Dragon, but she's still a slowpoke when it comes to the lounge." Butters smiled. He currently allowed a three-year-old to climb over his massive belly. Of everyone on SWAT, the big southerner was by far the most comfortable with kids.

The rest of the team stood awkwardly around the visitor's area of the children's hospital. She considered it a small miracle that Lyn Hernandez hadn't cussed out any kids yet. She was sure that she would, though, given enough time.

Currently, Hernandez stood silently in the corner, a long-sleeved shirt hiding her tattoos and a scowl on her face. It didn't remain in place for much longer. A small boy had snuck up on her and thrown the paper wrapper from a straw at her when she hadn't been looking. The two of them now conducted a clandestine projectile battle. The boy sat a few feet away from her with his back to her, but as soon as she raised a balled-up post-it note, he spun and giggled. She scowled at him and he only laughed harder and threw another straw wrapper at her. Kristen was impressed. She'd seen hardened criminals wither under that look.

"What's the lounge?" the girl with broken legs asked Butters. "Is that like police talk for jail or something? Is that like…like when you chase criminals into a standoff and you're all, like, 'get in the lounge, you piece of poop!'" The sniper laughed and Kristen joined him. Someone's mommy had let her daughter watch way too many cop shows.

"The lounge is where Butters gets all his donuts. Remember kids, watch what you eat," Keith said and nodded like he was on a public service announcement from the 1950s. He looked like the archetypal strait-laced cop—short hair, strong jaw, slightly narrowed blue eyes, and folded arms. Virtually everything he'd said had sounded like he was auditioning for the alter ego of a cheesy superhero. Still, despite his stiff posture and phony smile, the kids laughed at the mention of donuts.

Kristen smiled and stood. Butters and Keith really were better at this than she was. But they weren't the Lost Dragon or a steel dragon, so the newspapers cared little and less when they went to charity events without her.

Even there, in a ward for sick children in a hospital, her reputation had preceded her. Most of the kids knew who she was from the news and even those who didn't seemed to recognize her face. Not that she blamed them. A photographer currently snapped photographs of her smiling awkwardly instead of the little kid who clambered all over Butters or the two kids hanging off Drew's biceps.

The team leader wasn't much better at talking to the kids than she was, but at least he had a plan. He used the children as weights. Already, he'd bench-pressed an eleven-year-old boy who weighed far too much for his age and currently did curls with the two giggling children. They didn't seem to see him as human but more as a moveable jungle gym. That made sense to her. The man was massive. He stood well over six feet and had broad shoulders and a physique that indicated considerable time spent sculpting in the gym. She hoped they could keep him away from the kid in the wheelchair. It wouldn't be a surprise to see him attempt to squat her.

"Can I have your autograph?" a little girl asked Kristen.

"Sure, of course." She signed the cast on the child's arm. The patient appraised the signature and finally nodded. She seemed to want to be sure Kristen hadn't forged her own handwriting.

"Your steel means you can't break bones, right? I'm so jealous."

"You really shouldn't be," said Jim Washington, the Wonderkid.

"You shouldn't say 'should' to people," the girl stated matter-of-factly. "That's what my mom says."

"No, you should not," Jim said, no irony in his voice despite her using the contraband word. Kristen had to admit the Wonderkid was good at visiting with the kids, but that was hardly surprising. He was good at all things police work, even public outreach. That was why they called him the Wonderkid, after all. Her newest teammate would be exhausting if he wasn't so damn good at his job.

He was the black cop version of Keith's white cop, but while Keith looked kind of cheesy trying to smile and look stern at the same time, Washington looked at ease. The perfect balance of friendly professionalism—like the big brother who told you to do your homework but helped you the second you asked.

If he didn't keep glancing at the windows and the doorway, he might've looked friendly. But the kids noticed his paranoid mannerisms and mostly avoided him.

"Why shouldn't I be jealous?" the little girl asked.

"Because if the Steel Dragon walks past a magnet, it sticks to her," Jim said.

The girl nodded and considered this. Finally, she looked at Kristen with pity in her eyes. "Magnets are cool, miss. I'm sorry you can't play with them."

"Actually, as long as I'm—" She was cut off when the Wonderkid elbowed her in the ribs.

"It's a real pity, right, miss?" He raised an eyebrow at her. With a look, he was able to tell her not to pop the kid's bubble. Okay, so maybe he was better with children than she realized.

"Yeah, a real shame," she said, embarrassed that she had been about to tell a kid that she could simply turn her steel skin off when she wanted to. None of these children could do that with injuries. The weight of that sat heavily on her conscience. She had to use her abilities to protect people like this—people who couldn't protect themselves—even if she was as awkward as all get out.

The door to the visitor's room creaked open and Beanpole, the last member of their team, walked in. He was tall and lanky and looked at the kids the way a corndog might look at a flock of pigeons—equal parts terror and utter lack of comprehension.

"They're ready for you downstairs, Kristen." He didn't step any farther into the room than he had to. His discomfort made her feel better. Beanpole was an excellent SWAT member and yet children frightened him. She felt much the same way.

She nodded and trudged toward him. Despite her being awkward with kids, she greatly preferred their company to the press conferences the captain had made her do.

Since they'd driven Mr Black into hiding, the city of Detroit had experienced a period of relative calm. For the first week of the criminal mastermind's disappearance, SWAT had been on high alert, waiting for the dragon to retaliate with another team of thugs or mercenaries, but the expected strike never came.

After a few more weeks, Captain Hansen put Kristen on public relations detail. She'd already visited the homeless shelter, the home for battered women, a whole slew of events at community centers, the police gala, and now, the children's hospital. In all honesty, she much preferred being shot at to public speaking. At least her ability to transform into steel protected her from bullets. She didn't know what to do about rude journalists.

As she followed Beanpole down the stairs, she tried to tell herself that it wasn't all bullshit. She knew it was important to build goodwill toward the Detroit police department and that it was important for people across the country to see that the Steel Dragon was more committed to people than the other dragons who manipulated mankind from afar. Unfortunately, she couldn't help thinking about Mr Black.

He was still out there, no doubt plotting another way to throw the city into chaos. She should be out there finding him. True, she hadn't sensed his aura since Dragon SWAT had driven him out of his mansion, but that didn't mean he was gone. She had trained with him for weeks and she didn't believe he was the kind of dragon to simply abandon his plans.

"Are you ready for this?" Beanpole asked when they reached the first floor.

"Are you serious? Of course not. I sound as awkward as hell when I'm on TV. I'm glad they never play my whole speeches and only edit them."

"You're fine out there," he said and the encouragement sounded entirely phony.

"No, she's not. Kristen makes me look like a motherfucking poet laureate," Hernandez said and darted out the door from the stairway and into the hallway with them.

"You know, that's not exactly what I need right now," Kristen said.

"Whatever, Red. I'm only trying to help. If I can make you laugh, maybe you won't look like a damn deer in the headlights up there." The woman stuck her tongue out.

"And you being terrified of a room full of children has nothing to do with you coming down here?" she retorted sharply.

"I'm scared of the little shits. I can admit that. I'd take a bullet for one of them but fuck, did you see the snot on that one boy? I can only describe the color as radioactive. That shit's scarier than an M-16."

"They're not that bad," she said and tried to sound like she meant it, although she failed spectacularly.

"Right, yeah, and neither is public speaking. Come on, you've literally taken bullets, been exploded, and fought a dragon fist to claw. There's no logical reason why a crowd of rich fucking hospital donors who merely want to throw money around and feel good about themselves should freak you out, right?" Hernandez grinned. Oh, how she loved pestering her teammate during these events.

"You know, maybe you should go up there in my place," Kristen suggested. "Getting some Latina representation up there might be good for the force. Plus, you're a demolitions expert. You could talk about that gang we defeated. People still ask me for technical details about it."

"Yeah…see… Fuck that. For starters, there are real advantages to saying fuck every other fucking word. Captain Hansen used to ask me to make speeches about sexism and all that shit when I first started. She had this bullshit reverse-racism angle too, but I told her I wasn't fucking sure if I could control my shit-talking tongue and she stopped asking."

"What about you, Beanpole? Do you want to field the questions for me? At least you're well-spoken."

"Well, yes, er…that is, I don't swear like Hernandez does, but that doesn't mean I like crowds either. I'm with her. I'd take a bullet before I take a microphone."

"Gee, wow. You two are great at pep-talks." She gritted her teeth as they reached the functions room in the hospital. When she had first started attending these events, she'd thought that large rooms like these in hospitals or homeless shelters were wasteful. After seeing the money pour in after gatherings like this, however, she understood that they were actually a fundamental part of doing work for the less fortunate. Getting donors was the paperwork of the non-profit world—essential if less than glamorous.

"And here she is," Captain Hansen said into the microphone. "The Lost Steel Dragon, Kristen Hall herself!"

Scattered applause ensued. The captain had tried to combine her two nicknames, but Kristen hated the sound of it. The Lost Dragon was cool enough on its own. It reminded people that she'd grown up as a human and that there might be other lost dragons out there. Steel Dragon was also cool—and at least it was accurate—but Lost Steel Dragon made her sound like she'd misplaced something.

The Lost Steel Dragon took the stage.

"Thank you all for coming today," she began weakly.

"How does it feel to know that Mr Black, the criminal mastermind who almost threw this city into chaos and very nearly killed you, is still out there?" a reporter yelled from the back.

She sighed, unsure of how to address the outburst. Honestly, she hated that he was still out there. It gave her a trace of comfort that she had stopped his plans and discovered that he had tried to sway her to his side, but she absolutely hated that he wandered free where he could cause more trouble. More than anything, she wanted to hunt him with Dragon SWAT. She wanted to find whatever hole he'd burrowed into and smoke him out like the pest he was.

But those weren't appropriate talking points.

According to Captain Hansen, SWAT had done its job and gotten Mr Black, AKA Sebastian Shadowstorm—Kristen was supposed to connect the two names for the public—out of Detroit, and the city was doing better because of it. The statistics certainly backed the captain up. There had been fewer shootings and far less of the assault-rifle, explosives-driven activity that had been the hallmark of the beginning of Kristen's career.

It didn't matter to the captain that Mr Black was still out there. As far as she was concerned, the dragon was out of her jurisdiction simply because he was a dragon and wasn't breaking any laws in the city. But Kristen knew that was only temporary.

She knew that Shadowstorm was merely biding his time. He'd

been in Detroit for more than a century. There was no way he would abandon the city. He surely had hiding places and contacts across the entire Motor City, and considering how he saw humans as little more than cattle, she was absolutely certain that even if they did catch one of his minions, the monster would simply kill them and sever the loose end.

But the captain didn't want her to talk about any of those details. She wanted her to talk about new crosswalks, speed traps, and how the police force would hold a fundraiser gala. While the police officer in her could appreciate where her commanding officer was coming from, the steel dragon didn't care about any of that. She'd been to more than enough of these events.

It was time she addressed the questions people asked about the issues they cared about. Which meant that she needed to speak her mind. It was time for the world to really hear the Steel Dragon.

She cleared her throat and the microphone immediately blared feedback. Even that was preferable to the tame questions so many reporters normally asked.

The sound settled and she opened her mouth to tell the reporter that the Steel Dragon wanted to fight for her city. Before she could speak, however, pain blossomed in her left shoulder.

Startled, she looked up to where tinkling glass caught the light like drifting stars. The window above and across from her had broken even before she heard the shot.

CHAPTER FIFTY-THREE

By the time Kristen flung herself prone, she had already turned her skin into steel, but the pain didn't go away.

She thought the actual moment of injury should have hurt the most. While she'd been shot dozens of times, it had always been while she wore her steel skin. With it, bullets felt like nothing more than mosquito bites. Still, when she'd talked to the team about it, she had the impression that the moment the bullet hit hurt the most. It seemed she was wrong.

It had hurt when it entered her shoulder but now, sprawled with her head down, it felt far worse—as if something writhed and twisted in the wound like a centipede hungry for her flesh. It wasn't only her shoulder that hurt either. Her entire left arm and some of her chest ached as well. Her limb, especially, felt like the nerves had been replaced with sulfuric acid from a car battery and her hand spasmed inside her steel skin. The sight of her own metal hand twitching and trembling reminded her where she was and that her pain was irrelevant in the situation.

The Steel Dragon couldn't think of herself when people were in danger.

Tentatively, she felt the wound, pulled her right hand away, and looked at her palm. There was no blood. Despite the fact that the bullet had obviously punched much deeper into her body than the skin, her ability to turn into steel was able to stop the flow of blood. Even touching the wound didn't hurt too much.

The pain came from inside her, from the tissues that had already been damaged.

But if she wasn't bleeding, she wouldn't bleed out, which meant she could and must protect these people.

Grimly, she pushed herself to her feet and immediately regretted using her left arm. She wavered slightly but had no sooner regained her balance when another shot caught her squarely in the chest. It was stopped by her bulletproof armor this time and she barely felt it.

Kristen rarely wore bulletproof armor anymore. It was unnecessary given her abilities, and with her habit of drawing enemy fire, she often damaged the vests way more than a regular officer would.

She'd worn it today only because Butters had insisted that the kids would get a kick out of it. He'd been wrong. All they'd wanted to see was Kristen's steel skin, but part of her was thankful that it was on. The bullet in her shoulder hurt so much more than expected. She didn't know if that was because the rifle was so powerful or because there was more to the bullet than the typical lead alloy.

A moment later, the sharp report from the weapon carried into the hospital. Wherever the shooter was, he was damn far away and yet somehow, he'd managed to hit her not once, but twice.

"Butters, shots fired to the southeast," she said into her radio. "The asshole's gotta be way out there. The bullets arrive before the sound does." She had to yell to be sure he'd hear her over the sound of the screaming patrons of the hospital.

Drew and Hernandez already led the evacuation and guided people away from the broken window. Kristen looked around for signs of anyone injured, but she didn't see any blood. The sniper had targeted her.

"I'm on the roof, Kristen. I have a few possible locations. I'll keep you posted."

"And be careful. This guy is damn good. If you step out of cover,

I'll kick your ass myself," Kristen told him. He had seniority over her but she couldn't help but tell him to keep safe.

"Are you all right? Drew said you were hit."

"I'm fine," she lied and glanced at her shoulder. There was a dimpled spot where the bullet went in but it wasn't a mass of bloody carnage. Still, she touched the back of it and only felt smooth skin. There was no exit wound and she grimaced. This would hurt like hell later.

"Hall, get the fuck out of there," Drew ordered.

She ignored him. The room was almost empty but one or two civilians still stumbled toward the exit in panic. She was obviously the hostile's target, but that didn't mean they were safe. If she left, the sniper might consider hurting an innocent to bring her back in.

Obviously, that wasn't even vaguely an option.

The first bullet had struck in the brief moment of time before she had been able to hear the shot. The sniper must have known about her ability and planned the distance of the attack accordingly.

But now she knew there was a sniper out there, she wouldn't drop her armor.

"Kristen, I think I have a location for the sniper," Butters said over the radio. "Do you see a nine-story apartment from where you are? It has a big sign on the front that says, 'move in immediately.'"

"Yeah, I see it. Straight through the broken window. He's gotta be there."

"Great. Good, now get out of his damn sightline. He might be a good shot but there's no other building he can get to where he could take a shot. If you stand clear of that building, you should be safe."

Obviously, she would do no such thing.

Instead, she turned toward the hole and glared defiantly at the sniper in the distance, even though he was much too far away for her to see.

At a flash of light from one of the rooms on the eighth floor—the third window over from her right—she held her right hand up between her and the shot that had been fired. If she hadn't possessed dragon speed, it might not have worked, but since she did, she was able to move her hand into position before the bullet covered the hundreds of meters.

It struck her palm and it hurt like hell.

Kristen didn't look at the wound. Instead, she simply lowered her hand, squared her shoulders, and continued to stare resolutely at the window while the last few stragglers in the room moved into the hallway.

Only then did she move and reached slowly for her radio, all the while keeping her eyes trained on the window that had been the origin of the flash. Another gunshot didn't appear, so she activated the device. "Eighth floor, third window from the right. He must have taken all his shots from there."

"I can confirm. I saw the last shot," Butters said.

"You mean the shot Hall was too damn stupid and stubborn to dodge," Drew yelled into the radio. "Now get the hell off the stage, Hall. Do you hope he tries a rocket on you next? Take cover. That's an order!"

She shook her head. A feeling had come over her—one she'd felt before but only since she'd been a dragon. It was a feeling of possession, that someone had tried to take what was hers. She recognized it as a sense of loyalty she felt to the people who served her. At least, that was how Shadowstorm had described it. She was still a human, though, which meant people didn't serve her. It was her job to defend them.

"Hall. *Hall!* Get out of there!" Drew ordered.

Sharply, she shook her head once more, reminded herself that Drew was her superior, and left the stage to take cover.

The auditorium was totally trashed. Apparently, wealthy donors flipped chairs and created chaos when they were terrified as much as the less wealthy did.

When she stepped from the auditorium and into the hallway, Drew was on a radio, confirming that units were already on the way to the site to try to apprehend the shooter. She could tell from his tone of voice that he knew what she did—by the time Detroit PD arrived, the sniper would be long gone. There was no chance that someone with that kind of skill and experience would also wait around for the cops to drive there and ascend eight flights of stairs to apprehend him.

Kristen considered apprehending him herself. She was fast—damn fast—and her training with Stonequest, the leader of Dragon SWAT, had improved her skills. If the hostile was a dragon, there was a chance she'd be able to sense his aura the way Shadowstorm had taught her.

But in the next moment, Keith was in her face and she knew that if she ran off, her team would follow her. None of them had steel skin, so that was the last thing she wanted.

"Holy crap, Kristen, are you okay?" Her teammate's eyes were wide and he stared at the pockmark in her left shoulder.

"Yeah. We're lucky he only shot at me. I'm fine."

"Are you sure? It looks like that one got through." He grimaced like he'd been tasked with removing a piece of roadkill from a sidewalk rather than assessing her injury. The look was too much for her. It was so damn human.

It made her smile, then laugh. She dropped her tough visage. "No, Keith, I'm not sure. Actually, it fucking hurts like hell." She tried vainly to maintain the smile and felt tears well in her eyes. Reality began to sink in. She was hurt—hurt bad—by someone else who thought they could kill the Steel Dragon. Her worst nightmare had come back to haunt her.

Keith grinned. "Don't expect me to pity you. You may have been shot more than the rest of us, but it doesn't count unless it breaks the skin." He put a hand on her other shoulder—the uninjured one—and held her eyes with his for a second. His look said far more than his words did, that he knew that she worried for herself and her friends and the city. That he knew there was nothing he could say and that they'd both signed up for this crazy, selfless job knowing they'd face enemies like this and yet it was still impossible to prepare for it. He didn't say any of that, because it wouldn't do for the whole damn team to burst into tears. So instead, his hand on her shoulder would have to do. And instead of crying, she would have to quip in response.

"So that last bust we had where that bullet grazed your neck and left a burn didn't count?" It was a joke about fear. He could have died and they all knew it, and yet he hadn't. When you were on SWAT, it meant you had to joke about it, as scary as it was.

"I got burned in the neck by a bullet! Of course that shit counted."

Kristen laughed again, which was a mistake. The pain in her left shoulder and arm flared and she had to close her eyes and grit her teeth.

"Holy shit, Kristen." Keith swallowed. The lack of blood had made him think she was less injured than she really was. Now, he understood. "Doctor! We need a doctor!" He rushed to her side as she sagged.

There was no way a human—any human—could support Kristen's weight when she had her steel armor engaged, but Keith tried. This simply meant that instead of collapsing onto the floor, she tumbled on top of him.

"Doctor! I need a doctor!" he bellowed from beneath her bulk.

Drew was there before any doctor was. She looked at him and shook her head to try to clear the tunnel-vision brought on by the intense pain.

"Drew. I'm fine… I only… I need some air," she mumbled and told herself she would be fine. There was no other option. She'd be all right because she had to be for her friends and for the city.

"Stop talking, Hall. You've been shot. You're probably going into shock."

A doctor raced over with two nurses. Between the five of them, they managed to lift her steel body onto a gurney and pushed her down the hall.

"It hurts, Drew," she said.

"I know, Hall. Getting shot hurts," he responded calmly.

"Like it really hurts," she repeated. The shock he had mentioned made sense to her. She couldn't think much beyond the idea that she was in trouble.

"I know, but look, Hall—it'll get worse before it gets better." He clenched his jaw. "That first shot hit you, Kristen. It was aimed at you.

The hostile must have known you would take the stage and had that position planned in advance."

"Obviously." She laughed. Oh, that was a mistake. Fresh pain wracked her shoulder. Her tunnel vision closed in until she couldn't see anything, only hear the calm, quick voices of the doctors and nurses, the sound of the gurney as it rolled through the hospital, and the squeak of shoes on tile.

A red blob blossomed in the middle of Kristen's perception and her vision returned. At first, it was merely bright white until it resolved into a circle connected to some kind of arm—a light mounted to the ceiling.

When she could finally see clearly, she turned her head to take in her surroundings. They had pushed her into a room with way too many lights. Everything was bright and white, the scrubs of the doctors and nurses the only color she could make out in the fluorescent glare. She missed the children's ward with its carpet and brightly colored pajamas. Here, the sense of urgency was palpable. Every monitor on the walls seemed essential and every machine waited to spring into action.

A nurse had already activated one of these machines, attached it to the patient, and cursed under her breath. Kristen had seen enough medical drama shows to know that the machine should display her pulse and blood pressure, but it was designed to read human flesh, not dragon steel.

"You're gonna need something stronger than that," she grumbled to the woman, who jumped when she heard her. Obviously, she'd thought her patient was unconscious.

"Kristen, shut up and listen to me. Whoever this person was, they were obviously a professional. The distance is…well, it's insane. It looks like it's over two thousand meters. They knew the bullet would hit you before the sound and probably counted on it. Also, that first one missed your Kevlar. That might have been sheer luck for them or it might have been exactly what they hoped for. A rifle like that might have been able to punch through your armor. We simply don't know."

"It didn't," she said and pointed to the place where the second round had been stopped by her body armor.

She thought about the hand she'd held up to stop the bullet. While she didn't think the bullet had punctured her steel skin, she also didn't think there had been no damage. She wondered if the impact had broken any of the bones in her hand. If it had, the shots that struck her chest could have done even worse.

"Catch the asshole," she grumbled and looked around the room. Hospital staff washed their hands and put breathing masks on. A nurse drew a table up and placed some kind of a bag on it. She unrolled what was simply a long piece of fabric with pockets to reveal dozens of steel implements—pincers, pliers, scalpels, knives, and clamps. With practiced movements, she slipped some of these implements a few inches out of their pockets, ready for easy access, no doubt. Kristen didn't like the looks of the tweezers the nurse seemed focused on. They would have to go inside her and that was a painful thought.

"Hall, stop moving. You need to let the doctors work."

"I'll be fine."

"Of course you will if you let them work. Think about it. If that sniper made all those preparations, he might have used a different kind of bullet."

"What are you talking about?" She knew, though. It terrified her, but she knew.

"He might've used a bullet that could kill a dragon. Don't you remember what Shadowstorm said? Lead wouldn't kill him. This guy might have taken the same precaution. Whoever he was, he targeted a dragon and seemed to know how to get under your skin."

"Yeah, well, it didn't work," Keith said and forced a grin. She had totally forgotten about him and had lost track of him when her vision had faded briefly. Gratitude for her teammates suffused her.

"It might still be doing its job, though," Drew snapped at the Rookie. "Hall, there's no exit wound—do you understand me? The bullet's still in there. We need to get it out. That's what I told the doctors and they agree. They're not familiar with your uh…physiology, but that doesn't mean they can't recognize effects. Your left arm... Well...it looks like your veins are rusting."

Kristen looked around the room, which bustled with activity. A nurse continued to attach sensors to her, but the machine they were connected to provided no useful information. It read her blood pressure as over three hundred and her pulse at zero beats per minute. Two doctors argued in hushed voices while they watched Drew talk to her. A flash of a paranoia surged. What if they were targeting her? But that was insane.

Drew was right. There was a bullet inside her body—maybe something worse than a bullet. It had to come out.

"Yeah, fine. Get it," she said.

"You're still steel, Kristen. The doctors can't even get an IV in although they've tried. That's what I'm saying. You need to let the medical staff work on you."

She looked at her right arm as a nurse jammed a needle against her vein. The needle snapped like it was nothing more than a toothpick.

"No!" She snarled and jerked her arm away. There was no way for her to know what was in that bag of fluid. It could be drugs or it could be something that would stop her powers or even something that could let her powers take control of her. These people—these humans didn't know! She was a dragon—the Steel Dragon. How could humans think they could help her? The arrogance of the idea made her furious.

A flash of heat made all the nurses and doctors take a few steps away from her with looks of terror on their faces.

Only Drew stayed close. She trusted him. He was one of hers, so she hadn't made her aura affect him. But she hadn't meant it to affect the doctors either. She was losing control and was afraid that using the drugs or medicine or whatever the hell the doctors would do to her would make her lose even more control.

"Kristen, listen to me. These people need to help you. We need that bullet out, but we can't do that if you're wearing your armor. You need to turn it off."

"No!" Her steel skin was all that kept her safe and she was at her most vulnerable now. Even when she'd fought Shadowstorm—a full-blown dragon—her steel skin had been what had kept her alive.

Her aura rose inside her, an unbidden force, a tidal wave of fear that she could unleash on Drew to wash away his will and make him leave her alone. She fought the urge. Drew was her friend, not her servant or her minion to be ordered about as she saw fit.

"Kristen, if we don't get that bullet out, there's no telling what it could do to you. Drop the armor now. That's an order."

Strangely, him ordering her around helped. She had been raised by people and was a person, and Drew was not only her friend but also her boss. That grounded her and reminded her what she was and where she was from. She wouldn't use her powers on him. "He'll come for me! Don't you get it? This is what he wants. He wants me to be afraid of my powers."

"No, Kristen. Shadowstorm can't hurt you. We drove him from the city."

"Who do you think hired that sniper?" she retaliated acerbically.

The look on Drew's face said he'd already had the identical thought. "Even if he did, we have men scouring that building as we speak. You're safe now. I'll keep you safe."

She shook her head. Talking had become more difficult. Her throat and neck began to burn even worse than her left arm. She wanted to look to see if what Drew had said was true—she wanted to see if she was rusting—but she didn't dare. It took every ounce of self-control she had to maintain consciousness. If she saw her armor coming apart, she didn't want to think what her aura would do to the people who tried to help her. She had to turn her steel skin off, but if she did, she'd be as weak as any other human. In her moment of weakness, she couldn't do that. She couldn't risk her life.

"Kristen, if you don't drop your steel skin, you might die. If that happens, we both know that no one will be able to protect us from Shadowstorm. We need you, Kristen. We need your powers to keep us safe, but if you don't let me protect you while the doctors do their work, you won't be able to protect us ever again. We'll die."

Damn it, that worked. The idea of losing people got through to her. She couldn't let the sniper win, and if he had used some weird bullet that poisoned her, she had to let the doctors help her or there would be no one to protect her team, her family, or her city. If she died, she had no illusions about what would happen to Detroit. The devastation she'd put off would return. The Motor City would crumble to scrap without her. Nothing would survive but junkyard dogs.

Kristen couldn't let that happen. She clenched her teeth, took a few deep breaths through her nose as she nodded, and dropped her steel skin.

The pain doubled, tripled, and grew ten times as bad. She felt a twinge of something in her right arm and fought with every ounce of strength she had left not to turn back into steel. *It wasn't poison, it was medicine. It was only the IV.* Still, she clenched her teeth as the nurses pumped her full of drugs and the doctor looked at her shoulder.

"Scalpel," he said and his hand moved outside her line of sight.

She heard nothing more after that. Blackness seized her and she passed into a place of nightmares.

CHAPTER FIFTY-FOUR

It was beautifully cool flying above the clouds. They kissed her cheeks with dew and Kristen tried to embrace them and plunged into the billowy pillows of whiteness like a kid diving into a swimming pool.

She felt the coolness with her fingers, only to discover that she didn't have two arms, but four. Two of them were familiar—upper arm, forearm, wrist, and hand—except the fingers were longer, clawed, and scaly. These weren't human arms, but those of a dragon. She held them up and sliced through the clouds like a swimmer. Her scales were silver and delicate, more like those of a fish than a reptile.

It surprised her to realize that her other two arms weren't arms at all but wings. They had upper arms and forearms, but the fingers extended from the palm into long, delicate versions of themselves. Silvery webbing stretched between them like the wings of a bat. She found she couldn't control her wings the same way she could her dragon arms.

It required no conscious thought to flap them or when to simply coast. She didn't have to adjust them to the microvariations in air pressure. All she had to think was *faster, deeper,* and her wings responded. They worked as automatically as her lungs, an extension of her that gave her the skies.

It was an exhilarating and liberating feeling, an intoxicating sensation. She willed herself—her dragon form—to go faster and faster and her body obeyed her commands. With her arms and legs tucked against her scaled body, her wings pumped harder and faster until she burst from the top of a cloud and into a vista of blue skies, where the ground was nothing but a memory.

Mountains of clouds rolled in slow motion. She floated above it all.

Ahead of her, a single cloud seemed...different. Larger than the rest, it rose up from the table of fluffy white like a monster emerging from a pool of water. It was large, so much bigger than she was. It towered higher and higher and eclipsed the sun with its thick gray billowing shadow. Lightning cracked inside it, but she couldn't hear any thunder, only wind rising to buffet her.

Despite her wings functioning perfectly only moments before, they now seemed powerless to resist the wind. Great gales pounded against her dragon body, but they didn't come from the storm. Instead, they moved toward it. She was filled with the horrible sensation that she was being devoured—that this cloud would consume the steel dragon as easily as a blue whale swallowed krill.

It was a foe that strong armor would do nothing against, a force that sought metal the way animals sought water. She could not defeat water, wind, and lightning with steel. And yet, she couldn't escape.

Tendrils of wind sucked her inside the behemoth of a cloud.

Within, all was darkness. Wind battered her from all angles, so she immediately became disoriented. She couldn't find her way out and when she tried to flap her wings, great gusts of silver scales blew away. Each one left a tiny spec of exposed skin—human skin—and she began to hurt. She gritted her teeth, determined that she wouldn't let the pain consume her mind.

The lightning already did an excellent job of adding to her agony. It cracked louder and louder and great big bolts moved vertically and diagonally, within and throughout the cloud like nerve impulses in the brain.

Kristen felt that she knew what the cloud was thinking—horrible, malevolent thoughts that chilled her. It sought to rip her wings from her body like a cruel child would an insect and cast her to the earth.

She had to escape!

Despite her renewed attempts to find a way out in every possible direction, nothing freed her. Instead, she constantly found Sebastian Shadowstorm hiding in the clouds. He smiled at her and gave her false courtesies and sweet little lies while his dragon claws harnessed lightning and used it to blow her delicate scales off.

A bolt struck her. She expected it to feel hot and painful like the gunshot had but instead, it was as cold as ice. Rather than pain, she simply felt drained of all power.

In the next moment, she was in human form once more and plummeted earthward. She heard only two sounds—the rush of wind in her ears and Shadowstorm's laughter.

Dreams of falling weren't new to her, so she half-expected to wake before she impacted the apartment block that rushed to meet her. But either the drugs or the vibrancy of the dream kept her in it, and instead of waking, she pounded into the building.

Her momentum drove her through floor after floor after floor. Each shattered beneath the weight of her steel skin and concrete, tile, and metal girders tore like paper. None of it slowed her descent, though. She continued violently through the levels of the building until she reached the basement and landed in a swimming pool.

It was only a few inches above her head but she couldn't get out of the water. She tried to swim but she was too heavy. Her lungs began to burn and she had all but given in when a red-and-white buoy splashed above her. She caught it and pulled herself out of the water long enough to see her brother Brian holding the rope attached to it.

He pulled on it but despite his large frame, he yanked himself into the pool. In the next moment, it wasn't a pool but the Detroit River and she struggled to release the rope in which she was now tangled. As she sank deeper and deeper into the muck, she dragged him with her. Despite her burning lungs, she didn't drown. Her brother wasn't so lucky.

Her thrashing pulled his bloated body to her and she screamed and screamed and screamed. She could feel her aura affecting everything around her. The fish fled, people left the shores of the river, and the entire city of Detroit emptied out, all because of her. Her pain was their pain and her death would be their death. But rather than let the creatures of her domain perish with her, she forced them to flee and to abandon their master.

No one remained to bear witness to the monster that was the Steel Dragon.

There was no one left to help the person who defended the city.

She listened, but no one called her name.

"Kristen! Kristen, wake up. You're having a nightmare."

She woke abruptly and sat bolt upright. Her left arm ached from the effort, but her neck and chest felt better. She looked at her steel skin and, with effort, turned it off. Her transformation had already pushed out the IV that had been in her arm. The needle lay beside her and oozed watery-looking blood. She wished her steel skin could have forced the bullet out the same way it had forced the needle out.

"Smooth move, ex-lax. You turned your steel on and off, over and over. You probably short-circuited all their equipment."

Kristen looked over to identify the speaker. It was the Wonderkid, Jim, who leaned against the doorframe. He gestured at the now useless IV on the bed. She took a deep breath and forced herself to lay down in the hospital bed.

"Smooth move, really? What are you? Like seven?" She managed to say. It sounded snarky despite the fact that she still felt the terror of the nightmare tight around her throat. But this was how SWAT dealt with terror—you laughed in its face.

"Wow, I gotta say I'm impressed you can still talk shit. I thought that after the big bad dragon girl passed out from an itty-bitty bullet, you'd be all quiet and meek by now."

"You wish, Washington."

He smiled. "I don't. I really don't. And don't call me Washington, not anymore. We know each other too well for that."

That drew a responsive smile. He was right, of course. "Thanks for being here, Jim."

"No problem. Anyway, do you really think I'd miss this? Do you have any idea how much money I could make from the tabloids by selling what the Steel Dragon mumbles about when she has a bad dream?"

"You wouldn't."

Jim shrugged, entered the room fully, and sat on a chair next to her bed. "Maybe I would. Maybe I'd like to make an easy ten grand and go on a little vacation. I'm sure the dragons who run this world behind the scenes wouldn't have any problem with that whatsoever. After all, they respect human lives and all that." The sarcasm in his voice was palpable.

Before she could protest that not all dragons were like that, his tone changed. "Of course, I wouldn't piss off the only dragon I've ever met who really does care about people, so your secret is safe with me. But I am curious. Who is Brian? You said his name more than once."

She nodded. Of course she had talked in her sleep. She always had. While she was a dragon with powers unlike any other, she still mumbled in her sleep. No wonder the other dragons didn't ever seek her out. They must have found her entirely too human. Even her dreams ended up being human dreams. "Brian is my brother."

"Oh, right, of course. Drew mentioned that." There was something in his voice that set her on edge—like Brian was more than simply a name mentioned over beers and was maybe a detail to remember, a part of a case.

"Why did Drew mention my brother?"

He shrugged awkwardly. He was obviously holding something back from her.

"Jim, why did Drew tell you about Brian?"

Her teammate took a deep breath. "He sent a detail to your house as a precaution. No big deal. We think it's very clear that the sniper had targeted you and the identity of the Steel Dragon isn't exactly secret. You were out cold, so Drew and the captain thought it was better to take precautions. You know how it is."

"Has something happened?" Kristen demanded and saw right through his attempts to downplay the situation. She sat up again and a fresh wave of pain surged through her shoulder.

"Yeah, something happened. A sniper shot you in the damn shoulder. If you sit up like that again, you'll rip your damn arm socket to pieces. Take it easy."

Jim leaned forward and touched her wound tenderly. It was bound in gauze, but he still seemed to be able to tell something about the wound. He was a veteran, she remembered. He'd probably seen any number of dressed wounds.

She ignored his concern. "I need to check on my family."

He merely shook his head. "No, you don't. Not yet."

"Yes, I do." Her aura rose unbidden, ready to make him want to obey her desires and to feel what she wanted him to feel. She pushed the power down, determined not to use that, not now and not on her friends.

"Look, I know you have your fancy powers, so give me a second to check how fancy they are. Sit up slowly and let's see what's going on."

A little mollified, she nodded and sat with his help. It didn't hurt when she didn't jerk upright out of bed.

"Now, rotate your shoulder gradually…good. Exactly like that. Now, see if it's an ache all over or if you have twinges of pain."

She rotated her shoulder once again. "It aches, but honestly, it feels worlds better."

"Good. That's really good, Kristen. It means you're on the mend. Your freaky dragon powers are doing their thing to take care of your freaky self."

"Do you always talk to dragons so disrespectfully?"

"Only when they're injured." He grinned. "They can't chase me as well then."

Kristen wondered if he understood the seriousness of of that statement. She now knew there was much that Shadowstorm hadn't taught her, but healing power was one ability they'd spent a fair amount of time on. She called on it now and urged her body to focus on the wound and to use all her internal resources to mend the torn flesh and skin. Her teammate probably didn't realize how short the window was in which dragons were actually injured.

"I passed your little field test. Now, let me check on my family. Where's my phone?"

"I have it right here." He tapped the pocket of his shirt. "But there's more you should know. You weren't out long, but the situation has developed."

She stared at him, a little startled before common sense kicked in. Of course, she'd been unconscious, but the idea that the world had moved on and gone about its business while she was out filled her with a sudden pang of dread. This was her city filled with her people. She couldn't be out cold and dead to the world. "How long?"

"Only a few hours. The morphine should have kept you under for at least eight, but I had a feeling the Steel Dragon wouldn't rest easy."

Okay. That was better. At least she hadn't missed a day. "Did they catch the asshole?" she asked with way too much hope in her voice.

Jim shook his head and she nodded. She wasn't so naïve as to think that someone as skilled as that sniper had been would have waited around for the cops to arrest him.

"They found his position, though. It was the room you and Butters saw. They're combing through it now, looking for evidence, asking people on that floor if they saw anything—the usual, nothing a dragon needs to worry about."

"Great. So let me check on my family." She knew there were many things she could do that the regular cops couldn't, but collecting evidence was one area she didn't have any expertise in. If the sniper had left anything at all, she was confident that her team and Detroit PD would find it. Which meant she didn't need to worry about that.

It was Brian who sprang constantly into her mind, Brian she kept pulling underwater and into the murk and gloom of the river.

Her teammate looked around conspiratorially as if he didn't want to be overheard. He scooted his chair closer and reached into the other shirt pocket—the one that didn't have her phone. "There's more, Kristen. Look, I might get in trouble for sharing this with you, but… well, you and I were both working outside the law on that last mission, and it's a good thing we were."

"I was tracking you and you think that was a good thing?"

He shrugged. "If I hadn't had made that contact, we would never have exposed Shadowstorm, and if you hadn't followed me, I'd be dead. The way I see it, the only mistake I made was not telling you. I won't make that mistake again."

Kristen smirked. How odd it was to be such close allies with the Wonderkid. When he'd first arrived on the force, he'd hated her simply because of what she was and now, he wanted to recruit her for a clandestine operation? Almost dying together did things to people. In this case, it had brought them closer.

Jim pulled a plastic evidence bag out of his shirt pocket and put it on the table beside her. It contained what appeared to be a bullet, except it didn't resemble any she had ever seen. The shape was the same but beyond that, it looked like something from an Avengers movie.

For starters, it wasn't made of metal but of an orangey-red material that made her think of lava rock. There were cracks and fissures down the sides of it and the top of the projectile was deformed slightly, but to her, it looked remarkably intact. "Is that what…"

He nodded. "This is what they pulled out of you."

"What the hell is it?"

"It's a bullet, but one I've never actually seen before. I've heard of these, though. It's made from dragon scales."

"You're kidding."

"I certainly don't think it's funny."

"How did you get it?"

"As soon as they wheeled you out of surgery, they bagged it and gave everything to the police for safekeeping. It's a good thing you can trust police—you know, like me."

"This is supposed to be in evidence?" She was incredulous. Of course, she'd heard of cops stealing from the evidence locker, but never on Detroit SWAT. Captain Hansen ran a tight ship.

Jim shrugged. "No one knows it's missing yet. And it's not like I'll let you keep it."

She rubbed her face, not sure of what she thought about taking something from evidence and not sure if she even cared. This was bigger than SWAT. "Why dragon scales?" she asked after a moment.

"You know that I...uh, used to be fairly obsessed with hating dragons." He at least had the decency to look embarrassed but pressed on. "Well, they say dragons can't be killed with lead. Your physique is... well, different. I'm sure that if someone unloaded enough bullets directly into a dragon's heart or your brain, that would do the job, but it would take a ton of lead. These things interrupt the healing process or interfere with your immune system or something. Whatever it is, the Internet's fairly damn certain that a bullet made from a dragon is the best way to kill a dragon."

"What the fuck does that mean?"

"It means this guy not only knew where you were and what you were but had a damn good idea how to eliminate you."

"Did they recover the other two bullets that hit me?" she asked.

"Yeah, but I didn't bring them. There was no point. They weren't interesting enough."

"They weren't like this?"

"Dragon? No. They were armor-piercing rounds, though, and two different types if you can believe that. The asshole wanted to kill you with a single shot, but he was prepared in case he didn't. The other two shots were probably to test your steel skin."

Kristen peeked under her blanket and looked at her chest. There was slight bruising but nothing serious. The bulletproof armor had done its job. She held her right hand up —the one she'd use to block the third bullet—and looked at her palm. Already, a huge purple bruise had blossomed. That had almost broken through, which meant if the sniper tried stronger rounds, he might get through.

She focused her healing power on the bruise on her hand instead of her left shoulder. If she had to shoot a gun, she'd need her right hand. The purple began to fade away as her blood worked through her body to restore the damage.

The wound in her shoulder was more stubborn, no doubt because of what that bullet was made of.

"Well…that's better than three dragon rounds."

Jim shook his head. "I don't think so. I think that if it were three dragon rounds, we'd know Shadowstorm had simply given a marksmen a number of them. They're damn expensive—we're talking tens of thousands of dollars apiece—but I'm sure Shadowstorm could afford that unless there's a code about dragons not using them."

He eyed her and his old biases flickered in his gaze before he grimaced and shook them away. "No, what concerns me is that this guy is familiar enough with dragon rounds to know that they're not particularly good at shooting through metal. I've found some mentions of this idea, but it's difficult to acquire any solid info. I'm worried our sniper wants to conserve his supply of these so was looking for your other weaknesses."

"It's a good thing he didn't find them."

His frown remained in place. "That's true, but he also confirmed that he can get under your skin if he can get the bullet to you before you hear the bang and armor up. He's also eliminated two types of armor-piercing rounds to try. I don't like this at all, Kristen. I think we're dealing with someone who knows a fair amount about killing dragons."

"It's a good thing you did so much research into killing our kind. Hopefully, you can reverse-engineer a profile on this scumbag."

"Your kind, really?" He raised an eyebrow.

Kristen sighed. "I didn't mean that. It slipped out. My kind likes pizza with ham and pineapple and plays way too many videogames."

"What are you talking about? Pineapple on pizza? That sounds horrible."

"It's my brother's favorite topping, Jim. Now give me my phone so I can call him, please."

"Right, sorry. Here you go." He pulled the phone out of his other pocket and set it on the table beside the cracked dragon round. "Are you still worried about him even though it's most likely a dragon-killer out there? He should be fine, right? I thought your family was normal."

"They're definitely normal, but if this guy knows about dragons, he might come for them. That's why Drew sent a unit to my house. He knows Stonequest enough to know that… Well, you must know that dragons see humans as property?"

The man's scowl could not have been fiercer. "Yes. I do. Sometimes, I wonder if rich white folks would have enslaved my ancestors if not for their shithead dragon role models."

All she could do was shrug at that. It was impossible to speculate at what a world would look like without an incredibly powerful, self-centered ruling class. "Well, my family counts as the Steel Dragon's number one possession. If this person is really targeting me and not Detroit PD, they might set their sights on my family." She forced her voice to remain calm and didn't want to mention that she'd also dreamed that her abilities were killing her brother. That had merely been a dream. Dragons weren't prophetic, but that didn't make the nightmare any easier to swallow.

She unlocked her phone, opened her favorites, and touched the picture of her brother stuffing two pieces of pizza in his mouth. He didn't answer so she called again.

"It's around dinner time. I bet they're eating that gross pizza. I'm sure they're fine," Jim said.

Kristen knew otherwise. Her mom had visited her dad every single time he'd had to go to the hospital because of police work. She was always there before he'd woken up. Always. But she wasn't here now. Why?

"Did Drew tell them what happened?" she asked as the phone continued to ring. Each beep pushed her level of near-panic up a few notches.

"Yeah. The basics anyway."

A little distracted, she nodded and tried to stay calm but failed.

"They should be here. My mom has walked through police barricades for, like, thirty years."

"Try your brother again in a few minutes. Maybe he's in the bathroom."

"No. We have a code. Two rings within a minute means an emergency. And Brian always has his phone on him—always. Plus, he thinks farting into the speaker is hilarious so even if he's in the bathroom, he picks up."

Her brother didn't pick up.

She tried the house phone, also with no answer.

Something was wrong. Something was very, very wrong.

"We need to go. Now." A sense of urgency pushed her out of bed. She put her hand on the table to steady herself and her palm settled on top of the evidence bag with the dragon bullet. She closed her hand around it without thinking.

Jim certainly didn't notice. He was too busy trying to hide his smile when she stood and felt the cool breeze flowing up her legs and back.

"Damned hospital gowns." She growled in irritation. In that moment, she didn't care. She wasn't ashamed of her body and time was of the essence so she simply held her hand out. "Clothes. Now."

"Kristen, I—" He somehow managed to close his mouth, gather her clothes, and toss them to her.

She turned her back to him, undid the tie on the hospital gown, and let it fall as she yanked her clothes on.

"Mention this to Keith, and you die. Mention this to Hernandez, and you'll wish you were dead," she said as she put her bra and shirt on and dragged her pants on. When she turned, she could see that might have been a mistake. He had obviously been looking at her butt but so had the nurse who'd entered the room.

"Ma'am, you should be in bed," the woman said, obviously more accustomed to seeing partially naked people than the Wonderkid was.

"No," she responded quickly and flashed her aura. The nurse scuttled away, clearly nervous at her patient's ability but still determined to call a doctor. An aura couldn't change someone's nature, only heighten it, and a scared nurse ran for a doctor.

"Maybe you should do as they say. Your family's fine. I can check on them if it'll make you feel any better."

"If they were fine, they'd answer their phones."

Jim held his hands up in mock surrender. "Look, let me call the police on guard duty. They'll answer for sure. It's their damn job."

Kristen nodded. "Okay. Okay, fine, call them."

He complied quickly and a long, awkward moment of silence followed during which she watched his normally calm smile droop lower and lower as the phone continued to ring. Finally, he hung up.

His expression confirmed that he'd received no answer.

"We need to go. Now." She headed to the door.

A doctor appeared—a young woman with a last name she couldn't pronounce and a slight accent. "Ma'am, you need to lie down. Your physiology is different than a regular human's and we need to continue to monitor—"

She simply turned her body to steel and pushed past her.

"Ma'am! Ma'am, you should stop," The woman protested, but she didn't make a move to stop her. She must have understood there'd be no point.

As she entered the hallway and marched toward the exit, she wished, not for the first time, that she had wings. She wasn't entirely sure which hospital she was in and had never bothered to ask, but it didn't matter. There was no way any of her teammates had driven her car over from the SWAT station. She would have to catch a cab or, depending on her location, simply run the whole damn way. With her powers, that wouldn't be a problem, except she had an injured shoulder. Running miles and miles might not be the smartest thing to do right now.

"Miss, you need to check out," an overweight receptionist tried to tell her from behind her station, but she ignored her in the same way that she ignored the shouts from farther down the hallway behind.

"Hey! Hall! Damnit, Kristen, wait for me." Jim strode after her, a smile plastered on his face. He wouldn't run—not while in uniform and not unless he absolutely had to. A cop running through a hospital could trigger panic. This was the level of the Wonderkid's professionalism.

Kristen gave him a brief glance but didn't slow. She had no intention to wait for anything and stepped out the sliding glass doors and into the chilly afternoon. It hadn't snowed yet this year, but it would soon. She looked in all directions but there were no cabs waiting. Worse, she didn't immediately recognize the exterior of the hospital, which meant it was definitely not one of the ones closest to her parents' house in Dearborn.

The doors slid open behind her and her teammate exited.

"You won't stop me, Jim. You know that. I can knock your ass over if I want to."

He held his hands up in what she first assumed was surrender until she noticed the keys dangling from his finger. "There is no need to whack me, Miss Dragon. If you want my wheels, you got 'em, but I'm coming too."

After a moment, she nodded. She hoped she wouldn't need the Wonderkid as much as she hoped her family didn't need the Steel Dragon.

CHAPTER FIFTY-FIVE

The drive to her parents' house was painfully long. Jim didn't have a police car, only his regular wheels, so even though he pushed the speed limit they couldn't blow through red lights without the help of their sirens. Instead, they had to wait while jazz played quietly on the car stereo and Kristen was forced to think about what might be happening to her family. She'd tried Brian four more times and received no answer, not once. It required all her focus to stop herself from completely freaking out.

Her companion didn't help. "So...uh, that aura thing. I felt you do it to the nurse."

"Yeah, what about it?" she snapped.

He was a cop and was used to people snapping at him, so he didn't react to her hostility. "Do all dragons do that?"

After a moment, she shrugged and nodded. "Basically, yeah."

"Has Stonequest trained you how to use it?"

"No." She sighed. "No, he hasn't. Shadowstorm taught me about it, and he mostly focused on how to read other dragons' auras and how to keep mine under wraps or not. That's one of the reasons I'm worried he's still here. He was able to control his aura really well—

certainly well enough to hide from me. But, Jim, I don't really care about this right now. Is it relevant to my family?"

"No. Not exactly. It's only…well, when you do it, I can really feel it. You made that nurse damn nervous."

"That was the point."

"Sure. Yeah, I get that—"

"But?"

The light turned green and he found a gap between the two cars ahead of him and took it. Despite driving like he was in a car chase, his tone of voice was still casually professional. "Well, I could tell when you did it. I think that basically defeats the point of it."

"The nurse didn't think so."

"Right, yeah, I get that. You wanted her scared and she was scared, but… Well, I don't know. If you were a little more subtle about it, I think it would work better. People would be more willing to respond if they didn't know they were being manipulated, you know?"

The sentiment of what he said forced a smile onto her face despite the thoughts of dread surrounding her family. "Wait, did Jim Washington, self-proclaimed hater of dragons, actually give me advice on how to be a better dragon?"

He chuckled awkwardly as he hurtled around a mail truck. They were close to her parents' house now, less than five minutes away. "Yeah, well, you've kind of changed my whole perspective on dragons. Obviously, they're not all bad."

"Oh yeah? How many of us make the cut?"

"Well, you're okay, I guess. And Stonequest seems fine. Drew trusts him, anyway."

"Wow. The Wonderkid has found it in his heart to trust an entire two dragons. You do realize two is the second smallest number there is? Trusting two dragons isn't exactly magnanimous."

"I never said I wanted to be magnanimous to dragons." He said the word with enough sarcasm to make Hernandez proud. "Only that if we have one on our side, I'd rather she be as skilled with her abilities as possible. You might as well be as strong as you can be so you can stop the rest of those scaly, fire-breathing salamanders."

"I'll have you know my brother had a pet salamander." She had meant it as a joke but mentioning her brother's name had the effect of bringing bile up into her throat. They had to be okay. If something was wrong—if they had been hurt because of her—there would be hell to pay.

"Yeah, well, I think most dragons think of people in those terms. Pets that can be let off a leash." There was the old Jim—the marine with a chip on his shoulder and the soldier who'd seen what dragons could really do to people in a warzone.

"And you'd still want me to learn to control my aura? You know it doesn't really work on dragons, right? It's an ability that we—they—use to control people. If I learned to control it better, people would suffer for it."

"No, they wouldn't, Kristen. Not from you. Of course, people don't like being manipulated, but you could use it for good. If you could get a hostile to surrender without hurting hostages or get a perp to confess, well, that would help people. Think about it. This sniper is probably human. Most dragons don't fiddle with firearms too much. Stonequest can kind of handle a gun, but not really. Dragons use people as intermediaries or as pets or whatever. If you can control that ability, you could set them free."

"Or I could use it to get Hansen to send the whole damn force to my parent's house instead of a couple of measly cars."

Jim looked taken aback. He said nothing, but she saw distrust flash across his face. He couldn't think she'd ever do something so brazen with her powers, could he? Taking control of an entire police force wouldn't help her city but hurt it. And yet, at that moment, Kristen wanted nothing more than to bring the full force of the Motor City to her parents' house.

The sniper—whoever he was—had targeted her. He was after the Steel Dragon. That was painfully obvious. The bullet she had pocketed was a testimony to that. And according to what she understood of dragon culture, her family would be seen as nothing more than collateral damage.

He was right, though. If something happened to her family because of her, she would use everything in her power—every trace of every dragon ability and every speck of leverage she'd earned at Detroit SWAT—to obtain vengeance and make sure that whoever was terrifying her city wouldn't do so again.

Her teammate slowed as they reached her parent's street.

"What are you doing?" She hissed her annoyance. He was costing them precious seconds.

"The element of surprise might be the key. We'll drive past once and run a quick check, park a few houses down, and go from there."

"So you do think something is wrong?"

"You've called your brother's phone way too many times. It'd be stupid to act like that doesn't mean anything."

She nodded. At least they were on the same page.

They drove past the house. Two police cruisers were parked out front, their lights out. The outline of a person sat in the driver's seat of each one. One of them had a red mote of light near his face—a cigarette, obviously.

"Wilson must be smoking. That's a good thing," Jim commented.

"Oh yeah?"

"Dead people don't smoke."

She nodded but had paid more attention to her parents' house. The living room light was on, the blinds were closed, and the porch light was off. None of that was unusual, though. It was early evening, so her mom would no doubt be cooking and they often closed the blinds because the elderly couple who lived across the street regularly complained about her dad walking around without a shirt on.

Jim pulled to a stop a few houses down in front of Mrs. Ciskowski's house. She was an old Polish woman who used to make little cabbage-wrapped dumplings for Kristen and Brian. It was strange the things that came unbidden to the brain in stressful situations.

They exited the vehicle quickly. He unholstered his gun and she turned to steel. If they were walking into a trap, at least she'd be ready to fight.

Quietly and cautiously, they walked down the sidewalk in the fading light. A chill breeze picked up. She felt it through her steel skin but it didn't cut to her core like she knew the onset of winter could. Despite believing with almost every fiber of her being that something was wrong, she felt a sudden stab of hope that her family hadn't answered the phone because they were crowded into the kitchen, making hot chocolate.

They approached the cop cars and Jim cleared his throat. The innocuous sound should nevertheless have drawn the attention of the cops in the cruisers.

Neither one of them moved.

She moved toward the vehicle with the man smoking. Her gaze pierced the growing gloom and she frowned. His eyes were closed and the cigarette was jammed in his mouth, still smoldering.

"Fuck, Jim! Wilson's out cold."

When she turned, he had his arm inside the cop cruiser, his hand at the other man's neck. "Anders is too. He still has a pulse, thank God. Shit, Kristen. You were right."

He snatched the car's radio and called for backup. "We have injured officers at the Hall residence and reason to believe this is a hostage situation. Requesting immediate backup. We want Drew and Butters here if you can."

"I read you loud and clear, Wonderkid. Have shots been fired?"

"Not yet. The officers are unconscious but otherwise appear to be uninjured. We'll go in."

"That's a negative, Wonderkid. Hansen wants you to wait for backup. Repeat. Do not enter the Hall residence without backup."

"Are you saying that you want me to let the Steel Dragon go in alone?"

Kristen had already begun to approach the door. Her ears—sharper than they'd ever been when she'd believed herself to be simply human—could hear the angry protests of the dispatcher over the radio but the complaints fell on deaf ears. Jim followed her hurriedly and they moved silently across the lawn.

"Kristen, wait," he whispered.

"In your dreams."

"No, look."

She glanced behind her, frustrated by the delay, but he had taken one of the unconscious police officers' pistols and radio. After a moment's hesitation, she accepted them. A gun was a tool every bit as dangerous in her hands as her steel skin was. She'd be foolish to not have one.

"We take this slow, Kristen. These guys didn't kill those officers, even though that would have probably been the easier option. There's a good chance your family is alive and unhurt."

"Bullshit."

"No. Think about it like a human, not a damn dragon. They're concerned about their image or something or they aren't paid to kill cops. Whatever it is, leaving those officers alive is better than killing them. If you bust in there and start trying to rip people in half, you might make these assholes panic. When people panic, they do stupid shit. Now, there's gotta be a back door or something, right? Let's get close and see if we can see anything."

Tense with a mixture of fear and fury, she ground her teeth and glowered at him, but he made sense. So, instead of kicking the front door off its damn hinges like she wanted to do, they would sneak around the back. It wouldn't take more than a minute anyway, otherwise, she probably wouldn't have agreed to it.

Kristen moved in that direction but he put a hand on her shoulder. "You gonna be quiet like that?"

She understood that he was talking about her steel skin. If she tried to sneak with it, she'd undoubtedly snap branches and could even kick a chunk out of the concrete driveway if she wasn't careful.

But she couldn't go fully human either. If this was a trap—and she began to think it was—whoever was inside would be ready to hurt her. If she turned her steel skin off completely, she'd be in danger.

Clearly, a compromise was needed so she paused, concentrated on some of the lessons Stonequest had given her, and made her feet turn to flesh. She did the same with her hands. Changing them was simple enough but maintaining her body's armored state was more difficult. Still, she had practiced and she managed to stabilize. Her core and head remained steel, while her hands and feet were normal.

Jim nodded and looked impressed, and they proceeded.

The small gate was closed—another good sign—and she opened it barely enough for them to squeeze through. Any more, and it would squeak.

They eased past her mom's struggling azalea bushes, past her dad's soot-stained barbecue grill, and up the four steps to the back door.

Despite their careful scrutiny, they still hadn't seen a damn thing. All the window blinds were closed, and if anyone was in there, they kept their distance from the blinds.

Kristen put her ear to the door.

For a moment, she heard nothing but her dad spoke suddenly and, thank God, he sounded pissed off.

"Keep your fucking feet off the couch," Frank Hall grouched. A wave of relief washed over her. That sounded like her dad bitching her brother out for disrespecting the rules of the house, another regular night at the Hall residence.

She leaned in and allowed herself a smile as she imagined the tableau within and waited for Brian to either say something about the couch being twenty years old or her mom to chastise Frank for swearing.

But that wasn't what she heard.

"Please don't hurt him. He didn't mean to be disrespectful," her mom said, her voice high and shrill with fear.

The dull, meaty thwack of someone being struck followed and fury blossomed inside her.

In a blink, her hands and feet transformed to steel. She leaned back, ready to smash the door down and become a wrecking ball of vengeance but again, a hand settled on her shoulder and she hesitated.

"Wait, Kristen. That was only one punch. They're not roughing him up too bad."

"Not too bad? Can you even hear yourself?"

"Maybe these assholes will tell us something we need to know. Give it ten seconds."

Everything in her protested at any further delay, but ten seconds later, she had to acknowledge that the Wonderkid was indeed more experienced than her.

"We don't want to hurt you people, got it?" stated the gruff voice of a stranger.

"We're only here to keep you safe until we move you to a more secure location." The second voice was higher-pitched and more wheedling. She wondered if there were more than only the two.

"Do you expect us to believe you're here to keep us safe when you killed the cops out front?" Frank demanded, his voice thick. Kristen had a feeling he'd have a swollen lip from the blow. She vowed to do the same to every person in there.

"The cops are compromised, got it?" the voice that reminded her of a weasel said. "You can't trust them anymore, but don't worry, we didn't kill them either. Now, I'd kindly appreciate it if all of us simply sat quietly while we wait for our associates to arrive. It shouldn't be long now."

Silence descended on the Hall residence.

Jim leaned closer to her ear. "There's no reason to break your mom's purple door. Is it locked?"

She tried the doorknob. It wasn't.

"We go in together, on three. What's the layout like?"

"The back door opens to the kitchen and the open floorplan connects it to the living room. From back here, there are two bedrooms and a bathroom to the right. It sounds like my dad and mom are in the living room. Brian's probably there too. It's not like he would be anywhere else. I hear at least two hostiles, but my guess is there are more. If we're lucky, they'll have their backs to us."

"That it? Is there anywhere to hide?" he asked.

"There is a tiny pantry in the kitchen but I don't think anyone's gonna hide in there. It'd be damn tight. Plus, it sounds like they're waiting for a pickup or something and don't expect me at all."

"Really?"

"Yeah, really. What?"

"I thought the Steel Dragon would've come from nicer digs than a two-bedroom."

"Later, Wonderkid. Right now, I have skulls to crack."

"Right. We go in. You take point, obviously. If there's someone in the kitchen, ignore them and target whoever is on your parents. I'll cover you and take out anyone you blow past."

"All right. Are you ready?"

Jim nodded.

"Good. Here we go, in three. One… two…three."

She opened the door and they slipped inside.

CHAPTER FIFTY-SIX

Trevor Styx wasn't a bad guy. He'd merely made a few bad decisions.

That was practically one of the definitions of what it meant to grow up poor in the inner city of any major American metropolis. Not that he was angry or bitter. It was simply that he recognized there were many factors that had led him here, not all of which were within his control.

For example, if he had not tried to break into the same house as a group of criminals, he would never have met his current crew. It was an odd coincidence and at the time, one that he had thought would be fatal. The criminals had turned out to not be police, so that was something.

Although they had known so much more than he did. In retrospect, that alone should have been enough to clue him in to the stakes of the runs they went on.

For example, that house they'd all broken into at the same time—mansion was really a better word—wasn't merely a rich asshole's summer home but the residence of a bonafide dragon.

He hadn't known that. In fact, he hadn't had any idea, but the other three goons were quick to explain the situation once they'd given him a small but painful makeover. They had known what the place was and even known the name of the dragon—Ironclaw or some shit. While he had been after the silverware and maybe jewelry or antique coins, the other goons had known about the dragon's secret stash.

They'd befriended him once he'd made it quite clear that he wasn't working with the dragon who lived in the house. That hadn't been difficult for him as he'd always been good with words. In fact, words were about the only thing he was good with.

The thugs had taken him under their proverbial dragon's wing then and they'd all worked their way into the safe to find a collection of the weirdest shit he had ever seen.

Claws, teeth, scales—it was like someone had taken the dragon's bathroom trashcan and stashed it under lock and key. His new teammates had taken all of it but had been particularly excited about a finger—an honest to God finger—that had seemed to be made of cast iron.

He had simply tried not to think too hard about what was clearly seriously weird shit.

When they'd made their escape and returned to their getaway van, he accepted their invitation for a ride. His getaway plan had been the city bus, so everything about the situation seemed an improvement to him.

How wrong he'd been.

They'd gone to meet their boss on the top floor of a fancy hotel.

At first, Trevor had thought that even this was a stroke of good luck. Their boss had been smoking hot with a great fucking body all decked out in form-fitting black and technical gear. Black hair hung in front of one eye and she wore dark-red lipstick.

She'd beckoned for him to come closer in a voice as scratchy as Bob Dylan's. That appealed to him as well.

He'd told her what had happened and about how they'd robbed the same place. Ha-ha. What a great coincidence and all that.

The woman had smiled demurely and Trevor had almost lost it. There he was, meeting a criminal mastermind, and she liked him!

She invited him out to the balcony and Trevor remembered

fantasies playing through his mind. Maybe this woman needed a proper man, a man gifted in all things tongue for her team. Maybe she'd take him on as henchman lover and put him in charge of these other goons and maybe in charge of her finances. He was sure he could have negotiated her a better deal on the hotel room.

His first inkling of how royally fucked he was came when he saw what she'd left on the balcony. It was an entire damn armory—more weapons and more varieties than he'd ever seen.

Well, that wasn't quite true.

It was mostly rifles and the kind of scopes you'd need to see a moth's asshole from a mile off. She picked one of them up, handed it to him, and told him to find someone who was harming the city.

Trevor had put his eye to the scope and tried not to shake while he looked through the lens. Obviously, this woman had some kind of moral code that was somewhat in line with his. She robbed mansions—or the mansions of dragons anyway—and seemed to think guns were a useful tool. What did that mean, though? Someone who was hurting the city?

Warily, he scanned the ground far below while he tried to decide what counted as harm. A junkie was hidden in a back alley. Detroit had been through one hell of a period of growth lately but there were still junkies. Every city had junkies but now, they stuck to the back alleys.

But, as worthless as the guy was, he wasn't harming the city. He barely took up any space and didn't bother anyone. The dude looked so tweaked-out he wasn't even asking for change. His alleyway probably smelled like piss, but that wasn't a punishable offense.

His search continued.

For a moment, he settled on a family. He loved his mom, God rest her soul. Obviously, he didn't want to do anything to that one.

A firetruck drove past and he moved on.

Movement caught his attention and he paused. A police officer stepped out of a bank, talking animatedly with someone. He watched the conversation and a frown gathered on his face.

He couldn't hear the words, of course, but the expression made it clear to him what was going on. The cop was getting something from the banker, something that made him exceedingly happy. He pumped the other man's hand and grinned like he'd busted into someone's house and found a stash of emeralds.

The banker didn't look any more innocent. He nodded knowingly and added encouragement of some kind every now and then. Obviously, the two were in cahoots.

"In front of the bank. You have a dirty cop and a corrupt banker."

The woman took the rifle from him and aimed it at them. That was his first inkling that perhaps something was wrong. She wore gloves and seemed far more adept at handling the weapon than he was. He'd assumed she'd given him the weapon so he could use the scope, but now… Well, if something happened, his prints would be on it, not hers.

"How do you know the police officer is harming the city?" the woman had asked and annunciated each word carefully. She had a faint trace of an accent—something eastern European maybe? He didn't know, but the accent plus the figure plus the dark lipstick made him want to please her.

"Have you ever talked to a banker? They don't help anyone who actually needs it and are only interested in their damn shareholders. Do you know what shareholders do for this country? Nothing. Nothing at all. If he's working with a cop, that cop must be looking the other way for something—some sick fucking things bankers do in their back corners. Have you ever heard about those sex-rings politicians and their investors run? Apparently, little children aren't beyond their preferences. I'll bet that cop is delivering one or letting one slip through. Something horrible."

She nodded at his explanation and he smiled inwardly. He'd always been good with words and it seemed like she was as powerless to resist his charms as anyone else.

"I trust your judgment," she had said, and his heart had quickened. No one trusted him, not even his own sister. That was simply not a word used to describe Trevor Styx. Some people listened and even went along with him temporarily, but trust wasn't the word they used.

"Do you trust mine?"

"Your judgment?" he had asked. "Sure."

The woman fired the rifle as the cop's car drove into an intersection. They were so damn far away it actually took a moment for the bullet to strike. When it did, he breathed a sigh of relief. She'd missed. Thank fucking God, she'd missed. She'd hit the front tire instead of drilling a hole in the windshield.

His relief faded when the cop's car had swerved because its front tire was flat and drove in front of a bus going maybe forty miles an hour.

He saw the collision and the way the little green sedan had crumpled like a beer can at a party under a bridge. The man was dead. He had no doubt about that. Jesus Christ himself would have had to be seated in the passenger seat for someone to survive something like that.

"You have my trust, Trevor. This city is a better place because of your judgment."

"My judgment? I didn't tell you to kill the guy!"

"And I didn't. You did." She thrust the rifle into his hands.

He'd accepted it instead of letting it clatter to the floor. That might have been what he regretted the most. Why hadn't he simply run out at that moment?

"But I didn't know you would kill him."

"That's no longer relevant, Trevor. What matters is that I trusted you and now, you are in my trust."

The conversation had never really gone in his favor after that. Apparently, the woman had brought the crew into town and—lucky Trevor—they were working on a target on the police force.

The robbery where they'd found him had only been to obtain those weird dragon pieces and trade them for something. The stakes of this relationship had terrified Trevor. He'd thought he was working with a team of thieves so professional that they regularly robbed dragons.

It turned out that was their first attempt to rob anything larger than a pawn shop, and that their boss—the woman in black—

normally didn't conduct that kind of business either. She'd only accepted the gig because the contact had known the dragon who owned the mansion would be busy that night.

To make it all worse, she had explained that their mission was to kill the Steel Dragon herself. Apparently, the robbery that had brought him onto the team had merely been a part of that puzzle.

This had scared the shit out of him, but when he'd found it wasn't simply a dirty cop that this assassin was targeting but the goddamned Steel Dragon, what could he have done? Quit?

The worst part was that she was always watching. Every mission they went on, there'd be some crazy fucking moment where a bullet would come out of nowhere and shoot the lock of a door, or where a camera would burst into scrap immediately before it turned to look at him.

He had no doubt that if he'd tried to flee, there'd be a bullet in his brain to stop him.

Which made his current situation all the more troubling.

The goons—as he liked to think of his quiet, surly associates—had disabled the two cops in their cars before he even knew what the hell was going on.

In the next moment, they were inside, beating the shit out of some fat man and his fat kid. The mom had screamed at them to not damage the carpet with their blood and that her husband was an ex-cop and their little crew was royally fucked.

Trevor didn't particularly like hitting women. He understood that some men got a real kick out of getting a mouthy bitch to shut up, but he didn't fault women for talking. After all, he was chatty himself. But damn, had it felt good to get her to shut up with the back of his hand.

After barely a minute, they had the three fat fucks subdued and more or less quiet on the couch. Everything had seemed to be fine but now, they were there waiting. That was what bothered him the most about the whole damn operation. This was supposed to be simple. Go in, subdue the family—he hadn't known about the cops, but after his few weeks with the goons, he found most of them were rarely told the whole story—and wait for pick-up.

But it had been more than five minutes. That was a long time to wait with cops out front who could wake up at any moment.

One of the thugs had plopped down next to the fat kid's fat dad. He wasn't a kid really but a nineteen-year-old, privileged piece of shit. He told himself he didn't give a shit about some fatso who lived with his parents, had a roof over his head, and was well fed. That was more than many people had.

Everything had been fine until the idiot—Martin was his name—had put his feet on the couch.

"Keep your fucking feet off the couch!" the fat man had complained like he had any fucking right to talk.

Martin had looked at him once. He stood, dusted the dirt off the couch, then kneed the fat man so hard in the crotch that Trevor had actually seen his eyes bug out like a cartoon.

"Please don't hurt him! He didn't mean to be disrespectful," the woman had whined.

"We don't want to hurt you people, got it?" one of the other goons had told the woman but that hadn't calmed her. She looked around the room, no doubt for a weapon or a phone or something to change her situation. Trevor had recognized the look in her eyes—a mixture of desperation and resolution.

It wasn't a good look for an old bitch who was supposed to sit quietly on her couch.

"We're only here to keep you safe until we move you to a more secure location," he said.

Those were their mission parameters, after all. He had been glad to take this mission at first. The orders hadn't come from the woman in black but another man—well, not a man but a dragon. He was bigger and more obviously intimidating than the assassin and had to be her partner or something. The goons had listened to him when he'd given them orders, so he assumed they knew who he was. It had been nice to get out and do something. Even if it was kidnapping, it was better than being bored.

"Do you expect us to believe you're here to keep us safe when you killed the cops out front?" the fat man said, his voice both weak from being kneed in the crotch and a little thick from his bruised face.

"The cops are compromised, got it?" Trevor explained and walked toward the kitchen to get himself a beer or a pop. "You can't trust them anymore, but don't worry. We didn't kill them, either. Now, I'd kindly appreciate it if all of us simply sit quietly while we wait for our associates to arrive. It shouldn't be long now."

What happened next would be the moment that defined his life. He'd end up describing it more often than any other sequence of events, and yet he'd never quite believe it.

The first thing he noticed was that the doorknob turned extremely slowly.

He took a few steps back and moved past one of the goons who was in the kitchen. It was a little cowardly but he had no loyalty to these guys and besides, he was the mouth, not the muscle. He didn't need to be closest to the door.

Still, he thought that perhaps he should warn them and was about to say something when the door swung open.

"You're fucked now!" the fat kid had shouted and all three of the goons turned toward him instead of the open door.

Trevor alone saw the silver blur enter the house, race past the man getting a beer from the fridge, and slam its palm into Trevor's chest hard enough to catapult him over the dining room table.

A rapid gunshot felled the man in the kitchen. Before he'd even landed, a cop strode in through the open back door. The motherfucker had killed a man just like that, more or less in cold blood.

Dammit, he hated cops.

But the silver blur was what held his attention. It raced into the living room, caught the third goon—his name was Dorson—and lifted him into the air.

He saw then that it wasn't a blur but a woman.

She had stopped moving at that incredible speed to pick Dorson up. The woman had steel skin and obviously possessed superhuman strength. She lifted the man up and hurled him through the window of the living room with such force that when his head struck the window frame, the wood simply cracked.

This wasn't merely any woman but the damn Steel Dragon.

Trevor sat, raised his hands in the air, and spread his fingers wide. "I'm unarmed!" he shouted.

Martin had a totally different tactic. Rather than surrender, he yanked the fat kid to his feet and put a gun to his head.

"I know you're fast but you're not that fast," he said to the Steel Dragon and the whole room froze.

"Let him go," her partner said, a black guy with a thin mustache.

"Fat fucking chance," the thug responded, tightened his grasp on the boy's neck, and pressed the gun more firmly against his temple.

"We'll tell you everything," Trevor said. "Names, places, you name it. But don't kill us! Please. No one was supposed to get hurt. We didn't even kill the cops out there."

"Look at my father's face," the Steel Dragon bellowed. "Look what you've done to him."

Terror swamped him. Looking into her eyes was like looking into hell itself. There was nothing there but fire and fury and rage and he felt his bladder let loose. Still, he continued to talk. "That wasn't us! Honest! That was Dorson, that asshole you threw out the window. Please, ma'am, I'm telling the truth. We were supposed to pick these folks up and get them somewhere safe. I swear it."

"That's kidnapping," the black cop said.

"You two need to step the fuck into the back yard if you want this guy to live," Martin said and still held Brian tightly.

"Everyone needs to calm down," Trevor shouted. His hands were still raised. The black cop had his gun aimed at his chest now, while the Steel Dragon stared balefully at Martin and his hostage.

"He's right, Kristen. Now's not the time to do anything rash."

"Listen to the fucking cop," Trevor said.

She looked once at Trevor, disdain barely hidden behind her silver features, then drew her gun and put it on the floor. Unlike her clothes, the weapon wasn't silver. He assumed that meant it still worked.

"Look. We don't want anyone else to get hurt," she said and raised her own hands in the air. "We want to help you guys. It sounds like someone set you two up, right?"

"Damn right," he responded quickly. "We were supposed to be picked up by the boss. We thought the family wanted to get away from the cops. Seriously. This is all a misunderstanding. We don't want your family hurt any more than you do." One of his gifts was that he could lie as easily as he could tell the truth. He'd even passed polygraph tests. Most people felt something when they lied, but not him. Statements were categorized not into truth and fiction but into things he could say that would help him and things that wouldn't.

"Stop talking." The black cop gestured with the pistol still aimed at his chest and he nodded. He'd said his piece and hopefully, it would be enough.

Suddenly, he felt like it would be okay. A wave of relief washed over Trevor. His worry seemed to slowly seep away.

"We don't know what's going on here, but we really don't want anyone else to get hurt—not our people and not your people," the Steel Dragon said to Martin and took a step toward him.

"Bullshit," Martin said, although his voice lacked conviction.

"It's true, really," she said in a soothing tone. "We know you two didn't mastermind this whole thing. We have questions and you have answers. Let's work out something mutually beneficial. Like you said, you haven't killed anyone, so there are no charges that can't be worked out through a plea deal. Let's all relax and talk through this."

To Trevor's great surprise, the other man nodded at this—hesitantly at first but then with more feeling. He hoped the goon felt the great sense of relief and calm that he did and that these cops weren't there to hurt them, but to protect them. They wanted to know the truth, but that was only fair. He knew precious little about this whole operation, and he could empathize because he too wanted to know more about what was going on. Maybe he really could help the police.

"So take the gun away from Brian's head, drop it on the floor, and we'll all be fine."

Martin hesitated and for a moment, Trevor thought he saw the man battling the sense of calm. Finally, he relented and lowered his weapon.

The fat kid exhaled and fainted. His captor managed to slow his descent so he didn't crack his head on the coffee table. That, Trevor decided, was how he would describe the whole tableau if he ever stood in front of a jury. As soon as Trevor made that decision, his brain believed it to be the truth.

"We have more police coming, so we need to put you two in cuffs. It's for your own good. We don't want anyone to see those cops you hurt out there and get the wrong idea."

"Yes, officer. Thank you, officer." Trevor stuck his wrists out to the black cop. The man pulled him to his feet and cuffed his wrists behind his back. Even that felt strangely soothing to him. He felt like the chance for violence had passed. It was a huge relief. "We didn't hurt those police, by the way. It was Dorson—that's the guy you threw out the window—and Hector. That's the guy who you, uh…that's the guy in the kitchen." He only wanted to be helpful. Martin didn't need to take the fall for that. It had merely been orders.

"You too," Kristen said to the goon, who nodded and let her cuff him.

CHAPTER FIFTY-SEVEN

The smell of strong coffee and nervous sweat permeated the station. Kristen didn't think she'd ever seen so many officers jammed into the building before. There was no way they could all fit in the lounge so instead, they milled around the desks, argued about who the shooter could have been and what kind of monster would go after a cop's family, and generally gave Frank Hall one hell of a hard time.

She wondered if most families taken into protective custody felt the way her dad probably did. He'd been a cop for thirty years, and although he'd never made SWAT, he still knew a number of the officers there. Despite the fact that he'd been targeted in his own home, he acted like he owned the place, glad-handed people, and asked about their folks. Looking at him, it was easy to forget that he'd almost been kidnapped by an unknown enemy less than an hour before.

The rest of the family dealt with their stress in more predictable ways. Her mom nursed a cup of coffee despite the later hour and stared into the middle distance. Brian zoned into a game on his phone—typical behavior, but she'd have to talk to him later.

Captain Hansen came out of her office, climbed onto a desk, and waited for the room to quiet. It didn't take very long. "All right, so first thing's first—Officer Hall and Officer Washington, the force owes you a debt of gratitude. You saved the lives of two officers. Because of you, they get to go home to see their families tonight. Plus, I guess we're happy you saved the retired one. Some of us would've been sad to see him go."

The woman nodded at Frank as the crowd laughed and broke into applause and cheers. She waited for them to quiet before she continued. "Here's what I can tell you. Three hours ago, four hostiles tried to take our dragon's family hostage. She didn't let them."

More cheers followed.

"Kristen Hall and Jim Washington called into the station, confirmed orders, and went to Hall's residence—at least that's the story if any reporters come around. They apprehended three of the four hostiles. One was injured but seems to be stable, so good job there."

"The one Hall chucked out the window got away?" the Wonderkid asked.

"That's right. Because of all this, the Halls will be under our watch for a while. We obviously can't have the Steel Dragon hovering around them while this sniper is hunting her. Which brings me to my next point. Kristen Hall, you're on office duty until this is all resolved."

The cheers and humor were sucked out of the room as if by a giant vacuum.

"What? But that's ridiculous!" Kristen protested.

"What it is, is an order. And I'm telling the room so everyone understands that if you take Hall out, you risk your own life and your job. If she gets in a cruiser, you answer to me."

"This is bullshit." She was furious. A few other officers—those nearest her—took up her chant.

"If you have a problem, see me in my office. In fact, that's an order. You, Wonderkid, and Drew—my office. Now. Everyone else, get back to work."

A half-hearted cheer went up and was quickly replaced with grumbles about paperwork.

In the office, she quickly found that not everyone was as forgiving as the captain had seemed to be.

Drew wasn't normally one to show much emotion, but he showed it now. He paced like a wolf stuck behind a chain-link fence.

"Hey...Drew," she began haltingly.

"For the record, I recommended full disciplinary action against you two. The captain might not want to put a smudge on the Steel Dragon's record, but I disagree. Running off was reckless, stupid, and beyond dangerous."

"Yeah, but if we didn't do it, Hall's family would be dead," Jim replied.

That only earned a growl from the other man along with a reluctant nod. "I know. And really, I don't know what two regular cops could have done against four armed thugs. It's only... Don't you see you're being manipulated?"

"And what is my alternative?" She was on her feet now. "Let my family be taken prisoner?"

"Obviously not." Captain Hansen sat at her desk behind steepled fingers. "We won't dissect your actions, but we also won't let it happen again. This sniper is hunting you, Kristen. From here on out, you need to be a regular cop."

"A regular person won't be able to stop this killer."

"Kristen, look, I understand that protecting the people you love is a huge part of who you are." The anger had left Drew's voice and been replaced by a pleading tone that Kristen didn't quite know what to do with. "Until now, I've seen it as a huge strength."

Jim laughed. "I hear that. Going into a firefight knowing the Steel Dragon has your back is a great feeling."

The team leader smiled for half a second before his frown returned. "Not least of all because we know you'd do anything to protect us, but that's the problem."

"How is protecting my friends and family a problem?" she asked.

"Because this enemy is obviously smart and will try to turn your strengths into weaknesses," Captain Hansen said. "For all we know, that shot was aimed at your arm to get you to the hospital instead of kill you so they'd be able to snatch your family."

"Don't you think that's a little paranoid?" Jim raised an eyebrow.

"No, I don't, Wonderkid. I really don't. In fact, I think the smartest thing we can do is be as paranoid as possible. A piece of evidence has already gone missing, which is troubling in itself. I think the safest thing we can do is get Kristen out of here completely. I want you to check into a hospital in the suburbs until that shoulder is healed."

"Respectfully, ma'am, that won't be necessary," Kristen said and chose not to acknowledge the dragon-scale bullet in her pocket.

"It's well within my power to put you on medical leave."

"Even if I'm unhurt?" She yanked the bandage off her shoulder.

The two men's gasps were yet another reminder that she was no longer human.

"Don't be ridiculous Hall. It's been less than twenty-four…" Captain Hansen trailed off, her mouth agape.

"The wound… It's already closed?" Drew was incredulous.

Kristen nodded. "It's still stiff but it won't be by tomorrow morning."

The captain recovered first. "That changes nothing. There have been multiple attacks against you and your family. We need to discover how they're connected before you or your family are hurt again."

"Do we know anything about the kidnappers yet?" Jim asked.

Drew nodded. "They are a small 'thug for hire' team. We've seen them before and think about half of them are still at large, but we have people looking for them. We'll catch them."

"The shooter is another matter," Captain Hansen stated.

"Did you find any clues in his nest?" Jim asked.

The team leader responded first. "We did, but you're not gonna like it. For one thing, those shots were fired from about two thousand, six hundred meters away."

The Wonderkid whistled at the distance. "Damn."

"Most snipers are listed with a maximum of one thousand, eight hundred to two thousand meters. Two-six is... Are you sure?" she asked.

"Positive," Drew confirmed. "And I didn't realize you were a gunhead."

"I'm not, but my brother plays a ton of video games. He can tell you the specs on almost any weapon ever made, whether or not you ask him. But even in games, you can't make those kinds of shots."

"Our shooter can. She has the chops." Captain Hansen flexed her jaw.

"Wait, we know who the shooter is? That's good!" A desire for vengeance flared inside her. She saw the same emotion pass over everyone else's face and immediately reminded herself that she really had to get that under control.

"It's really not." The woman dug in her desk and withdrew a shiny silver half-circle about the size of a quarter. "She left her calling card." She tossed it to Kristen.

She caught it and turned it over in her hand. "It's...a dragon scale?"

Drew shook his head. "No, only a little silver made to look like one."

"The assassin's name is Death. Most of our sources say it's a 'she,' but we really don't know for sure. This scale has been found at multiple crime scenes across the world. Almost any time a dragon has been shot and killed in the last twenty years, one of these silver scales is there."

"And no one's ever caught her?" She was amazed that such a tiny, beautiful thing could symbolize murder on a global scale.

"No one's really tried." The captain sighed. "Killing dragons is out of human jurisdiction the world over. You know how they are and how they hate us to pry into their lives. All we know is that Death has an impressive kill list. If the dragons know more, they're not telling us."

At that moment, the door to the office opened and Stonequest entered.

He glanced at the scale in her hand, then at her. "So, it is Death." He didn't look any more pleased to know who the shooter was than the captain was.

"Tell us you've been holding out on the intel," Drew said and a weak grin slid onto his face.

Stonequest shook his head and crushed any hope that might have built. "All we know is that when Death chooses a target, she doesn't stop until she succeeds. She's damn resourceful and beyond dangerous. Kristen, this means your training can't be at your pace anymore."

"What do you mean?"

"I mean that we need you to have every possible dragon ability available to you. If Death is hunting you, she no doubt knows what you can and can't do. You've still never taken your dragon form. I have no doubt that she knows this and is operating around it. We need to unlock your abilities if you're going to live through this. We've never had a steel dragon before. This might be the opportunity we've waited for."

"What does that mean?"

"It means you're coming with me."

He nodded at Captain Hansen and Drew who both nodded to acknowledge Dragon SWAT's preeminence over human affairs.

"What about my family?" she asked.

"We'll keep them safe—change hotels, armed guards in their rooms, the works," the captain assured her.

"That might not be enough," Kristen protested.

"With respect, if you can't activate more of your abilities, I know for a fact there's nothing these humans can do to keep you safe."

She glared at the other dragon but she followed him out of the office and into the night.

Her logical assumption was that they'd get into a car or something because Stonequest took her to the top of the parking garage. Once there, however, he approached the edge and turned to her.

"We're practicing here?" she asked.

"No, but it's easier to start a flight from up high." No sooner had Stonequest finished speaking than he transformed. First, his skin seemed to flake away to reveal stone beneath but the flaking continued. More and more thin fragments of stone and dust fell off him as he doubled in size, then doubled again and again. Wings burst from his back like bones made of lava rock. A tail erupted from his spine to spray more stone and dust across the roof. A membrane, clear as crystal, spread between the bones of his wings and he flapped them once. Dust and debris blew across the top of the parking garage but in a moment, it was all gone, vanished to wherever it had come from.

"I really need to learn how to do that." Her mouth was agape.

"Some dragons learn by simply leaping from a building and activating their powers in a moment of need."

Her expression wary, she peered over the edge. The parking garage was high but not that high. "I think I could survive that landing in my steel form."

Stonequest sighed, a truly odd thing to see a dragon do. "This would be easier if you could transform too," he grumbled. "But until then, climb aboard and hold on tight."

The ride out of the city was a heady, surreal experience. Despite apparently being made of rock, he flew gracefully and barely flapped his wings as he reacted effortlessly to the changes in the cold air.

Kristen longed to be able to do it as well, but not enough to jump from his back and test his theory about necessity being a good teacher.

They flew for close to an hour, and by the time they reached their destination, she was exhausted.

It was a mansion of some kind. Stonequest said something about "our finest palatial manor," before he took her to a bed and told he'd fetch her at dawn.

She nodded and was asleep the moment her head touched the pillow.

CHAPTER FIFTY-EIGHT

Kristen awoke and stared in bemusement at a beautiful ceiling. It was an odd sensation because prior to this moment, she hadn't ever thought that ceilings could be beautiful. In her experience, they either came in white with little popcorn-like things on them or maybe dingy tiles like in an elementary school. The roof above her bed was auburn with gold lace painted in a delicate pattern. She rubbed her eyes and assumed she was having a beautiful but boring dream, but the ceiling persisted.

A little more awake, she pushed up and favored her left arm but quickly discovered she didn't need to. She seemed to be fully healed. The room itself was as beautiful as the ceiling above it. Two antique chairs and a roll-top desk could only ever be described as presidential.

She got out of bed and discovered a pile of neatly folded clothes on one of the chairs. It appeared to be some kind of training outfit much like something used for martial arts.

Fresh clothes made her think of a shower. The thought had no sooner manifested than a knock came at the door. She answered it.

"Would you like a hot bath, ma'am?" asked a short-statured woman wearing black and white and a headscarf that completely eclipsed her hair.

"Uh, yes, please? But...um, where is Stonequest, and—not to be rude—but who the hell are you?"

"Stonequest is meeting some of his allies. He told me to send you to him when you were clean and fed." There seemed to be something more that the woman wanted to say, though. She wondered if it was something Stonequest had said about a stinky human riding his dragon form. Before she could ask, the woman cleared her throat. "My name is Farah. I am a housekeeper at the Dragon Retreat. I can take you to the baths and help you wash your hair."

Struggling to take it all in, she simply nodded and followed the woman to the most elaborate bathroom she had ever seen. Truly, after seeing the space, she didn't think she'd ever actually been in a bathroom before. Her dad's preference for the word 'shitter' seemed a better description for all the tiny rooms with toilets that she had previously thought of as bathrooms.

This room was something else.

Every inch of it boasted tile the shade of eggshell with little blue, pink, and green flowers painted into the tiles. Sinks and showers were positioned around the room, but what held her attention most was the massive pool in the center.

It was a circle perhaps ten feet in diameter with three gargoyles spaced around it. Steaming water bubbled from the throat of one and two of the most beautiful women she had ever seen were seated in the water.

One of them lounged against the wall, her breasts above the water and her eyes closed as another woman in a headscarf massaged shampoo into her scalp.

The other woman's hair was wrapped in a towel, and her eyes shot daggers at the newcomer.

"Your clothes, Lady Steel?" Farah said.

She hesitated for only a moment before she stripped down. While she might be the new kid in town, she wouldn't let this woman—a dragon, no doubt—intimidate her.

Farah led her to a shower where she washed off the grime that came from being an officer for SWAT. Once her skin was a well-scrubbed pink, she returned to the bath.

As she settled into the steaming water, knots of tension that had been in muscles for months melted away.

While her helper washed her hair—a truly decadent experience—one of the dragon women continued to stare at her. The moment might have been perfect if not for her constant sneer. She was about to say something to her, but the woman spoke first.

"So, you're the steel bitch, huh?"

"Excuse me?" she said, shocked at the imperiousness of this other woman.

"We all know who you are. You've plastered your pretty red hair all over the television, haven't you?"

"That wasn't my idea—"

"You haven't shied away from the camera either. Know this, steel bitch. You're not a dragon. You may do the little trick with your metal skin, but for all we know, you're merely a dragonling whose egg should have been cracked. Until you can transform, you won't be anything more than a curiosity."

Before she could respond, the woman stood and the water wicked away from her body. It wrung itself from her hair, pushed itself down her naked body, and formed in waves where it held and waited to crest against her legs.

"How did you—" Kristen began.

"You're not the only one of us with unusual abilities. There are mages who can do little parlor tricks like yours. Do yourself a favor and walk home before you waste more of Stonequest's time."

With that, she stepped from her side of the pool and the water surged to fill the void she had created with her abilities. A servant brought her a garment much like a karate gi and similar to the one Kristen had found in her room.

"I apologize for Lady Aqua," Farah said and rinsed her hair. "She has not been kind to a new dragon for centuries, but she will come around when she sees what you are capable of."

"There's no point in delaying the training, then."

"Yes, my lady."

She stepped from the bath and Farah fetched her a towel. Once dry, she put on the gi and was relieved that it fit well but was still loose enough to allow her a full range of motion. It made a perfect training outfit, really.

From there, she was led to a dining room with the largest spread of breakfast she had ever seen. Every kind of fruit she knew was on offer, plus a few others that had to have been imported from well south of Michigan's border. There were breads of every kind, bacon, sausage, and ham, and a chef would cook eggs to order, omelets or otherwise.

Kristen noticed with growing delight that everyone in the dining room ate with the gusto of a Hall. Despite the men having chiseled arms devoid of body fat and the women all being narrow-waisted, they ate like the buffet might run out of food at any moment. This was a piece of dragon culture that she could participate in.

Her enthusiasm returned and she attacked the breakfast buffet without delay. She ate six pieces of avocado toast, a four-egg omelet crammed with sausage and olives and topped with an absurd amount of crème fraiche and more bacon than she could count. Between it all, she tried the various fruits and savored the perfect texture of each one. All in all, it was the best breakfast she could remember eating. Better even than the platter of breakfast tacos she had once had when she'd visited Austin, Texas, with her family.

While she ate, the dragons ignored her and she did the same. She hoped that outside of the bathroom, there would be some sense of decorum and the dragons seemed to respect this.

Finally sated, she pushed her chair back and belched. That drew a look of disfavor from the other dragons, but she didn't care.

"Lady Steel, if you're ready?" Farah said and startled her as she hadn't seen her return. "Stonequest is waiting for you."

"Oh, right, sorry! I thought with the bath and the meal that I'd have more time."

"His orders were to see that you were bathed and fed. If you're satisfied on both counts, I am to bring you to him." There was a tinge of fear in the woman's voice. Kristen didn't like it but wondered if that was the price of working for beings who could eat a human as easily as they could a pile of bacon.

"Let's not keep him waiting." She pushed herself from the table. While she didn't think that Stonequest would punish Farah—he seemed more interested in the welfare of human beings than most dragons—he didn't run this place either. She would feel horrible if the woman were punished because she had taken her time to nurse a cup of coffee.

They moved quickly through the hallways of the manor and past oil paintings and marble sculptures. Many of them were of humans—or at least dragons in human form—but a few of the paintings were of dragons in front of castles or on fields of battle. Like everything else there, the collection was beyond impressive.

Her guide led her to a huge hallway. This one had marble floors instead of carpet and seemed to be the entryway for the residence. Honestly, she didn't have the vocabulary to describe it. The room was as large as a ballroom, with curved staircases that led to the upper floors. A grand entryway? A dancing hall? Whatever it was, it was beautiful, but she didn't have much time to appreciate it as Farah led her between the staircases and out the back door.

Outside, the grounds were as beautiful and well-maintained as the palace itself. Perfectly trimmed grass was interrupted only by beds of flowers in bloom despite the cold weather. Gazebos dotted the landscape to provide shade for quiet conversations. On a hill toward the back of the grounds stood a pillared structure that looked like it belonged in ancient Greece, not outside Detroit. Between the mini-Parthenon and the palace lay a huge rectangle of sand.

Within it, dragons sparred in both dragon and human form with weapons both ancient and modern. She saw swords, crossbows, and guns. They used all of it on each other, seemingly without fear. It made SWAT's gym and shooting range look like it was made for preschoolers.

"Farewell, Lady Steel," Farah said as she scuttled back to the palace.

"Thank you!" Kristen yelled at her retreating back, which seemed to draw the ire of a few dragons who'd strolled quietly across the immaculate grounds.

"Kristen! It's about time." Stonequest jogged toward her from the sandy rectangle. A servant tossed him a towel and he dried off before he pulled a shirt on. A good thing too, she decided, as he looked like his human body was chiseled from marble by a hand as skilled as the ones that made the sculptures inside the manor. He was less distracting this way.

"Morning, Stonequest. Sorry for being late."

"It's fine. We have a long day ahead of us, so I wanted you to be fed. Are you good to skip lunch?"

She nodded before she knew what she was doing. That possibly explained why the dragons had eaten so much. Halls didn't skip lunch.

"Good. Are you enjoying it here?" he asked and gestured for her to walk with him.

"Uh…mostly."

"Mostly? Most of us are amazed the first time we come to the Dragon Retreat. It's hard to get the European style right in this country."

"The place is great, seriously, but everyone is a little…cold?"

He grimaced. "Try not to worry about them. They'll all change their tune once you have your wings."

"Do you really think you can teach me how to transform into a dragon?"

"You already are a dragon and have all the hallmarks of a dragon in human form. We merely need that last piece. You've made great progress so far. I'm sure you can do it with a teacher who actually wants to unlock your abilities."

"I hope it doesn't take long. That sniper is still at large. Did you hear that some thugs targeted my family as well?"

Stonequest nodded, his grin gone. "I did, yes. Which is all the more reason to train, and train hard. I understand how…fragile human families can be."

Kristen didn't really know what to say to that, so she merely nodded.

"I did have some questions about what happened that night, though. Can you tell me your version of events? The police report said the thug who had a gun to your brother's head surrendered. Is that true?"

"It is." She told him the whole story, careful to include all the details of her dragon abilities—how she could transform only parts of her body into steel if she wanted to, her increased speed and strength, and her night vision. But he was most interested in how she'd disarmed the man with the gun.

"It sounds like you activated your aura on that guy."

She nodded. "I wondered if that was what happened. Shadowstorm talked often about sensing auras, so I've done some study there, but I'm still not really sure how to control it directly. I think there have been a few times when I've made people angry because I'm angry or made them agree with me, but well… It's not always pretty."

"Our aura is one of our most powerful abilities, especially as it relates primarily to humans. It doesn't take a ton of control to be able to shield yourself from other dragons, so we won't focus on that too much, but its effects on other species can be huge."

"Are you saying that humans are other species?" she asked and while she tried not to sound confrontational, she failed dismally.

Stonequest shrugged awkwardly. "We're different but that's not what I meant. Our aura can do far more than make an angry mob or quell one. Watch."

He closed his eyes, took a deep breath, and raised both arms. She felt something emanate from him, but it wasn't an emotion exactly, more like an…interest? It was hard to describe.

She understood that she couldn't make sense of it when a bird landed on his finger. It was a gorgeous little thing, entirely red with a thick orange beak, black mask, and a little tuft of feathers at the top of its head.

"Wow! Is that a robin?" she asked.

"What? No!" The look of disdain on his face was palpable. "This is a northern cardinal. Seriously? You thought this was a robin? Robins are the state bird of Michigan and have a puffy red breast, a yellow bill and—"

"Is learning about birds an important part of my training?"

"No. It's only—you're right. Never mind. This is a cardinal. A male. I'm using my aura to make him think of me as a friend. If I tweak it only a little…"

The bird sang a song.

"Or I can have it fly off and return."

It flew about twenty feet away, came back, and sang on his finger again.

"Or make it think you're a predator."

The bird flapped its wings and attacked her face, chirping angrily as it did so.

She held up her hands to defend her face but the bird had already landed on his finger.

"The trick with auras is that you make the subject feel a certain way. Animals have simpler emotions than we do—most animals, anyway, and don't get me started on using an aura with a sperm whale—so they're easier to control. The hard part is matching the emotion to an action. You can't simply tell the bird 'land on my finger.' You have to make the bird want to land on your finger if that makes sense."

Kristen nodded. In theory, that made sense. "So, it's not mind control but emotion control."

Stonequest nodded. "Yes…well, kind of. You don't really control anything but rather simply nudge one way or the other. It's easier if you actually try it yourself."

He waited while she focused on the bird. The cardinal? She tried to make it think her finger looked like a great perch. When that brought no response, she tried to make it afraid of Stonequest. Finally, she tried something that he'd already done and attempted to make it think her face looked like a monster.

"You can try whenever you're ready," he said.

"I am trying!"

"Oh. Sorry. Normally, the bird does something. Are you sure you're trying?"

"Yes!" She focused harder on the bird and willed it to feel happy, sad, terrified—anything. It chirped once and cocked its stupid little red head to the side.

"Most dragons start by simply scaring it. Nudge it to think you're a hawk."

Feeling like a fraud, she tried a nudge and it simply chirped sweetly.

"Look, this doesn't make sense to me." She rubbed her face. "Maybe it's because I don't see how it can be a good thing to control other creatures' minds."

"Emotions."

"Whatever. Isn't it an abuse of power to take control of what's inside another being's head?"

"Using your aura can be an abuse of power. Throughout history, many have used it to subjugate the weak-willed," Stonequest said.

"So, it is bad."

"Not necessarily," he countered. "It's a tool, like a pen or a hammer or a handgun. All tools can be used either for horrible purposes or to elevate our existence. How it's used determines its ethics."

"Okay...but isn't controlling someone else's emotions inherently worse than all those things?"

"I would argue that handguns are worse than our aura. Even in the hands of police officers, they often kill. Our auras don't do that. But the fact is it's an ability that dragons possess. It's as integral to us as venom is to a spider. We've used it for thousands of years and will continue to use it. I understand if you're uncomfortable with it and I think that coming at it from the human perspective might be a good thing for more dragons to think about, but it doesn't change the fact that if you ignore it, it's a tool you won't have. It could even be the decisive factor against Death."

"So you think the sniper is a human, then?"

He nodded. "I do. I can't imagine a dragon mastering a gun like that. It's a human tool, not really our speed."

"But you think I can learn an aura?"

"You're not human."

She raised an eyebrow at that.

Stonequest chuckled. "This is why I want you here for periods of training. Your perspective is so interesting. Now come on, get this bird to land on your finger before the big bad dragon takes advantage of it."

Kristen nodded. While she still wasn't entirely comfortable with the idea, if she mastered it, at least she could use her aura to stop other dragons from using theirs.

Once again, she focused on the cardinal perched on his finger. He had said it worked by nudging its emotions, so she tried to nudge. *Be happy, little birdy. Be so happy you want to land on my finger.*

The bird chirped.

Perhaps it was time for a different approach. She tried to feel its emotional state. After a minute of probing with an inner awareness she hadn't even known she'd possessed, she sensed a small mote of feeling. The tiny bubble seemed to be contentment and not much else. She tried to feel the emotion and immediately thought that Stonequest was totally trustworthy.

Okay, so she was closer.

She tried to extend that feeling of comfort to herself and the bird turned to her. It cocked its little head and flew off. She cursed under her breath but flexed the nudge to calm the bird and make herself feel like an ally, someone who would protect it.

To her delight, it circled her once before it landed on her finger.

"Oh, wow!" For a moment, her reservations faded completely from her mind. She'd actually communicated with a different species. That was amazing!

Then, the bird pooped on her hand. "Ahh!" She dropped her hand, lost the aura, and the bird flew away as she wiped the poop on her training gi.

"Did you do that?"

"If you had full command of your aura, you'd already know the answer to that question."

Kristen struggled not to roll her eyes. He sounded a bit too mystical for her taste.

Then, Stonequest's visage cracked into a grin. "But enough of that for now. Let's get to work."

CHAPTER FIFTY-NINE

"We have a robbery in progress. Requesting units to the comic bookstore on Library Street. I repeat, requesting units to the Vault of Midnight. Someone made off with forty thousand dollars' worth of rare comics."

Kristen had been back at the station for a day and had a while to wait before her next training session. For some reason, Stonequest insisted that she alternate time between her human team and the dragon training. She bolted up from her desk and rushed to the gear room. She had to go on this one. If Brian found out she had saved comic books, he'd be beyond amazed. There were no doubt people in peril too and she didn't forget about them, but it was pleasant to have something come up that wasn't about people getting shot or blown up or taken hostage.

She raced through the halls and reached the gear room to find Drew there, geared up and with his arms folded. "You're grounded, remember?"

"But…the comic books," she protested.

"Take it up with the captain. She said to send you to her office if you came here."

"Okay. Okay." She sighed. "But try not to ruin the comics, all right?"

"Whatever you say, Hall." He snorted a laugh as she trudged through the station and toward the captain's office.

"Where did you think you were going?" Captain Hansen yelled as soon as Kristen stepped inside. The only thing worse than being yelled at by the captain for trying to do her job was that she was being reprimanded in front of Stonequest. He sat in one of the guest chairs and wore a broad smile.

"I only… Comics can't be that dangerous. It's probably only some nerds trying to get rich. How is SWAT even going out for that one?"

"The crooks made off with a Spider Man #1. People would die for that comic—or kill," the captain stated matter-of-factly.

She raised an eyebrow. "Ma'am, are you a nerd?"

"What I read in my free time is none of your concern," the woman snapped in response. "The fact remains that we have an assassin at large. And until Death is brought in, you will not leave your desk. I don't even want you near the windows."

"So, you did put me at that desk on purpose?"

"Of course, I did. Not everyone on SWAT operates on instinct like you always try to."

"But ma'am, I need to be out with my team. Death obviously knows who I am, which means she might target my teammates. Right, Stonequest?"

"I have to say I agree with the captain. Death hasn't targeted any other police officers, so thinking that she will is purely conjecture. Plus, your training hasn't progressed enough for you to handle a major threat like that. Dragon's flame, I'm worried about taking her on with my team from Dragon SWAT. If it were only you, especially without your dragon form, you'd be killed."

"But I have steel skin," she protested.

"Which Death knows all about. Sorry, Kristen. I'm with the captain." He folded his arms.

"Ugh. Fine. Can I go back to my desk, then?"

"But of course," Captain Hansen said.

She cursed inwardly because she had hoped that Stonequest was there to whisk her away for more training. Worse, it seemed that the two captains simply swapped notes, so there went any chance she had to deliver her planned monologue of protest about the hypocrisy of her being grounded. Damn.

Kristen didn't think she'd ever experienced time pass as slowly as it did for the next three hours. What made it even worse was that when her team returned, they almost bounced off the walls with stories to tell.

"I could not believe when you hit their trunk and popped the lock," Hernandez said to Keith.

He made no response aside from a hearty laugh.

The team moved to the break room, so she left her desk and fell into step to follow them.

"It was like a confetti of wizard cards," Butters said.

"Wizard cards? You mean Magic the Gathering?" she asked.

"That's the one." The sniper snapped his fingers when he recognized the title. "They'd filled their trunk with these things. Apparently, the comics were too valuable to keep out of sight. Anyway, the Rookie got a lucky shot off—"

"It was not lucky," Keith protested.

"It was mid-pursuit. It's not like you can make shots like that on the regular. No one can," Drew said.

Keith huffed and folded his arms. "Whatever. I did aim for the trunk."

"Anyway…" Butters took the narrative back. "These cards scattered everywhere, and what did the perps do? They swerved and stopped and tried to pick the things up."

"Not all of them." Hernandez laughed. "One of them stayed in the back seat, reading comic books as fast as he could until we cuffed him."

Everyone laughed at that, the demolitions expert so hard she had to wipe a tear from her eyes.

"So, Red, what have you been doing here?" she asked.

"Paperwork." Kristen sighed.

"There's more of that to come. The comic shop is throwing the book at us. Apparently, all that crap was insured and they argue that by failing to respond fast enough and then chasing the crooks, we endangered their livelihood." Drew smiled. "If you want to help, we'd be happy for it."

"I don't mind talking to the comic shop," Keith said and grinned. He'd found a mop in the corner of the breakroom and thrust it into Kristen's hands. "Hall has stuff to do here to be useful. The station won't clean itself."

Everyone laughed and she joined in, although hers was a rueful chuckle.

As soon as the Rookie's mouth closed and his grin faded to hide his teeth, she slapped him across the face with the dirty mop.

"What was that for?" He wiped dirty water from his face.

"You said to clean. I simply looked for the dirtiest thing handy."

Hernandez leaned in and sniffed him. "Sorry, Rookie, but Red has a point. You stink."

CHAPTER SIXTY

A call came in for a mission and Drew assembled his team. Part of him felt bad that Hall wasn't allowed to join them, but he agreed with the captain. Death was too dangerous to mess around with. That aside, it was also pleasant to run missions with only regular people.

He had been on SWAT for years and was good at his job. Damn good at it, if he was honest. And it wasn't that Hall wasn't good as well. Really, he loved her like a sister and thought she was a damn good cop. But there were times when it was nice to be more than back-up for the Steel Dragon.

Well, not nice. Dealing with armed criminals was never nice, but it was what he knew how to do, and he did it well.

They loaded into the van with him at the wheel and headed out.

"What's the mission, Drew?" Butters asked.

"It's fairly basic." He raised his voice and spoke over his shoulder so those in the back could hear. "A couple of robbers hit a convenience store. They have a hostage, but the place is locked down and the officer in charge says things are looking good to get them to surrender. They only want us as back up in case it doesn't go well."

"We can handle that without the Steel Dragon," Hernandez said.

"She'd probably rush in there and snap their necks before they could even piss themselves."

Everyone laughed but it was forced. Without Kristen on missions, their team didn't feel complete. All too often, he'd have to remind himself how pleasant it was to be a team of normal humans—exactly like he'd done a few minutes earlier—but the truth was that he missed her as much as they did. He didn't know how the hell they would catch Death, but he hoped they did and that it was soon.

Drew appreciated that his team had to work harder and be more precise with Hall grounded, but he didn't like what her being stuck at the base did for his team's morale. Steel Dragon or not, she was part of them now. Not having her there felt as odd as it had to lose Jonesy. He rarely entertained the thought that if they didn't catch the sniper soon they might lose her as well.

He issued the standard basic orders—Butters and Beanpole on sniper duty, the Wonderkid and the Rookie headed around back—and after a few minutes, they arrived at the convenience store.

What was it about those kinds of establishments that criminals loved? He would never understand it. They seemed to attract the slightly insane and mostly incompetent. After they'd arrived and assessed the scene, he could tell that this situation was no different than most.

Two guys had tried to steal cash and maybe some scratch-offs and hadn't escaped quickly enough. When the cops showed up, they took the clerk hostage. It was almost pathetic how common a story it was but his job wasn't to ponder societal ills. They were there to save lives.

He could see he'd need to do that today. One of the crooks stood in the doorway with the hostage in front of him and a handgun held to the man's temple.

"Where's the other one?" Drew asked over the radio.

"Inside behind a shelf. You can see his shoulder poking up," Butters replied.

"All right. I'm going in," he said to the officers who'd called in the situation. "Cover me and be ready to move in. This guy wouldn't stand in the doorway if he didn't want to talk. I'll go radio silent.

Hernandez, if Keith and Jim find an entrance, it's your call whether they go in."

"Yes, sir."

He nodded, drew his handgun from its holster, held it in the air, and placed it on the pavement at his feet. "I'm unarmed, see? They called me in because I like to talk," he said to the man. The trick with talking to criminals in these kinds of situations was to be loud enough to be heard over their own heartbeats pounding in their ears but to not sound like you were screaming at them. His low, booming voice worked well.

"Talk is cheap, pig," the robber yelled in response.

Typical. They often liked to start with a line from a movie, especially if there was more than one of them.

"You're right. So is robbery. With the right lawyer, you might do less than a year. If you hurt that man, though, you'll find yourself facing far more time. No one likes a murderer." As he spoke, he approached the convenience store slowly with his hands raised.

"I'm not a murderer."

"I know you're not. Believe me. We've seen monsters and you don't seem like one, merely a man down on his luck." He made it a few steps closer.

"You don't know the half of it, pig." There was desperation in the man's voice. That could be good if properly channeled but could also be extremely dangerous.

"Luck changes. Yours can change. What's your name?" he asked as soothingly as he could.

"Fuck you! You assholes will only feed me to your fucking pet dragon."

"That isn't true." He took another step forward. "And anyway, she's not with us today. It's only us humans. My name's Drew, by the way."

"Not another step closer." The man shoved the pistol against his hostage's head. "They call me Dogface."

He could see why. The man's face was so badly pockmarked it looked like whiskers, and one of his ears was damaged. The top half of it hung down like a bulldog's. Drew frowned inwardly. Dogface probably wasn't the best name to negotiate with, but that was what he had.

"Look, Dogface, I'll be straight with you." Fortunately, he didn't have to raise his voice as much now as he was about ten paces away. "You won't walk away from this. We have you surrounded. You'll face a jury of your peers—people like you. What story do you want to tell them? That you were down on your luck and you messed up, but at your darkest moment, you let a man live? Or that you're a killer?"

"I'm not a killer." His pistol raised marginally from the hostage's skin and lowered slightly. Drew had him. The man simply didn't know that yet.

"Good. That's good, Dogface. Now, here's what we'll do. You'll lower that weapon to the ground and kick it toward me. I'll tell your lawyer all this was your idea, of course. Then, you'll tell your buddy to do the same, and you guys will come out of this looking like victims of circumstance. All right?"

"Al-all right," Dogface stammered. He lowered his pistol a little more.

No sooner did he lower the weapon than a red hole appeared in his forehead and his brains blew back into the convenience store.

Dogface fell back, very clearly dead.

The hostage screamed and stumbled forward.

A moment later, Drew heard a gunshot in the distance.

Shock gave way to reality—Dogface had been shot.

"That's the sniper! Find cover people. The asshole's behind us." Drew immediately fell prone. There wasn't any cover available close by. He was in the parking lot between the police cars and the convenience store. Still, he scooted forward and realized as he did so that the bullet that might end his life could already be on its way to kill him.

He glanced up to where the cops scurried behind their cars. Hernandez had got them to come to the correct side anyway. Thank God for that.

The sound of broken glass was followed and a scream from inside the convenience store a second before the report of another shot cracked from behind them.

Drew turned his head as the other robber staggered out from his hiding place in the aisle, a hand clamped around his neck in an effort to stop the blood that gushed from his wound.

The sniper had got him. Through a window, a shelf, and a bag of chips, the sniper had still found her target.

He reached the front of the store before his hand slid from his neck and he collapsed next to his partner.

The hostage stumbled past and screamed in terror, so Drew did what he did every day at work. He pushed to his feet and helped someone—threw his arm around the man and led him to the police cruisers. They slumped behind a door and waited.

The clerk was crying, thanking his God, thanking Drew, and thanking the police. The SWAT team leader heard none of it. He waited for another shot. While he didn't think the sniper could hurt anyone through a police car, that shot into the convenience store through the window was all but impossible. If they could do that at a distance far enough for there to be a delay in the sound, the regular rules didn't seem to apply.

After a few minutes and no more shots, he felt confident enough to step out from behind the police cruiser.

He stood, faced the direction the shots had come from, and looked for a flash of light. If he saw one, he'd have a millisecond to dodge before the bullet killed him and seconds before he heard the weapon.

No shots came and everyone seemed to draw a collective breath of relief.

"I think we're in the clear," Drew said into his radio. "I want helmets on and Butters, keep your eyes in the direction those shots came from. Still, I think we're in the clear."

"You already said that, sir," the Wonderkid said over the radio.

He tried to force a smile. This was a new sensation for him. Normally, he operated under the assumption that he could do his job because he had been better-trained than the common criminal and had a team that could protect him. With Death on the other end of the sniper rifle, neither was the case. It was a profoundly uncomfortable feeling.

What was worse was that they needed to do something about the bodies. He called an ambulance, but that simply meant he had to stick around and make sure no one else was hurt.

He sent in a team to investigate where the sniper had been as well, but there were multiple apartment blocks in that direction. It would be basically impossible to find her.

It was also impossible to know if Death was simply waiting for them, which created additional stress.

But they went about their jobs, blocked the crime scene off for forensics, and ensured that EMS had what they needed.

Despite all the activity, no more shots were fired.

"What the hell do you think that was all about?" Hernandez asked as EMS left with the two bodies. She too was jumpy. Her gaze darted constantly toward where they had heard the gunshots come from.

"I think that was her way of saying she's watching us." Drew hadn't realized he'd been sweating until he wiped his brow and found it slick.

She nodded. "She could have taken us out instead of the robbers."

"I know. She chose to let us live."

"What does that mean?" she asked.

"It means she thinks she owns us."

"And what the fuck are we supposed to do about that?"

He sighed. "I have no fucking idea."

CHAPTER SIXTY-ONE

"Oh, thank God you're all right." Kristen had never been so relieved to see anyone walk through a door as she was when they entered the lounge. She'd followed the incident at the convenience store over the radio. It had taken everything in her power not to rush out after them, but given all that had happened, she saw now that it was good that she hadn't.

The sniper could have shot her in the back of the head and there wouldn't have been a thing she could have done about it.

But for some reason, Death had spared her team. For that, she was grateful, albeit confused. However, she could deal with confusion. She rushed forward—windows be damned—and hugged each one to make sure they knew she was happy they were okay, even Hernandez.

"Nice to see you too, Red," the demolitions expert said. Those casual words were an admission of terror she had never before heard from the woman. Lyn Hernandez didn't do nice. Facing your own demise had a way of humbling people.

"Hall, Drew, I want you in my office," Hansen said.

"Ma'am?" Keith asked.

"Oh, for Christ's sake. Bring the whole team."

A moment later, they all crammed into Hansen's office and looked at a manila folder the contents of which were surely far more important than the bland exterior.

The captain appraised her officers. "Obviously, we need to find this assassin or whoever hired them."

"It's Shadowstorm, it has to be." Kristen's tone brooked no argument.

Her superior raised her hands in a gesture that indicated frustration. "Well, if you can find him, Hall, by all means, bring him in for questioning. It went so well the last time we brought a dragon in."

"Do you think the sniper's a dragon now?" she asked.

Captain Hansen shook her head. "I have no idea. I don't want to make any damn assumptions, but I can't imagine dragons paying humans to kill dragons."

"Captain, with respect, you didn't call us in here to talk about the sniper."

"Perceptive as always, Drew. You're right. We don't know shit about the sniper. The asshole operates on a whole other level. There has been a further complication, though."

"What is it?" Kristen asked.

"Those thugs who tried to kidnap your family? They don't know a damn thing. They said their boss made all the contacts and that they only followed orders."

"Business as usual, then." Drew sounded tired.

The boss scowled and nodded.

"Can't you simply catch the boss, then? The toad can't be that hard to find," Keith said.

"You're right about that, Rookie. In fact, we already found him—and the rest of the team too."

"But that's great!" Kristen said. "I can pump them for information and put the fear of the Steel Dragon into them." Suddenly, the idea of having an aura that could make people feel things didn't seem like such a bad thing.

"Don't get ahead of yourself, Hall. We found the team because they're all dead. Each one was eliminated with a single bullet fired from a high-powered rifle. Perfect fucking executions." Captain

Hansen looked disgusted. "No one even called the cops on the damn crimes."

"And none of the ones we have are talking?" the Wonderkid asked.

"Oh, one of them is talking. Styx, the scrawny one. He won't shut up, actually. I get the feeling he'd give us his buddy's social security numbers if he knew them, but that's the problem. They don't know a damn thing, and half of what he says is false. I don't think he even realizes he's lying. My guess is that Death ordered it like that so the part of the gang doing the kidnapping wouldn't know anything about her—or him. That way if it went wrong, well…"

Everyone nodded. It had gone exactly as Death had wanted it to.

"I don't think we'll solve this with regular police work," Kristen said finally.

The captain sighed. "You're probably right. There have been assassinations like these in a dozen countries and on multiple continents. If no one else could catch her, I don't know why we'll be able to."

"Because we have a dragon," Keith said and sounded optimistic despite the evidence that suggested he should feel otherwise.

The truth of that struck her like an arrow to the heart.

"We're only in this situation because Hall is a dragon," Drew said.

"No, no, Keith is right. If I can unlock more of my abilities—those Death doesn't know about—I can beat her. That's the whole reason for me training with Stonequest, but I need to focus more intensely on it. Originally, we all thought it was a way to protect myself, and it is, but it might also unlock abilities that enable me to track her and defeat her when I find her. I have to. We don't have any other choice."

"Are you're sure leaving the station is safe?"

"We trained at a mansion out in the country with, like, fifty dragons. If Death can get me there…well, we're all beyond screwed."

Captain Hansen snorted a chuckle at that. "All right. Sure, it's better than anything I have right now. Call Stonequest and keep away from the damn windows until he gets here."

"Yes, ma'am."

After a phone call to Stonequest and thirty minutes of waiting,

Kristen once again flew out toward the dragons' palatial manor on the back of a dragon.

He said nothing on the journey, which gave Kristen time to think—something she both desperately needed and wished to avoid at all costs.

She couldn't see a future in which she didn't realize the entire spectrum of her dragon powers. Shadowstorm—she was quite confident that the dragon was involved in all this—wouldn't stop throwing enemies at her until either he'd been defeated or she was dead. The latter would be inevitable unless she learned to transform.

She would have to fully become a dragon to save her friends and family.

And yet, what would be the cost of that? Unlike any other dragon she had met, she'd grown up as a human. She identified as human and her friends were human but now, if she was to protect that world, she needed to become something else—something more. It occurred to her that until this moment, she'd believed she could be both—a human dragon, and not merely in words but in reality. She'd somehow envisaged herself as a human who could also become a dragon when the need arose. The reality, though, was that it worked the other way. She was a dragon who could also be human. In this situation, being human was not enough and she would have to take that final step and become more than that.

It had already begun to happen. While she had always been protective of her family and close friends, she now felt personally responsible for them in a way she never had until she'd found out that she was a dragon. Her emotions didn't always feel like her own, which seemed even stranger because she could now more easily affect the emotions of others.

At the root of this was the fact that she didn't want to lose who she was. Perhaps the fear that she might lose that was the reason why she hadn't yet managed to transform. It was an interesting thought. The who she was had always been defined by her belief in her humanness. Yet part of her had always wondered if there was more to her life. She had chalked that up to youth and assumed that many people felt that way. As things turned out, there had been more to little Krissy Hall. Now, she still wanted to belong to both worlds.

Kristen felt like she knew what she had to do. Her family had already been attacked and that made her choice for her. The implications of that—of what she needed to become—was exhilarating but it was frightening as well.

She could see that with more power—the power that was her true dragon birthright—she might be able to better protect her people, her family, and her city. With that, she could stop this threat and root out Shadowstorm.

It wasn't a choice, really. She knew that she must become what she was born to be. And yet, if she fully embraced her powers, she would also accept that she wasn't human but was something more powerful and more deadly. What would happen to the person she had been?

CHAPTER SIXTY-TWO

After a decadent dinner, a night of rest, and a massive breakfast, Kristen and Stonequest were in the sandy training arena again. They had spent the morning meditating, but despite the fact that she enjoyed the process, her mentor had been less than impressed.

"I'll attack you. Defend yourself." He removed his shirt and revealed the chest that really did seem to be carved from marble.

"Human or dragon?"

"Is that a question you'll ask all your enemies?"

"No, of course not—"

Her protest died when he launched into the attack. His fists pounded into her gut and she catapulted away and tumbled through the sand.

She pushed herself to her feet, thankful that she'd practiced activating her steel skin so many times.

Before she could so much as dust herself off, he was on her again. This time, he swept her legs out from under her and in the instant before she fell, threw one hell of an elbow into her chest.

The hard landing winded her and she gasped for air. Steel skin protected her from puncture wounds, but she could still have the wind knocked out of her.

"Will you give me a minute?" she pleaded.

In reply, he kicked her in her steel gut and she somersaulted through the sand.

All right. Enough was enough. Now, she was pissed.

She pushed to her feet and raced forward to rain a flurry of punches and kicks on her opponent. He blocked them and barely flinched at the blows. She couldn't really tell because of her steel protection, but it seemed like his skin was more mottled than it had been. Maybe he could armor his human form in stone the way she could turn herself to steel?

The time spent thinking about anything except how to pummel him cost her dearly. Stonequest struck and caught her in the neck with a karate chop that bowled her over.

Kristen rubbed her neck. "That could've killed me."

"We are facing Death. It's time to act like it."

"What is your fucking problem?"

"My problem is that you have a vast reserve of power at your disposal and you refuse to access it." He glared at her. "I can feel you holding yourself back."

"I'm not trying to."

"Enough whining." He launched himself into a flying kick. It would have been an impossible move for a regular human, but dragons in human form were far from regular. Still, she had seen more than enough kung-fu movies. She caught his leg and hurled him away from her.

He began to transform into a dragon before he even fell. A gale of dust and chips of stone resolved into a dragon with skin of mottled marble.

She tried not to think about when she'd last fought a dragon in her human form—not an easy thing to do. Her battle against Shadowstorm had been in an arena exactly like this. He would have killed her if not for her friends, but none of them could help her now.

"This isn't fair."

"Tell that to Death." With a pump of his wings, Stonequest propelled himself forward and pounded into her with a claw as big as her chest. She struggled to break his hold but couldn't and he crushed her into the sand as if to grind her like a cigarette butt.

"Fight me, dragon!" he roared.

"Fuck…you!" She spat sand and managed to slide from his grasp.

Kristen turned to run in an effort to get beyond his reach. She made it three steps before his tail whipped around and struck her in the back.

Once again, she tumbled helplessly through the sand before she finally stopped and pushed herself up.

Already, Stonequest was there. He plucked her up in his front claws, flew fifty feet into the air, and dropped her.

The wind raced past her as she fell. Now was the time to transform. She knew that but still, she didn't. Instead, she made sure her steel skin was on.

When she impacted, sand spewed around her and her muscles screamed in protest.

"Stop it," she pleaded.

He ignored her, tucked his wings, and plummeted toward her.

The dragon was so large, she couldn't even roll clear of his shadow before he barreled into her with the force of a semi-truck focused into a fist the size of a cannonball.

She blacked out for a half-second.

When her brain began to work again, she was in his talons. Compared to him, she was merely a doll. He shook her viciously.

"Is this how you protect your friends?" Stonequest roared and thumped her head against the sand. "Is this how you save your family?" He pummeled her with his other fist. "Is this how you die?"

He hurled her like a piece of discarded trash, useful no longer. She plowed through the sand and tried to get her hands and knees under her. Even that was a struggle and tears came unbidden. She'd trusted him and he intended to kill her.

"What is your fucking problem?" she screamed and forced herself to her feet.

Kristen looked across the arena and saw through her tears that Stonequest was in human form once more. He ran to her, put an arm under her shoulder, and helped her to her feet. She flinched at his touch.

"What the fuck is this?"

"Kristen, I'm sorry. Really."

"Bullshit!"

"I should have explained but I was worried it wouldn't work if I did. Obviously, it didn't either way."

"Worried what wouldn't work?" She choked out a sob.

"The first time you activated your powers, it was because someone had fired a rocket at you. In a moment of great crisis, your body instinctively saved you. I…I hoped to brute-force your transformation, I guess."

He led her to a bench beneath a gazebo. A servant appeared from nowhere with a pitcher of cold water.

"That kind of training…it's inhumane," she said and fought to keep the fury out of her voice. The result was that she simply sounded scared and she hated that. She'd rather have Stonequest know she was pissed.

Still, he balked at the word. That he took it as an insult to be called inhumane was a small comfort. "I see that now, and I'm sorry. It's only—well, you're being hunted and I don't want Death to win."

"So your plan was to nearly kill me?"

"I won't do it again. I merely thought that with enough duress, you'd transform."

"Maybe I don't have that kind of power yet."

Stonequest shook his head. "You have more than enough power."

"How can you possibly know that?"

"Your aura. Everyone walking the grounds of this manor can tell from your aura that you should be able to transform. Honestly, I think that's one of the reasons so many of the dragons treat you so coldly. You have more raw power than most of them, and yet you refuse to transform."

"I'm not refusing anything," Kristen protested.

He sighed. "I don't mean it like that. But with the power I feel coming off you, transformation shouldn't be difficult. If anything, it ought to be natural. Our winged, scaled form is our true form after all."

"Maybe for you." She looked away, out across the landscape that was so obviously designed for humans to walk. Despite them growing ever closer to winter, it was still warm there. Flowers still bloomed. On second glance, she saw that this place wasn't for humans at all. It was unnatural, governed by different laws than her mom's azalea bushes.

"I think that maybe that's the problem. You still haven't accepted that you're a dragon."

"Yes, I have! I take bullets for my team. I use my speed and strength to stop criminals."

"But those are human affairs, and human ways of fighting."

"What's wrong with that?"

"You're not human," Stonequest retorted. "You're something far more powerful. You're clinging to your human form, augmenting it, strengthening it, but not setting it aside like you need to. I think you might be unintentionally repressing the transformation. You have a mental block that's trapped you in that body, limiting your powers and your true essence."

Kristen stood and whirled on him, her bruises forgotten as anger coursed through her. "Can you even hear yourself? You sound like him—like Shadowstorm! You think being in my human body means I'm trapped? That this form is inherently weaker than you?"

He didn't have to answer. She could see it on his face. He obviously thought humans were weaker than dragons and she hated the part of her that knew he was right—and that so much of what he said dovetailed with her own thoughts on the matter.

"This is the whole damn problem with dragon kind. You think that you're better than humans."

"We are better than humans," he stated as a matter of fact. "We're stronger, faster, and live longer, which means we can study things in far more depth."

"But none of that means you're better. You're more powerful, sure, but that doesn't mean you're better than mankind. It was our weak night vision that drove us to master the electricity that lights your mansion. It was our inability to fly that led us to invent the airplane. We might not live as long, but we really live. We're part of this world in a way that you're not. We share far more in common with the animals than you do."

"Can you even hear yourself, Kristen? All this talk of we and you makes it sound as if you're not a dragon at all. But you are. You're one of us. You'll outlive your family by centuries and you can already destroy even the strongest human in any contest of strength. I know that you're young but in time, you'll grow to see that humans can't fully understand the world in the way you can. Already, you shrug bullets off. How can you still identify with the creatures who invented war and the atomic bomb and ignore their own polluting filth?"

Kristen grimaced as if she'd been struck. "Just because people aren't perfect doesn't mean you get to control them."

"Yes! There it is, Kristen. This is what you need to see! Humans are a them. You are different from them. You are a dragon. Realize your power and you can help us change our broken systems. But first, you need to realize your power."

She had heard enough, and her own inner conflict raged with the same ferocity as their outward debate. Angry with him and angry with herself, she turned her back on him and marched across the grounds. She went to her room, changed into her regular human clothes, and pulled out her human phone.

By some stroke of luck, her rideshare app showed that someone was nearby. She ordered a ride and went out front to wait.

Stonequest found her there as the car made its way down the long driveway to the mansion. "Kristen, you don't need to do this. It'll take you hours to get back to the city."

"Once it would have taken people days to cover this distance. I see a few hours as a triumph of mankind's, not an inconvenience."

"I'm sorry I was harsh on you, but don't leave. We need to keep training."

"There's already somebody trying to kill me in Detroit. At least if

I'm there, I can protect the people I love. I'm sorry if that seems like a liability."

"I want you to transform so you can protect them. Don't you see that?"

"I do," Kristen said. "I'm not even really angry with you anymore. But I have to do this my way."

"Even if your way gets you killed?"

"Look, I gotta go. It's not polite to make people wait." She got into the car, checked with the driver that he wouldn't mind the drive into the city, and they left.

Thankfully, the man recognized her need for silence and she was able to nap on the ride home and let her body heal from the pummeling she'd received. She'd meant what she said to Stonequest. His heart was in the right place, maybe, but his methods? They plain sucked.

She was a dragon and knew that deep inside. But she was human, too. He wasn't wrong about her needing to find her power. But her gut said she had to handle that in her own way.

CHAPTER SIXTY-THREE

They met at a place of Shadowstorm's choosing on the roof of an abandoned apartment block slated to be demolished in a few days. Although he'd only given the assassin less than an hour to reach the location, she'd still beaten him here.

He might have been impressed if the Steel Dragon were dead.

"Perhaps it's time you changed your moniker," he said to the other dragon. Both had arrived in their true forms. His body was dark, the color of bruised clouds, with flickers of lighting that played across his scales. He seemed to drink in the light, being one of the few dragons who drew from more than a single elemental force for his magic.

Death's dragon form was dark as well, with scales that bordered on black. He couldn't tell exactly what her power was, but no one could. Already, she'd transformed into a human form—a thin woman with dark hair and dressed in black. Obviously, she didn't want him to glean any information from her dragon body. She'd made a career of killing dragons. One couldn't do such a thing by giving away information about oneself.

Although to be a successful assassin, one was expected to actually kill the target.

"Her death will come as it did for every other dragon I have ever targeted," she said.

It bothered him that she knew who he was. Not long before, he could have operated behind the guise of Mr Black, but now that the Steel Dragon had outed him, everyone knew his identity. The only advantage of this was that he could conduct meetings in dragon form.

Dragon to dragon, Shadowstorm was quite large, but dragon to human, he was beyond massive. And yet Death didn't seem intimidated at all. She held herself with a self-assured arrogance he found obnoxious given that she'd failed.

"I paid you well to solve this problem," he complained.

"And solve it I will."

"When?"

"As soon as possible. The Steel Dragon is proving harder to kill than I expected. Her skills are fair in her human form, and that steel skin is a tricky thing."

"I warned you about her steel skin. The entire human news apparatus warned you about her steel skin," he roared. He hadn't meant to lose his temper but it was so fun to roar at human-shaped beings.

"Yes, true, but you failed to fully brief me on her team. They are more than competent."

"I told you they were police."

"Even for human peacekeepers, they are exceptionally skilled. Plus, there's Stonequest."

Shadowstorm growled at the mention of Stonequest. "He's hardly around."

"And how close did you let him and his precious dragon SWAT get to you before you tucked tail and went into hiding?"

He sneered at her. "You tell me all your reasons for failure, and yet you have not returned the treasure I gave you for this job."

"Because I have a plan. You see, the Steel Dragon does have a weakness. Her humanity."

"I tried to turn her already. It wasn't possible. Something tells me she won't listen to a killer."

"I won't need to convince her of anything. I've found where her human family is nesting."

Hope bloomed inside his chest. It was the same feeling as one he'd had when he'd discovered a new human settlement centuries before. There was a power to knowing about unconnected humans. They were strong together but isolated, they were laughably weak.

"So snare them!"

Death had the audacity to laugh in his face. "Don't insult what I do, and I won't insult whatever mess you've got yourself into with the Masked One."

"How did you—"

"You hired an assassin, Shadowstorm. Do you think I accept simply any contract? There are many dragons out there who would like me dead. It's good to know I'm not the only one of us with enemies."

Shadowstorm took a deep breath and exhaled. Smoke and steam came from his nostrils and made swirling clouds around her. The gesture terrified humans, but despite her form, she didn't seem intimidated in the least.

At least I'm not working with a coward, he reassured himself.

"If you get the family, the Steel Dragon will come to save them."

"Your little kidnapping gambit with those thugs I'd found failed. There's no reason to think I could find thugs that are any more competent, especially considering this is supposed to be your city."

Anger surged and he growled, a low, almost subsonic sound that he was quite sure Death understood despite her human form. If she insulted him again, they would fight. Honor demanded it. Even in the world of dragons that existed outside the Dragon Council and their petty dragon SWAT, there was honor that must be defended.

She held up her hands in a placating gesture. It was the first sign of deference to her employer she'd shown all night. "I won't stoop to kidnap humans, no matter the price. Things have happened in the past—messy things—and it's simply not worth the hassle."

"So why even concern yourself with their location?" He had begun to grow frustrated. Yes, Death was an assassin—a master of ending the lives of dragons—and yet, there she was, a few feet in front of him and still in her human form. This was not how she hunted dragons. He could attack her now and snap her little human neck before she could even transform. If she didn't start talking sense, he would too.

"I won't fetch them, but I'm not above using them," Death said, her tone a purr.

"How?"

"If I put them in jeopardy, do you believe the Steel Dragon will come to their aid?"

"It's all but a certainty. As long as she knows they are in peril, she will be unable to resist."

"Then imperil them I will. She'll come running, and I'll finish her off in the confusion."

Shadowstorm shook his head. "This sounds needlessly convoluted. You won't capture them, but you'll make attacks on their life? You're letting the human police decide where you battle the Steel Dragon."

Death shook her head and clicked her teeth like he was nothing but a disobedient servant. "I know my trade. The Steel Dragon will die. Tonight."

He nodded. While he certainly wouldn't trust Death with his life, he felt he could trust her to end Kristen's. She was an assassin, after all, and if her price were any indication, the best in the world. Besides, he didn't really care about the details of the plan, only that it came to pass.

The Steel Dragon must die if the Masked One was to be appeased. And he must be appeased if Shadowstorm wished to keep his life.

CHAPTER SIXTY-FOUR

The carshare ride was a long one, and when the driver neared the destination, Kristen would still have a few blocks to walk. She didn't want anyone to have the address of her parent's safe house in their phone. She tipped well—after all, it had been an hours-long drive—exited the vehicle, and found her bearings.

Her parents were staying in a honeymoon suite in a pleasant hotel. They were on lockdown so they couldn't come and go. She thought it was a fairly safe location. The cops had first recommended a safe house in a rundown hotel. It even had undercover cops stationed there, but her mom had balked at the prostitutes on the street so they'd been sent to a nicer establishment. She was sure her parents didn't mind.

As she wound through the streets and moved steadily closer to the hotel, she watched her backtrail constantly with her dragon nightvision the entire time. She had to be sure she wasn't followed. Her family had already been put in danger once because of her and she would not let that happen again.

Although a part of her wondered if such thoughts were naïve. Could her parents ever return to their quiet suburban life? They'd already faced droves of reporters, news vans, and now kidnappers. Perhaps it was childish to think they'd ever be safe again.

It was a somber thought and left her a little despondent as she showed the receptionist her badge.

The woman nodded politely and told her to wait, but instead of telling her the room number, two police officers came over. Some people might've been worried at the reception, but she was pleased to see they were taking their jobs seriously. She recognized one of them and waved. He nodded and led her to the elevator.

The officer used a key to access the floor her parents were on. Without it, the elevator wouldn't allow anyone entry.

"Has anyone else asked to see my folks?" she asked casually, even though if someone had asked that it would mean this place wasn't secure.

"No, ma'am."

They rode up and stepped out to where two more men stood on guard outside the room. She showed them ID since she didn't personally know them, and they let her in.

Inside, she found what she'd expected. Her mom and brother were passed out—Mom in the bed and Brian in front of a TV that someone had long since muted.

Her dad was awake, though, and chatted to the two cops in the room.

"Krissy!" Frank Hall said when Kristen entered. "I wondered if you would visit your poor family. Do you know we've already eaten everything on the room service menu? Johnson here says he won't even go get me a pizza from Buddy's. Can you believe this shit?"

Johnson held his hands up to protest the accusation. The other cop laughed and Frank smiled.

"You didn't—that's not honest to God beer, is it?"

She pulled the six-pack out from behind her back, glad that she'd stopped at a liquor store on her walk over. Part of losing any possible tail, she'd told herself, but really, she'd only wanted to be able to have a drink with her dad.

"Bell's Oberon Ale."

One of the cops grinned at that, so she opened four bottles and passed them out.

"We shouldn't," Johnson said.

"The Steel Dragon's here. We'll be fine," Frank proclaimed and took a sip. "Aw, goddammit, Krissy, you got this fancy wheat-beer microbrew shit?"

"Dad, this is good."

"Not as good a cold can of PBR."

"I'm sure you can get crap beer from room service."

"Yeah, for six dollars. Six, dollars, Kristen. For a god damn PBR." He shook his head in disgust and seemed more appalled at the expensive room service than the fact that someone was actively hunting his daughter. But then, that was Frank Hall.

"Well, if you don't like it, I can drink yours."

He waved her away. "I'll make do, Krissy. Now, tell us, what on earth is the Steel Dragon doing keeping her old man up on a work night?"

"Keeping you up? It looks like you're doing fine here."

Frank laughed, but she heard his voice crack. "There's a goddamn assassin out there hunting you, Krissy. I'm sure you'll be fine. Your mother is scared shitless, but I know better. Still, do you think I can simply pull the covers up and sleep when we have armed guards watching us fart?"

Kristen didn't laugh at the joke. In fact, it took almost everything she had not to break down into tears. Her dad could read her like a book, though. He put his beer down and gestured at the two cops to give them some space. They both retreated to the doorway so father and daughter could talk.

"What's going on, Kristen?" he said, stood quickly, and fixed her a cup of coffee.

Despite opening the beer, Kristen was relieved that he fixed her coffee. Her mom had made it a rule for as long as she could remember for him not to drink alcohol when he was stressed. Frank—being a cop—had seen what alcohol could do to people who were already stressed, so had honored his wife's wishes. It was nice that he honored them even when she was passed out.

She took a sip of coffee and managed not to grimace. It was horrible. Her father had never learned how to use enough grounds.

"Is it the assassin?" he asked.

Kristen uttered a single painful guffaw. "Believe it or not, no, not really."

He grinned at that. "Well, what the hell could put you on edge more than some super-sniper?"

"Okay, that's part of it, for sure. I've been training with Stonequest, mostly so I can be ready to defeat Death."

"Death?"

"That's the assassin's code name."

"Isn't that like a firefighter's nickname being hose?"

"Dad!" She glared at him and he merely grinned in response. Frank Hall was a man who believed in using humor to defuse a situation. She tried to maintain her glare but finally, a smile broke through. At times like this, she simply couldn't help it.

"Go ahead, sweetie. I'm only making sure my little girl's still in there."

She looked down and noticed she'd turned herself to steel, something she hadn't meant to do. "See, this is exactly it. Stonequest is trying to train me to take more control of my powers. I want to be in more control. I really think I need to."

"So, what's the problem? You have super-speed and stuff. Big deal. Your brother has a super-fat mouth and he's absolutely shameless about it."

"It's not those powers, dad."

"Then what? Are you worried you'll have to start dressing like the rest of those douchebags? You know I saw one of them dragons the other day wearing an ascot. Honest to God."

Kristen snorted. Leave it to Frank to see the big issues. "Well, yeah, that's kind of it, actually. I haven't transformed yet."

"Sure, you have. You're steel right now."

She made her skin revert into flesh and acknowledged that she'd let it get away from her because she was stressed. "But I haven't turned into a dragon. I've already felt myself changing. I don't have to worry about getting hurt like regular people. I have an aura that can affect other people's emotions—"

"Use that one on your mother for me sometime—"

"Dad!"

"Sorry, sweetie. Go ahead."

"I have all these powers that I never expected, and they're already changing me. I take risks I wouldn't have taken without them and do things that would have terrified me before, but now… Well, it's simply a way of life. Plus, there's this sense of…of loyalty."

"Loyalty?" He sounded almost comically disbelieving.

"Yeah. Kind of? That doesn't really begin to explain it, honestly. Like the idea of you or Mom or Brian getting hurt makes me feel…" She grunted, unable to express herself. "I simply can't let that happen. It's the same with my team. None of you can get hurt because of me. You're all my responsibility now. I've already changed so much. I'm scared that if I do actually transform into a dragon body, I'll lose who I was. I'm scared that I'll be governed by what it feels like to be a dragon and forget who I am. I'm scared that I'll have to give up who I am—that the Kristen Hall you know will vanish if I change."

Frank took a sip of coffee and studied her for a moment. He set the cup down and took her hand. "Krissy. I don't know much about dragons. You know that, of course. Even when I was a cop, I wasn't on SWAT or anything. I know more about parking meters than I do the Dragon committees—"

"The Dragon Council," she corrected him.

"Whatever. My point is that I don't know them, but I do know you. You're my little baby and I might know you better than you know yourself."

"You didn't even know I was a dragon."

"I did so."

"No, you didn't."

"Will you stop taking after your mother for five damn minutes and let me talk?"

She smiled. Marty never let Frank finish a sentence either.

Her dad took another sip of coffee. "I may not know dragons, but I knew you were one. Listen to things you're describing. Taking risks? Kristen, you tried out for every damn sport there was. Your whole fucking childhood was risk after risk. And loyalty? You once beat a kid up because he said Mario was better than Donkey King and it made your brother cry."

"Donkey Kong."

"Let me finish."

Kristen nodded and sipped her coffee.

"The point is, if you're a dragon, you've always been one. If other dragons are brave, loyal, and stubborn, then it makes sense you are too."

"I didn't say anything about stubborn."

"Well, maybe that one you get from your old man. Plus, you have your mother's iron will. I know this is all crazy. I'm merely your fat old man, watching you do all this amazing stuff. It's crazy, but I still have my fat gut. For you, it's gotta be…well…" Frank shook his head, speechless for a rare moment. "But, honestly, when the news came in that you were a dragon? I wasn't surprised."

"Oh, come on."

"Really, Kristen, I wasn't. And you know what, neither were you."

"Yes, I was. I was shocked."

He shook his head firmly. "Maybe you were surprised—maybe. But what did you do when you transformed? You sprang into action. You took risks to protect those you loved. You did what you've always done, only with more power than you had before. The truth is, you've always been a dragon."

"Well, yeah. That much is kinda obvious."

"I don't only mean in your DNA, Krissy. I mean in your heart. You're worried about all this changing you, but what I see is it's simply made you into more of what you already were."

"I don't know, Dad…"

"Well, I do. You've always been driven—special. Your mother and I always knew you'd exceed our wildest dreams."

"All parents say that about their kids."

Frank laughed and hooked a thumb at Brian, passed out and snoring on the couch. "Your mother and I would be pleased if this one got a damn job. He's special, sure, but not like you, Kristen. I'm sure this is crazy for you, but you're not becoming anything you weren't. You're simply discovering a part of yourself that's always been there."

Kristen nodded, wiped a tear, and stood. "I should go, Dad. I should keep training."

"That's my girl!" he said and beamed. "But don't you want to drink these beers and spend the night?"

She grinned. "I do, really. But I can't, not until you guys are safe."

"I'll tell your mother you stopped by. You know she'll be pissed for you not waking her up."

"I know."

"Well, all right, then." He enveloped her in a hug.

When she left the room and rode down in the elevator, she felt better—like a veil had been lifted. She had to do this—for her family and for herself. Stonequest had been right about that, at the very least. Maybe he'd been right about everything he'd said in his little speech to her. She needed to come into her full dragon strength if she wanted to be at all useful to her friends and family. But that didn't mean giving up who she was. The only part of her that she had to leave behind was the part of her that doubted what she was capable of.

And now, with her family's support, she thought she could finally do that.

CHAPTER SIXTY-FIVE

Death couldn't believe how lucky her night had turned out to be. First, Shadowstorm had let slip that he had been in contact with the Masked One. That had been a bluff on her part, but he had confirmed it before he could cover his surprise. One never knew when such information might come in handy. Now, to top the day off, the Steel Dragon herself had arrived to visit her parents.

The assassin had thought she was still at the dragon's manor in the countryside—one of the few places she didn't dare to go—but it seemed that had changed.

Her plan had been to wait for one of the family members to leave, wound them in the leg, and wait for the Steel Dragon at the hospital, but the process could be simplified.

She was in the building visiting her family. When she left, she would wait for her to be alone on the street, kill her with her usual efficiency, and move on to her next contract. There was no need to bother with the humans. That was good. She hated dealing with humans. It was embarrassing for someone of her talents to have to work directly with the cattle who ran the background of the dragons' world.

As she sat with her rifle aimed at the door, she did nothing but think. She knew there were assassins who didn't watch through their scopes, but she found this laughable. Her job was to kill, which meant her work was to be ready for the killing moment. She couldn't do that with a pair of binoculars.

She hadn't accomplished all she had by being anything but patient.

And she had accomplished so much. Wars had been avoided because of her work.

Dragons didn't normally go to war with each other. For thousands of years, there had been a more or less civil peace between them. They still fought proxy wars, of course, using the humans who lived in their territories, but that was totally different than dragons actually plotting to murder each other.

Physical combat was the main way for dragons to solve their disputes. A duel of the gods, it must seem to humans, and indeed it was. Dragon combat often ended in death, and because of this, there were dragons who didn't wish to participate in it.

Their powers weren't uniform. All had the same basic abilities—flight, increased speed and strength, and aura. But from there, their abilities varied. Most could breathe fire, but there were variations to those powers too. Some dragons could control flame for example, while others spat acid.

Some of these found themselves in disputes with dragons who had a particularly powerful skill set. When this happened, the weaker dragon often discovered that physical combat was a barbaric, demeaning thing—not to mention a surefire way to reduce their own life expectancy. If they felt this way, they would hire professionals like her to deal with these disputes.

That's what Death was—a problem removal specialist. She stabilized the world, helped those with powers that didn't translate into combat skills, and pruned the dragon family of its more bloated, obnoxious branches.

Truly, she would work for anyone who would hire her. It took a special kind of dragon to see the wisdom of assassinating a foe instead of airing their grievances and resorting to pummeling each other. Most of the time, the wisdom of the client to hire her was all the commitment she needed, but she had to admit, there was something wrong about this Steel Dragon.

It wasn't her obsession with following human laws. Law itself was an interesting construct and all dragons—even Death—had codes of honor they believed in. And it wasn't her unusual abilities. She was always interested in the unusual. What affronted her sensibilities about the target was that she saw herself as human, which was an affront to all of dragon kind.

The Steel Dragon had to be destroyed, culled from the herd and weeded from the garden before she could spread her disgusting ideas about humanity having rights.

Merely thinking about it was enough to make her aura begin to pulse. She quickly snuffed that out, though. It was an ability she rarely used and it wouldn't do for other dragons to sense it. But forcing it down all the time meant that she had exquisite mastery over the tool. There weren't many dragons who could kill one of their own kind and not ever let their heartbeat elevate or their aura spill out in either pride or guilt. She was as cool-headed as they came, and yet something in her boiled and she wished to slay this Steel Dragon tonight.

And then, as if the flames themselves smiled down upon her, Death had her chance.

Her target stepped out from the first floor of the hotel. This was the moment. She took aim. Last time, she'd merely tested her target's power with a shot to the shoulder. Now that she knew her scale-tipped bullets would work, there was no reason for further trial.

That was the secret to her success, something that almost no one knew. When she hunted dragons, she tipped special rounds with fragments of her own scales. Much like a dragon claw or tooth would wreak great damage on another dragon, her scale-tipped bullets did what mere lead could not.

They put dragons down.

There would be no more tests. She aimed for the Steel Dragon's head and was about to pull the trigger when Kristen turned and spoke to someone inside.

The assassin waited. She could give this girl a few more moments of life. It would cost her nothing, while firing too soon would ruin her entire attack.

She doubted that even the dragon's steel skin could withstand the bullet she had loaded into her rifle. The weapon itself was incredibly large and super-high caliber—a custom job that most humans couldn't ever hope to handle.

The bullet was even more special than most of her rounds. In addition to the scales, this bullet was diamond-tipped and the most powerful she'd ever created. Certainly more powerful than the one she'd first tried on the Steel Dragon. This particular combination of gun and ammunition had killed eleven dragons. It took extraordinary measures to eliminate one of her own kind. With incredible healing abilities, dense muscles, and scales as tough as metal, a round had to not only pierce the dragon's body but also destroy either the heart or the brain.

The brain being the better option, of course.

It was easier to kill a dragon in human form, but even that wasn't a sure thing. Most dragons transformed the moment they sensed danger, and those transformations changed the location of hearts and brain.

The Steel Dragon turned to the street again. The door to the hotel closed behind her and she began to walk.

Death could see her face. She looked happy and totally oblivious to what was about to happen. Her quarry wouldn't even hear this shot. By the time the sound reached her, the shot would have already splattered her brains on the sidewalk behind her.

The assassin took a breath and held it, steadied her weapon as she led the target, and was about to pull the trigger when she heard something on the roof behind her.

She cursed. Her intended target would have to wait a moment. She'd placed alarms, magic and otherwise, on the roof exactly as she always did. They were complex things, and they should have slain anyone who came near. That they'd failed to do so meant the person up there was a threat.

Despite having the shot lined up, she took her eye away from the gun and transformed into her true body.

Some dragons' transformations were flashy things of smoke and fire. Others vanished into clouds of dust and debris.

Death simply extended. One moment, she was a woman and the next, her fingers were claws, her arms were scaled, and wings emerged from her back.

She wasn't particularly powerful in her dragon form—not like her client Shadowstorm, who really was an impressive specimen—but she was more than competent with her abilities. It would take a considerable fight to best her.

Her night vision easily pierced the darkness of the roof but she saw no dragon. She stared intently but still, encountered no fiery breath boiling and primed to erupt or bolts of lightning carefully parsed and ready to crack. All she saw was a human.

And a woman with a handgun, of all things. One of the dinky little things that they liked to brain each other with.

The assassin laughed at the tiny weapon aimed at her chest. "That can't hurt me."

Even in her human form, the weapon would have done little damage. Dragon muscles were tough. It would take something special to crack through them and obliterate the heart. Simply injuring one wouldn't be enough. A dragon's heart could heal unless it was destroyed completely. In this form, her dragon form, she would be practically invulnerable to most weapons. A handgun was a particularly laughable threat.

It was curious that the human had made it past her alarms, though. Was she a mage, perhaps? That might explain it.

"How did you get up here, little thing? You should have felt terror unlike anything you've ever experienced." Not to mention that there should be holes in her body and her flesh should be burned to a crisp.

"I don't fear you, beast."

Death grinned at that. Beast? Really? Who was this impetuous little insect? Well, she would find out soon enough. She flexed her aura and used it like a laser to unravel this puny human's will. Soon the human wouldn't fear her but instead, would want to please her. She'd tell her everything she wanted to know.

"Who are you?"

"Merely a human who has had enough," the woman said and fired her little handgun.

The assassin laughed at the bang but almost instantly, something changed. She looked down. The bullet had penetrated her scales and it hurt badly. It was, she thought, like being gored by a dragon's claw, but far worse.

"How did you—"

Death never got her answer. The human stepped forward quickly and before she could say another word, fired her gun three more times in rapid succession. Each bullet ripped a hole in her scales and each shot inflicted a wound. She teetered on the edge of the building and toppled over to fall toward the street below.

"You never should have gone after her," the strange human said.

Constance Vigil watched Death tumble from the rooftop. It seemed a shame to let the dragon go to waste—something akin to killing a bison and simply letting the meat rot. She could have killed hundreds of dragons with the bullets made from Death's corpse.

But she didn't need to kill her. She only had to keep the assassin from killing Kristen Hall—who would likely show up in only a few moments. That reminded her that she didn't have long to get out of this building before the Steel Dragon arrived.

She ran.

Really, the Lost Dragon was why she'd had to stop this assassin. Death—as Constance had been told this dragon was known—had targeted Kristen, and that simply wouldn't do. Stopping her was a priority.

In all honesty, she didn't know any more about the Steel Dragon than any of the other mages in her circle, but debates swirled around her existence and her arrival in the same city in which they'd conducted their own experiments. Could the now-famous Kristen Hall be one of the experiments their mages had designed? It was quite possible, but if she was, how had she gotten loose in the world? The girl should have been locked up with all the other dragons they'd created.

Constance had to remind herself that no one had all the answers.

She smiled to herself. Being part of a clandestine society of mages intent on taking the yoke of power from the dragons that controlled the world had given her a very specific skill set. She'd had the magic ability to disarm Death's traps and the practical experience to plan an escape route.

A quick rappel down a rope brought her to ground level, this time on the far side of the building from where her quarry had fallen. A quick peek around the corner told her that Kristen and Death had already encountered one another. She didn't have any doubt that the Steel Dragon could prevail in this fight. The assassin might be a dragon, but she was a dragon with several dragon-scale bullets inside her, each one weakening her powers and sapping her strength.

For a brief moment, she wondered if she'd look back on that moment one day with fond memories or shame. Maybe the Steel Dragon would join their fight or maybe she would prove to be as dangerous to mankind as the other dragons. If that happened, perhaps her body would prove capable of making bullets that could truly destroy any dragon.

Constance hoped that wasn't the case, but hers was a position in the world that offered no comforts. One way or the other, her organization would act. Only time would tell what that would involve.

She also hoped the Steel Dragon would see what had happened—that someone had saved her life, an ally stronger than a dragon.

CHAPTER SIXTY-SIX

Kristen heard a gunshot and instinctively, flung herself prone and turned her skin into steel. In the same moment, she realized that by the time she'd heard the gunshot, it would have been too late for her abilities to protect her.

But the projectile never came. Nothing struck her, nor did any piece of nearby pavement shatter from an impact.

"Did you hear that, Hall?" the officer at the door of the hotel yelled.

Before she could answer, three more gunshots rang out. She tried to pinpoint the source of the sound with her heightened dragon abilities. It was closer than she had thought—the top of a building only a few blocks away. Then she saw an enormous shape fall from the roof and smack into the side several times before it impacted with ground-shaking force. A dragon! But who? Was it Stonequest, keeping an eye on her? Or someone less friendly?

"Call for backup and send them there." She pointed at the building and the officer nodded. He was already on his radio.

Kristen ran with every ounce of speed her dragon powers gave her. Snow pelted her face as she ran. It appeared to be some kind of fancy apartment building like those that appeared all over Detroit. Not for the first time, she cursed her inability to fly. If she could turn into a dragon, she would be there already. She knew she'd have to transform and that she could keep her identity, but something about pursuing a gunner was so human. It hadn't occurred to her to try to transform until that moment. She covered the few blocks in less than a minute and reached the building.

She brushed the thoughts of unused powers away as she studied the scene.

It was a dragon that had fallen, all right. But it wasn't Stonequest, Sebastian, or any other she had seen before. Its dark-red scales glittered as it rolled itself slowly upright. Blood poured from several wounds. One was in the chest, but the others all seemed to be in various limbs.

"Are you all right?" she asked.

"No," the strange dragon replied. It was a woman's voice. "Not really."

"Help's on the way," she told her as she stepped closer. Strangely, the wounds weren't healing. They continued to bleed and slow trickles of liquid dribbled down the massive body.

A glittering flash caught her eye. Something on the ground sparkled as it reflected the lamplight. At first, she wasn't sure what she saw. Then she realized the reflections were made by scales—small, silver dragon scales. They'd poured from a black leather pouch that must have been torn free from the dragon as she fell.

She knew those scales. They looked exactly like those Death used as her calling card. She glanced at the dragon quickly and saw those dangerous eyes staring balefully at her.

"What a shame. I had hoped to avail myself of that help you offered and worry about killing you later," she told her. "But I suspect you've realized who I am."

"Death."

"Just so." The dragon heaved herself onto her hind legs. Her claws raked the air where Kristen had stood, but she had already moved left and into a roll that carried her away from the slash.

"I've been looking for you," she said as she found her feet. She punched out with a steel hand to deliver a powerful blow to an already injured rear leg. The assassin roared with pain and whipped her head around.

Jaws snapped closed inches away from her head as she ducked the attack. She drove a right uppercut into Death's jaw. The dragon's head jerked away from the attack.

"It doesn't have to be like this," she said. "You can come quietly, and we'll get you medical attention."

Her adversary laughed. "Oh, I don't think my employer's employer would like that. I appreciate the offer, but I would like my hide to remain intact, thanks."

Quickly, she weighed her options. Help was coming, but it would probably be human police, not Dragon SWAT. Humans would merely give the dragon additional targets to threaten. She needed to finish this fight before anyone else was hurt. That was a problem because she'd never beaten a dragon in its real form. Stonequest had assured her that doing so was simply impossible.

But this dragon was hurt, bleeding, and limping. Rather than closing, each of those wounds seemed to be growing slowly worse. Spotted lines of bright red seeped from each injury. She recognized that right away.

"You had a taste of your own medicine, did you? Someone used dragon bullets on you," she taunted.

"And it hurts like hell," Death agreed. She flapped her wings once and became airborne, then crashed down again where her opponent stood.

The Steel Dragon didn't move this time. She held her ground, her guard up, and hammered a blow into the massive chest as the dragon bore down on her. Death bellowed with pain and tumbled back.

Kristen didn't waste a moment. She lunged forward and used the massive forelegs as steps to climb up onto her neck. Once she was there, she clamped her steel arms around the dragon's throat and began to squeeze. Death coughed, bucked, and even rolled over completely in attempts to dislodge her attacker, but she clung tenaciously even when the massive bulk rolled over her.

"It doesn't have to end like this," she said through gritted teeth. "You can surrender."

"Never." The assassin hissed her fury. "I took a contract. I finish it or I die."

"It's your call."

She now felt she'd given her attacker more than enough chances and tightened her grasp around the sinewy neck. The dragon tried to cough, no longer able to breathe. She wound her steel arms even tighter and increased their pressure until vertebrae began to crack. All the emotional turmoil from the past few days emerged in a single inarticulate cry of rage.

The release surged through her and she poured all her fury into her arms and yelled in triumph when something snapped inside Death's neck. The dragon toppled and was still. She rolled off to one side and came up in a fighting stance, ready in case her enemy was still alive.

Cautiously, she approached, but all her senses told her the dragon was dead. It was completely still, a difficult feat for a creature with lungs that must have been larger than an entire person. No sound came from its body either, but most importantly, she sensed no aura. Even when dragons weren't actively trying to influence something, they always radiated an aura. This one didn't. That could only mean it was dead.

She looked at the wounds on her adversary's chest. They were tiny holes. On the dragon's huge body, they looked like punctures from a pellet gun. She shivered. That was the fate Death had intended for her. She must have waited for her on the roof, ready to fire when she left the hotel. But who had shot Death, then?

Kristen knew her team was on the way so she'd have backup soon, not to mention a forensics team. But that made her think of Stonequest. He'd been very involved in this case. Surely he'd get wind of it and when he did, he'd no doubt take over the crime scene. That meant if she wanted answers, she had to get them now.

She returned to the dragon's corpse, made a hasty circuit around its body, and located the black pouch again. After a quick glance around her, she retrieved the bag and stuck her hand inside.

The first thing she felt was more of the little scales. The next thing she found was a smartphone.

Her smile was one of triumph. To a dragon, the phone might have been nothing more than a curious bauble, but to a human, it was the greatest source of clues one could hope for.

Quickly, she took the phone out and examined it, hunched over it to block the snow—that now fell faster and faster—from touching the screen. It was a cheap Android phone, obviously something Death had bought recently and intended to dispose of. She tried to open it but it was locked and had a button for a fingerprint.

Kristen wondered how paranoid the dragon could be. Would she have used her human form or dragon form to unlock the phone? The human form would have been more obvious perhaps, but if Death could turn only part of her body into her dragon form, that might be even more secure.

After a moment's thought, she picked up the dead dragon's clawed hand and hoped that she had been like all the others she had met—supremely confident in her own abilities.

It turned out she was. The phone unlocked at the touch of the dragon's thumb. It was a good thing her dragon form wasn't that big. If she'd have been as large as Shadowstorm, it would have had to be her human hand that unlocked the phone.

She wondered about that. Since she'd died this way, did that mean she would forever remain in her dragon form? What would happen if Kristen died with her steel skin activated? Would she be impossible to cremate? If she was buried, would rust dispose of her body instead of microorganisms? It was an odd and perhaps unsettling thought but irrelevant at the moment.

Right now, she needed to go through the phone as quickly as she could. She knew that either her team or Dragon SWAT would be there momentarily. Dragon SWAT seemed to have an uncanny knack for arriving at dragon-related crime scenes.

There wasn't much on the smartphone. It was obviously a burner with a VPN and a secure browser but nothing useful. But, if the assassin had used the phone at all, they might be able to trace where it had been by using GPS coordinates.

Kristen called the station using Death's phone. She asked for computer forensics and once transferred, asked them to run the number and IMEI through the GPS search. The operator told her it would take a minute, but once he had the information, he'd send it to her personal phone.

Once she'd thanked him and hung up, she went into the building and sprinted up the first stairs she could find, taking steps four and five at a time in her haste to reach the rooftop. Maybe the shooter was still there, maybe not, but there could be something.

For the next forty seconds, she tried to scour the roof for more clues but found little. Snow had begun to accumulate in patches here and there, but it had barely started. There were no footprints but there was some kind of a spherical device set up near the door. She thought it might have been magic, but she couldn't tell. A huge crack down the middle of it suggested that whatever it had once done, it no longer functioned.

She also found a tripwire connected to a flash grenade at the top of the stairs, but that too had been disarmed. That was good luck. She knew her steel skin was impervious to grenades, but her eyes could be blinded as easily as any human's.

Still, it all left her with more questions than answers. Who had made it past these traps? Who would have knowledge of both magic traps and tripwires? Was it a person who did this or a dragon? A single culprit—perhaps mourning the loss of one of Death's victims—or a team working together?

There was nothing else to see up on the rooftop and she could hear approaching sirens. The police would gather around Death's body soon, and she assumed she should be there when they did. She bounded down the stairs and stepped into the cold air to find her team already moving toward her.

"Do we have hostiles?" Drew shouted and sounded breathless.

"Only one. Dead." She pointed at Death's body.

"Holy fucking shit! Red killed a dragon," Hernandez cried.

"But that's… Kristen, that's amazing," Butters sputtered.

Beanpole and Keith said nothing. The former was wide-eyed but cool-headed, while the Rookies mouth hung open with the corners still somehow turned up into a grin.

"Nice job," the Wonderkid said with a nod.

"Thanks, but it wasn't only me. Death was injured when I arrived," she said. "Shot with dragon bullets."

"Dragon bullets?" Drew asked.

"Like the one Death hit me with. Someone gave her a taste of her own medicine."

"Any idea who?"

She shook her head. "The shooter was on the roof with Death, who was up there ready to take a shot at me. But whoever it was, they were long gone by the time I got there."

"Well, shit. You did this, though? You killed her?" the team leader asked.

Kristen merely nodded. She tossed Drew one of the silver scales she'd pulled from Death's bag. "I found that."

"Anything else?"

"Her gun's up on the roof, aimed at the entrance of the hotel where my parents are—a big damn thing. Other than that, only her cellphone."

She took it out and waggled it at her team. Everyone's eyebrows raised appreciatively.

"Doesn't that belong in an evidence bag?" The Wonderkid winked.

"Dragon SWAT won't know what to do with it. I already called the station. They're running its history as we speak. I'm hoping for GPS data."

Everyone nodded, then split up to cover the scene. Before another minute had passed, Dragon SWAT arrived. Stonequest was in the lead with three other dragons behind him. They flew between the Detroit skyscrapers and through the falling snow, their wings pumping to create flurries in their wake. Massive beats of their wings as they landed scattered the traces of snow that had accumulated.

With four concurrent flurries of energy, the dragons transformed so four beings in the shape of people stood with the team.

"Well done, Kristen! Is this your work?" Stonequest pointed to the dead dragon.

"Yes."

He studied the huge corpse. "What are those strange wounds from?"

"Someone shot her," she replied. "With dragon-scale-tipped bullets, I assume. Like the one Death used on me."

"But that is Death, right? Someone else fired those shots?" he asked.

Kristen nodded.

Stonequest nodded. "All right. So, we have a killer's killer to find. Clues?"

"Her gun, a few traps, a bag of silver scales she wore around her neck, and this." She tossed him the locked phone and he obviously didn't know what to make of it.

"It unlocks with her fingerprints," she said helpfully.

Stonequest nodded and gestured for two of the other dragons to join him. The three of them made a triangle around Death's corpse and began to chant in unison. The wind picked up, the stars seemed to glow through the clouds, and she was a dragon no more but a human woman wearing black tactical gear.

A sudden burst of fear rose in her chest. She'd thought the dragon was dead, locked immutably in its bestial form, but seeing it transform was a reminder that there were more than dragons in the world. There were dwarves that ruled Canada, pixies with unpredictable magical powers and alien to humans, and even mages—human beings who'd mastered magic.

But it wasn't only the magic that put Kristen on edge. It was seeing the form that had tried to kill her. This slender female body was the one who had targeted her from afar and hunted her across the city while she had been going about her life. After seeing Death in her real body, it seemed wrong that this was the form in which she had tried to kill her— the one to fear. It was all the more frightening that her body lay in the dry silhouette of a dragon's frame. The snow that had landed had melted and made an outline around her dragon body. In moments, though, the illusion was gone as snow landed in the dry space and instantly melted.

Kristen had to turn away.

"The damn thing won't open," Stonequest said.

"Try her dragon form?" Hernandez said casually.

He nodded, muttered an incantation over Death's hand, and it transformed into a claw. That unlocked the phone and he stared at it in obvious confusion.

"Stonequest…" Drew began.

"Dragon SWAT appreciates your help, but we'll take it from here. Dragons killing dragons is our jurisdiction." Despite having worked together for months now, his response sounded canned and impersonal.

"Right," the team leader said and sent Kristen a look that said, *let's go.*

She agreed and they wandered to the SWAT van without protest.

They piled in with Drew and Butters in the front and the others in the back.

"Arrogant pricks," Jim said.

"Too bad, too." She held her phone up. "I have the GPS map."

Drew and Butters clambered out of the front seats and joined the team in the back. Together, they poured over the data.

It was like viewing a convoluted obstacle course, a maze made up of the streets of Detroit. The first thing that became obvious to Kristen was that Death never went anywhere twice. She said as much to her team and they all nodded.

"She must have been crazy paranoid," Keith murmured.

"With good reason," Butters pointed out. "Can you imagine your job description being to hunt down the greatest cop Detroit's ever seen? She must've been scared silly of our Steel Dragon."

Hernandez mimed gagging at the compliment but Kristen didn't mind.

"Wait, look there," Beanpole said. "She's been there twice."

"That's where we are right now," Kristen said. "That doesn't help us much."

"There's another place, though. Look, both times, she went to that other place before coming here," he continued.

"Do you think that's where she received her orders?" Jim asked.

"It must be. Other than that, there's no pattern at all to her movements. She's as cautious as hell but still had to get her missions from a boss with a different kind of paranoia," Drew said.

"Do you still think its Shadowstorm?" she asked.

He nodded. "I do, but we'll need more evidence."

"Then let's go get it." The Wonderkid sounded downright eager.

"Should we tell Dragon SWAT?" Keith asked.

Drew and Kristen shared a look. She broke the silence first. "We gave them the phone. They should be able to figure it out."

Beanpole shook his head. "I don't want to go in without backup. This guy—Shadowstorm or whoever it is—might be there."

"I don't think we have a choice," Kristen interjected. "Do you remember the last time we had Shadowstorm cornered? We called SWAT in and he fled as soon as he sensed them. He's incredibly perceptive when it comes to auras. If we call in Dragon SWAT, he'll simply run off again and find a new hole to hide in."

"Well, won't he sense your aura or whatever?" Hernandez asked.

"Yes, probably. I'll try to suppress it as much as possible, but I don't think I'll be able to hide it from him."

"Then won't he run off?" Keith asked.

"He might," she agreed. "But he might not. The last time we fought, he almost killed me. I think that if he senses me coming and only me, he'll try to stay and fight. I don't know why, but I think I'm a real threat to him. Hiring Death was extreme and I'm willing to bet he wants me dead badly enough to fight me."

"But Kristen, the last time he fought you, you almost died." Drew avoided eye contact. It was never pleasant bringing up when someone else almost died.

"That's true, but things have changed since then."

"You didn't tell us you could transform," Keith said. He truly was the dragon fanboy.

"I can't, not yet, but I think I know what's stopped me. I was scared that I'd become someone else, but I don't think that's true anymore. I think I'll simply become me."

Hernandez groaned. "That's so cheesy, Red."

Everyone laughed.

"Are you sure you can do it?" Drew asked once the laughter had died down.

Kristen grinned. "Nope, not at all. But we have to risk it. There's a good chance Shadowstorm's not there, anyway. If that's the case, we'd be letting evidence get away for no reason. And if he is there, then yes, I want to destroy him or die trying."

No one laughed at that. She grimaced. While she tried to keep her aura from affecting her team, she'd apparently tried too hard. None of them felt her confidence, her certainty in herself, or her devotion to her city.

But that was okay. That was what it was like to be human. And if she died protecting the people she loved, that would be a very human way to go. And if she did manage to find Shadowstorm, she'd push herself to her very limit. She'd either die fighting him, ridding the city of a parasite that had lived off it for decades, or she'd win. Either way, she would end this, once and for all.

CHAPTER SIXTY-SEVEN

The crystalline sphere on Sebastian Shadowstorm's desk began to glow—first a mild yellow, then a dull orange. The device had been made by a mage and could sense auras even better than he could. It meant a dragon was approaching and looking for him. It wasn't Death, either. The orb would have remained yellow instead of turning amber if it had been her.

There was no one who knew where he was hiding save the assassin. He hadn't even shown his thuggish minions his current hideout. It meant that not only had Death failed, but she'd also done so in spectacular fashion. He had no doubt which dragon now approached. It was Kristen, the Steel Dragon, traitor to her kind. It couldn't be anyone else.

For her to have discovered his whereabouts, she must have bested Death, either killing her or beating her so badly that she was apprehended by dragon SWAT. That meant there would be no one to punish and no one to torture for their mistake. The Masked One wouldn't see it that way, though. He'd still very much have someone to place all the blame on. Shadowstorm grimaced when he thought back to the dancers forced to waltz through the gore of their own kind. He didn't believe humans were any more than cattle, but there were still limits to what should be done when slaughtering meat. Nevertheless, he understood his allies. He'd chosen them, after all.

Working with the Masked One simply meant he couldn't fail.

Although he was disappointed that Death had not met expectations—the amount of resources he'd expended on her fees was embarrassing to even contemplate—he wasn't entirely surprised at her inability to kill the Steel Dragon.

Kristen Hall was a feisty, stubborn little being. She had stood against him in combat despite not activating her dragon body. And then there were her pesky allies. While his alarm didn't indicate that any dragons accompanied her, he assumed she'd bring her human police. In fact, he counted on it.

While Death had pursued her through the city, Shadowstorm had quietly prepared his base for a final showdown with the Steel Dragon.

Although the Detroit Renewable Power facility had been officially shut down due to licensing and permits, no one seemed to have noticed that the steam continued to run.

Well, that wasn't entirely true. He chuckled smugly. His contact at the Detroit Free Press said one of the reporters had asked questions, but he'd been shot down and sent to cover the water treatment situation in Flint. The dragon hadn't simply wasted more than a century in Detroit. He was a part of this city, a hidden master who knew where all the strings could be pulled.

For example, despite the Renewable Power facility being shut down, trash was still delivered for incineration. The transformer station was still operational—even though there had been unusual spikes in its energy consumption. And while the building was devoid of workers, no one had bothered to lock the network of tunnels that started beneath the facility and radiated out into the city.

That was where he headed now, down into the tunnels beneath the facility. These were the blood vessels of Detroit that delivered hot steam to the city that was spawned from its own burning garbage.

Shadowstorm didn't doubt that Kristen would find where he had gone. In fact, his plans required that she do so. But she wouldn't find the way down to his lair easily either. He had grown increasingly paranoid since being summoned by the Masked One and no longer relied on people to protect him. Once they'd set up the web of traps, he'd had them executed. That was one of the other reasons he knew she had found Death. There simply wasn't anyone else alive who could possibly know where he was.

The Steel Dragon would come to the facility and that would be her downfall. She would either be snared like an insect in a web or, if she somehow did make it all the way into the tunnels where he was waiting for her, she would die at his hands.

He knew that if this happened, he'd not only have the advantage of centuries of experience but that the deaths of her pathetic human allies would weigh on her as well.

While he wasn't stupid and hated that she saw herself as a human, he also accepted it. He could use this weakness to his advantage. She had some kind of traitorous sense of loyalty to the lesser species and would risk her life for the humans she cared for.

By the time she reached him—if she reached him—she'd either be exhausted from protecting her humans or mourning their death. Either way, he would be able to destroy the pathetic excuse for a dragon and take back the city that the insolent little whelp had inadvertently pried from his hands.

Shadowstorm almost relished meeting with the Masked One. He'd explain the careful traps he'd set and the way he'd quickly and efficiently dispatched Kristen's allies, and the powerful dragon would only stare. He was old, but the Masked One was positively ancient and wouldn't understand the dangers of steam tunnels, the power that humans had harnessed and put into their machines, or the sheer mass of garbage humans created.

But that would come in time. First, he would destroy the Steel Dragon. Then, he would celebrate.

CHAPTER SIXTY-EIGHT

The SWAT van eased to the curb outside the Detroit Renewable Power facility.

"This is the place?" Butters asked.

Kristen nodded. "That's what it says on the phone."

"What is it?" Keith asked.

"It's basically an incinerator for garbage." Jim stepped from the back of the van and studied the gate in front of them.

"That's disgusting." Hernandez frowned.

"The city council agrees," the Wonderkid continued. "I read that they voted to shut this place down. It releases particulates into the air, for one thing. Plus, there are all kinds of weird rules about who pays how much to get their trash burned. I won't get into it because we have a dragon to kill but apparently, it's not a great deal for Detroit."

"What do they do with all the burned garbage?" Drew asked as he took out an assault rifle and checked the magazine.

"They use it to make steam, which they send around the city to heat many of the buildings downtown. It's why we have all those grates that spit steam all the damn time. Those are leaks. I guess there's a whole network of tunnels under the city and has been since 1903."

"I thought that was sewer gas or something," Hernandez aid.

Jim laughed. "This city would smell far worse than it does if all that came from the sewers."

"But if it shut down, how come there's still steam coming from that smokestack?" Butters gestured to the towering brick smokestack that protruded from the white-and-red block of a building.

"Because Shadowstorm is expecting us." Kristen had no doubt that this was true.

"Are you sure we shouldn't call your boy Stonequest?" Keith sounded nervous.

She was glad he did, though. It would give her an opportunity to deal with her team.

"I'm sure. He'll run."

"There has to be a whole mess of tunnels down there for him to choose from," Jim pointed out.

With her back turned on the facility, she faced her team. "I'm also sure this won't be an easy fight. Shadowstorm wants me dead, obviously. His assassin failed, so I have no doubt that we'll walk into a real death trap. I think it would be better if all of you went home."

The response was instant.

"Are you out of your mind?"

"Fuck off, Red."

"Under no circumstances."

Kristen couldn't track who'd said what, only that they'd all refused. "I'm serious. Last time, it was all of you that exposed him. He won't forget that. I…I can't lose you—any of you."

"So what, we're supposed to watch you walk in there without backup and let Shadowstorm grind you to pieces?" Drew said.

"I've been training—"

"So have we," Hernandez cut in. "We've all done this far longer than you, Red. You forget you're still the newbie on the team and that we all signed up for this crazy job because we know that someone's gotta risk their fucking life."

"Hernandez is right." Jim nodded. "You have a way better chance to defeat him if we have your back, which means this city has a better chance."

"This city is my responsibility," she protested.

"With all due respect, Kristen, no, it's not." The words were especially surprising coming from Keith. He was generally her biggest supporter. "This is our city as much as it's yours. We're glad to have a dragon on our side, but it's still ours. I'd rather risk my life than have dragons duke it out like we're nothing but a prize to be fought for."

For a moment, she was speechless. She simply didn't know what to do with her friends' courage. None of them had her strength, her speed, or her steel skin, yet they were all willing to venture into a place that would put their lives at risk simply so she could try to defeat Shadowstorm? It was too much.

"Oh, Jesus, Red. Stop crying, you'll rust," Hernandez said.

She nodded and wiped her eyes. "Okay. Let's do this. Drew, bolt cutters for the gate?"

"They won't be necessary," Beanpole said. "The gate is not locked."

Kristen nodded. Of course it wasn't. They pushed the gate open and entered. Inside the fenced-off area was a massive parking lot dotted with various buildings—cooling towers and a few others that were probably offices or something similar. Garbage trucks, a few dumpsters, and a massive pile of garbage cluttered the lot and in the center was a massive red-and-white building. It appeared to be the heart of the operation and looked like it had recently been expanded to house the tower of bricks that probably comprised the smokestack of the incinerator.

"All right. Beanpole, watch our back. Butters, I very much doubt this asshole will give us vantage points to snipe from but if he failed to notice one, I want you there. Hernandez, are you packing explosives?" Drew's eyes never left the facility.

"Does a bear shit in the woods?"

"Good girl. Now, I don't want you to bring this place down on our heads, obviously, but once we see Shadowstorm, look for exits. He doesn't have a problem with running off when he loses a fight, so if he reaches one of these tunnels, make him regret it."

"What about me, sir?" Keith asked.

The team leader grinned and tossed him an assault rifle. "You, me, and Jim? We'll watch Kristen's back. We have the fun job of shooting a dragon with bullets we know won't hurt it."

The Wonderkid shot her a knowing look and she felt the bullet that had punctured her shoulder in her pocket. She didn't know what she would do with it but leaving it behind seemed like definitely the wrong answer.

They pushed forward into the Detroit Renewable Power facility, a building she had only ever previously heard about on the local news. It now seemed to possess the importance of an ancient European castle.

Slow and careful progress brought them about halfway across the parking lot that surrounded the red-and-white building. The entire team startled when the electric transformers in a corner away from the facility itself crackled. Bolts of electricity arced between them like a tesla coil gone mad.

"The dumbass missed us," Hernandez said.

"I'm not so sure about that," Kristen said. She could feel the electromagnetic energy pulling at her steel skin. It was getting stronger and stronger and in a moment, it would drag her across the parking lot and slam her into one of the massive transformers, where she'd be crucified with electricity.

She turned her steel skin off and the tug stopped.

Keith laughed. "That was a weak trap."

"I don't think it was only for me. What about your guns?" she asked.

Drew answered first. "Mine's getting pulled for sure. Double time toward the facility."

"Ahh!" Beanpole yelled. His weapon had already slipped from his hand and clattered across the parking lot toward the transformers. He cursed and bolted after it but was too slow.

Everyone else raced toward the facility before the magnets could rob them of theirs.

"Beanpole, get back to the van and keep your radio handy. It would help to know if anyone else shows up—mages, thugs, even Dragon SWAT," Drew yelled at the other man as he ran. "And for Mom's sake, don't approach the malfunctioning electrical transformers. There are more guns in the van."

"Yes, sir. Sorry, sir!" Beanpole yelled and adjusted direction toward the vehicle.

Kristen led them to a door, concerned that this was exactly what Shadowstorm wanted, but the rapid fire of a machine gun peppered the ground ahead of them with a line of bullets. It seemed that he didn't want them to use this door after all, but that didn't mean she could allow them to be shredded by the barrage.

She turned and led the team away from the door and toward a massive pile of garbage outside the facility.

"Do we have a sniper, Butters?" Drew asked.

"No, sir. It's an automated system, looks like. I can't tell if its magic or machine-powered."

"Can you take a shot?"

He lifted his rifle, aimed, fired and cursed.

The gun started to fire in return.

They ran farther from it and closer to the garbage.

"Either it's one hell of an AI or magic, but either way, it's firing through a tiny slit. I can't target the gun itself and I don't know where the sensors are." Butters looked downright ashamed that an automated system had already bested him this early in the fight.

"I think we need to assume its magic," Kristen said. Everyone nodded—an agreement of necessity.

"There's an entrance." Keith pointed to open hangar doors. A conveyer belt led inside them and a giant claw looked like it normally deposited trash on it but was currently still.

"We can go in with the trash," she said. "I don't think Shadowstorm would think a dragon would sink that low."

They moved toward the conveyer belt and the stench of garbage became more acrid as they approached.

"This plan stinks," Keith joked. No one laughed. That would have involved breathing far too deeply.

They had reached the base of the garbage pile when the crane activated. She saw no operator seated at its controls, but the massive machine began to move all the same. Its boom arm swung out and a dangling claw of metal gnashing teeth hung below it. "Go, go, go! Up the pile!" she said. She stayed on the ground near a giant circle with an X painted on it, no doubt the claw's typical target.

It probably wasn't smart, but she thought she could totally destroy it.

Instead of targeting her, however, it tracked the Wonderkid up the garbage heap. She cursed, turned on her dragon speed, and reached him as the claw descended. Its massive metal jaws closed around them both and she activated her steel skin.

The machine was strong but the Steel Dragon was stronger.

"What do you want me to do?" Jim asked as she held the jaws apart so they couldn't close.

"Get inside. Hernandez!" she bellowed. "Blow the controls for this fucker."

He obeyed and scurried up the garbage heap, his legs sinking into the trash up to his knees as he did so.

Kristen tried to hold the jaws of the claw at bay but it was too much. They slammed shut. Her head, arms, and torso were now inside the clawed scoop and her legs dangled out. If she was a human, she'd no doubt be dead.

She was forced to wait, blind and deaf as her prison carried her to who knew what.

After an agonizing thirty seconds, the expected explosion—dulled from her being enclosed in metal—stopped the mechanical claw's movement.

Impatient, she kicked her legs but her prison remained shut.

Something pinged off the claw, followed rapidly by another. After the third, it opened and dumped her into a pile of garbage inside the facility.

The team stood above the pile in the massive open hangar doorway. Butters settled his rifle on his shoulder. He must have shot the release for the claw—a damn hard shot, but he had done it in three tries.

"Where's Hernandez?" she asked, tried to push herself up the pile of muck, and failed. She was impressed her team had not only scaled the garbage pile but reached the doorway.

"She blew the controls. She's on her way," Drew called.

The door to the facility began to slide closed from either side with the team trapped in the middle. Already, the catwalks that led around the trash pile were blocked.

"Hernandez, see if you can find another way in without getting shot!" Drew yelled over his shoulder as he turned his back to the outside and scrutinized something in the building.

"Fuck that!" Hernandez yelled but it was obvious from how faint it sounded that she was too far. She wouldn't make it.

"Everyone else, jump!"

"No!" Kristen yelled but the others ignored her. They all flung themselves into the garbage pile. Butters and Drew did so with disgusted resignation, but Keith and Jim almost looked like they enjoyed it. She couldn't let them go it alone, so she turned her dragon speed on and raced up the pile. At the top, she discovered another garbage pile inside the building and she jumped into it with her team.

They plunged into the trash and she immediately realized they'd fallen into another trap.

The stack began to writhe and convulse like some great beast had been asleep at the bottom and had now awoken.

"Stay near the top," Jim shouted. "I saw a video online about this place. Those are giant metal corkscrews down there. They'll grind us up like hamburger meat."

That instruction was easier said than done. As the trash was pulled into the garbage grinders, lighter items were pushed toward the top while heavier things—like people—seemed to sink through the mass like pasta in boiling water. Already, they'd sunk six feet, and the top of the wall was out of reach. No one could jump that high, and even if they could, the footing was so poor that it gave instead of providing a springboard. She had to turn her body back to skin instead of steel to avoid sinking through it all.

"How deep you think this pit is, Jim?" Drew asked.

Kristen turned to him as well. He was the only one of them who seemed to have any idea about the specs of this place.

"How the fuck am I supposed to know? I've seen this place on the news once or twice and Googled it, but it's not like I know the goddamn engineering plans!" There was panic in his voice and she couldn't blame him. They were way too close to those grinding screws.

Chunks of garbage spewed—coffee grounds, popped diapers, and the leftovers from kitchen sinks. The screws continued to grind, and they sank even deeper.

"We need an idea!" Butters shouted. Despite his weight, he wasn't any deeper in the garbage than the rest of them, but there was real panic in his voice. She had to do something—anything—if her team was going to survive this.

She pushed toward the surface and again, the mass of garbage threatened to swallow her. An extension cord wound around her neck. It seemed both ends were already stuck in the grinder below. She tried to pull herself free but had an idea. A dumb, dangerous idea, but an idea all the same.

After a deep breath, she dove into the garbage. Moving down through it proved to be much easier than staying afloat in it. Yes, the smell was almost unbearable. It was dark, although not pitch-black thanks to her night vision, but at least she could head down. It made it easier that she'd turned her skin to steel again, so she basically sank through the muck. She wondered if—in all of Earth's history with its dragon overlords—a single dragon had ever willingly dived into garbage. From what she could tell, not getting their hands dirty was maybe rule number one of being a dragon. Swimming through trash had to be a serious no-no.

When she reached the bottom of the pit, she confirmed that Jim had been right. Massive screws spiraled to churn the garbage and break it into tiny pieces. She had no doubt that they would do the same thing to a human body—grind it up beyond its constituent parts.

Fortunately, her body was not human. She'd already activated her steel skin to make her descent faster.

Having reached the bottom of the pit, she rotated herself so her feet pointed down and jammed her steel-skinned legs between the screws.

The pressure was immediate, like the world's worst shiatsu massage chair. Her skin held, though, and didn't break. She hadn't thought it would—she could withstand bullets, after all—but a wave of relief surged all the same. The screws continued to grind against her body but failed to damage or dislodge her and after a long moment, an odd pop sounded from somewhere hidden in the walls of the pit and the pressure stopped. She had done it. Her intervention had prevented them from being crushed into fuel for the incinerator.

"Kristen!" She heard them call, their voices muffled through the trash. Their obvious anxiety spurred her into action, and she dragged her arms through the garbage in an effort to clear the surface away from her head. With her legs still trapped, she had to dig her face clear rather than simply scramble through. Bags split and rained muck on her and she grimaced but hauled herself upward. Still, the trash in her hair and on her face was worth it when she felt a hand catch hers.

Another pair of hands and another appeared in her vision, digging garbage furiously away from her. After a moment, she could see again. Drew, Keith, Butters, and Jim looked at her and grinned like fools.

"Steel Dragon? More like trash snake," Keith said.

Everyone groaned.

"That was a golden opportunity, and that's what you did with it?" Butters joked and slapped the Rookie on the back of the head.

"If it was such a good opportunity, let's hear what you have," he countered.

The sniper paused. Everyone laughed despite almost being crushed. He had nothing.

"I thought Princess Leia was tough. She has nothing on the Steel Dragon," Jim quipped.

Everyone smiled and nodded, Kristen included, but no one laughed. They'd laughed once in the face of death because they'd had to. Almost dying on the job regularly brought out the gallows humor in people, but to do so twice seemed downright arrogant.

"Not to bring the mood of this trash party down even further, but we're still stuck in a garbage pit," Drew said and didn't release her hand. "Do you have a plan to get us out of here Miss Steel Dragon?"

"I do, actually. Do any of you see an extension cord?"

Keith, Jim, and Butters didn't have to look far to find the cord that had caught her and given her the idea. The Wonderkid located it first.

"We can use this to climb out."

She nodded and winked, which caused some kind of slime to run out of her hair and into her eyes.

"The only problem is that both ends of this are stuck." Keith grimaced. Despite his complaint, he'd obviously worked out how to solve this particular logistical problem, although he seemed determined not to voice it. She did it for him.

"One of you tough SWAT boys has a knife on you, right?"

Drew and Keith both reached for theirs.

"Well, get down there and get us this repurposed rope," she said.

His expression resigned, Keith nodded. He didn't want Drew to let go of Kristen any more than the team leader did.

"If you guys keep calling me Rookie after this, you can all go fuck yourselves." And with that, he dove into the garbage.

They waited for what seemed like forever before he reappeared with one end of the extension cord. Somehow, he'd managed to get it with the plug still intact.

"It was wound around the metal screw." He said every word while exhaling and obviously tried to keep as much filth out of his mouth as possible.

"Halfway there, Rookie," Butters said.

"Listen, you fat fucker, why don't you get the other half? Whales are supposed to be able to hold their breaths for like an hour, right?" the man retorted with a solid dose of vitriol.

No one laughed harder than Butters.

Keith grinned. He'd obviously prepared the joke but he didn't press the point. With a deep breath heavy with resignation, he dove back into the garbage. He surfaced maybe twenty seconds later with the other end of the extension cord. This one, he'd had to cut with the knife.

"Nice," Kristen said. "Now, find a piece of pipe or something, tie that cord around it, and throw it around one of those handrails up there so we can climb out."

He nodded and he and Jim went to look for a pipe. They found a piece of PVC without too much work, ran the cord through it, and knotted it. Thereafter, they took turns to hurl the makeshift grappling hook up toward the handrail. After a few attempts, the Rookie managed to loop it around.

With a triumphant, "What do you think of that Wonderkid?" He climbed up.

It almost came loose once, but he did a weird little flip trick with the cord and it held. Once at the top, he held it so Jim could climb up. His teammate wasted no time and his experience in the military was obvious in the way he raced up the cable.

"You next, Drew," Kristen told him.

"If you think I'll climb out of here while your foot is still trapped in there, you're fucking crazy." Drew shook his head.

"You have to. The Wonderkid and the Rookie will be eaten alive without you, Drew."

"We're all dead without the Steel Dragon."

"It's okay. I have a plan."

He took a deep breath and his face soured at the smell, but he nodded and released her. She had been a little worried that she would be yanked back into the twirling screws despite hearing something that had sounded like the motor had broken. There was no way to be sure that was the case but either way, her steel legs did far more to stop the screws than him holding her hand had and she didn't move.

The team leader ascended and looked like a veteran rock climber every step of the way.

Only Kristen and Butters were left.

"All right, then, Miss Steel Dragon. What's the plan?"

She swallowed and forced a smile.

"You don't have a plan, do you!"

"Not exactly, no. But I think I can get out of here. Go ahead and climb up and I'll meet you there."

He folded his arms and shook his head. "We both know that cord won't hold me. For our team to survive, you have to make it up before I try."

Kristen nodded. She'd tried not to think about that, but he was right. It was a small miracle the wire had held Drew. She very much doubted it would hold Butters.

But that didn't solve the more immediate problem of her steel legs being stuck between the massive screws. When she tried to jiggle them, they didn't move an inch. She tried flexing, twisting, kicking, and every movement she could think of, but nothing worked. Without a doubt, she was trapped.

"Kristen, not to rush you but…uh…" Keith didn't have to finish.

Flashes of light were visible through the windows to the facility. Shadowstorm was summoning a storm. She didn't think his control was enough to actually strike any of her team with lightning bolts or anything so dramatic, but she also had a feeling that she'd had only a glimpse of his power.

The thought of hurricane-force winds coalescing on downtown Detroit came to mind. He could bring wind damage, lightning, and maybe a blizzard given the conditions outside. His extreme weather could destroy the city if she didn't get her leg unstuck. What was worse was that she didn't understand his powers any better than she understood her own. What if she defeated him but took too long and the storm lingered? Maybe once he set it in motion, it would be self-sustaining. If that was the case, she really was out of time.

"Kristen, what do we do?" Butters asked.

She knew what she had to do. The answer was obvious. Stonequest had tried to get her to do it and her father had said she needed to. Even Butters must know she had to become the Steel Dragon. She had to transform.

The problem was she didn't know how.

Perhaps if she concentrated and thought about how she was stuck and how if she could transform, she could simply break the machinery and be free... Despite her focused attempt, it didn't work.

"Come on, Kristen!" Drew yelled. "Something started rattling down below. We need to go."

A little panicked now, she tried again but with no result. She remained stuck, which meant Shadowstorm would have free reign over her city. He'd be free to hunt her family and kill her father, her mother, and Brian, for no reason beyond their relationship to her. But he wouldn't stop there. He'd kill her teammates one by one, no matter how hard they tried to fight him. She knew they wouldn't be able to stop him. He was simply too powerful and would take everything away from her.

"Yes, Kristen! Yes!" Butters shouted.

Something shifted inside her. Suddenly, her leg was no longer human but something with power unlike anything she had ever experienced.

There was no time to consider it, though, as she realized her legs were free. She moved quickly and climbed to the top of the garbage pile, grinning like a fool. Something had changed and she'd activated a power she'd never used before. She looked at Butters, expecting to be congratulated.

Instead, he frowned and studied her human body with disappointment and without apology. "That was, uh...anticlimactic."

"Whatever." She shrugged and waded toward the cord.

Butters followed, chuckling. "What did you do—make your leg into a tiny dragon leg or something?"

"Like you'd even understand. Foolish human," she joked.

"Oh! Perhaps you have become a dragon then," he called after her as she clambered up the orange extension cord. She reached the top without issue. Jim and Drew caught her arms and pulled her up beside them.

"All right, Butterball, try not to let your greasy fingers slip," Keith called down to their teammate.

"Hardy-ha-ha. You know, I may not be the strongest, pound for pound, but if you think I can't climb a rope you have another think coming. In fact, I once singlehandedly climbed the rope hanging from the bell in the church's steeple because the preacher said we couldn't eat until it chimed and a swarm of paper wasps had taken up residence. The things were damn surprised when—"

The cable snapped.

He plummeted into the garbage.

"Butters! Kristen called.

"I'm all right. I'm all right. But I landed funny on my—oh, dear God. Why?" He gasped when he rolled over to find he'd landed on his rifle and had snapped it in half.

"Are you okay?" Drew asked. He had to raise his voice as something in the facility had begun to make considerable noise.

"I'm fine. I'll live, but I won't be much help now. I broke my baby. Oh, cruel mistress Hostess and unfair Colonel Sanders, why must you taste so delicious?"

"Are you blaming twinkies and fried chicken for your fat ass?" Keith hollered.

"Can't a man have a moment to grieve?" he protested.

"No," Drew said and drained the humor from the moment. "It's getting hotter in here. I think Shadowstorm activated the incinerator."

"Butters, you have to hurry." Jim was looking around the top of the garbage heap from up on the ledge. "There has to be another cord down there—a rope, some clothesline, something."

The sniper shook his head. "You need to leave me here. Without my rifle, I'm not much good. You need to hurry and stop Shadowstorm before this storm gets out of control."

"We can't leave you here." Kristen's words emerged as a growl and she was surprised at the ferocity of her own voice.

"You have no choice. Besides, Hernandez will find a way in here. I'm sure she's already placing explosives. I'll be fine. But you have to end this tonight."

She nodded. While she hated herself for it, she understood the wisdom of what he argued for. She had to leave him behind so she could save him.

"Is there anything you want me to tell Shadowstorm for you?" she asked.

"Tell him he's a plucked turkey."

That teased a grin from them all as they left their friend in the garbage pit.

It was difficult not to think about the missing three when she turned to the remaining members of her team. Had this been Shadowstorm's plan? To stop her teammates and eliminate them as allies so she would be forced to face him alone?

But no, it couldn't be. He would definitely have planned to kill her friends, not keep them away. Which meant she was winning. And if she wasn't? Well, she had to believe that she was.

"Do we have a plan?" she asked the others.

"He's not anywhere in the facility. I checked the offices and don't see anywhere else he could be hiding," Drew stated.

"There's a ton of places in here he could be!" Keith protested.

The team leader shrugged. "True, but you really think that's his style? He'll simply hide behind a trash compactor and pop out at the perfect moment?"

"No way. Not with his ego." Kristen scanned the room to try to determine where he would have gone. The incinerator ran at full capacity now and made the room hot. Steam began to build in pressure and seeped from leaks in pipes throughout the room.

"The tunnels." As soon as she said it, she knew that was where he'd gone.

Shadowstorm had been in Detroit for a long time. He undoubtedly knew more about the tunnels beneath the Motor City than most. In addition, he'd probably also had more than enough time to boobytrap them.

"If he's down there, it won't be easy to find him," Jim pointed out.

Kristen closed her eyes and felt for Shadowstorm's presence. It didn't take long before she touched it. It was a white-hot presence, a ball of fury and hate hotter than the steam from the boiler that issued into the room.

"I have him." She looked across the facility and immediately located a grate in the floor. It didn't take a detective to guess that it would be conveniently unlocked. "But you guys can't come with me. Shadowstorm wants to kill you all so I'll lose focus. It'll be better for everyone if y'all stay here. Get Butters out and get to safety."

"And give Detroit to the winner of a dragon battle? Fuck that!" Jim protested.

"Yeah, that's bullshit! I want to cap this motherfucker." Keith slapped the side of his assault rifle. "It would be fucking awesome to have that on my resume."

Drew only stared at her and silently challenged her to tell him to go away again. She was brave but not that brave.

"All right, then. Let's move."

They descended a staircase to the floor of the facility, approached the grate with their weapons raised, and found—unsurprisingly—that it wasn't locked. Keith pulled it open while the others trained their weapons on the entrance.

Nothing emerged and, after a few moments of waiting, they entered what was surely Shadowstorm's greatest trap.

CHAPTER SIXTY-NINE

The first few minutes in the tunnel were almost tedious. Nothing attacked them and nothing fired at them or threw sparks or anything like that. The lights even worked on that first level.

To navigate, Kristen followed the seed of rage she felt she knew could only be Shadowstorm. Her aura couldn't make her a map of the maze of tunnels, but that didn't matter because mostly, she could sense that he was below. Down was therefore the main direction in which they went.

They followed the tunnel to a stairway and descended there, then traversed that one to another stairway and went down again.

"You can feel the weight of the city on our shoulders," Keith murmured.

"That's why we call you Rookie, Rookie," Drew murmured in reply. "You should feel that weight every time you put your badge on."

"I don't know, Drew. I like working under pressure, but this is something else," he said and sounded like he wanted to say more.

"We have action." Jim was all business.

The lights above them went out first and plunged them into darkness. Kristen didn't mind it as she could see with her dragon abilities, but everyone else activated the lights on their guns.

They froze in readiness but nothing attacked. Instead, one of the pipes along the sides of the tunnel rattled as if some beast had passed through it. The disturbance moved beyond them and before it reached the stairs they'd come down, it burst out of the pipe.

They simply stood and stared in something close to astonishment at a jet of steam that had emerged rather than the expected attacker.

"He doesn't want us to leave," Kristen said.

"No, it's fine. It's only a little steam. Haven't you ever been to a sauna?" Keith let his gun drop to his side and extended his hand. There was something dreamlike to his tone of voice.

"No, Keith!" She tried to flash her aura to make him fear the steam, but she was too late. He stuck his hand into it and screamed.

"Fuck!" He yanked his hand out quickly and the dreamlike tone of voice was gone. When he grasped his weapon, he cursed. He'd burned his palm. "I'm sorry, you guys. I don't know what the hell happened. I had this feeling like I used to when I was a kid and we'd all go to the sauna and I... I'm so sorry."

"Don't' be." She squared her jaw. "It was Shadowstorm. He used his aura on you. It's my fault. I should've been able to protect you."

"From my own feelings?" Keith—for the first time since she had discovered what she was—looked terrified to work with the Steel Dragon. He didn't understand what she was becoming. No one did.

She gritted her teeth. "We have to keep moving."

They crept down the narrow passage and the steam billowed behind them until they reached another stairway. This one took them down to another tunnel that immediately opened into a three-way intersection.

Kristen chose a direction at random, Shadowstorm was still below them—waiting for them, no doubt. She assumed he wanted to use the steam to tire them, but she felt certain that he wanted to face her. Apparently, she'd made the wrong choice. As soon as she started down the left path, another wave of energy seemed to surge through the pipes and burst one of those directly ahead.

Steam immediately filled the tunnel.

"Let's push through," Drew shouted over the hiss of steam.

"No!" she yelled and turned the other way.

"He's herding us to him," Jim protested.

"Better that than being cooked like dumplings," she responded and strode on. There was no need to explain that she felt sure he was guiding them to him and that she intended to go along with it.

The team followed until one of the pipes in that tunnel also erupted. She had been damn close to it at that moment and immediately turned her skin to steel but could still feel the heat through her protective layer of metal. There could be no doubt that one of her teammates would have second- or third-degree burns if they'd been the ones to lead.

"Turn back," she ordered.

"I saw a stairway though there," Keith hollered.

"It's too dangerous. Turn back."

"But—" She ignored his protests and turned quickly, caught him by the arm, and dragged him from the steam-choked passage. She didn't want to use her aura on her team—partly because it would split her focus and make it harder to track Shadowstorm, and partly because she thought they deserved better than that—but she was sorely tempted. Her adversary wouldn't have had any reservations about using his aura to keep humans from danger. In fact, he'd probably think that not using his aura would be wrong. Like letting a killer walk free when you had many jail cells.

But Kristen wasn't him, not yet anyway. So she avoided the temptation to make her team feel terrified at the prospect of facing a dragon made of shadow and storm that had the knowledge to control the steam veins of the Motor City. Instead, she treated them as equals, and they pressed on.

She led them down the third tunnel. They made it perhaps thirty yards when they discovered the end blocked by fallen rubble. She was dumbfounded as she'd honestly thought Shadowstorm was leading them to him. Why send them down a collapsed tunnel?

"We need to go back," Drew said, stating the obvious before anyone else could.

They spun to begin their retreat but one of the pipes in the tunnel they were in ruptured and filled the tunnel with steam.

"Shit!" she cursed. "This is my fault. I thought he was leading me down there for a fight."

"Why fight the Steel Dragon when you could simply steam her alive?" Jim asked morosely.

"We have to take those stairs that Keith saw." Drew gestured down the tunnel and then toward the left.

"How the hell can we get through that?" Keith rubbed his head. "It's like pea soup. I can't see through it at all. Plus, it'll steam us like broccoli."

"The pipe ruptured on the left," Jim said. "I think if we stick to the right, the temperature shouldn't be that bad."

"Then we follow the wall with our hands until it turns to the right, hold hands, and cut across to where Keith saw the stairs." She tried to keep her voice calm despite the rising temperature in the tunnel.

"That sounds good," Drew said and took point.

"Sure, if by good you mean it sounds like a great fucking way to end up on a dragon's plate next to a cup of melted butter," Keith said but he fell into step behind the team leader.

Kristen let them go first. If she led the way with her steel skin, she wouldn't be able to tell if it was safe for humans.

They entered the steam. Even with her night vision, she could hardly see through the billowing clouds of heated vapor so it wasn't much of a surprise when Keith vanished.

It was terrifying—definitely and unequivocally terrifying—but not a surprise.

"Rookie!" she called into the superheated mist.

"End of the line, Steel Dragon," Keith said, and she found that he was right. Her hand reached the end of the tunnel. It was time to leave the guiding brick wall and move out into the steam.

"Here we go, Wonderkid," she said over her shoulder and stepped forward.

It was a supremely disorienting experience. Although Drew and Keith talked loudly to maintain audio contact, it was easy to lose a sense of where she was. By the time she touched the opposite side of the hallway, she was drenched in sweat and practically hoped Shadowstorm would attack her there and then.

But, of course, he didn't. He understood human emotions better than people did—after all, he'd exploited them for centuries. That knowledge was a tremendous advantage as he undoubtedly knew that her fear, anxiety, and exhaustion would be the first blow against her. Although, as she moved through the steam and her lungs began to burn and her breath turned ragged, she began to wonder if he really did want a fight. Boiling her alive under the city seemed like it might do the job for him.

She tried not to lose herself to these thoughts, but it was a struggle. If any of her team passed out, she wouldn't even be able to find them in the steam. The horrifying thought seemed to echo in her mind.

But ultimately, the fear was needless. She made it through to where Drew and Keith waited for her. Footsteps from behind her told her when Jim emerged. All of them were sweating, red-faced, and exhausted but alive.

"I don't think we'll make it through much more of this." The Rookie tried to catch his breath.

"I have a feeling we won't need to go much farther." Kristen could feel Shadowstorm. He was close—so close—and unbelievably angry. She somehow knew that he could sense Keith, Drew, and Jim in a way that she could not. Their survival did not please the callous dragon.

"All right, let's go." Jim nodded toward the stairway.

"Hold up." Drew touched the pipes that ran through the tunnels. She hadn't realized there was more to this subterranean warren than only the steam pipes. Electricity was present, cable, and even fiber optics by the look of it. He passed over each in turn before he settled on a larger pipe than the others. "You guys know I love this city, right?" He touched the selected duct tentatively with a finger.

"Not as much as Kristen and I do, but yeah, sure." Jim raised an eyebrow. "Why, what do you plan to do?"

"Take water away from way too many people." Drew stepped back from the pipe, raised his rifle, and fired three times. The first bullet didn't break it, nor the second, but the third cracked it and water began to spray on the wall beside them.

"All right. You're all hot and you stink. Hit the showers."

She didn't need to be told twice. As she passed through the cold spray of water, she turned her skin off briefly so she could better appreciate the refreshingly cool and—best of all—clean, water.

The team all did the same and looks of relief settled on their faces.

All except Drew. He didn't look proud of what he'd done.

"It's gonna be all right, big guy." Keith patted him on the shoulder.

"I know. Its only…it's a school night."

Jim chuckled—more of that laughing in the face of death. "It's damn near one in the morning. Any kids still up to take a shower probably won't go to school tomorrow."

The team leader actually smiled at that—a rare sight to see—and nodded. "Let's do this damn thing. Are you ready, Steel Dragon?"

"As ready as I'll ever be," she said and tried to sound like she meant it.

They descended the stairs to a landing, reversed direction, and continued.

When they finally emerged in a tunnel, it soon opened into some kind of underground station. Kristen had no idea what the room was for. Perhaps it had once been used for trains or perhaps this was where the construction equipment that must have dug these tunnels had been housed while the workers slept.

Either way, it was a large, cavernous room, close to the size of a basketball court. Compared to the passages they had been in, it seemed practically endless and could easily have accommodated something the size of a rec center. The floor was surfaced with old tiles, some cracked here and there. The walls were brick, although sections had been tiled over long before—lending credence to the abandoned train station theory, even though Detroit didn't have a subway. The ceiling was raw stone crisscrossed by wires and pipes. Wooden scaffolding lined most of the walls, abandoned decades before. Bare bulbs hung above them but barely illuminated the space.

Pillars dotted the room to support the tons and tons of stone and brick they'd passed through.

There was, however, still sufficient light to see Sebastian Shadowstorm standing in the middle of the space. He wore a black gi with a red sash across his waist and his trademark black gloves piped in red. His arms were folded across his enormous frame. In the stark light of the naked bulbs, he seemed to be more shadow than man, his shoulders so large they eclipsed his legs from the light. Only the red of his belt gave any hint that he had the body of a human. His hair was pulled into a tight ponytail, and his goatee framed the cruel rictus that defined his face.

"Kristen. You made it," he said, his voice cold and humorless, so different than the kindly tone he'd used when they'd trained together. Of course, she now understood it wasn't really training but a dissection of her abilities.

"Sebastian," she replied and attempted to sound as cold and furious as he did.

The flinch of his scowl told her she had at least partly succeeded.

"We've wasted time enough, don't you think? Come now. It's time you died."

CHAPTER SEVENTY

Kristen raced toward Sebastian. She couldn't wait for him to attack. If he struck one of her friends even once, they'd be dead.

He anticipated her attack, of course, and swung a massive right hook into her gut as soon as she entered range. She careened across the room and against a wall of tile that immediately shattered and revealed the raw brick behind it.

Before she could scramble to her feet, he launched his assault. His arms blurred as they struck her ribs repetitively and pummeled her ribcage like it was nothing more than a punching bag. If she were human, she'd be dead.

But she wasn't a human.

She kicked off the ground and pounded her steel forehead against his skull.

He reeled back, dazed by the blow.

Using the brief moment of advantage, she pushed off the wall and tackled the larger man, who fell heavily. He was obviously unaccustomed to facing a foe who could do such a thing and she was able to batter him a few times before he managed to throw her aside.

His strength was unimaginable. Despite the fact that she was made of steel, he hurled her with ease. She twisted in midair like a cat and came down on her feet hard enough to crack the tile.

"Ah, Steel Dragon, I miss our little sparring matches. I forget what it's like to fight a foe more massive than myself. A fun little challenge." He chuckled but the sound cut short when bullets raked his chest.

Drew had fired a couple of rounds.

Shadowstorm cursed but the weapon had done nothing to him. Instead of blood, shadow itself seemed to leak from the wound.

Kristen couldn't let herself gawk, though. Instead, she bounded forward, vaulted up, and caught him in the chest with her steel knees.

He toppled back but unfortunately, she wasn't able to stay on top of him this time.

She landed beyond him. In the time it took her to turn, he was able to kick her in the small of the back.

The blow felled her, and she gasped as pain seared along her spine. He really did know how to hurt her despite her skin. She couldn't believe she'd actually trusted this monster. While she had thought she'd been the one learning, it was him discovering her weaknesses.

When she turned and lashed another kick, Shadowstorm had gone.

He stepped from the shadow of a pillar behind her, his hands clasped together, and struck her across the shoulders.

Her dazed mind reeled at what she thought she'd seen as she sprawled and struggled to stand. It looked like he had moved from shadow to shadow…but that was impossible, right?

"What are you?" She finally managed to push herself to her feet.

"You insolent little bitch, I am your better."

Bullets caught him in the shoulders and he roared and turned.

Jim had obviously been the marksman and he simply ran off, sticking to the perimeter of the room, and grinned like a child who'd stolen a slice of pie before Thanksgiving dinner.

Kristen noticed that again, blood didn't issue from his wounds but some kind of black smoke. It looked like blood did under water, only jet-black.

Though it wasn't blood, she still karate-chopped the injury with every ounce of her strength behind it.

Shadowstorm roared in pain and stumbled forward. The blow hadn't knocked him over but it had hurt. That might be better.

Unfortunately, when he turned to her, she could see the wounds from the first bullets had already healed. She often forgot about dragons' legendary healing abilities. So much of her own powers were spent avoiding any injury at all. This was possibly the worst way to be reminded that she wasn't the only dragon who could shrug bullets off.

But not all bullets…

Her thoughts immediately turned to the bullet in her pocket. She couldn't fire it, but maybe she could still use it as a weapon.

Thinking in the middle of the battle cost her dearly. Her adversary vanished into another shadow and reappeared beside her friends.

"Keith!" she shrieked as the dragon picked the Rookie up like he was nothing more than a soccer ball.

Images of him ripping her teammate in half flashed before her eyes but apparently, humans were below even this level of notice. Rather than tear him limb from limb, he hurled him at her.

Kristen caught him—she had to, or he'd snap his neck—but when she did, Shadowstorm raced forward and slammed his fist into her gut.

She doubled over in pain but as she did so, she fumbled in her pocket and retrieved the cracked dragon-scale bullet. She could use this. If she could only wear him down a little more she could—

A massive uppercut connected with her chin. The dragon struck her with such force that she rocketed into the ceiling. She plummeted amidst a rain of stone and prepared for a hard landing.

But while the rocks struck the floor, she didn't have the opportunity. As she approached, her opponent kicked to arc her across the room once more.

She impacted hard with the tiles and sensed that this was it—he would move in to finish her now—when gunshots erupted in a concerted barrage that echoed almost painfully loud in the underground chamber.

Shadowstorm roared.

Drew, Jim, and Keith had managed to triangulate him. Despite the Rookie's burned hand, he managed to fire as well. The dragon seemed momentarily distracted as if he didn't know what to do about the onslaught of projectiles.

He whirled constantly in an attempt to target his attacker, but each time he faced one of the three men, they moved and left the other two to fire. Soon, he was draped in a cloud of his shadow blood.

This was Kristen's moment—her single opportunity—and she grasped the bullet in her hand with the point protruding through her steel knuckles. She'd punch him in the temple or the chest, whichever was open, and hope that he felt the same burning she had from the terrible weapon.

There was no time to think it through. She raced toward the cloud of blood and toward Shadowstorm's screams of pain. Her fist raised, she leapt high and let gravity add even more momentum to her finishing blow.

A dragon's tail lashed out from the cloud and struck her across the chest. She pounded into the tiled floor and rolled.

He began to laugh. She could hear him clearly as her friends had evidently run out of ammunition and had to reload.

"A cute battle, certainly, but enough is enough," he roared from the cloud of shadow-blood.

She slid her hands under her and pushed herself to her feet. When she looked at her adversary, he wasn't shrouded in a cloud of blood but the energy he put out when he transformed.

The light seemed to leach from the room as the form in the center grew larger and larger. A nightmarish cloud of teeth and claws, lightning and storm clouds, spawned the dragon that stood amongst them a moment later, deep under the heart of the Motor City.

Her heart sank when she realized that she'd dropped the bullet. She looked around frantically while her mind reminded her that the tiny point of dragon claw was her only chance against this beast.

"Are you looking for an exit, Kristen?" Shadowstorm rumbled, his tone amused.

"More like an end to this battle." She located the bullet. It was her only hope now that she was trapped facing this monstrosity. She shifted closer to where it had rolled against a pillar and was lodged between a tile and the ground.

"There is but one end, you worm. If you hold still and surrender yourself, I can give it to you more quickly."

Shadowstorm—in the largest dragon body she had ever seen—attacked.

CHAPTER SEVENTY-ONE

He struck Kristen with the force of an eighteen-wheeler. The space wasn't large—not by dragon body standards—but there was still enough for him to pump his wings once and propel himself into her. She catapulted wildly into some scaffolding. Instead of the heaviness of steel, she seemed to weigh what a pebble would compared to the monster she now faced.

She pushed herself out of the equipment but more of it collapsed around her as she tried to untangle herself. Shadowstorm caught her in one of his claws and plucked her from the tangle of broken wood like a farmer would pluck an apple from an orchard.

"I like your steel body, Kristen," he taunted and squeezed her in his fist. He flexed his aura and tried to make her feel terror in every fiber of her being. Obviously, he thought her less than dragon if he believed that would work. "It has more heft to it." He hurled her across the station again. Her momentum carried her through a pillar and she struck a second with her shoulder, stopped, and fell.

Gunshots rang out as she pushed herself to her feet. Her friends were trying to buy her some time and she hoped it didn't cost them their lives.

Her adversary roared and exhaled a huge wash of flame toward the team. Curses came as her friends—she couldn't see who—managed to evade them. Some of the scaffolding caught on fire and Shadowstorm laughed.

She rolled behind a pillar and pushed herself to her feet.

"Little Steel Dragon, where are you?" He chuckled. In his dragon form, there was a low tone beneath it like the rumble of a lion. "Oh, wait, you're not precisely a dragon, are you?"

His tail whipped around the pillar she had hunkered behind. If she had still been there, it would have pounded her face into the concrete. She made a note to avoid the tail—and another to avoid the jaws, claws, fire-breath, and whatever other bizarre abilities the dragon had.

"Backup's on its way," she shouted and her voice echoed off the walls.

"We both know that's not true, little tin human."

Instinctively, she screamed when his massive dragon head appeared beside her. She didn't run and instead, drew her fist back and punched him in his teeth with every ounce of strength she had.

He recoiled—slightly—but snapped at her and she was no longer sure if she'd even hurt him or if he'd simply readied a strike like a heron hunting a minnow.

In the next moment, his bulk moved around the pillar and she faced a full-grown dragon. He raised his claw and tried to crush her like a bug.

Kristen moved toward his wrist, getting within his reach with her dragon speed, and avoided being pinned.

Shadowstorm hissed and tried to stab her with his other claw. She dodged again. This was one move, at least, that Stonequest had helped her practice against.

The dragon abandoned this tactic and—now that she was so close—simply tried to eat her. That might have been the end, but she managed to get a foot on his bottom jaw and her hands on his top jaw.

He tried to close his mouth but her steel form was too strong. She briefly entertained fantasies of forcing his jaw back and cracking his skull open, but the inferno that boiled out of his throat rapidly snuffed that idea out.

Flames engulfed her and she was blown from the dragon's mouth. Once again, she encountered the far wall amongst more scaffolding that he had ignited when he'd expelled her from his mouth.

She stood shakily and almost blacked out from the heat. Her skin didn't hurt—it would take more than that to burn her, apparently—but the heat seemed to be cooking her brain inside her skull.

Utterly disoriented, she stumbled out of the burning scaffolding and tried to get her bearings. The entrance was…behind her?

Her curse was echoed by her teammates. Shadowstorm had now turned their exit into a wall of flame.

"Everyone needs to get out," she shouted over the crackle of flames.

In response, more gunshots chattered.

Gallows humor until the end. She had to force a grin at the sheer arrogance of even attempting to shoot the dragon.

"A good point, tin human," her adversary said from across the room. She expected him to vanish into shadow and reappear close enough to obliterate her with his tail, but instead, he turned.

"You'd better run," she shouted, and it sounded like her mouth had a swollen lip. Okay, so he was able to hurt her through her steel skin. That was good to know.

He merely laughed before his tail whipped at the entrance to another tunnel into the room. It collapsed as if he were a toddler and the structure was nothing but wooden blocks. "I'm having so much fun, tiny tin human. Let's not lose our audience now." Another gout of flame erupted from his throat, then another. Soon, all the equipment in the room was ablaze. She could feel the heat through her steel skin and knew that while she might survive, her friends were only human.

"You monster," she screamed and raced forward in a burst of dragon speed. She had to fight back and had to defeat him. Without thinking, she caught hold of his tail and tried to yank him away from her friends but held on too long. He flicked it and catapulted her through the ceiling and into the roof of a tunnel filled with steam.

Kristen's arms flailed as she attempted to grasp the ledge of the hole she'd created. She barely managed to hold on with her fingertips. This only brought more laughter from Shadowstorm.

"I spy, with my dragon's eye, the legs of a human." His clawed hands curled around her and yanked her through the hole.

He swung her into the floor, then a pillar, the ceiling, and another pillar. Between each strike, she moved so fast, her vision closed in and her stomach twisted. Finally, he smashed her into the tiled floor. He didn't release her and instead, ground her face into tile like she was nothing but a cigarette butt.

"You know, I think I'll eat your friends first, then come back and kill you. It's been so long since I've tasted the flesh of man. A couple of months, at least, but it feels like years."

She struggled to stand. Her muscles protested and seemed to prefer the quick passage of death to a continued fight against this fire-breathing monster of an enemy.

Her gaze was drawn to the bullet that nestled in a pile of rubble that moments before had been a pillar. She summoned a deep well of strength and dragged herself toward the tiny weapon.

"Where are those little humans, though?" The dragon moved through the flames and his tail swished like that of a cat hunting a mouse.

His targeting her friends gave her a burst of strength. She couldn't let him kill them. Somehow, she stumbled to her feet, managed the couple of steps required, and retrieved the bullet. It took concentration to put it between her knuckles and finally, she made a fist.

"I'm the only human you get to kill today," she shouted.

Shadowstorm laughed maniacally at that. "What great words to die by!"

He pumped his wings once and the gust of air fueled the flames that now ringed the room and made them burn blue instead of orange before he drove into her. She once again clattered to a painful stop on the hard tiles and gasped for breath.

The dragon bounded toward her. With the constraints of the

room, it took only a single leap before he towered over her where she cowered below him on the floor.

He rumbled a satisfied laugh as he raised a clawed hand to crush her. Her training with Stonequest said she should dodge but she ignored the instinct. Instead, she clenched her fist and aimed it at his palm.

His claw swung and immediately recoiled, and he grasped one hand with the other.

She knew it wouldn't kill him, not in the palm, but she had to save her friends.

"Drew! Jim! Keeeeeeith!" she shouted as he thundered around the room and his frenzy shattered pillars and hurled flaming scaffolding everywhere.

"Hall!" Drew yelled in response. He and Jim had the unconscious Rookie between them, an arm over each of their shoulders. They were as close to the wall as they could be, but with the equipment on fire, they had exactly zero cover from the dragon that continued to demolish the room.

"I'll clear a path for you," Kristen called.

"Finish him off," Drew ordered with his boss-cop voice.

"I can't. Hurting his palm took everything I had. We have to get out of here."

"Through the steam tunnels? We'll never make it. This is it, Kristen."

"No, no we can do it If we make it to the van—"

"He'll pick us up and drop us in the river. You have to face him, Kristen."

The sound of an avalanche behind her made her turn quickly to see that most of the ceiling had collapsed.

In the moment that followed, she realized she could hear her own breathing over the crackle of the flames. Shadowstorm had stopped moving. Was he trapped under the rubble? Had he broken a bone? Was he dead?

Through the smoke, the hulking shape of his human form

appeared. His hands were clasped together in front of him but he was laughing.

"That was dragon's flesh? Clever, clever little human. Considering you aren't one of us, you sought to use our bodies against us? Too bad you didn't hit my throat or heart with it. As it is, my hand will take days to heal." He held the bullet up in his two fingers and crushed it.

"No—" She choked on the protest.

"Was that your—what's the human expression—ace up your sleeve? I must say, I expected more from Stonequest's little protégé. No matter. You've proven yourself as pathetic as the apes who now cower behind you. Step aside as I consume their flesh."

"You're bluffing," she said. "You can't transform now."

He chuckled, a low, dark sound that grew lower as he approached and became a rumble that filled the room while his body once again took the shape of a dragon.

"No, I am quite hungry—healing powers and all that," he growled, whipped his tail, and flung her through the flames.

Before she could fall, the tail snapped again and pressed her against the wall. In horror, she realized he intended to force her to watch while he ate her friends.

And there was nothing she could do. It was over and she'd lost. He would destroy this city, starting with her friends, then her family. Once he'd revenged himself on those she loved, he'd take the city and it would be as if she had never existed.

Shadowstorm had won.

CHAPTER SEVENTY-TWO

"The only question left is which of these steaks I eat first," the dragon said with mock deliberation, "and if I should eat them rare or well-done."

Tears poured down Kristen's face, strangely soothing in the smoke-filled chamber. She would die there but with the knowledge that he would kill everyone she loved.

"Bring it, you fucking alligator." Drew spat in the dragon's direction.

"I'll find the sack of rocks you need to eat to digest your food, you overgrown fucking chicken, and I'm gonna take a shit. Every time you eat, you'll taste my asshole." Jim smiled mirthlessly.

The team leader barked a laugh at that.

"It looks like it'll be this one, then." Shadowstorm took the Wonderkid in his claw and began to squeeze. "It appears you need an anatomy lesson."

Keith coughed and shifted briefly through consciousness as his brain fought to wake him fully.

"The Steel Dragon will…fuck you up," Keith managed before he passed out again.

She actually laughed at that. It was so insane. Her friends were about to die because of her, and what did they do? They didn't cry or rage or quit, they simply laughed in the face of death.

But they weren't laughing at death, not really. Even in the dragon's grasp, Jim looked at her, hope naked on his face. Drew also looked at her, his expression grim but not dire. And Keith had awoken only to say he believed in her.

There would be nothing worse than letting her people die. She couldn't fail them.

Her people.

Before, she had thought of that as a bad thing, but that's what they were. They were her people.

Dragons weren't the only ones who had people they protected and cared for, people they thought of as their own because they wanted them in their lives. Her mother and father thought of her and Brian as their own, and there was nothing wrong with that. People spoke of "my husband" or "my grandmother." Yes, there was possession to that, but that didn't make it wrong. In fact, it made perfect sense.

Something solidified inside her like molten steel touching water and a sense of purpose took shape.

Kristen realized that she had looked at being a dragon all wrong. She had thought her power would make her a danger to the people in her life, but that wasn't the case at all. People had only survived dragons and wars and malaria because they cared about each other. They wanted the people they loved to stay in their lives so badly, they'd seize any power they could do keep them there.

Yes, some abused their power. There were monsters who walked the Earth, but just because she had power didn't mean she had to abuse it.

She could use hers selflessly. It was a way she could protect those who needed protection from monsters like the lying beast of shadows who now threatened her friends.

It started in her heart, which was a surprise to her. She'd always thought it had been a mental block, but when her chest doubled, then tripled in size, she thought maybe she'd had it wrong from the start.

Steel scales burst from her chest, raced down her arms and legs, and altered her steel skin from the smooth nearly hairless texture of a human to the scaly armor of a dragon.

Her limbs extended and her legs grew another joint. Claws extended from her hands and feet. Wings emerged from her back and with barely a thought, they pushed her off the wall and she slid from Shadowstorm's grasp.

The Steel Dragon landed on all fours, although her neck was now long enough that she could still see her enemy in front of her. Her spine extended and another appendage came into existence in her mind. She had a tail—a wickedly long tail with a barbed tip like that of a halberd. The word for the weapon came to her in her brother's voice.

She breathed in through a longer snout. Thousands of tiny silver particles reabsorbed into her body. Apparently, her transformation shrouded her in silvery glitter. She was one hundred percent cool with that.

A great heat surged in her chest like a forge or an engine—no, a nuclear reactor.

Shadowstorm tossed Jim aside and growled at her.

Her new senses told her there was more to the sound than simply a threat. There were unspoken words. An emotional language revealed itself to her. She could sense his rage, his desire to destroy her, and, like sour milk in a cup of coffee, his fear.

The knowledge told her that he could taste her emotions as easily as she could his. He could taste her resolve, her courage, and her unwillingness to let him live and didn't like any of this.

Kristen smiled a dragon's grin before she attacked.

She pounded into her adversary, unprepared for her own strength. Her steel body outweighed the larger dragon and she plowed over him. The two of them bulldozed through the rubble in the middle of the room.

Though Shadowstorm was afraid, there was also a sense of purpose in his aura. He had fought dragons before and had killed dragons before. That lent him confidence she had yet to learn. They rolled together and she attempted to end up on top but he thwarted her and gained the advantage. She'd forgotten to use her wings.

He bit at her throat to sever her jugular but she struck him with her tail. The blade at its tip sliced his face and slit the scales that would have been his cheek if he'd been human.

With a bellow of pain, he fell back, stumbled, and staggered through the rubble. Apparently, the tip of her tail was as effective as the tiny bullet if not more so. She decided that she liked being a dragon.

"Kristen! A little help," Drew yelled.

She turned to locate him. Keith was still unconscious, but the team leader was strong enough to carry him. Jim had made it to them but was limping. At least he still had his gun. She cleared the burning scaffolding from their exit with a single swoosh of her tail and didn't even feel the flames.

"Wait for me," she told them as Shadowstorm attacked, brandishing both claws.

Kristen dug her rear talons into the tile so instead of tumbling, she only slid.

He brought his tail around and snapped it at her face. She dodged it but he had anticipated this. He used her movement to snap at her neck once again and managed to get his jaws around her before she retaliated with a claw swiped along his throat. She shoved him off.

Her adversary roared and she smiled, exuding confidence. She'd cut his neck and could tell from his aura that the wounds burned.

"The neck, huh?" she said, pumped her wings, and flung herself at him. She over-calculated and he was able to dodge. Her momentum carried her into the far wall and the impact shook the entire room and more of the roof rained down around them.

She could tell from Shadowstorm's aura that he had become more frightened. If she'd caught him with a strike like that, she could have knocked him out long enough to savage his throat and end this battle.

Unfortunately, she couldn't do that again. Her friends were in the tunnels above her.

The thought seemed to occur to him at the same moment it occurred to her, for he billowed into a shadowy mist and flew up through the hole in the ceiling and into the dark steam tunnels where her friends had fled.

CHAPTER SEVENTY-THREE

Whatever Shadowstorm's shadow powers were, they didn't allow him to simply vanish. With a pump of Kristen's silvery wings, she followed him into the tunnel above them. His massive bulk blocked the passage ahead of her.

Gunshots resounded around him, almost muffled by his girth.

She clamped her jaws on his tail and pumped her wings to drag them both back.

He mewled like a cat as she yanked him from the passageway. As soon as his arms and legs were free, he clawed and scratched at her, screaming something about her not knowing how to fight with proper etiquette.

In response, she kicked him with her back legs and hurled him into the chamber where they'd originally fought.

"Get up and out of here," she told her friends, using her aura to assure them that she would be safe.

"The steam," Drew replied.

When she studied the pipes, she could see the heat like she wore infrared goggles. There seemed to be a main pipe that fed the other smaller pipes. This one was the size of a man instead of an arm. She struck it with her tail, severed it, and gave the steam an easier path of escape than the relatively tiny, twisting veins that ran through the tunnels.

"You should be safe now. Most of the steam is flowing into the room below us. Get up top and get to safety."

"We're not leaving you," Drew said.

To save time, she pulsed her aura to him so he would understand that he wouldn't be leaving her but saving Keith and Jim.

He nodded as emotional understanding resonated with him far faster than thoughts could.

Kristen scrutinized the broken chamber below her, now filled with smoke, fire, and steam.

A fitting setting for the Steel Dragon to end the terror Shadowstorm had inflicted on the Motor City.

Satisfied that her friends were now safely on their way, she dropped into the steam and smoke and landed effortlessly with a pump of her wings.

Shadowstorm was waiting.

He emerged from the vaporous cloud in a whirlwind of claws. She tried to block his attacks with her claws but found his dragon body was simply too big to stop with her arms alone. His claws raked her belly, a sharp pain she felt even through her steel skin. He knocked her on her back and attempted to rip her stomach open.

She tried to push him off and discovered that her back legs were much stronger so she forced them under his bulk and shoved him off. Her tail darted out and nicked him as he staggered into the steam. She looked at her belly, fearful that she'd see her guts spilling out, but she wasn't so much as bleeding and couldn't restrain a grin.

"Hey, Shadowstorm. You're fucked!"

Kristen righted herself and tried flicking her tail. It was much faster than her arms and legs. He attacked from the steam again but this time, she defended herself with her tail. It arced and sliced one of his forearms, then the other as he tried to get past the darting blade. It seemed her tail worked almost completely by reflex. She thought *block* and her tail blocked. She thought *stab his eyes* and her tail did its damnedest to stab his eyes with its pointed tip and ax blade. Seriously, she liked her tail.

Once again, he vanished into the steam but this time, she followed him. She pumped her wings, cleared the obscuring vapor, and revealed her enemy, who hissed like an animal cornered in its burrow.

Obeying a deep inner impetus, she leapt forward, used her wings to carry her even farther than her muscles could, and attacked him with both claws and her tail.

Apparently, that was how dragons were supposed to attack. He defended against her claws and her tail, but he couldn't stop her jaws. She pushed through his swipes and latched her teeth around his neck. His flesh gave beneath her bite. This would be the end of the monster who tried to destroy her city.

Shadowstorm turned insubstantial and slipped out of her bite.

For a second, Kristen thought he'd vanished completely but saw that he'd simply turned into his human form and slipped through her jaws and claws.

So, his shadow power wasn't that special, then. He had merely learned how to use his transformation in an unusual way.

She turned and followed him and was alarmed to realize that her instincts very much liked pursuing a human. That was more than a little odd and she'd have to remember it. But there was some kind of perfect justice to ending him while he was in human form.

Too bad he had other plans.

As soon as he reached the massive opening in the ceiling, he transformed into a cloud of shadowy smoke. Two dragon wings emerged from the cloud, pumped a few times, and elevated him into the tunnels above them.

Kristen followed. At first, she grinned at the knowledge that she'd put this arrogant dragon on the defensive—until she realized that her team was probably still trying to get out of these tunnels.

She landed moments after him but he was already gone, vanished into the gloom and the steam that still seeped through the subterranean passages.

Immediately, she called on her aura. She felt him already another level above her. The coward was trying to escape. She could feel the fear in his chest and the terror at facing another dragon.

There wasn't enough time to race down the tunnel, transform into a human, and run up the stairs to the next level, so she simply powered through the two ceilings above her. She found him there, but he wasn't cowering.

Instead, he was coiled like a spring. As soon as her body was in range, he struck. He was a master of his aura and he'd used it to trick her.

Her stupidity drew a loud curse. She was halfway through the floor so she couldn't dodge. Still, her steel skin would protect her.

Or so she thought.

Seconds before his claws touched her chest, the tips turned into black clouds of shadow. Instead of merely raking across the surface, they penetrated her steel skin and somehow reformed inside her and raked at the muscles in her chest.

Kristen roared in pain and managed to smash her tail through the ground and slice him across the chest. Otherwise, she very much thought she might be dead.

He didn't give her time to recover or pull herself free but attacked again and again. His relentless assault forced her to all but demolish the tunnel in a poor attempt to defend herself.

The latest assault had scared her. He could somehow get his claws through her skin. What was to stop him from stabbing her directly in the heart? A vision of him reaching into her chest and plucking her heart from her filled her mind. She felt a pulse from his aura and knew her death was his intention.

A volley of gunfire erupted from the end of the hallway, and Shadowstorm spun toward it. "Your friends die today!" he bellowed and ran down the hallway.

Something above them exploded, and the hallway between the two dragons collapsed. An avalanche of bricks thundered on top of him.

"Meet us up top, Red!" Hernandez yelled. The woman had obviously made it inside the facility.

The Steel Dragon pulled herself free and moved into the collapsed hallway. Hernandez had blown the bottom of the first tunnel they'd been in, so she could see lights from the facility now. But she didn't go up yet. Her adversary attempted to extricate himself from the wreckage.

She pounced, landed on the bricks, and drove them into his wounded body.

"It's over, Sebastian. Stop fighting now and I'll take you in alive," she growled and flexed her aura to show him that she had reserves of strength left.

Beneath her, the bricks shifted and collapsed as Shadowstorm once again became insubstantial and freed his body from the rubble.

Kristen swiped viciously and tried to catch him with a claw when he became human, but he never fully did. Instead, he took his mist form once again and attempted to boil past her.

He tried to flee down the hole she had created but before he could, light flooded the space and his shadowy form dissipated to reveal the human-like Sebastian.

Blinded by the light, he glanced around quickly and stepped into the shadow.

"It's not a fair fight anymore, Shadowstorm. I have backup. You won't get out of here."

"This was never a fair fight," he hissed, surged forward, and transformed into his dragon form once he was in the shadow. She was ready for him, parried his tired attacks, and pushed him toward the blinding light.

Shadowstorm tried to turn to mist again but this time, she was prepared. As soon as the edges of his form blurred, she called upon the furnace she'd felt in her belly since she'd transformed.

White-hot flames erupted from her to trap him in her hands in his human body.

But even being incinerated at close range wasn't enough to kill him. He struggled against her grasp, unable to use his transforming ability in the bright light, but the flames themselves didn't hurt him.

That might have frustrated her if she was alone, but she knew she had backup. She clenched her fist tightly around him, ran directly below the light, and hurled him up and into the facility.

The reports of assault rifles rang out. She could tell that Beanpole had made it back from the van with guns for everyone.

She paused beneath the hole, pumped her wings, and elevated through it. The team had fired at Shadowstorm when he'd reached the top of his ascent. He'd transformed into a dragon and stayed low.

"Incinerate that piece of trash," Drew yelled. He stood beside the hole she had come through and near one of the dozen massive lights that pointed into the aperture.

If that wasn't code, she didn't know what the hell was. She nodded.

In the facility, though, it was much harder to corner her enemy. She had the sense that this was how dragons truly fought—in the air.

He raced around the room and his slow wingbeats hardly explained his great speed. She followed and realized that up there, without walls so close around her, she could really move.

He was tired, while she was exhilarated, and she was gaining on him.

Kristen caught him and they exchanged blows from claw and tail. He managed to thrust her off and resumed his flight around the facility. As he altered his trajectory toward one of the windows, he began to turn insubstantial again. They were large but not so big that he could fit his dragon body through them.

"The lights!" she yelled, but her team had already understood the importance of them. Three lights illuminated the window and in his weakened state, Shadowstorm couldn't transform. Instead, his head shattered the glass, his wings and shoulders impacted the brick frame, and he tumbled into a writhing pile of claws and black scales.

She swooped to land on top of him and pounded into his chest with her claws like a cat pouncing on a toad.

He cried out in agony as she ripped at his chest with her steel claws but she could tell that wouldn't be enough to finish him. His aura showed pain but it didn't weaken at all. His healing powers would keep him alive unless she destroyed his heart or his brain.

Or his throat, she thought grimly.

Her dragon form had few reservations about biting through an enemy's jugular. She snapped but once again, Shadowstorm became insubstantial and squirmed out from her hold.

Down on the ground, the lights the team was using couldn't penetrate every corner.

He slipped through one of the paths of shadow between the equipment.

It seemed the others were ready for this eventuality as well, though. Once he was in human form, a furious barrage of assault rifle fire once again drew more curses from the enemy.

"If I can't kill you, I'll have to settle for them," her adversary yelled and raced toward the gunshots.

When she tried to follow, she was immediately stopped because of her size. She transformed into her human body in a flurry of silver dust and raced after him.

They sprinted between conveyor belts and towering equipment. She attempted to gain on him as he followed the gunshots to their source. Bullets struck him and drew more of his dark, shadowy blood from his body, but he didn't seem to care. He merely raced forward, hungry for death.

The shadow dragon didn't realize he was drawing ever closer to the incinerator, but then, why would he?

Kristen rounded a corner and saw the flash of gunshots from inside the incinerator.

Hernandez's voice yelled from inside the tower of bricks. "Bring it on, you fucking lizard."

Shadowstorm roared and raced forward, transformed into his dragon form once more, and extended his massive head inside the structure.

No sooner was his head inside than lights flared and the tower exploded.

She watched in awe as five stories of brick almost a century old collapsed onto his head in the cleanest demolition she had ever seen. It was even well-lit. The lights her team had used to limit his power illuminated every brick as they plunged onto the dragon to crush first his head, then his entire body under the destruction.

"Hell yeah! I always wanted to do that," Hernandez shouted from behind her. She had a radio in one hand and a detonator in the other.

"Are you're all right?" Kristen yelled over the clatter of bricks rather than the more appropriate, "How the hell did you get out of there?"

The other woman answered the unspoken question, though. "The dumbass really didn't think nearly enough about tech. I left a radio strapped to a bundle of C4 in there."

Kristen laughed and turned to the rubble and the defeated dragon.

The bricks moved and somehow, in defiance of the limits of what she could even understand, Shadowstorm pushed himself free.

He roared, his dragon form intact but broken. Both wings were hopelessly mangled. His tail worked and swished in fury, although there were kinks in it like a cat that had its tail slammed in a car door.

Although he was missing teeth and blood wept from many of his interlaced black scales, he wasn't dead.

"Humans…death to humans," he growled and inhaled in preparation to incinerate everyone in the room.

In an instant, she transformed into a dragon once more and raced forward to drive her full weight into his gut before he could release the flame.

With another roar, he collapsed onto the pile of brick. She body-slammed him again.

When they'd been in the air, there had been a kind of poetry to their fight—like eagles fighting over a fish or dragonflies over a pond, perhaps. What followed was far less elegant.

Despite possessing the body of a dragon, she felt more like an elephant seal as she and Shadowstorm pounded their bodies against each other again and again. They tumbled through the rubble and scattered it with their claws as they hurled their bodies together and each tried to find purchase on the other's neck with their jaws.

"You could have ruled with me," he hissed as she knocked him back.

"Why would I wish to rule nothing but the ash of the city I love?" she retorted.

"Love?" He said the word with the same disdain most people reserved for the words, "genocide" or "torture." "You can't love humans and be a dragon."

His tail caught her, although he was too weak to knock her away. All he could do was slow her long enough to inhale and breath fire into the room. Garbage ignited, the paint on the walls burst aflame, and even bricks began to melt.

She considered pulling back. The flames were hot—intensely hot—but out of the corner of her eye she saw the fire started down in the tunnels had spread too. The flames had greedily followed remnants of trash and wooden scaffolding until they too had reached the recycling facility. Instead of only the center being on fire, every wall was.

"Kristen!" Keith shouted. "You have to get out of here."

That steeled her resolve. "If humans can care for dragons, we can care for them."

With new resolve, she pushed forward through his flames and felt the heat through her steel skin, feared it would melt, but no longer cared. She wouldn't allow him to hurt her friends. She couldn't, so she pressed forward despite the pain and the heat that threatened to pop her eyeballs like grapes. Finally, she reached him.

Kristen sliced his gut with a claw in the moment that the fire stopped, but he writhed, opened his jaws again, and breathed more fire on her.

The intelligence and cunning behind his eyes was gone. Instead of guile and false charm, she saw only hatred and rage burning hotter than the fire that spewed from his guts.

She lunged forward and used every ounce of her dragon speed to knock him back, but even then, the flames didn't stop.

Left with no choice, she did what Shadowstorm had done to her. She had to if she wanted to save her friends. With whip-like speed, she uncoiled her long sinuous neck—the strike of a snake or a heron—and closed her steel teeth around his neck.

He didn't try to turn insubstantial or fade into shadows or even attempt to escape. Instead, he twisted in an effort to position his mouth to spray flames at his adversary. When she closed her jaws and felt his windpipe crush and his jugular tear, she felt no guilt. She felt more like she'd put down a rabid beast than a human adversary.

But that had been Shadowstorm's point until the very end. He wasn't a human but something different.

Kristen stepped back and scrutinized his broken body. He was dead. She'd almost severed his head and apparently, that was enough to kill a dragon. He lay amongst the brick and the flames, dead on the throne he'd tried to carve from her city.

"Hall! A little help!" She turned quickly at the sound of Drew's voice. He and the team had climbed onto a piece of equipment and were now trapped. Flames licked at them from all sides. They'd probably be dead already except the broken windows and the hole in the ceiling where the incinerator had been let out the smoke that would otherwise have choked the room.

They had little time to spare. She pumped her wings and was there beside them in a moment. "Climb on my back," she ordered and wondered how many times, if ever, this had happened. Did dragons use their abilities to save human lives? she didn't care whether they did or didn't. She was a dragon and she would use her abilities as she saw fit. Today, that meant saving the people who cared about her.

They complied, all six of them—Drew, Keith, Hernandez, Jim, Beanpole, and Butters.

"Butters, did you stop for a snack?" she asked. The rest hadn't felt like anything, but he felt like someone had loaded her shoulders with sacks of grain. She smiled at the absurdity of the comparison she had made. A sack of grain would now be a trifle.

"You can come back for me," the sniper said and shifted as he tried to get off. That was a lie, and he knew it. If she left him behind, he'd roast like the turkey he was named after.

"Sit still," Kristen said and used her aura to calm her friends despite the inferno that roared all around them. They calmed—she could feel their emotions now as easily as she could see the heat of the flames all around her—and she pumped her wings to push herself above the flames.

Unfortunately, she couldn't simply soar out. The superheated air wasn't thick enough to support a steel dragon burdened with so many humans. But she honestly didn't know what else she could do. She couldn't simply bulldoze through a wall, not if she wanted her friends to survive.

"Can you turn off the steel, or what?" Keith shouted.

She smiled and changed her body from steel dragon to only dragon.

Instantly, she felt lighter and when she pumped her wings this time, the force was enough to lift her higher. She flapped through the flames and made a quick, tight circle before she glided through the hole in the ceiling that had once been where the incinerator stood.

They cleared the roof not a moment too soon as the flames inside reached a cache of propane or perhaps a tank of methane. She would never know the exact mechanism, only that something exploded in the heart of the facility, and that was enough to destabilize one of the walls. Once one wall on the decades-old building went down, two others followed.

The force of that much brick collapsing on a network of tunnels was enough to avalanche the entire building, industrial equipment and all, into the pit where the two dragons had begun their battle and that Hernandez had further weakened with her explosives.

In a moment, all that was left of the garbage sorting and burning portion of the facility was a blazing pit and a single brick wall. The upper half of galvanized steel had melted away into nothing.

"Thanks for saving us, Red, but I'm not dressed for this shit," Hernandez shouted over the wind.

"Can you take us out for coffee?" Jim asked.

Kristen smiled. Below them, Shadowstorm's body burned in a grave he'd dug for himself, but all around them, snow was falling. This high, there hardly seemed to be any sense to the movements of the flakes. They drifted this way and that, pushed about by her wingbeats as much as by the wind itself.

She didn't feel cold, though. Inside her chest, a fire roared, a furnace of power that fueled her abilities. She realized she knew that feeling. It was the same sensation that had made her stand up for her brother when he'd been bullied. This was her dragon heart, and it had always been a part of her.

It was an easy choice to share the warmth she felt and she nudged it into the hearts and minds of the humans on her back. She felt them all relax. Despite being high above Detroit, they all now understood that they wouldn't die. They understood that they were safe and that she cared for them and would do anything in her power to protect them.

"Kristen, I think I speak for all of us when I say that we appreciate the warm-and-fuzzies you're giving us right now," Butters shouted over the wind, "but if you don't land and let us put goddamn hats and scarves on, we're all gonna freeze to death up here."

"Right, sorry." She swooped into a slow descent toward the city. Her dragon's heart might keep her warm, but the humans on her back were still regular people. She found that comforting but also knew that they'd all prefer to be comforted with a glass of something steaming.

She flew them carefully into the city they all called home.

CHAPTER SEVENTY-FOUR

In her dragon body, Kristen found she could sense auras far more easily than she could when she'd been stuck as a human. It was as if her gleaming silvery scales were conductors for the ability. When she landed outside the Detroit Renewable Power facility, she could tell that Stonequest and six other dragons were already headed toward them.

It was almost a surprise when Drew cleared his throat and asked about them. "Let's call the station and get backup. This place needs to be cordoned off. The fire and steam in the snow are screaming special news bulletin."

"It's out of our jurisdiction," she said, a little startled that as a dragon, she spoke slightly slower than she did with a human mouth. It was still her voice, but it was slightly lower and more melodic.

"What do you mean? This place is definitely in Detroit." Keith folded his arms.

She pointed a claw at Dragon SWAT. The seven dragon forms were close enough now she could easily make out their silhouettes against the clouds glowing with light from the city.

No one else seemed to be able to see them, though, until they landed one by one and there were so many around them that the snow ceased to fall on them. The seven dragons were so hot that together, they created a bubble of heat against the cold.

"Kristen Hall, the Steel Dragon," Stonequest said by way of greeting. Normally, he transformed into his human form, but now he remained in his dragon body and circled around her silvery body. She still hadn't turned to steel, but she did so now. In the blink of an eye, she went from silvery dragon with whitish, slightly leathery skin between her scales, a mane of white hair, and horns the color and texture of ivory to completely steel.

He didn't answer verbally but he did flash his aura at her. It seemed he was pleased and impressed that she could transform and completely unsurprised. The feeling he gave her reminded her of how her dad had felt when she finally rode her bike down the block without training wheels.

"We defeated Shadowstorm," she began to explain but Stonequest and the other dragons' auras told her that they knew this already. But of course they did. They were undoubtedly there because they'd sensed the battle. In the end, Sebastian hadn't controlled his aura at all. Every dragon within fifty miles might have felt his rage.

"He's over there?" Stonequest gestured with his long neck toward the burning pit that spewed smoke and steam into the snowy night.

Kristen nodded.

"How did you finish him?" There was something in his aura that made her worry she'd done the wrong thing.

"We fought, then brought the incinerator down on him. Even though he was defeated, he tried to burn my friends, so I snapped his neck in my jaws." She expected to be reprimanded. In the heat of battle, it had seemed the natural thing to do, but saying it now seemed grisly.

He nodded. "It's good to know he's finished."

"You thought he wasn't?"

"Shadowstorm is a master of his aura. We could all sense it from miles away—yours too—during the battle, then it snuffed out at the same moment that yours burned hottest. I assumed he was dead but needed to be sure you delivered a finishing blow."

"You mean he could have survived?" She was incredulous.

"Not if you crushed his neck. A dragon's bite is a powerful thing, and we need our heads connected to our bodies as much as any other creature. To defeat him, you either needed to pierce his brain or his heart or sever his jugular."

She knew the power in the bodies of dragons. The bullet that had been made from one had worked as effectively as a taser on a human body.

"All right, team. I want this mess put away and I want it done yesterday."

"That will not be an easy thing to do, Stonequest," a purple dragon replied. Her aura was strange to Kristen. It lacked the straightforwardness of Stonequest's or the layers of Shadowstorm's. It felt… smoky, maybe?

"Even with the mages helping?"

"I won't tell you how to do the job without using the tools," the purple dragon snapped in response.

Ah, that was what she had sensed in this dragon's aura. She was a particularly adept magic-user. She realized that there were also three mages on her back. From her aura, she could tell that the dragon thought of these humans as hers. To harm them would be a personal insult to her, to which she would retaliate. She found it comforting that this dragon made it known that to hurt these people would result in a dragon battle, but it was weird that she thought of them as hers.

Kristen sighed. She supposed this was how she thought of her friends too.

"Can you clean it up or not?"

The purple dragon smiled. "We might not fix the machines, but bricks and beams are not a problem."

"Fine, Timeflash, do it."

Stonequest followed Timeflash toward the burning pit.

The dragon and her three mages each stood near a corner of the demolished building. A purple light erupted from Timeflash's eyes, mouth, and hands and a moment later, it was mirrored by her three assistants. Kristen could sense from the dragon's aura that the mages were augmenting her power.

After that, though, she wasn't able to do anything but gawk. Her dragon jaw dropped open when the purple dragon and her people repaired the building she and Shadowstorm had so completely demolished.

The fire withered and steam began to seep back into the hole.

Unbelievably, the incinerator repaired itself with a roar like an avalanche as the bricks sorted themselves and stacked themselves into the tower. At first, she could only hear this happening, but in a moment, they cleared the roof of the red-and-white building and continued higher. Smoke and steam continued to pour past them as they returned to the tower from which they'd come and which—until a moment before—had been destroyed.

Once the tower was done, the metal walls of the building pulled themselves into place, straightened the bends and kinks caused by the heat and explosions that had occurred in the building, and resumed functioning as the walls as if nothing had happened.

A glass window repaired itself and it was as if the facility hadn't been damaged at all, at least from the outside.

Timeflash sagged when it was finished and the purple light left her and her mages. The three humans raced toward her and magic flared from their fingers. The spell they wove turned into a massive net of energy which caught her before she fell. She looked paler than before. The effort of fixing the building had obviously wearied her.

"Wait, some dragons can turn time back?" Kristen was incredulous.

Stonequest chuckled. "It looks like that and it's why she named herself that, but no. It's as impossible to turn time back as it is to bring someone back from the dead. So don't worry. Shadowstorm's body is still in there."

"But then how—"

"She can sense how objects touched by humans fit together. If she can act quickly enough, she can repair things that were destroyed.

Tests have proven its not time magic, more like following instructions with a type of telepathy."

Her mind spun. Shadowstorm had seemed to possess powers the likes of which she couldn't understand—not least of which being the snowstorm that now blanketed the city. She didn't know if he had called it into existence or simply hastened its development and now, she assumed she'd never know.

"But then, she could repair bombed cities and fix car crashes." The possibilities seemed endless to her.

Stonequest shook his head. "Not really, no. Her powers are limited. Even to do that building, she needed those mages to assist her, and they didn't fix the machines inside. Regular mechanics will need to do that. But don't worry. You'll learn about all this kind of stuff once you're on dragon SWAT."

"Yeah, right, whenever that is."

"Now, Kristen. That was an invitation."

She laughed until she saw that he merely smiled gently. He wasn't joking? "You're joking," she stammered. It was all she articulate.

"No, I'm not. You're one of us now. You activated your dragon form and I don't think anyone on the Dragon Council would dispute your powers. I knew you'd be powerful, but this? Defeating Shadowstorm in a lair of his own devising would have been a mighty challenge, even for me. You've done incredibly well. I have the right to recruit the dragons I choose to, and right now, I'm recruiting you."

"But my team—"

"Were fine before you arrived and will continue to do their excellent work after you've moved on," he said. He looked at the human team leader. "Am I correct?"

Drew nodded. His eyes looked a little sad but he smiled. "We knew this day would come, Hall."

"I'm more than only a dragon, though," Kristen said. She felt disagreement from Stonequest's aura and smiled. "Okay, yes, I am a dragon, but that's not all I am. I'm still human. I was raised by humans and I grew up as a human. That will always be a part of me, and even if I could pretend like I wasn't, I don't want to. Being human…being human rules."

"Hell yeah!" Keith said from behind her.

Stonequest nodded. "I won't argue. After all, you may be the first dragon in history who has spent decades more time in her human form than her dragon form. But still, there is training that must be done. Things that you must learn about being a dragon. Your time working with people in this capacity is done."

Kristen glanced at Drew again, seeking permission, guidance… something. He nodded, still grinning. That gave her courage enough to take the next step. "When do we leave?"

"I assume you'll want to see your family again."

"And that they'll throw a barbecue before you go," Butters suggested.

"Tomorrow then," Stonequest said.

She nodded and he dismissed her and her team. Quickly, she transformed into her human form and entered the van. Together with her team for perhaps the last time, they drove back to the station.

The barbecue started out so normally it was almost surreal. Despite the snow that had fallen the night before, Kristen's dad still wore shorts. The snow hadn't stuck to the ground—because Shadowstorm had died? she wondered—but that didn't mean it wasn't cold. Still, Frank's pale, knobby knees would not be hidden on barbecue day.

"Frank, are you sure that'll be enough pulled pork?" her mom asked for what had to be the fortieth time.

"For Christ's sake, Marty, it's twenty goddamn pounds of pig and another six chickens."

"Yeah, but Dad, dragons might be here. Dragons," Brian said cryptically. He'd done nothing to help the entire day, which was entirely normal for him. Instead, he'd spent his time playing videogames and begging his sister to transform.

She'd done so once, which had made her dad release such a stream of profanities that she'd actually been proud until she'd realized he wasn't swearing in amazement but at what she'd done to his front lawn. Her mom had only been able to cry. When she had reverted to her human form, Marty had crushed her in a hug so tight she thought it might have been capable of asphyxiating dragons.

"Brian, we're out of pickles," the woman now said. "Run to the store. You can take the car."

"Moooom! Seriously? Kristen can fly there. I've almost beat the boss."

"I'm not using my dragon abilities to get pickles," she snapped at her brother. She'd sat down with him and told him she'd be away for a while training, but he had only shrugged.

"And Kristen's friends are showing up," her mom added.

At that, she rolled her eyes. Leave it to her mother to ignore magic dragon powers but be concerned about proper hosting etiquette.

"Ugh, fine!" Brian scowled. "But mark my words, Steel Dragon, if you eat any pickles, you answer to me."

Her parents shared a look that said *what went wrong?* Then, Marty opened the door. Jim Washington stood there with a bouquet of flowers.

"Good afternoon, Mrs. Hall. I brought some flowers for your lovely home."

"Oh, you must be the Wonderful kid," she said and managed to embarrass a steel dragon of unimaginable power for possibly the ninetieth time that day.

"They call me the Wonderkid, ma'am," he said as she took the flowers.

Kristen showed him through the house and out to the backyard, the opposite path to the one they'd taken the last time he had been here.

"Nice to see you, sir," Jim said to Frank, who currently removed chunks of pork shoulder from his smoker.

"Yeah, likewise. It's nice to have Kristen bring cops over when it's not a kidnapping."

"Yes, sir."

"If you two will excuse me," her dad said and took his pork inside.

For a moment, the two said nothing and simply watched their breath steaming in the crisp winter air. Then, he cleared his throat and spoke. "You know, I learned a lot from you."

"Jim, we don't have to do this," she protested.

"No, we do. When I met you, I hated you simply because of what you were, and I didn't even know what you were. I thought all dragons were cruel, callous beings and believed you were the same. I'm proud to say that you changed that in me. And now, you can transform." Jim shook his head. "I want you to know I'll always appreciate that—"

"What the fuck's going on back here?" She turned when Hernandez appeared at the side gate with Keith in tow.

"Are you two having a heart to heart?" The Rookie grinned.

"No—" she tried to say but Hernandez noticed Jim's watery eyes and grinned.

"Holy shit, this is pathetic. You're not even drunk yet, Jim. Grow a pair." The woman laughed and Keith joined her.

"Thanks for coming out, Hernandez," Kristen said.

The demolitions expert shrugged. "Eh, I wasn't doing anything important and who can say no to free barbecue?"

"Nothing important?" Keith's eyebrows almost raised completely off his head before he turned bright red.

"Wait a minute…" Kristen looked from his embarrassed face to Hernandez's wicked grin. "Are you two—"

"Banging? Yeah, obviously," the woman said. He only blushed more fiercely.

Jim frowned. "I thought you were…uh…"

"A dyke? You can go fuck yourself, for starters. No, I'm not a dyke. I'll bang anything. Bombs, boys, and bimbos."

"Class act, Hernandez," Drew said as he descended the steps from the house. "It's good to know your work ethic goes all the way down."

She shrugged and actually looked proud of herself.

"Drew! You made it," Kristen said.

"I almost decided to stay home so you'd feel guilty and come visit us." He smiled.

"Nothing like that Steel Dragon guilt," Keith added.

"I'll visit as much as I can, but I'm still glad you made it."

"Of course. I wouldn't miss it. Your dad has the best stories about the old-timers on the force."

She smiled. Drew, even off-shift, was still one hundred percent obsessed with being a cop.

"Wow. Here for the Steel Dragon's fat dad. That's a new one," Hernandez said.

Kristen might have balked at someone calling her dad fat once—even though it was true—but she was so damn pleased that the people who'd seen her transform and fight a dragon to the death were there and still thought of her parents as her parents.

Drew smiled awkwardly. "I've gotten to know one Hall. They're cool. I don't want to lose that."

"It's not like I'll vanish forever! You guys talk about me like I'm moving to another planet. We see Stonequest on the regular. I'll be around."

Eye-rolls all around met this statement. Hernandez went so far as to snort in derision. "Yeah right, Red—maybe I should call you Steel now, though—like you've ever had any chill at all. I can't exactly see you facing an existential threat to dragon kind and clocking out at five and stopping by for airsoft with us." By the time she had stopped talking, the humor had drained from her voice.

"Yeah…yeah, I guess you're right," she said. Suddenly, the air felt way colder than it had been. "Do you guys want to head inside?"

"Aren't you going to do tricks or something? Show us dragon moves?" Keith tried to joke but given the moment, it felt forced.

"I can't. My dad will kill me if I mess the grass up."

That earned some chuckles, at least. By the time they went in and removed their jackets, the awkwardness had passed. Until Butters burst in the front door with Beanpole trailing behind him.

"Kristen! Come hug me before I get all covered in sauce."

He stumbled forward and threw his arms around her. She smelled alcohol on his breath. "Has he been drinking?" she asked Beanpole.

The man shrugged, then nodded quickly. "He said he couldn't say goodbye sober."

"And now I won't have to," the sniper said and crushed her tightly in his grip.

"Dude, let go before she has to turn into steel," Keith shouted from the kitchen.

Butters released her and rubbed his eyes.

"I want you to know that if Dragon SWAT gives you any trouble, you can count on us."

"Ha!" Hernandez laughed. "To do what, exactly?"

"I saw that sniper lady. I'll shoot holes in their wings. I'll step on their tails, and I'll…I'll…"

"Dinner is served!" Kristen's mom shouted and Butters changed demeanor immediately.

"I'll have to fill my plate." Kristen forgotten, he lumbered through to the kitchen. He led the charge, much to her mother's delight, and stacked his plate high with pulled pork, chicken, pasta salad, coleslaw, and a couple of buns to cram it all inside of.

The others followed, then Kristen. Brian arrived as they sat and complained loudly about the injustice of being sent for pickles only to find that they weren't actually needed. Marty consoled her son by chopping them and putting them on his plate, which only made all the cops at the table laugh and pleased her son not at all.

"A toast!" Frank Hall said, raised his half-finished can of beer, and waited for the swearing and storytelling to pause. "To Kristen. Your mother and I always knew you were something special. You might be the only person in the world whose parents weren't surprised to find out you were actually a dragon. You're amazing, Krissy, and now you've beat a dragon, and well, I'm so… That is…" He had been doing well but now, the tears began to run.

Her mom tried to salvage the speech. "We're proud of you, honey, and we'll always be here for you."

"Even with them people breaking in here?" Jim asked. Obviously, he'd had a beer too many. That question was a little too rude for the normally perfect demeanor of the Wonderkid.

"We're not moving simply because some dickholes thought they could scare us, especially not now that my sister can turn full dragon."

Everyone laughed at Brian's joke and Kristen finally felt like it would be okay. These people—her people—would be able to go on without her. They were strong, brave, and capable of things she needed dragon abilities to accomplish. She was proud to know them and knew that each of them in their own way defined who she was.

The party went late into the night and her coworkers indulged so much that they crashed on the couch and slept over. Marty wouldn't let anyone who'd so much as sipped a beer head home.

In the morning, when Stonequest arrived in the falling snow to take Kristen to join Dragon SWAT, all the people she loved were there to say goodbye and wish her well.

As she transformed into her dragon body—careful to do so in the street so as to not damage her dad's precious grass—she thought of all they'd given her. Confidence. Courage. Strangely good reflexes when it came to playing fighting games. She might have still become a dragon without them, but she wouldn't have been the person she'd become. Being the person they all, in turn, cheered for, insulted, looked up to, or came to trust was her favorite person to be.

It was with a strange lightness in her heart that Kristen took flight with Stonequest and waved goodbye to the people she loved. She knew she'd see them again—to deny herself would be like denying that she was a dragon and a failure to see the world as it was.

"Will you be okay?" Stonequest asked over the wind. He'd no doubt sensed her aura.

"Thanks to all those people down there, I think I will be."

The Steel Dragon and Stonequest flew off into an unknown future.

STEEL DRAGONS BOOK TWO

Available Now at Amazon and through Kindle Unlimited.

Kristen Hall grew up a human – but she's not. She's a dragon.

And dragonkind will never be the same.

She's achieved some mastery over her powers and even defeated an enemy dragon.

But nothing she has done has prepared her for what's coming next. Kristen has been invited to join Dragon SWAT – a force of dragons which serves to keep order among their species. But not every dragon is happy with the status quo; some see humanity as a threat which should be eliminated. They're not alone. A growing number of humans feel the same about the dragons.

Forces are moving in the world to bring both races into a final conflict. The prize? Survival of their species and control of the Earth.

Powerful humans and dragons are playing chess with the future of the world. But Kristen was a piece none of these beings anticipated. She could swing the balance of power in either direction.

The Steel Dragon has plans of her own, though. Armed with the sense of honor instilled in her by her human parents, she's going to have to dig to the bottom of the mysteries at play if she hopes to have even the smallest chance of averting a catastrophic war!

Available Now at Amazon and through Kindle Unlimited.

KEVIN'S AUTHOR NOTES

OCTOBER 20, 2019

Wow, this book was a long time coming! Michael Anderle and I have talked about doing some sort of work together for ages. Finally, late last year, we realized the only way we were going to properly brainstorm ideas for a new series was if we got together in person and sat down to do the work.

Cue one airplane flight for me from my Boston home to Las Vegas! On Spirit, no less.

That actually turned out better than I'd feared. I upgraded my seat to their "extra space", which put me in the front of the plane. It was, believe it or not, one of the more comfortable flying experiences I've had. A pleasant surprise, since I'd heard a lot of negative things about Spirit before.

Ah, Vegas. I've been out that way for author events before, but never just to meet and hang out with one person like this. Vegas can be pretty fun, it turns out, even if you have precisely zero interest in gambling. (My math skills are too good for gambling to be that much fun.) It's a cool place. I was able to experience much more of it than I had before, thanks to Michael touring me around a bit.

Mike and I spent several days powering through a bunch of different story ideas, working them over to see which ones we both liked. I think there were concepts for at least three other series which were tabled — at least for now. Someday those other ideas might see the light of day, too.

But by day two we were already pretty set on Kristen's story: The Steel Dragon. It hit all the right notes for both of us. We had a strong protagonist who's a 'fish out of water', exploring a world that is wildly unfamiliar to her. Over the course of my visit Mike and I blocked out no less than fifteen potential storylines for the Steel Dragon series.

You've got three of them in your hands now.

Once we had the rough idea down, it was time to spin out the beats for the book. That part was my job; plotting is one of my strong points, and I had a lot of fun figuring out all the trials and tribulations our hero was going to face. Once I finished the beats for each tale they went over to Michael, who sent back a draft.

Then I went over the draft and tweaked it here and there, adding a few scenes, expanding on others... The usual stuff. If I did my job right you'll never be able to tell which scenes I wrote and which ones were straight Michael Anderle. You'll have to let me know!

The LMBPN beta reader team was absolutely instrumental in making these stories the best they could possibly be. With their help we refined and enhanced Kristen's tale in ways that the two of us could never have done alone. I want to shout out to those readers with a VERY special 'thank you!'

Oh, did I mention that there's more where this came from? Yes — volume two is coming down the pipe as soon as the LMBPN hamsters (kidding, they use guinea pigs now) have it ready. Kristen's adventures are only just beginning.

Thanks for taking the voyage with us!

MICHAEL'S AUTHOR NOTES

OCTOBER 21, 2019

Thank you for reading this story, and perusing these author notes at the end of the book!

I'm presently flying back from Frankfurt (went there for the 2019 Frankfurt Book Fair) back to the USA. I'm somewhere over the Atlantic I'm guessing. All I can see are the white clouds below us (someone up in the cockpit mentioned we are cruising at 32,000 feet) so I have no idea where we are.

This publishing business is so vast, it is sometimes hard to comprehend all of it, but I am trying.

A little bit about my collaborator, Kevin McLaughlin.

If I was asked to name 'one thing' that I find unique about Kevin, it is that he has worked as a nurse and knows his stuff when it comes to medicine. This was evident one time at a convention when an author's daughter was ill. I heard about the story in the morning (it happened the night before) and when I was getting the story I found out Kevin had visited their room and helped the child.

Since I hadn't really associated Nursing with Kevin before (it was a factoid, but not something which was front and center for me) I remember being confused for a moment. The person I was speaking to MUST have noticed the confusion on my face and mentioned he was a nurse.

That was when it snapped into place. *Of course he would know how to help!*

If you get a chance to meet him, his desire to help people damn near oozes out of him.

While I want to help people, I admit I have a huge aversion to blood. Not necessarily my own (I asked for a mirror at 10 years old to watch the doctor sew up my lip that had a tree trunk slammed into it.)

But he deals with it professionally and yet retains his compassion.

Kevin was in the Army (I'm assuming for one four-year stint? I don't know and now I'm scratching my cheek trying to figure out how come I never asked.) We used some of that knowledge creating the Steel Dragon Universe.

Now for some Behind the Fiction Dirt.

Kevin and I enjoy talking shop and stories, so it seemed like working together would be a fantastic next step. Both of us love the Indie publishing scene, great books, and telling stories so why would it be a challenge?

But, it was.

We had met a few times in person (at various 20Booksto50k events and Boston Fantasy-Fest. Plus, he and Liz took Judith and I to dinner in Boston one night as well. He's outgoing, fun, smart and likes to laugh.

And damned opinionated.

The opinionated part had never been a real problem in our many previous conversations, so I didn't think anything of it. Not until we tried to hammer out this story did this aspect become challenging. We tried a few times to work out the story concepts over video calls but it just wasn't jelling for us.

So, I pitched him coming out to Vegas in (December?) of 2018 and he took a flight and we setup in a conference room and hashed out this series. It was hard, damned hard. He would come up with something and it didn't work for me. I would come up with an idea, but it wouldn't work for him.

By hashed out, we beat each other up with ideas and counter ideas. It was like watching a tennis match.

All day we went back and forth and I was wrung out creatively by the end of day one. Fortunately, I think we got somewhere on the big picture for Steel Dragon the last hour of the day, so that I went into day two with a bit of positivity. By the end of hours and hours of work, we had the story that is coming to your hands now.

I can say that with assurance because I know damned well Kevin wouldn't settle. There is no give in that man at all.

;-)

If you get a chance to talk with him, do it. He is a uniquely qualified author that brings so much knowledge of the industry (including being a part of it since he was like…10 I think?)

However, out of all of the aspects I'd talk about if asked - I would point to him and say, 'He is one of the most compassionate guys I know.'

The rest is just dressing.

WITCH OF THE FEDERATION

If you loved Steel Dragon, you might also enjoy the Federal Histories series, from Michael Anderle. Book one is Witch Of The Federation and it's available from Amazon and through Kindle Unlimited.

The future has amazing technology. Our alien allies have magic. Together, we are building a training system to teach the best of humanity to go to the stars.

But the training is monumentally expensive.

Stephanie Morgana is a genius, she just doesn't *know it*.

The Artificial Intelligence which runs the Virtual World is charged with testing Stephanie, a task it has never performed before.

The Earth and their allies, may never be the same again.

Will Stephanie pass the test and be moved to the advanced preparatory schools, or will the system miss her? Will the AI be able to judge a human's potential in an area where it has no existing test data to compare?

Available now at Amazon and through Kindle Unlimited.

BOOKS BY KEVIN MCLAUGHLIN

Adventures of the Starship Satori (Space Opera blended with military SF)
Finding Satori - prequel short story, available only to email list fans!

Book 1 - Ad Astra: Book 2 - Stellar Legacy

Book 3 - Deep Waters

Book 4 - No Plan Survives Contact

Book 5 - Liberty

Book 6 - Satori's Destiny

Book 7 - Ashes of War

Book 8 - Embers of War

Book 9 - Dust and Iron

Book 10 - Clad in Steel

Book 11 - Brave New Worlds (2019)

Book 12 - Warrior's Marque (2020)

The Ragnarok Saga (Military SF)
Accord of Fire - Free prequel short story, available only to email list fans!

Book 1 - Accord of Honor

Book 2 - Accord of Mars

Book 3 - Accord of Valor

Book 4 - Ghost Wing

Book 5 - Ghost Squadron

Book 6 - Ghost Fleet (2019)

Valhalla Online Series (A Ragnarok Saga Story)
Book 1 - Valhalla Online

Book 2 - Raiding Jotunheim

Book 3 - Vengeance Over Vanaheim

Book 4 - Hel Hath No Fury

Blackwell Magic Series (Urban Fantasy)

Book 1 - By Darkness Revealed

Book 2 - Ashes Ascendant

Book 3 - Dead In Winter

Book 4 - Claws That Catch

Book 5 - Darkness Awakes

Book 6 - Spellbinding Entanglements

By A Whisker (short story)

The Raven and the Rose - Free novelette for email list fans!

Dead Brittania Series:

Dead Brittania (short prequel story)

Book 1 - King of the Dead

Book 2 - Queen of Demons

Raven's Heart Series (Urban Fantasy)

Book 1 - Stolen Light

Book 2 - Webs in the Dark

Book 3 - Shades of Moonlight

Other Titles:

Over the Moon (SF romance)

Midnight Visitors (Steampunk Cat short story)

Demon Ex Machina (Steampunk Cat short story)

The Coffee Break Novelist (help for writers!)

You Must Write (Heinlein's rules for writers)

BOOKS BY MICHAEL ANDERLE

For a complete list of books by Michael Anderle, please visit:

www.lmbpn.com/ma-books/

All LMBPN Audiobooks are Available at Audible.com and iTunes

To see all LMBPN audiobooks, including those written by Michael Anderle please visit:

www.lmbpn.com/audible

CONNECT WITH THE AUTHORS

Connect with Michael Anderle and sign up for his email list here:

Website: http://lmbpn.com

Email List: http://lmbpn.com/email/

Facebook:
www.facebook.com/TheKurtherianGambitBooks

Made in the USA
Coppell, TX
14 November 2020